THUNDER
OF
EREBUS

Books by Payne Harrison
STORMING INTREPID
THUNDER OF EREBUS

THUNDER OF EREBUS

PAYNE HARRISON

CROWN PUBLISHERS, INC.
NEW YORK

Published by Crown Publishers, Inc.,
201 East 50th Street, New York, New York 10022.
Member of the Crown Publishing Group.

CROWN is a trademark of Crown Publishers, Inc.

Manufactured in the United States of America

Library of Congress Cataloging-in-Publication Data
Harrison, Payne.
Thunder of Erebus / Payne Harrison. — 1st ed.
p.   cm.
I. Title.
PS3558.A6718T48   1991
813'.54—dc20   91-2337
                                                              CIP

ISBN 0-517-58405-0

10 9 8 7 6 5 4 3 2 1

First Edition

This book is dedicated to my mother,
Mary Beth Garrett Harrison
—also known as
The Steel Magnolia

············
ACKNOWLEDGMENTS

Being an author is a bit like being an astronaut, in that the person who rides the rocket has all the fun and glory, but behind him (or her) is a vast network of people who provide unceasing support to make it happen.

In writing *Thunder of Erebus,* I am indebted to many fine public affairs officers in the U.S. military, but would like to single out a few who went more than the extra mile in extending their assistance: Chuck Canterbury and Maj. George Lennon of the 6th Infantry Division (Light); El Ahlwardt of the Naval War College; and Maj. Chuck Pope of the U.S. Army Field Artillery Center.

Through the courtesy of Maj. Gen. Harold T. Fields, Jr., I had the opportunity to visit the 6th Infantry Division (Light) and see first-hand the extraordinary men and women of his Alaska-based division. During the course of my visit I was able to drive a SUSV snow vehicle (I didn't wreck it), crawl into a snow cave (I didn't dig it), and see two night parachute drops in twenty-below weather (I was on the ground). I was impressed all along the way with the caliber of men and women I met, and the candor with which they spoke. During the course of my visit, Maj. Gen. Samuel E. Ebbesen and Col. Thomas J. Lawrie were most kind in making arrangements to ensure my research efforts brought in a fruitful harvest, and I thank them both.

Much of my time with the division was spent with the "Northern Watch" of the 106th Military Intelligence Battalion, and I will be forever indebted to Lt. Col. Hal Stevens, Maj. Ron Burgess, and Maj. Kim Chapman for the time and hospitality they extended to me. Lt. Karen Gibson introduced me to the charms of military skis and kept an eye peeled for any rogue moose that might have interfered with my progress (or lack thereof). I would like to thank Cmd. Sgt. Maj. John T. Bergeron for insuring I had proper survival gear in the wilds of Alaska, and I would like to thank Sgt. Frank A. Socha for insuring I survived.

During the time I spent with the Long Range Surveillance Detachment of the "Northern Watch," I found superb soldiers and superb leadership at every level. Capt. John Knie and SFC James Storter were in charge of this extraordinary group. They and their men were most generous with their valuable time—visiting with this rather overweight, out-of-shape civilian who asked a lot of stupid questions. I am indebted to the LRSD as a whole, but would like to mention SSG Mike Martens, SSG Bill Mounce, SSG Steve Menard, SSG Robert Espiritu, Sgt. Alan Wika, PV2 Matt Grucella, PV2 Jim Hayes, PV2 Chris Scarborough, and PFC Richard Whitley.

Lt. Col. Shep Snow and his crew at the Northern Warfare Training Center were selfless with their time, showing me the nuances of snow shelters, and briefing me on their school and vital rescue operations. (If you're ever lost in the mountains, these are the guys you want to search for you.)

To Lt. Alan McArthur, who escorted me throughout my visit in the Alaska hinterland, my wife sends her heartfelt thanks for bringing her husband back alive.

I would also like to extend my thanks to: Lt. Col. Les Grau of the U.S. Army's Soviet Army Studies Office, Prof. Ilya Mamantov, and Melissa Robol for their insights into Russian language and culture; Craig Beck and my "Baker Street Irregular" Bob Gates for their comments and ideas; Rick Wright for his expertise on the C-130; "Buzz" and Richard for their insights into naval surface warfare; Col. Don Borden for his briefing on Alaska and Fort Greely; Maj. Walter Olson for his briefing and tour of the permafrost tunnel of the Cold Regions Research & Engineering Laboratory in Alaska; Bob Regan for his valued help and advice; my sister Karen and my research assistant Charlotte Thomas for their careful and meticulous work; Guy Gutheridge at the National Science Foundation's Division of Polar Programs for his kind assistance; Mike Baile and Anna and Carlos Burbano for their logistical support; Tom Sharp and Alan Altick for giving me a place to roost; and my friends who briefed me on the "Night Raptor" vision system.

To my agent Jan Miller, her right hand Sandra Burrowes, and left hand Katie Hazelwood; and the crew at Crown Publishers: Jim Wade, Betty Prashker, Alan Mirken (emeritus), Michelle Sidrane, Chip Gibson, Allan Eady, Carl Apollonio (emeritus), Laurie Stark, Andrew Martin, Jim Davis, Deb Rowley, Bob DuBois, Kent Holland (emeritus), Cathy Collins, Ken Sansone, Vaka Pereyma, Gail

Shanks, and Victoria Heacock; I would like to say "thanks" for teaching me that writing and publishing a book is a genuine team effort.

My wife, Paula, and I celebrated our tenth wedding anniversary while *Thunder of Erebus* was in progress. I look forward to relying on her love and support during future endeavors, as I have in the past.

Finally, to Walter Boyne, the dean of American aviation writers, I must say I am indebted and honored for his unselfish advice, counsel, and encouragement.

As evidenced by this roll call, I received a tremendous amount of help along the way, and any errors that remain in the manuscript are mine and mine alone.

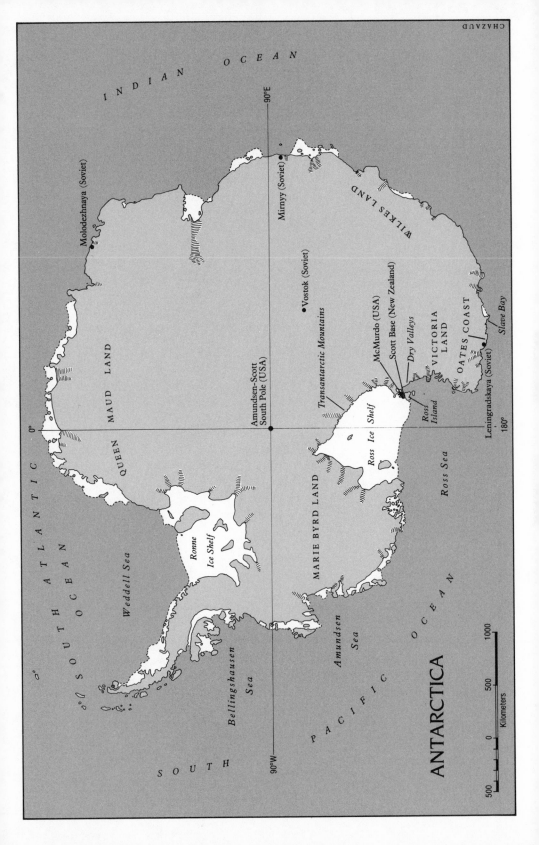

CHAZAUD

ANTARCTICA

INDIAN OCEAN

Molodezhnaya (Soviet)

Mirnyy (Soviet)

90°E

Vostok (Soviet)

WILKES LAND

McMurdo (USA)
Scott Base (New Zealand)
Dry Valleys

Transantarctic Mountains

VICTORIA LAND

OATES COAST

Slava Bay

Leningradskaya (Soviet)

180°

Amundsen-Scott
South Pole (USA)

MAUD LAND

QUEEN

0°

Ross Island

Ross Ice Shelf

Ross Sea

MARIE BYRD LAND

SOUTH ATLANTIC OCEAN

Weddell Sea

Ronne
Ice Shelf

Bellingshausen
Sea

Amundsen
Sea

PACIFIC OCEAN

SOUTH

90°W

1000

500

0

500

500

Kilometers

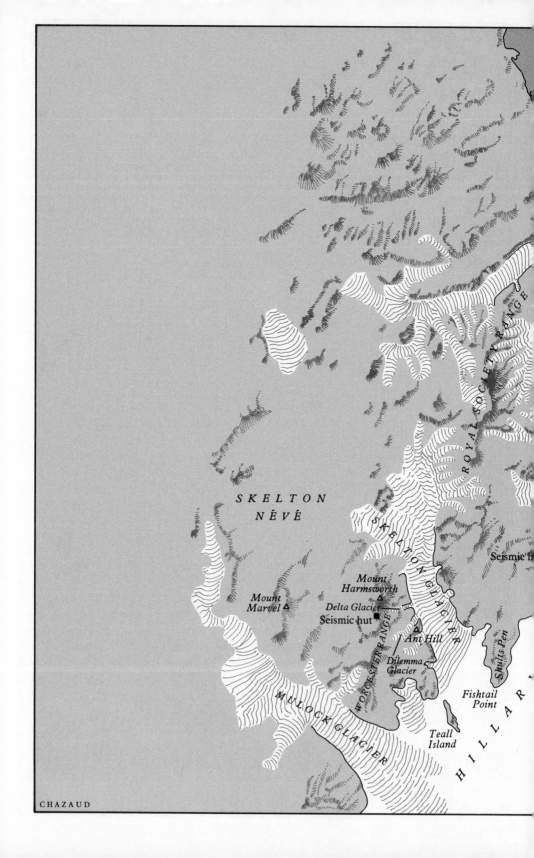

ROYAL SOCIETY RANGE

Seismic h

Skull's Fen

SKELTON
NÉVÉ

SKELTON GLACIER

Mount
Harmsworth

Delta Glacier

Seismic hut

Mount
Marvel

Ant Hill

WORCESTER RANGE

Dilemma
Glacier

Fishtail
Point

MULOCK GLACIER

Teall
Island

HILLAR

CHAZAUD

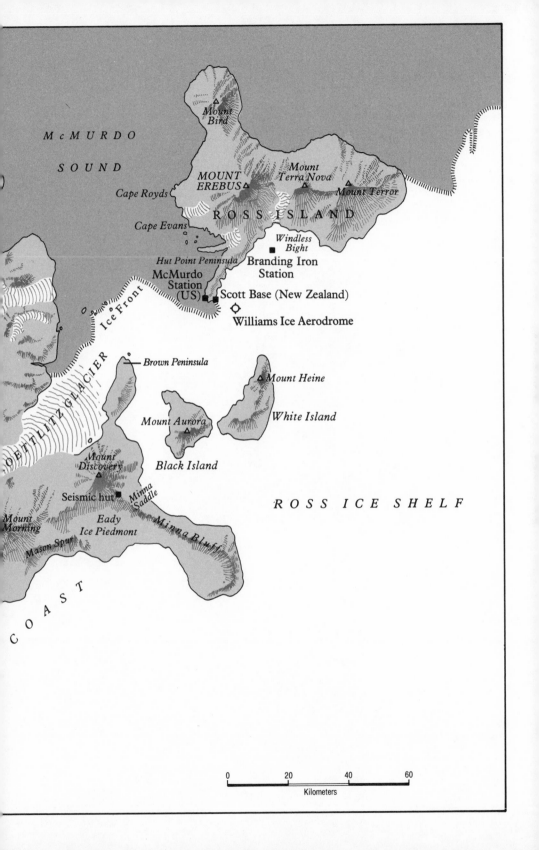

M c M U R D O

S O U N D

Mount
Bird

Cape Royds

Mount
Terra Nova

MOUNT
EREBUS

Mount Terror

R O S S   I S L A N D

Cape Evans

Windless
Bight

Hut Point Peninsula

Branding Iron
Station

McMurdo
Station
(US)

Scott Base (New Zealand)

Williams Ice Aerodrome

Brown Peninsula

Ice Front

Mount Heine

KOETTLITZ GLACIER

Mount Aurora

White Island

Mount
Discovery

Black Island

Seismic hut

Minna
Saddle

Mount
Morning

Eady
Ice Piedmont

Minna Bluff

R O S S   I C E   S H E L F

Mason Spur

C O A S T

0   20   40   60

Kilometers

THUNDER
OF
EREBUS

Erebus:

In Greek mythology, the son of Chaos and Darkness, the brother and husband of Nyx (the night).

Also known as that region of funereal darkness through which lost souls passed on their way to Hades—or, the lower world.

1

. . . .

THE GENIE

In northeastern Wyoming, the rugged grasslands along the Powder River Basin stretch gently westward until they rise up to form the Bighorn Mountain range. This vista of sagebrush and scrub grass is magnificent in its desolation, providing a natural counterpoint to the neighboring uplift of the Bighorns. Indeed, so empty is this landscape that it is difficult to believe it possesses a history that is starkly compelling. For it was here, on this desolate windswept plain, that the United States government lost a war fought on its own soil.

To provide access to the new promised land of the American West, the United States Army began construction of a road along the Bozeman Trail, which skirted the eastern rim of the Bighorn Mountains. It was a simple construction project, but by taking such an action the Army unwittingly lit the fuse to a powder keg—for the road the Army was building cut through the territory of the Oglala Sioux and Cheyenne Indian nations. To the Sioux and Cheyenne, this grassland east of the Bighorns was not simply another piece of real estate. It was one of their prime hunting grounds—their food source.

The powder keg blew, and for over two years the fury of the Cheyenne and Sioux nations rained down upon the white man in a clash of arms across the Bighorn territory. It was a conflict chilling in its savagery. Savage to the point that the United States government finally capitulated and signed a treaty in 1864, whereby the Bozeman Trail road was abandoned and the Bighorn territory was ceded as Indian land, closed to white settlement.

The chief who led the Sioux and Cheyenne nations in their fight to retain their Bighorn territory was a warrior of great temerity, yet he later became a champion of peace between the Indian and the white man. He was a noble savage, who remains to this day the only Indian leader to emerge victorious in his war with the United States.

His name was Red Cloud.

**KWAJALEIN MISSILE RANGE, MARSHALL ISLANDS,
WESTERN PACIFIC—November 18**

"Red Cloud Base, Red Cloud Base, this is Arrowhead One. Coming up to the drop zone IP in about nine-zero seconds. Are we go for curtain drop?"

The tactical action officer (TAO) aboard the USS *Red Cloud* listened to the static-laced voice through his headphones and shot a glance to the civilian beside him. The civilian had also monitored the transmission and held up a finger to the TAO, indicating that he needed a moment. The civilian was a sallow-faced man with a full beard and thick spectacles, who had unruly dark hair that seemed a stranger to a comb, he was wearing a borrowed navy blue jumpsuit that covered his unremarkable physique like so much sackcloth.

The two men were sitting in front of a large screen in the Combat Information Center (CIC) of the *Red Cloud,* which was an *Arleigh Burke*–class destroyer cruising through the Pacific waters west of the Marshall Island chain. It was shortly after 3:00 A.M., and the tension was building in the CIC chamber.

The tactical action officer was a thirty-four-year-old lieutenant commander who was extremely thin despite the good food served on board. So thin that his polyester uniform seemed to be draped on a coat hanger instead of a human frame. He was the focal point of considerable stress in the ship's nerve center, causing him to twitch in his seat continually, and to ask the civilian once more—somewhat testily this time, "How about it, Dr. Sharp? Are we ready?"

Garrett Sharp, Ph.D., the civilian guest aboard the *Red Cloud,* murmured into his headset one more time, then lowered his finger and said, softly, "The Scimitar is armed. Go for it."

The TAO nodded and turned his attention to one of four large display monitors that dominated CIC. The *Red Cloud*'s SPY1-D radar swept the airspace for 180 miles around the ship, while its UKY-1 computer translated the return impulses into display characters that peppered the screen. The TAO toggled his mike switch to transmit and said, "Gas Passer Flight, this is Red Cloud Base. We are green for test. I say again, we are green for test. Drop the curtain."

"Roger, Red Cloud," came the reply. "Turning to one-eight-three now."

The TAO watched the three green circles on his screen—denoting

Gas Passer Flight—as they turned onto a course of almost due south. This route of travel was perpendicular to, and slightly ahead of, the course of the *Red Cloud.*

Five thousand feet above the ship, the pilots of Gas Passer Flight finished out their formation turn until the digital compasses on their instrument panels read one-eight-three. The three aircraft were specially modified versions of the C-17 transport, and for this mission the term "Gas Passer" was not a misnomer, for each aircraft's cargo bay had been fitted out with a single gigantic pressure tank, and the rear loading door had been replaced with a nozzle about the size of a pickup truck. The pressure tanks were filled with highly compressed, negatively charged krypton gas.

The navigator on Gas Passer One watched the readouts from his chronometer and the satellite global positioning system, then poised his hand above the valve switch while droning, ". . . Four . . . three . . . two . . . one . . ." His hand came down on the switch as he said, "Dropping curtain now."

In the rear of each aircraft a nozzle valve turned, and a cloud of colorless krypton vapor spewed from the tails of Gas Passer Flight. Because it was almost three times heavier than the surrounding atmosphere, the gas billowed lazily down toward the ocean in an invisible curtain.

On the bridge of the *Red Cloud,* Capt. Darrell Odum looked out the window on a beautiful Pacific night. The ocean was tranquil with a mirror surface, and the stars formed a brilliant canopy as the vessel moved slowly along, traveling barely fast enough to maintain steerageway. Despite the beautiful evening, Captain Odum was in a foul mood—as he had been for the better part of the past year. He was a middle-aged man with dark hair, glasses poised above full cheeks, and a slightly paunchy waistline. So frequent were his foul moods that his crew now called him "Teakettle" behind his back, because he was steaming all the time. The *Red Cloud* was supposed to have been the capstone of Odum's twenty-seven-year naval career; however, for ten of the past eleven months the vessel had been in the Newport News shipyard, undergoing a high-tech facelift to install the super-secret Scimitar system, which transformed the *Red Cloud* from a warship to a seaborne experimental laboratory. The ship's rear missile deck and helicopter pad had been peeled off and replaced with a mysterious, elongated dome that possessed a single window on its starboard side. And on the starboard prow of the *Red Cloud* was a special, triple-pronged missile launcher that resembled Neptune's trident. Captain Odum was incensed over these mutations. This ship, *his ship,* had been commandeered and raped—yes, *raped*—by a brigade of silicon-chip snake-oil salesmen. Needless to say, the captain's interest level in this particular test mission wasn't very high, and he had only a vague idea of what it was all about. He loathed all the little techno-medicine-show intruders that were underfoot and crawling over his ship, he didn't understand half of what they said when they talked, and yet, according to his orders, he had to "extend the civilian guests every courtesy" while they executed this . . . this . . . *experiment.*

"Lord," Odum grumbled to himself. "Instead of a warship captain, I'm a mother hen to a two-billion-dollar floating guinea pig."

"Bridge, CIC," squawked the intercom.

Odum leaned over the arm of his captain's chair and brutally smashed the talk button. "Bridge."

"Captain, the curtain is dropping," said the TAO.

"Terrific," growled Odum. "Wake me when it's over." Then he announced to the men on the bridge, "Get your damn goggles on," as he fumbled with his own.

What was unfolding on the plot screen of the Combat Information Center was the culmination of two years' preparation. And as disinterested as the captain might be, all eyes in CIC were focused in rapt attention on the symbols dancing across the tactical display.

As the yellow triangle representing an aircraft called Arrowhead One moved past its IP (initial point) and entered the drop zone, the TAO hit his mike switch and said, "Arrowhead One, Arrowhead One, this is Red Cloud Base. You are go for egg drop."

"Roger, Red Cloud," came the reply. "Dropping eggs now."

Forty-seven miles south of the *Red Cloud,* the bombardier aboard the aging B-52, which was Arrowhead One, hit a series of switches on his armament panel, and almost immediately six sausage-shaped, air-launched cruise missiles dropped from the pods slung underneath the bomber's wings. The missiles continued free-falling from their nine-thousand-foot altitude until their wings deployed and their Williams F107-101 air-breathing turbofan engines came to life. Then, following the instructions programmed into their inertial guidance systems and radar altimeters, the six missiles continued their descent before pulling up at thirty-five hundred feet. Here the projectiles leveled off and fanned out until they were roughly abreast of each other on a line about two kilometers wide. They were all harmless, without warheads, and on a course that would directly overfly the *Red Cloud.*

Upon releasing his load, the pilot of the B-52 put his aircraft into a harsh right turn and pushed the throttles up to their stops.

Back in CIC, the anorexic-looking tactical action officer—who was the maestro of the operation—watched the screen intently as Gas Passer Flight continued their head-to-head course with the six cruise missiles. When their krypton tanks were empty, the C-17s also banked sharply to the east. "Is the Scimitar still armed?" queried the TAO nervously.

Garrett Sharp, looking remarkably calm behind his thick glasses, merely nodded.

On the screen, the *Red Cloud* was passing under the northern edge of the krypton curtain, while the cruise missiles were rapidly approaching from the south.

The TAO made a conscious effort not to glance at Sharp. Trying to figure out what the bespectacled genius was thinking was useless. The guy was impossible to read. So the TAO studiously ignored him while lightly tapping the safety cover on the firing switch for the Highwire missiles.

The tridentlike launcher on the prow of the ship held three custom-made missiles, code-named Highwire. They were simple devices, without guidance systems. Once they were fired, they would follow a trajectory to the south, each one playing out a spool of thin copper wire that remained anchored to the ship. Perhaps this was the reason for their code name.

In a complex air and sea ballet, the *Red Cloud* was on a perpendicular track to the downward-sloping krypton gas curtain, sliding under its northern fringe, while the six cruise missiles from the B-52 were twenty-seven miles out and rapidly approaching the curtain from the south. The Highwire missiles were poised on the starboard prow and ready to fire on a southerly trajectory.

The idea was to have the cruise missiles fly into the upper end of the krypton curtain as the rest of the gas cloud sloped down toward the ship—at precisely the right instant, under perfect atmospheric conditions.

On the CIC display screen, the six red triangles representing the cruise missiles crossed the green line of demarcation that denoted the southern fringe of the krypton gas curtain. "They're inside," the TAO said softly.

The cruise missiles continued on, plunging deeper into the cloud of vapor as the northern edge rapidly descended toward the decks of the *Red Cloud.*

The TAO flipped up the safety cover on the firing button and decided to give his companion another verbal nudge. "They're in the green zone, Dr. Sharp."

Garrett Sharp scanned his instruments for a final check and replied, "Scimitar is slaved to optical trigger . . . it's yours."

Without hesitation, the tactical action officer mashed the red button and immediately a vibration rumbled through the CIC compartment.

On the prow of the ship, the Highwire missiles roared off their trident launcher and raced into the southern night sky, just as the cloud of negatively charged krypton was approaching the decks of the *Red Cloud.* The positive electrical charges in the surrounding sea began their siren's song, coaxing the negative charges in the krypton cloud to come down and touch the sea in the Pacific night. They continued coaxing and coaxing, until finally the attraction was too great and the negative charges in the krypton curtain leapt through space, jumping onto the missiles' copper wire and racing toward the ship in a giant arc of man-made lightning. The air along this electrified channel heated to sixty thousand degrees Fahrenheit in an eyeblink, causing it to expand and smash into the neighboring layers of colder air, creating a natural cymbal-crash of thunder.

Captain Odum had to pace the deck of the specially insulated bridge by memory, because his goggles blocked out what little light there was. Odum despised the infernal goggles. Although they were supposed to fit over his eyeglasses, they did so only by mashing the frames into his face.

When the Highwire missiles launched, the bow of the *Red Cloud* erupted in flame. Through his goggles, Captain Odum could just barely make out their tail plumes as they quickly rose into the night. The plumes grew smaller and smaller in the distance, until everything appeared dark once again. Odum started to shake off the initial shock of the launch and relax, but then he experienced a prickly feeling that began teasing his neck and spine. Rapidly it became more pronounced and he started to scratch himself—then the hair on his scalp started to rise, just as a flash of white light enveloped the bridge and the windows shook with a thunderclap *BOOM!* The light was not just blinding, but penetrating, consuming, piercing—an intimate brush with the naked power of nature. Odum reeled back against the bulkhead in a reflexive spasm. A few seconds elapsed before he could regain his equilibrium and take a couple of deep breaths; then, when his senses had sufficiently cleared, he took a personal inventory and was grateful to find he was unharmed. "Damnation," was all he could mutter as he pulled off the goggles and pushed his glasses up on a nose turned slick with sweat. "Damnation . . . I . . . I haven't seen anything like that since a night-firing exercise on the *Missouri.*" He tried to mask the tremor in his voice as he asked the deck officer, "Course and speed?"

The dazed young officer held on to the instrument bin for reassurance as he pulled off his goggles with his free hand and said, "Course zero-nine-three. Speed three knots, Captain."

"Damage?"

The lieutenant murmured into his headset to the damage-control center of the ship and replied, "Negative, Captain."

Odum turned and looked out the window. Some ripples on the mirrored sea were dissipating, but everything else was calm, the night a canopy of stars. "Damnation," he whispered softly to himself. "Damnation."

In CIC, the Highwire missiles were being tracked on the display screen when the TAO and Garrett Sharp heard a muffled thunderclap, followed by a high-pitched whine.

Instantly, the six red triangles of the cruise missiles vanished from the screen, as if brushed away.

Stunned, the TAO ordered, "Air radar check."

A nearby petty officer punched a circuit test button on the console of his air radar scope, then looked up and announced, "The spy radar is working fine, sir."

The remaining officers and sailors in CIC were deferentially quiet. Although they'd worked on this project for almost a year, they were still amazed—and perhaps a little frightened—by what they'd just witnessed. The silence continued until Garrett Sharp said, in his soft monotone voice, "It worked."

2

. . . .

THE BOTTLE

ROSS ICE SHELF, NEAR THE U.S. SCIENTIFIC BASE AT McMURDO SOUND, ANTARCTICA—April 16

The drilling rig looked strangely out of place, as though it belonged somewhere in the West Texas oil fields instead of here, on the tundra-like setting of the Ross Ice Shelf. Particularly since it was covered with red canvas that made it resemble a teepee on the pervading whiteness of the Antarctic ice.

The gentleman who bore the time-honored title of "mud logger" unzipped the red canvas door of the drilling rig to step out of the cold and into the warmer chamber. He was wearing a red handlebar mustache and looked somewhat childlike in the parka that was draped over his elfin frame. His coat was worn open, with no gloves, because in the waning days of daylight in the austral autumn, the temperature had skyrocketed to a balmy fourteen degrees Fahrenheit. He approached a bear of a man who was helping guide a dangling section of drill pipe along the derrick's monkeyboard. This linebackerlike gentleman wore mud-spattered coveralls, a checkered wool shirt, a black beard over pink cheeks, and—like everyone on the derrick—a hard hat.

The mud logger tapped his friend's massive shoulder, causing him to turn and break into a wide grin. "Ah, Theodore." (He pronounced it *Tay-oh-door.*) "What do you have for me?"

The mud logger held up a plastic Baggie and shouted over the cacophony of the diesel engines and rotary drill, "You might want to shut it down, Ivan. Looks like we've hit a new formation."

Ivan Telenko nodded and turned to the "driller" standing in front of a console of controls. Ivan drew his finger across his throat to indicate he wanted the rig shut down. The driller fiddled with his instrument panel and the rotary table quit turning the "kelly" of the drill stem.

At first glance, one might assume this drilling derrick was hunting

11

for oil, but it wasn't. It was hunting for knowledge—searching for another tiny piece of geological data that would push back, if only by a small notch, the mystic veil that covered the Antarctic continent. And the men who populated this specially heated drilling derrick were probably the most highly educated group of roughnecks who ever pushed a rig tool, for they were part of the Soviet-American Antarctic Geologic Exploration Expedition that was jointly funded and operated by the U.S. National Science Foundation and the Soviet Academy of Sciences. The co-directors of the expedition were the mud logger with the red handlebar mustache, Dr. Ted Brendan, and the Siberian, Dr. Ivan Telenko. The two men could not have been further apart in appearance and upbringing, yet they were kindred spirits who had developed a close personal and professional friendship—keeping in touch through letters and professional conferences during the freezes and thaws in U.S.-Soviet relations over the past few years. Their own friendship had been struck at a conference on paleomagnetism in Prague, during the early period of Gorbachev's *glasnost* era. They had weathered the superpower freeze after Gorbachev's untimely demise, but now the ice was thawing anew—and the two geologists had exploited it to put together a joint project in a place that held their mutual fascination—Antarctica. And, sorrowfully, their expedition was coming to an end, along with the daylight hours of the austral autumn.

Dr. Theodore Brendan, of the University of Minnesota Geosciences Department, shook the rock chips in the Baggie and said, "Looks like we've broken through that basalt-trachyte strata and punched into another sedimentary level." He checked his watch and sighed with regret. "What say we push one more core and make it a wrap?"

The Siberian's brow furrowed as his mind searched for the right translation. "What is it?" he asked finally. "A 'wrap'?"

Brendan chuckled. "That means we're finished, old friend. For this season anyway. One last core, then you saddle up and head back to Vostok."

Telenko's eyes danced. American slang fascinated him, and catching the correct nuance always made his massive chest swell even more. "Saddle up? That mean pack bags. No?"

"Yes." Brendan smiled. "I'm afraid you have to leave, old buddy. If you stayed here any longer you'd turn into a U.S.-government-certified, apple-pie, hot-dog, and baseball American boy."

Telenko was entranced by the possibility. "You really tink so?"
The elf nodded. "Oh, yes, Ivan, I honestly *tink* so. No question.
Now let's pull the pipe up and get our core."

The Siberian bear and a couple of Brendan's strapping Ph.D.
candidates began the laborious process of plucking up the drill pipe
and moving it, piece by clanging piece, onto the monkeyboard so
they could move the coring bit into place.

The Ross Ice Shelf is a mammoth slab of ice—much of it floating—that is about the size of France or Spain, and ranges in depth
from a few tens of meters near landfalls, to almost a thousand meters
at its thickest known point. The shelf is something of a transitional
zone between the ice cap of the Antarctic continent and the open sea,
for although the shelf appears stationary, it is not. It is fed by
snowfall, by sea water freezing on its bottom, and by glaciers flowing
through the sievelike barrier of the Transantarctic Mountains. When
the continental ice passes through these mountains and becomes one
with the shelf, it then begins a snail-like journey toward the open sea,
moving five to ten feet per day. Where this cliff of ice reaches the
open sea, it forms a kind of natural colossus: a sheer face of ice that
looms two hundred feet above the surface of the water and looks—as
the explorer James Clark Ross noted—like something akin to the
white cliffs of Dover.

It is the body of these impressive cliffs that fracture and calve into
the great tabular icebergs, which are then nudged by ocean currents
toward the warmer, lower latitudes where they finally complete their
life cycle and melt into the sea water from whence they came.

The Soviet-American drilling operation on the Ross Ice Shelf had
bored through 562 feet of ice and into the lava apron that originated
from the volcanoes on Ross Island and spread underneath the ice
shelf. The drill bit had passed through the hardened lava and several
other geologic layers—before being plucked up by Ivan and Ted for
the final "coring."

Taking a core sample from the earth is conceptually simple. A
special dual pipe with a diamond cutting-rim bit is lowered into the
bore hole, then the plug of earth is extracted—much like a cork from
a bottle. This plug was 432 feet below the point where the ice rubbed
against the lava apron uplift in the sea floor. Once the core sample
was brought to the surface, it would be divided between the U.S. and

Soviet teams and shipped back to their respective countries, where
it would be dissected and analyzed. And a small piece of the puzzle
that was Antarctica would be revealed.

* * *

The activity hall at the U.S. scientific station at McMurdo Sound
was a simple wooden structure that often doubled as a gymnasium.
Behind the basketball goal was a small kitchen that was serving as
a bar on this particular occasion. Wooden structures fared well in
Antarctica because the cold and the extremely low humidity provided the right atmospheric conditions for the wood's longevity. A
hut constructed during Robert Falcon Scott's discovery expedition
was not far away—still relatively intact from the time it was built in
1902.

In the activity hall that "evening" (there was very little daylight
now) two large flags hung from the ceiling—one Soviet, one American—in honor of the joint enterprise that was coming to a close. A
couple of hundred people from the base populated the party, most
of them young to middle-aged male academics, but a few of the
partygoers were from the Navy logistical team, and fewer still were
women scientists. Some Warren Bernhardt jazz music drifted lightly
through the air as the scientists talked shop, discussing their work
and the research papers they planned to publish when they returned
to civilization. Research papers with esoteric titles such as *Terrestrial
Gyroscopic Effects and Gravity Tides,* or *Mesozoic Conchostrachan
Fossils,* or *The Sedimentology of Fine-Grained Permian Clastics.*
Soon the polar sun would disappear to mark the end of the scientific
season, and like a summer resort, the population of McMurdo Sound
would soon shrink from its apex of 1100 to its wintertime skeleton
crew of 180.

As the music played on, Ivan Telenko moved through the crowd
like an incumbent mayor on the hustings—laughing, hugging, backslapping, and reminiscing about his five months in this icebound
American enclave. He had become immensely popular around the
Sound because of his gregarious nature, and if there had been a
mayor's race at McMurdo, the big Siberian would have won hands
down.

But there was no mayor at McMurdo. The head honcho at the
base, and for all American interests on the continent, was the senior
U.S. representative—a tall, gangly-looking gentleman named Desmond Voorhees, who had spent the better part of the last nineteen

years in Antarctica, first as a graduate student, and later as a teacher of Antarctic meteorology. In spending so much time on the ice continent, he finally decided to join the staff of the National Science Foundation, where he worked his way up through their bureaucracy to become senior U.S. representative. Voorhees was six foot four, with thinning burnt-orange hair, and he had a curly beard that followed the pronounced jawline of his narrow face. He suffered from an extreme case of farsightedness, and as a result wore thick, metal-framed glasses that made it seem he was looking at you from behind a couple of ice cubes. Although a trifle eccentric, Voorhees filled the role of senior rep superbly, having to be scientist, arbitrator, polar accountant, ambassador, hard-ass manager, father confessor, and charming host, all rolled into one.

Telenko felt a hand come down on his shoulder as a familiar voice said, "Ivan, we're going to miss you." The Siberian turned and grinned. "Desmond!" (He pronounced it *Days-moon.*) "I shall miss you as well. Perhaps you come to Vostok next year?" Vostok was the Russian Antarctic station on the interior ice cap, some 750 miles away.

"Love to," replied Voorhees. "Perhaps you and Ted can put together another proposal for next summer. I'll see that it gets a fair hearing at NSF."

Telenko nodded with enthusiasm. "Excellent. I fly tomorrow with our core samples. It be interesting what we find."

"I'm sure it will. Please convey my respects to your colleagues at the Academy. I appreciate their funding half the cost of the drilling expedition."

"No problem," replied Ivan, smiling. The Siberian enjoyed exercising the horses in his stable of American slogans.

"So where does the Russian bear go from here?" queried a feminine voice. "Back to Siberia? Trading one icebox for another?"

Telenko turned again, this time to face a petite blonde who was wearing jeans, hiking boots, and a wool Pendleton shirt, and was holding a cocktail glass. "Dana!" he cried, while eveloping the woman in one of his hugs, almost causing her to spill her drink. She did not resist as his giant arms swept her in, and even let the embrace linger a bit longer than social etiquette required. But upon her release, Dana Harrow deliberately stepped back and smiled her wry smile. Her blond hair was cut in a pageboy style, and her nose had a slight upturn. Her body was small, but with definite curves, and

if you saw her for the first time the word *pert* would come to mind.
"Sorry to see you go, Ivan," she said. "Maybe we'll run into each
other again next season."

Telenko's left eyebrow formed an arch. "You come back next
year?"

Harrow swirled her Scotch and water while contemplating the big
Siberian. "You bet I come back next year. My project is only half
finished."

"Ahhh, of course. How I forget? Well, perhaps next year will
present us with another, ah, opportunity."

She smiled demurely. "Perhaps."

Women were in short supply at McMurdo Station. But conversely,
if you were an attractive woman—as Dana Harrow certainly was—
the available supply of men tended to be a bit too cerebral, too
test-tube-oriented, often married, and too consumed by their work.
That was why the manly Telenko and the comely Dana had been
attracted to one another—an attraction that had almost led to a
romantic interlude. But conflicting schedules, demands of research,
and curious colleagues had always seemed to get in the way. So their
mutual attraction never blossomed into a love affair.

The Siberian looked at her thoughtfully, then moved the conversation to a professional level. "And how is your project?"

Harrow shrugged. "It's been a struggle, but I finally have my
remote sensing posts installed. If they don't get blown away, they
should crank out some good data. At least until the batteries give out
or the recording discs fill up. I should have some solid information
to match with the deformation readings when I return next summer.
How about you?"

He scratched his graying beard and replied, "I hope core samples
will tell us more about composition of seabed geology under the ice.
But we shall see." Ivan held her smile for some moments before being
diverted by some other well-wishers.

After the party died down and the activity hall slowly emptied,
Ivan Telenko exited the building and walked down the graded road
to the motor-pool depot. An assortment of bizarre transports greeted
him as he made his way to the small Sno-Cat that had been assigned
to him. He fired up the diesel engine and dropped it into gear, causing
the hard rubber tracks to start churning through the volcanic ash.

McMurdo Station was sited at the end of a peninsula that stuck out from the southwestern corner of Ross Island. That is to say, the base was built on a volcanic formation, and several months of the year the snow melted away to leave a black, gritty ash underfoot. Telenko continued on, driving past the hodgepodge of austere and ugly structures that made up the base—a mixture of everything from Quonset huts to functional low-rise buildings. The Sno-Cat left the volcanic grit and drove onto the Ross Ice Shelf, heading for Williams Field, which was the iceborne airfield that serviced the base. It was about five miles away, as the crow flies.

Upon reaching the ice apron alongside the runway, Telenko turned his Sno-Cat toward the four C-130 Hercules cargo planes that were parked side by side with military precision—hard to miss with their distinctive orange tails and ski landing gear. Ivan figured the tails were painted orange to make them easier to locate after a crash. A comforting thought.

He drove along the ice apron until he found his core samples being loaded into the cargo bay of one of the aircraft. It was this Hercules that would take him back to the Russian station at Vostok. He got out and spoke with the Navy crew chief to ensure that all of his precious samples—which had been split fifty-fifty with the Americans—were accounted for. Once satisfied that they were, Telenko climbed into the Sno-Cat to head back to his dormitory room and grab some sleep before his departure. He would pack his personal gear tomorrow, say goodbye to Ted Brendan, and take off. But shortly after leaving the taxiway the Russian glanced at the sun and figured he had some daylight left, so impulsively he turned off the road and struck out across the white expanse of the ice shelf toward the Windless Bight.

The mass that is Ross Island—fifty-five miles long and twelve miles wide at its narrowest point—is dominated by the volcanoes Mounts Erebus and Terror; the former active, the latter extinct. The northern shore of the island faces out to the Ross Sea and its attendant pack ice, but the southern shore of the island—which is concave in shape—faces out to a region called the Windless Bight. The concavity of the island's southern shore acts as a kind of catcher's mitt to the northwestern tip of the Ross Ice Shelf, and it keeps the movement of the ice in the Windless Bight down to a crawl. While exploring the area, Brendan and Telenko had found a small rise in the ice shelf, indicating an uplift of Ross Island's submerged lava apron. They took a radar sounding that confirmed that the floating ice shelf was, indeed, grounded at that spot. This made it a good place for drilling because the ice movements at the site were minimal, and they would not have to contend with a layer of sea water between the ice and the lava apron. So it was in the Windless Bight that Ivan and Ted had decided to sink their hole and see what they could find.

Telenko's Sno-Cat kept cranking across the white tabular ice shelf, following the previously made tracks where he knew there were no crevasses. It was against the rules to go off the established roads alone, but since he was on a quasi-established path, Ivan felt he was just bending the rules, not breaking them. Eventually he spied the red canvas cover of the derrick house, and upon reaching the teepee-like structure he killed the engine and clambered out of the cab. With its diesel engine stilled, the drill site was majestically quiet. In the next few days, Ted Brendan's crew would break the derrick down and haul it back to McMurdo for storage through the long, dark, cold polar winter.

As Telenko circumnavigated the derrick, kicking up little puffs of snow crystals along the way, he thought fondly of his diminutive friend Ted Brendan, of Dana, and of the time he'd spent among the Americans. There was no question in Telenko's mind that these had been the happiest five months of his life—for here, in this remote and pristine land, the natural affinity between Russians and Americans came to the surface and flourished. The two peoples held much in common, in that they were both considered uncivilized brutes by the Europeans that geographically separated them. America had the Western frontier, Russia the Siberian taiga. The United States was an ethnic melting pot, the Soviet Union—or Confederation, as it was now—was even more of a mixed bag. No one liked the superpowers, but they were both grudgingly respected. And they had been allies during two world wars. Had it not been for the historical spike wedged between the two countries by Joseph Stalin, the natural relationship between the two peoples might have come into flower. But Stalin—whose evil eclipsed even that of Adolf Hitler—had painted America as his enemy, and that mind-set had continued through his long string of successors. The warming of Soviet-American ties had begun during Gorbachev's reign, but had been derailed with his death. Now, however, they were back on track, on an upward swing, and the Siberian bear found himself the beneficiary. Here, at the bottom of the world.

Telenko halted and listened to the primitive stillness of the ice.

There was hardly a breath of wind on this side of the island. He chuckled and said to himself, in English, "No wind. Perhaps that why they call it Windless Bight." He continued listening, but the silence was almost deafening. It was so remote. So still. And in a way it reminded him of his Siberian village. His journey from that remote village of Olenek to this point on the Ross Ice Shelf had been the product of hard work, a prodigious mind, fortuitous luck, and his mother's party connections. By practicing his geologic trade in the Siberian taiga, he'd struck upon a vast kimberlite deposit that had yielded a treasure trove of gem-quality diamonds. This discovery, which came to be known as "Telenko's Find," had catapulted him into membership in the Soviet Academy of Sciences. And now he was here. On the bottom of the world. Drilling a hole through a giant slab of ice and working with a gaggle of Americans. He was blissfully happy, and was so sad that it was coming to an end.

They were on the downside of the austral autumn now—the sun dropping below the horizon for twenty-one of every twenty-four hours—and soon McMurdo Sound would plunge into total darkness as nature closed its icy grip around the continent.

As Ivan Telenko immersed himself in the majestic vista of Mount Discovery, rising in the southwest, the sun slowly passed behind Mount Erebus—moving the volcano's shadow, inch by inch, across the ice field until it crept over the drilling derrick and the big Siberian standing alongside it.

A strange chill, not born of the temperature, came over the Russian, causing him to turn and face the volcano's darkened silhouette. Against the dusky, crystalline sky, Mount Erebus no longer seemed the benign presence it had been before. Somehow its countenance had been transformed—imparting to the human intruder a feeling that was malevolent, forbidding, colder than cold.

A wind from the seaward side of the island lifted up a cloud of ice crystals and spun them into the air, creating a whirlwind that was backlit by the unseen sun. As the light beams passed through the swirling ice crystals, they were both reflected and refracted, creating a dazzling sun pillar that hypnotized Telenko as it danced along the ridgeline of the mountain's silhouette. He remained there, mesmerized by the confluence of light, sky, ice, and mountain. But then, as quickly as it had appeared, the sun pillar vanished behind the ridge, leaving only the darkened silhouette of the volcano.

Involuntarily the Siberian pulled his parka closer, seeking some refuge from the chilling shadow that was now draped over him. The air seemed different somehow, having assumed a disquieting, even a sinister timbre. He longed for the sun pillar to reappear and provide him some solace, but it refused to obey his unspoken supplications. He was left alone on the ice—a silent, solitary figure, standing in the shadow of Mount Erebus.

3

· ·

THE DRY WELLS

**THE KREMLIN, MOSCOW, RUSSIAN REPUBLIC OF THE
SOVIET CONFEDERATION (RRSC)—June 21**

"Antarctica?"

To Minister of Defense Yuri Timoshenko, that word, spoken from
his own lips, seemed to sink into his chest like a steel spike, causing
his knees to go slack. He fell back into the overstuffed leather chair,
where he remained impaled for some moments, trying to regain his
equilibrium. Then, slowly, his dark brown eyes recovered a semblance of clarity and he leveled them at the wiry little man sitting
across the expansive desk. "Antarctica?" he repeated softly, the
shock almost too great to absorb. "Minos . . . are you certain? Are
you absolutely certain?"

The diminutive Minos Konstantos—Greek by blood, Georgian by
birth, physicist, member of the Soviet Academy of Sciences, and
(something of a rarity within the Soviet Confederation these days)
a Communist to his marrow—replied, "Yes, my dear Yuri Ilyanovich, there is no question whatsoever. The materials were analyzed
carefully, and I went over the test results myself to ensure the data
were correct. The core samples taken during the U.S.-Soviet geologic
expedition a few months ago indicate a substantial reservoir of the
carnallite mineral, which happens to contain an astonishing amount
of the rubidium-96 isotope. As a physicist, I have carefully followed
the research papers published by the Americans concerning their
gamma-ray laser research, as well as material supplied by the state
security committee's Technical Directorate." Konstantos took a moment to sip some of the Earl Grey tea from his glass, being careful
not to spill any on his black goatee. "Unfortunately, our ability to
conduct gamma-ray laser research has been virtually nil, for our
geologic teams have been unable to find a source of rubidium-96
within the Soviet Confederation. It was bad enough that the Americans had such a commanding lead in this field, but now to find that

21

they have a rich source of rubidium-96 just a veritable stone's throw from their base at McMurdo Sound; well, to say the least, it is frustrating. . . . And the fact that we helped underwrite this discovery is a most bitter pill to swallow."

Yuri Timoshenko leaned forward on his sledgehammer fists and pushed himself up from his chair. He took a few steps to the window of his office, which was on the second floor of the Council of Ministers Building in the Kremlin, and gazed out at the scene. It was a lovely summer's day, and the onion domes of St. Basil's Cathedral were peeking over the Kremlin wall, imparting a feeling of tranquillity and beauty. Ordinarily it would be a perfect time for Timoshenko to leave the office early, doff his uniform with its strangling gold braid and medals, and stroll along the Moskva River in comfortable civilian clothes. He might smell the flowers, feed a squirrel, feel the sun on his face, or perhaps glimpse the thigh of a young Russian girl as the breeze lifted her skirt just the right way. But now, with the news his Georgian-Greek friend had brought him, all thoughts of relaxation, or peace, had vanished. This news was serious. Deadly serious. "It is more than a bitter pill, Minos," he confided in a voice that quivered with genuine fear. "Your information goes far beyond being distasteful. This is a . . ." Silence hung in the air as Timoshenko searched for the proper word. "A cataclysm."

Konstantos was unsettled by his friend's reaction. The social circles of scientists and military men overlapped, but Konstantos had found Adm. Yuri Ilyanovich Timoshenko—former commander of the Red Banner Black Sea Fleet and now Minister of Defense—a man of striking abilities. Timoshenko was of medium height, but of ample girth, with large hands and feet, and his round head of thinning, dark, wavy hair rested upon the neck of an ox. He was, quite simply, of peasant stock with a peasant's body; but he possessed a suppleness of mind that consistently caught his friends, his superiors, and his subordinates off guard. He could recite Pushkin in Russian and Lamartine in French; and depending on his audience he could talk intelligently on plasma physics, soccer scores, Rachmaninoff's compositions, or missile guidance systems. Over the years, Timoshenko and the Georgian-Greek had grown close, acting as each other's confidant, friend, and sounding board. Because of this intimacy, Konstantos knew the defense minister's intellectual waters could take a sounding of remarkable depth, therefore the anxiety in Timoshenko's voice made him anxious as well.

"I do not understand, Yuri Ilyanovich, how could this discovery—at the South Pole, for God's sake—be such a cataclysm? Do we not have a treaty with the Americans outlawing space weapons? As a physicist, I know that this gamma-ray laser device will not work in the atmosphere. This is due to a phenomenon called—"

"The Compton Effect. Yes, I know, Minos, I know. You have read the open American papers on the gamma-ray laser, and I am quite sure you have seen the data provided by KGB's Technical Directorate, but have you seen any"—he was reluctant to continue—"any information concerning a secret American test in the Pacific late last year?"

Konstantos shook his head.

The admiral contemplated his friend. Although their backgrounds and upbringing were, indeed, poles apart—one a sailor, the other a scientist—the Russian knew they both shared a common gift, and that was their ability to recognize and seize upon two seemingly alien and inconsequential strands of information, then twist them together and view their refraction through a common prism. Timoshenko was looking through such a prism now, and the image he saw was fearsome. He needed this little Georgian-Greek. Needed his candor. Needed his support. Needed his wizard-like scientific mind to confirm his worst fears. Therefore he must be told.

The admiral went to a large cabinet in a corner of his spacious and ornate office. Half of the cabinet was a depository for wines, liqueurs, and vodka, while the other half was an electronic safe. He opened the rosewood door and punched in some numbers on a keypad. There was a hum and a click, then the steel door came open. He extracted a file and passed it to his friend with the terse comment, "Read this."

Konstantos took the red file, which was marked in bold black lettering:

OMICRON SECRET
ACCESS LEVEL:
MAIN MILITARY COUNCIL
STAVKA
ORIGINATION:
GRU, DIRECTORATE THREE

The *Glavnoye Razvedyvatelnoye Upravleniye* (GRU, or Chief Intelligence Directorate), which authorized the document, is organized into a number of departments, called directorates, and these are staffed and operated to serve the intelligence needs of the Defense Ministry's General Staff. The GRU includes such divisions as the Cosmic Directorate, which collects and analyzes photo imagery from spy satellites, an archive department that keeps track of the voluminous encyclopedic data an intelligence service is prone to gather, and the Sixth Directorate, which gathers electronic intelligence.

But the GRU's mainline spying operations on foreign soil—"human intelligence"—is handled by its First, Second, Third, and Fourth Directorates, and focuses on collecting foreign military data—everything from the circuit design of a French Exocet missile, to dossiers on regimental commanders in the British Army.

It is the GRU's Third Directorate that is responsible for human intelligence in the geographic regions of North and South America, the United Kingdom, Australia, and New Zealand.

When operating in a Third Directorate country, the GRU organization is referred to as a *Rezidentsiya,* and the GRU officer in charge is the legal *Rezident.* He is "legal" in the sense that he enjoys diplomatic immunity and possesses an embassy title like "military attaché" or "Ministry of Trade representative." The identity of the GRU *Rezident* in Soviet embassies is often an open secret, but many of the officers on his staff are harder to ID and keep consistently under surveillance. This is particularly difficult in a democracy of the Western Hemisphere, such as Mexico, where GRU officers enjoy ideal conditions: diplomatic cover, limited surveillance by host-country authorities, and easy access to the defense industry heartland of the United States. As a result of these superb circumstances, the Soviet Embassy in Mexico City is absolutely teeming with GRU officers who work unceasingly to identify and recruit "illegal" agents working in the military or defense industry along the American West Coast. Potential targets like TRW, Vandenberg Air Force Base, Northrop, Hughes Aircraft, Boeing, and the American naval base at San Diego—to name but a few—are enough to make any GRU *Rezident* salivate, regardless of the prevailing diplomatic climate. So tempting is this intelligence gold mine that the GRU places many of its top people—the best of the best—in its Mexico City *Rezidentsiya,* one of whom was a legendary figure named Tamir Zaporozhian.

Zaporozhian was a Cossack by birth, and with his swarthy looks and prodigious language skills he could, and did, pass for anything from a Mexican businessman to a Lebanese goatherder. Zaporozhian became the deputy *Rezident* of the Soviet embassy in Mexico City, and it was he who struck upon the strategy of not developing agents directly in the United States himself. Instead, he focused on developing agents within the Medellín drug cartel, which turned out to be a painfully easy thing to do. All it took was a lot of money and a little patience. By working through his drug proxies, he was able to follow the distribution chain of Colombian cocaine through Mexico and into California, then down through the "wholesale" and "retail" levels. His proxy agents carefully and methodically built up a list of retail customers served by the distribution chain, then step by step they assembled information on those customers—things like age, education, occupation, appetites, and habits. Most of these customers were, of course, useless to Zaporozhian, but his painstaking efforts brought a few precious pearls to the surface. And when that happened, Zaporozhian would personally intervene and "handle" the target.

One such target was a male word-processing clerk at the Lawrence Livermore Laboratory who had once been a regimental clerk-typist in the Marines, and had been hired by Livermore because of his efficiency and security clearance. The young man had come from a Midwestern background and was schooled in traditional values, but the hedonistic enclaves in California had seduced him, pulling him into the mire of cocaine addiction. When Zaporozhian took him over, the young clerk-typist had only been up to his ankles in cocaine. But the GRU man pretended to be his friend, doling out larger and larger packets of the white powder at lower and lower prices until the ex-Marine was sucked into the vortex of absolute addiction, and Zaporozhian owned him, lock, stock, barrel, and security clearance. From that point forward, every comma that went into the young man's Livermore word-processor file also went into a dead drop earmarked for a GRU pickup agent.

What Minos Konstantos was reading with rapt attention in the Kremlin office of the Soviet Minister of Defense was a verbatim translation of Garrett Sharp's after-action report on the Scimitar graser test in the Western Pacific.

TO: John Fairchild, Assistant Secretary of Defense, Defense Advanced Research Projects Agency, Pentagon, Washington, D.C.

FROM: Garrett Sharp, Chief, Scimitar Development Project, Lawrence Livermore Laboratory, California

SUBJECT: After-Action Report, Scimitar Operational Test, Kwajalein Missile Range

ABSTRACT

Historical Review

As you are well aware, the Strategic Space Defense Limitation Treaty curtailed any further space-based research on the gamma-ray laser (graser) for strategic missile defense. That same treaty, however, allowed "terrestrial research" on the graser to continue. Under the direction and funding of your department, Livermore has continued research on potential terrestrial applications of the graser, and in view of the Scimitar test in the Pacific, I think I can say our results have been nothing less than astonishing.

Compton Effect

Due to its incredibly short wavelength, the graser releases an energy pulse equivalent to thousands of megatons, but when this energy wave is discharged in the atmosphere, its wavelength immediately begins to lengthen. This phenomenon is called the Compton Effect, and it rapidly saps the power of the graser pulse—to the point that it would be virtually useless as a ground-based weapon. However, because outer space is a vacuum, the graser held incredible potential as a space-based defense system because there was no atmosphere to produce a Compton Effect. The Space Defense Limitation Treaty curtailed this research, but in continuing the terrestrial research, some extraordinary breakthroughs were made that led to the Scimitar Project.

Scimitar

In the laboratory we found that if the graser was fired within, and at the precise moment of, an electrostatic discharge, the Compton Effect was dampened to a small degree. In essence, it is like a Western gunslinger kicking open the swinging door of a saloon and firing his six-shooter. During the brief moment the door is open he has a clear shot, but then the door rapidly closes and blocks his fire.

The detailed results of the Scimitar test are included in the body of this report, but the essence of the test is this: We successfully slaved the firing of the graser within an artificially induced lightning discharge, which delivered an energy blast equivalent to two megatons that destroyed a number of aerial targets at a range in excess of nine miles.

We cannot explain why such a discharge dampens the Compton Effect. We can only observe it.

Significance of Scimitar Test

The ramifications of this test are beyond measure, for if a deployable terrestrial graser weapon can be developed—and I am confident that it can—it would alter ground warfare as we know it. A graser weapon mounted in an aircraft could destroy a brigade of attacking tanks in the blink of an eye. In effect, it would provide the destructive power of a nuclear weapon without nuclear fallout. Whoever had such a device could control, say, the Persian Gulf—for they would possess the ultimate conventional weapon.

Strategic Reserve

The downside of all this is that our supply of rubidium-96 (Rb-96) is virtually depleted. When Rb-96 is treated in a nuclear reactor it becomes the isotope Rb-98, which is the only isomer substance we have found that has the requisite properties for the graser. It has a half-life of fourteen months, which means roughly every year our supply is slashed by half.

Our only source of Rb-96 has been a deposit in the Sawtooth Mountains of Idaho, but that has played out. If a new supply of Rb-96 could be secured, it would enable us to continue research on the terrestrial graser and pursue peaceful applications as well, which include medical imaging and semiconductor manufacturing. . . .

Upon finishing the report, the little Georgian-Greek slowly closed the red file and ran his fingers over the black lettering. Then with an ashen face he looked up at Timoshenko and asked, "Yuri, how in God's name did you obtain this document?"

Timoshenko, who had four sons and was not insensitive to the document's history, replied, "By the most distasteful means you could imagine, Minos." The defense minister sighed and surveyed his sumptuous office with its ornate desk and luxurious appointments. Timoshenko thought of his prestigious position, his bemedaled uniform, his Zil limousine. Then his gaze fell upon the manicured, peasantlike hands hanging out of his tailored, gold-braided sleeves, and he realized how dirty those hands really were. "Yes," he murmured softly, "by distasteful means . . . but that is my problem, dear Minos, not yours. I must know, what is your scientific interpretation of this document?"

The Georgian-Greek was fidgeting in his chair, now looking at the problem through the same prism that had frightened the Russian admiral. "I . . . I can't say for certain, but on this first reading I find it chilling. The power of a nuclear weapon without the drawbacks of fallout? . . . That would mean . . ."

"That would mean our conventional defenses would count for
nothing. And I mean *nothing*. . . . And that would mean . . ."
Although the room was climate-controlled, Timoshenko found himself sweating. He took out a white linen handkerchief and wiped his
face, then he returned to the cabinet safe and withdrew another red
folder and took it to his desk. His voice was quivering now. "Minos
. . . what I am about to show you is even more sensitive than what
you have just read. You must not reveal to anyone that I have
disclosed this to you. But I must have your counsel. I am at a loss
as to what to do."

With a trembling hand, Minos Konstantos took the file that had
an equally potent warning emblazoned upon it, and opened it to the
first page, which read:

OPERATION TIGER'S CLAW

TO: Minister of Defense

FROM: Operations Staff, STAVKA

Overview

In response to the extraordinary report furnished by the Minister of
Petroleum, you were directed by the Confederation Cabinet to prepare an
operations plan, code name "Tiger's Claw."

The Petroleum Minister's report shows unequivocally that due to the
devastating reserve shortfall in the Tengiz oil fields, the Soviet Confederation's domestic production of oil will fall ten percent per year over the
next five years. Exploration and production of oil, even with Western
assistance, has not kept pace with national requirements. This year the
Soviet Confederation will cease being an exporter of oil. Next year we will
have to import as much as we can afford. Two years from now we will
face extraordinary shortages—just as our domestic automobile industry
is to be taking root. Three years from now our economic progress will
be irreparably harmed and the fabric of our new Confederation may
begin to disintegrate.

While new reserves of natural gas have been found and brought on
line, these new resources are earmarked for export to provide foreign
currency that is fueling our economic development. Also, our industrial
base does not have the time or the resources to retool from oil to natural
gas.

The inescapable fact is that our domestic oil shortfall will reach devastating proportions. Our wells are running dry and new reserves are

scarce, while, at the same time, our domestic demand is growing. We cannot afford to buy foreign oil. We cannot afford to lose Western capital and technical assistance. But if we do not gain access to a new supply of oil, our economic rebirth will be stillborn just as our people are growing accustomed to an improved standard of living.

Operation Tiger's Claw is designed to address these issues.

Tiger's Claw: Operational Summary

The crux of the Tiger's Claw operational plan is to:

1. Implement a combined airborne, armored, and motor rifle thrust into the major oil-producing territories of Iran.

2. Using thirty-two divisions, we will seize the major oil-production facilities, neutralize the remaining Iranian armed forces, and install a friendly political regime.

3. Immediately announce and implement a policy of keeping the Strait of Hormuz open to free and innocent international passage, and provide assurances to Western powers that their oil lifeline to other Persian Gulf countries will remain open.

Western Response

The position paper provided by the Foreign Minister regarding Tiger's Claw anticipates diplomatic outrage and perhaps some economic sanctions from Western powers, but with vigorous assurances from the Soviet Confederation, no military response is anticipated for the following reasons:

1. As demonstrated in the Gulf War with Iraq, Western lines of communication are extraordinarily long, and transporting a vast armed force to a combat zone in the Middle East would take Western powers a matter of months, not weeks. By that time the Iranian situation will be secured.

2. The Soviet Confederation's lines of communication to the Persian oil fields are short: we share a common border with Iran.

3. While Western military forces are qualitatively proficient, they have shrunk substantially. We enjoy numerical superiority, even with our major reductions. If the West was to engage the Soviet Confederation in combat on a broad level in Iran it would require:

—A much larger call-up of reserves than occurred during the Gulf War. This would give any Western leader pause.

—Civilian airlift and sealift capacity would have to be appropriated on a much larger scale than occurred during the Gulf War.

4. Iran has long been hostile to the West, particularly the United States, therefore the Soviet Confederation's presence may even be considered an improvement by some Western political leaders. Therefore, if

any economic sanctions are imposed on the Soviet Confederation, they would probably be lifted after a politically acceptable timeframe.

In summary, it is the Foreign Minister's view that *as long as the oil continues to flow to the West,* they will not respond militarily.

The detailed operational plan of Tiger's Claw is outlined herein.

Minos Konstantos read a few more pages before slapping the file closed. He was both enraged and stunned. "Yuri, this is insane! I cannot believe you have endorsed something like this."

Timoshenko stood and leaned forward on his fists once more. "Of course I do not endorse this lunacy! You think I learned nothing from Afghanistan? From Iraq? This is not so much a military plan as it is a political document." The defense minister took his handkerchief and ran it over his forehead again as he collected his thoughts. "Minos, you know as well as I that the only thing that is holding this Confederation of ours together has been our economic progress, which has been fueled by investment capital from the West. But in the face of this progress, many of my comrades are bitter. Their careers have been shattered. There are many in the army and the government who would embrace this insane plan as a means to go back to the old ways. The reason I am here, in this post, is that I supported Chairman Kostiashak in his reforms, but I know his position is fragile. Together, he and I were able to dissuade the Confederation Cabinet from implementing Tiger's Claw . . . for the time being. That is because I was able to convince them that an invasion of Iran would not be the simple exercise envisioned in this document. The Iranians have virtually no air force, but they do have a thousand serviceable tanks—which we sold them, by the way. And I think it would mean a fight with the West, particularly the Americans. Such a fight would be costly, but I feel we would prevail over the Americans for the reasons outlined in the Tiger's Claw plan. But the point, dear Minos, is that this discovery in Antarctica changes everything."

The little Georgian-Greek was puzzled. "How can that be?"

"Because if the Americans are able to secure this supply of rubidium and can fashion an effective terrestrial graser weapon, they *could* stop our invasion of Iran in its tracks. . . . But if we could secure the rubidium supply for ourselves and build a graser weapon, then no one could stop us from taking the Iranian oil fields. It would be a seductively easy option for the Cabinet to embrace. I know the Cabinet, Minos. It is very much like the old Politburo. The way they see it, if we do not seize a new supply of oil, then this Confederation will fragment, and we will descend into civil war—and those in the Cabinet will personally lose everything."

Konstantos pulled on his goatee for some seconds before replying. "If we were able to secure this source of rubidium, we could possibly use it as a means to forestall an invasion of Iran. The gamma-ray laser has extraordinary potential for energy generation. Although it would take some time to develop, in the long term it could potentially alleviate much of this oil-supply problem—of which I knew nothing. Possessing a rubidium supply would perhaps placate the Cabinet. At least for a time—time enough to find another solution to this oil dilemma. Another solution besides a second Afghanistan."

Timoshenko sat back down. "So, it is a two-edged sword. If the Soviet Confederation were to gain control of the rubidium supply, we could possibly develop a new energy source and not face the horror of an Iranian invasion. But if the Americans extract the rubidium for themselves, then we lose a potential energy source and the Americans can prevent us from seizing the oil fields."

Konstantos thought for a few moments, then nodded. "I would say you are quite correct."

Timoshenko buried his face in his enormous hands and softly murmured, "Then the Cabinet will not allow the Americans to take that rubidium deposit for themselves. . . . Oh, Minos, I tell you, if there were any way I could suppress your report on that Antarctic discovery, I would."

Konstantos gulped. "If . . . if you feel it necessary, my friend, then do so. You may rely upon my . . . discretion."

Timoshenko was humbled by his compatriot's loyalty. "No . . . no, Minos, they"—he jerked a thumb toward the ceiling, indicating the Cabinet conference room on the floor above—"they must be told. Everything. It would only be a matter of time before they found out anyway. Russia has not changed *that* much."

Konstantos nodded. "Very well, Yuri Ilyanovich, as you wish. But perhaps you are making too much of this."

The Russian admiral, who knew the Cabinet from the inside, as his Greek friend could not know it, replied, "I think not, Minos. I think not."

UNIVERSITY OF MINNESOTA, MINNEAPOLIS—June 25

. . . The tectonic compression of the eastern and western continental plates thus created the uplift that formed the Transantarctic Mountain range along the Shackleton-Hillary-Scott Coast. In contemporary times, volcanic activity has occurred in other areas of the Antarctic continent, but in the region mentioned above, the only remaining activity is the Ross Island volcano of Mount Erebus.

Dana Harrow stretched and leaned back in the chair of her office—or, rather, the glorified broom closet that served as her office. As with most graduate students in most universities, the graduate teaching assistants at the University of Minnesota Geosciences Department were consigned to tiny offices. Harrow's cubbyhole provided her with little room, except for her desk, her word processor, and the surrounding bookshelves that were crammed with a mélange of geologic texts and journals.

Dana grimaced at the stack of ungraded test papers on her desk—a product of the summer school sophomore geology class she taught. She sighed and tried to remember when she was a sophomore. After pondering the question for some moments, she decided it must have been sometime during the Paleozoic Era.

Dana grew up as the stereotypical California girl. Only child. Middle-class family. Generic high school routine, except that she was a cheerleader. She attended the University of California at Davis, where she picked up a degree in nursing and a philandering husband. Divorce followed, and she settled into the single-woman-nursing routine at San Francisco General Hospital. Intensive care. Grew up fast. The hours were long, the work sometimes rewarding but mostly grueling, the pay good, the cost of living high, and she watched a lot of people die.

She might still be slugging away there, instead of here, had she not taken that trip to Hawaii. The Big Island. Saw an eruption of Mauna Loa and was never quite the same again. The natural violence of the earth in upheaval mesmerized her and fired her imagination as nothing else had, and from that moment forward she knew what she wanted to do. Upon deplaning at San Francisco International she immediately began tracking down graduate fellowships and tallied up the required credits for a Ph.D. in geophysics.

So here she was, six years later, thirty-three years old, in hock up to her eyeballs in student loans, and pounding a word processor in a closet at the University of Minnesota. But at the end of the tunnel was a Ph.D. sheepskin and a position as assistant professor at the University of Hawaii—teaching more basic geology, but also giving her a chance to pursue research in her chosen field of volcanology.

A face sporting a large red handlebar mustache poked through the door. "Say, Dana, you still here? It's seven-thirty."

Harrow looked up at Ted Brendan and smiled, then pointed at the stack of ungraded test papers on the desk. "Afraid so. I still have to grade those for the troglodytes"—her standard epithet for sophomores—"so I'll be here a while yet." Brendan nodded, recalling his own graduate-school days. He had become her mentor, friend, and sponsor in her quest for the Ph.D.—and he was also her connection to Antarctica. "Did you get the NSF form? I put it in your in-box. We have to get that returned pronto."

Harrow reached into another stack of papers and extracted a thick printed form. "Right here. I was going to get to it this weekend."

Brendan nodded. "Okay. Don't stay too late. Afraid I gotta go. Have to read the kids a story before bed."

Harrow waved him off and he quickly vanished. Ted was such a super friend, she thought. Wistfully she wondered why all the good guys were already married. She sighed once more as her gaze fell upon the National Science Foundation form, which would be her ticket back to Antarctica and the harvest of data for her dissertation.

As the thought of the ice continent filled her mind, it triggered a feminine reaction, causing her to pull open her desk drawer. She extracted a small vanity mirror, pulled back the blond bangs of her pageboy haircut, and minutely inspected her face. Dana was a beautiful woman who possessed a distinct jawline, high cheekbones, and a slightly turned-up nose. But ever since she was thirteen she'd suffered from chronic skin problems. Been to every zit doctor on the West Coast, and tried every medicinal cure from clam juice to retin-A in an attempt to clear up her complexion—all to no avail. As a result, she often wore thick makeup to cover her problematic blemishes. She hated the makeup intensely because it gave her face an opaque quality and made her look like something of a loose woman. But then, in Antarctica, something bordering on the miraculous had happened. Perhaps it was the pristine air, or the globs of sunblock she rubbed on to guard against the sunshine; but whatever the reason, her skin had taken on a new vitality and cleared up until it was as smooth as a baby's backside. For the first time since she was twelve years old, Dana had chucked her makeup and faced the world with an unblemished face. It was intoxicating.

When she'd returned to civilization, though, the blemishes had returned—but with only half their intensity. As she inspected her face, she remained hopeful that a second Antarctic treatment would clear up her skin totally, once and for all. That, alone, was worth freezing her ass off for a few months.

She stretched again, then leaned over the word processor to take another small step on the long road that was her dissertation.

. . . Mount Erebus is the sole remaining active volcano on Ross Island. The island's formation is the result of intersecting extensional fractures that produced coalescing masses of lava. . . .

4

· · · · · · · · · · · · · · · · · · · ·

OVER THE SEA

THE KREMLIN—June 30

Minister of Defense Yuri Timoshenko ran his fingers along the hull of the ship that occupied a corner of his sprawling office. The hand-carved rosewood replica was almost four meters long, and the admiral thought it a beautiful thing; for it was an exact scale model of the Soviet Union's first supercarrier, the *Tbilisi*—a magnificent ship of seventy thousand fully-loaded tons that was roughly on a par with the *Forrestal*-class of American supercarriers. Like its U.S. counterpart, the *Tbilisi* possessed the angled flight deck and a starboard-mounted conning tower. But unlike the newer class of American *Nimitz*-class carriers, the *Tbilisi*'s belly was fired by fuel oil, not by a nuclear reactor. Timoshenko's feelings for the vessel were obvious as he lovingly caressed its keel, then picked up one of the hand-carved models from the flight deck. Gently he toyed with the replica of the twin-tailed Sukhoi-27 Flanker interceptor in his enormous hands, and for only the twenty-third time that day he wished he were on the deck of the magnificent ship instead of stewing in this confining office.

Admiral Timoshenko had come up through the officer ranks of the submarine corps, and the submarine—of all classes and sizes—had long been the capital ship of the Soviet Navy. Timoshenko knew submarines. Knew their power, their mystery, their capabilities—and their limitations. In spite of his love for the underwater vessel, he had long envied the Americans' marriage of air power and sea power in the form of the supercarrier. He knew such a hybrid possessed many shortcomings, but also some compelling strengths. If the Soviet Navy ever clashed with the U.S. on the open sea—out of range of the Soviet Navy's land-based long-range bomber force—Timoshenko knew his chance of victory would be close to nil. Therefore, he had lobbied the Navy for much of his career to build a vessel like the *Tbilisi,* and in so doing had antagonized much of the senior nautical staff. So forceful was his advocacy of the carrier that he had placed his career in jeopardy—to the point of becoming a pariah, a Russian Rickover of sorts. Indeed, Timoshenko might have finished out his career commanding a coastal patrol boat out of Vladivostok, had someone not heard his cry in the wilderness—and that someone was a man named Col. Gen. G. A. Kuznetsov, commander of the Soviet Navy's aviation arm. A politically astute man, Kuznetsov sensed the value of having a junior submarine admiral as an aviation advocate, and Kuznetsov became Timoshenko's mentor. Then, as the carrier idea took root in the Navy, Timoshenko's star rose rapidly until he became commander of the Red Banner Black Sea Fleet, where he supervised the laying of the *Tbilisi*'s keel in the Nikolayev shipyards.

As the Cold War wound down, the political leadership wanted a committed reformer at the helm of the Defense Ministry, and Timoshenko got the nod. It was not a position he sought. Wrestling with defiant generals in the Red Army while cutting their appropriations was, quite simply, a bitch. To keep the Defense Ministry from falling apart, he'd doled out the shrinking military budget with an eye on politics as well as strategy. Yet, as the force structure shrank, he still insisted on retaining the best men and equipment in the military, and on fostering improvements in their training. He also labored incessantly to enhance their morale. To do all of that while keeping the supercarrier program on track was a Herculean task that would have overwhelmed a lesser man.

But Yuri Timoshenko was not a lesser man. The admiral picked up the model of the Flanker and balanced it on his massive upturned finger. The wooden plane wobbled slightly, but remained suspended on its perch. *So many things are balanced now*, he thought. *There is so much promise, yet so much peril.* Russia was at last making genuine economic progress. Not "smoke and mirrors" advances, but real, food-on-the-table progress. Given the time, Timoshenko felt the economic reforms would become entrenched; but one little hiccup, one ill-blowing wind, and the fragile control of the Cabinet over the new Confederation would unravel, and the *Rodina* would lose its balance to plunge back into the abyss of the old ways.

And now that ominous abyss loomed before him, in the most imponderable of places—the godforsaken wastes of Antarctica.

There was a knock on the door and Timoshenko grabbed the model as it teetered off his finger. The admiral's aide poked his head through the opening and said, "Academician Konstantos to see you, Defense Minister."

Timoshenko nodded, grateful to have a friendly shoulder upon which he could lean. The energetic Georgian-Greek joined the admiral beside the model of the *Tbilisi* and immediately sensed that his friend was troubled. The scientist's goatee twitched as he asked, "Tell me, Yuri Ilyanovich. What were the results of your meeting?" And he pointed to the ceiling, indicating the Cabinet conference room on the floor above.

Timoshenko looked as if he were studying the Flanker model, but his mind was elsewhere as he replied, "Not good, I am afraid, Minos. Not good at all. The Cabinet grasped at once the significance of the rubidium discovery on the ice continent, and they do not know what to do. Some want to seize the place at once, while some say it is not worth the danger, and others cannot make up their minds. But all are afraid. Even the Chairman. I could see it through his grandmaster's mask. A fearful Russian is a dangerous thing, Minos. A most dangerous thing."

Konstantos nodded in understanding. "You are quite correct, Yuri Ilyanovich. But what was their decision? What are you going to do?"

The admiral sighed. "The decision was to do nothing . . . for the moment at least. Let sleeping dogs lie, as the saying goes. The rubidium is under almost two hundred meters of ice, so one hopes that will deter the Americans. I have been told to watch the site carefully, and if the Americans do nothing, we do nothing."

Konstantos pondered the admiral's reply for a few moments, then asked, "But what if the Americans try to mine the rubidium?"

Timoshenko's broad shoulders sagged. "Then, my friend, we must be ready to strike—quickly and forcefully, to take that damned frozen spot on the bottom of the earth for our own . . . at least long enough to extract a hundred metric tons of ore for ourselves and create a stockpile. On this the Cabinet would not yield a centimeter. Not even the Chairman could restrain them."

The scientist's goatee twitched. "But perhaps if we went to the Americans and tried to negotiate some sort of settlement of this issue . . ."

The admiral waved the model in the air and said, "The Cabinet dismissed that out of hand, Minos. If we tried to negotiate, we would alert the Americans that we wanted what they had. Then they could suspend their observance of the Antarctic SCAR Treaty and fortify their base at McMurdo Sound. At this moment they have no defenses there. . . . And who can say, perhaps they do not even know the rubidium is under their very noses."

The physicist shook his head. "Yuri Ilyanovich, I am frightened of what this could mean."

In frustration, Timoshenko raised his voice. "I know what it can mean, Minos. But I have my orders. If the Americans move, I must prepare the armed forces of the Motherland to strike!" And with that he slapped the model airplane down on the flight deck of the wood-sculpted *Tbilisi.*

THE BLACK SEA—July 1

The Su-27 Flanker interceptor slammed down onto the angled flight deck of the *Tbilisi,* its tail hook kicking up sparks as it grabbed the arresting wire pulled taut across its steel surface. "Wire" was really a misnomer, for it was really a hawserlike steel cable that was snagged by the aircraft's tail hook. As the Flanker hurtled forward, the wire played out through a pulley system and engaged a hydraulic piston that ultimately reined in the twenty-ton aircraft.

On the conning tower bridge, *Vitse* (Vice-)-Adm. Gavriil Strekalov smiled with approval as the Flanker pilot raised the tail hook, then followed the hand signals of the deck master and taxied his aircraft to the waiting elevator that would take the interceptor to the hangar deck below.

As deputy commander of the Red Banner Black Sea Fleet, Strekalov was always enthralled with the balletic precision of flight-deck operations, and he relished his perch on the bridge of his flagship. The *Tbilisi* had a separate flag bridge for him, but he didn't care for it. He preferred to be on the ship's bridge, and surprisingly, the captain of the supercarrier enjoyed having him there—to the point that he'd ordered a second captain's chair installed alongside his own for the admiral's use. Strekalov couldn't view the flight deck very well from a stand-up position. He was only five foot five, but as a former weightlifter he was built like a fireplug. His head was shaped like a rugby ball with close-cropped hair, and his arms were so muscular it seemed he would have difficulty bringing them to his sides when standing at attention. And although small in height, he was tall in stature in the eyes of his men.

The *Tbilisi* was cruising almost dead center in the Black Sea, heading due south into the wind at twenty-one knots to launch and recover her aircraft. Strekalov leaned over and said to the captain, "Dmitri, it is a beautiful day. I think I will go outside."

Captain, First Rank, Dmitri Vaslov, tall, blond, and as handsome as his superior was not, smiled and replied, "Very well, Admiral. Do not forget your ear protectors."

Strekalov laughed as he hopped out of the swivel chair. "You are worse than my wife, Dmitri. But whatever you say, Captain. He is your ship."

Strekalov left the buzzing activity of the bridge and walked out onto the flying bridge. He handed his hat to a senior seaman, then put on a pair of ear protectors that looked like a set of stereo headphones, and stepped up on the little platform that had been welded onto the deck just for him. The admiral rested his arms on the rail, and as the salt air hit him in the face, he inhaled deeply, entranced by the cloudless sky, the blue sea, and the magnificent ship being propelled through the water by 200,000 shaft horsepower turning its four giant screws.

On the prow of the *Tbilisi,* two Su-27 Flankers were being prepared by the deck crew for takeoff. Unlike her American counterparts, the *Tbilisi* did not use steam catapults to launch her aircraft. Instead, the Flankers were held fast by a deck clamp as they powered up their twin Lyulka AL-31F turbofans and kicked them into afterburner. When adequate thrust was achieved, the clamp was released and the aircraft shot forward, yanking a small lanyard that ran from the tail of the aircraft to the clamp on the deck. The lanyard triggered a small expendable rocket engine that was sandwiched between the aircraft's two turbofans, and this booster blasted the Flanker up a twelve-degree takeoff ramp, leaving a white cloud of cordite-smelling smoke in its wake.

Through his ear protectors, Strekalov could hear the engines of the Flankers howl up to full military power, and as the launch master began leaning down with his arm extended, the afterburners kicked in, creating a din that seemed to shake the entire ship. Then, finally, the launch master touched the deck, and the starboard-side Flanker lurched forward. A burst of white smoke erupted from the tail and the fighter shot off the ramp and into the air, followed two seconds later by its wingman. Once again the admiral admired their precision as they banked to starboard and came together in a loose formation.

The rocket-booster/ski-ramp launch system had been perfected at the Saki Naval Air Test Center in the Crimea. The Soviets had labored long and hard to develop a reliable steam catapult system like the Americans', but it had simply eluded them. The *Tbilisi*—the first true Soviet supercarrier—had been launched on December 5, 1985, from the Black Sea shipyard of Nikolayev. By comparison, the Americans had operated supercarriers for decades. There were some things—like the steam catapult—that only experience could bring. Nevertheless, his flagship was a formidable vessel—the centerpiece of a battle group that consisted of nine other surface ships, three submarines, and sixty-two aircraft.

In another year, a second supercarrier would finish its sea trials and join the fleet, bringing the number of battle groups to two. A third Russian supercarrier had been scrapped due to budget cuts. Two groups were still a far cry from the nine groups the Americans still possessed. But the way things were going between the superpowers, many Russians were questioning the need for that second and very expensive carrier. The Americans had already scaled back their carrier groups from fourteen to twelve. And then from twelve to nine. Due primarily to cost.

The hatch to the bridge opened, and Captain Vaslov beckoned Strekalov inside. Doffing his ear protectors, the firepluglike admiral came inside and asked, "What is it, Dmitri?"

Vaslov handed him a small scroll of teletype paper. "This just came in for you, Admiral."

Strekalov's muscular hand took the paper and he rapidly scanned it.

The blond captain noticed the puzzlement on his superior's face, causing him to ask, "Something interesting, Admiral?"

Strekalov shrugged and said, "I have been summoned to Moscow."

SAN MATEO, CALIFORNIA—July 9

The seedy bar was dimly lit, yet the slender young man was wearing sunglasses. He told people he wore them because of the constant eyestrain from the VDT word processor screen, but in fact his retinas had become hypersensitive to light. His dark hair was unkempt, and his skin—which had once been bronze from the sun—was now white and pasty. He sat in the farthest booth from the entrance, facing the door, with a beer in front of him; but he wasn't drinking. His eyes remained fixed on the entrance, waiting for his benefactor to appear. His hands couldn't remain still, and they seemed to dance everywhere—adjusting his glasses, nipping and tucking his windbreaker, scratching his ear. He was a man on the hair trigger of a total breakdown. He thought about retiring to the men's room—or the head, as the Marines used to call it—and take a quick whiff of that white powder. But he didn't want to risk missing his benefactor. He checked his watch. Twenty-five minutes past the rendezvous time. The benefactor had never been late before. Had he missed the signal? Had he been captured? Or, worse, had the benefactor abandoned him? The hands danced a more frenetic dance.

The door opened, allowing a probing beam of sunlight to slash through the bar. The young man shielded his eyes, then the door closed and the dim, dingy lighting returned. The benefactor had appeared.

He was of medium height, stocky, with dark, swarthy looks. He was wearing a laborer's clothes, like the other men in the bar this afternoon. He might have been a migrant worker, or a Navajo Indian. It was hard to tell. But whatever he was, there was a presence about him. He had the aura of a . . . predator.

The benefactor surveyed the bar for some moments, allowing his eyes to adjust to the dim lighting. Then he found his quarry and walked to the back of the bar, quickly sliding into the booth across from the young man. With a predator's eyes he looked over the young man while lighting a cigarette. Finally, Tamir Zaporozhian stuffed the cigarette pack into his breast pocket and gave the young man a beneficent smile. "I am so glad you waited. My flight from Mexico City was delayed and I barely made it. So, my friend, what was the nature of your distress call? Have you expended your supply of that white powder already? You are such a naughty boy. But no matter. I will see to it you have all you require. We are friends, are we not?"

The ex-Marine's hands were vibrating now. "No . . . it's not that. It's . . . it's . . ."

Zaporozhian sensed this was danger of some kind, and he had to find out what it was. "Come now, my friend. There is nothing you cannot share with me. Tell me, what is wrong?"

The young man's hands clasped the glass of beer. "It's Livermore," he said, almost choking. "I got a notice . . . in the inter-lab mail. . . . I have to take a urine test next Wednesday. They'll find out about the coke. They might even start an investigation. It will blow everything." He lowered his head and tried to stifle the sobs.

Zaporozhian reached out and patted the ex-Marine's arm. "There, there, my friend. You need not worry. You did exactly the right thing in contacting me." He reached into his other breast pocket and took out a small plastic vial. He opened it and tapped out three large white-coated pellets onto a paper napkin. "You think we did not foresee something like this? You think we have been 'asleep at the wheel,' as you Americans say? Certainly not." He pointed at the pellets. "You simply take these little jewels four days before the test. Stay off the coke until then, and drink lots of water. It will mask the testing of any drug. You say your test is on Wednesday?"

The young man nodded.

"Excellent. You caught me just in time. You should take them now, without delay. . . . By the way, have you left anything for me?"

He reached into his windbreaker pocket and pulled out a 3.5-inch computer disk. "Yeah, I brought this with me. Some files I got on Friday before I left."

Zaporozhian looked at the disk as if it were a coiled viper, and the predator in the man quickly came to the surface. "You fool!" he growled in a hushed voice. "Have you learned nothing from what we taught you? You *never* carry the merchandise with you to a meeting. You leave it at the dead drop!" The Cossack shot a glance around the bar, then grabbed the disk and stuffed it in his pocket. "Never do that again, do you understand?" he said, while regaining control. "Forgive me. But I am used to following proper procedures. You are a former Marine, so I am sure you understand. . . . But why should we worry about such things? Our two countries are friends now, are they not? Soon we will be sharing such information openly. But until then, my friend, you are too valuable for us to lose." He rose to leave. "I must go," he said, pointing to the pellets. "Remember. Take them without delay, and drink lots of water. No coke until after the urine test. You will pass with flying colors." He patted the young man on the arm, and quickly strode from the bar.

The ex-Marine word-processing clerk at Lawrence Livermore Laboratory—feeling like the poor wretch that he was—called for a glass of water from the bar to wash down the white tablets.

AN F/A-18 HORNET OVER THE PACIFIC

"Okay, Blackjack, you've got the ball."

The pilot finished out a slow, banking turn under a moonless night and watched the flight deck of the USS *Carl Vinson* slide into its proper place, ahead of and beneath him. As he swept the scene with his eyes, the ocean and sky appeared to be different hues of gray and the ship a stark white. Sort of like a black-and-white TV picture. That's because it *was* a TV picture.

On the nose of the Hornet, just in front of the canopy, there was a little dome with a grapefruit-sized ball inside it. The grapefruit was a Texas Instruments Forward Looking Infrared sensor mounted on a gimbal mechanism that could rotate on three axes, and this was synced to the helmet the pilot wore. The head-steered infrared image was then projected onto two disks called "dual optic combiners," suspended in front of the pilot's eyes. If the pilot turned his head to the left, the grapefruit rotated left, and the same to the right, up and down, and tilt. It allowed the pilot to turn his head freely and peer into the moonless night.

The landing beacon of the amber-colored "meatball" on the *Carl Vinson* shone brightly through its Fresnel lenses. If the Hornet strayed too high or low from the glide path, the amber beacon that was centered between two horizontal lines of green lights would move up or down, telling him he was out of the landing groove. At this particular moment, however, all of the lights—green and amber—appeared white; but through training and experience, the pilot knew which lights were which as he followed them down for a touchdown on this, his fourth fly-by. He hit his mike switch and said, "Roger, Golden Eagle," to the landing signal officer, "we're coming home on this one."

"Whatever you say, Blackjack," replied the LSO. "You're a little high."

"Roger, Golden Eagle." Blackjack kicked in the automatic actuators that put his variable-camber wings into the correct position for the prevailing flight conditions, then he dropped his landing gear and tail hook. Once they were down and locked, he cut his airspeed a tad and monitored the meatball carefully to make sure it was in the right place, which would put him on a four-degree glide slope.

With its gear and flaps down, flying a little above stall speed, the F/A-18 Hornet didn't look like a hornet; rather, it resembled a duck coming down for a landing on a lake, with its webbed feet dangling below its body. But warplanes, being what they were, had to have macho-sounding names like Tomcat, Falcon, Intruder, and Vigilante. So, even though it looked like one, the F/A-18 wasn't called a "Duck." It was a "Hornet."

Blackjack tensed as the deck of the *Carl Vinson* rushed up to meet his plane, and there was a whining-skidding-scraping sound as aircraft met seaborne vessel in a controlled crash. He shoved the dual throttles to the max, preparing his aircraft to "bolt" from the deck and get airborne again should the Hornet's tail hook miss the arresting wire. But Blackjack was pitched forward against his shoulder harness—the true indicator that he had been "trapped"—and he immediately cut power. He looked to the left and down, and the ball in front of the canopy mimicked his head. He could clearly see the deck crewman motioning him to the giant elevator that would take him to the hangar deck.

Lt. Michael "Blackjack" Pershing was enthralled by the image he was receiving from the Night Raptor vision system. It had eased much of the raw fear normally associated with a pitch-black night carrier landing, and that was enough to capture his endorsement.

The elevator took the Hornet down to the hangar deck, where a seaman hooked a small tow cart onto the aircraft's nose wheel and pulled the fighter to a parking position. Once his experimental aircraft was tied down and secure, Blackjack raised the canopy, extended the ladder, and carefully unplugged all the wiring and hoses that were his umbilicals to the airplane and the Night Raptor system. Then, with the help of a crewman, he took off the helmet and exited the aircraft. When his foot touched the deck, one of the squadron's maintenance chiefs appeared behind him and said, "Bossman wants to see you in the ready room, Mr. Pershing. Pronto."

Blackjack nodded and said, "Right away, Chief," then headed down the hangar toward the passageway that would take him to the ready room of the VFA-171 "Rough Riders" Squadron.

Upon looking at Blackjack Pershing, the first word that came to mind was *gangly,* for he was tall (a quarter-inch under the Navy maximum limit of six-foot-six for pilots), sinewy, bowlegged, and his arms seemed to dangle out from his fairly broad shoulders in an arc. Had he not been an aviator, he probably could have pursued a career as a scarecrow. His hair was a kind of muddy brown and his features somewhat gaunt, and he often wore an "aw, shucks" kind of smile. To look at him, you'd think he was brought up on a ranch in West Texas, but he wasn't—it was more like south central Texas.

Blackjack made his way through the narrow passageway and down two flights of steps that were too steep to be called a stairway, but not exactly a ladder either. They were particularly difficult for someone of his height to negotiate, and he'd banged his noggin on the flight of steps above more times than he would've liked to count.

He walked into the Rough Riders' ready room, which was empty except for its rows of overstuffed leather chairs, and the commanding officer of VFA-171, who was sitting on the briefing table, studying a clipboard. Cmdr. George "Bossman" Barstow was a man of medium height and build, with curly reddish brown hair and thin lips. As always, his demeanor was crisp, military, and unsmiling. You could tell without a second look that Barstow was Annapolis. Career with a capital *C.* And as Blackjack entered the room, the squadron commander's resentment of the younger man was cloaked only by the thinnest of veils.

"Your report, Lieutenant." Barstow never called Pershing by his call sign of "Blackjack" unless they were in the air.

Blackjack just kept on smiling. "This Night Raptor system is sweet, Commander. It lights up the whole scene real pretty. Much better situational awareness than a fixed Flir screen or radar image on the instrument panel. Made the landing a breeze. Caught a three-wire, in fact. I bet you could even handle a nighttime dogfight with this baby."

Barstow remained stonefaced while scribbling something on his clipboard. "The Navy is not interested in making wagers, Lieutenant. The Navy is interested in cold, hard data upon which to make a sound procurement decision. I want you to write up a full report on your objective observation of the Night Raptor system and have it on my desk by ten hundred hours this morning."

Blackjack looked at his aviator's watch. It read 0114, or 1:14 A.M. He didn't need another shovelful of paperwork piled onto his pregnant-looking in-box—and putting an ultrashort time fuse on the Night Raptor report was just another cheap shot by Barstow. But Blackjack just kept on smiling and said, "Whatever you say, Commander."

Barstow nodded. "That will be all, Lieutenant."

Blackjack turned and headed out the hatch, and as he did, Barstow had a hard time suppressing his internal fury, for Michael Pershing was everything the squadron commander despised: Irreverent. Unpolished. Unmilitary. Unkempt. And a Blue Angel.

Blackjack was to flying what Mozart was to music, for his skills in the air went beyond the extraordinary. His initial duty assignment in the Navy had been as a pilot of the F-14 Tomcat, but then he had applied to the Blue Angels and made the team after his first interview. The F/A-18 Hornet was the Blue Angels' aircraft, and for two years Blackjack had flown that supercharged machine in aerobatic shows across the country. He was so taken with it that when his tour ended, he decided to transition permanently into the Hornet. He received further schooling in the F/A-18 at the Navy Strike Warfare Center at Fallon Naval Air Station in Nevada, where he learned to drop bombs with uncommon precision. Then, upon graduation, he was assigned to the Rough Riders Squadron on the *Carl Vinson*— which dropped him squarely into Barstow's lap.

And for Barstow, having Blackjack in his squadron was the bitterest of pills to swallow; for Barstow had planned, nurtured, stroked, and fine-tuned his own naval career like a virtuoso. The son of an admiral, Barstow had been to all the right service schools. Been the admiral's aide. Been a congressional briefing officer. Been to sea. Flew in the Gulf War. Been to the Naval War College. Been a squadron commander. He'd snagged every gold ring on the career ladder—except the one he coveted most. Three times he'd put in his paperwork to the Blue Angels. Three times he'd gone through their interviews. And three times they'd said no. Those rejections were the only times in his entire gilt-edged career when Barstow had been told he didn't measure up.

Blackjack had made it. First try. One of the youngest pilots ever to do so. . . . Those simple facts forced Barstow to confront his only failure every day; and as a result, the squadron commander hit Pershing with every cheap shot he could think of. But the gangly Texan simply would not be provoked. Blackjack just kept coming back with that smile. That damned, fixed, infernal, taunting smile that said, "I made the cut with the Blues, and you, Bossman Barstow, didn't."

The stillness of the ready room cracked as the pencil held between Barstow's fingers finally snapped under the pressure.

Blackjack eased the door of his stateroom open, being careful not to make any noise. "Stateroom" was a grandiose term for a cubicle that included a couple of bunks, lockers, and fold-down desks. He paused and heard the rhythmic snoring of "Sweet Thang," his room-mate, then eased himself in and snapped on the small directional desk lamp. Gently he opened his locker and hung up his pressure suit, then sat down and powered up his laptop computer. He began typing up a report on the Night Raptor system and unconsciously started humming his favorite Marty Robbins tune, "Big Iron," a ballad about an Arizona Ranger in the Old West who takes on an outlaw gunfighter. As he hummed along and concentrated on his report, the smile that had been on Blackjack's face slowly trans-formed into a countenance that was tightly set and grim. He didn't know what Barstow's problem was, but knew that if he ever took the bait on one of the commander's cheap shots, it would be a victory for the Annapolis prick. That's why Blackjack just kept on smiling at Barstow. Smiling all the time, no matter how deep the manure was piled on top of him.

Blackjack's humming grew a bit loud, causing a stir in the neigh-boring bunk.

"Ummmphh."

"Oh . . . sorry, Sweet."

"Mmmmmphh." A sleepy face—angular and black—appeared from under the covers. It was slowly followed by a muscular torso that came up on one elbow. "Ummm . . . what you doin' up, man? You know what time it is?"

"Yeah, Sweet, I'm sorry, but Bossman laid some cheap-shit paper-work on me after I flew that test. I wanna zing him by beating his deadline by about two hours."

"Uhhhh," mumbled Sweet Thang as he collapsed back on his bunk. "That sucker sure has got your number. What's his problem, anyway?"

Blackjack kept on typing and shrugged. "Dunno. I guess it just goes to show that all Annapolis grads are pricks."

Sweet Thang raised his hand up to flash his own Naval Academy class ring, and said, "Only the white ones."

Blackjack chuckled, then resumed his typing. When the slow, rhythmic sound of Sweet Thang's snoring returned—as he knew it would—he softly renewed his humming of the ballad of "Big Iron."

SAN MATEO, CALIFORNIA

It was 2:38 A.M. on Sunday, and the proprietor of the dingy bar was
closing the place up. He was a late-middle-aged man with greasy
gray hair and a heavyset torso, who looked overly bored from doing
this sort of thing too many times. The last few patrons had stumbled
out the door and to their pickups for the semidrunk drive home that
would be fraught with peril. The proprietor never stopped to wonder
about the body count caused by his customers heading home from
his saloon.

As he closed the door he heard somebody call his name. He turned
around and saw it was Consuelo, his butterball of a cleaning lady and
sometime waitress, calling him to the back of the room. The proprietor sauntered on back and saw a crumpled, slender young man
half-lying, half-sitting in the booth. Wearing sunglasses. The proprietor groaned. Another drunk to dispense with. "Come on, buddy, let's
go," he said irritably. There was no response as he repeated, "Come
on," and grabbed the young man's elbow.

But the arm seemed as stiff as a board.

The autopsy would later show that the death of the ex-Marine
word-processing clerk was caused by the direct ingestion of pure,
uncut cocaine.

5

. . . .

UNDER THE SEA

RED BANNER NORTHERN FLEET SUBMARINE BASE, GUBA ZAPADNAYA LITSA, KOLA PENINSULA, RRSC—August 9

Like a long black eel, the *Kharkov* slinked along the surface of the inky waters, gliding past a row of other submarines moored beside the concrete pier. On the bridge of the *Kharkov*'s sail stood three officers, wearing their navy blue greatcoats, who were carefully guiding the vessel through the deep channel of the bay. This base of the Red Banner Northern Fleet was some 150 miles east of the Norwegian border on the Kola Peninsula, and because it was warmed by the Gulf Stream current, it was free of sea ice year-round. But in spite of the warm waters that came up from the south, and the August sun, which was shining brightly, a cold and wet wind was howling out of the Arctic. It whipped the bay waters into small whitecaps and chilled the naval officers—who were topside on the sail bridge—to their bones.

Ahead of the *Kharkov* loomed the sheer face of a rocky cliff, and at the base of this cliff were two arches that resembled the reptilian eyes of an alligator, poking just above the waterline. As the *Kharkov* drew closer, one of the alligator's eyelids began to rise, revealing a lighted interior beyond. The "eyelid" was, in fact, an eighty-ton blast door designed to protect the valuable vessels inside from a nuclear explosion.

The *Kharkov* glided through the 'gator's eye and into a cavernlike chamber of immense proportions—a chamber that enclosed more cubic meters than the New Orleans Superdome and Seattle Kingdome combined. The innards of this seaside cliff had been blasted out over a period of years to create the world's largest attack-hardened submarine pen, which served as home port to a number of the Soviet Confederation's nuclear missile and attack submarines. The thick, rocky exterior and heavy blast doors of the submarine pen offered protection and concealment to the exotic vessels, while the interior chamber was a maze of channels, docks, and catwalks, plus cranes for loading missiles, torpedoes, and stores—all under the illumination of garish, high-intensity floodlights that peppered the ceiling.

The *Kharkov* slowed even further as it made the necessary turns to reach its appointed berth. This was not an easy task, for the *Kharkov* was a ballistic missile submarine, half again as long as a football field, carrying sixteen SS-N-23 missiles with a total of forty-eight multiple independently targeted reentry vehicle (MIRV) warheads. In other words, this one vessel possessed enough firepower to, say, blow away the East Coast of the United States.

To accommodate all of this firepower, the *Kharkov* possessed an odd appearance. Indeed, it looked as if an immense shoebox had been grafted onto the dorsal side of the vessel. This turtleback shape enabled the boat to carry the large SS-N-23 missiles, but it also brought forth the nemesis of all submariners, and that was: noise. The water flow around the boxy shape created a gurgle that could be heard for miles by the sensitive underwater ears of American hunter-killer submarines. But for the *Kharkov,* noise was less of an issue than it might seem, for he was not built for running the gauntlet of the American underwater listening posts along the Greenland–Iceland–United Kingdom SOSUS line. Instead, the *Kharkov* was designed to cruise under the Arctic ice cap. If a war order came, then it would find a *polyn'ya*—an opening—through the ice, then surface and launch its missiles.

The interior submarine pen, through which the *Kharkov* was now traveling, had been designed with channels wide enough and deep enough so the boats could maneuver without tugs or harbor pilots, and make a hasty exit if need be. But even so, putting a submarine into this subterranean berth was a navigational chore that required a deft hand and solid judgment, and the man on the bridge of the *Kharkov*'s sail possessed ample supplies of both. *Kapitan Pervogo Ranga* (Captain, First Rank) Kasimir Bodin watched the channel banks like a hawk as he passed instructions to the deck officer, who in turn repeated the orders into his headset for the helmsman below. Meanwhile, a *starshiy* (senior) lieutenant began barking commands through a bullhorn to the linesmen who were scrambling out of the hatches in the bow and stern.

"Stand by your lines!" came the electronic voice from the lieutenant's bullhorn, and the sailors fore and aft assumed their positions along the deck. A crew of linesmen stood directly across from them on the concrete pier, ready to heave the mooring lines over.

As the *Kharkov* slowly backed into its slip, something on the catwalk above caught Captain Bodin's eye. It was a lone, uniformed officer, watching the submarine intently as it passed underneath him. Bodin recognized the hulking figure instantly, and the recognition caused him to smile—if only briefly—before ordering, "Ahead slow."

"Ahead slow," echoed the deck officer into the headphone, and almost immediately there was a slight wash astern as the twin propellers reversed their pitch to break the rearward momentum.

"Send lines over," ordered the captain.

"Send lines over!" barked the bullhorn, and simultaneously four messenger lines were thrown from the pier and pulled in by the sailors, who quickly wrapped them around recessed cleats on the side of the *Kharkov.*

"All stop," ordered Bodin.

"All stop," repeated the deck officer.

The lieutenant lowered his bullhorn and said, "Mooring secured, Captain."

Bodin nodded and pointed up to the catwalk that spanned the slip. "Well done, Comrade Lieutenant. I am sure the Minister of Defense was impressed with your seamanship." Startled, both junior officers looked up to see Yuri Timoshenko—wearing his Admiral of the Fleet greatcoat and saucerlike hat—grinning down at them. "Move smartly, comrades," ordered Bodin. "Go below and tell the first officer to have all division leaders prepare their exit log reports, and to meet me in the wardroom at eighteen hours. We will commence liberty shortly afterward."

"Aye, Captain."

"Aye, Captain."

The two young officers nearly dove through the hatch, as did the sailors on deck. Word that the Minister of Defense was topside would flash through the length of the *Kharkov* in about eleven seconds.

When the sail bridge was cleared, the captain returned his gaze to the admiral on the catwalk. The two men contemplated each other in silence for a full thirty seconds, allowing unspoken but understood communication to channel back and forth between them. Finally it was Bodin who broke their wordless communion with, "Yuri Ilyanovich, you have been too long without a deck under your feet. Come down and have tea with your old shipmate."

"It has not been as long as you think, Kasimir Sergeievich. It may surprise you to know I have been on many a submarine without you at my elbow—and survived."

"That is because I trained you well, you old swine. Now get down here and have some tea."

Timoshenko grinned and clambered down the catwalk ladder to the dock, then up the gangway to the forward hatch, where he squeezed his girth through the small hole with difficulty. Not so for Bodin, who went down the sail hatch like a gymnast. Timoshenko moved down the passageway to join Bodin in the central control room, leaving a wake of bulging eyes and spines snapping to attention as he went past. The former submariner noted that the boat and its men were clean and crisp looking, even after a four-month deployment. This impressed but did not surprise him, for he expected nothing less from the ship of his old first officer.

The defense minister and the captain made their way down to the next level and entered the *Kharkov*'s wardroom, where Timoshenko doffed his greatcoat and giant saucer of a hat, then swung his bulk onto the leather-covered bench seat. Bodin, too, took off his coat and hat, then poured two cups of steaming tea. After taking a seat across from the admiral, he moved the tin cup around in his hands, enjoying its warmth. Timoshenko raised his own cup and said, "To the *Kharkov*'s successful deployment."

Bodin clicked his cup to the admiral's and echoed, "To a successful deployment."

Both men gulped, then Admiral Timoshenko said, "Four months, Kasimir. A long time under the sea."

Bodin nodded. "You and I have been under longer, Yuri Ilyanovich." He studied his teacup for some moments, then said, somewhat wearily, "I heard a rumor before we sortied that the Confederation is cutting a dozen more submarines. . . . I sometimes wonder why we go out anymore."

Kasimir Bodin had served as first officer—*starpom*—to Timoshenko on three separate submarines; but when Timoshenko's career star began to rise, Bodin had chosen not to follow as his deputy. The fifty-year-old bachelor preferred to remain at sea, where he was now a captain of the first rank (equivalent to a Western full colonel) and doing exactly what he wanted to do—commanding a submarine at sea. For four months at a time the *Kharkov* would prowl under the Arctic ice cap, weaving around ice keels, its crew searching for a *polyn'ya* through which they could surface and practice their drills— or be resupplied by air if the need arose.

Physically, the two men were starkly dissimilar. While Timoshenko had his heavyset peasant's body and gargantuan hands and feet, Bodin possessed the lean body of a fencer. But atop this fencer's body was a most distinctive head. The high, balding forehead sloped back at an angle that was in line with the long, sharp, pointed nose. There was not much of a chin—due to an overbite—nor were there any lips to speak of, and his eyes were small, black, and beady. In short, Kasimir Bodin had the head—and some would say the manner—of a shark.

"So what brings you to my ship, *tovarisch?* Is the *Kharkov* to be decommissioned?"

Ah, Kasimir, thought Timoshenko. Always to the point. That is why you are my best submariner. And that is why I am here. "I have something to tell you, old friend. You will find it impossible to believe, but believe it you must," and he went on to explain what had been found on the Antarctic continent.

When he finished, it took a few moments before Bodin could find his voice to blurt out, *"At the South Pole?"*

Timoshenko shook his head. "No. Not at the Pole. On the periphery of the continent. Near the American base at McMurdo Sound."

Bodin's normally controlled face remained dumbfounded, but he recovered enough to ask, "Why are you telling me all this?"

Timoshenko carefully studied his tin cup before saying, "Because, my dear Kasimir, if the Americans do nothing, then *we* do nothing. But if the Americans attempt to mine out the rubidium ore, then we must strike."

Bodin fidgeted, refusing to believe what he was hearing. "What do you mean, 'strike'? Strike and do what?"

Timoshenko leaned forward on his massive forearms. "Strike and hold the area long enough to extract the rubidium for ourselves."

Bodin continued staring at him. "But, again, why are you telling me all this?"

Timoshenko studied his cup and said, "Because if we strike, the Americans will not sit still. They will try to reclaim their territory. And when they come, they will come with their carrier battle groups.

For certain. That means we must have all of our conventional resources on station to neutralize them. And *that* means we must have
the *Zimorodok* missiles operational."

Bodin was again incredulous. "The *Zimorodok?* I thought that the
entire system had been scrapped. The boats. The missiles. Everything. Budget constraints I was told."

The Minister of Defense nodded. "It *was* shelved. But as of last
week the missile production was revived. Within four months we will
have enough missiles to arm three submarines."

"But the *Zimorodok* submarines were canceled. You cannot build
three subs in four months." As the clarity of his own statement sunk
in on him, Bodin stammered, "You—you do not mean to put the
Zimorodok missiles on the *Kharkov?*"

Timoshenko nodded.

Bodin almost came out of his seat. "But the *Kharkov* is not a
hunter! It is a standoff ballistic missile submarine. A *noisy* standoff
ballistic missile submarine. The Americans will hear us coming two
hundred kilometers away. I will not expose my crew to such fool-
hardy danger, Yuri Ilyanovich."

The defense minister raised a hand to calm his friend. "We have
to make do with your class of boat because its tubes are large enough
to accommodate the *Zimorodok* missiles. The only alternatives to
your Delta-IV-class boat are the Typhoons," said Timoshenko, referring to the Soviet Confederation's largest state-of-the-art submarine.
"And they must be held on station."

"You mean they are too expensive to be expendable," snapped
Bodin.

Timoshenko regretted it, but he had to assume an admiral-like
tone of voice with his friend. "As far as our political leadership is
concerned, Kasimir, we are *all* expendable. But do not dismiss your
old shipmate out of hand. Hear me out."

Bodin sighed, then grudgingly nodded.

Step by step, Timoshenko outlined his plan, and it seemed to
mollify the *Kharkov*'s captain, if only slightly.

"You give me your word we will have that much air cover?"

"Absolutely, Kasimir. I doubt if we would ever have to use the
Zimorodok, but if we do, I must have my best submariners at the
helm. That is why I am here."

Bodin knew it wasn't flattery. It was simply the truth. He sighed
again and said, "Very well, Yuri Ilyanovich. As always, I will

carry out your orders. The *Kharkov* and her crew will not let you down. . . . Tell me—what do we do now?"

Timoshenko nodded. "Take some leave. Restore yourself. The *Kharkov* will go into the shipyard to be fitted with the special navigation and guidance electronics for the *Zimorodok* missiles. When your crew returns, they—and you—will be drilled on their use. When the missiles are ready, the *Kharkov* and the other ships will return here for loading. . . . I fervently hope this will turn into nothing but a meaningless exercise."

Bodin shook his head. "Meaningless, Yuri? This is insane. Joining the United States in battle on an ice continent to dig out some mysterious mineral? Insane."

Timoshenko tossed the rest of his tea down and said, "Let me put it to you this way, Kasimir. Suppose, just suppose, there was only one source of uranium in the entire world, and that source was in Antarctica. Do you think we would fight to secure that sole source of uranium for ourselves?"

Bodin fidgeted again. "I suppose so."

"Then believe me, Kasimir. This rubidium isotope is ten times more valuable than uranium. Perhaps a hundred times. We cannot let it fall into American hands. . . . Our economic survival depends upon it, Kasimir."

The *Kharkov*'s captain stared at the dregs of his teacup and remained silent.

WILLIAMS FIELD ICE AERODROME, NEAR MCMURDO STATION, ANTARCTICA—October 3

Desmond Voorhees was not a happy man as he watched the flight of three orange-tailed C-130 Hercules aircraft circle into a landing pattern. It was early October now, and the last two months of his life had been sheer misery. The thirty-knot wind whipping ice crystals into his face did not improve his foul mood, to say the least, and he estimated the temperature was minus twelve degrees Fahrenheit. The temperature wasn't that bad, really. But the chill factor—well, only God knew. All Voorhees could say for certain was that the wind was blowing hard enough to freeze the behind off an old polar veteran like himself. His metal-framed glasses felt cold on his nose as he pulled his parka tight around his tall, skinny frame. He hoped the airplanes made it down okay. His life had had enough upheaval

for the time being. Voorhees—the senior U.S. representative in Antarctica—simply could not understand why an edict had been handed
down by the higher-ups at the National Science Foundation, ordering him to cancel two-thirds of his research grants and make room
for three hundred "guests" at the McMurdo facility. No explanation
was given, and he was firmly told not to ask questions.

"But grants and slots have already been awarded," he'd protested.
"We're already booked solid for the austral summer."

Cancel them, came the order. Give them apologies. Make it up to
them later. Just get the billets ready and render all assistance to the
leader of the team you'll be receiving—an Army colonel named
Ernest Battelle.

Voorhees glumly watched the lead C-130 touch down and taxi on
its skis to its station on the ice apron. A cloud of snow and ice
bloomed behind the aircraft as it throttled up to make the final turn
into its parking slot. Shortly thereafter, the pilot feathered the engines, and the rear cargo door emitted a whine as it was lowered to
the ground. Inside the cargo bay was a military man wearing an olive
drab parka and holding a clipboard in his mittens. His fur hood was
pulled over a fatigue hat that was worn slightly askew, and his
Army-issue spectacles seemed an ungainly counterpoint to his ab-
surdly bucked teeth. He bounded down the ramp and asked, "Dr.
Voorhees?"

"Correct," replied Voorhees, extending a mittened hand.

The new arrival grabbed it clumsily and said loudly over the wind,
"Ernie Battelle, U.S. Army Corps of Engineers. How ya doin',
Doc?"

"Er, fine, I suppose, Colonel Battelle. I would like to welcome you
to McMurdo, and I hope you will find your stay worthwhile. I've
been instructed to offer you every assistance."

Battelle nodded. "Thanks, Doc. Just give us a few hot meals and
a place to bunk, and me and my boys will be fine. We're bringing
everything else with us. Snow vehicles, equipment, fuel, the
works."

Voorhees tried to smile charmingly as he leaned forward to speak
lower, yet still be heard against the wind. "As you may know,
Colonel Battelle, I have been told absolutely nothing about the purpose of your visit here."

Battelle's bucktoothed grin expanded as he clapped a mittened
hand on Voorhees's shoulder. "That's as it should be, Doc. Don't

worry yourself about it. We won't be in your way. Afraid all of this is classified."

Voorhees was shocked. "*Classified?* You mean like military-type classified? How on earth could anything in Antarctica be worth keeping secret? Everybody here works like hell to get their data published. I know we're currently operating without a treaty, but the old SCAR document specifically prohibited 'any measures of a military nature' in Antarctica. In lieu of a new treaty, the U.S. has continued to observe the defunct SCAR agreement. Your activities may be in violation of that provision. Perhaps someone has made a mistake."

The toothy grin reappeared. "Like I said, don't worry yourself, Doc. We know all that. You may recall that the old treaty does not prevent 'the use of military personnel or equipment for scientific research or for other peaceful purposes.' That's why we came here unarmed. I got six MPs with sidearms to keep the peace, but that's all. Sorry I can't say more, Doc. I'm sure you'll understand. Gotta get my other planes unloaded. We'll depot our gear here until our vehicles arrive on a later flight." Battelle turned and walked toward the second C-130 that had just parked, leaving a dumbfounded senior U.S. representative in his wake.

"And I'm supposed to be in charge here," Voorhees mumbled to himself as he looked once more into the cargo bay of the C-130. A group of parka-clad soldiers were unstrapping crates of equipment for unloading, and from behind one of the crates emerged a small figure wearing a red handlebar mustache. He exited the airplane and walked down the ramp while pulling tight the drawstring on his parka hood.

"Ted!" shouted Voorhees against the wind. "Ted Brendan!" And the two man embraced each other. "What in the world are you doing with this crowd?" asked Voorhees. "You're the last person I expected to see after I cut your grant. Or, I should say, after I was *told* to cut your grant."

Brendan shook his head ruefully and shouted over the wind, "I must say, I'm a bit bewildered myself, Desmond."

Voorhees watched Battelle barking orders into the cargo bay of the neighboring C-130, then turned back to Brendan. "Ted, can you tell me what the hell is going on here? I've had to ax three hundred slots this summer and I have no earthly idea why. Can you shed any light on this at all?"

Brendan shrugged. "Desmond, I'm sorry. I'm totally at a loss myself. All I can tell you is that I was summoned to the office of the university president, told to gather up all my research from last summer, and report to this Colonel Battelle. The president said all—and I mean *all*—of the university's federal funding would come to a screeching halt unless I cooperated—and kept quiet. I linked up with this Battelle in New Zealand last week, and that's about all I know."

"Your research? The drilling project?"

"Yeah. Only there wasn't much data to bring. After I got back to the States last year, I sent the core samples to the U.S. Geological Service assay center in Denver for analysis—and they never came back."

Voorhees was totally perplexed now. "This is major-league crazy. And my name is mud in the entire polar science community. I've become 'Mr. Butcher' by cutting so many grants at the last minute, yours and Ivan's included. . . . How is Ivan taking all this, anyway?"

Again, Brendan shrugged. "Haven't heard word one from him since I cabled that our project had been scrubbed."

Voorhees shook his head.

"It's okay, Desmond," Brendan comforted him. "I'm just glad you could bring Dana back. She'd have been in a pickle if she couldn't have finished collecting the data for her dissertation."

"No problem. She'll no doubt be glad to see you. She's scheduled to arrive next week."

Brendan shot a glance at Battelle. "That could be a problem, Desmond. Except for you, we've been told to keep ourselves away from the rest of the contingent here. Battelle ordered everyone to keep to our dormitory when we weren't working, and he said he'd arrange for separate hours in the dining hall. Sort of a quarantine."

6

. . . .

THE ROCK

GIBRALTAR—October 29

Flight Lt. Neil Sexton of 899 Naval Air Squadron eased the throttle forward on his Sea Harrier jump jet to taxi onto the runway. The Gibraltar airfield serviced both military and civilian aircraft, and Sexton's Sea Harrier had just emerged from the Royal Navy's Fleet Air Arm maintenance hangar. Since his ship, the HMS *Illustrious,* was in port, he was pulling a tour of "scramble duty" while his shipmates were off carousing in Spain on shore leave.

"Gibraltar Tower, this is Victor-Lima-seven-one-five. Request clearance for takeoff, over." During the ensuing pause, Sexton ran his eyes over the instruments and, because it was a warm day for October, activated the aircraft's water-injection system for the Pegasus engine.

"Roger, Victor-Lima-seven-one-five," came the reply. "You are cleared for takeoff. Wind is out of the west-southwest at seven knots. Please make it quick. There's a Cessna coming in behind you."

"Roger, Tower," said Sexton in his clipped British accent, "and thanks." He double-checked the vector stop setting to ensure it was at the sixty-degree position, then moved the nozzle lever to the ten-degree mark, causing the two thrust nozzles on each side of the Sea Harrier to rotate slightly downward from their horizontal placement. Sexton then pushed the throttle all the way forward while keeping the aircraft's brake on. Even though he had plenty of runway, the slender, dark-haired young officer—who looked like Timothy Dalton's kid brother—treated every takeoff as if it were from the flight deck of the *Illustrious.* When his pilot instincts sensed the thrust buildup was about to push the tires into a skid, he released the brake and let the fighter roll. It quickly gained speed, and when it passed the ninety-knot mark he shoved the vector lever to its stop setting of sixty degrees, causing the nozzles to rotate sharply downward and push the Sea Harrier into the western sky. He flipped his radio to a different flight-com frequency and toggled the mike switch. "Iris Base, Shutterbug One is up."

There was some static in his earphones, followed by, "Ah, very good, Shutterbug. So glad you could join us this morning." It was the sarcastic controller aboard the Nimrod radar plane. "I do hope we didn't interrupt your beauty sleep."

Sexton sneered at the controller under his rubber oxygen mask, then rotated the engine nozzles to their full horizontal position, which propelled the Sea Harrier into conventional level flight. "I deeply regret the delay, Iris, but we had to load some fresh film into the pod. I'm sure you understand."

"Quite. What say we go to work, Shutterbug? Come to bearing one-zero-seven. Your target is a hundred twelve miles out on the surface. You can't miss it. Take some nice snaps and then home to mother."

"Roger, Iris. I'll make them artsy-craftsy and, if you're lucky, perhaps even in focus. Keep in contact if you please."

"Whatever you say, old man."

"Cheerio."

Having taken off into the west, Sexton banked his Sea Harrier back around to the east and streaked above the sheer limestone face of "the Rock"—an imposing geologic formation that rose up 1,398 feet out of the Mediterranean Sea.

As his Sea Harrier climbed to a cruising altitude of eleven thousand feet, Sexton watched the limestone cliffs of Gibraltar recede in his cockpit rearview mirror. It was a crystalline day, and the Med was an azure blue. The beauty of the sea and sky enraptured the young aviator as he took time to enjoy a couple of barrel rolls. And because it wasn't carrying a heavy weapons load, the aircraft was delightfully responsive.

"Shutterbug One, Iris Base," crackled in his earphones.

"Go, Iris," he replied.

"We make you fifty-two miles out from target. Be advised, looks like you will have company shortly. Approaching your one-o'clock position at angels twelve-five. Speed approximately six hundred knots."

"Roger, Iris." Sexton scanned the airspace ahead of him, but it was difficult to see anything because he was headed into the morning sun. Finally, he caught the image of something zipping high above his canopy, but he couldn't tell what it was. No matter, he thought.

He'd see it again shortly, and the thought of the upcoming encounter dispelled his cheerful mood.

About fifty seconds later a twin-engined fighter—sporting missiles under its wings, and a red star on each tail—pulled abreast of the Sea Harrier on its starboard side. Sexton quickly examined the dartlike projectiles hanging under the Russian's wing, then took both hands off the controls and raised them above his head to signify his aircraft was unarmed. He pointed downward to indicate the reconnaissance pod slung underneath the fuselage, and said to himself, "Now don't get excited, Ivan. I just want to take a picture."

The Russian nodded, indicating he recognized the recon pod. This reassured Sexton, so he put his hands back on the controls and toggled the mike switch. "Iris Base, Shutterbug One."

"Go, Shutterbug."

"I have an escort. A Sukhoi-27 Flanker with Atoll and Aphid missiles."

"Roger that, Shutterbug. Proceed with caution and use your discretion on approach. You're on track for the target. Dead ahead, twenty-eight miles. If the Flanker splashes you, rest assured we've got your transmissions on tape. We'll use them to file a vigorous diplomatic protest."

"That is a great comfort, Iris," replied Sexton icily. "Shutterbug out."

Sexton turned to his Soviet wingman and pointed down again. Might as well be courteous, he thought, as he eased back on the throttle and put the Sea Harrier into a gradual descent. The Russian stayed with him down to twenty-five hundred feet, where Sexton saw his target in the distance—the *Tbilisi,* cutting through the gentle swells of the Mediterranean. It was an impressive sight, and Sexton brought his Sea Harrier onto a course that would take him parallel to the approaching ship, about a quarter mile from its starboard side. This, however, was too close for his Russian wingman, who quickly maneuvered himself closer to the Brit and motioned assertively—indicating that Sexton should take a wider track.

"Oh, come on, old man. Be a sport, will you? You chaps do it to us all the time with your bloody Bear bombers."

But the Russian kept waving him off, and Sexton did not have the means to protest. He cut his speed further, to three hundred knots, and banked away from the ship until he was three miles out on a parallel, head-to-head course with the carrier. This seemed to mollify the Soviet wingman, who ceased his gesticulations.

As the Sea Harrier flew past the *Tbilisi*, Sexton turned on the side-oblique cameras and lustily admired the magnificent vessel. "Nice piece of work, that," he murmured enviously. "Yes, Ivan, very nice, indeed. I just wish Her Majesty had one like it. A shame you won't let me get closer. Might as well not have come out. We'll probably get a better picture with our cameras on the Rock. . . . I'm disappointed in you, Ivan. Over breakfast I read in my newspaper that you were going to make a goodwill visit to Cape Town before you put in at Cam Ranh Bay. And here you're being nasty. How uncivilized." The British pilot was, in fact, quite miffed that he was being shortstopped from getting a good picture . . . which gave him an idea.

Sexton continued on past the stern of the ship for some miles, then began a long, sweeping bank to bring his Sea Harrier around 180 degrees—all the while easing his throttle forward and climbing, bit by bit. The Soviet Flanker stayed with him initially, then fell behind, then caught up, then fell behind, then caught up, fell behind, caught up. By the time Sexton finished out his turn, the Sea Harrier was up to seven thousand feet and on a dead approach to the *Tbilisi*. If he didn't alter his course, he would overfly the full length of the carrier.

Again the Russian pulled alongside the Sea Harrier's starboard wing and gestured wildly, this time giving his Flanker's wings a waggle to indicate his displeasure. As the stern of the carrier rapidly approached, Sexton waved an acknowledgment, then banked the Sea Harrier slightly to port and pushed in his throttle until his airspeed indicator read 520 knots. Now the Russian was like a racehorse trying to catch up to another horse on the outside of a curve. He had to increase his power to stay on the starboard wing of the Sea Harrier and keep himself positioned between the Brit and the *Tbilisi*—just as Sexton hoped.

Unlike the Sea Harrier, which had poor visibility to the rear, the Flanker aircraft had excellent 360-degree visibility from its bubble canopy. The Brit was aware of this as he yanked his shoulder harness tight, released the preset stop on the vector setting, and pushed the throttle forward.

As the Sea Harrier pulled away again, the Russian goosed his Flanker's engines to keep up, and in so doing he began to overshoot his quarry. Sexton waited for the precise instant when the Russian's view of him was blocked by the Flanker's left tailfin, then the Brit stiffened his neck muscles, rolled the Sea Harrier onto its back, and jerked the vector lever all the way back to the ninety-eight-degree mark. The nozzles of the Pegasus engine spun around, savagely braking the aircraft and pushing it "up"—which was presently down. Sexton was slammed forward against the harness as the speed of his aircraft violently bled off and it began plummeting toward the sea. As the Mediterranean replaced the sky in his canopy view, Sexton rotated the nozzles back into their horizontal position, which put the Sea Harrier into a powered dive. He pulled up hard, groaning under the five-G maneuver, and leveled off just in time to skim the surface of the waves—and to see the *Tbilisi* looming in front of him. He shoved the throttle to the max and engaged the cameras, and as the ship raced toward him he pulled up and crossed the bow at a mere three hundred feet altitude with the shutters clicking away. Once past the vessel, he kept the throttle at its max setting and started a gradual climb as he turned to head for home.

By the time the Soviet pilot discovered the Sea Harrier wasn't there anymore, and had finished turning his Flanker around to search for it, he received a searing message from the *Tbilisi*'s "air boss" that an unescorted British fighter had just screamed over the carrier's flight deck. Upon hearing this, the Russian aviator radioed back that he wanted to pursue the Sea Harrier, but he was ordered to land.

THE *TBILISI*

Vitse- Adm. Gavriil Strekalov and Captain, First Rank, Dmitri Vaslov both instinctively dropped their binoculars and ducked as the British Sea Harrier roared over the *Tbilisi*'s forecastle. Captain Vaslov quickly left the flying bridge to go inside, then returned and said, "Our fire-control team had a target solution computed on the British aircraft a hundred kilometers out, Admiral. Had this been a genuine wartime situation, that Sea Harrier would have never gotten this close."

As he watched the aircraft disappear into the western sky, Strekalov said, with a twinge of nervousness, "I hope you are correct, Dmitri. . . . I hope you are correct."

THE SEA HARRIER

"Shutterbug One, Iris Base," radioed the controller on the Nimrod.
   "Go, Iris," replied Sexton.
   "We cut that one a bit fine, didn't we, laddie?"
   "Ah, had a bit of a problem with my nozzles, Iris. Almost splashed before I got it sorted out."
   "I'm sure. If you were monitoring Ivan's radio, you would get an entirely different impression, I should think. See you at home."
   You mean see me on the carpet in the old man's office, don't you, Iris? You bloody twit. Sexton knew that hot-dog flying around any carrier—of any nation—while flight operations were under way was *verboten*, and that Her Majesty's government did not need one of her warplanes having a midair collision with a Soviet aircraft in international airspace. Sexton also knew his squadron commander would undoubtedly give him eighteen different shades of hell about the evasive thrust vectoring and low-level pass over the *Tbilisi*'s flight deck . . . at least until the film was developed. Despite the Cold War being over, the Royal Navy couldn't ignore a Russian supercarrier passing through the Strait of Gibraltar for the first time. The young pilot had no doubt the pictures would be most welcome at the Admiralty, and this thought caused a slight, confident smile to cross his face as the Rock began peeking over the horizon.

ROSS ICE SHELF, ANTARCTICA

Col. Ernest Battelle was a competent Army officer—and a social pariah. The sort of person who could disperse an officers' club cocktail party faster than someone yelling "Fire!" Battelle's uniforms never fit, his glasses were thick, and his buck teeth seemed to amplify his loud scratchy voice and boisterous manner. But the funny thing about it all was that Ernie didn't notice. Indeed, he was oblivious of his status as a social outcast.
   Despite his repellent persona, Battelle possessed one redeeming skill: he could assess an engineering problem at a glance, and whip out the solution like a Cray supercomputer. On the rubidium extraction problem, he was given carte blanche by the defense department to come up with the means to dig out a hundred tons of marine salts from beneath 562 feet of ice and 234 feet of earth. All under top-secret status.
   In ninety days, Battelle had accomplished what he called "a mini-

Manhattan Project." He'd designed the equipment, supervised its fabrication, and assembled his team of three hundred engineers, miners, and technicians. The results of his labors were now sprawled across the ice shelf where the Soviet-American Geologic Expedition had drilled its exploratory hole a year ago.

Battelle's derrick was poised on the very spot where the Brendan-Telenko drilling rig had stood, but his contraption was of a different design and three times as large.

Suspended from the derrick's superstructure by four steel cables was the centerpiece of Battelle's creation. A cylinder with rounded ends, it looked like the containment vessel of a nuclear reactor. Several thick electrical cables and hoses ran into the top of the vessel, which was sixteen feet in diameter, while on the bottom was a hole about twelve inches across.

Battelle stood on the deck of the derrick, admiring the results of his handiwork. He clapped his mittens against the cold, then he turned to his executive officer, Lt. Col. Samuel McClure, and barked an order. "Okay, Sammy, let's make Branding Iron Station operational. Fire her up!"

Lieutenant Colonel McClure—who was also in the Corps of Engineers—cringed at the sound of Battelle's voice. It was like scraping a hacksaw across a blackboard. But he mumbled "Yessir," and spun his finger in the air to signal the sergeant manning the control panel.

Shortly thereafter, the still Antarctic morning was broken by the howl of four diesel generators coming to life. It wasn't long before steam started to billow off the lower half of the vessel, to rise and dissipate in the colder ambient air. Slowly the metallic surface of the vessel began to change color. First to a dull red. Then to a bright red. Battelle and his exec, who were cold just moments before, stepped back from the heat. Battelle said, "Lower away!" and the exec nodded to the sergeant, who threw a lever.

Four winch spools holding the suspension cables slowly began playing out, and the vessel started to disappear through the hole in the floor of the derrick's superstructure. Lower and lower it went, until its red-hot surface hit the ice with a distinct *pssssssttttt.* The bulbous bottom of the vessel formed a watery, steamy depression in the ice where a pool of water collected and started to boil. This caused more ice to melt, and as more ice melted, the vessel was lowered slightly. As the vessel was lowered, some of the water was pumped through the hole in its bottom to pass through a heated hose until it was sprayed out onto the ice shelf a hundred yards away.

Battelle's creation was a combination of heat exchanger and suction pump. It transformed the ice into water, then transported the water out of the hole. Inch by inch the vessel would melt a kind of elevator shaft through the ice until it hit solid earth 562 feet below the surface of the Ross Ice Shelf. Barring problems, the heat exchanger could melt through thirty feet of ice in a twenty-four hour period. Having brought the whole project to fruition in a matter of months demonstrated that Battelle was indeed competent, if not a genius.

A mitten pounded on the exec's shoulder, followed by the exclamation, "It's a-workin', Sammy! It's a-workin'!"

McClure cringed again.

DEFENSE MANUFACTURING CENTER, VOLGOGRAD, RRSC— November 8

The spit-shined toe of Kasimir Bodin's shoe connected with the ample rear end of the plant manager, sending the corpulent man into a rack of spare-parts trays that went over in a crash. The heavyset manager extracted himself and spun round, his fleshy cheeks turned crimson. "You cannot do this to me!" he screamed. "I work directly for the Deputy Minister of Defense for Production! I will have you arrested!"

"And *I,*" countered Bodin, "am working directly for Minister of Defense Timoshenko. And until I get my missiles built and built correctly, I will plant my foot in your fat ass as often as I please!"

The exchange between Bodin and the plant manager was taking place along one of the production lines of the Defense Manufacturing Center where the *Zimorodok* missiles were being assembled. Production was behind schedule, and the defense minister had sent the shark-faced Captain, First Rank, Kasimir Bodin to Volgograd to break up the log jam.

Two dozen workers had watched with relish as their plant manager—whom they despised—was humiliated by the sinewy naval officer. (Armament factories were still run the old way in the new Soviet Confederation.)

"Now you listen to me, *Comrade,*" fumed Bodin. "You were to have completed production of *eight* missiles by now, and yet not one—not *one*—has been completed." He waved at the horizontal missiles lying along the assembly line. "What is the holdup?"

The tubby plant manager straightened his white laboratory coat, trying to regain some of his shattered dignity. "Some critical supplies for the manufacture of the missiles have been lost from our inventory. We had to resubmit our requisition for those supplies, and that takes time."

"*What* supplies?" snapped Bodin.

The plant manager cleared his throat. "A critical component that is used as an electrical conductor in the circuit boards of the guidance system."

"*What* critical component?" Bodin's patience was at an end.

The plant manager cleared his throat yet again. "As you know, the guidance system for the *Zimorodok* missile is ultrasophisticated. It pushes our technology to the absolute limit. The circuit boards are custom-designed and -fabricated, and we were instructed to use only the finest materials. . . . And as I said, some, ummm, critical materials have been lost from our stores."

Bodin growled, "For the last time, *what* supplies?"

The plant manager gulped, and said in a whisper that was barely audible, "Gold."

Bodin was stunned. *"Gold?"*

The white-coated manager nodded. "Gold is used in the electrical contacts of the circuit boards. Our inventory of two kilograms went missing from our secure stores area. An investigation was conducted, but it could not be found. I have submitted a requisition for resupply."

Like an ocean swell, Bodin rose up and grabbed the hefty manager by the lapels of his laboratory coat, then shoved him against the booster stage of one of the prone *Zimorodok* missiles. Then, with a cold, menacing voice, he said, "Now you listen to me, you disgusting tub of lard. I know where that gold went. It went into your pocket! I do not care how you do it, but you get those golden circuit boards finished and into those missiles, and they had better work *perfectly*. Do you understand? Because if they do not, Comrade, let me tell you what is going to happen to that fat ass of yours." Bodin tightened his grip on the lapels and brought the manager's face to within an inch of his own. "You see, you do not understand with whom you are dealing, you fool. I was the *starpom* under Admiral Timoshenko on three submarines. I know what kind of man he is, but you obviously do not. Once we had a fire on board the *Sakhalin*. A small fire in the circuitry that controlled the nuclear pile of our vessel. The *starshiy* lieutenant who was supposed to be monitoring the instruments was found drunk at his post. We saved the ship, but do you know what Yuri Timoshenko did with that drunken *starshiy*, who was the grandson of a Central Committee member? He took that worthless piece of slime—slime like you—ordered him out on deck, closed the hatch, and submerged. We heard him pounding on the hatch as we went under, but Timoshenko did not so much as blink an eye. That is the kind of man you are dealing with, Comrade. Now unless you want to try to walk back to Volgograd from the middle of the North Atlantic, I suggest you move your lard ass and get these missiles *finished.* And I don't care who you know in the ministry. They cannot save you now." Bodin released the manager, who glared at the naval officer with a mixture of anger, hate, and undisguised fear. Fear won out, so he turned and began walking toward his office. The manager was wrestling with the bitter thought of returning the gold when the *thwack* of Bodin's shoe connected with his ass once again, causing him to break into a lumbering run.

When the manager disappeared around the corner, Bodin looked around at two dozen smiling faces that had witnessed the spectacle with rapt attention. "What are you staring at?" he barked. "Get back to work, and these missiles had best not fail, or you will all have to deal with me, too!"

The workers returned to their labors with a frenzy that would have amazed even the Japanese.

It was all Bodin could do not to smile.

BRANDING IRON STATION, ROSS ICE SHELF—December 4

The control panel operator noticed that the tension on the heat exchanger went slack. So he rewound and played out the cable several times—only to get the same result. Then he checked the length of the cable in the shaft against the radar-image depth chart of the ice shelf. They tallied. He picked up the phone and punched a button to ring Battelle. When the other end answered, he said, "Colonel, looks like we've hit bottom."

The heat exchanger had broken down a couple of times, but other than that it had performed well—melting through 562 feet of ice. Battelle's crew now had to get the rail guides lowered for the elevator. Fortunately, they were in the "catcher's mitt" of the Windless Bight, where ice movement was minimal.

THE *TBILISI*—December 27

Through his binoculars, *Vitse-* Adm. Gavriil Strekalov watched Cape Town sink below the horizon in the *Tbilisi*'s wake. Their goodwill visit had gone well, in the sense that it took place without incident. The Russians and South Africans had been very correct with each other, neither side daring to stray from the carefully defined protocol. Strekalov didn't think the visit had done much to dispel the natural distrust the two countries had for each other, but in a way their goodwill visit was like chicken soup for someone with a cold—it didn't hurt.

Such a strange place, this South Africa, he thought. So beautiful, so economically advanced, yet with an undercurrent of fear that reminded Strekalov of his youthful days in Stalinist Russia. He sensed the country was polarizing along ethnic and racial lines, and the little admiral shuddered at the thought. He was glad to be rid of the place.

Ahead lay the Indian Ocean and a passage through the "Roaring Forties" and "Furious Fifties"—the southern latitudes known for their horrendous weather. Then the ship would steam around the southern coast of Australia and New Zealand before turning north for Vietnam. If everything in Antarctica remained quiet, as Strekalov hoped it would, then the *Tbilisi* would put in at Cam Ranh Bay before traveling on to Hong Kong, Taipei, and Tokyo. He did not want to think about the alternative.

The admiral panned his binoculars away from the receding outline of Cape Town and turned them forward. Soon they would be rounding Cape Point, where the Indian and Atlantic oceans met. The little Russian had seen it many times before, and silently he agreed with the assessment of Sir Francis Drake that the Cape of Good Hope was "the fairest Cape in the whole circumference of the earth."

The two South African coastal patrol boats escorting the carrier tooted their horns and turned back toward Cape Town, indicating the *Tbilisi* was outside the twelve-mile boundary of territorial waters, and almost immediately two Su-27 Flankers roared off the launch ramp to take up their positions on routine combat air patrol.

Strekalov sighed with relief, reassured by the knowledge that Captain Vaslov was a prudent man.

CAM RANH BAY, VIETNAM—December 28

Lance Cpl. Vladimir Porsov was dripping with sweat as he walked along on his tour of guard duty. This tour of the guard had given the term idiocy new meaning, for he was "guarding" a row of uncovered, unshaded, and unoccupied cinder-block bunkers near the large air base runway at Cam Ranh. The slight and slender Porsov, who was red-haired and freckle-faced, tried to fathom some reason why he had volunteered for the Red Army; for it had taken him eight thousand kilometers from his hometown of Minsk and plunked him down in this slime pit of the world. It made him wonder why the Americans had wanted this shithole of a base in the first place. But his toad-faced sergeant had given him the order to guard, so here he was—walking, guarding, and sweating while cursing under his breath. Idiocy.

But then Porsov heard a low drone wafting through the air, causing him to halt and look up toward the western horizon. A flock of specks appeared in the sky and began to grow. His eyes widened in amazement. He'd never seen anything like this. There were always aircraft at the base, but they usually came and went in small flights of two, three, or four. As this group drew closer he counted sixty to seventy specks that slowly turned into aircraft of all types and sizes: transports, tankers, a Mainstay radar plane with its rotodome on top, and dozens of small fighters. The lead element of three transports landed and turned onto the taxiway, and as they rumbled past, one split off and parked at Porsov's row of bunkers. The engines were killed and the rear door lowered, disgorging a ground crew and some service vehicles—small vehicles that ran on tracks, not wheels. That was curious, he thought.

Then, as the transport was unloading, a string of eight MiG-29 Fulcrum fighters landed and taxied over, trailing their drogue chutes and sending waves of heat into the air from their engine exhausts. The ground crewmen quickly took up their posts to guide the Fulcrums into position so the towing vehicles could later push them, backwards, into the roofless bunkers.

Porsov was enthralled by this activity, and he figured this massed flight more than doubled the complement of planes at Cam Ranh.

Upon a signal from the ground crewman, the pilot of the lead Fulcrum cut his engines and raised the canopy as a ladder extended from underneath the fuselage. While the pilot was extricating himself, Corporal Porsov noticed a small, multicolored rectangle painted on the side of the Fulcrum, just underneath the canopy. The young soldier drew a bit closer, and his eyes widened as he recognized that the tiny rectangle was an American flag.

The pilot of the Fulcrum dropped to the ground and returned the smart salute of his crew chief. They talked briefly for a few moments, then the crew chief shrugged and pointed to Porsov. With his sweat-soaked blond hair pasted against his forehead, Capt. Fyodor Tupelov walked up to Porsov, causing the young man to snap to rigid attention. "Comrade Corporal," said Tupelov easily, "it is a long flight from Vladivostok. Could you direct me to the nearest latrine?"

Porsov gulped and pointed to a wooden shed a hundred meters away. The pilot nodded his thanks and strode off. But Porsov had to satiate his curiosity. Tupelov had only taken a few steps when Porsov called after him, "Excuse me, Comrade Captain?"

Tupelov halted and turned. *"Da?"*

Porsov cleared his throat. "Yes, sir. Excuse me, sir . . . but are you the pilot who shot down that American bomber some time ago?"

Tupelov smiled, gratified that his celebrity status extended all the way to Vietnam. "Why, yes, Corporal. If circumstances permit, perhaps I can tell you about it sometime."

Porsov was staggered that someone famous like Captain Tupelov would even talk to a lowly corporal like himself, and this caused his spine to become even straighter. "Yes, sir. Thank you, sir."

"Don't mention it," replied Tupelov as he strode off to answer nature's call.

Porsov immediately began a rigid march up and down the line of aircraft, as if he were a KGB ceremonial guard in Red Square, goose-stepping in front of Lenin's Tomb. If any intruder tried to so much as touch Captain Tupelov's plane, he would shoot the bastard on sight.

But as the sun began dropping below the horizon, Porsov's inquisitive mind began wondering why all these aircraft had landed in this remote outpost. At the end of one marching tour, he asked one of the crew chiefs, "Excuse me, Sergeant, but can you tell me why so many planes have come here together, at one time? Is this some sort of exercise?"

The crew chief snarled back, "You are to guard these aircraft and not ask questions, Comrade."

Chastened, Porsov continued marching, but the question kept nagging at him. Why are they here? Why, why, why? He knew the Soviet Confederation's presence in Vietnam had been shrinking for years, until last year when the trend had been reversed due to the Chinese civil wa— China! That must be the reason. The Chinese civil war had gone crazy. He'd read in *Krasnaya Zvezda* (*Red Star*), the Soviet Army's newspaper, that the Chinese army had splintered into personal fiefdoms controlled by the warring commanders. And there was a rumor that one renegade general was threatening to invade Vietnam to expand his personal empire. Porsov had thought it was all bluster by the Chinese, but apparently not. China had conquered and ruled Vietnam for a thousand years before the first Vietnamese dynasty was established in 1009. And in modern times—1979, to be exact—China had engaged Vietnam in a bloody border clash.

Now something must be afoot once again.

But Captain Tupelov would stop the Chinese, should they try anything. Vladimir Porsov was certain the famous pilot had traveled to Cam Ranh to protect this vital Pacific base of the Motherland from imminent invasion, and the thought caused the young corporal to become even more vigilant in his duties.

Vladimir was wrong.

7

. . . .

THE CASINO

WOOMERA PROHIBITED AREA, SOUTH AUSTRALIA—
January 3

The morning sun was just peeking over the eastern hills of the valley as Arlan Kendrick stepped out of his dormitory building. The beams from the shining yellow orb caught him squarely in the eyes, causing him to raise a hand to shield his vision. He guessed it would be another oppressive scorcher in the Nurrungar Valley.

As a young boy on a summer's night back in Arkansas, Arlan would often be found lying on the back lawn of his home, hands clasped behind his head, staring up at the stars. In those reflective evenings of his youth, he'd often wondered what it would be like to cross the void of outer space and land on the moon. Now that he was posted in the Nurrungar Valley, Arlan wondered no longer. That was because this piece of desolate, uninviting, arid real estate seemed very much like a lunar landscape—or Martian, really, for the omnipresent iron-oxide dust gave the rugged terrain a reddish coloring.

The tall, blond-haired Kendrick, who had the graceful moves of a gazelle, was part of a small colony of Americans, Brits, and Australians in this barren region of the Outback. Having spent Christmas at Nurrungar, the former University of Arkansas basketball player groaned at the thought of another day in this place. But a holiday was coming, and he would soon take his leave. Only seventeen days stood between him and his trimonthly rotation back to Adelaide. Green, lush, civilized, seaside, female-populated Adelaide. Seventeen days. To go. He sighed and began the short walk toward another concrete building in the compound—a concrete building that was as banal as the one he'd just left. All the structures in the Nurrungar Valley were, without question, unremarkable—except for the four geodesic domes that rose out of the dusty red landscape, giving it the appearance of a space colony. As far as Arlan was concerned, the only redeeming feature of Nurrungar was the lighted

73

basketball court that he frequented after the sun went down and the valley cooled off.

"Mornin', mate. Care for a little roundball this evenin'?"

Arlan stopped and turned, and saw that he was being followed by Jeremy Grimshaw, his Australian liaison officer. Grimshaw was shorter than Arlan, but wiry and quick on the court. And he had a deadly jump shot.

Arlan smiled in reply, and said, "You got it, mate." Grimshaw caught up with him and together the two men walked into the building known as the Casino.

The high-tech colony that was Nurrungar began emerging from the valley floor in 1969 under the auspices of a secret agreement between the United States, Great Britain, and Australia that dealt with the sensitive subject of acquiring and sharing signal and satellite photo intelligence. To get in on this agreement and share in the lucrative intelligence "take," Australia had an equally lucrative card to trade: its real estate. Australia was a superb location for such a hush-hush enterprise. It was an island, it was isolated, it was thinly populated, and it was ideally positioned to pick up errant Soviet radio signals that bounced off the atmosphere and back to earth. But by 1969, another one of the island nation's hidden charms had come to the surface.

In the late 1960s the U.S. Air Force was planning to bring a new, more sophisticated early-warning satellite system on line that was known by the unremarkable designation of Defense Support Program 647, or DSP-647. Physically, this satellite resembled a squat, mirror-coated barrel with shiny paddles and a long snoot attached. The long snoot contained an infrared telescope that could detect the tail plumes of ascending ICBMs, while other sensors on board had the ability to pick up the telltale signs of an underground nuclear test.

In order to "paint" the Asian continent with these sensors, the U.S. Air Force placed a DSP-647 satellite in a geosynchronous orbit over the Indian Ocean between the Maldives and the Seychelles, 22,300 miles above the earth. This provided excellent coverage of the Soviet Union—and China as well—but before the program could bear any fruit, there was a stumbling block to overcome. The Air Force needed the means to download this sensitive imagery to a secure location, then relay it to North American Aerospace Defense

Command (NORAD) headquarters in Cheyenne Mountain, Colorado.

Thus, Nurrungar. It was perfect for a downlink station, in that the small valley was within transmit range of the DSP-647 satellite and it was one of the most secure locations in Australia, residing inside the 73,000-square-mile Woomera Prohibited Area—an installation similar in many respects to the American White Sands Missile Range in New Mexico.

Since its initial construction, the facilities at Nurrungar had gone through an evolutionary cycle, changing missions and becoming higher and higher tech. The DSP-647 satellites had long been retired, replaced by the newer Teal Sapphire birds that were so sensitive they could even detect and track aircraft or cruise missiles in flight. And although it still retained an emergency backup communications system, Nurrungar was no longer needed as a primary downlink or relay station. That was because data from Teal Sapphire was transmitted directly to a Real Time military communications satellite, which bounced the signal to Cheyenne Mountain.

Yes, the old days were gone, but the colony at Nurrungar had found a new purpose.

The Casino had gone digital.

Arlan entered his office, with coffee cup in hand, and sat down in front of the VITec image processor. He checked the reflection of his image in the blank screen, taking note of his distinct blond widow's peak and slightly crooked nose—the result of an elbow on the court in Arkansas some years ago. He set down his cup and powered up the machine, then like a virtuoso he cracked his knuckles and began to play the keyboard.

As part of the secret intelligence-sharing agreement between the United States, Great Britain, and Australia, the National Reconnaissance Office (NRO) had farmed out a portion of its imagery-analysis duties to Nurrungar. A similar operation existed at the NSA monitoring station at Menwith Hill, just west of the town of Harrowgate in Yorkshire, England.

Kendrick was a one-time Razorback basketball star who supervised the American team of imagery analysts stationed at Nurrungar. It was their job to keep a spaceborne eye on a large chunk of the earth. Specifically, everything south and west of Japan, and south and east of Bangladesh. That was a huge territory to cover, and Arlan knew it. His team, like most photo interpreters, were buried in data. Hi-tech gizmos like the VITec processor helped; but in these times of budget cuts he had to cover the same ground with a smaller staff, and they were all overworked.

As he did almost every morning, Arlan was in the process of calling up the "hot sheet," which listed the imagery his team of analysts had flagged for his attention. The first digital pictures were from the new KH-13 Keyhole satellite that had recently made a pass over the east coast of China and Southeast Asia. Arlan ran through the pictures, which showed a significant increase in the Chinese military presence just west of Hong Kong, and along the coast of the Taiwan Strait. Arlan paused and shook his head. That Chinese civil war had turned into a real nightmare for the Russians, the Indians, the Vietnamese, the Taiwanese, and what was left of the British Crown Colony of Hong Kong. Since the People's Republic of China no longer existed in a coherent form, the British Prime Minister had announced Her Majesty would retain her crown colony of Hong Kong "until such time as a legitimate Chinese government emerges with which we can negotiate in good faith." Arlan had no idea when a legitimate government would emerge. Nor did the Brits. Hong Kong had been turned into a garrison, and China was nothing less than a rogue elephant. No one could tell who was in charge, or when one of the renegade army commanders—in madness—would strike out across the border. Arlan didn't give Hong Kong much of a chance. About the only people left in the place were British soldiers and Hong Kong citizens who couldn't get a visa or afford a plane ticket out, or both. It was a grim price the Brits were paying for a long-dead empire. Arlan sighed and earmarked the imagery of the troop buildup for delivery to his Australian and British liaison officers, and for transmission to the National Reconnaissance Office headquarters in Washington, D.C.

The next item on the hot sheet was the imagery from a KH-13 pass over Cam Ranh Bay, in Vietnam. This caught his interest because, as the analyst had noted, the number of aircraft on the base had increased dramatically from only a week ago. The airfield was crammed with transports, fighters, tankers—even some Mainstay radar planes with their rotodomes clearly in view. Having once been an Air Force photo-interpretation specialist, Arlan paid close attention to this development. With the monitor's cursor he drew a rectangle around one of the smaller planes parked between some revetments and hit the zoom command. The twin-tailed fighter grew and grew until it filled half the screen. Next, Arlan called up the KH-13's infrared imagery on this particular aircraft and merged it with the optical image. It was obvious this Soviet fighter had landed shortly before the KH-13 pass, because the infrared picture showed the twin engines were still hot. Arlan pegged the aircraft as a Fulcrum, and to confirm his opinion he typed in "Identify" and hit the Transmit button. This queried the imagery data bank at National Photographic Interpretation Center in Washington via the Real Time military communications satellite. About ninety seconds elapsed before his inquiry was answered with:

```
Mikoyan MiG-31 Foxhound
Two-seat, all-weather interceptor
Length: 72.5 feet
Wingspan: 46 feet
Power Plant: Two Tumansky RD-F turbojets
Max Takeoff Weight: 90,500 pounds
Max Combined Thrust: 64,000 pounds
Max Speed: Mach 2.4
Ceiling: 75,000 feet
Armament: Four   AA-9   radar-guided   air-to-air
          missiles, plus cannon and other mis-
          siles.
```

A MiG-31 Foxhound? Arlan silently felt chagrined that he'd made such an error and pegged it as a MiG-29 Fulcrum. From an overhead view the two aircraft were similar, but the Fulcrum's wings were tapered into the fuselage while the Foxhound's were boxy around the air intakes. That was the giveaway, and he'd missed it. . . . But wait a minute. What was a Foxhound doing at Cam Ranh? He'd never seen one in this neck of the woods before. He couldn't put his finger on it, but subliminally he felt there was something out of kilter here . . . something that didn't dovetail. His curiosity aroused, Arlan called up another picture of the same aircraft, but from the parallax of a forty-degree side-angle view. He drew a rectangle around its tail, then hit the zoom command, causing the tailfin to grow until it filled most of the screen. The image was a bit blocky from the enlarged pixels, so Arlan hit the ENHANCE button and the edges became a bit more distinct. It was barely discernible, but he could just make it out—right below the red star on the tail were some large block letters that read "8/11."

He typed in "AIRCRAFT: MIG-31 FOXHOUND. TAILMARKING: 8/11. IDENTIFY." It took several minutes this time, but it came back with:

```
Unit: 11th Interceptor Regiment, Soviet ADF

Headquarters: Archangel

Aircraft Type: MiG-31 Foxhounds

Strength: 40 aircraft

Commanding Officer: Colonel Boris Ludenov (For
                    dossier, access level 07 re-
                    quired.)

Responsibility: The 11th Interceptor Regiment
                is assigned to the 34th Air De-
                fense Division of the ADF. The
                division is responsible for
                strategic airspace defense of
                sector 17-C, which covers the
                port and city of Archangel.
```

A few moments elapsed before it finally triggered within Arlan's mind. *ADF. That* was it! In the Soviet Armed Forces, the ADF—the Air Defense Forces—were a separate and distinct branch of service from the Air Force. The ADF operated from fixed bases and had the specific mission of protecting Soviet airspace from American strategic bombers. The regular Soviet Air Force, by contrast, was more of a mobile force, organized to provide close air support and air cover to the Red Army when it was on the move. The Foxhounds were part of the ADF. They operated from permanent air bases inside the Soviet Confederation and never left them.

Until now.

The pace of Arlan's pulse ratcheted up a notch as he called up the original imagery of the Cam Ranh airfield. He moved the picture around on the screen until he counted thirty-eight Foxhounds. Wow!

They'd brought in the *entire* regiment. Arlan went back to his data request and hit the ENTER key for more data.

```
Notes:  The 11th Interceptor Regiment is one of the
        highest rated units in the Soviet ADF. Last
        spring the regiment's pilots won the White
        Rose Trophy during an air-to-air combat
        competition at Novosibirsk. (The White
        Rose Trophy is named for Lilya Litvyak, the
        female World War II Soviet fighter ace who
        scored twelve victories against the Ger-
        mans and was known as the "White Rose.")
        The White Rose competition is analogous to
        the U.S. Air Force's William Tell exercise
        held every two years at Tyndall AFB,
        Florida.
```

Arlan's chair squeaked as he leaned back and clasped his hands behind his neck in a thoughtful pose. What in the world, he wondered, were the Russkies doing by transporting their "top gun" interceptor regiment to Vietnam? The Eleventh was trained to provide static defense of Archangel. It wasn't geared to go traipsing halfway around the world. Moving those Foxhounds contradicted decades of Soviet doctrine and policy. Arlan closed his eyes and murmured to himself, "Why, why, why?" Until inside his brain a light bulb clicked on, causing his pulse to ratchet up once again.

Excitedly, Arlan moved his chair over to another computer in his office and keyed in the proper coding, ending with "Cam Ranh" and "Search."

This time his request went via the real time satellite to the communications center of the National Reconnaissance Office, which in turn routed it through a fiber-optic cable to an "encyclopedic" data base at the Central Intelligence Agency headquarters in Langley, Virginia.

An army of analysts at the CIA scoured mountains of "open" press reports from around the world, reading articles on a mind-numbing array of subjects—some in languages you never knew existed—and entered them into a massive data base. Arlan's second computer was wired into this data base and he could access certain files up to his 05 security clearance level. But what he was looking for now was low-level stuff—something he'd read in a newspaper a week or so ago. When the response to his request popped up, Arlan scrolled through the newspaper entries on Cam Ranh Bay. Most of them were different versions of the same story about the transformation of a former U.S. base into a Soviet outpost. But finally he found an entry that was on the mark:

CAPE TOWN UNION LEADER (12/28) The Soviet Confederation's new super aircraft carrier, called the *Tbilisi*, departed here yesterday morning after completing her goodwill visit. The ship will continue on to the Soviet base at **Cam Ranh Bay** in Vietnam before resuming her extraordinary goodwill voyage to Hong Kong, Taipei, and Tokyo.

Vice-Admiral Gavriil Strekalov, the officer in charge of the ship's visit, remarked that by visiting South Africa the Soviet Confederation wanted to demonstrate its desire to have open communication with all nations, of all persuasions, without regard to old prejudices or the state of a nation's internal affairs. . . .

Arlan sat still for a few moments, pondering whether or not to go through the bureaucratic gymnastics of getting access to the Navy's White Cloud satellite data on Soviet ship movements. He quickly dismissed the idea. To get the Navy to cut loose with its coveted White Cloud data was like pulling teeth from an oversexed dragon. So Arlan came up with another angle. He spun his chair back to the VITec monitor and punched in some codes. A three-dimensional globe of the earth with latitudinal and longitudinal grids came up on the screen. He rotated the globe until the southern tip of the African continent was centered on the screen, then he put the cursor on coastal waters by Cape Town and typed in "KH-13, 12/27." Electronically he flipped through the pictures provided by the KH-13 satellite, but was frustrated by the thick cloud cover—cloud cover that also degraded images from the infrared scanner. Muttering epithets under his breath, Arlan typed in "LACROSSE, 12/27," which brought up data from the Lacrosse radar imaging satellite. Arlan knew that radar could penetrate cloud cover, but the images it provided—particularly of moving targets—were somewhat fuzzier than optical pictures. Be that as it may, he was soon flipping through the radar imagery. He got faked out by a couple of supertankers before he found his target, but finally he was able to bring it up on his screen. The green radar picture showed the *Tbilisi*'s massive flight deck in fuzzy relief, and as he gazed at the display he quickly outlined what he knew.

First: British and, surprisingly, Taiwanese banks and companies had taken huge positions in underwriting the Soviet transition to a market economy. Second: Arlan knew that the Russians, the Taiwanese, and by now the British, were pretty much of one mind when it came to the Chinese threat. Third: The Soviets had moved some of their best air defense units into the Pacific Theater—air units that were trained to defend *fixed* positions, like a city—plus their new supercarrier was on the way.

What was the real price tag the Russians had to pay for the economic help of London and Taipei? Why had the Brits and Taiwanese taken such big positions in Soviet joint economic ventures? America wouldn't fight to protect Hong Kong, and Taiwan was fifty-fifty. Not good odds by anyone's measure. To stave off potential invaders, Britain and the Nationalist Chinese would look for help from someone with a common interest—preferably a superpower. And that superpower would obviously be . . . Arlan was dumbfounded. Was there some sort of secret quid pro quo agreement between the Brits, the Taiwanese, and the Russkies? Protection of Hong Kong and Taiwan in exchange for economic development? . . . Was an agreement already in place? . . . And *we* don't know about it? Instinctively Arlan looked over his shoulder, thinking of his British colleagues in the next office. But then he shook his head. Naw . . . no way. Something like that just couldn't happen without our knowing about it. Could it? As incredible as it seemed, he had some pretty strong evidence right in front of him. And if the Brits and the Taiwanese were nothing else, they were clever. . . . Hmmm. The very idea of a Soviet supercarrier defending Hong Kong from the Chinese was as improbable as, say, *the Berlin Wall tumbling down.*

That did it.

Arlan got up from his chair and locked his office door. Then he sat down at the other computer and started banging out a top secret memorandum to his boss at NRO headquarters. He succinctly outlined the evidence and his hypothesis about a possible Soviet-British-Taiwanese link. He then encrypted the memo on a one-time cipher disk and then transmitted it to the NRO communications center. The com center staff would ensure the message was deposited into his boss's classified electronic mailbag, waiting for retrieval when the sun came up over Washington ten time zones away.

As he got up to unlock his door, Arlan felt very pleased with himself. The one-time Razorback basketball star felt he'd pulled off a brilliant piece of detective work by bringing together divergent strands of information and drawing a picture of what was really happening. That was first-class intelligence work, he told himself, absolutely first-class, and he gave himself a pat on the back.

Arlan was wrong.

ALTITUDE: 175 KILOMETERS ORBITAL INCLINATION: 88 DEGREES—January 8

The explosive bolts on the anchor brackets fired, separating the descent canister from the mother spacecraft, which was Kosmos satellite number 2237. An instant later the small hydrazine engine engaged and the canister plummeted toward the upper reaches of the earth's atmosphere.

Bit by bit, the heat from the reentry friction increased, burning away the canister's ablative shield, and turning it into a fiery spectacle that looked like a torch against the inky, star-filled sky. Down and down it went, until the denser atmosphere slowed it to a point where its drogue chute could be deployed. The drogue caused the canister's speed to bleed off even more, and then at the proper moment it yanked out the main chute. The onrush of air immediately caused the larger canopy to blossom out and rein in the payload for a landing on the Kazakhstan steppes.

Upon impact, the release of tension on the parachute lines triggered a radio locator beacon, and it wasn't long before a Soviet Mil Mi-17 helicopter was hovering overhead.

Inside the canister was a roll of fine-grained exposed film, sixty centimeters wide and twenty meters long.

8

THE EDGE OF THE ENVELOPE

THE USS *CARL VINSON*—January 9

". . . and finally, as for Saltshaker Flight, the USS *McKean* will be cruising a hundred twenty miles to the northwest of Golden Eagle in the vicinity of three-one-five. She will be carrying laser target panels that will record any hits from your target designators. Further, the *McKean* will have gun cameras calibrated to their close-in weapons systems, so they'll be able to tell if she makes any hits on you."

Cmdr. George "Bossman" Barstow was concluding his briefing on the morning's combat exercise, which involved his squadron, the Rough Riders. They had been assigned four "aggressor" targets, which were in reality four escorts of the *Kitty Hawk*'s carrier battle group that were scattered around the *Carl Vinson* in various locales, all waiting to engage the Hornets of the Rough Riders in mock combat.

"The elements of Saltshaker Flight," Barstow continued, "will be Otter, Jazzman, and Pershing as lead. You will be directed to your target by Hummer Two. Vector to final IP at angels three, then go combat on the deck at Hummer's command. Otter will approach from the south and exit to the north. Jazzman and Pershing will approach from the west. Jazzman will exit to the south and Pershing to the east. Return to Golden Eagle on individual vectors. You may encounter air-to-air from some *Kitty Hawk* aggressors following your drop. I will be in the area as an observer." He checked his watch. "Launch is at ten-forty hours." Barstow looked around the room imperiously. "Any questions?" None. "Very well. Dismissed." As a group the squadron rose and began filing out the door toward Flight Deck Control.

Blackjack walked out beside a short, pipsqueak-looking guy with red hair—almost orange, actually—that was worn in a bristly crewcut. The little guy also played a mean clarinet, which had earned him the call sign of "Jazzman."

83

"So it's you and me, kid," said Jazzman with an impish grin. "You just fly us in, and I'll stay on your wing real tight."

Blackjack put his hand on the little guy's shoulder. "Okay, Jazz. Sounds good. Just do me a favor, if you don't mind. After you hit your exit point, keep your altitude level for two minutes and turn your jammer off."

Jazzman looked at him funny. "Level for two minutes? Jammer off? How come?"

Blackjack pulled him into an alcove as everyone else surged past. "Just think about it. We'll be over the target at eleven-fifteen hours. You exit to the south, Otter goes north, and I go east—"

"Right into the morning sun," said Jazzman, finishing the sentence for him.

"Uh-huh. I got a feeling somebody wants to bounce me with the sun to his back."

"Somebody like who?" asked Jazzman.

"Like an 'observer,' maybe."

Jazzman nodded. "Okay. I dig. Straight and level for two minutes, but no more than two minutes. Mind if I ask what you have in mind?"

"Make it easy on yourself and don't ask."

The clarinet player shrugged. "Awright. Just don't put my ass in a sling. Bossman isn't exactly in love with *me*, either."

"I hear ya. Just make it straight and level, like a statue, for two minutes."

"Like a statue. I promise."

They left the alcove and went to Flight Deck Control, where they handed over the tags denoting the takeoff weight of their aircraft. These data would be used to set the steam catapult at the correct pressure for launch. Blackjack spied his roommate, Sweet Thang, whose angular black face looked, as always, impatient to get airborne. Sweet Thang flew the F-14 in the VF-51 Screaming Eagle Squadron. Blackjack Pershing had been with the Eagles before he went to the Blue Angels and then transitioned, which was to say "defected," into the F/A-18 Hornet. Blackjack pulled his roomie aside.

"Say, Sweet. What they got you doing on this drill?"

Sweet Thang shrugged. "Just the northern CAP." (Combat Air Patrol.) "Why?"

Blackjack scribbled something on his notepad and handed it to his roomie. "You remember that guy who kept me up all night a while back? Well, we're dumping our load on a tin can named *McKean* about a hundred twenty miles northwest of here. My flight is coming in low from the west and south of her. My exit point is east. I'll buzz you on this freq at button five. If Wrangler sees something that smells like a rat, let me know, okay?"

Sweet Thang figured he was doing something he would regret later, but he did, quite literally, have to live with Blackjack. So he sighed and said, "Okay. I just hope nobody's listening."

Blackjack punched him in the arm. "No chance. There'll be so much chatter on this exercise, nobody will notice."

Blackjack watched Sweet Thang's F-14 Tomcat roar off the number two catapult of the *Carl Vinson*'s flight deck, leaving little wisps of steam escaping through the catapult slot. The jet blast deflector lowered and Blackjack eased the throttles of his Hornet forward in response to the wand movements of the yellow-shirted taxi director. Blackjack steered his aircraft's nose wheel into proper alignment with the slot as a green-shirted crewman duckwalked beneath the fuselage to strap on the catapult hook. At the same time, another greenshirt held up a plastic board denoting the Hornet's 31,370-pound takeoff weight. Blackjack acknowledged with a circular motion of his flashlight, confirming that it was the correct weight for the catapult setting.

The precision ballet of ship, aircraft, and deck crew working together never failed to enthrall Blackjack. All those bodies. All that effort. Just to get him up in the air. He shot a glance over to catapult number one, half-expecting to see Jazzman, but Jazzman was still one back in line. Straight across from Blackjack, like a racehorse in the neighboring gate, was "Bossman" Barstow. The squadron commander wore a distinctive black crash helmet with gold lightning bolts painted on it.

For his own helmet, Blackjack rejected the lightning bolts, checkered-flag patterns, and other rakish symbols that were so popular with most fighter pilots. Instead, he wore a white helmet with a block **A&M** in maroon letters, making him look like a football player from his alma mater, Texas A&M.

For an instant, with their sun visors raised, the eyes of the two men locked, and the loathing each one had for the other was transmitted across the flight deck on a primal frequency that only they could decipher.

While an airplane is a machine that relies on the laws of physics to get itself airborne, the art of flying that airplane is just that—an art form, like the ballet. What talents, then, must a naval aviator possess? They are difficult to define, except that some of the same skills used in ballet come into play. Hand-to-eye and foot-to-eye coordination. Spatial awareness. Empathy with one's partner (or, in this case, one's wingman). And an artist's flair.

Qualifying as an aviator of the F/A-18 Hornet was much like qualifying for the Kirov Ballet, in that to make the cut you had to be good. *Better* than good. In the Kirov Ballet the competition was so stiff that even the dancers who made up the chorus were superb athletes and artists. Truly superb. It was only once in a generation that someone like a Nijinsky or a Baryshnikov came along—a dancer who so outclassed everyone else that his performances took on mythic dimensions.

Cmdr. George "Bossman" Barstow, the squadron commander of the Rough Riders, was an excellent pilot. He really was. A fine dancer for any chorus, you might say. It was just his hard luck that Lt. Michael "Blackjack" Pershing happened to be the naval aviation equivalent of Vaslav Nijinsky.

In rapid sequence the two catapults fired and unleashed the Hornets into the air. Blackjack banked left toward his assembly point, while Barstow trimmed out his aircraft, retracted his gear, then climbed toward the north-northwest. It was a clear day, except for a squall line of thunderheads looming far, far in the distance.

* * *

Fifty-two miles out and 31,000 feet up, Sweet Thang's F-14 Tomcat was flying a racetrack pattern with another Tomcat from his squadron. Alternately one F-14 would scan the airspace in front of the ship with its powerful AWG-9 radar, then circle around as the other Tomcat took its place.

Sweet Thang toggled his mike switch. "Hummer Two, this is Eagle Three on station at angels three-one. We're in the pattern."

"Roger, Eagle Three," replied the controller on board the E-2C Hawkeye radar plane, which was designated as "Hummer Two." "Sending data link over now."

Hummer Two was cruising near the Tomcats, painting the airspace and ocean surface with the radar in its rotodome. The data link enabled Hummer to share data on radar contacts with the F-14s, and pass it down to the Combat Information Center on the *Carl Vinson.*

"Wrangler," who was Sweet Thang's backseat radar intercept officer, flicked a switch on his display screen and received the electronic data link from Hummer Two showing all of the air and surface targets in his sector. He quickly noted the four ships from the *Kitty Hawk*'s battle group that were strung out in a rough semicircle one hundred to one hundred fifty miles north of the *Carl Vinson;* then he picked out the Hornets of the Rough Riders squadron as they formed up in their attack elements for the practice strike and moved out. Wrangler saw the *McKean* in the far northwest corner of the semicircle's arc. He raised his head and looked over Sweet Thang's shoulder and figured it was on the other side of that squall line.

Blackjack, Jazzman, and Otter were flying under the squall line in a loose "stacked" formation, with Blackjack in the lead. They were approaching the *McKean* from their IP to the southwest of the target, and raindrops were streaming over their canopies.

"Saltshaker Flight, Hummer Two."

"Go, Hummer," radioed Blackjack.

"Your target is thirty-eight miles out at zero-three-eight degrees. Go tactical. Out."

"Roger, Hummer," replied Blackjack, and he switched to another frequency. "You copy, Otter?"

"Roger, Blackjack. See you back at Golden Eagle." Otter peeled off from the bottom of the stack and headed due east in a descent. His inertial navigation system was tweaked so he would know when to turn due north and head for the *McKean;* he hoped to get there just as Blackjack and Jazzman arrived. Otter—who really did look like one—knew nothing rattled the "ship drivers" like a bunch of hostile aircraft appearing out of nowhere simultaneously.

Blackjack and Jazzman turned north, and as they flew out from under the squall line, the water droplets on their canopies quickly dissipated. Blackjack gave his wings a waggle to signal Jazzman, and together they descended from three thousand feet to their tactical altitude of fifty feet above the water. Skimming over the waves at 440 knots can be an unnerving experience, and it was a demanding task even for Blackjack.

Without taking his eyes off the water, Blackjack punched his radio button number five and clicked his mike switch twice to let Sweet Thang and Wrangler know he was listening. There was a pause before a voice came over the radio—with no identification—and said, "That, ah, package you inquired about is at angels two-eight in a racetrack at your five o'clock, thirty miles out. Looks like he's hidin' in the top of that squall line of thunderheads. That is all."

Blackjack clicked his mike again twice, thinking that Sweet Thang couldn't disguise his voice very well. But no matter. The radio waves were heating up with chatter as the first elements of the Rough Riders finished their bomb runs over the targets and were bounced by Tomcats from the *Kitty Hawk.* Blackjack made an instinctive scan of the airspace above him, then checked his inertial navigation once more. When he reached the proper point he waggled his wings carefully, then slowly banked to the east with Jazzman in train on his left. They continued on for some minutes, then Blackjack hit radio button two and said, "Okay, Jazzman. Combat spread."

Jazzman said, "Rog," and peeled his Hornet off to the left until the two aircraft were traveling abreast with three hundred yards between them.

At 28,000 feet, Squadron Commander George "Bossman" Barstow was flying a "racetrack" pattern, whipping along the tops of the squall clouds that concealed him from any visual scan below. The western perimeter of the billowy clouds ended abruptly, like the face of a cliff, so the late-morning sun, which was rapidly approaching its zenith, bathed the *McKean* and the surrounding ocean for miles around. It was a perfect setup.

As he continued his racetrack pattern, Barstow turned the planar antenna of his APG-65 nose radar nearly sideways in order to scan the *McKean* some thirty miles to the north. He was monitoring the transmissions of Saltshaker Flight, and his respiration rate was increasing in anticipation of what was to come. Finally, *finally,* he would nail that bastard Pershing right between the eyes and wipe that smug smile off his face once and for all.

He banked his Hornet and whipped around to the backstretch of his racetrack pattern, and in so doing his radar image of the *McKean* was blind until he could rotate the planar antenna back to the other side. When Pershing flew over the *McKean* and made his exit to the east, Barstow planned to sprint quickly north to get the sun behind him as he visually acquired the exiting Hornet. Then he'd bounce the sonofabitch and put him in his gun camera. And when the tape was replayed for the entire squadron, it would show them that Pershing—the high and mighty Blue Angel in the Rough Riders, *his* squadron—wasn't such a hot-stick pilot after all. Barstow felt his grip on the Rough Riders was slipping because of Pershing. The men seemed to respond to the young Texan naturally, deferring to his judgment and leadership in the air. "Blackjack would do it this way. Blackjack would do it that way," was becoming a constant refrain. It seemed to Barstow that he was having to pull rank more and more to command respect within his own squadron. But that was going to come to a screeching terminal halfstop. And soon.

He sucked in a little gasp as his radar acquired three blips converging on the *McKean*. . . . Yes. It would be soon now. Very soon.

As the sea rushed underneath his Hornet, Blackjack scanned ahead and saw the mast of the *McKean* poke above the horizon. He keyed his mike and said, "Tally," then heard two clicks from Jazzman in reply as he pulled back on the stick. As the aircraft ascended in the targeting "pop-up" maneuver, he kicked in his jammer, then fired off chaff bomblets and flares to confuse the ship's radar and infrared sensors. Then he rolled the Hornet over and pulled the aircraft into the crest of an arc, which brought the *McKean* into view at the top of his canopy. With his prey in sight, he pulled back farther on the control column and the Hornet went into a shallow inverted dive, causing the *McKean* to move squarely into the frame of his head-up display. Rolling the aircraft right side up while maintaining the dive, he reframed the *McKean* in the display, just as Otter screamed over the ship lengthwise. Blackjack saw the square target reflector on the destroyer's fantail and started lining up the target designator recticle through the head-up display as he fired off more chaff and flares. Once his quarry was pegged by the recticle, he triggered the laser beam from the Hornet's targeting pod and it zapped the reflector on the destroyer's stern.

Dropping a laser-guided bomb was like dropping a marble into a funnel. If you dropped the bomb anywhere within the top of the funnel, the weapon's guidance system would adjust the tailfins on the bomb so it would follow the funnel down to its tip—which was the point being illuminated by the laser beam. There were two pods slung under the Hornet's fuselage. One was a laser target designator that

Blackjack was aiming through his head-up display, while the other was a Laser Spot Tracker/Strike Camera that sensed where the bottom of the funnel was and passed that information to the bombs just prior to release. But there were no bombs on this run. It was just for practice, and the *McKean*'s reflector panel was being scanned by the pod's 35-mm panoramic strike camera and recorded on video-tape.

As he began pulling up from his arcing dive, Blackjack got the RELEASE prompt in his head-up display. Perfect. He killed the video recorder from the strike camera, and fired off his final barrage of flares and chaff bomblets as the blurred image of the *McKean* whipped underneath him.

Bossman Barstow was watching the CRT screen of his cockpit display very carefully. The three blips converged on the target, and the screen went bonkers as the attacking pilots activated their radar jammers and fired off chaff bomblets. That was expected. Barstow's APG-65 Doppler-pulse radar would soon reacquire them when they killed the jammers. He was fixing to kick his Hornet into afterburner for his sprint to the north when the images came back into focus. There was Otter, headed north. Jazzman, headed south. And . . . where was Pershing? Barstow moved the antenna around, searching. Still no Pershing. Barstow felt his throat go dry. What had happened? Had the vaunted Blackjack crashed? Augured into the sea? No. Not Pershing. Not him. Not the Blue Angel. But where was he? *Where was he?*

If you put a yardstick to it, the distance between the belly of Jazzman's Hornet and the top of Blackjack's twin tail stabilizers was about thirty-two inches. Any closer, and the airflow around the fuselage of Jazzman's Hornet would have caused control problems for Blackjack. But from his instinct and his aerobatic experience with the Blue Angels, Blackjack knew how fine he could cut it. Being so close and under Jazzman would mask him from the radar above, and just as long as Jazzman flew "like a statue" as he'd promised, then everything should be all right—even though the margin of error for the two aviators was virtually nonexistent. Blackjack was screaming along at a mere thirty-six feet above the wave tops. With any kind of air turbulence, what he was doing would have been suicidal. He should have been tense, but he wasn't. It all felt so natural to him.

As they passed under the squall line, the sunlight turned to shadows, and once again water droplets began streaking over their canopies. He hit his radio button five and clicked his mike switch again. There was a pause before Sweet Thang's voice came through. "If you are where I think you are, your package is above you at angels two-eight, two miles out at your nine o'clock, heading away at zero-eight-three. Nobody else around." Blackjack gave him another two clicks in reply.

It was time to go.

He kicked in his radar jammer again and eased back on the throttles to let Jazzman pull ahead. Then he put the Hornet on its tail and lit the dual afterburners, which responded with a rapid-fire *whump-whump,* shooting the Hornet upward like a spurred racehorse and shoving Blackjack back against his seat. There was such a controlled violence about it all, yet it seemed to fulfill his instincts as nothing else did. He was at ease with himself and the elements around him, and as the Hornet plowed into the ceiling of squall clouds, he found himself humming the gunfighter ballad of "Big Iron."

Barstow was becoming frantic. He was whipping his radar antenna this way and that, trying to acquire the missing Pershing. His prey couldn't have augered in. Someone on the *McKean* would have seen it, and the radios were mute on that score. *Where are you, Pershing? Damn you! Show yourself!*

Blackjack's Hornet was still accelerating in the vertical climb when it popped out of the clouds and into the brilliant sunshine. He immediately killed his afterburner and jammer, then craned his neck back and rolled his upright Hornet 360 degrees to scan the cloud tops. To the east he spied a gray speck against the white fluff, so he pulled his Hornet into a tight loop, then rolled upright and leveled off until he was skimming along the cloud tops. He cut in the afterburner to close the gap.

Bossman Barstow was totally baffled. Jazzman and Otter were out of range now. The exercise was winding down, and all he could get on his screen was the *McKean.* Pershing had vanished, and Barstow felt his triumph slipping from his grasp.

As Blackjack reeled in his quarry over the cloud tops, he was careful not to overshoot. He killed the afterburner and applied a little air brake as he brought his aircraft up behind the "bogey," whose tail markings left no doubt it was Bossman Barstow. He eased his Hornet up to about sixty feet behind and a little below Bossman's plane, and stayed with him for a few moments, savoring what was about to happen. Leisurely he turned on his gun camera, then flicked the switch to illuminate his own Hornet's radar.

The *screeeeccch!* in the headphones from the radar warning receiver was so loud that Barstow winced. Then he whipped around and could just make out that somebody was behind and below him. Someone from the *Kitty Hawk*? He had to shake him, so he went to full military power and climbed into a vertical rolling scissor switchback, but the bogey stayed with him. Then he tried a gut-wrenching high-G barrel roll, but the bogey stayed with him. Finally he flew out from over the squall line and put his Hornet into a split-S dive down to the ocean deck, but the bogey refused to be shaken.

So Barstow gave up. He pulled up to five hundred feet and flew straight and level, a signal acknowledging he was beaten.

The aircraft on Barstow's tail slowly pulled around and drew up alongside him. Teasingly slow, or so it seemed to the squadron commander. Barstow just hoped none of this would get back to his underlings in the Rough Riders squadron. He had appearances to maintain, after all. They didn't need to know that he'd been nailed by someone from the *Kitty Hawk*. Who the hell was this guy, anyway?

When the distinctive **A**Ⓣ**M** lettering on the helmet came into view, Barstow's throat constricted as if he'd swallowed a chicken bone—sideways.

Back on the *Carl Vinson,* Blackjack, Jazzman, and Otter were standing at rigid attention against the bulkhead of the Rough Riders ready room, while Cmdr. George Barstow paced up and down. The Bossman's face was nearly purple, and contorted to such a degree that it resembled a raisin. "All right, you people!" he bellowed. "I want to know what happened out there, and I want to know *now!*" He shoved his raisinlike face as close to Blackjack's as he could, but the younger man was almost a head taller. "Now then, Mr. Pershing," he demanded in a low, guttural growl. "Just how did you drop off my radar screen and then magically reappear on my six? Just tell me how you did that."

Blackjack was the picture of innocence. "Well, Commander, I don't really know. I just made my bomb run as laid out in the brief, then I took off on my exit point to the east. I saw you—not knowing it was you—and figured I was gonna get bounced, so I went up the north face of the squall line and happened to find you in a vulnerable position."

Barstow was breathing through his teeth. "You saw me thirty miles out, at twenty-eight thousand feet!? What a joke! Even *your* eyes aren't that good, Mr. Pershing. Besides, I was in the clou—" He cut himself off, realizing too late he'd admitted the whole thing was a setup. And having made such a gaffe, Barstow *had* to nail Blackjack now. So he turned on the other two. "Otter, Jazzman, did you see Pershing after he made his pass over the tin can?"

"No, sir."

"No, sir."

"Then why the hell did he drop off my screen!? I had all of you covered."

Jazzman shrugged. "Well, sir, I can't really say. You know that Doppler radar. Maybe Blackjack was flying at a right angle to your position and you couldn't pick him up." Jazzman was referring to the drawback of the Doppler-pulse radar: aircraft flying at right angles to the beam might not be detected.

This caught Barstow off guard, and made him start to rethink the layout of the exercise. But then he saw a smile start to creep onto Blackjack's face, and this shoved Barstow's fury into afterburner. The commander's voice was almost a whisper as he said, "Okay, you people. Okay. We'll do this your way. Follow me."

In the Combat Information Center of the carrier, Barstow stormed in with three lieutenants in tow. He accosted the burly chief in charge of the air threat radar screens and said, "I want to see the tape of the exercise we ran this morning."

The chief shrugged and said, "Aye, sir. I just took it off the spool. I'll put it on another machine and you can watch it on one of the viewer screens."

"Right," said Barstow, as he continued to glare at the three lieutenants, who remained at attention.

The chief sensed the commander was about to herniate some vital organ, so he quickly loaded the large reel-to-reel tape and went over to one of his operators sitting at a small green screen. "Take a break, Kaminsky," he said curtly, and the young seaman promptly exited his chair. The chief sat down in his place and punched some buttons. "Okay, sir, this is the data-link feed from Hummer Two." And a bunch of blips came on the screen.

"I want to see the strike over the *McKean,*" demanded Barstow.

The chief pointed. "That's the *McKean* there." He rotated some knobs and the *McKean* centered on the screen. Then he ran the tape through fast forward until three blips appeared to the southwest of the vessel, flying very close together. The chief slowed it to playback speed, then reached up and adjusted the volume on the speaker. "I recorded the mission frequency."

"Saltshaker Flight, Hummer Two," said a static-filled voice through the speaker.

"Go, Hummer."

"Your target is thirty-eight miles out at zero-three-eight degrees. Go tactical. Out."

"Roger, Hummer." A brief pause. "You copy, Otter?"

"Roger, Blackjack. See you back at Golden Eagle."

One blip separated from the group and took off on its own vector, then they all traveled a bit farther before turning to converge on the *McKean.*

"Okay, Jazzman. Combat spread."

"Rog."

The two blips traveling close to each other spread out.

"Tally."

Two staticky clicks followed, and the three blips turned into fuzzy circles, leaving smaller fuzzy circles in their wake.

"Jammers and chaff," said the chief.

The fuzziness continued for some seconds as they passed over their target, then it went back to normal and the *McKean* reappeared. One small blip was traveling rapidly south of the vessel, the other north. There was no blip traveling east, where Blackjack was supposed to be.

Blackjack gulped, and figured the jig, as they say, was up. His jammer wouldn't totally conceal his separation from Jazzman. When Blackjack's fuzzball pulled away from Jazzman's blip and started climbing, it would show up on the green screen—and Barstow would have him nailed. He never figured the squadron commander would take it this far.

Barstow leaned closer, hungrily sensing that something was about to appear on the screen that would, at the very least, enable him to bust Pershing out of the Navy; or, at best, lock him up in the brig. But then the screen went bonkers—turning into a jumbled mass of green lines and fuzz.

Barstow turned on the chief. "What happened?"

The chief shrugged. "We're not quite sure about that, sir. Somehow the data link with the Hummer got messed up for a minute or so. We figure maybe some Prowler jammer from the *Kitty Hawk* was pulling our chain. Don't know exactly what happened."

When the screen cleared, it showed two blips climbing, diving, and weaving like crazy, then flying level together as Blackjack administered the coup de grâce to his squadron commander.

Barstow became stiff, then he stared at Blackjack with a wildness in his expression that the young Texan could only remember seeing in the eyes of crazed horses. After a few moments of tense silence the squadron commander's raisinlike face turned from purple to ghostly pale, and he stormed from the room.

Blackjack draped his long, lanky frame over the chair in his stateroom and scratched his muddy brown hair as he finished his story. "Then the jamming quit and there we were on the screen. Just Bossman and me, goin' up, down, and all around, with him trying to shake me. After it was over I thought he was going to have puppies, but then he left CIC without saying a word. I mean to tell you it was sweet, Sweet. I owe you and Wrangler one for that. I still can't figure out how the Hawkeye's data link got jammed, though."

Sweet Thang, who was still wearing his green flight suit, leaned against the door and shrugged. "I dunno. Sometime I'll have to ask Wrangler how he did that."

Blackjack sat up straight. "Wrangler jammed it?"

Sweet Thang nodded. "Yeah, you know Wrangler. A regular electronics wizard. He figured you'd need cover to get to Barstow, so he garbled the data link."

Blackjack whistled. "Listen, Sweet. I didn't want you guys to go that far out on a limb."

Sweet Thang shrugged again. "In for a penny, in for a pound. Besides that, Barstow was asking for it. He ruined my beauty sleep the other night."

Blackjack grinned. "And you do need your beauty sleep, don't you, Sweet?"

Sweet Thang threw a towel over his roommate's head and said, "Not as much as you, fart face. I gotta go. They want me in the maintenance shed. See you at chow."

Blackjack pulled off the towel and said, "Right," as his buddy left. He continued smiling, recalling Bossman's ghostlike face in CIC. The man looked as if he'd had an embolism, or whatever the hell you call those things. Blackjack chuckled, forgetting too easily that he'd broken a bundle of rules and come within a whisker of destroying his naval career. Yet, even in his triumph, Blackjack was at a loss to figure out what Bossman's problem was—why the squadron commander always had a burr under the blanket as far as he was concerned. The younger man wasn't looking for a fight, but he'd be damned if he was just going to sit back and let Barstow bounce him. "Piss on it," he mumbled to himself, while grabbing a paper off the top of his in-box. He leaned back in the creaking chair, carefully crossing his long bowlegs as he propped his feet up on the fold-top desk.

Michael Pershing had been brought up on a small ranch outside Burnet (pronounced "Burn It"), Texas. And since he was literally raised on horseback, his long legs had always looked something like a wishbone. He probably would still have been in Texas, punching cows on the family ranch, had his dad not bought that used Cessna years ago. And once Blackjack was airborne in his Daddy's plane, the younger Pershing's life was forever changed.

He sighed and tried to put the morning out of his mind by concentrating on the safety memo in his hand. He was reading the first paragraph when a knock came on the door.

"Yeah?"

The door opened and there stood Lt. Cmdr. Samuel F. B. Morse (no kidding, his real name), who was the *Carl Vinson*'s deputy communications officer. He was of medium height, more than a little paunchy, and always wore a dark beard that was grown to the limit of Navy regulations.

"Say hey, F.B.," greeted Blackjack. "What brings you down to these parts?"

Morse didn't say anything. He simply tossed a small object into the air that landed on the fold-down desk with a clatter. Blackjack took his feet off the desk and leaned forward to take a closer look, and saw that it was a cassette tape. He picked it up and asked, "What's this?"

Morse remained immobile and replied in a flat voice, "That's a recording of a transmission one of our scanners picked up on four-three-six-zero-point-five kilohertz. Piss-poor radio procedures were used. Something about a 'package' at angels two-eight, up in the squall-line clouds. Know anything about it?"

Blackjack looked at the tape as if he were holding a dead mackerel in his hand. Shit. He was nailed. This was all Bossman needed to run his ass out of the Navy, and the good commander would certainly do just that. Blackjack just hoped he could protect Sweet Thang and Wrangler and Jazzman from the fallout. Apparently it was time to come clean. He sighed and said, "Yeah, I know about it, F.B. . . . It was all my idea. I conned some other people into helping me. Mind if I ask who else knows about this?" he said, while holding up the cassette.

Morse sniffed. "Just you, me, and the guy in my shop who snagged this stuff off the air. As far as I'm concerned, that's where it ends. I hear that Barstow is a real prick."

Blackjack went limp with relief.

"But I'll tell you something, Mr. Pershing," continued Morse, "you fuck around on the radio waves again and I'll personally run your gonads up the flagpole to see if anybody salutes. Got it?"

Blackjack gulped and nodded. "Got it, F.B."

Morse said nothing more, and closed the door behind him.

Blackjack took a few deep breaths to get his pulse down to a hundred fifty beats per minute. He'd pushed his luck to the absolute edge of the envelope, and perhaps a little beyond. No more, he told himself. Whipsawing Bossman Barstow wasn't worth trashing his own naval career.

There was a cracking sound as Blackjack's powerful hands broke the cassette in two.

McMURDO STATION, ANTARCTICA

Dana Harrow pulled on her parka and walked out of the Icebreaker Lounge. The wind was brisk and the sun was shining through a thin veil of high cirrus clouds. The days were getting longer now, and it never really got dark anymore. Just a slight twilight after midnight. She looked toward the vista of the Transantarctic Mountains, then turned back to inspect Mount Erebus. The volcano seemed to be belching more fumes than normal, so she struck out across the mixture of snow, ice, and volcanic ash toward the seismograph lab. She walked briskly, saying "Hi" to some of her compatriots who were headed toward the lounge after a long day of research.

She entered a cinder-block building that contained the geophysical gear for her volcanism study, as well as equipment for the other geophysicists and their projects. She was alone. Activity on the base was muted this year because three hundred members of McMurdo's normal summertime population had been supplanted by the group working on the "Secret Project." You couldn't get three people together at McMurdo without the conversation turning to the damned "Secret Project." Speculation was rampant as to what it was all about; some said it was a huge oil discovery, while others claimed they'd found evidence of extraterrestrial life. It all sounded totally gonzo as far as Dana was concerned. And the crew on the project was weird, too. They refused to mingle with the other people on the station. They ate during separate shifts in the dining hall, slept in a sequestered dormitory, and most wore Army parkas. Gonzo.

Dana had found her first trip to Antarctica an exciting adventure in a wild and ethereal land. But now the thrill had worn off. There wasn't much to do except monitor the readings from her seismic sensors and help some of the other guys with their experiments. It was becoming a little tedious. All that, and she missed Ted—and Ivan.

The door opened and a small figure appeared, wearing an oversized parka and an ice-encrusted handlebar mustache.

Dana's eyes popped open as she cried, "Ted!" and ran toward him. They gave each other a healthy hug, and as she drew away, her face remained full of astonishment. "This is incredible! I didn't even know you were here. When did you get in?"

Brendan looked back to check his rear, then closed the door and talked in the hushed tones of a conspirator. "I got in shortly after

you did, but I've been with the project out on the ice shelf. A couple
of MPs have been keeping an eye on me to make sure I stay in
quarantine. I guess they didn't trust me, and I guess they were right
not to. But they finally let down their guard and I managed to slip
away. Can't stay long, though."

Dana was incredulous. "MPs? Military Police? Quarantine? Ted,
what is going on out there?"

Brendan threw up his hands in exasperation. "Beats the hell outta
me, Dana. All I know is that they have this contraption that's
burning a big hole through the ice. I asked the guy in charge, some
guy named Battelle, why I was press-ganged for this project when
nobody will tell me what it's about. He just said, 'We may need to
call on you.' But nobody calls. I'm sitting around with nothing to do,
and not a clue as to why." He propped himself against a stool,
looking more downcast than she'd ever seen him. She placed a reas-
suring hand on his shoulder and suggested, "Maybe you could ask
Desmond about it."

"Ha!" he barked bitterly. "That's something else. Desmond
doesn't know squat about it. Do you believe that? The head man
knows nothing. I don't like this, Dana. I don't like this one damn
bit." Like many old Antarctic hands, Brendan felt a kinship with the
continent, as though he were a self-appointed protector of its fragile
ecosystem and scientific treasures. He didn't look kindly on a bunch
of secretive invaders violating his turf. To take his mind off it, he
changed the subject. "So how's your research, anyway?"

Dana sighed. "Pretty routine now. I've got four remote units
placed. One in the dry valleys, one each on Mount Discovery, Mount
Morning, and Mount Harmsworth, plus the deformation monitors
up on Erebus. They're all transmitting okay. I just record the readings. The big job will be sifting through the data when I get back to
school."

Brendan nodded in understanding. "Listen, I better get back. If
I can, I'll slip away again. I told Desmond I'd try to get us all
together sometime. On the sly. I hope we can."

They embraced once more, and Brendan departed, keeping his
parka hood low over his head.

Dana watched him walk down the road, then closed the door on
his receding figure and frowned, more puzzled than ever before. And
as she pondered the quirkiness of it all, she absently reached into her
parka pocket and drew out a compact mirror. Carefully she opened

the small looking glass and inspected her face. It didn't take long for a smile to replace the frown, as she confirmed for the eighth time that day that the Antarctic magic had worked, and once again her skin was as smooth as a baby's backside.

THE KREMLIN—January 10

The face of Minister of Defense Yuri Timoshenko was acutely downcast—one could even call it mournful—as he tossed the satellite photos across the desk to Dr. Minos Konstantos. "There you have it, Minos," he said wearily. "Indisputable proof that the Americans are going to mine out the rubidium for themselves. It is with profound regret that I inform you I have been ordered to implement Operation Snow Leopard."

The wiry physicist picked up the photos and rapidly flipped through them, his dark beard twitching as he did so. In view of all the equipment strewn across the ice cap, there was no question that something on a large scale was taking place. "Are you certain this is the same location as the geologic drill site?" he asked.

"Precisely the same," replied Timoshenko.

Konstantos squirmed. "Are you quite sure there is no other way, Yuri Ilyanovich? It has forbidding ramifications, and it will surely destroy our new relationship with the Americans. With all of Western Europe, in fact. We will be taking a giant step backward into the darkness. Perhaps if we went to the United Nations and—"

Timoshenko cut him off. "We have been over this a dozen times, Minos," he said wearily. "The Americans need but a hundred metric tons of these rubidium salts, and our ability to seize the Iranian oil fields is torn asunder. A mere hundred tons. If we go hat in hand to the United Nations, asking for some settlement, the Americans will stall long enough to extract those hundred tons. Time is the issue, Minos. Time. It won't take long for the Americans to scrape out that amount of material. Besides, the austral summer does not linger. If we are to succeed, we must act swiftly. The Cabinet voted twelve to one to go forward with Snow Leopard, with one abstention. I cast the only dissenting vote, and the Chairman, if you can believe it, abstained. . . . But I must say that when some on the Cabinet questioned my resolve to prosecute this operation, the Chairman shielded me. Called me a patriot, in fact. So it is in my hands, Minos. I must go forward."

Konstantos tossed the satellite photos back on the desk and sighed. "Well, if it must be, then I suggest you take your time before launching your operation—what did you call it? Snow Leopard?"

Timoshenko's bushy eyebrows came together, indicating his puzzlement. "What do you mean, take my time?"

The Georgian-Greek shrugged. "You might as well let the Americans do the work."

For the first time in a very long time, Yuri Timoshenko chuckled. Such a clever man, this little Georgian-Greek, he thought to himself. "I am afraid, Minos," he replied wearily, "that the Cabinet will not respond to such compelling logic. Waiting is out of the question."

CAM RANH BAY, VIETNAM

The sun was rising on yet another sweltering day as Lance Cpl. Vladimir Porsov watched the task force pull out of the harbor. In all, ten ships—a cruiser, two destroyers, four frigates, and three support vessels—had raised their anchors and were heading east toward the rising sun in the South China Sea. It was a stirring sight—all that power cruising out of the bay.

Vladimir could never find out exactly what was cooking with all the ships and planes buzzing around the base, but he knew it must be something big. And, seeing the ships depart, he inexplicably found himself wanting to go along.

BRANDING IRON STATION, ROSS ICE SHELF

The roar from the torch's nozzle was like the howl of a jet engine, requiring everyone within the ice chamber to wear ear protectors. The pressurized oxygen and acetylene ran through the eight-foot-long steel barrel and leaped out in a tongue of flame that melted ice like butter. The operator worked the tripod-mounted torch over the face of the ice until his supervisor clapped him on the shoulder. Then he cut the valves and took off his goggles and ear protectors.

"That should do it," said the supervisor. "Wrap it up in a tarp and store it along with the others."

Using seven of these devices, Battelle's crew had hollowed out a large dome under the ice, some eighty feet high and 190 feet across, as a vacuum hose pumped the meltwater to the surface. Four struts that guided the cagelike elevator rose up from the ground and disappeared into a hole at the top of the dome, as did the umbilicals that

carried electrical power and ventilation down from the derrick
above. The ground under the working party's feet was ruddy black
lava rock—part of the lava apron that had once flowed from the
volcanoes that created Ross Island—and it was covered with a fine
layer of mucky silt.

Scaffolding rose up at various places from the floor, supporting a
network of floodlights that illuminated the scene, giving it an eerie,
almost lunar quality.

Battelle's men were hustling to and fro, preparing eight jackhammers that would be used to cut through the lava apron before the
digger drill could be brought into play to excavate the precious
rubidium-filled salts some 234 feet below.

The men had doffed their parkas, and some had donned their rain
ponchos. Due to the heat from the torches, the air in the dome had
risen to fifty-two degrees, and the melting ice caused a slow drip of
water, like raindrops, over the mining site. But now the torch operation had been brought to a close and the temperature would soon
drop below freezing again.

It was the opinion of Battelle's engineers that the ice that formed
the dome was, essentially, a contiguous block—like a single piece of
wood—and that there were no stress fractures within or near the
dome that would cause the roof to crack, fracture, or cave in. Nor
were there any fissures that would allow sea water to flood the site,
which was well below sea level. Nevertheless, Battelle knew the Ross
Ice Shelf moved, even though the movement in this vicinity was
minimal and slow. And the fact remained that the ice above the dome
weighed tons upon tons. In view of these titanic forces, Battelle had
ordered jack supports installed at various points around the dome to
guard against cave-ins, and had ordered the radar sensors—which
could take an electronic sounding through the ice—to continually
scan the area topside, looking for fissures that might allow sea water
to enter the dome.

Battelle had taken every precaution he could think of to make
Branding Iron Station as safe as possible. But the precautions did
little to console the men working on the floor of the icedome when
the eruption occurred.

9

. . . .

ROCKET'S RED GLARE

On the night of September 12, 1814—during the War of 1812—four thousand British troops were put ashore near Baltimore, Maryland, and the next day the British fleet sailed up the mouth of the Patapsco River in preparation for a bombardment of Fort McHenry, which guarded Baltimore harbor. The attack commenced during the day of September 13 and continued on until late into the night. In what must have been a stupendous display, the British lobbed some 1,800 rocket-bombs against the battlements of Fort McHenry.

On the night of the bombardment, a Washington lawyer named Francis Scott Key was on the deck of a British sloop, having been detained after negotiating a prisoner's release. Key was certainly anxious, because he knew Fort McHenry was thinly defended. The bombardment finally ceased and dawn came, but owing to the smoke, haze, and drizzle, the fort could not be seen—and the fate of McHenry remained unknown to him. But at last the mist parted, allowing Key to gaze upon the oversized American flag still flying over the ramparts. Seized by emotion, Key pulled an unfinished letter from his pocket and began scribbling down the verses of what would ultimately become "The Star-Spangled Banner."

One of the British vessels that hurled those rocket-bombs against Fort McHenry—the type of munitions that provided Key with the "rocket's red glare" for his poem—was a ship specially designed as a launching platform for the fire-spitting projectiles.

It was named the Erebus.

McMURDO STATION

Dana Harrow was reaching for her coffee cup when it shimmied off the edge of the table and shattered on the floor. Almost simultaneously she heard something that sounded like a low growl, or maybe distant thunder, wafting through the air. After a few moments of shock, she realized what had happened and ran outside without her parka. There was a gusty wind, and since she was without her thermal silk longjohns, the twenty-five-degree cold easily penetrated her woolens and raised goosebumps on her skin. She folded her arms tight against her body and looked toward Mount Erebus, thirty-seven kilometers away. A gray-black cloud was rising rapidly above the volcano's caldera and moving southeast in the wind. Mesmerized, Dana could only stand there shivering and murmur, "Wow, wow, wow." This was different, somehow, from the Mauna Loa eruption she'd witnessed in Hawaii. Here the desolation and the white stillness of Antarctica that served as a backdrop to such a violent upheaval, was intoxicating. She stood there—watching the cloud of volcanic ash rise into the air—and wondered about the gold. Erebus was called "the golden volcano," for its ash contained minute particles of pure gold that accompanied its eruptions. Not enough gold to bring prospectors to Antarctica, but enough for scientists to track its distinctive ash plume.

Eventually the cold penetrated Dana's euphoria, causing her to mumble, "What am I doing?" And she ran back into the seismic lab to check her instruments. She looked at the recordings on the deformation meter and, sure enough, six hours previously there had been a 2.2 centimeter deformation in the crust of Mount Erebus.

Alone in the lab, she howled, "This is great!" to no one but herself. This was a made-to-order capstone for her dissertation. Actual hard deformation data—*her* data—on an Erebus eruption that she could match with the seismograph readings from her remote locations. A smaller eruption than the one in 1984, but probably the biggest one since then. This would definitely put her dissertation over the top. Maybe she could even jack up her starting salary at the University of Hawaii.

The phone rang and she grabbed it. "Hello. . . . Yes, yes, Desmond. I'm looking at the readings right this minute. I'm getting surface wave magnitudes of one-point-five to one-point-nine. What? . . . Yeah, you bet it got my attention. . . ."

BRANDING IRON STATION

The initial reaction at the bottom of the icedome to the eruption of Mount Erebus was markedly different from Dana Harrow's. It wasn't exactly panic—but it was close. The men had felt the tremor, and the vibrations caused shards of ice, some of them as large as baseball bats, to fracture off the ceiling and fall to the ground. Two men were struck by the falling chunks—one on the shoulder, the other on the head—and both were felled by the impact. The soldier hit on the head was knocked unconscious, but his hard hat kept his brains inside his cranium.

The only route of escape out of the dome was the single elevator, which was presently on the surface. Sixty-three men gathered at the bottom, crushing against Lt. Col. Samuel McClure, the executive officer, who was on the phone to the derrick above.

"C'mon, Colonel!" shouted a young lieutenant as he pushed against his superior. "Get us outta here! This place could cave in any second!"

McClure shoved him back and shouted, "Get ahold of yourself, Lieutenant! You're setting a piss-poor example for your men. We'll get them out as soon as possible."

Seeing one of their officers crack caused the men's anxiety to flare into genuine panic. More shouts were heard, and the group began transforming into a mob that McClure felt he could not control. Bodies crushed against him, and the receiver was yanked from his hand. He was shoved around, and had to fight his way to the periphery of the mob for fear of falling to the ground and being trampled. Once free, he backed off to watch the crowd of surging and shouting men. A couple of fights were starting to break out over who would hold the lifeline of the telephone. McClure looked on, appalled at what he saw and powerless to do anything about it. Where the hell was that damn elevator? Why was it taking so long? More shouts filled the air and the mob was working itself into a frenzy when they at last heard the elevator coming down from the surface.

It seemed to take forever before the cage descended through the hole at the top of the dome, but down it came, foot by agonizing foot, until it stopped just above the crowd below.

During the elevator's journey down, the crowd had turned quiet; but when it stopped above them, just out of reach, shouts of "Get down here! Don't stop!" rose up until the cagelike doors slid back to reveal Col. Ernest Battelle.

Standing with his hands on his hips, he bellowed, "All right, listen up! I just got off the radio with Dr. Voorhees over at McMurdo. Apparently we've had an eruption of the volcano, Mount Erebus, on Ross Island, but the resident geologist says the worst is probably over for the moment. We're going to pull you out of here in a quick and orderly fashion. After everyone is out and we get a clean bill of health from the geologist, I will send down an inspection team to ensure that the dome is structurally sound. Now line up in single file. I want those who need medical attention to go up first. Everyone else line up by rank in ascending order—lowest rank first, the executive officer and myself last. Now move it—in an orderly fashion."

Lieutenant Colonel McClure watched the men as Battelle's words exerted a calming effect, and once more they transformed, this time from a mob back into soldiers. Quietly and efficiently they formed up in a line as the colonel had ordered.

McClure looked up at Battelle, standing in the elevator with hands on his hips in a commanding posture, his glasses glaring like a couple of headlights. "Hmmm," he murmured to himself. "Maybe this guy Battelle isn't such a horse's ass after all."

THE MAGMA CHAMBER BENEATH MOUNT EREBUS

Think of a champagne bottle . . . with an ultra-long neck . . . that has been shaken *very* hard. The carbonation bubbles struggle to get out, and when the gas pressure becomes too great, the cork pops.

This is similar to what happened in the eruption that Dana Harrow witnessed.

Like a primal oven, the molten rock, or magma, stewed in a gigantic chamber beneath Mount Erebus. Prior to the eruption, the magma congealed and plugged the vent near the surface of the volcano's caldera. When the steam pressure in the magma chamber became too great, it blew the plug out of the surface caldera—like the cork from that bottle of champagne—and filled the air with a spurt of smoke and ash. When this type of explosion occurs in the vent column of a volcano, a wave of back-pressure can travel back down the vent column and keep the gases within the magma chamber in a solution state. But when the back-pressure wave dissipates, the magma and gases can expand and be expelled through the vent—like champagne rushing out of that uncorked bottle.

But in this particular eruption, the back-pressure wave dislodged a secondary plug of what volcanologists call "country rock" at the bottom of the magma vent. This acted as a second cork that sealed off the magma chamber and kept the gases in solution.

For the time being.

ALTITUDE: 696 MILES ORBITAL INCLINATION: 63.4 DEGREES

Hurtling around the globe in the dark emptiness of space were three small, boxlike objects, flying in a triangular formation behind a mother craft. Each spaceborne box weighed less than a hundred pounds and was separated from its sister vessel by a distance of thirty-one miles. The mother craft was endowed with a cylindrical body that was sandwiched between two large solar panels, and it flew about sixty miles ahead of its offspring. As they orbited the globe, momma satellite and her three children carried some of the most sensitive technology the United States Navy possessed.

These were the White Cloud satellites—one of three sets of orbiting vessels that scanned the seas with their passive and active sensors, enabling the Navy to locate and track Soviet surface ships wherever they might travel on the world's oceans.

The three smaller satellites that flew in a triangular formation were essentially electronic ears tuned to pick up radio and radar emissions from Russian vessels; and once an emission was acquired, the three offspring would communicate with each other and with mother, then beam the information to the Current Operations Department of the Navy Operational Intelligence Center (NOIC) outside Washington, D.C. A Cray Y-MP supercomputer would digest the data—correlating satellite speed, orbit, and altitude, as well as target speed, signal source bearing, and the like. Then the Cray would spit out the ship's location and it would be displayed on a large, luminescent screen in the NOIC's situation room.

In essence, the creators of White Cloud had taken the classic locator techniques of radio triangulation to an ultrasophisticated spaceborne level. Additionally, the mother craft used an infrared system to track the engine heat and exhaust emissions of Soviet ships, and this capability led to speculation that White Cloud could track the warm-water wakes of submerged nuclear submarines.

But there was more. White Cloud's tour de force was the mother craft's millimeter-wave radar. This radar did not have the range of the radar aboard the Lacrosse satellite, nor could it penetrate cloud cover as well. But the millimeter-wave radar was somewhat better at detecting slow-moving targets, like ships; and the equipment was much less bulky, which meant it required a much smaller and less expensive launch vehicle than did the Lacrosse satellite.

With all three elements—electronic, infrared, radar—working in concert on three separate sets of satellites, the White Cloud array could track ships for nineteen hundred miles on either side of their orbital track. With that range, and their high orbital inclination, every square inch of the earth's oceans were "painted" by the White Cloud system on a timely basis, making the Navy confident that Ivan's surface ships had no place to hide on the open sea.

FAR SOUTH PACIFIC 57°18' SOUTH, 164°34' WEST, THE *TBILISI*—January 15

Wrapped in his parka, *Vitse*-Adm. Gavriil Strekalov stepped carefully onto his ice-encrusted footstool, welded to the deck of the *Tbilisi*'s flying bridge, then waved to the Royal Australian Air Force P-3 Orion as it flew overhead. On Strekalov's order, the combat air patrol of Su-27 Flankers had been told to allow the lumbering, propeller-driven RAAF reconnaissance plane to overfly the ship without restriction. The short but muscular admiral wanted the Australians to get a firm fix on the Russian carrier's course and speed, so he was making it easy for them. As the Orion banked to the northwest and climbed back into the clouds, Strekalov wondered if the Aussies had seen him wave.

The sky was overcast, and the *Tbilisi* was plowing through ten-foot swells in a stiff gale. Flight operations were extremely difficult to execute in any weather, but this cauldron of wind, ice, and water made them doubly so. His pilots possessed little experience in rough-weather launchings and recoveries, and they'd already had two near catastrophes. But the only way you gained experience in foul-weather flight operations was by operating in foul weather. And ever since he'd received the unbelievable confirmation message from Red Banner Black Sea Fleet headquarters in Sevastopol, there was no question in Strekalov's mind that the *Tbilisi* would soon be conducting combat flight operations—in abysmal weather.

War at sea, he mused. War in a polar sea. Who could have predicted such a thing? It was madness on a global scale. He'd attended the briefings. Seen the hard facts on that mystery isotope under the ice. Ten times more valuable than uranium, they said. A hundred times. It would alter our world. Go forth, Gavriil Strekalov, said the politicians. Go forth with your ships and men and save the Motherland.

Oh, Lord, what he would not give if just once those same politicians should have to go upon the sea and "save the Motherland," instead of the young men whose lives were now in his hands. But, he told himself, if you refuse the politicians, they will replace you, Gavriil Strekalov. Replace you with someone more politically reliable, but much less capable. And the lives of these young men, the ones you love like your sons, will be endangered even more than they are now. The little admiral sighed. He could bring himself to take off the flag-rank shoulder boards he wore so proudly. He could turn his back on the Soviet Navy and leave his career in ashes. He could even find the steel within himself to tell the Cabinet to go to hell. But to leave his command and place his men, such young men, in greater jeopardy? That he simply could not bring himself to do. Strekalov took a deep breath of cold sea air, allowed himself one more moment of self-reflection, then pushed open the hatch to the bridge, leaving the stormy weather and his lamentations behind.

Upon closing the heavy metal hatch, he stomped the ice from his feet while a seaman took his parka and placed a steaming cup of tea in his hand. The admiral then joined Captain Vaslov and the ship's skinny and high-strung navigational officer at the plot board. Admiral Strekalov took a gulp of his tea and said, "If nothing else, that damned Australian plane is persistent. He has shadowed us every day, sometimes twice a day, since we were two thousand kilometers west of Perth."

Captain Vaslov put his hands on the plot board and leaned against it as he said, "That is correct, Admiral. But the Australians are seeing a Soviet supercarrier for the first time. They are naturally curious."

"And they always seem to find us," observed Strekalov with a grim face.

After its departure from Cape Town, the *Tbilisi* and its two supply ships had taken a slow, deep southerly course across the Indian Ocean—plodding, day by day, to a higher and higher latitude. Ostensibly the ship was taking a long training loop underneath Australia and New Zealand before heading back north toward Cam Ranh Bay, then on to Hong Kong for its goodwill visit. Strekalov had sent the supply ships on to Vietnam two days ago, and had ordered the *Tbilisi* to turn north that morning, wanting the RAAF Orion to see for itself that the Soviet warship was playing out its public-relations script.

The navigator was interrupted by a *starshiy* lieutenant, and the two officers conferred for a few moments. The navigator took two slips of paper from the young man and turned back to his companions at the plot board. "Admiral, Captain, I have just received word that our investigation team is en route back to the ship. Their inspection reveals that the candidate we spotted yesterday will do nicely. It is twenty-two kilometers to the east-southeast, bearing zero-nine-seven."

The admiral contemplated their position on the chart and watched as the navigator penciled in the location of the candidate. "What about the cloud cover?"

The navigator grabbed one of the phones dangling from the edge of the plot board and talked to the ship's meteorologist for a few moments. Then he looked up and said, "Although it does not appear so, the cloud cover dissipates rapidly to the west. We could sail out from under it in about thirty minutes if we turned and increased speed to maximum."

Strekalov nodded, then asked, "When is the next overflight of the American satellite?"

This time the navigator turned to a computer terminal and tapped on the keyboard. He scrutinized it carefully before replying, "We will be coming under another White Cloud pass in sixty-three minutes, Admiral."

Quickly a multitude of issues raced through Strekalov's mind— the *Tbilisi*'s current course and speed, the distance to its target, the cloud cover, the time window between the White Cloud overflights, would the Australian Orion return?—and all the foggy what-ifs with which a commander had to contend. Finally he gulped down his tea and nodded to the tall, blond Captain Vaslov. "Very well, Dmitri. Now is the time, and let us make sure the Americans know we are here. Proceed west at maximum speed to get us out from under the clouds, then turn north again and recover all aircraft. Turn on every radio, navigational, and target-acquisition radar we have. Put half a dozen Flankers topside with their engines at high idle to heat up the deck. After the satellite passes over us, turn back toward our candidate at flank speed, shut down all electronics, and hose down the flight deck with fresh water."

Vaslov nodded. "Understood, Admiral." And he immediately began barking orders.

Within seconds, the force of 240,000 horses began pushing the 70,000-ton supercarrier into a sharp ninety-degree turn to the west.

WESTERN PACIFIC OCEAN, NORTH OF NEW GUINEA

At the same time as the *Tbilisi* was executing its turn, the task force of ten ships that had left Cam Ranh Bay five days previously rendezvoused with five warships from the Soviet naval base in Vladivostok. They formed up around their flagship, which was the smaller 38,000-ton carrier *Minsk,* then turned southeast toward the Strait of Magellan, at the tip of South America.

According to stories planted in various Soviet naval periodicals, these ships were being rotated out of the Red Banner Pacific Fleet to allow their crews to spend some time in the Soviet home waters of the Black Sea. They would be replaced by a similar complement of ships from the Red Banner Northern Fleet that were, at this moment, crossing the equator in the Atlantic, headed south.

On their respective courses and speeds, the two task forces would reach Cape Horn at just about the same time.

McMURDO STATION

"Dammit!"

Dana Harrow's epithet had a hard edge to it as she twiddled the knobs on the transceiver.

To gather data for her dissertation on Antarctic volcanism, Dana had placed a string of seismic sensors on Mounts Discovery, Morning, and Harmsworth, plus one in the dry valleys west-northwest of McMurdo, and the deformation instruments on Mount Erebus itself. The remote seismic information was collected onto a Refraction Technology seismic data recorder, then transmitted to McMurdo via radio at predetermined intervals. The normal sequence for the "batch" transmission was once every three hours, but since the eruption of Mount Erebus five days ago, Dana had reprogrammed the data transmission for once every hour. The Ref Tek device was ideal for her research, but somewhere there was a glitch. The data from the three mountain stations strung out to the southwest of McMurdo were transmitted by line-of-sight VHF radios. But since two of the three stations were over the horizon and out of sight, Dana had used a set of radio repeaters to relay the signal back to the McMurdo seismic lab. There was no signal coming in at all, which meant the first radio in the chain—the one on Mount Discovery— was busted somehow. Maybe an antenna had blown down. Maybe there was a malfunction in the power supply. Maybe it was something else. Who the hell knew? But whatever it was, it had to be fixed, and fixed quickly. Desmond Voorhees had asked her to keep a close eye on the activity of Mount Erebus, and that meant she had to have her whole system up and running. She fiddled with the knobs some more, then put her hands on her hips and fumed. Besides complying with Desmond's request, there was a much darker and more personal cloud pressing in on her: her critical data were in jeopardy. No data, no dissertation. No dissertation, no Ph.D. No Ph.D., no University of Hawaii.

She grabbed her parka and headed out the door toward the motorpool.

THE *TBILISI*

As its twin-coaxial rotor blades cut through the icy air, the Kamov-27 aircraft began to shimmy and shake as only a helicopter can.

This was going to be a short hop, but even so, the pilot was scared. The ceiling had dropped to a mere hundred meters. Heavy, wet flakes of snow were falling, and the air was clammy with humidity. The fear that gripped him was the same fear aviators had faced for generations: icing. If ice formed on any of the Kamov-27's six rotor blades, it could destroy their aerodynamic lift and drop his aircraft onto the deck, onto the target, or worse, into the ocean. Given the temperature of the water, he figured the odds of him and his crew surviving were about three cuts below zero. Earlier in the day his helicopter had flown the inspection team out to the candidate and back to the ship, and the icing conditions were marginal then. Now they were worse. Much worse, even though the wind had died down. It was so bad that Captain Vaslov had ordered the rescue helicopter to stand down because of potential icing. "But no stand-down for us," cursed the pilot under his breath. In view of their uncomfortable situation, the pilot and copilot were monitoring the helicopter's engine temperature, rpm, and torque settings like a couple of expectant fathers, looking for any telltale signs of icing.

After several minutes of idling, they were given the takeoff signal by a green-jerseyed deck crewman, and in response the pilot twisted the motorcycle-style throttle on the collective stick. The engine spooled up to full power and the pilot pulled up on the collective, causing the coaxial blades to take a bigger bite out of the air. Water and bits of ice on the deck bloomed away in the propwash as the twelve-ton helicopter lifted off. It hovered for a moment, then pivoted and moved slowly away with a heavy-gauge steel cable slung under its belly. It was the fourth time, and thankfully the last, that the pilot would have to ferry a cable over to the sailors waiting atop the giant tabular iceberg that was drifting alongside the *Tbilisi.*

On the flying bridge of the supercarrier, *Vitse*-Adm. Gavriil Strekalov and Capt. Dmitri Vaslov pulled their parkas close against themselves as they closely monitored the progress of their ship's mooring to the iceberg.

Typically, Antarctic icebergs are created when they separate from the giant ice shelves on the periphery of the continent, and they can vary vastly in size. Some are little more than glorified pack ice, while a select few can approach, or even exceed, the size of Luxembourg. Most of the bergs, however, fall between these two extremes—like this one, which had been calved from the Ross Ice Shelf. The iceberg's topside was two and a half times as large as the *Tbilisi;* and while its freeboard was roughly equal to the carrier's, below the waterline it easily dwarfed the ship. Strekalov was familiar with the icebergs that calved off the Greenland ice sheet, but those tended to be craggy, dome-shaped structures. He was amazed at the smooth, straight lines of this tabular berg. Its shape was quite like an aircraft carrier chiseled out of ice.

Following the plan conceived in Moscow, Captain Vaslov was in the process of lashing the ship to this mammoth frigid object. Although a consummate sailor, he had never attempted anything like this before, and knew of no one who had. Therefore, with no precedent to guide him, Vaslov had to rely on his experience and intuition. He was mindful of the *Titanic*'s fate when it was slashed asunder by a deadly iceberg, and he did not want a similar disaster to befall his ship. Therefore, he'd approached his quarry gingerly, peppering it with sonar scans to ensure that the *Tbilisi* would not be damaged by a bezel of ice lurking below the waterline. Fortunately, this berg had calved cleanly from the ice shelf, and a sheer wall of ice extended over two hundred meters below the waves.

The wind and the swells had eased quite a bit, but the motion of the sea was still a problem. Vaslov had ordered four mooring cables to be ferried across to the berg. Two were hooked up to power winches along the port side of the ship, while the other two lines were being pulled in the old-fashioned way by a couple of hundred sailors. The young men were working on two ice-free patches of the deck, and as they grappled with the lines, they looked as if they were in the midst of a giant tug-of-war. And in a sense, they were.

Peering through his binoculars, the tall, blond Vaslov looked every inch a ship's captain as he ordered, "Halt forward winch!"

"Halt forward winch," echoed the officer of the deck to the helmsman.

"Halt forward winch, aye."

A mere thirty meters separated the two hulking forms, and the cables were going slack and taut with the action of the swells. The captain guessed they were now too close to the iceberg for the propellers to be damaged should the ship pivot, so he ordered, "Forward and aft winches ahead dead slow."

The orders were repeated, and inch by inch the port side of the carrier's angled deck approached the ice cliff, until a swell brought them together with a low groaning and scraping sound.

"Halt all winches! Make all lines fast and tie them down!" ordered Vaslov, which sent the sailors on deck into a flurry of activity as they pulled in the remaining slack and secured the cables. With his binoculars, the captain saw that some of the docking fenders—which had been installed for this special purpose—were crumpled, and part of the catwalk on the port side was damaged; but other than that, Dmitri Vaslov had successfully moored the *Tbilisi* to the tabular iceberg.

He lowered his binoculars and exhaled for the first time in what seemed years. Then he turned to Strekalov and said, "Mooring secure, Admiral."

Strekalov gave him a quick nod. "Superb seamanship, Dmitri. Douse the utility helicopter with cold water quickly. Also douse the deck area where the deck hands were pulling in the lines."

Vaslov passed on the orders to his officer of the deck, then called for his navigator.

The navigational officer poked his head outside and said, "*Da,* Captain?"

"How long until the next pass by the American satellite?"

The navigator disappeared inside, then reappeared. "Three minutes, Captain."

When the White Cloud satellite flew over the *Tbilisi* again, the satellite's radar would show just another iceberg floating in the polar region of the Pacific Ocean. The infrared sensor—if it could penetrate the cloud cover—would see the carrier's frozen deck as an extension of the berg, and the elint sensor wouldn't pick up so much as a bleep from the ship's electronics.

Strekalov and his men had successfully hidden a 70,000-ton warship.

McMURDO STATION

"Aw, come on, Danny. Cut me a little slack, will you? I don't have time to rustle up a partner. I won't be gone all that long, and I need to get my equipment fixed *now.*"

Daniel O'Dell, chief mechanic and bottle washer of the McMurdo motor pool, leaned up against the doorway of the maintenance garage and fired up a Marlboro, cupping his hands to protect the flame from the wind. After taking a puff, he exhaled, and the Marlboro dangled from his lower lip like a rock climber teetering on a ledge. The ear flaps of his fur cap were untied, giving him the appearance of a flop-eared dog. And when he spoke, his head moved in such a way that the dangling cigarette and the drooping ear flaps seemed to bobble up and down in a kind of balanced unison. "Sorry, Miz Harruh," he said consolingly, "but yew know thuh rulz. Nobuddy goes out on the ice shelv by thinselvs. I eithuh need Doc Voorhees's approvul, ur yew need a partnuh. Is that simpul."

Dana stamped her foot. "But, Danny, *listen.* I need the data *now.* You have no idea how critical this is. You may recall we had an eruption a few days ago? If Mount Erebus was going to blow its stack, you'd want to know, wouldn't you?" Dana felt the threat from Erebus was nominal at the moment, but the danger of losing her data was acute. "Desmond is visiting the Kiwis over at Scott Base today," she continued. "I don't have time to go track him down. If he were here, I'm sure he'd give his approval. Besides, I'll have a radio in the Sno-Cat. I'll be in range of the com center almost the whole time in case I get in a jam. . . . The radios in the Sno-Cats do work, don't they?"

Under three days of stubble, Danny's cheeks turned crimson and his Mississippi drawl took on an edge. "All the radios on mah rigs work jist fine, Miz Harruh. But rulz iz rulz, and that means no rig fur yew if yur alone. Sorry, but I gots tuh git back to wurk," he said, with Marlboro bobbling. He walked back into the garage and shut the sliding door with an air of finality.

116   T H U N D E R   O F   E R E B U S

Facing the sheet metal door, Dana growled, "Good*bye*, Mr. O'Dell," and strutted off, her face red with a mixture of rage and frustration. Passing a row of vehicles, she turned behind one and kicked its hard rubber tracks in despair. Then she simply stood there as the absurdity of her situation caved in on her. Here she was, in Antarctica of all places, watching her career go into a tail-spin because of some little electronic glitch—on a remote mountain she couldn't reach. She didn't know whether to laugh, scream, cry, or do all three in concert. She uttered a low groan and kicked the tread again. There was nothing to do now but track down Desmond or find some companion who was available to make the trip with her. All the while her data could be evaporating. She kicked the rubber track one last time, crunching her toe. And as the pain traveled up through her foot, leg, and spine, and into her brain, it seemed to cut loose an idea. She needed a Sno-Cat. In front of her was a Sno-Cat. She opened the door. The keys were in it. She looked around, then climbed into the cab. Turning the key, she checked the fuel and saw that it was topped off. The spare jerry cans strapped to the side were undoubtedly full as well, but she wouldn't need those anyway. Without hesitating, she slammed the door and fired up the diesel engine.

The Sno-Cat consisted of a boxlike cab resting on top of two hard rubber tracks. It had an automatic transmission and was steered with two joysticks instead of a steering wheel. Pulling on the left joystick would slow the left track and put the vehicle into a left turn, and vice versa. Dana dropped the machine into gear and yanked on the right joystick to pull out of the motor-pool lot. In a matter of seconds it was crunching over the volcanic ash that formed the McMurdo roadbed. She looked into the rearview mirror, half-expecting someone to come chasing after her. But no one did. . . . Damnation. Maybe she could get up to the sensor hut, fix her gear, and return this rig to the motor-pool lot before anyone knew it was gone. But if somebody did find out, well then, maybe Desmond would cover for her. And if not? Dana sighed, and wondered if anyone had ever been arrested in Antarctica for Grand Theft Auto.

BRANDING IRON STATION

Once again, Col. Ernest Battelle stood in the doorway of the cagelike elevator, using it as a perch. But this time there were no nervous troops to quiet. Instead, the elevator now served as the means to survey the mining site under the icedome.

After the eruption, Battelle had ordered the inspection of every square foot of ice for cracks or instability. The two significant cracks his engineers had found had been shored up with jack supports, but no one could tell exactly how deep the fissures ran.

The temperature in the ice chamber had dropped below freezing again, causing the "rain" from the melting ice to cease; and the men on the floor could see their breaths as they worked under the flood-lights. These pockets of illumination on the dome ceiling gave the scene something of a surreal quality. It was as if the men were working on the surface of an alien world that was hostile to their intrusions. Perhaps the eruption had been a warning.

Battelle was not insensitive to these troubling elements, and nei-ther were his men. It seemed they always worked with one eye on the elevator, mentally gauging the time it would take them to cover the distance to that slender lifeline to the surface. Battelle shared their fears. He was worried for his men. And worried about time. They'd lost five days from the eruption, and they still had to sink this shaft 234 feet and extract a hundred tons of ore before the onset of winter. Would they have enough time? He couldn't say. There were simply too many variables.

The ice chamber was filled with the ripping sound of a half-dozen jackhammers working in concert, breaking up and sinking a hole through the hardened lava apron. Fortunately their mining site was on the outskirts of the lava apron that surrounded Ross Island, and it was only thirty-three-feet thick at this point. Once his men had punched through the black, crusty mass with their jackhammers, they could bring the giant drill tool into play, and that would bore a hole through the softer sedimentary earth much faster.

Battelle absently bit his lip. It was still quite a ways before they hit pay dirt.

WHITE STRAIT, ROSS ICE SHELF

Dana Harrow looked at her watch. She'd been on the road—which was to say, the ice—for over an hour, growing tired of the constant grind of the diesel engine. On the flat ice shelf the Sno-Cat could cruise at a little over twenty miles per hour, and she was now about halfway toward the location of her sensor station, passing through the strait between Black Island and White Island, which were shallow landfalls that protruded through the ice shelf. They were both unremarkable and much smaller than Ross Island, and for some reason—Dana guessed it was wind patterns—the westerly Black Island was almost bare of snow and ice, exposing its dark rock face to the world, while White Island seemed to retain its mantle of snow and ice through much of the austral summer.

Dana was familiar with the route to her sensor station, but was leery of crevasses just the same. The fissures that opened up in the ice could be small and shallow, or deep, dark, foreboding, and large enough to swallow a Sno-Cat whole. Sometimes snow would build up on the lips of a crevasse, growing closer and closer together until the chasm was spanned by a bridge of snow, making it invisible and deadly to anyone passing over it without a tether line. She knew where the crevasses were supposed to be, and gave the danger area a wide berth. Even so, she kept a sharp lookout.

After passing through the strait, she turned her Sno-Cat to the southwest, toward Mount Discovery. Now that it was high summer, part of the mountain's rocky face was free of snow, providing a counterpoint to the magnificent white backdrop of the Royal Society Range. But Dana's mind was not attuned to the view, for she was mentally running through a dozen technical scenarios. Suppose the equipment on Mount Discovery couldn't be fixed—then what? Suppose Desmond Voorhees found out about her sortie onto the ice and blew a gasket? He had said it was vital to monitor the seismic activity of Mount Erebus, but just how vital? Vital enough to break the rules? She grumbled and kept the Sno-Cat churning toward the Minna Saddle, more than an hour away.

From the southeastern slope of Mount Discovery, a peninsula of land called the Minna Bluff extends out into the ice, and the depression between the peninsula and the mountain proper is called the Minna Saddle. Dana had set up her monitoring station across the saddle on the far slope of Mount Discovery, while the radio antenna was higher up on the ridgeline so it could link up with both her home base at McMurdo and the station to the west on Mount Morning. Dana spied the radio antenna up on the ridge and was grateful to see that it appeared intact. She crested the saddle and turned up the ridgeline, urging the Sno-Cat forward as far as it would go until the exposed ground became too steep. She put on the brake and killed the engine, then zipped up her snow parka and pulled on her balaclava stocking cap and mittens. Since it was high summer, the temperature was up to thirty-four degrees, but there was a stiff breeze coming out of the west. She hadn't put on her parka pants that morning because it was warm, but was glad that for some reason she'd pulled on her long-handled silk thermal underwear. When she stepped out of the heated cab, the cold wind immediately whipped at her clothes and sent a chill to her skin, but she knew the walk would soon warm her up. She grabbed an ice ax and a hand-held emergency radio out of the cab and set off on the short climb.

The remote sensing unit was housed in a hut set in a small depression on the side of Minna Saddle, where it enjoyed a measure of protection from the violent winds. Dana had spent the previous summer installing it and similar units on Mount Morning and Mount Harmsworth, plus one in the dry valleys.

She took a switchback path that required some huffing and puffing, as well as some nimble footwork to keep her balance in the brisk wind; and because she was walking on exposed ground she was not wearing crampons. It was with a sense of relief that she saw her hut come into view. Although it was windy, she was grateful the sky was clear and she didn't have to contend with any ground-hugging clouds, storms, or whiteouts. But the weather in Antarctica could always change, with swiftness and savagery. Perhaps that was why no one was supposed to go out on the ice shelf alone. The thought made her quicken her pace.

The hut was nothing but a twelve-foot-by-twelve-foot prefab plywood structure. It possessed the radio transceiver/repeater, the Ref Tek data acquisition device, and the seismic sensor, as well as emergency rations, a down sleeping bag, an emergency radio, flares, a first-aid kit, a small cooking stove, Blazo fuel, and a cot.

The Ref Tek device could function for a month on a single twelve-volt car battery, and that was how Dana had designed it to work. Two shelves held six batteries each, and the wiring from all the batteries funneled to a central timer-switcher device. At three-week intervals the switcher ratcheted over to the next battery in line to provide fresh power to the system. But because batteries don't work well in extreme cold, the hut also had an automatic thermostat and a butane heater that was set underneath the battery racks. Keeping the batteries warm was less of a problem during the austral summer, when temperatures near McMurdo could actually exceed freezing. It was during the winter that the cold dropped to absurd levels.

Before entering the hut, Dana raised the plywood cover on the storm window and secured it; then she stepped inside, grateful to be out of the wind. First she sniffed to assure herself that the pilot light hadn't gone out and the room wasn't full of butane gas. Then she inspected the automatic thermostat and heater to ensure that they were in good shape, and was grateful that everything seemed in order. The thermometer said it was twenty-eight degrees above zero in the hut. Absolutely tropical. The thermostat was set at twenty-five degrees. The heater probably hadn't been used all that much. Next she took an electrical gauge—the kind one would find in a gas station—and tested the battery that was on line. The needle didn't flicker, showing that the power supply was a dud. She tested the remaining batteries and found all to be in working order, then she manually ratcheted the switch to the next battery, which caused the liquid crystal displays on the Ref Tek device and the radio repeater to come alive.

So that was it. Just a dead battery. A pain in the ass, but at least she was now back in business, and overjoyed she didn't have to rebuild the antenna farther up the hill. She exited the hut and—since she was there—checked the guy wires holding the hut in place to make sure they were taut. Then she looked at the butane tank and saw that it was more than half full, which should last the rest of the summer. Dana took a moment to survey her handiwork and wondered what would happen to her seismic stations when her research was completed and she left Antarctica. The parts for their assembly had all been ferried in by helicopter, and she'd built them with borrowed help from her colleagues during the last austral summer. Her grant had not included any money to break the sites down, but Desmond Voorhees had told her not to worry. The NSF would either continue operating the stations or take responsibility for their disassembly.

Desmond. Sheesh. The Erebus eruption notwithstanding, he was probably going to kick her ass back to Minnesota, or wring her neck, or both. She sighed as she lowered the plywood cover over the storm window. Then she zipped up her parka, grabbed the ice ax and radio, and headed back down to the Sno-Cat.

OFFICE OF NAVAL INTELLIGENCE, THE PENTAGON

"Whaddaya mean, you *lost* it?"

The bookish, ascetic-looking naval lieutenant (junior grade) cleared his throat and tried not to stammer as he said, "Ah, well, sir, we had a firm fix on the *Tbilisi*'s position from that RAAF recon plane, and we confirmed it two orbits ago with all three White Cloud sensors—IR, elint, and mil-radar. She was about seventeen hundred miles southeast of New Zealand. Her decks were hot from flight operations, and electronic emissions were shooting off every which way. Bright as a float in the Macy's parade. But then on the next orbit she was gone. Vanished. Same results on the next orbit. Nothing. It was like she sank without a trace."

The naval captain—who was operations officer for the Office of Naval Intelligence—had the looks and disposition of a retired umpire. Bald head, sandpapery skin over a basset-hound face, and two dour black eyes that seemed to say the formula for bureaucratic success was: "Don't make waves." He looked up at the officer, who was so thin, so young, so . . . frail. He continued staring as he drummed his fingers on the desk and asked, in a bored tone, "How old are you, kid?"

Affronted, the young officer held himself erect and said, "Twenty-six, sir."

"And where'd you go to school?"

"Tufts, sir."

The fingers continued to drum. "Probably majored in something I can't pronounce."

The bookish officer adjusted his horn-rimmed glasses and replied, "Computational mathematics, sir."

"Uh-huh. . . . Other than your officer training, you ever been to sea?"

The lieutenant (jg) cleared his throat again and replied, "Well, not actually. That is to say, no, sir."

The rough-looking fingers, which were attached to a crease-lined hand, stopped drumming as the captain said, "Supercarriers, whether they be Russian or American, do not sink in peacetime—in fact, they're damn hard to sink in a war. If there had been an explosion or fire, don't you think we'd have picked up a distress call? Don't you think they'd be burning up the radio circuits talking to their HQ back in Sevastopol?"

"Yes, sir."

"Have you checked with the spooks at NSA to see if there was any radio traffic out of Sevastopol or Vladivostok that might indicate the *Tbilisi* had a problem?"

The lieutenant (jg) brightened. "Yes, sir."

"And was there any?"

He darkened. "No, sir. Perhaps I should get in touch with NRO and see if they'll let us use the Lacrosse satellite. Maybe we could—"

The captain slowly shook his head and murmured, "Fuzzy thinking, Lieutenant."

The young man was lost. "Sir?"

The acerbic captain, who had twenty-eight years in service, emitted a muffled "Harrumph," and decided to take a different, more educational approach with the young man. "Sit down a minute, son."

The lieutenant (jg) did so.

"Do you know who the deputy chief of the General Staff for Intelligence is? The big G-2 in the sky, so to speak?"

"Admiral Gainesborough, sir."

The captain smiled, then leaned back in his squeaky chair and put his feet up on the desk. "That's right, old Sadie Gainesborough. Your boss. My boss. Now our Sadie is not a happy man. He has seen his beloved Navy castrated by budget cuts, and seen the old Joint Chiefs structure ripped apart and put under this General Staff horseshit, which allows those Army and Air Force coneheads to muck around in the Navy's playpen. But old Sadie doesn't give up easy, and he took it upon himself to start reversing this unhealthy trend. Made it a personal mission, you might say. He went up to the Hill and stroked some senators and such, and got funding for your precious White Cloud satellites. Then he knocked heads with the administration to transfer White Cloud from the National Reconnaissance Office to the Navy's control. Which is to say, *your* control. And he did that by telling everybody—the Congress and the President—that the Navy is *special.* Now, then, if it leaks out that our one-point-eight-billion-dollar satellite system can't find a Russkie supercarrier, the biggest jerkoff ship they've got, then everybody is going to say, 'Hey . . . this Navy ain't so special after all.' And if that happens, our dear patron and sugar daddy, Admiral Gainesborough, will have a stroke, and control of your darling White Cloud satellites will go back to the NRO, I'll be forced into retirement, and you, perish the thought, will have to go to sea. So you go back downstairs, Lieutenant, and you find me that *Tbilisi.* Prove to me, prove to the admiral, prove to the Congress and the President, that the Navy is *special.* Am I getting through now, Lieutenant?"

The bookish officer gulped and replied, "Yes, sir." The thought of going to sea nauseated him.

ROSS ICE SHELF

Dana Harrow was weary now, and glad her seven-hour round trip was almost over. As the Sno-Cat traveled across the ice shelf toward McMurdo, she toyed with the idea of trying to sneak the vehicle back into the motor pool. But upon reflection she decided to make a clean breast of everything to Desmond Voorhees. She'd first explain that "borrowing" the Sno-Cat and going out alone enabled her to keep the seismic stations on line so she could continue to monitor Mount Erebus per his instructions . . . then she would lamely admit she was worried about her dissertation. No sense in trying to fool him.

But right now she was too tired and hungry to care about Desmond's reaction. She would stop by the seismic lab on her way to the motor pool and check her equipment, turn in the Sno-Cat, grab something to eat, 'fess up to Desmond, and hit the rack. She looked at her watch. It read 9:34 P.M., McMurdo time. Even though the sun was out twenty-four hours a day now, and there wasn't a cloud in the sky, the base would soon be turning in for a good "night's" sleep. Maybe she would wait and talk to Desmond tomorrow.

The hard rubber tracks of her vehicle were churning across the talcum-powderlike snow of the ice shelf, and Dana was about three miles south, and a little east, of McMurdo—roughly equidistant between the base and the Williams Field ice aerodrome. The tip of Hut Point peninsula—where land, ice, and sea all converged—was shaped like an arrowhead. Dana could see the small American McMurdo base on the western sea side of the arrowhead, and not quite two miles away was the smaller New Zealand installation— called Scott Base—on the eastern side that faced toward the ice shelf.

Her eyes followed the line of the peninsula to the base of Mount Erebus, then up the slope to the craggy black dome that was now covered with a mottled epidermis of snow, ice, and volcanic ash from the eruption. The sky was clear and the wind had gone still, allowing a thin skirt of clouds to lie undisturbed along the lower slopes of the 12,444-foot mountain.

The excitement that Erebus usually kindled in Dana was absent, for she was bone-tired. And it was her fatigue, along with the rattle-trap noise of the Sno-Cat—the rolling treads, the diesel engine, the creaky seat springs—that kept her from hearing the sound until they were almost directly overhead. It began as a high-pitched drone, but soon grew into a wail that pierced her fatigue and the noise of the groaning diesel engine. At first she thought something was wrong with the Sno-Cat, but then one of their shadows whipped overhead and they popped into view, filling the windshield.

They were airplanes. Three large jet airplanes, painted a tan color and flying in a kind of V formation as they turned onto a course parallel to the runway of the ice aerodrome. God, they were flying low, thought Dana. Must be fixing to land.

But these planes did not land. Instead, they pulled up and gained a bit of altitude—just before little dark puffballs began falling from their tails, drifting down to the waiting white expanse of the aerodrome.

Dana brought the Sno-Cat to an abrupt halt and peered intently through the windshield at what was unfolding before her. She left the engine running and jumped out of the cab, and as she hit the ground, another formation of planes roared overhead, causing her to duck. This time there were six of the large, jet-powered transports, and they broke into two smaller formations—four planes heading for McMurdo, and the other two heading for the nearby New Zealand Scott base. Again, a multitude of puffballs fell from their tails and began drifting toward the earth. Dana's fatigue quickly vanished as she realized what those puffballs were.

They were parachutes.

Again she involuntarily ducked as six more of the tan-colored aircraft roared over her, heading past the aerodrome toward the Windless Bight of the Ross Ice Shelf.

Dana felt her stomach turn into a cold vessel, where fear supplanted hunger—for when the last group of transports flew over her, she could see a marking on one of the tails that was unmistakably a big red star.

10

....

SNOW LEOPARD

Columbus had been dead for 313 years before mankind first laid eyes on the enigmatic Terra Australis Incognita—*the unknown southern land.*

The leader of the expedition that made the initial sighting was led by an able explorer and seaman whose achievements could be ranked alongside those of Columbus, James Cook, or Ferdinand Magellan. Yet unlike Columbus, Cook, or Magellan, this explorer's seminal journey into Antarctic waters never received the recognition it deserved.

Who was this daring explorer and superb sea captain who led two ships of 188 officers and men on a dangerous two-year expedition? His name was Faddei Gottlieb von Bellingshausen, and he laid eyes upon the Antarctic mainland (not knowing what it was) on January 20, 1820, when he spied an "ice field covered with small hillocks."

Although von Bellingshausen was born in Estonia and possessed a Germanic-sounding name, his true allegiance belonged to neither country.

He was an officer in the Imperial Russian Navy, in service to Czar Alexander I.

McMURDO STATION

Maj. Gen. Mitrofan Tromso had barely released his parachute harness when his radio operator shoved a handset in front of his face. Tromso ripped off his hard leather headgear (for some strange reason, Soviet paratroopers wore the same headdress as Red Army tank crewmen) and grabbed the receiver to say, "Leopard Six, this is Leopard One. Give me your status at once!"

A few seconds of static were followed by "Leopard One, this is Six. My team is on the ground and assembling. We will begin advancing within seconds."

"*Speed,* Leopard Six," urged Tromso. "Speed is critical. We do not know which structures house the American and New Zealand communications equipment, but we know the antennae for both installations are consolidated in a fenced area up on that hill." Tromso looked up at Crater Hill, which rose above McMurdo on Hut Point Peninsula. "Find them and cut the connections!"

More static. "My team is moving out now. We have a target in sight. Leopard Six out."

Tromso lowered the handset and took a moment to get his bearings. The general was just the sort of man you would expect to find as commander of the Soviet 103rd Guards Airborne Division. Slightly under two meters tall, trim, athletic, and close-cropped brown hair with a sprinkling of gray. He was a veteran of Afghanistan, and his judgment was quick and rarely forgiving. He was not particularly liked by his men, but was thoroughly respected. Rapidly he ran through the reconnaissance photos and maps that were imprinted on his mind, then he methodically began matching them up with the landmarks he now held in view. No matter how great the preparation, he mused to himself, it always seemed different once you got on the ground.

"Leopard One, this is Leopard Four," crackled through the radio, followed quickly by, "Leopard One, this is Leopard Three."

Tromso keyed the mike and said, "Wait one, Three. Leopard Four, report."

"My troops are assembling and preparing to move out. No resistance thus far and we have already taken some prisoners."

Tromso quickly responded, "Remember, Leopard Four, speed is essential, but use force only as a last resort. These people are scientists, not soldiers."

"Understood. Leopard Four out."

Tromso knew that Leopard Four understood. He was a reliable but overly cautious battalion commander. That was why his unit was chosen to sweep through McMurdo Station and Scott Base and collect the scientists. He would make sure his men followed orders. "Leopard Three, report."

Static. "This is Three. The airfield is secure. It was deserted except for two C-130 aircraft and a few technicians."

"Excellent, Three," replied Tromso. "Radio our aircraft on the assigned frequency. Tell the second stick to bring in their aircraft and deploy their troops after landing."

"Leopard One, if I may," responded the voice, at once supplicating but firm. "Our pilots have limited experience with ice runways and ski landings. I recommend our troops jump according to plan. Then, if the pilots crack up on landing, our people will not be on board. Besides, my men in the second stick want to jump."

Tromso smiled. Leopard Three was one of his best battalion commanders. Maybe *the* best. He knew a paratrooper had no desire to land in enemy territory as if he were on an airliner. "Agreed, Leopard Three. Carry on, and set up the radio relay with Leopard Five with all possible speed."

"At once, Leopard One."

Tromso's radio was a line-of-sight FM tactical set. His troops landing on Branding Iron Station were on the other side of Hut Point Peninsula—out of sight and out of radio range.

BRANDING IRON STATION

The staccato sound of jackhammers mixed with the growl of compressors reverberated through the icedome, and Lt. Col. Samuel McClure had to shout to be heard over the din. "We're almost completely through the lava apron now, sir. It would've been a lot faster if we could've blasted our way through, but we couldn't do that for fear of dropping the dome on us."

While walking toward the elevator, Col. Ernest Battelle nodded his agreement. "I know, Sammy. Using half a dozen jackhammers at once is a screwy way to do it, but like you said, we couldn't take a chance on the blasting. We've had enough surprises." Battelle stepped inside the elevator.

"Yes, sir, but digging through with jackhammers sure eats up our time."

Battelle closed the cagelike doors. "We'll just have to press on. I'm going topside and call it a day. I'll be back to relieve you at zero-six-hundred."

"Very well, sir."

The elevator began its ascent, and as it disappeared through the hole at the apex of the icedome, the utility phone rang—the same phone that had been the cause of mob violence only five days before. The executive officer took it and said, "This is Colonel McClure."

The voice on the other end was frantic. "Sir! Get Colonel Battelle up here fast!"

McClure became alarmed. "He's on his way up now. What's the

problem, trooper? . . . Hello? . . . Hello? . . . Trooper, what's the problem?"

Ernest Battelle opened the cagelike doors of the elevator and looked directly into the muzzle of a Kalashnikov AK-47 assault rifle. With a single glance Battelle took in the rifle, the Red Army paratrooper, the deflated parachutes out on the ice shelf—and knew immediately what was happening.

Funny thing about Ernie Battelle. Besides being a horse's ass and a social pariah, he was also utterly fearless. He grabbed the muzzle of the AK-47 and yanked it upward so that it was pointing into the air, and as the startled paratrooper held on to the weapon, it rattled off a few rounds that ricocheted around the derrick's tower. Then, as the Russian pulled on the rifle to reclaim it, Battelle shoved it forward so the butt slammed into his enemy's stomach. The paratrooper reeled back, but held on to his weapon as he fell back onto the deck. He was stunned and unable to breathe or move, and his vision took on a slow-motion quality as he watched the American grab a large Stilson wrench off a tool shelf and bring it up to strike him. He felt for the grip of his rifle, but he was moving too slowly. He was going to die.

The wrench was coming down when a half-dozen AK-47 slugs ripped through Ernie Battelle's chest and dropped him, dead, onto the deck of Branding Iron Station. The platoon sergeant bounded up the remaining steps and ran over to inspect his victim. It was the first time since the American Expeditionary Force withdrew from Siberian soil during the Russian civil war in 1920 that a Russian soldier had killed an American soldier in combat.

As the platoon sergeant knelt down over his victim, he had the same surrealistic feeling he'd experienced in Afghanistan so long ago. He never took any joy in killing. Particularly in killing an unarmed man. But a member of his platoon had been in peril and he'd done what he felt he must. He moved from Battelle's body and pulled the private to his feet, yelling, "Into the elevator, Klasov! Quickly! They may have heard the shots!" Then he turned and saw the other members of the platoon running toward the derrick as fast as they could through the ankle-deep snow.

McMURDO STATION

When the U.S. government gets its hands on something—anything—you can usually multiply its inherent complexity by several orders of magnitude. And that complexity extended even to Antarctica, in that the head man at McMurdo Station was Senior U.S. Representative Desmond Voorhees, who was from the National Science Foundation and acted like a kind of ambassador. But logistical support for McMurdo Station was provided by the U.S. Navy and the Coast Guard. Needless to say, this bureaucratic mishmash invited disaster if the senior rep and the head Navy man didn't get along. But fortunately, Desmond Voorhees and Navy Capt. John Benton got on very well, and treated each other as colleagues and friends. They often shared a high-profile drink at the Icebreaker Lounge, sending a subtle message to their subordinates and visitors that if the two top guys at McMurdo could be buddies, then there needn't be any cause for conflict among the different factions.

But besides the visible cocktails, they sometimes enjoyed a fast game of chess—as they were doing now. Desmond Voorhees, in deference to his position, had the largest quarters in the dormitory building, which included a bedroom, a small living room–study area, and a tiny kitchen.

In contrast to the tall and angular Voorhees, Benton was almost a foot shorter and rather paunchy. He wore a white-sidewall haircut on a bald head, had a lightbulb-shaped nose, and enjoyed wearing turtleneck sweaters. The only similarity between the two men was that they both smoked pipes. Benton puffed away on his while he moved his black bishop to take a white pawn.

Voorhees studied the board and said, "Sure I can't talk you into coming back next summer, John? Things sure seem to run a lot smoother when you're around."

Benton kept an eye on the board as Voorhees toyed with his queen's knight. " 'Fraid so, Desmond. This tour is going to be a wrap on my career. I'll spend another year in Washington or Norfolk, and then muster out."

The knight moved. "What do you think you'll do when you get out? You're only fifty-five. Surely there are a few miles left in the old jitney."

Benton smiled to himself and replied, "A couple of things, actually. I've been offered a teaching position at the Coast Guard Academy, which is attractive, but there is—"

Benton halted in mid-sentence, and both he and Voorhees turned their heads to look at the closed door. There seemed to be some commotion coming from down the hall. The noise grew louder and louder, and it eventually became distinct as muffled shouts and slamming doors. Benton and Voorhees looked at each other for an explanation, but neither had one. Finally, Voorhees said, "What on earth?" as he and Benton started to rise from their chairs. But then the door burst open to reveal a Soviet paratrooper leveling an AK-47 at them.

"Hands up! *Vy zaklyuchonny!* You are my prisoner!"

Neither man moved, because neither could mentally accept what they were seeing.

The muzzle motioned to the ceiling. *"Ruki vverx!* Hands up!"

This time they got the message, and two pairs of hands went into the air.

"Put on coat. Come with me. *Bystro!* Fast!"

BRANDING IRON STATION

Lt. Col. Samuel McClure was still holding the receiver in his hand, trying to raise someone on the derrick above. What could have happened? He kept trying until he heard the elevator start descending again, and this gave him a sense of relief. He would soon learn what the problem was. The cage continued its approach, and when it dropped into view, McClure could see through the metallic semiveil that it held about half a dozen strangers wearing strange garb and holding tools. . . . Wait, those weren't tools. They were *rifles!*

The door burst open and the Guards platoon sergeant shoved his AK-47 in McClure's face with the words, "You are prisoner!"

ROSS ICE SHELF

The last puffball had long since fallen to the ground, and the airplanes had turned out to sea and disappeared; but Dana Harrow's boots remained bolted to the ice as she tried to deal with the consummate shock of what she'd witnessed. She probably would have stayed in place for quite a time, had another flight of six transports not come up behind her and roared overhead, heading toward the ice aerodrome. As they cruised over the ice field and emptied their bellies, the sky beneath them became almost black with parachutes blossoming into the air.

This second wave was like a mental slap to Dana, causing her to jump back into the Sno-Cat and turn on the radio. Grabbing the mike, she pressed the keying switch and said, "McMurdo Base, McMurdo Base, this is"—she looked at the label on the transceiver—"this is unit nine. Can you hear me? . . . Over." She remembered you were supposed to say, "Over."

There was a brief pause before the reply came back with, "Unit nine, McMurdo Base. Where the hell have you been? The guys at the motor pool have been running around trying to find their missing Sno-Cat, and I've been trying to raise you. Where are you at? Over."

Dana thought she recognized the voice. "Barry, is that you?" Barry was the McMurdo commo chief, and a techie if there ever was one.

"Yeah, that be me. Who be you? And *where* be you, too? Over."

"Barry, this is Dana Harrow. Listen to me. I am a few miles out from McMurdo on the ice shelf. I have just seen, so help me, a bunch of parachutes falling on McMurdo, on Scott Base, and on Williams Field. Barry, I think they were Russian planes. And I think they were dropping—are still dropping, in fact—what do you call them? . . . Paratroops."

There was more than a moment of silence before the radio said, "I'm not quite sure I understand you, unit nine. Say again."

"I *said* a bunch of goddamn Russian paratroopers have fallen on McMurdo, you jerk! Go to the window and see for yourself!"

A chuckle came back through the transceiver. "That might be a little difficult, dear. I'm in the basement, you know. But that's an interesting story. I've heard some of the survival kits in the Sno-Cats have medicinal brandy in them. Sounds like you found one of those. Why don't you just come on back and sleep it off?"

Dana mashed the button. "Listen, you dumb ass, I'm not drunk and I'm telling you a bunch of Russian paratroops have just dropped onto McMurdo! You better notify Desmond and Benton and the Kiwis and anybody else you can think of pretty damn quick!"

"Sure, sure, Dana. I think you better just bring the Sno-Cat back to the motor pool and go to the dispensary. Hypothermia can be dangerous if . . ." The radio squawked and the transmission was replaced with static.

She mashed the mike button again. "Barry? . . . Barry, can you hear me? Hello? . . . Barry, come in."

Static.

Dana looked through the windshield. The last parachute had hit the ground, and the six transports were heading out to sea like the others. Fear was rapidly supplanting confusion in her mind, but Dana forced those feelings aside and made herself think. She knew that something unbelievable was happening. Something she could not comprehend. But her instincts told her that McMurdo was to be avoided at all costs. She needed some time to sort things out and figure out where to go from here. To drive into McMurdo now would be crazy so she fired up the diesel and turned the Sno-Cat back toward Mount Discovery.

McMURDO STATION

As they had done in rehearsals, the paratroopers of the 103rd Guards Airborne Division swept through the buildings of McMurdo Base like a bunch of hungry ferrets, digging out their quarry and forcing them out into the roads. All over the base the scene was repeated, where men and women—with hastily pulled-on winter gear—were formed up into ranks. They all looked at each other with gazes of complete bewilderment, asking each other what was happening, but no one had an answer—except, perhaps, the crew members of Branding Iron Station. And they weren't talking.

The biggest group was formed up outside the main dormitory building, where the collective gazes fell upon Voorhees and Benton. As they lined up next to each other, the senior U.S. representative felt the massed eyeballs of his colleagues and subordinates boring down on him, silently begging for an explanation. But he had no explanation to give. Voorhees felt completely impotent as he leaned down and whispered to the Navy captain, "These soldiers are Russians."

Benton nodded carefully.

"This must have something to do with that damned . . . that damned . . . whatever the hell it is out on the Windless Bight." Voorhees looked around. "Where is that Battelle?"

Benton surveyed the scene too. "I don't see him."

As the whispering up and down the line grew in intensity and became audible, a Guards captain strutted up and down the line yelling, "*Molchat!* No talking!" Everyone hushed up as the captain turned to his top sergeant and said, "Move them out."

Because no one was armed, the prisoners were allowed to lower their hands as they were marched off in the direction of the ice wharf.

After a rapid climb, Maj. Gen. Mitrofan Tromso stood atop Crater Hill and surveyed the antenna complex that was the linchpin for McMurdo's communication with the outside world. He turned to the commander of his signal battalion, who was Leopard Six, and asked, "Are you certain all communications have been severed?"

Standing atop Crater Hill, they could feel the wind coming off the Sound, and the signal officer had put his parka on over his utility uniform. "For this location I am certain all communications have been broken," he said. "However, our intelligence briefing said there were some amateur radio operators in the American and New Zealand villages. Leopard Four has been told what kind of antenna to look for, and my men are monitoring the appropriate radio bands with their scanners and direction finders. If someone is transmitting, we will triangulate on their position and cut them off in short order."

"Is our communication with the *Mirnyi* and *Arktika* established?"

From a radio set positioned on a tripod stand, the signal officer took a handset and passed it to the general, saying, "Affirmative, sir."

Tromso took the handset and said, "Sea Leopard, this is Leopard One. Rendezvous Diamond. I say again, rendezvous Diamond."

"Roger, Leopard One. We are en route. Sea Leopard out."

He tossed the handset back to his signal officer and climbed up to the rim of Crater Hill. He raised his binoculars to view Branding Iron Station, and could see that some of the commandeered vehicles were starting to move out. He lowered his glasses and walked along the rim to the seaward side of the crater, then turned his binoculars on the ocean to try to find the *Mirnyi* and the *Arktika*. He couldn't see them yet, but they would be along soon. Looking down the hill, he saw the lines of prisoners moving toward the ice wharf.

The shoreline along the seaward side of Hut Point Peninsula, near McMurdo Base, forms a small inlet that is called Winter Quarters Bay, and it is here that ships dock and unload their stores and scientific gear for summer research projects. To accommodate this sea traffic a pier was needed, so the inventive Americans decided to use locally available materials to build one. Ergo, the ice wharf. It was quite simple, really. They constructed a rim of ice about two feet deep in a rectangle and flooded it. Then they let it freeze and built another rim on top of that, flooded it and let it freeze, and so on and so on, until they had a pier made of ice. It was reinforced with steel and covered with some dirt on top to provide insulation, but essentially it was a stack of ice rinks built on top of one another. And it worked.

Desmond Voorhees and John Benton were on the front rank of the middle pack of prisoners who were traveling in a loose march toward the ice wharf. As they approached the pier, a Guardsman came walking down the road, shouting in broken English, "Wher iss Verheez? Wher iss Verheez?"

The senior United States representative to Antarctica waved his hand and said, "I am Voorhees."

The Russian motioned with his rifle and said, "You come with me."

Voorhees shrugged at Benton and followed the paratrooper up the rise beside the road. He approached a man who was clearly in charge, for three radio operators were hovering around him. Voorhees's escort ran ahead and jabbered something to the man in Russian, and the tall Guards general beckoned his visitor to step forward. "You are Voorhees?" he asked in stilted but correct English. "Desmond Voorhees, senior United States representative here?"

"That is correct. And I demand to know the meaning of this outrageous act! This is kidnapping! This—this is an *invasion!*"

The tall Russian, who was still an inch shorter than Voorhees, raised a hand to cut him off. "You will listen to me, Dr. Voorhees. I am Major General Mitrofan Tromso, commanding officer of the 103rd Guards Airborne Division. The Soviet Union is exercising a legal claim on the whole continent of Antarctica, and we are now evicting foreigners who are trespassing on our sovereign territory."

"*Legal* claim? What legal claim? The Soviet Union was a signatory to the SCAR Treaty."

Tromso nodded. "You are quite correct, Doctor. But as you will recall, that treaty is no longer in force, and no other has taken its place. Therefore, the Soviet Union is free to exercise its claim based on a historical expedition."

"What historical expedition?"

"The initial sighting of Antarctica by the expedition of Faddei von Bellingshausen of the Imperial Russian Navy."

Voorhees nearly lost his balance. *"Bellingshausen!* That was almost two hundred years ago! I'd say your claim was a bit stale, General. That's like . . . like Norway trying to claim New York City because the Vikings landed in America first. I don't know what kind of joke you're trying to pull here, General, but you're not going to get away with—"

"I assure you it is no joke, Doctor Voorhees, but I do not have time to argue over legalities. I am here to inform you that you and your people will be transferred to a ship for transport to a neutral port, where you will be released for repatriation to the United States. You will travel in safety and comfort, and if you and your people cooperate, no harm will come to you or to them. But I must warn you—any attempt at resistance will be dealt with harshly."

Desmond Voorhees had never felt so impotent, and he could feel the acid building up in his stomach from the frustration. "Very well. We are not in a position to offer resistance. Where are you taking us?"

"You will know when you arrive there. . . . Captain!"

A Guards captain stepped forward and Tromso said, "Dr. Voorhees, this is Captain Savinykh. You are to designate one of your people to remain behind and help us collect the scientists from their field research locations. Upon collection, they will be ferried by helicopter to the transport ship."

Desmond didn't say anything, mentally trying to grope for some way he could fight back.

Tromso left no opening. "I must add, Dr. Voorhees, that any field crews we recover will be treated well. But any unidentified people that are found by our helicopter patrols will be fired upon without warning. All research crews are to be recovered. Do I make myself clear?"

"Quite clear," Voorhees replied acidly. "Captain what's-his-name here . . ."

"Savinykh," offered the young officer.

". . . can work with my communications chief. He has a list of the locations and staff of each field crew. There weren't many research parties this year."

"I'm sure," said Tromso knowingly.

Voorhees continued to glare at him. "This is about that business out on the Windless Bight, isn't it?"

Tromso raised his field glasses and looked out at the Sound. "Farewell, Dr. Voorhees," he said.

WILLIAMS ICE AERODROME

The massive Antonov-124 Condor transport touched down on its ski landing gear and engaged the thrust reversers, slowly bringing the leviathan craft to a halt. It then turned onto the ice taxiway, passing another Condor that was preparing to take off. The transport did not even kill its engines as the rear cargo bay doors yawned open and the loading ramp extended down to the ice. A large tracked vehicle fired up its diesel engine and pulled a train of pallets out of the cargo bay. Once the train was on the ice, the loading ramp retracted, the doors closed, and the Condor pulled away to taxi for takeoff—just as another Condor was landing.

The ice runway at Williams Field required the aircraft to use ski landing gear. But Operation Snow Leopard was going to require a great many fighter aircraft, for which it was impractical to use ski landing gear that could not be retracted. So, immediately after the aerodrome was secure, the Condors began landing with their cargo pallets.

At the end of the runway a sergeant major was screaming at a bunch of airmen who were working with antlike intensity to break the pallets down. Once that was done, the combat engineers would start assembling the aluminum-alloy plates into a two-thousand-meter runway that would be laid down on top of Williams Field.

The first runway would be completed in twelve hours, and the fighters could begin to land.

ICE WHARF, McMURDO STATION

The nuclear-powered icebreaker *Arktika* nudged the ice wharf and then reversed its engines to back out and clear a path for the *Mirnyi,* which was traveling in its wake, two kilometers behind.

It was high summer, and there was only a thin film of pack ice across McMurdo Sound this year. The *Mirnyi* probably could have made it alone with no sweat, but the operational plan for Snow Leopard called for the icebreaker to clear a path—so the *Arktika* was there, clearing a path.

In the annals of icebreakers, the *Arktika* held a singular position, for on August 17, 1977, it became the first surface ship to break its way through the polar ice cap and reach the geographic North Pole. But that was over twenty years ago, and the ship was old now, reaching the end of its serviceable life. Which was to say it was expendable if need be.

As the aged *Arktika* pulled back, it was replaced by a gleaming ship that was as resplendent as a bridal gown, and this vessel was definitely not expendable. Built in the Gdansk shipyard, the white-skinned *Mirnyi* was a world-class pleasure cruise ship that had been put on the water to serve the burgeoning tourist industry of Antarctica. Only a year old and equipped with sonar to detect the underwater formations of icebergs, it normally steamed along the coast of the Antarctic peninsula. But now it had been pressed into service for something else.

A gangway was extended onto the ice wharf, and the Americans and New Zealanders were herded up into the hold. As Voorhees and Benton shuffled along toward the gangway with the rest of their group, a short, dignified man with white hair wedged through the crowd to pull Voorhees's sleeve. He was Reginald Bloom, the head man at the New Zealand Scott Base. "Desmond. What is happening here? These are Russian soldiers."

"I know, Reginald. I mean, I know they're Russians, but I don't know why they are here. It's my guess it has something to do with that project out on the Windless Bight."

This did not satisfy Reginald Bloom. "You *guess?* Don't you know?"

Voorhees shrugged. "I have no idea, Reginald. Word of honor."

"But that is absurd! You are the senior U.S. representative here."

" 'Absurd' is the perfect word, Reginald. But I simply do not know what's out there."

"*Speshite!* Move fast! Keep moving," ordered the Guards paratrooper.

And they filed up the gangway.

MINNA SADDLE

Dana Harrow drove the Sno-Cat through the Minna Saddle, where she had been six hours previously. She was trying to cope with a kaleidoscope of feelings, from bewilderment to incredulity to raw fear, all intertwined with overpowering fatigue.

Paratroops. Russian paratroops. Here in Antarctica. Beyond belief, she kept telling herself. It *had* to be that "Secret Project" out on the Windless Bight. Had to. But what could there possibly be in this frozen wasteland worth sending paratroops after? Oil? No. That didn't make sense. The Persian Gulf was a lot closer to Moscow. Diamonds? Couldn't be that. Ivan Telenko had discovered diamonds aplenty in Siberia. Gold? Uranium? As a student of geology, Dana knew the Russians possessed those commodities as well. What then? The black monolith from *2001: A Space Odyssey?*

Completely baffled, Dana parked her vehicle and killed the engine. She grabbed the binoculars and the ice ax from the back of the Sno-Cat, then started back up to the hut nestled into the slope of Mount Discovery. Her pace was labored, reflecting her weariness as she continued to trudge past the seismic hut and up toward the crest of the ridgeline. Upon reaching it, she raised the binoculars and surveyed the scene. McMurdo was still the same . . . but wait. She spied the sterns of two ships heading out of the Sound. What were they? She turned the glasses onto Scott Base, and everything there looked the same. Then she turned them onto Williams Field. What in the world? . . . One, two, three, four new planes. She guessed they were some of the ones that had flown over her. But there were also two giant planes. God, they must be *huge.* Even from this distance she could see that they dwarfed the other Russian planes and the two American C-130s that were there. Dana watched as one of the gigantic aircraft took off and headed west, just as another was coming in from the east for a landing. Arms tired, she lowered the binoculars and started back toward the hut in a zombielike trance. She entered the plywood structure and couldn't decide if her hunger or her fatigue was going to gain supremacy. Clumsily she unfolded the cot and unrolled the down sleeping bag on top of it. She turned the thermostat up to sixty degrees, and the butane heater under the battery shelves came to life. Then she pushed the window open a crack for ventilation. After giving the slip to a bunch of Russian paratroopers, she didn't want to die from asphyxiation. She rummaged in the emergency rations box for something to eat, and found some granola bars that were frozen hard. She put them on the battery shelf and sat down on the cot to wait while they thawed out. As fatigue consumed her, Dana slowly leaned over to put her head down on the cot, and by the time her cheek touched the sleeping bag she was already asleep.

BRANDING IRON STATION

"Damn!"

Maj. Gen. Mitrofan Tromso grimaced as he viewed the olive drab body bag containing the remains of Col. Ernest Battelle. "I was hoping something like this would not happen."

"It is regrettable, General," replied the battalion commander in charge of securing Branding Iron Station. "But unfortunately it was unavoidable. He was about to dispatch one of my men with a wrench when he was shot."

Tromso grimaced again. "And you think he was in command?"

The battalion commander said, "We believe so. His insignia show that he was an American colonel. We did not have time to interrogate prisoners, of course, but we found no one of higher rank. So we assume he was in command."

Tromso shook his head and then looked out on the ice shelf to see something gleaming in the sunlight a hundred meters away. "What's that?" he asked, pointing.

The porky chief engineer, who was a civilian and had arrived on a Condor flight, explained—trying without success to mask his nervousness at being drafted for this operation—"The Americans used an ingenious device to melt a passage through the ice shelf. The water from the melted ice was apparently pumped through a heated pipeline to that location. It appears the men in charge of water disposal took the opportunity to fashion an ice castle of some kind."

Tromso shrugged, then grabbed the civilian engineer by the arm and said, "Let us have a look at our prize."

The elevator doors opened, allowing Tromso, the pudgy engineer, and the battalion commander to step into the icedome. The Guards general was genuinely impressed as he surveyed the scene. It had a quality about it that was eerie, otherworldly.

"This way," said the engineer.

Tromso noticed that the uneven floor of volcanic rock was pitted and scarred—from ice abrasions, he assumed—and was covered with a film of silt.

"This is the shaft the Americans were sinking," the engineer explained. "It would have been more convenient if we had allowed them to do more of the work, but of course we had no way of knowing how far they had progressed. They were just beginning to punch through this lava apron. We must finish this task, then dig through approximately seventy meters of sedimentary rock, then a second lava apron, and then we should be at the rubidium deposit."

"How long do you estimate it will take?"

The engineer continued gazing at the hole. "Once we sink the shaft, we must then cut a side tunnel to excavate the salt deposits that contain the rubidium. Working around the clock, I would estimate three to four weeks to reach the salt deposit level. Then another one to two weeks to extract a hundred tons of the deposits and get them to the surface. You must remember we only have the single elevator to work with."

Tromso gazed into the open pit and pondered his situation. Four to six weeks. The timing could have been better. Might have been worse. Had the Americans been alerted? His signal officer had said there were some amateur radios in the villages. If their security was still intact, how long would it be before the Americans learned of their presence? Could this engineer really produce as fast as he said he could? The first two weeks were critical. He had to build the runways and bunkers and get the aircraft in place. Tromso had brought only one regiment of the 103rd Guards Airborne Division with him, for three reasons: there had been no significant military opposition to overcome on landing, any subsequent conflict was going to hinge on air superiority, and when it came time to leave McMurdo he could extract a single regiment a lot faster than a whole division.

Whether or not the Americans had received a warning, Tromso knew it would take time for them to respond. Time to figure out what was happening, to activate their forces, then travel thirteen thousand kilometers from the American West Coast and deploy—possibly in hostile weather. All that would definitely take significant time. In two weeks he would have a thick, thick blanket of air cover that he felt would be virtually impregnable. If Tromso got his two weeks, then the engineer could have that and three more. But that was it.

"You have five weeks, Comrade. No more. I will not put my people in jeopardy for longer than that. And Moscow can be damned. Five weeks."

RED BANNER NORTHERN FLEET SUBMARINE BASE, GUBA ZAPADNAYA LITSA, KOLA PENINSULA—January 16

Captain, First Rank, Kasimir Bodin was perched like a restless hawk on the catwalk spanning his Delta-IV-class submarine, the *Kharkov.* He was watching the final *Zimorodok* missile, which was suspended by a crane, being lowered into the launch tube on the submarine's turtleback. Eleven missiles had already been loaded. This last one would make it an even dozen, leaving four of the *Kharkov*'s sixteen launch tubes empty. But it was all Bodin could do to get thirty-six missiles cranked out of that miserable factory, which made it twelve missiles apiece for the *Kharkov,* the *Smolensk,* and the *Magadan*— all Delta-IV-class submarines slated for the deployment. Bodin had little faith that the *Zimorodok* missiles would work at all, but he was stuck with the axiom that all military men must come to grips with: orders were orders.

The sound of heavy footsteps coming up the metallic stairs made Bodin turn to see Admiral of the Fleet Yuri Timoshenko climbing the steps to join him on the catwalk. The admiral was wearing his greatcoat and the giant saucer of a hat that was encrusted with gold braid—and he carried a large envelope under his arm. Timoshenko stood beside Bodin, and neither man spoke as they watched the loading proceed on the *Zimorodok* missile. It was cold within the cavernlike base on this January morning, and the two submariners could see their breath.

"Our men have landed," said Timoshenko finally. "Thirteen hours ago. No resistance, of course, except for one casualty. As far as we can tell, no warning has been sounded as yet."

Bodin breathed deeply. "We should have been on station before this Snow Leopard business started, but the missiles . . . that worthless factory . . ."

"I know, Kasimir. I know."

Bodin shook his head and continued, "I must leave with all possible speed before the Americans can increase their surveillance of our naval movements." Timoshenko said nothing as Bodin's eyes remained fixed on the *Kharkov* and the missile being loaded. "Twenty-three thousand kilometers from Kola to the Ross Sea," said Bodin. "A long voyage. Traveling at maximum cruise, I anticipate it will take us at least three weeks to arrive on station. But traveling at maximum cruise is noisy, Yuri Ilyanovich."

Timoshenko took the envelope from under his arm and handed it over, saying, "Four weeks, Kasimir. It is all in your orders."

Bodin took the envelope with an expression of surprise, then returned his gaze to the sub. "Why four weeks? The sooner I get out of range of the American sensors, the better."

The defense minister nodded. "Quite true, my friend. But we do not know when the Americans will learn of Snow Leopard. Therefore, we must ensure that the *Kharkov,* as well as the *Smolensk* and the *Magadan,* will evade any American submarines once you are past their SOSUS line." Timoshenko instinctively looked around to make sure he could not be heard, then lowered his voice. "You are to use the Passage."

Bodin jerked his head round. "The Passage? So *that* is why a new periscope mast was installed. I was wondering why . . ." Once the words were past his lips, the ordinarily self-confident Bodin realized his faux pas and found himself stammering. "By that I mean . . . I mean to say that . . ."

Timoshenko chuckled wryly. "What you mean to say, my dear Kasimir Sergeievich, is that you are not supposed to know anything at all about the Passage. I reviewed your file before those orders were cut. You were never cleared for information on the Passage. You were never briefed on the Passage. You should not even know that the Passage exists. Yet Kasimir Sergeievich Bodin knows. How did such a breach of security come to pass, my old friend?" Timoshenko chuckled again, taking pleasure in outfoxing Bodin, if only by a small measure.

Bodin cleared his throat, then once more returned his gaze to the *Kharkov.* "There are no real secrets among submariners, Yuri Ilyanovich. You know that as well as I. We go under the sea for months at a time. Men come to know each other better than they know their own families. They talk. Like all Russians, they have secrets to share. Crews transfer. They talk again. They go on leave together and get drunk and boast. All the time talk, talk, talk. We all know that happens, Yuri Ilyanovich."

Timoshenko nodded. "*Da,* Kasimir. You and I know better than anyone that there are no secrets, but for the sake of the *Kharkov* and your brother vessels, I hope the secrets of the Passage have not fallen upon the wrong ears."

"As do I," agreed Bodin. The *Zimorodok* missile had almost disappeared down the tube now. "I will be prepared for departure within the hour. What about the *Smolensk* and the *Magadan?*"

"They should be leaving from Polyarny as we speak. You will rendezvous with them under the ice north of Spitzbergen before turning south to pick up your escort."

"Escort?"

The defense minister smiled again. "It is all in your orders, Kasimir. Your departure is timed to ensure that the American satellites will track you as you leave the harbor. You are simply another Delta-IV submarine, en route to a routine deployment under the polar ice cap." Timoshenko looked down at the submarine and saw an officer walking up the gangway with a tightly packed grip in his hand. He pointed and said, "Your pilot for the Passage has arrived. He is a proficient officer. You may rely on him to get the *Kharkov* through."

"Very well, Yuri Ilyanovich." Bodin extended a hand as their eyes met. "I bid you farewell, old friend."

The admiral took the hand of his former *starpom* and held his gaze for some time. "Goodbye, *tovarisch.* May God go with you."

Bodin lowered his gaze and replied, "I do not feel God will smile on an enterprise such as this, Yuri Ilyanovich."

MOUNT DISCOVERY SEISMIC STATION

Dana Harrow came awake with a start, and sprang into a sitting position on the cot. For several seconds, in that disjointed time between sleep and true consciousness, she had no idea where she was or how she'd gotten there. But slowly the shock dissipated and gave way to recollection, and then fear. Had she dreamed it all? Was she crazy? Or had Soviet paratroops actually landed in McMurdo? As her senses came into sharper focus, the bewilderment and fear rapidly gave way to hunger and thirst. She stared at one of the granola bar on the battery shelf. It had defrosted in the sixty-degree temperature, so she ripped off the paper covering and began to devour it, realizing also that she was thirsty to the point of dehydration. She ventured outside to fill up a canteen cup with snow, then came back in and fired up the little camper stove. The snow melted rapidly, but it didn't make much water, so she made several trips until she had a full cup. She downed it and repeated the process. Dehydration was a constant threat in the cold, dry climate of Antarctica, and if she was to stay alive, she must remain healthy. Her thirst quenched, she wolfed down three more granola bars, then sat there and contemplated her predicament. There wasn't much to contemplate. What the hell could she do? Go back to McMurdo and give herself up? That held little appeal. Sit tight and wait to be rescued? Who knew she was here to be rescued? She felt grimy and dazed, and could have used a shower, but more than anything, Dana could not sit still. She had to do *something*.

Leaving the hut with binoculars and ice ax in hand, she headed for the ridgeline. After huffing and puffing, she made it to her observation post, where she could see Williams Field. It was overcast as she trained her binoculars onto the runway and saw two of the giant airplanes, plus three smaller ones, and the two C-130s. She put down the field glasses. So it wasn't a dream. She reached into her pocket and pulled out a little notebook and pencil and wrote down the time, date, and her observation of Williams Field. There was no particular reason for her to do this, but she was a scientist, and making notes of her observations was part of her nature. Besides, it gave her something to do.

She started back down toward the hut and upon seeing the brightly-painted orange Sno-Cat, Dana knew she had a problem. The hut was a light brown color that did not exactly blend in with the surrounding black volcanic rock and white snow and ice, but it didn't stick out, either. The orange Sno-Cat stuck out. Like a beacon. With all those planes buzzing around, someone might see it from the air. Dana knew that if she was to remain hidden, she had to get that Sno-Cat out of sight.

Fortunately, she knew how that could be done.

THE ROSS SEA—January 17

Desmond Voorhees and Navy Capt. John Benton were sitting in the posh dining room of the luxury ocean liner *Mirnyi,* staring out the window. The sky was overcast and the sea choppy, but in the distance they could see a helicopter approaching. They figured it was probably bringing in another research crew at gunpoint.

As the drumbeat of the rotor blades drew closer, Voorhees turned to Lt. Col. Samuel McClure and asked, "Now am I to understand, Colonel McClure, that you knew nothing about the nature of the material you were excavating out on the Windless Bight?"

McClure put his coffee cup down and said, "That's correct, sir.

Only Colonel Battelle knew everything about the Branding Iron project. I tried to feel him out a dozen times, but he always brought the curtain down. We had no idea what we were going after. As you can imagine, speculation was rampant among the men as to what was down there. Nobody could figure it out. All that Colonel Battelle would say was that we were after some mineral deposits." McClure's camouflage fatigues were cleaned and crisply starched, having just returned from the ship's laundry. The prisoners were receiving red-carpet treatment from the vessel's crew. He stared at his cup and said mournfully, "The Colonel took the secret to his grave."

Voorhees looked out the window again, brooding. The helo was approaching for a landing on the ship's fantail. "We have to get word to Washington," he said finally. "Somehow. The Soviets could keep us incommunicado on this luxurious brig for days—even weeks. Colonel McClure, how long was it going to take your crew to dig out whatever it was you were after?"

McClure shrugged. "We guesstimated anywhere from four to eight weeks to go, depending on the strata we encountered. But the Pentagon may already be alerted. Sort of."

Voorhees and Benton leaned forward while McClure whispered, so as not to be heard by the English-speaking waiters. "Every forty-eight hours we sent an encrypted progress report via our own communications gear to the National Military Command Center in the Pentagon. When we miss a couple of communications windows, that should put them on the alert."

Voorhees nodded. "Yes, and when our base in New Zealand and Amundsen-Scott Station at the Pole, and even NSF headquarters in Washington try to reach us and there is no answer, that should alert someone as well."

John Benton rolled his coffee cup around in his hands and said, "I'm not sure I agree with that thesis." Benton was also attired in recently laundered clothes, wearing the same pants and navy blue turtleneck he had been wearing at Desmond's chessboard when he became a prisoner.

Voorhees scratched his burnt-orange beard and asked, "How come?"

"For two reasons. Whether you're talking about the Pentagon or the NSF, you're talking about bureaucracies, and things move slowly in bureaucracies. Despite the broken communications, it's going to take time for someone at some level to make a decision as to what to do. A key decision-maker might be on vacation and the problem could lie in his in-box for who knows how long. A committee might be formed to study the problem. The farther you get away from Washington, the slower things work. And we're at the South Pole, right? Nobody behind a desk in Washington could possibly conceive what has happened to us—what *is* happening to us—so don't count on any expeditious response there. The second reason that help may be slow in coming is *maskirovka.*"

Voorhees was puzzled. "What is *maskirovka?*"

Benton set his coffee cup down and started tamping tobacco into the pipe he'd received gratis from the smiling clerk in the ship's store. "It's a Russian term for deception, guile. That sort of thing. I should think the Soviets would try to forestall any American military response by keeping up a false *maskirovka* front for as long as possible."

Benton's analysis made Voorhees feel even more helpless. "Then what can we do?"

Benton fired up his new pipe. "I think we have to find some way to blow the whistle on this whole thing. Do something that will bypass the bureaucracies and get things rolling. And fast. If we don't, the Russians will be up and out of McMurdo with the prize—whatever the prize is—before we can stop them." Benton looked around. "Regardless of these comfortable surroundings, as an American naval officer I find it most distasteful being a prisoner of war."

"You got that right," agreed McClure.

Voorhees surveyed the elegant dining room. It had obviously been the scene of formal dinners for wealthy Western European, North American, and Japanese tourists—bringing in foreign currency to fuel the improving Soviet economy. The dining room could seat five hundred people, easy. Lunch for the prisoners had long since finished, but a few stragglers lingered here and there, trying to provide each other with some mutual comfort and psychological support. Everyone had fine accommodations on the ship. Voorhees and Benton each had their own suite. The Russian crew was treating them in grand style, trying to wash away the bitterness of their forced incarceration. But the crew's good cheer could not take away the sting of the armed KGB guards scattered around the ship. It was hard to get in the mood for a fast game of shuffleboard when someone was standing behind you with a pistol belt. Voorhees turned back to Benton. "You said we would have to blow the whistle on this thing. Bypass the bureaucracies. How? Get word to the White House?"

Benton shrugged. "Maybe. But the White House has its own bureaucracy, too. And they're in the middle of a transition, don't forget."

Voorhees took off his wire-framed glasses and pinched his nose. He had an idea. "John, you know a little something about ships, don't you?"

"I should hope so."

"On a vessel like this, where would you expect the communications gear to be? Radio, telex, radiotelephone. That sort of thing?"

Benton thought for a moment and said, "The ship's crew would have their bridge communications and probably a separate communications room nearby. And since this is a pleasure liner, there would probably be another commo room for passenger use. That would be near the bridge as well."

Voorhees nodded. "What means of communication would a pleasure boat like this have?"

Benton mulled that one over. "Civilian commercial circuits, I would think. From what I saw in my suite, it looks like this ship is possibly wired for a link-up with the International Maritime Satellite, or the Comsat Maritime Satellite, which would provide direct-dial capability almost anywhere in the world. Of course, the phone is dead in my suite."

"Mine too," observed Voorhees as he looked out the window. The clouds seemed to be breaking up a bit. "Colonel McClure, our commo chief is still at McMurdo. Do you have some commo people on your crew? Somebody who knows the intricacies of radios, maybe even satellites?"

McClure looked over at one of the tables and said, "Mr. Gronski, I need you over here."

A large, barrel-chested man with deepset eyes and bushy eyebrows got up from the table and walked over. Like McClure, he was wearing camouflage fatigues.

"This is Mr. Gronski, our signal warrant officer in charge of crypto and communications. He's the one who transmitted our status reports."

Voorhees looked at the W2's anvil-like shoulders and said, "Yes, I think Mr. Gronski is just what we're looking for. Please sit down. I have something to propose."

And the four men went into a huddle.

When Voorhees was finished, McClure turned to the signal man and said, "You're the key guy on this gig, Ski. I can't order you to do something like this."

With the fastidious hands of a surgeon, Gronski opened a cellophane package of crackers and meticulously spread one cracker with a pat of butter while saying, "I'm game, sir."

"Good," replied Voorhees. "Now we need to reconnoiter that part of the ship very carefully. Get as close as we can to—"

"Desmond!"

Voorhees turned to see a familiar face with a red handlebar mustache rushing toward him. "Yes, Ted, what is it?"

Ted Brendan was breathing heavily. "Most of the field crews have been retrieved by helicopter. I've talked to them all and looked high and low through the ship. I can't find Dana anywhere."

AMUNDSEN-SCOTT STATION, GEOGRAPHIC SOUTH POLE

"McMurdo Station, McMurdo Station, this is Amundsen-Scott. Do you copy, over?"

Static flowed through the speaker before a voice came through. "Yeah, yeah, Amundsen-Scott. This is McMurdo. We read you, over."

The radio operator at the American base at the South Pole sighed with relief. "Where the hell have you guys been? You've been off the air for I don't know how long. Over."

"Yeah, sorry about that, Amundsen-Scott. We've had a real disaster here. A sewer line from one of the upstairs toilets burst and we had shit-laced water coming into the commo center like an upside-down geyser. It was a mess. All our gear got soaked and our circuits shorted out. We're just starting to get things repaired. Over."

"Oh, no. Sorry to hear that, McMurdo. We were starting to get worried. Is that you, Barry? It doesn't sound like you. Over."

"Naw. My name's Freddie. I'm new here and just walked into this shit. Literally. Also, Barry took sick. Came down with some kinda virus and is in the dispensary. Over."

"Sounds like everything came down at once. Listen, Freddie. I need to know about Crandall's research team that was supposed to take those measurements on the ozone depletion. They were supposed to arrive yesterday. Over."

"Oh, yeah. I think their C-130 had some kinda engine problem or something. They're deadlined for a while. Listen, buddy, I gotta go. I still have a bunch of crap to clean up. We'll talk later, okay? McMurdo out."

"Uh, yeah, sure. Later. Amundsen-Scott out."

WILLIAMS ICE AERODROME—January 17

Maj. Gen. Mitrofan Tromso exhaled with relief as the first MiG-31 Foxhound fighter touched down on the aluminum runway and was directed onto a taxiway that led to a snow-packed bunker. Although approaching exhaustion, Tromso was pleased with the progress thus far. His engineering crew had worked feverishly to get the first runway in place and were now working on the second. Eventually there would be five, but the first was the most critical. He clapped his stocky combat engineering officer on the back and said, "You have done well, Colonel. Your men are to be commended."

"Thank you, General. My crews have worked nonstop and are getting tired, but we will not stop for rest until the second runway is completed."

"Excellent," Tromso replied as he looked at the big-wheeled bull-dozers building the protective revetments for the fighters. "And the bunkers? How are you progressing there?"

"They are taking longer than the runway construction. That is why we delayed the arrival of the initial fighters. I need ten days to two weeks, but by that time I will have a bunker, taxiway, and runway system in place that will allow dispersement and protection for all of the fighters, yet also provide them with the ability to scramble and get into the air rapidly."

Tromso nodded. "Make sure the pilot and crew shelters are located next to each aircraft's bunker."

"Certainly, General."

Tromso now turned to the officer in overall charge of air and anti-air defenses. "Your status?"

The brigadier general in the Soviet Air Defense Forces was parka-clad like the engineer, but he was slender and above average height, and he had a magnificent Gallic nose. He might have been from Dijon, rather than the small Siberian town of Uray. "My ground defense people have installed radar and missile units near the sum-mits of Mounts Erebus and Terror. That will provide us with excel-lent coverage out to sea and over our airfield here. The Gadfly sensors and missiles will ring the airfield and bunkers for close-in defense. My mountaintop radar stations will feed their signal to the command bunker being set up at the New Zealand base. Once the Mainstay radar planes are on station, we will have an eight-hundred-kilometer radius of surveillance with constant air patrols."

Two Condors were parked on the taxiway along with three Illyu-shin-76 Candid tankers, and another MiG-31 was landing. Over the howl of the engines, Tromso said, "Transmit to Moscow that I want the Mainstay radar aircraft here without delay, but the *Tbilisi* is to be kept"—Tromso chuckled to himself—"the *Tbilisi* is to be kept on ice until it is needed."

The two subordinates, as if on cue, chuckled also. Then Tromso looked up at the overcast sky and said, "We are fortunate the Americans have no optical satellites that orbit this far south."

"Indeed," agreed the air defense brigadier.

"I have set up my quarters in the American base," said Tromso. "I am going to get some rest. You may reach me on my personal radio net should you require me. Take proper rest yourselves."

"Yes, General."

"Yes, General."

BRANDING IRON STATION

The Russian jackhammer operator almost fell on his face as the tool bit broke through the hardened lava apron and plunged into the softer sedimentary rock. The operator hefted the tool bit out and cut a wider breach in the lava to be sure, and when he was certain, he shouted over the din of the other pneumatic hammers to the chief engineer standing on the edge of the pit. "We have broken through!"

The pudgy civilian engineer, who was middle-aged and looked slightly beleaguered, had spent most of his career in the Siberian coal fields. He yelled to his assistant, "Make the digger drill ready!" The chief engineer did not want to be under this icedome. Who knew if the roof would collapse? Who knew if the sea would break through? It was a most uncomfortable situation.

At least he was getting to use some American equipment.

KOETTLITZ GLACIER

The clouds were coming out of the west, snaking through the Transantarctic Mountains like a stream weaving its way between tall,
craggy rocks. As the foggy morass approached, Dana Harrow knew
she would soon be encased by a whiteout, in which sky and snow
would merge into an amorphous envelope to rob her of the horizon.
Whiteouts could be so disorienting that even birds had been known
to lose their equilibrium and fly straight into the ground.

One thing in her favor was that Dana had become familiar with
this area scouting locations for her remote seismic stations. She had
driven the Sno-Cat back over the Minna Saddle and turned westward
up the Koettlitz Glacier—a large river of ice that fed into the Ross
Ice Shelf. As the cloud bank rolled toward her she stopped the
Sno-Cat and hopped out. With a compass she took a quick but
careful azimuth on the summit of Mount Discovery so she could find
her way back to the hut.

After a few moments the fog enveloped her, and Mount Discovery—along with the other mountains, and the sun and sky—were
replaced with a hazy, impenetrable gray veil. She pulled the survival
backpack out of the rear of the Sno-Cat and set it on the ground, then
peered ahead; but of course she could see no more than thirty yards.
Even so, she felt she was in the right place.

Dana returned to the rear door and lifted out a heavy volcanic
rock she'd loaded prior to her departure from the seismic hut.
Laboriously she carried it to the driver's cabin and dropped it to the
floor with a *clunk.* Then, while holding the door open, she heaved
the rock onto the accelerator pedal, and the bright orange Sno-Cat
lurched forward. Dana leaped back so as not to be swept along by
the machine as it churned through the snow and plunged into the
veil of fog. After it disappeared, she stood in place with the backpack
at her feet, listening to the fading sound of the tracks and diesel
engine. Softer and softer it became until there was a low cracking,
growling sound, followed by a kind of *whoosh* and a rumble, and
when it was over the glacier was left in a ghostly quiet. Dana assumed
the diesel engine was killed when the Sno-Cat hit the bottom of the
giant crevasse.

She had driven the Sno-Cat up to a field where the glacier was
known to have yawning fissures in its body. The cracking and
whooshing sound came when the heavy Sno-Cat broke through a

snow bridge and tumbled to the bottom of the crevasse.

She hefted the survival pack onto her back with difficulty, then took a bead on her compass, using the azimuth to Mount Discovery as a reference point. She had a long journey before her—over twenty miles as the crow flew. As she trudged off through the ankle-deep snow and into the fog, she was grateful the temperature was up to twenty-eight degrees.

11

. . . .

BOLD HORIZONS

WASHINGTON, D.C.—January 20

". . . to protect, honor, and defend the Constitution of the United States. So help me God."

The septuagenarian Chief Justice lowered the Bible and extended his liver-spotted hand with the words, "Congratulations, Mr. President."

The inaugural assembly in front of the Capitol cheered as the new Chief Executive received his congratulations from the jurist, then turned to the crowd and waved. It was a cloudy day, crisp and cold, with the wind blowing his auburn hair into a swirl—but as always, Jonathan Blakely's coiffure seemed to fall back into place. As he absorbed this extraordinary moment in American politics, he mused to himself that he had come a long, long way from Bakersfield.

Fresh out of college with a communications degree, Jonathan Blakely started his broadcasting career as a weekend weatherman on a UHF station in Bakersfield, California. The ratings of the station were so low they didn't even register on the Arbitrons. So with nothing to lose, he started doing the weather while wearing a raincoat, a parka, or sometimes—if it was a sunny day—just a pair of swim trunks, a mask, and a snorkel. Ratings grew. So much so that management moved him to weekend news anchor. Then to main anchor. (Blakely just ripped the news off the wire and read it because the station had no local news staff.) Ratings increased.

It was at this particular juncture that something fortuitous happened. One of the anchors on a network affiliate in L.A. got sacked, and Blakely got the nod. He was twenty-six years old and the anchor of a major market station. Ratings climbed again, and it was here that Blakely honed his natural magic. Like an electronic sorcerer, he became master of the twenty-second sound bite. He would read the snapshot news stories in such a way that he seemed to share some

mysterious umbilical, some intimate link with the viewers. He connected with them on a primal level—empathizing with their gut
sense of outrage, pity, humor, bitterness, or grief. That flawless face
was overpowering. On camera he was the image of the fantasized
boyfriend, husband, brother, or son that so many longed for.

The network signed him to an anchor slot, of course, and ratings
soared again—to the point that the New York *Daily News* pro-
claimed Blakely had "eclipsed the Cronkite legend." The jealousy
and ridicule he received from his newsroom colleagues were only
surpassed by the fealty paid to him by the network executives. But
by now he had tired of the broadcasting game. He was thirty-nine,
and he decided it was time to take a higher aim.

Blakely ran for United States Senate in the state of New York
against a three-term incumbent who was a former economics professor at NYU. The old professor had served on the Federal Reserve
Board, sat on the Senate Finance Committee, and was a master of
financial and tax policy.

Blakely was master of the twenty-second sound bite.

The professor never had a chance.

Blakely went to Washington and spent one term in the Senate. He
never introduced a single piece of legislation, but he introduced
himself at countless fund-raisers across the nation, and at the end of
six years he had an IOU from every other county chairman in the
country.

It was time to go national.

He had the money, the connections, and, most important, his
national constituency.

He spent two years running for the presidency, and at the end, the
election was a joke. After all, who could compete with a handsome
man who had visited millions of voters in their living rooms every
evening and spoke with such . . . such . . . *sincerity*.

So here was Jonathan Blakely now. The President. On the Capitol
steps. A man envied by prime ministers and potentates. A man
adored by millions. A man who was Commander in Chief of the
United States Armed Forces . . . A man who had never managed so
much as a candy store.

As the cheers finally quieted down, Blakely began his inaugural
address in that resonant voice, and spoke about the new era of peace
in the world, about the reduction of long-held tensions and growing

partnership between the superpowers. But he said America still had to have a national agenda. . . . For Roosevelt it had been the New Deal. For Kennedy it was the New Frontier. And for the administration of Jonathan Blakely, America would seek out and press onward to "Bold Horizons."

If you listened to his inaugural address in its entirety, it sounded somewhat stilted. Almost jerky. But if you broke it up into twenty-second increments, you'd realize how well it would play on the evening network news.

THE *MIRNYI*—January 21

The KGB guard was leaning against the bulkhead, trying to cope with complete boredom, when the raucous sound of laughter came down the stairwell, followed by a stumbling noise.

Four men, in various degrees of stagger, were quasi–falling down the stairs that led to the Starlight Bar on the deck above. The tall one with the wire-framed glasses and red beard said, "Whooooops. Washit, fellas. You kin *hiccup* kill yerselves if you urnt careful."

As they stumbled onto the landing, the KGB guard grumbled to himself that Russians apparently did not have the exclusive franchise on drunkenness . . . and this guard knew a great deal about drunkenness. Yes, indeed, he knew a very great deal about drunkenness. He found it particularly galling, even cruel, to be standing guard just a deck below a palatial bar that was stocked to the rafters with liquor of every description.

"Ohhhhhhh," moaned the big man with the bushy eyebrows, who was wearing camouflage fatigues. "Ohhhhhhh," he repeated while going down on one knee. "My stomach . . . I feeeel sick, *burp* . . . gotta puke."

The other fatigue-clad figure grabbed his elbow and said, "Hang . . . hang in there, Ski *hiccup*. We'll get you to the . . . the toilet."

The tall man with the red beard stumbled over to the guard and mumbled, "Say . . . lishen, buddy. We was upshtairs, inna bar, see? . . . Had a little party. Might as well have a little party since we're cooped up on this bucket (sway) and the booze is free, right? You Rooskees have been downright hospudable, I really muss say. . . . My fren here . . . heez sick. Can you let us use the toilet in there?" The drunk pointed to the door.

"You go," ordered the guard sternly. "This bridge area. You not permitted here." He made a shooing motion with his hands. "You go."

"Ahhhhh, come on, buddy," coaxed Red Beard. "Let us use the head and I'll give you a swig of this." And he pulled a half-liter bottle of Stolichnaya vodka from inside his jacket.

The guard looked upon the little bottle the way someone in the Sahara would look upon an oasis. Drinking was forbidden on this mission. Absolutely forbidden. . . . But then everything seemed to be forbidden. He couldn't remember when he'd last tasted vodka—the magic Russian elixir. He looked around and almost rejected the offered bottle. But then he paused. It had been so long. So painfully long. With a quivering voice he softly said, "One drink." He took the bottle and turned it upside down, letting the liquid gush down his throat in a generous swallow. He brought the bottle down, and as the hundred-proof liquor burned into his stomach, he felt as if he'd just come up for air.

"Go ahead, buddy," urged Red Beard. "Have another."

The Russian needed little prompting this time. He upended the bottle again, and when he was in the middle of his third gulp a massive fist slammed into his solar plexus. The Russian's lungs emptied, forcing the vodka at the back of his throat up into his sinuses. The searing, choking, burning feeling caused him to reel back, but Voorhees caught him. The Russian reached for his gun, but John Benton already had his hands on it. The Russian tried to struggle, but Gronski had him by the waist and wrestled him to the ground. Finally the Russian tried to scream, but he had no air in his lungs. Benton got the automatic pistol out of the holster and handed it to McClure, who chambered a round and shoved the barrel against the Russian's nose.

"I'll keep our host company," said McClure. "You go find it."

"Don't we need the gun?" Voorhees asked.

Benton said, "Leave the gun with McClure," as he cracked open the door that the Russian had been guarding and peeked in. Just as he'd thought, there was a passageway that led to the bridge. Benton hoped that the *Mirnyi* was like most modern pleasure liners, where microcircuits had replaced helmsmen, leaving the bridge sparsely populated. "Come on," he whispered.

Benton, Gronski, and Voorhees tiptoed down the carpeted passageway until they came to a door with a Russian-language sign, and the symbol of an antenna between two lightning bolts. "I bet this is it," whispered Benton. The three men filed in.

It was a small room crammed with electronic equipment, with a lone, white-uniformed officer sitting behind a counter. "We would like to send a message," Benton said calmly as he walked through the waist-high swinging door. The ship's officer was stunned, and started to stand up and scream for help when Benton pulled something out of his pocket that flashed open with an authoritative click.

With the switchblade at his throat, the radio officer slowly sat back down. Benton looked at Voorhees, who was gazing at the knife. "A little something I confiscated from a white hat a long time ago," Benton explained. "Sure glad we weren't searched when we came on board. You two go to work."

Gronski sat down at the neighboring chair and inspected the equipment. There were three vertical panels of dials and switches, with a phone in front of each. Gronski pointed at the equipment and asked the ship's officer, "InMarSat?"

The Russian said nothing, but Benton knew that since he was a communications officer he was bound to speak English. The Navy captain pressed the switchblade into the man's throat a little harder and said, "We mean business, friend. You can answer his question or never talk again. What'll it be?"

The Russian pointed at the center panel and said, "*Da.* InMar-Sat."

Gronski studied the set up a moment longer, then looked at the Russian and pointed at a phone booth by the entry door. "The booth?" he asked.

"*Da,*" said the Russian.

"Go in that booth, Dr. Voorhees," Gronski ordered. "Pick up the phone and dial zero." Desmond did as instructed, and a light came on at the base of the middle phone. Gronski picked it up and put the receiver onto a spring trap device that held the receiver onto the face of the equipment panel, sort of like a wall phone. Gronski rose from the chair and told Benton, "Sit him down."

In a moment the Russian was in the other chair, Gronski on one side, the switchblade on the other. "Now listen carefully, friend," explained the warrant officer. "I need you to patch that phone in the booth into the InMarSat bird. I'm a commo man, just like you, so we understand each other. But your stuff is in Russian and I need you to take us the last step. Now go ahead and patch us in, but if you try anything funny, I will become very angry. And my buddy with the blade here will become very angry. And I don't think you want us to become angry, do you?"

The Russian carefully and slowly shook his head so the switch-blade wouldn't bite, then he threw some switches.

"Now?" asked Gronski.

"*Da.*"

"Okay, Dr. Voorhees. Hang up and lift the receiver again. You should have a dial tone."

Voorhees did so and said, "I've got it."

"Okay," said Gronski, "if our friend here is telling the truth"—he turned to the Russian—"and you are telling the truth, aren't you, friend?"

The ship's officer nodded, again just enough so as not to be cut by the switchblade.

"If our friend here is telling the truth, this should tie us into the InMarSat. You can dial direct. Punch in zero-zero-one for the U.S. country code, then the area code, then the number."

"Here goes nothing," mumbled the senior rep. "I hope I don't get a recording."

ALEXANDRIA, VIRGINIA

Ringggg!

"Mmmpfff."

Ringggg!

"Uhhh . . . wha . . . ?"

Ringggg!

"Ummm . . . answer it, will you, honey?"

"Uh . . . yeah." (Fumble, fumble.) "Hello."

"Woltman? Seymour Woltman, with the Associated Press?"

"Uhhh . . . yeah, who's this?" He looked at the bedside clock that read 3:18 A.M. "Christ, you know what time it is?"

"Never mind that," the voice said urgently. "Just listen. There isn't much time. This is Desmond Voorhees, senior United States representative to Antarctica."

"*What? Antarctica?* What is this, some kinda stupid practical joke?"

"Shut up and listen! I'm calling you because you're press. We met about six months ago at a party at the New Zealand embassy. You gave me your card and I remembered your home phone number because you made a joke that it was the same as Independence Day."

"Yeah, that's right. Seven-oh-four, one-seven-seven-six."

"Listen to me. The Soviets have taken over McMurdo Station in Antarctica by force. I repeat. The Soviet Union has taken over McMurdo Station by force. They dropped in paratroops. Do you understand me?"

Pause.

"Okay, who is this? A Russian invasion at the South Pole? What are they after? Penguins? You must be getting an early start on April Fool's Day, fella."

"Not the South Pole! McMurdo! We were all taken prisoner and put on a Russian cruise ship called the *Mirnyi*. Put this story on your wire immediately! This is Desmond Voorhees, and I'm telling you the Soviets have taken over McMurdo! Call the White House! Call the Marines! Call the—"

"Okay, fella, that's about enough. Who the hell are you, anyway? . . . Hello? . . . I said, who are you?"

Static.

Woltman slammed the phone back on its cradle.

His companion asked, "What was that all about? . . . The South Pole?"

"Nothing, baby," he murmured, while gently patting her bottom. "Just some lunatic or practical joker. Go back to sleep. I've got an early day tomorrow . . . today, rather. Gotta go up to the Hill and interview some senators about this 'Bold Horizons' crap."

"Ummm," she mumbled, and soon her breathing assumed a slow, steady rhythm.

But Seymour never went back to sleep.

A C-130 HERCULES OVER THE ROSS SEA

"McMurdo Base, McMurdo Base, this is Navy eight-three-one-niner. We are twenty minutes out from Willy Field. Do you read, over?"

Nothing.

Navy Lt. Cmdr. Herb Curtis was totally frustrated with the commo situation. The U.S. Antarctic program base at Christchurch, New Zealand, had been trying to raise McMurdo, but had only received a strange report about a busted toilet line and a flooded radio room. But that shouldn't have caused the air traffic control tower at Williams Field to go off the air. The tower sort of looked like a small grain silo, painted orange, with a glass aquarium on top. It was portable and could be moved around on the ice shelf whenever safety required.

Curtis was a pilot in VXE-6, the Navy's Antarctic Development Squadron 6 (known as the "Puckered Penguins"). In the bureaucratic slumgullion stew that made up the American presence in Antarctica, the seven C-130 transports and six Huey helicopters that comprised "the world's southernmost airline" were actually owned by the National Science Foundation, but they were flown by Navy pilots of VXE-6.

Curtis was a three-year polar veteran who had made the 2,200-mile trip from Christchurch to Williams Field more times than he could count. He needed a weather report on conditions at Willy Field and he wasn't getting it. If the aerodrome was socked in, he would have to divert to another station or put the Hercules down on an alternative landing site. The landing situation didn't look good, because he could just barely make out Mount Erebus in the distance, its mottled dome poking out of a skirt of ground-hugging clouds. Curtis was thinking about the silent control tower, and about a long-overdue dinner, when his copilot rapped him on the arm and pointed at the portside window. "Herb! Look at that!"

Curtis looked out and saw a fighter plane flying alongside them with its landing gear extended and a red star on each of its twin tails. The absolute shock of seeing something so alien in this part of the world made the pilot freeze at the controls for a few moments.

"What is it?" asked the copilot.

Curtis shook his head and blinked, but the twin-tailed fighter was still there. "Tha-that's a Russian fighter aircraft. An Su-27 Flanker." The Soviet pilot began pointing to Curtis and then to Mount Erebus. "I think he wants us to follow him," said the copilot. As the shock wore off, Curtis reached the only logical conclusion he could reach. He switched from the C-130's VHF air-traffic radio to the long-range HF radio that was set to a distress frequency monitored by the American base back in New Zealand. "Mayday! Mayday! This is Navy eight-three-one-nine! Kiwi Base, do you read, over?"

A staticky, broken response said, "We . . . ead . . . ay . . . gin."

"I say again, Mayday, Mayday, this is Navy eight-three-one-niner!

We're twenty minutes out from Williams Field over the Ross Sea. We are being shadowed by a—"

The left wing of the Hercules aircraft disappeared in a flash of orange and yellow flame, causing the nose of the aircraft to spin around and smash into some of its own debris.

The last thing Herb Curtis would remember was the icy wind howling through the shattered windshield. He could still feel the penetrating cold on his lacerated face, long after he'd lost the swirling image of sea-sky-sea-sky-sea-sky.

A MIG-29 FULCRUM OVER THE ROSS SEA

Capt. Fyodor Tupelov watched the C-130 Hercules as it tumbled down toward the icy water. It was so completely helpless, and Tupelov took no satisfaction in witnessing its death. Shooting down a warplane was one thing. This was different. Something akin to murder. But the electronic warfare officer on the Mainstay radar plane had said "Splash it," and there was no time for argument. The American was transmitting.

As the Hercules hit the waters of the Ross Sea, Tupelov turned away, almost sick. "Why did you have to transmit?" he asked in a whispered moan.

CBS NEWS STUDIO, NEW YORK—January 22

The set director held up his hand and said in a commanding voice, "Ten seconds!"

Behind the desk on the news set, the anchorwoman rapidly scanned the rap sheet that outlined the pecking order of stories for the upcoming newscast. Her blond hair was complemented by a yellow blazer, and contrasted by a black turtleneck and a black handkerchief in the breast pocket. She had the cheekbones of a *Vogue* model and the eyes of a deputy sheriff, and when she read a news story there was a coolness about her—an aloofness of sorts—that seemed to make her a bit, well, judgmental.

But then, she'd once been a Texas judge.

"Intro!" yelled the set director.

The CBS "eye" logo was keyed over a wide-angle shot of the news set as the intro music played and the announcer intoned, "This is 'The CBS Evening News,' with Catherine Crier."

The picture cut to the anchorwoman and she took the cue as the TelePrompTer began scrolling down in front of the camera lens.

"Good evening. In reports filtering out of China this evening"—a map of China appeared in the upper right-hand corner of the screen—"it appears that the forces of Field Marshal Wan Chee have retaken the city of Shanghai. The opposing forces of General Lin Foung captured Shanghai two months ago in some of the bloodiest fighting in the Chinese civil war. In its first foreign-policy statement, the Blakely White House said it was watching the situation carefully and—" She was interrupted by the noise of studio sound doors bursting open. The managing editor breached on-air protocol and lunged past the set director to hand her a printout from the news wire. "Just came in," he said breathlessly. "Go with it now."

Crier took the short printout and quickly scanned it while holding up a finger to the audience—like a judge who needed a moment to render a decision on a complex point of law. But nothing in her career as a judge-turned-journalist had prepared her for a story like this. With a look of perplexity she faced the camera and said, "Ah, ladies and gentlemen, I have just been given a bulletin, straight off the Associated Press wire, that says . . . Soviet troops have landed . . . and occupied the American . . ." She scanned the printout again to insure the piece of paper actually said what it said. ". . . the American scientific base at McMurdo Sound in . . . Antarctica." She gave the camera an expression that seemed to say, *It sounds as crazy to me as it does to you.* But then, like a judge dealing with a bizarre flare-up in the courtroom, she regained her poise and said, "I repeat, we have an AP story that reports Soviet military troops have landed at and occupied the American scientific base at McMurdo Sound in . . . Antarctica." Setting the paper aside, she said, "We'll, ah, try to get more on this for you later, ladies and gentlemen, but that is all we have at the moment. Back to our lead story this evening on the Chinese civil war. . . . Forces under the command of Field Marshall Wan Chee have recaptured the city of Shanghai. . . ."

And she continued to read. But instinct told her that the piece of paper she'd just set aside eclipsed the story she was reading by tenfold.

Or perhaps twenty.

12

· · · · · · · · · · · ·

AURORA

In March 1908, six men from Ernest Shackleton's Nimrod *expedition made the first successful ascent of Mount Erebus. In the climbing party was a twenty-six-year-old Australian geologist named Douglas Mawson, who took the opportunity to measure the volcano's caldera (it was 2,640 feet in diameter and 900 feet in depth).*

Less than a year later, Mawson was among a group of three men who were the first to arrive at the South Magnetic Pole—a grueling round-trip journey of 1,260 miles that they covered on foot, pulling sledges, without benefit of dogs.

After Shackleton's Nimrod *campaign came to an end, Mawson—a most capable man—returned home and started to mount his own expedition to chart the coastline of Antarctica directly south of Australia. He was successful in putting the enterprise together, and on December 2, 1911, his expedition ship sailed from Hobart, Tasmania.*

It was during this expedition that Mawson set out with two companions to explore the territory along the coast. The exploration party was 315 miles from its base camp when one of Mawson's colleagues and a supply sled fell into a giant crevasse. This placed the two survivors in a perilous position, short of supplies and dogs. Their journey back toward their base was arduous as they faced blizzards, frostbite, starvation, and exhaustion. Mawson's second companion died en route, and he barely survived—but he did reach the base camp.

Upon his return to Australia, Mawson resumed his academic career and went on to become a professor of geology—also making two more voyages to explore the Antarctic coast. He died in 1958, one of the last great giants of Antarctic exploration.

The saga of Mawson's survival during his famous expedition was truly epic, but there were two aspects—"sidebars," if you will—to his foray into the polar realm that bear mention. Mawson was a scientist, and he had an interest in applying new technology to the art of exploration. On his expedition he brought with him the first airplane to touch Antarctic soil (or ice), and the first radio to transmit from the

southern continent. The aircraft—a flimsy Vickers REP Aeroplane—
was damaged even before Mawson left Australia, and it never got off
the ground after its arrival at his Cape Denison base camp. It did,
however, see some limited use as a propeller-driven tractor for hauling
sledges. A more encouraging result was obtained from the radio. Al-
though the winds at the Cape Denison camp played havoc with the
antennae, intermittent contact was made with the outside world, via
a repeater station Mawson had set up on Macquarie Island, some 850
miles from Hobart.

It was perhaps ironic, then, that the ship of Mawson's expedition—
the first vessel to bring both aviation and electronics to Antarctica—
was named the Aurora.

A KC-10 TANKER, 37,000 FEET ABOVE THE SOUTH PACIFIC,
NORTH OF THE SOCIETY ISLANDS

As the sun dipped out of sight, the sky along the far horizon turned
a deep violet, and the tail-boom operator in the arse of the KC-10
tanker could see the planet Venus twinkling in the indigo twilight
just above the purple spectrum. When dusk eventually turned to
night, he knew Venus would be joined by a spattering of stars,
shining majestically against the canvas of a nocturnal Pacific sky. He
allowed himself this metaphysical interlude, then turned his attention back to the matter at hand as he mashed his face against the
telescopic viewer—and began searching the horizon for something
other than stars.

"See anything, Boomer?" asked a voice through the intercom.

Boomer panned the lens across the sky. "Nothing yet, Skipper."

The voice came back, testier this time. "Well, they were supposed
to be here seven minutes ago. I've got better things to do than hang
around in a holding pattern, waiting for them to get their act together. The next thing you know, those prima donnas will be wanting
us to serve them in-flight cocktails."

"Yessir," replied Boomer in a tired voice. He could recite the
Skipper's litany of complaints by memory.

The KC-10 had taken off five hours previously from Hickam Air
Force Base in Hawaii, and the whole mission hinged on this very
special KC-10 tanker being at the right place at the right time. That's
because this particular airborne filling station did not carry regular
jet fuel. Instead, it carried a bellyful of liquid methane at minus 272

degrees Fahrenheit. There were only five of these methane tankers in the world, and they were scattered over the globe in strategic locations—dispersed so that they could provide timely refueling to a mysterious flying object that required an unconventional diet.

Something twinkled in the viewer, and it wasn't a star.

"I think I see him, Skipper," said Boomer. "He's got his navigation lights on."

"About time," grumbled the pilot.

Boomer paid no attention to his boss now, for he had become mesmerized by the flashing green and red strobe lights in the viewfinder. They were approaching the tanker at astonishing speed. Unbelievable speed. He wondered if they were going to overshoot, but then they began to slow perceptibly. Slower . . . slower . . . He raised his face from the viewer, and with his naked eyes he watched the navigation lights draw closer and closer until he could see a dim outline against the dusky horizon. No matter how many times he saw one, it never failed to amaze him. A black, sinister-looking object— resembling an elongated manta ray—was barely discernible against the darkening purple sky. It dropped below the rear end of the tanker, then slowly rose up to the tail boom, like a trout coming up to nibble a baited hook. Once in position, the manta ray held itself steady, and a little rectangle of white lights appeared on its dorsal side.

With a hand controller, Boomer aimed the laser beam at the rectangle, then flipped a switch to the ON position. Almost immediately he heard a clear voice come over the secure channel, saying, "Hello, Mother Bear. Sorry we're late, but some jerk in a Piper wandered into the airspace at Dogpatch. We had to stay in the shed until air traffic gave us the all-clear. Then after we were airborne, our GPS had some kinda glitch. I think it's okay now, though."

Boomer recognized the voice. "Glad you could make it, Catman. The Skipper was getting impatient."

"Roger. Let's go. Guide us in, we're thirsty."

"No problem. I've got an in-flight cocktail for you." With deftness and experience, Boomer orchestrated the refueling, placing the boom into the dorsal vent of the flying black manta ray and starting the flow of liquid methane.

After the manta ray drank its fill, the pilot said, "That's it. Shut her down."

Boomer cut the fuel flow and retracted the boom.

"Thanks, Mother Bear. See you on the way back."

"You got it, Catman. Don't run into any penguins."

There was a pause before the manta ray's pilot said, "I guess you figured out where we're headed. You must be a genius."

"No genius, Catman," confessed Boomer. "I just listened to the news on my way in to work this afternoon."

"I guess there are no secrets. See you later. Catman out."

"Mother Bear out." Boomer killed the laser channel.

The two aircraft were traveling due south as the black manta ray fell behind, then began a slow climb over the tanker. Boomer watched the navigation lights on the mysterious aircraft as it gained speed and flew overhead, passing from his field of vision. The KC-10 then began a slow, banking turn to take up a northeasterly heading toward the next rendezvous point, where it would meet the manta ray for a refueling stop on the journey home. As the rear end of the tanker swung around to the southwesterly view, Boomer put his face against the telescopic viewer to see if he could find the navigation lights against the deep purple sky.

But the Aurora was already gone.

THE AURORA

After climbing to 75,000 feet, Lt. Col. Felix "Catman" Griggs leveled off the flying black manta ray and ran through a final instrument checklist. Or, rather, the on-board computer ran through the checklist. Whereas the old SR-71 Blackbird had possessed an instrument panel of gauges based on 1960s technology, the Aurora's flight management system was displayed on three plasma viewer screens. The computer ran a diagnostic program through the innards of the manta ray, sensing everything from fuel consumption to engine rpm to skin temperature, and displayed any notable aberrations on the orange plasma screen.

"Ready, Pretty Boy?"

Maj. Thomas "Pretty Boy" Floyd, the reconnaissance systems officer (RSO) in the backseat, scanned the readout of the Global Positioning System (GPS) and the magnetic compass heading. "Hold on a sec. I wanna check this damn GPS again." The Aurora had a primary and backup GPS receiver that took in the signals from the NavStar navigation satellites and computed the aircraft's position and altitude to within ten meters—when the contraption was working correctly, that is. If both primary and backup showed the same reading, then that usually meant it was functioning properly. But if there was a discrepancy between the two, as there had been earlier in the mission, that meant one of them was out of whack, and the RSO had to use an old-style astro-tracker to figure out which one. "Awright, Catman. I've got identical readings on the GPS. I guess it's working again. Come to vector one-eight-seven, then bring her up to one-twenty and go to cruise."

"Rog." Catman Griggs made the minor course adjustment, then brought the nose of the manta ray up for the 1,800 mph climb to 120,000 feet.

The Aurora spy plane was the follow-on to the aging SR-71 Blackbird, and like its predecessor, it too was a product of Lockheed's famous "Skunk Works." Aurora really did look like a kind of elongated manta ray, in that it possessed a body that tapered into the wings. Indeed, it was difficult to discern where the fuselage ended and the wings began. This blended wing-in-body design made the Aurora a hypersonic surfboard, so to speak. As the spy plane accelerated into the realm of Mach 5, it had to push the air out of the way as it traveled along. And as the air was forced aside it became compressed, forming a shock wave along the manta ray's underbelly. This shock wave pushed up against the underside, providing lift, and because Aurora rode this shock wave like a surfboard, it was deemed a "wave-rider."

Catman Griggs leveled off at 120,000 feet, and saw that his airspeed indicator was at 2,060 mph. He toggled his intercom switch and said, "Okay, Pretty Boy, here we go."

"I'm right behind you," replied Floyd.

"Yeah. You always are. Yuk, yuk. Let's go find out what Ivan is up to."

Pretty Boy Floyd, a man who could win an ugly contest without difficulty, said, "Yeah. This has got to be a drill, right? I mean, this can't be for real? A Russian invasion at the South Pole?"

"Not the South Pole," corrected Griggs. "McMurdo Sound."

"Whatever. Let's hang ten."

"Rog." They were already at full military power, so Griggs advanced the throttle into afterburner. The dual conical spikes on the underside engine intakes retracted slightly, allowing greater airflow into the compressor. Simultaneously, the bypass ducts behind the compressor blades opened and allowed the air to travel past the engine core and into the tailpipe, just ahead of the afterburner. When the compressed air and raw methane fuel mixed in the twin infernos of the tailpipes, two giant tongues of blue-white flame leapt into the night, catapulting the Aurora across the Pacific sky like a shooting star.

As the airspeed indicator went past 2,500 mph, Catman Griggs was pushed back into his seat and the manta ray's black titanium-aluminide skin began glowing a dull red from the air friction. The short, wiry, catlike pilot, who possessed a bristly mustache and darting eyes, caught a glimpse of the stars just before the heat shield extended up and over the windshield to "button up" the cockpit. He never liked this part, because he now had to rely completely on instruments as the Aurora continued to accelerate past 3,000 mph . . . then 3,500 . . . 3,600 . . . 3,700 . . . and finally 3,800 mph. The hypersonic wave-rider was "hangin' ten."

McMurdo Sound was about four thousand miles away.

The Aurora would be there in a little over an hour.

THE *TBILISI*

The noise from the howling engines of four Su-27 Flanker aircraft wafted over the deck and up to *Vitse*-Adm. Gavriil Strekalov, who was standing atop his footstool on the flying bridge. He was grateful for the ear protectors as the screaming engine exhausts of the Flankers noisily and rapidly melted the ice that had encased the flight deck for the last seven days. The little admiral looked toward the launch ramp and watched the crewmen release the final cable that had tethered the Soviet supercarrier to the tabular iceberg. Since linking up with the iceberg, the *Tbilisi* had drifted slowly north to warmer waters, and Strekalov had been surprised at how fast the giant berg had started to disintegrate. The ice on the deck had melted quite a bit during the day, so, to keep their ice "camouflage" in place, the crew had resprayed the deck with fresh water each night so it would refreeze when the sun dipped out of sight for a few hours.

But now the deception had ended.

Strekalov left his footstool and entered the bridge. He doffed his parka and ear protectors while Captain, First Rank, Dmitri Vaslov—tall, blond, and commanding in presence—was surveying the growing gap between berg and ship with a pair of field glasses. As his short and muscular superior approached, Vaslov said, "We are drifting away from the berg, Admiral. As soon as we have safe clearance, I will engage the engines and put us on a course for our station in the Ross Sea."

"*Da,* Dmitri. Very well. I only hope those miners can dig out that damned mineral, whatever the hell it is, so we can be finished with this business. Our *maskirovka* did not last long. The American carriers will be here soon. I am quite sure of that."

Vaslov tried to comfort his admiral. "But once we are on station, we will have air cover in depth. And a double cordon of escort vessels."

Strekalov nodded. "True enough. And the Americans will be far from their support bases. Just as we are." Strekalov looked out the window. He estimated the wind was blowing at a five on the Beaufort scale—roughly twenty knots—creating a field of chilly whitecaps as far as the eye could see. And he could see a good distance because the sky was clear. "At least our little deception was successful," he mused. "If the American satellites had located us, that Australian observation plane would have been on top of us long ago, no doubt."

The wind had pushed the ship and the iceberg fifty meters apart. Captain Vaslov dropped his field glasses and ordered, "Back one-third. Rudder amidships."

"Back one-third, rudder amidships, aye," echoed the officer of the deck.

The ship rumbled as the giant propellers came to life, and the *Tbilisi* began pulling away from its concealment.

The little admiral reached into his pocket and read once more the brief, terse message from Sevastopol. He took a deep breath, then mentally put all of his reservations, misgivings, and revulsions about Snow Leopard behind him. If he was to bring his men safely home, they needed a task force commander who was a total warrior. He shoved the message back into his pocket. "Once the deck is clear of ice, launch the combat patrol with two An-26 radar planes aloft at all times. I want alert aircraft on the ramp and prepared to launch at a moment's notice. Come to general quarters at the slightest provocation. Get us to the Ross Sea and under the air umbrella as fast as you can, Dmitri. From this moment forward, the *Tbilisi* is on a war footing."

"Understood, Admiral."

THE AURORA

Catman Griggs brought the hypersonic manta ray out of afterburner, and as the spy plane decelerated to 2,500 mph, the heat shield retracted, allowing him to gaze upon the stars once again. The aircraft's ground-track had passed from darkness and into the land of the midnight sun, but at an altitude of 120,000 feet, the stars were still visible.

Although Griggs had shut down the liquid methane feed into afterburner, he kept the air flowing through the bypass ducts and into the tailpipes in order to mask the spy plane's infrared heat signature.

In the backseat, RSO Pretty Boy Floyd powered up his surveillance gear. Depending on the mission, the Aurora could mix and match various reconnaissance pods—infrared, photo, radar, video, you name it. On this trip Floyd had a television camera, plus an elint (electronic intelligence) pod and an infrared sensor. He checked the primary and backup GPS readouts, and found that they tallied. "We're about four hundred miles out. Let's drop down and take a look."

"You got it," replied Griggs, and he put the Aurora into a shallow descent. "Your crystal ball tell you anything yet?"

Floyd flicked some switches to activate the elint scanner, and the symbology quickly appeared on the orange plasma screen. As he examined the readout, Floyd felt an onrush of adrenaline flow into his bloodstream. "Catman, we're picking up a periodic scan in the India-band. . . . About every nine seconds I'm getting a sweep."

"India-band? Nine-second interval? You figure a Mainstay?"

Pretty Boy swallowed and said, "Yeah. That's what I make it." There were some moments of silence before Floyd said, "This must be for real, Catman."

"Yeah. Must be. Make it good on one pass, Pretty Boy. We don't have enough fuel to loiter."

"Roger."

Griggs pulled up at 83,000 feet and kept the speed at a steady 1,725 mph—which meant the Aurora was traveling a mile about every two seconds.

As it was with the SR-71 Blackbird, so it remained with the Aurora—in that the RSO in the backseat was an incredibly busy person. He drove the mission by operating the navigational and recon systems, feeding instructions to the pilot, and making sure the sensors brought in a fruitful harvest. Floyd was running checks on the external sensors now—a recon version of "clearing the guns." He made sure the elint pod recorder was functioning properly, started the infrared scanner, then engaged the video recorder and brought the TV picture up on his backseat monitor. He was so busy, in fact, that he failed to notice that the primary and backup GPS readouts were beginning to digress.

A blanket of low-lying clouds hugged the seaward face of the ice cliffs and extended out into the Ross Sea, so Floyd was faked out for a few minutes before he could discern the demarcation line where the white fluffy clouds ended and the ice began. He was about to figure out he'd made a mistake when Griggs asked, "Shouldn't we be powering down pretty soon now?"

"Wha—? Aw, shit! This damned GPS! Power down now, Catman! Go subsonic!"

Griggs pulled back on the throttle as fast as he dared, while Floyd frantically punched the buttons to put the optical system on full automatic.

WILLIAMS ICE AERODROME

Maj. Gen. Mitrofan Tromso felt refreshed after five hours of uninterrupted sleep, but he had been awakened by the message that the *maskirovka* was over and he could expect hostile action at any time.

The sky above Williams Field was clear, but the wind was brisk and cold as he watched yet another flight of Fulcrums make their landing approach. With the arrival of each additional fighter, his confidence grew proportionally, for he knew that Snow Leopard's success would hinge on three things: air superiority, air superiority, and air superiority. Two of the aluminum-alloy runways were completed now, and the third was near completion. A third of his fighter cover had arrived, but his engineers had been unable to keep pace with the construction of the snow-packed revetments, leaving some of the aircraft parked in the open. Tromso turned to the slender brigadier of the Soviet Air Defense Forces, and said, "I must speak with my combat engineer. I want all of your aircraft in bunkers."

"*Da,* General," replied the ADF brigadier. "I am keeping a close eye on this situation. I would prefer not to bring any more aircraft in from Cam Ranh until we have more bunkers constructed and the third airstrip is completed."

Tromso nodded and said, "Very well."

Willy Field was a scene of frenetic activity now. Two Ilyushin-76 Candid tankers and two Mainstay airborne radar/tanker aircraft were parked on the ice apron, while groups of Fulcrums and Fox-hounds were lined up along the two completed runways. Big-wheeled bulldozers were still scraping out taxiways and constructing bunkers. Canvas tent living quarters were popping up next to the bunkers to provide the pilots and ground crews immediate access to their air-craft in a scramble, and already smoke was appearing from a few of the smokestacks poking through the canvas tops.

"I have two Mainstays on constant patrol," observed the ADF brigadier, "giving us an eight-hundred-kilometer radial sweep, and I have fighters and a tanker on continuous combat air patrol. With that kind of warning and with five runways eventually operational, we should be able to scramble the entire complement of aircraft before any unwelcome visitors arrive."

Tromso nodded. He knew everything the slender ADF general was telling him was true, but he could not shake the tension that came from being a static target. "What about fuel?" he asked.

"The oiler is unloading at the ice wharf as we speak. It brought along several tanker trucks to transport the fuel to the aerodrome here."

"Good," sighed Tromso.

The ADF commander pointed again. "The runway construction crews are about to drop from exhaustion, General. I suggest we let our combat engineer give them a rest period. The two existing run-ways will suffice for now."

Tromso was about to give his consent when a *boom!* punched through the air. After a moment of shock, Tromso demanded, "What was that!?"

Without replying, the ADF commander sprinted to his Sno-Cat and motioned Tromso to jump in, just as pilots and crews tore out of their tents and started running pell-mell toward their aircraft in a scramble.

Tromso and the ADF brigadier churned across the ice to their command post near Scott Base. They left the Sno-Cat and bounded up the metal steps of the operations van, where they entered a darkened room filled with radar screens and technicians. The brigadier asked the shift commander, "Was that a sonic boom?"

The shift commander pushed his headset microphone out of the way and said with a grim face, "Not from any of our aircraft." He leaned over a technician and pointed at various specks on the screen. "These are our aircraft. They are some distance from us and all are traveling at subsonic speed. These are the scrambling aircraft."

"Are you tracking anything else?" demanded Tromso.

The shift commander shook his head. "*Nyet,* General. We have no bogeys of any kind on our screen." Groping for straws, he added, "Perhaps it was one of those ice quakes we were told about."

When the titanic forces of the Ross Ice Shelf pressed against each other—like a geologic fault—a shift or rupture could occur, much like an earthquake. The resulting noise from one of these "ice quakes" could be unsettling on the normally quiet ice shelf.

"That wasn't any damned 'ice quake,' " growled the ADF brigadier. "I know a sonic boom when I hear one."

No one spoke for some seconds. "One of their stealth fighters or bombers, perhaps?" suggested Tromso.

The brigadier shook his head. "They are both subsonic aircraft, General. . . . Sergei, try the close-in air-defense group. Did the Gadfly radars pick up anything?"

The shift commander muttered into his headset, then looked up and said, "Nothing, sir."

Like water coming in under the door, fear crept into the command post as the three men realized *something* had caused the sonic boom. But what? They had not seen it, and none of their sophisticated sensors could find it. Tromso was reduced to relying on instinct. "Go find the engineering officer and tell him to kick some butts! I don't care if the construction crew falls asleep on their feet! I want that third runway finished *now!*"

The ADF commander exited the van to go tell the engineering officer to kick some butts.

Tromso grabbed the shift commander by the arm and growled, "Notify my aide to send a message to Moscow. Tell them I want more fighters in here immediately!"

THE AURORA

Catman Griggs finished out the long, sweeping turn and put the Aurora on a northern vector. "Did you get the pix?"

"Yeah," said Floyd curtly. "That cloud bank didn't extend over the target, so we got a clear shot." Neither one said anything for what seemed a very long time—until Griggs asked, as gently as he could, "Think we left a footprint?"

Sheepishly, Floyd said, "Sure to have. . . . Sorry, Catman."

The Aurora was a stealthy craft, designed to conceal itself from radar while traveling at hypersonic speeds. Its wing-in-body design, along with its stubby, canted-in tail stabilizers, provided a low profile that greatly reduced its radar signature. The titanium-aluminide skin was not particularly stealthy, but this was mitigated by the treatment of its leading edges—the part of the airplane where a lot of radar energy is reflected. The manta ray's leading edges were coated with a reinforced carbon-carbon (RCC) material that could withstand the heat from kinetic friction as the Aurora was "hangin' ten" in hypersonic drive. But in addition to this, the RCC material was fashioned into tiny honeycomb patterns that acted like a hall of mirrors. When a radar beam entered the honeycomb, it was reflected from side to side as it traveled down a channel that sapped most of its energy. And last but not least, the spy plane's engines were buried in the body to conceal the spinning turbine blades, which were highly reflective of radar energy.

Combining all of these stealth characteristics gave Aurora a radar signature that was bigger than the stealth bomber, but smaller than the B-1. Yet the benefits of that radar invisibility counted for little if the spy plane lowered a sonic boom over the target. That's why standard mission procedure called for the Aurora to fly over its target at subsonic speed.

"Don't get down on yourself, Pretty Boy. The GPS broke down, that's all. Just use the backup to get us back to Dogpatch."

"Roger. Come to zero-zero-five and hang ten."

"We're on our way."

In an hour and ten minutes the Aurora would be refueling once again from the back end of Mother Bear. An hour after that, it would be on the ground at "Dogpatch," which was Area 51 of Nellis Air Force Base in Nevada—home to many of the Air Force's black programs.

The Aurora would be landing at night, of course.

THE PENTAGON

"Whaddaya mean, you *found* it!?"

The naval lieutenant (junior grade) stammered as he said, "Ahem, well, sir, it, ah, just popped up out of nowhere about two thousand miles southeast of New Zealand. We went back through the tapes and couldn't figure out where it came from. It just appeared."

The operations officer for the Office of Naval Intelligence rubbed the temples of his basset-hound face as he looked through the venetian blinds at the sun coming up. What the hell was happening? He'd just arrived home last night when the phone rang. On the other end of the phone was his fire-breathing boss, Adm. Sadie Gainesborough, asking what the hell was this news story about a goddamn Russian invasion at the goddamn South Pole? The chief of staff had turned around immediately and returned to the Pentagon, along with everybody from Army and Air Force intelligence and the Defense Intelligence Agency. Lights had burned throughout the night at Langley and Fort Meade, as well as the Pentagon—a sure sign that the intelligence community was trying to come up with some answers to the incendiary phone calls coming from the White House.

Now that Russian supercarrier had reappeared out of nowhere. A stone's throw from Antarctica. What the hell was happening?

"What about those Soviet ships at the Strait of Magellan?" he asked, groping for something.

"Well, sir, they had passed through the strait a few days ago and were on a heading for Vladivostok. The latest White Cloud pass shows they have all come around to a southwesterly heading," said the lieutenant (jg) as he unrolled a map. "If you take the *Tbilisi*'s course and the new bearing of those Russian ships, they intersect here." The lieutenant (jg) tapped a spot on the map that read ROSS SEA.

"You mean to say they're going to have an entire carrier battle group assembled down there in a few days?"

"If they maintain their current courses and speeds, rendezvous should take place in about ninety-two hours . . . sir. And the task force of fifteen ships in the South Atlantic, including the ASW carrier *Minsk*. You know, the group we thought was on its way from Cam Ranh and Vladivostok for rebasing at Murmansk? Well, that group has turned around and is heading back the way it came."

The operations chief gulped. "Oh, Lordy. What have we got in the area?"

"Ah, well, sir, I checked with ops just before I came over, and we have one *Los Angeles*-class sub shadowing each task force. Other than that, all we have that is remotely close by is the destroyer *Bledsoe* off the west coast of Chile, en route for some drug-interdiction duty off Peru; a couple of guided-missile cruisers in western Samoa; and a tender and a couple of frigates in Brisbane. And that's about it . . . sir. Everything else that we have in the Pacific is currently north of the Equator."

"You mean in very short order the Russkies will have a supercarrier battle group of thirty vessels in the Ross Sea, including a *Kiev*-class ASW carrier, and all we have even remotely close by are five surface warships, two subs, and a *tender?*"

"Yes, sir," replied the lieutenant (jg), noting that grace under pressure was not his superior's long suit.

The operations chief rubbed his temples again. Old Sadie Gainesborough was going to herniate when he heard all this. He reached into his desk drawer for a roll of antacids.

13

. . . .

ASSEMBLY

PEARL HARBOR, HAWAII—January 24

The CH-53 Sea Stallion helicopter slowly cruised over Ford Island, passing above the *Arizona* Memorial where the remains of the ship and 1,177 sailors and Marines were entombed. The memorial structure was suspended over the vessel, resting on underwater pilings. The fourteen open-air windows on its sides and the seven windows in its ceiling represented a perpetual twenty-one gun salute to those who died there on the morning of December 7, 1941. The structure is an understated monument, moving in its simplicity, and it rarely fails to strike an emotional chord within the legions of tourists who flock to see it—many of whom are Japanese.

But as the Sea Stallion passed over the *Arizona* on this February morning, the memorial seemed conspicuous by the absence of tourists.

The base had been closed to civilian traffic, for Task Force Beowulf was assembling.

The green-shirted deck crewman guided the Sea Stallion onto the landing zone of the USS *Carl Vinson* with a series of arm movements, and upon touchdown, the rotors slowed to an idling beat. A strapping Marine corporal—part of the ship's security detachment—ducked slightly as he approached the side door of the rotary-wing aircraft, then he came smartly to attention. He looked "strack" in his white billed hat, khaki shirt, blue trousers, spit-shined shoes, and sidearm. He was to be the escort for the VIP.

The door of the Sea Stallion slid back, and the corporal saluted as the passenger hopped down onto the carrier deck. The corporal looked down . . . then down some more . . . and blinked with a look of incomprehension. There must be some mistake. Somebody had sent them a dwarf in a Marine uniform. The VIP who had exited the helicopter had a bald head with white sidewalls, a generous nose adorned with military-issue spectacles, and a waifish body. The corporal remained in semi-shock until the sun glinted off the three stars on the dwarf's collar. And if that wasn't enough to dispel any remaining doubt, the little guy put on his soft cap—which had the Marine insignia on one side, and three more stars on the other. The dwarf returned the salute.

"Welcome aboard, sir!" shouted the corporal over the blades. "I'm to be your escort."

"Very well, Corporal," said the diminutive general in a voice that was barely audible. "Please take me to the flag bridge."

"Yes, sir."

As the hulking corporal walked off, Marine Lt. Gen. Myron Tharp followed, but at a slower pace, somewhat surprised at the relative minor activity taking place on the deck of the *Carl Vinson*. A maintenance crew was working on a Sea Sparrow air-defense missile emplacement, and some other technicians were working on the "meatball," but other than that and a couple of Marine guards on the perimeter of the deck, there was nothing happening. That was because all of the aircraft were on the ground at Naval Air Station Barbers Point. They would join the ship shortly after it put to sea.

Myron Tharp was born in Great Neck, Long Island, the only child of a dentist and a doting mother. Something of a bookworm as a youth, he was abysmally bad at sports. His parents were Reform Jews, but devout, and they (especially his mother) envisioned a life for him in academe, perhaps even to attend the Yeshiva.

But Myron was not what he seemed to the casual observer. He attended New York University, but then to his parents'—particularly his mother's—horror, he enlisted in the Marine officer training program. When he signed up, it was all the recruiter could do not to snicker. The kid weighed a hundred twenty-eight pounds, *just* made the minimum height requirement of five foot two, and looked like a librarian. The recruiter figured the little Jewish kid would wash out in the first week—maybe the first day.

For the next two summers, before his junior and senior years at NYU, Myron traveled to Quantico, Virginia, for eight fun-filled weeks of heat, sand, mosquitoes, pugil sticks, no sleep, and all the high-grade misery upon which Marine drill instructors had built their reputations. The soft-spoken little Jewish kid was, of course, a particular target for harassment. A couple of DIs made a side bet he'd be dead meat in two days.

But at the end of the first summer, Myron Tharp was still there. Still quiet. Still soft-spoken. Still physically small. And still there. Through hard work he'd made himself wiry and tough, like a jockey. The second summer came and went, and Myron Tharp was still there. The tougher the training, the more resilient he became. He turned into something of a tar baby for the Marine DIs. They simply couldn't break him.

That was because under Myron's deceptively delicate veneer beat the heart of a warrior.

He went into Marine aviation. Shipped out with one of the first F-4 squadrons deployed to Vietnam. Caught some ground fire. Ejected. Picked up. Sustained an eye injury that took him off flight status and saddled him with glasses. Fought like an Indian to stay in the Corps as an infantry officer. Vietnam was rolling—big time. Got his wish and wound up as a company XO in a Marine garrison located at a place called Khe Sanh.

From Vietnam he progressed through a variety of staff and command positions that make up a military career, including a stint as chief of staff of the Naval War College. For someone like Myron Tharp simply to survive in the Marines was remarkable in itself, but his entry into flag rank entered the realm of the astounding. Just think of it. A squirty little Jewish guy named Myron Tharp, a general? A *Marine* general?

Ridiculous.

How did he do it?

Desire and determination? Certainly he had those qualities, but they alone did not carry someone like him to flag rank. No. There was something else. What set Myron Tharp apart from his peers was that his persona possessed one attribute that outweighed his liabilities—an attribute that enabled him to surpass many of his fellow officers and pin three stars on his collar.

Myron was smart.

Tharp's escort took him through the labyrinthine passageways and stairways of the *Carl Vinson*'s tower toward the flag bridge. The activity within the ship, unlike that on the deck, was frenetic. People brushed past him without taking notice of his rank. The sailors' movements betrayed an undercurrent of electricity, of sublimated fear—which was to be expected of men about to go into battle.

Tharp thought to himself that it was incredible how a single news story could trigger such a frenzy of activity. The Marine general did not know Navy Capt. John Benton or Desmond Voorhees, but he would have admired their strategy of using the press to kick the lumbering national security bureaucracy into high gear.

"Myron!" boomed a baritone voice from down the passageway. "Myron Tharp!"

The Marine general turned to see a tall, barrel-chested figure rushing up the passageway toward him. "Hello, Bart," he said, smiling.

A giant hand enveloped his, while the other pounded him on the back, almost knocking his glasses off. "Myron, am I glad to see you! Things have gone crazy. Absolutely crazy. Come on up to the flag bridge."

Tharp turned to the young corporal and said, "You can take off now, son. Admiral Rumley will look after me."

The corporal split.

"I'll take good care of you, Myron. No doubt about that. Come on. I got somebody I want you to meet." And with a giant hand on his back, Tharp was ushered toward the flag bridge.

Vice-Adm. Hobart Rumley was everything Myron Tharp was not. Six foot four, barrel-chested, a jawline like a T-square, and a thick mane of white, impeccably groomed hair. He wasn't a "blue water" admiral, but, God, did he look the part.

Career military officers tend to fall into three categories: politicians, bureaucrats, and warriors. Politicians play any given situation to enhance their career advancement—going to sea, or to the field, just long enough to get their tickets punched so they can return to Washington for "high visibility" in front of defense department officials and Congress. Bureaucrats will bend themselves into pretzels to avoid making waves. And warriors are warriors.

Hobart Rumley was a third-rate sailor but a politician par excellence. His only command slot had been during peacetime as the captain of a frigate, which he'd managed to keep in one piece. Barely. With such dismal seamanship skills, it looked as if his career had nowhere to go—until he was assigned as a liaison officer to the House Armed Services Committee. And it was there that his career broke loose and ascended like a Poseidon missile. Rumley became the perfect point man for hearings—specifically, budget hearings. If Congress killed a weapons system, the Navy would send Rumley up to the Hill. He would walk into that hearing room, wearing that uniform like a glove, gold braid dripping off it. The Navy would always lean on the networks for coverage whenever Rumley appeared. Unlike some of the grizzled, gravel-voiced generals and admirals who gave grudging monosyllabic testimony (which was devastating on TV), Rumley was different. He was not confrontational. It wasn't his style. His silky baritone voice and off-the-cuff humor could charm the socks off almost any tight-fisted congressman.

As the Red Menace retreated from Eastern Europe and other places around the globe, the fiscal ax swung heavily on the armed services as Congress searched for a mythical beast called the Peace Dividend. In this bloodletting, Rumley was personally credited with saving two carrier battle groups, and keeping their number from falling below nine.

Rumley was chosen as commander of Task Force Beowulf because he was politically acceptable to a nervous Congress that was, in just forty-eight hours since the initial AP story, questioning the wisdom of an open military conflict with the Soviet Confederation in Penguinland. But on a live news conference from the Pentagon, the Secretary of Defense had laid out the whole story on Branding Iron Station and what was at stake. In an emergency meeting of the UN Security Council, the United States ambassador accused the Soviet Confederation of violating sovereign American territory, and demanded an immediate withdrawal and a return of American prisoners. The Soviet delegate replied that the prisoners would be returned forthwith. But as for the demand of a withdrawal, the Soviet Confederation was exercising a historic claim on its sovereign territory, and as far as the Soviet Confederation was concerned, the American ambassador could, diplomatically speaking, piss up a rope.

The world was shocked.

The Congress was nervous.

The White House was . . . confused. But while the President's pollsters were figuring out which way to play this one, and the legal boys were scratching their heads over a defunct treaty, the Defense Department started the ball rolling on the premise that McMurdo was sovereign U.S. territory . . . and we were taking it back.

To reassure Congress, the Pentagon chose Rumley as commander of Task Force Beowulf. He was a political asset. But the problem was, he knew precious little about running a combined operations task force. His entire combat experience consisted of a single cruise as a junior line officer aboard the carrier *Oriskany* in the Tonkin Gulf during the Vietnam War.

So he was joined by Myron Tharp. No one in the military had a better overall grasp of air power, sea power, and land combat than the little general. That's why he was chosen as deputy commander of Task Force Beowulf.

And that's why the admiral was glad to see him. Rumley knew his own weaknesses, and he knew Myron Tharp's strengths. The two men had forged a bond when Tharp was a colonel and Rumley a captain under the old Joint Chiefs system. They had been brothers in arms within the office of the Secretary to the Joint Chiefs. Together they had looked after the four-star brass, making sure their appointments were kept, coffee cups filled, pencils sharpened, and paperwork routed. Not wanting to look like a fool where military strategy and tactics were concerned, Rumley quickly learned how to tap Myron's brain for insightful comments about amphibious landings, fighter plane bomb loads, or a snappy quote on what Sun Tzu said about siege warfare. With Tharp's brainpower and Rumley's polished delivery, the two forged a solicitor-barrister relationship that enhanced their mutual career advancement.

Tharp gave more than he got from the relationship, but like most everyone else, he found that he enjoyed being charmed by Bart Rumley. He also knew that charm had its limitations.

The two flag officers made their way up to the flag bridge and entered the adjoining conference room. Standing there, leaning over a table, was a man in camouflage fatigues. He was of medium height, middle-aged, with a hawkish-looking face that—like Tharp's—sported military-issue spectacles.

"Josh," said Rumley expansively, "I want you to meet Myron Tharp."

Army Maj. Gen. Joshua Pfeiffer extended his hand and said, "Good to meet you, General Tharp. Admiral Rumley has told me a lot about you. Sorry we had to meet under these circumstances."

Joshua Pfeiffer was commanding general of the Alaska-based Sixth Infantry Division (Light). The parenthetical "Light" meant they were a light infantry division, and they were known as the

"Arctic Light Fighters." Like Tharp, he was a quintessential war-rior. Pfeiffer looked as if he would have made a good linebacker in his youth—which was exactly the case. At Fordham. His torso was bulky but solid. He'd developed his skills in the art of war with a single-mindedness that was extreme. He didn't relate to the civilian world very well. When his peers would start talking about retirement or mutual funds, he'd be lost and turn the conversation to Slim's Burma campaign or Wellington's logistics at Salamanca. He was uncomfortable in civilian clothes and hated to come back from the field. He'd worn his hair in a spike haircut long before it was fashion-able. The Army wouldn't let him near Capitol Hill—wouldn't let him near Washington, for that matter, or even station him on the East Coast. But with a Vietnam battlefield record like his (three tours), they couldn't retire him either. So he wound up in Alaska.

As they gathered at the table, this was the *troika* that would lead the American Task Force Beowulf into battle across the Antarctic Circle—Rumley the politician and task force commander, Pfeiffer the warrior who would lead the ground forces, and Myron Tharp—warrior, vice-commander, and linchpin who would have to bring everything together and make it work.

"Admiral Rumley and I were going over some fresh Aurora photographs that just came in from Eye-Pac," said Pfeiffer, giving the acronym for Intelligence Center Pacific (IPAC)—an interservice group in Hawaii that acted as an "all source" clearinghouse for intelligence data throughout the Pacific Theater.

Tharp methodically went through the photos.

"I must say it doesn't look good, General," said Pfeiffer while pointing out the planes and runways. "The air boys have gone over these already. As you can see, four runways are completed and a fifth is under way. So far we've been able to count twenty-three MiG-31 Foxhounds, twenty-six MiG-29 Fulcrums and Su-27 Flankers, seven Il-76 Candid tankers or transports, two An-124 Condor transports, two Mainstay radar planes, and thirteen Backfire bombers. Those are the ones we can count, and there may be some under the covered bunkers that are out of sight. Fortunately the Aurora caught the sun at the right angle so the bunkers displayed their shadows. The ana-lysts figure there are some Mainstays and fighters in the air on defensive patrol."

Tharp ran through the numbers in his mind. "So we're talking roughly seventy fighters and bombers already in place."

"Yes, sir," said Pfeiffer, "and more are arriving all the time. The ground crew is working like a bunch of ants building more bunkers and taxiways."

"And their supercarrier, the *Tbilisi,* is in the Ross Sea," said Rumley. "That's another sixty aircraft right there. One smaller *Kiev*-class carrier and twenty-eight escort ships will be on station soon, so they have the sea approaches covered pretty damn well. Now, Myron, I've been thinking, and I've decided we should go after that *Tbilisi* first. Then we land the Marines to establish a beachhead and—"

Tharp shook his head. "That won't work, Bart. We're dealing with a very strong force of land-based aircraft, and the *Tbilisi* battle group is sure to be under their air umbrella. I'd be willing to bet that the number of Backfire bombers are going to double. With those Main-stays in the air, they'll see us coming five hundred miles out and come after *us* with the Backfires. Whoever put this plan together was very clever. They've got the Foxhounds for static defense, and the Ful-crums and Flankers to engage our carrier-based fighter cover and clear a path for their Backfires. And the sea approaches are covered by the *Tbilisi* task force. Yep, very clever, indeed. Before we do anything, we must first neutralize the land-based aircraft on the ground. Then we'll worry about the *Tbilisi.* "

Rumley was scratching his chin.

Pfeiffer felt himself already taking a shine to this little Marine with the soft voice named Tharp.

"Well . . ." said Rumley, groping, "if we have to nail 'em on the ground and get through the Mainstay radar fence, how about we get SAC to send in some stealth bombers?"

Again, Tharp shook his head. "No, Bart. There are only sixteen stealth bombers in existence—barely half an operational wing. They're all subsonic. The Russians, as we've said, are bound to have patrols in the air, and it's perpetual daylight down there now. On a white background those black bombers are likely to be acquired visually. Besides, we can't guarantee that all sixteen would be ser-viceable at once."

Rumley was feeling uncomfortable. As the task force commander, he thought he should direct the war planning. This was a lot different from congressional testimony. "Well, uh, Myron, have you got any ideas?"

Tharp inspected a map of the McMurdo area that was on the table, then looked at the photos again, this time with a magnifying glass. Finally he placed his hands on the table and said, in his soft voice, "Admiral, may I suggest . . ."

When Tharp was finished, no one said anything for quite some time, until Pfeiffer spoke up. "That's a helluva line of dominoes that have to fall down in order for this to work, General."

"That's very true," admitted Tharp. "But everything hinges on air supremacy. We have three carrier battle groups in Task Force Beowulf. We can't commit any more for the operation. We'll be operating far from any friendly bases, and we simply won't have the firepower to engage over a hundred hostile aircraft in an air battle. We've got to nail them on the ground, or our battle is over before it starts."

The two warriors had taken over now. Rumley might as well have not been in the room.

Pfeiffer picked up one of the photos again. "Well, sir, if this plan of yours is going to work, we're going to need some men on the ground."

Tharp nodded in agreement and pointed to an object in the blownup photograph that Pfeiffer was holding. Essentially the object looked like four darts laid down on a tray. "These Gadfly air-defense missiles are deadly," said Tharp. "They can throw up a close-in air defense that's devastating. I saw a DIA report that had some CIA source data in it. Soviet field tests on the Gadfly were extraordinary. If we're going to nail them, we have to clear the Gadflys out of the way. And to take them out we're going to need someone on the ground. Have you got some people in your division that are geared to handle something like this?"

Pfeiffer tossed the photo back on the table and said, "I've got 'em."

THE DENMARK STRAIT—January 25

As the *Kharkov* cruised out from under the ice pack that covered much of the Denmark Strait between Iceland and Greenland, a small buoy was released from the rear of its turtleback, which pulled a thin wire toward the surface. This was the antenna to the *Kharkov*'s very-low-frequency (VLF) radio that enabled the ship to communicate with a Bear communications aircraft circling above. The aircraft, in turn, relayed the submarine's signal to the Red Banner

Northern Fleet Headquarters in Polyarny. The *Kharkov*'s VLF antenna was 510 meters long and vibrated as it was pulled through the water, thus creating an acoustic signature that could be detected by sonar. But for now, noise didn't matter, because the *Kharkov* was 120 meters below the surface, flanked between two old, dilapidated November-class attack submarines—the only two of their kind remaining in the Soviet fleet. The Novembers were the very first class of nuclear-propelled attack submarines in the Soviet Navy, and their underwater stealth characteristics were roughly similar to those of the Grambling University marching band. What better way to advertise your presence than to be escorted by two of these rattletrap vessels?

Twenty miles behind the *Kharkov* came its Delta IV sister ship, the *Smolensk,* and behind that came the *Magadan.* Each of them were escorted by two old and noisy Echo II–class boats. This underwater version of "seventy-six trombones in a big parade" was traveling through the Denmark Strait, stepping loudly upon the Greenland–Iceland–United Kingdom (G-I-UK) SOSUS line. The underwater sensors lying on the seabed couldn't help but pick up the clatter-bang-rumble-din of the submerged convoy.

But that was the intention.

In the radio room of the *Kharkov,* the teletype printer slowly tapped out the message with a relentless *blip . . . blap . . . blip . . . blap . . . blap . . . blip.* The advantage of VLF radios was that they could transmit and receive messages under water. The down side was that the lower the frequency, the slower the data transmission.

When the message was completed, the machine emitted a *beep-beep,* and the communications *michman* (warrant officer) ripped it off the printer and retired to the closet-sized encryption room where he closed the door. He opened the safe and took out a one-time pad and laboriously began deciphering the message.

The missile-fire-control room aboard the *Kharkov* was a horseshoe-shaped desk of panels—peppered with a multitude of lights, switches, and dials. If the launch order came, the fire-control officer, a *kapitan tretyego ranga* (captain, third rank), would sit in the middle of the horseshoe, flipping switches and pushing buttons to fuel and arm the sixteen SS-N-23 missiles in the turtleback compartment. All of the launch procedures would normally be performed under the watchful eye of an armed KGB guard who was precisely drilled on the procedures to be followed upon receipt of the firing order. If the fire-control officer deviated from the proper sequence, he would be dispatched by the guard's revolver and replaced by his backup. That was the positive check. The negative check was that in order to fire the missiles, the fire-control officer, the *starpom* (executive officer), and the captain all had to insert and turn special keys in control boxes simultaneously.

Incredibly for a submarine, the SS-N-23 ballistic missiles were liquid-fueled. But those had been stripped out of the *Kharkov*'s tubes and replaced with the solid-fuel *Zimorodok* missiles. All the new firing circuitry was wired into the fire control panel, so only a single key on the U-shaped console was needed now.

Captain, First Rank, Kasimir Bodin stood over his fire-control officer and asked, "Now do all of your people understand that we did not have sufficient time to wire the guidance system into the master panel here, therefore the targeting data will have to be entered into each missile individually as it is received by the communications room?"

"*Da,* Captain. That is understood. My division has been briefed. We have completed our diagnostic check on each *Zimorodok* guidance system. They all functioned properly, except one, and the factory technician is repairing it now in the electronics shop. We will begin launch drills within the hour, with one man stationed at each missile tube. I will pass the targeting data to them through a system of telephonic headsets I am having installed."

Bodin grimaced. Not a terribly sophisticated method, but it would have to do. "Drill your men until they can do it in their sleep. If the attack order comes, we must act swiftly or lose our quarry."

The radio *michman* came though the hatch and handed Bodin a file folder containing the deciphered message that had been received over the VLF radio. "This just came in for you, Captain. I decrypted it myself."

Bodin opened the file and scanned the message, which read:

1-1823GMT/24/01

TO: KHARKOV, SMOLENSK, MAGADAN & ESCORT VESSELS

FROM: STAVKA, STRATEGIC SUBMARINE FORCE COMMAND, RED BANNER
NORTHERN FLEET, POLYARNY

FLASH   FLASH   FLASH

TWO NIMITZ-CLASS CARRIERS—CARL VINSON AND THEODORE ROOSE-
VELT—DEPARTED PEARL HARBOR 1422 GMT THIS DATE ON SOUTHERLY
HEADING.

SURFACE TASK FORCE DEPARTED SAN DIEGO 1238 GMT THIS DATE,
HEADED SOUTHWEST FOR PROBABLE RENDEZVOUS WITH PEARL HARBOR
CARRIERS.

NORFOLK-BASED NIMITZ-CLASS CARRIER EISENHOWER, ESCORTS, AND
AMPHIBIOUS TASK FORCE IN NORTH ATLANTIC ON MANEUVERS. HAVE
TURNED SOUTH AND SHOULD CROSS EQUATOR APPROX 2130 GMT THIS
DATE.

INTELLIGENCE INDICATES HOSTILE ACTION OUTSIDE AMERICAN DE-
CLARED ZONE OF EXCLUSION—60 DEGREES TO 90 DEGREES SOUTHERN
LATITUDE—POSSIBLE BUT NOT, REPEAT NOT, PROBABLE. DO NOT ENGAGE
HOSTILE FORCE OUTSIDE EXCLUSION ZONE UNLESS FIRED UPON. PRO-
CEED ACCORDING TO SEALED ORDERS.

END MESSAGE

Bodin handed the folder to the fire-control officer and said, "It is
no longer *if* we receive the attack order, but *when*. We may already
be too late. We should have been on station before this damned Snow
Leopard business commenced." Bodin slammed his fist into his palm
and spat, "That damned worthless pigsty of a factory. They cost us
too much time." Bitterly he shook his head and said, "I will be in
central control."

And he took the folder back.

The central control room of the *Kharkov* was the nexus for all of
the ship's sensors, systems, and weapons. From here the captain
could talk to his sonar, commo, missile, engineering, or torpedo
divisions, consult with his navigator, or look through the attack or
search periscope. His missile key station was located here as well.
There was hardly a space that was not crammed with switches,
gauges, LED displays, or cathode-ray tubes. Two helmsmen—one
who operated the diving planes and another who operated the rudder—sat at a panel of airplanelike controls, watching TV monitors
that projected a computer-generated picture similar to what you'd
see if you were traveling beneath a long elevated highway. The
helmsmen—supervised by the trim officer perched on a seat behind
them—were holding the vessel steady until the VLF antenna was
reeled in.

Bodin entered central control and beckoned to his *starpom* executive officer, Avraam Ryback, and the pilot, Toomas Mizim.

Kapitan Vtorogo Ranga (Captain, Second Rank) Avraam Ryback was fashioned from the same stripe as Captain Bodin in that he was sinewy and energetic, but much shorter than the captain, and he wore spectacles on his narrow face. He was clearly the kind of *starpom* earmarked for command.

Kapitan-Leytenant (Captain-Lieutenant) Toomas Mizim—the pilot assigned to take the *Kharkov* through the Passage—was nothing like Bodin and Ryback. He was of medium height, and his slightly overweight body appeared soft, lacking any muscle definition whatsoever. His large brown eyes had the forlorn look of a cat that had just been dunked, then pulled out of the water. Bodin guessed he was one of those academic types who gravitated to submarines, but would probably not make the cut for command.

"This just arrived from Polyarny," said Bodin as he passed the message file to the two officers. They scanned it, and their expressions betrayed their discomfort. "Has sonar picked up any American or British submarines trailing us, Avraam?"

The *starpom* Ryback shook his head. "*Nyet,* Captain."

"Well, you can be assured they are there—in view of the fact that we are stepping on their SOSUS line while traveling between two tambourines." Bodin had long envied the silent capabilities of the American and British submarines. The newest class of Soviet attack submarines—the *Mikhail*—was quieter owing to a smoother design and better propellers, and was on a par with the *Los Angeles–* and *Trafalgar-*class subs. The *Mikhail's* improved propellers were due, in part, to advanced milling technology provided by Japan's Toshiba and Norway's Kongsberg.

But the *Kharkov* was a Delta-IV submarine, an updated version of the basic "Yankee class" design that was over thirty years old; and although an improved design, the Delta-IV was certainly detectable by American subs and sensors. And since it was flanked—as Bodin mentioned—by two underwater tambourines, there was no doubt the Americans were out there, tracking them in force.

"Since we are to proceed according to our orders," said Ryback while looking at his watch, "it is almost time for another scatter maneuver."

"Proceed, Number One," replied Bodin.

The *Kharkov* was 120 meters below the surface, cruising at eighteen knots. Ryback went to the helm station and checked his watch against the ship's chronometer. At the prescribed instant he ordered, "Slow to eight knots."

"Slow to eight knots, aye," replied the trim officer.

Bodin felt his vessel decrease in speed as Ryback went to one of the multitude of hand receivers hanging from the ceiling like straps in a subway car. He grabbed one that seemed indistinguishable from the rest. This was the acoustic telephone that would digitize the sound waves of his voice and transmit them through the water to the escort subs. At the precise moment he keyed the microphone and said, "Scatter."

Immediately the portside November-class escort increased its speed to twenty knots, leaving an acoustic signature like a nail scraping on a blackboard. Simultaneously it turned to cross the beam of the *Kharkov* at an angle, while ascending fifty meters. The starboard escort did the same thing, except that it descended fifty meters. The two escorts would crisscross in front of the *Kharkov*'s bow four times, turning as sharply as possible, to make as much additional noise as possible. Once the maneuver was completed they would resume their original escort positions. The *Smolensk,* the *Magadan,* and their escorts would execute identical maneuvers over the same spot of the ocean floor as they passed it in sequence, and the same drill would be repeated several times over the next two days.

"Conn, sonar."

Bodin mashed the intercom button. "Sonar, conn, aye."

"We obtained a faint contact on the towed array at bearing zero-nine-seven. Range unknown. Nationality unknown, but I would suspect it is a *Los Angeles*– or *Trafalgar*-class submarine that turned somewhat sharply after the scatter maneuver began."

Bodin smiled. "Apparently we flushed one of the invisible American or British submarines. Very good, sonar. Keep me advised of further contacts."

Bodin turned to Toomas Mizim. "As you heard, Comrade Pilot, we have at least one adversary shadowing us. Probably more. Do you think we will lose them through the Passage?"

Mizim's forlorn expression remained unchanged as he replied in a soft voice, "Without question, Captain."

Bodin thought this officer was one of the most enigmatic submariners he'd ever met, which was saying something—because almost by definition submariners were enigmatic. "How many times did you say you had been through the Passage, Comrade Pilot?" It was the fourth time Bodin had asked.

"Many, many times in the simulator at Polyarny, and as a junior officer I was on the original survey team that charted the Passage. Once you are inside, it is no problem, except for the Hump approximately midway. The exit point is not a problem, either. It is the entry point that is the most difficult—and dangerous."

"And tell me again how many times you have navigated the entry point?"

Mizim did not betray his irritation at being asked this question yet again. Once more his soft voice replied, "As I said, many times in the simulator. Eight times with myself at the conn. Twice in *Mikhail*-class submarines, six times in *Alfas*."

Bodin pulled on his sharklike nose. "Eight times is not many, Comrade Pilot."

Mizim nodded. "True, Captain, but navigating the entry point of the Passage is not something anyone rushes to embrace. It is extremely difficult going in, and virtually impossible to use as an exit point. Every sub that has attempted an exit course through it has sustained significant damage. Without the small two-man submersibles to chart the entry point, it is likely the Passage would not have been explored."

Bodin nodded. "Has a Delta-IV sub ever been through the Passage?"

Mizim shook his head. "*Nyet,* Captain. The *Kharkov* will be the first. Only submarines with titanium hulls—like the *Alfas, Akulas, Mikhails,* and the newer class Delta-IVs—can withstand the depths. In particular, the Hump."

Bitterly Bodin said, "So the *Kharkov* is to be the first. Such an honor . . . Number One."

Ryback left the navigational plot to join the captain and the pilot.

"Avraam," said Bodin, "ensure the Comrade Pilot receives all of the practice on handling the *Kharkov* that he desires. I will be in my cabin if you require me. Notify me of any future sonar contacts with American or British subs or surface warships."

"*Da,* Captain."

Bodin half-stepped, half-slid down the ladder to the auxiliary control room on the deck below, then he went forward through the passageway to enter his cabin. The captain's quarters on the ship were bigger than the other officers' quarters, but not by much. The big difference was that Bodin did not have to share his tiny abode with another body. Only the captain, the *starpom,* and the chief engineer enjoyed private accommodations. The doorway of the spartan quarters opened to a narrow aisle. On the left was a bunk recessed into the bulkhead, with cabinets above it. On the right was a small washbasin, and a tiny desk that was also recessed into the bulkhead. Off to one side of the desk was a small TV that was wired into the periscope, and above the alcove were a cabinet and two phones on wall cradles—one black, one red. The black phone was a ship's intercom. The red phone was a secure voice-channel to fleet headquarters in Polyarny, but it could only be used if the sub surfaced and the transmission was relayed via a satellite or a Bear communications aircraft.

Bodin opened the desk cabinet and revealed two safes with combination locks. One safe ordinarily held a backup set of launch codes, but it was empty on this voyage. The other safe was a catchall for sensitive items, and this was the one Bodin opened. He hesitated, then slowly reached in and withdrew a silver-framed photograph that pictured an eight-year-old girl. Blond hair. Blue eyes. Coquettish smile. Every father's dream. Her name was Marlenya, and she was Kasimir Bodin's only child. As always, her image caused the captain's hard features to soften in the lamentation of remembrance.

Eleven years ago he'd returned from a long deployment to find that his wife had taken Marlenya and vacated their meager apartment in Murmansk—leaving not so much as a note of farewell to acknowledge the end of their bitter marriage. He'd tracked them down, of course. To Volgograd. She'd married some party hack and was living in a comfortable apartment. Bodin could carry on without his dead marriage, but the little Marlenya had captured his heart, and he told his wife he intended to take the child with him. She didn't try to fight him. Didn't even raise her voice, in fact. All she did was ask him a single, simple question: What could he, as a submariner, offer his daughter except long, oppressive periods of loneliness? Kasimir Bodin realized he had no answer, and walked away.

He returned to Volgograd only once after that. From a distance he watched Marlenya in the schoolyard, playing with the other children after classes were finished for the day. His wife, or ex-wife to be exact, had appeared with her new husband, and when little Marlenya had run to the strange man's embrace it was like a knife sinking into his heart.

He had returned to the sea, seeking whatever solace such a consuming mistress could give.

Even now he could not bear having Marlenya's picture in view, so he kept it in the safe. With moist eyes, the hardened submarine captain replaced the photograph, then took out a slim binder that had been in the envelope Defense Minister Yuri Timoshenko gave him upon the *Kharkov*'s departure. Bodin clicked on the fluorescent desk lamp and made himself as comfortable as possible in the spindly chair. Then, for the fifth time since the voyage began, he opened the binder and began to read the secrets of the Passage.

OMICRON SECRET
STAVKA
STRATEGIC SUBMARINE FORCE
RED BANNER NORTHERN FLEET
ACCESS ONLY BY AUTHORIZATION OF
SSF COMMANDER

This document was prepared by the operational staff, Hydrographic and Oceanographic Fleet, under the direct supervision of the Fleet Commander, and in coordination with the Commander, Strategic Submarine Force. Contents of this report are classified Omicron level and are not to be released except with the specific written permission of the SSF Commander.

Overview

In order to gain access to the strategic lines of communication in the North Atlantic between the United States and Western Europe, the Soviet Navy has long faced the nettlesome task of negotiating the Greenland–Iceland–United Kingdom gap. This has long been troublesome for our submarine force, owing to the sensitivity of American and British submarines, and the underwater sensors of the American Sound Surveillance System (SOSUS) line. The route through the Rekjanes Ridge, southwest of Iceland, provided our forces with limited concealment for a time, but in recent years the Americans have increased the number of SOSUS sensors in the Rekjanes formation, negating its effective concealment to a large degree.

While making a routine hydrographic survey in the area of the Rockall Bank, the survey vessel Akademik Oparin discovered an extraordinary geologic formation that can provide concealment to certain vessels of the Soviet submarine force once they are past the SOSUS line.

Location

This underwater formation lies 315 kilometers northwest of Donegal Bay on the western Irish coast. In this vicinity, the sea floor of the Hebridean Shelf falls off sharply into the underwater depression of the Rockall Trough. This trough has a maximum depth of 3,000 meters and is approximately 100 kilometers across. The western edge of the trough rises with a sharp grade into the Rockall Bank plateau, which has an approximate average depth of 600 meters. (The only surface evidence of the Rockall Bank plateau is the tiny Rockall Island at 57° 35'N, 13° 48'W.) This plateau lies on an axis of northeast to southwest.

The southeastern perimeter of this underwater plateau—where it falls into the Rockall Trough—is an area of great geologic complexity known as the Feni Ridge. The top of the Feni Ridge appears to meld into the plateau, while its base goes down to the bottom of the trough. The Feni Ridge is approximately 500 kilometers in length, and although it appears to be a contiguous geologic formation, *it is not.* Throughout its length, the ridge is largely hollow—a chamber of mammoth proportions, with a ceiling-to-floor dimension that exceeds the depth of Lake Baikal (the deepest lake in the world) more than twofold.

Geologic Formation of the Feni Ridge Chamber

The fleet's chief oceanographic geologist is uncertain as to how this chamber came to be formed within the Feni Ridge, but based on the available geologic data, the following is his professional opinion: Approximately 300 million years ago the British Isles were located near the Equator, and the plateau wall of the Rockall Bank—where the Feni Ridge now stands—was on the periphery of what is now the Eurasian continental plate. When such a plate pushes against the sea floor, something must yield, and the sea floor is pushed under the plate in a process called "subduction." The subduction phenomenon can create a deep ocean trench—such as the Marianas Trench in the Pacific—or it can cause magma vents to be formed in the earth's crust that can result in the buildup of volcanoes. In the case of the Feni Ridge, both events apparently occurred, resulting in an ocean-floor topography sequence of plateau-trench–volcano string. As the British Isles drifted to the north, stress fractures occurred in the sea floor, causing a transform fault to shear this long spine of volcanoes lengthwise. Slowly, over time, one-half of the sheared string "fell" into the trench. The second half was going to follow (and, geologically speaking, it still is), but the plateau has acted as a kind of restraint to the second half of the volcano string that was cleaved in two, and it came to rest against the wall of the plateau in a "lean-to" fashion, covering the deep trench.

Over millions of years, silt has covered the Feni Ridge, making it appear that it is a contiguous mass with the Rockall Bank plateau.

The underwater tunnel that runs underneath the bulk of the Feni Ridge is geologically extraordinary in the extreme—i.e., the roughly uniform size of the volcanic spine that runs its length for 500 kilometers, the deep ocean trench that is quite narrow, the movement of the continental plates. All of these elements had to come together to form this subterranean chamber, which the survey team has often referred to as "the Passage."

Entry and Exit Points

As the survey progressed, a number of vents into the Feni Ridge Chamber were discovered, but mostly they were quite small, not large enough for a submarine to negotiate. Only two points have been found that can accommodate a submarine. (A third potential entry/exit was found that could be enlarged by blasting, but underwater blasting would attract undue attention.) The entry point is at the northeastern extremity of the ridge, and the exit point is 325 kilometers to the southwest. For all intents and purposes, transit through the Passage can only be accomplished one way, from the northeastern entry to the southwestern exit (see appendix and schematic diagram for navigational details).

Strategic Value

The entry point to the Passage lies approximately 750 kilometers south of the closest American SOSUS sensors, near the Faroe Islands. The depth of the entry point is 428 meters, which approaches the maximum operational depth limits of Western submarines. The ceiling of the main channel has an average depth of 733 meters, which is well below the diving capabilities of Western submarines, but still within the operational parameters of our own titanium-hulled vessels—Alfa, Mikhail, Akula, and some Delta-IVs. Almost midway through the Passage, there is one area of danger known as "the Hump"—a geologic protrusion that reaches down from the ceiling to a depth of 1,157 meters (again, see appendix and schematic drawing for details). Although our titanium-hulled vessels have withstood the pressure at this depth, it should be pointed out with great clarity that our engineering studies have indicated the margin for error is slight.

Once inside the Passage, our submarines will be totally concealed, and after they transit the exit point they will be sufficiently out of range of the SOSUS sensors to preclude the Americans or British from obtaining an accurate fix on their positions. Only if a random American or British ASW vessel or aircraft is near the exit point as our submarines leave the Passage will they be discovered.

The Passage provides the Soviet Union with limited but extraordinary strategic and tactical advantage, but it will remain effective only as long as operational security is maintained. If the exit point is ever compromised to the Americans or British, then the Passage will have lost its value. Secrecy is therefore paramount.

The staff would mention that the cost of charting the Passage was high. During the survey, the Rodina lost the *Tashkent,* an Alfa-class vessel, with all hands. Cause unknown. The remains of ship and crew most probably lie at the bottom of the ocean trench, some 5,000 meters deep.

Kasimir Bodin closed the binder. Once again the sea had elicited his awe and fear. The idea of taking his vessel through the Passage was at once fascinating and terrifying. And to get him through, he would have to rely on a forlorn-looking, enigmatic pilot named Toomas Mizim. To reassure himself, Bodin once more pulled from his breast pocket the note he had found paper-clipped to the schematic diagram in the binder. It was handwritten, almost indecipherable, but Bodin was more than familiar with the rough-styled script. It simply read:

Mizim is the best.
Yuri

MOUNT DISCOVERY

Dana Harrow fell through the door of her seismic hut, half-frozen and barely alive. With a shaky, mittened hand she reached up and turned the thermostat to a high temperature to warm up the hut. She feared she was slipping into hypothermia as she reached out with her numbed foot to push the door closed against the howling wind. Lying there on the floor, she was too exhausted to move, but knew that she must.

After dropping her Sno-Cat through the crevasse, Dana had started back on foot toward the hut, taking a shortcut over the backside of Mount Discovery. The snow on the mountain slopes and on the glacier was shallow, so she had left her snowshoes back at the hut. But on the way back, a blizzard had closed in on her and she had stumbled into a snow-filled ravine, which encased her in a chest-level snowdrift. She'd struggled out, only to become disoriented by the storm, and she fell again. She'd dug out a shelter in the snow and climbed into her sleeping bag to wait out the blizzard. It had lasted three days, and when it finally broke, it took all of her strength to climb out. By the time she got moving again, Dana was almost out of food and water, and already exhausted.

Now she lay on the floor of the hut, having covered a twenty-mile trek on foot in some of the worst winds she'd ever encountered. She was afraid of frostbite, and leaned over to put her face as close as she dared to the gas heater.

THE *CARL VINSON*

There is nothing quite so awesome as a supercarrier battle group, on line, cutting through the sea. The floating steel fortress of the carrier exudes strength and power as it flings its warplanes into the air like Thor unleashing his lightning bolts, while the escort vessels—cruisers, destroyers, frigates, submarines—swarm around the steel island like drones supplicating to the queen bee.

Although it carries a stupefying array of firepower, including the nuclear kind, if you place the carrier battle group (CBG) under a magnifying glass, the initial impact of its image starts to fade, and its vulnerabilities come into focus—the most salient of which is its lack of conventional offensive punch. That is because the bulk of the CBG's firepower is geared toward protecting the carrier. The F-14 Tomcat interceptors, the E-2C Hawkeye radar planes, the S-3 Viking antisub aircraft, the escort vessels, the Sea Sparrow missiles, the Standard missiles, the chaff missiles, the Phalanx close-in missile-defense Gatling gun, the antisub helicopters, are all geared primarily for the defense of the carrier.

While the escort vessels do have a standoff offensive capability with their Tomahawk missiles, a CBG's offensive punch is concentrated, by and large, in its thirty-six strike aircraft, consisting of twenty-four F/A-18 Hornets and twelve A-6 Intruders.

The fearful array of hardware—ships, planes, and missiles—that make up a nuclear CBG cost about $18 billion, plus about $1 billion a year to operate. All that for an offensive punch of thirty-six aircraft.

When all of them are serviceable, that is.

As Marine Lt. Gen. Myron Tharp stood on the portside perimeter of the *Carl Vinson*'s flight deck, watching the Pacific sky and ocean meet at the horizon, he was well aware of the vulnerabilities and limitations of his task force. In a set-piece battle on the open sea, Tharp felt confident that Task Force Beowulf could overcome and sink the *Tbilisi*. But he knew that trying to overpower the land-based Soviet warplanes at Williams Field—which Aurora photographs now showed to be in excess of 220—with only his carrier aircraft would be improbable if not impossible. That's why Myron Tharp wasn't even going to try. If his Beowulf plan did not work, then Tharp felt the battle was lost and the Soviets would have their prize—which would enable them to develop graser weapons. And by just possessing such weapons, the intel assessments said the Russians could probably control the flow of Middle East oil without having to fire a shot.

There was a lull in flight operations on the *Carl Vinson* now. Two E-2C Hawkeye radar planes were airborne, as well as two F-14 Tomcats and two F/A-18 Hornets on combat air patrol, plus a KA-6D Intruder tanker to refuel them in flight. The sub screen encircled them, listening for their enemy counterparts on sonar, and being assisted by the S-3 Viking sub-hunter aircraft. On deck were Tomcats poised on catapults one and two, ready to race skyward at a moment's notice. A few more Hornets and Intruders were parked on the flight deck, but the bulk of them were on the hangar deck, and there were no launchings or recoveries taking place. Tharp was wearing his utility uniform with a camouflage hat, standing on the flight deck near the catwalk, taking a moment to admire the beautiful day.

"Excuse me, General. Got a minute?"

Tharp turned to see a man with rather unkempt hair and a paunchy middle, wearing a polyester uniform with no insignia except for a plastic tag on the breast pocket that said PRESS.

"And you are?" queried Tharp.

"Seymour Woltman. Associated Press. I'm with the Pentagon press pool."

Neither man made a move to shake hands as Woltman looked out to sea and said, philosophically, "Incredibly peaceful, isn't it? Hard to believe there's a war on."

"Appearances can be deceiving, Mr. Woltman. What can I do for you?"

Woltman shrugged. "Oh, nothing much. I just have about twelve thousand questions I would like to ask the vice-commander of this task force. Wondered if you could spare me five minutes."

"Make it three."

"Okay, three. Is this ruby stuff—"

"Rubidium."

"Yeah, is this rubidium stuff really worth going to war over?"

Tharp sighed. "Mr. Woltman. We cannot win a conventional war with the Soviets for the Middle East oil fields. *Cannot win.* The Soviet forces are too great—even with their massive reductions they still have eighty-seven active divisions. We have cut ours to fifteen. Their lines of communication are short, ours too long. Even if Israel and Western Europe came in totally on our side, which is doubtful, we still could not prevail. We cannot win in the Middle East five years from now, but we might win in Antarctica now. With the rubidium we can fashion graser weapons that could even hold the Soviet Confederation at bay and ensure that the flow of oil to the West continues. That's why we're here. Our dependency on foreign oil is greater than it ever has been, I'm afraid. If we don't dislodge the Soviets from McMurdo, then you better park your car and get used to walking."

"But everybody in the country is in a state of shock over this thing. Can't it be settled somehow?"

Tharp pursed his lips. "Now that Soviet paratroops have entered the picture, I would say negotiations were remote at this point."

"So when does the shooting start?"

Tharp adjusted the hat resting on his bald head. "We're maintaining a five-hundred-mile exclusion zone around each carrier battle group in the task force until we cross the sixtieth parallel. Then it's a free-fire zone."

"Won't the Russians be tracking us with their satellites?"

Tharp shrugged again. "I suppose so."

"You *suppose* so?"

"Time's up, Mr. Woltman. Please be careful not to be sucked into one of the jet intakes while you're on deck. The turbine blades can turn you into strawberry jam rather quickly." And with that, Tharp began walking toward the conning island on the starboard side of the ship.

"But, General," Woltman called out. "I thought everything was peaches and cream between us and the Russians. Everybody thought so."

Tharp turned and called back, "That reminds me of something my grandmother used to tell me."

Woltman cocked an ear. "And what was that?"

Tharp crossed his arms in a moment of remembrance. "She used to say, 'All the fools aren't dead yet.' Good day, Mr. Woltman."

The Marine general resumed his march across the deck, but before entering the conning island he paused and looked up at the forest of antennae that bristled around it. . . . And that started Myron Tharp to thinking.

For almost twenty years before his arrest in 1985, a naval warrant
officer named John Walker had dealt an espionage blow to the U.S.
Navy that was so complete in its devastation that had war ever come
between the United States and the Soviet Union, the balance of
power on the high seas may well have been seized by the Soviet Navy.

After his capture, Walker confessed something to the FBI that was
particularly frightening: During a meeting in Vienna, Walker had
told his KGB "handler" that his contact at Alameda Naval Base
(another naval warrant officer, named Jerry Whitworth) was having
difficulty obtaining data on the Navy's newest and most secret cryptologic system, the KGR-77.

The KGR-77 series was the most advanced cryptologic device
then in existence. It was able to encrypt and decrypt several different
levels of Navy message traffic—everything from routine supply orders to the highly sensitive "Blue Channel" message traffic between
senior Navy commanders. When Walker had told his KGB handler
that Whitworth was finding it impossible to obtain keylists and
technical data on the KGR-77, the KGB handler told Walker *not
to bother with it.*

The implication of that statement from the KGB handler was
clear—that the Soviets *already had access* to the secrets of the KGR-
77 series, that Moscow was already reading Blue Channel traffic, and
that Walker was not the only spy purloining the most closely
guarded cryptologic secrets of the National Security Agency.

The KGR-77 series remained in use for a number of years after
this disclosure while the NSA went back to the drawing board to
come up with a better machine. They finally did, and it was anointed
the KSP-57.

The KSP-57 used a system of "binary" custom computer chips
instead of a keylist system, and the technical people at NSA took a
blood oath that the machine was absolutely impregnable. Each KSP-
57 had an internal logic structure that was fitted with a distinct,
custom-made "female" computer chip unique to that particular machine. Every twenty-four hours a "male" chip was changed—a chip
that would work with any "female" counterpart. The crux of this
binary system, however, was that each unit was "addressable," in
that a secret message could only be deciphered by the particular
KSP-57 machine(s) it was addressed to. The enemy could possess the
"male" chip for that particular day, but unless they possessed the
custom "female" chip for that particular machine, they couldn't

break the cipher. Cranking out so many chips was an expensive process, but it had two advantages: the hands-on operators of the KSP-57 had no knowledge of the chips' internal logic, and unlike keylists, computer chips could not be easily photographed or duplicated.

As Myron Tharp contemplated the forest of antennae that covered the *Carl Vinson*'s conning island like a hairnet, he wondered if the new KSP-57 machine and the Blue Channel message traffic were genuinely secure. Or were the high-level NSA secrets still being compromised somewhere along the line? Tharp maintained his gaze on the antennae, then decided he was going to find out. He entered the hatchway of the conning tower and made his way to the communications center.

An hour later an encrypted Blue Channel message was transmitted from the *Carl Vinson* to CinCPAC (Commander in Chief Pacific) in Pearl Harbor, outlining the exact time and place at which Task Force Beowulf was going to cross into the zone of exclusion at the sixtieth parallel.

An hour after that, a Grumman C-1A supply plane was launched from the number-two catapult and headed toward Pearl Harbor, carrying a sealed message for CinCPAC in its hold.

14

. . . .

THE PASSAGE

THE *KHARKOV*—January 27

Under the starry, moonlit night of the North Atlantic, the ocean swells were cresting into whitecaps as the sail of the *Kharkov* broke through the surface and extended its satellite receiver mast into the air. The icy ocean winds buffeted against the man-made intruder in their midst, but to no avail. The receiver mast extended to its full length into the night sky and immediately began pulling in signals from the Soviet Global Navigation Satellite System, or "Glonass." Once the signals were processed by the navigational computer, the *Kharkov*'s position would be fixed to within thirty meters.

As the Glonass transmissions were coming in, a cover on the top of the sail slid back and a bulblike object rose out of the hole. This was the submarine's "Cod Eye" radiometric sextant—a device that identified specific stars in the North Atlantic sky by measuring their electromagnetic intensity. The Cod Eye's primary role was to provide the submarine's SS-N-23 ballistic missiles with a navigational fix before launch. But the SS-N-23 projectiles had been yanked out of the *Kharkov*'s tubes and replaced with the *Zimorodok* missiles. Even so, the pilot had ordered a star shot taken with the radiometric sextant as a backup to the Glonass system. Stars had guided ships for millennia before satellites had soared into the heavens, so perhaps Toomas Mizim took some comfort in that.

In the central control room of the *Kharkov,* the tension was increasing as the *starpom,* Avraam Ryback, stood at the navigational plot—his sinewy, energetic body hopping back and forth, checking the readouts from the Glonass system and the Cod Eye radiometric sextant. Ryback then compared the figures against the ship's inertial navigation system, which was not in harmony with the other two systems. That was because the inertial device had not been calibrated since the *Kharkov* submerged on the initial leg of the voyage to go under the Arctic ice cap on a feint. Ryback, who was acting as navigator for the transit, was preparing to read off the latitude and longitude figures—down to the minutes and seconds—for the pilot, Toomas Mizim, who was resting with one hand against the periscope column.

Capt. Kasimir Bodin stood at a nearby panel, holding the handset of the acoustic telephone. He was struck by how passive, almost docile, the pilot seemed to be. Mizim just stared ahead with those forlorn cat eyes of his.

"Position readings as follows," called out Ryback. "Glonass: fifty-five degrees, forty-two minutes, eighteen seconds north; fourteen degrees, fifty-eight minutes, twenty-two seconds west. Radiometric sextant: fifty-five degrees, forty-two minutes, twenty seconds north; fourteen degrees, fifty-eight minutes, twenty-three seconds west."

"Calibrate inertial guidance between the two readings," ordered Mizim. "The Glonass system is not as accurate in the northern latitudes as it is in the tropics."

"Aye," replied Ryback as he punched in the numbers on the keyboard of the inertial guidance system. Once the data were entered, he double-checked them and said, "Done."

"Retract antenna and sextant," ordered Mizim. "Come to course two-six-seven and submerge on a twenty-degree plane down to four hundred ten meters. Ahead one-third." Once the compass reading on the periscope column came to two-six-seven, Mizim said, "Captain, commence the maneuver."

Bodin keyed the mike and said, "Scatter," and the ancient November-class escorts began their high-speed crisscross. Bodin quietly speculated that their convoy of Delta-IV-class boats and noisy escorts had attracted a school of American and British attack submarines, undoubtedly puzzled by the rattletrap procession.

Mizim left his post at the periscope and took a position beside the trim officer, who was perched above the helmsman and planesman sitting at the airliner-style controls. The pilot watched the inertial readout above the TV monitors as the trim officer intoned, "Depth, four hundred meters . . . four-zero-five . . . four-zero-eight . . . four-ten meters . . . trim to horizontal."

"Maintain course at two-six-seven," ordered Mizim.

"Maintain two-six-seven, aye."

Bodin noticed a change start to come over the pilot. He seemed a bit—what was the word?—energized.

The *Kharkov* had left the deep Rockall Trough in its wake and was now cruising over the Feni Ridge, approaching the entry point.

"Reduce speed to five knots," said Mizim.

"Speed five knots, aye," echoed the trim officer.

The pilot now seemed mesmerized by the latitude and longitude figures on the inertial readout as he intoned softly, "Course two-six-five, ahead dead slow."

"Two-six-five, ahead dead slow, aye."

The digits on the readout slowed their rate of change, and Mizim remained transfixed by the numbers. There was a period of silence until he ordered, "Come to one-nine-two, then all stop."

Bodin felt the vessel turn, then the trim officer said, "Bearing one-nine-two, all stop."

Mizim had positioned the *Kharkov* slightly to the south of the entry window in order to compensate for the current of the North Atlantic Drift. He had also aligned the ship with the largest gap in the entryway, so that during the descent it would drift with the current and pass through unscathed. His margin for error was small.

"Incline sail planes and aft planes to ninety degrees vertical," ordered Mizim.

"Sail and aft planes, incline to ninety degrees vertical, aye."

On the *Kharkov*'s sail and stern, the diving planes rotated until they were pointing straight up.

Mizim returned to the periscope station. "Flood main buoyancy tank to eighty percent negative."

The diving officer flipped some switches and said, "Main buoyancy, eighty percent negative, aye."

As water rushed into the center belly tank of the *Kharkov,* the vessel went from neutral to negative buoyancy and began sinking.

"Up periscope," ordered Mizim in a voice that was losing its soft timbre. The tube rose and Mizim yanked down the brass handles as he mashed his face against the rubber eyecups of the viewer. Curtly he said, "Illumination."

On the bow, sail, and stern of the submarine, searchlights stabbed their beams into the black depths, and Mizim clicked on the light-amplification viewer in the periscope. This device allowed him to follow the beams a greater distance into the darkened waters, even though the image it provided had a greenish hue.

"Position?"

"Precisely on track," replied Ryback.

"Depth?"

"Four hundred twenty meters," replied the diving officer. "Four-two-five . . . four-two-six . . . four-two-seven . . . four-two-eight . . ."

Mizim could see the green image of a craggy ridge rising into his periscope view. The effect was much like moving between floors in a descending elevator with the door open. The craggy wall continued to move past, uncomfortably close to the bow of the submarine, but then it disappeared, replaced by nothingness.

They had entered the Funnel.

"Depth four-three-five . . . four-four-zero . . ."

"We are past the entry point and into the Funnel," announced Mizim.

The entry point to the Passage was a small oval aperture through the Feni Ridge, which quickly flared out into a large chamber shaped like a funnel—wide at the top, and narrowing to a spoutlike tube near the bottom. As the *Kharkov* continued its vertical descent, Mizim's face remained mashed to the periscope viewer, searching for the telltale sign of the Funnel's bottom. Faintly at first, then with greater definition, the craggy wall of the Funnel slowly came into view. In the subdued red light of the control room, Bodin watched the periscope view on a nearby TV monitor as Mizim ordered, "Sail and aft planes horizontal."

"Sail and aft planes horizontal, aye."

"Ahead dead slow, come to two-one-two."

The trim officer leaned over the planesman and helmsman and said, "Ahead dead slow, course to two-one-two, aye."

"Depth?" Mizim's voice was sharp.

"Five hundred ten meters . . . five-one-five . . ."

As the green image of the Funnel wall became sharper in its resolution, sweat trickled off the pilot's forehead and onto the rubber eyecups of the viewer. "Funnel narrowing," announced Mizim. "Blow main buoyancy tank. Come to neutral buoyancy."

"Neutral buoyancy, aye."

There was a hissing and popping sound as the water in the central buoyancy tank was displaced by air.

"Depth?"

"Five-three-three meters."

"Heading and speed?"

"Bearing two-one-two, ahead dead slow," replied the trim officer. The descent was rapidly slowing, but the Funnel wall was closer than it should be. "Back one-third," ordered the pilot.

"Back one-third, aye."

There was a mild whiplash as the propulsion reversed.

Once the neutral buoyancy became greater in its effect, the descent of the *Kharkov* slowed to a crawl, then halted just as a black hole appeared in the green craggy wall. Mizim ordered, "All stop."

"All stop, aye."

They had reached the opening of the spout tube.

Mizim took advantage of the pause to yank a handkerchief from his pocket and wipe his face and the rubber eyecups. "The entry to the spout channel is dead ahead, Captain," announced the pilot, in a voice of extraordinary firmness.

"Proceed," said Bodin.

"Ready on the planes?" Mizim queried.

"Ready on the planes, aye," replied the trim officer.

"Ready on the tanks?"

"Ready on the tanks, aye," echoed the diving officer.

Once again Mizim mashed his face to the viewer and said, "Ahead at five knots." To Bodin, the pilot seemed like an actor in a theater where the curtain had just been raised.

"Ahead five knots, aye."

The spout tube veered off the bottom of the Funnel in a downward-sloping angle of thirty-one degrees for about six hundred meters before going into a harsh dogleg turn to the left—at a shallow angle of descent. To negotiate the spout tube, the *Kharkov* would have to maintain the correct angle of descent and the precise speed, otherwise it could strike the bottom, top, or side of the tube—or worse, become wedged in the rocky channel. Ordinarily a submarine would dive or ascend by turning the diving planes up or down like the control surfaces on an airplane, while maintaining neutral buoyancy. But a submarine had to maintain sufficient speed in order for this to work. The spout channel was closely confined, so the *Kharkov* would have to dive *and* sink at the same time by using the diving planes in conjunction with the buoyancy tanks. Everyone on the ship was aware of this navigational maze, and that was why everyone—in the subdued red light of the control room—had dark wet patches at the armpits of their uniforms.

In Mizim's periscope viewer, the spout hole approached. It always seemed so small. And as the ring closed around his field of vision, the pilot yelled, "Dive angle on planes thirty-one degrees! Flood forward trim and central buoyancy tank to fifty percent negative! Blow aft trim tank to fifty percent positive!"

"Aye!"

"Aye!"

Bodin grabbed a railing as he felt the deck pitch forward and heard the tanks venting and blowing simultaneously. The *Kharkov* was now in the spout tube, and Mizim was trying to keep the vessel equidistant from the ceiling, deck, and sides of the rocky channel. His angle within the tube was correct, but the ceiling was too close, to the point that he was in danger of clipping the extended periscope. To compensate, he had to sink the vessel even farther in the channel while maintaining the dive angle.

"Down scope, halfway. Central buoyancy tank to sixty percent negative."

"Halfway, aye."

"Sixty percent negative, aye."

Mizim kept his eyes against the viewer as he knelt down on one knee in concert with the descending scope. The ceiling came excruciatingly close, but the additional negative buoyancy took effect and lowered the *Kharkov* into the midstream of the channel. He must not overcompensate. "Blow central buoyancy to fifty percent negative."

"Fifty percent negative, aye."

The submarine was well positioned in the tube now, but Mizim remained down on one knee.

The easy part was over.

A dark streak of sweat appeared along the spine of Mizim's cotton uniform shirt, for they were fast approaching the dogleg turn. He'd never attempted the dogleg with a sub of the *Kharkov*'s enormous dimensions, and he knew it was going to require a deft hand to adjust the ship's tanks while—at the same time—executing the perilously sharp bend to port and retrimming the diving planes.

"Blow forward tank to fifteen percent negative! Aft tank to fifteen percent positive! Central tank to ten percent negative buoyancy and planes to eleven degrees down angle!"

"Aye!"

"Aye!"

Hissing and popping.

Mizim licked his lips. The bend was approaching. "Ahead one-third! Left full rudder! Reverse port engine!"

As Captain Bodin felt the vessel begin to turn, his eyes remained riveted on the television monitor. The green wall of the dogleg loomed at him on the screen . . . it was coming closer . . . it was approaching too fast. They weren't going to . . .

"Reverse starboard engine! Full power to both screws! Hard right rudder!"

"Aye!"

There was a slight pause, then everyone lurched forward as both propellers bit into the water with their reverse pitch and broke the *Kharkov*'s forward momentum. Then, as the reverse thrust gained a toehold and the water began flowing over the rudder from aft to forward, the stern of the vessel began swinging around. Mizim crawled around to point the periscope to the rear, where the aft lights were illuminating the stern. The rocky wall was closing in on the rudder assembly. "Forward both engines!" Mizim screamed. "Full power! Left standard rudder!"

"Aye!"

Another pause, and the *Kharkov* lurched again. On the monitor screen, the rudder assembly and the craggy wall seemed close enough to kiss, but then the rudder pulled away.

Mizim spun around once more, looking forward. "Ahead five knots. Rudder amidships."

"Ahead five knots. Rudder amidships, aye."

Toomas Mizim had handled the *Kharkov* as if it were a bus in a tight turn—stopping it, then turning the wheel and backing up, then driving forward again. They had made it, and now they were in the Corkscrew.

The Corkscrew was a spiral-like tunnel with a three-quarter curving turn. It was set in a plane that was slightly inclined and terminated at the Narrows, which was a kind of cattle chute that led into the Passage proper.

"Decline planes seven degrees," Mizim ordered. "Central tank to thirty percent negative."

"Aye."

"Aye."

The channel ceiling was higher in the downward-sloping entry of the Corkscrew, causing Mizim to say, "Up scope," with relief.

"Up scope, aye."

The Corkscrew would follow a spiral down to starboard, then up, and up some more, and then to port, then down to port and into the Narrows.

"Ten degrees right rudder."

"Ten degrees right rudder, aye."

Bodin watched the monitor as the ceiling fell away into nothingness.

"Incline planes to twenty percent. Forward trim tank to twenty percent positive, aft trim tank to twenty percent negative, central buoyancy to thirty percent positive. Rudder amidships."

"Aye."

"Aye."

Hissing and popping.

Mizim swiveled the periscope head upward, and when the ceiling started to reappear he turned the viewer to port to see the channel wall start falling away. They were approaching the top of the Corkscrew.

"Planes to horizontal. All tanks to neutral buoyancy. Ten degrees left rudder."

"Aye."

"Aye."

Hissing and popping.

The *Kharkov* ceased rising and cruised over the top of the Corkscrew spiral. Mizim was grateful for the width of the channel, for that would change soon. Very soon.

The ceiling was coming closer as they approached the final strait to the Narrows. Mizim licked his lips again. A droplet of sweat trickled into his left eye and it stung, but he couldn't take the time to flinch. He couldn't see it through the light amplifier, but he knew it was out there. With instinct, intelligence, and experience guiding him, he prepared himself to put the *Kharkov* into the final leg of the journey.

"Rudder amidships! Thirty percent dive angle on the planes! Ahead flank!"

"Aye!"

Bodin grabbed the rail again as the vessel's bow dropped once more. There seemed to be an electric charge around the pilot now. An aura of sorts. He was in absolute command of the vessel.

When the *Kharkov* reached the proper angle of attack, Mizim ordered, "Planes to horizontal!" and the sub remained at a thirty-degree inclined dive. As the propellers increased their revolutions, the walls of the channel whipped by Mizim's field of vision and began to narrow, as if he were racing down a cattle chute. The portside wall was too close. A correction was needed. "Five degrees right rudder!" That was enough. "Rudder amidships!"

The cattle chute terminated in a window that was just large enough to accommodate the *Kharkov,* but it was oval-shaped and canted at a starboard angle—something akin to the doorway of a dilapidated house that leaned to one side, almost to the point of collapse. To get through the doorway, the *Kharkov* would have to lean over, too.

"Ready on the planes!" Mizim screamed.

"Ready on the planes, aye!"

In the periscope, the craggy window of the Narrows rushed toward him, beckoning like the jaws of a shark. The pilot's primal instinct and nerve came into play at this moment as he mentally gauged the distance, track, and momentum to his only escape from the Narrows. There was no possible way to turn back now. Closer . . . closer . . . closer . . . the channel walls were pressing in . . . closer . . . the window hurtled toward him. . . . *"Now! Decline starboard planes five degrees! Incline port five degrees! Down scope!"* He slammed the brass handles against the periscope tube and leapt back as the viewing port dropped to the floor.

Bodin felt the deck cant to starboard, like an aircraft rolling to the right. Then the *Kharkov* shuddered as it displaced water from the opening, and Bodin heard an eerie *screee . . . screee . . . screee,* as a rocky outcropping of the Narrows window caressed the keel of the vessel.

Then, like a moray eel leaping from its lair, the *Kharkov* shot through the window and into the vast chamber of the Passage—unscathed except for some scratches on its hull.

As the rolling of the vessel continued, Bodin became alarmed, until Mizim ordered, "Reverse angle on the planes! Slow to one-third, then trim us out, helm."

"Aye."

"Depth?"

"Eight hundred eight meters, sir."

Mizim sagged against the periscope tube. "Continue on this course for two minutes, then bring us about and all stop. Have sonar listen for the *Smolensk* and *Magadan.*" Mizim's uniform shirt was sopping as he looked to Ryback and asked, "Damage control, was there any breach in hull integrity?"

Ryback muttered into the intercom phone, then shook his head and said, "No breach in hull integrity."

With relief, Mizim turned to Bodin and said, "The *Kharkov* is now in the Passage, Captain. Your crew performed flawlessly. We took the Narrows window a bit too close on the port side, which resulted in the hull being scraped. But I take responsibility for that. I now transfer the conn to you."

Bodin stared at the sweaty pilot, then at the blank monitor, then back again. "Transfer accepted, Pilot. I believe you have earned yourself a shower."

"Thank you, Captain. I will take you up on that suggestion while we wait for our brother ships to appear."

As Mizim brushed past him, Bodin touched the periscope tube, then said, "Pilot Mizim?"

As Mizim stopped and turned, the sweaty streaks on his uniform appeared black in the subdued red light, and his forlorn eyes had circles around them where they had been pressed against the rubber eyecups. "*Da,* Captain?"

Bodin turned and gave him a deferential nod—a kind of homage—and said, "That was the most incredible piece of seamanship I have ever seen."

"Conn, sonar."

Bodin mashed the intercom button. "Sonar, conn, aye."

"The *Magadan* is through and is approaching our position, Captain."

Bodin, Ryback, and Mizim—who was now wearing a clean uniform—all sighed with relief.

"He is cutting power now," squawked the intercom.

Bodin took the acoustic telephone and keyed it in order to speak with the captain of the *Magadan,* whom he knew well. "Welcome to the Passage, Alexei Andreievich."

A few moments passed before a fuzzy but shaky voice came through the speaker. "I never want to go through anything such as that again, Kasimir Sergeievich. We clipped our stern against the channel wall as we negotiated the dogleg turn. I was afraid we would become wedged in, but our pilot brought us through."

"As did ours," replied Bodin, while looking at Mizim. "How bad is your damage?"

"We can maneuver, but once we are through the Passage, I will have to send out divers to inspect it. What about *Smolensk?*"

"Our brother vessel sustained some damage to the portside aft diving plane as he passed through the Corkscrew. He, too, can maneuver, but may have to make repairs en route. The *Kharkov* only sustained minor scrapes on his hull."

"You were lucky, Kasimir."

Bodin shot another glance at Mizim. "Luck had nothing to do with it, Alexei. Prepare to move out. *Kharkov* in the lead, then the *Smolensk,* then the *Magadan.* Cruise at fifteen knots. Allow ten minutes' spacing between each vessel."

"Aye. *Magadan* out."

"*Kharkov* out."

As Bodin replaced the acoustic telephone in its cradle the intercom squawked again. "Captain to sonar."

Bodin hit the button and said, "On my way." Then he nodded to Ryback. "You have the conn, Number One. I will see you and our pilot at breakfast."

"Very well, Captain."

Bodin left the central control room and went aft through the passageway to the second compartment, which held the sonar suite. It was bathed in a low blue light to enhance the displays on the computer monitors. There were three *michman* operators sitting side by side, with a chubby *starshiy* lieutenant standing over them. He was holding a headphone to his ear as he said, "We have something, Captain. Very faint. Coming from the direction of our entry point into the Passage."

Bodin took the headphone and pressed it against his ear. He heard it, too, and it was extremely faint. Barely discernible.

A pinging sound.

Bodin smiled. "The Americans are searching near the entry point with their active sonars. They lost us and they cannot understand why. Undoubtedly our decoys covered our disappearance. They would not use their active sonars unless they were desperate." Bodin's hard features broke into a grin. "What I would not give to be a fly on the wall at their SOSUS headquarters when the American boats report that we have vanished."

BRANDING IRON STATION—January 28

The portly chief engineer looked on with satisfaction as the small skip loader took shovelful after shovelful of earth from the mouth of the mine shaft and moved it over to the periphery of the icedome. The skip loader had been disassembled, brought down piece by piece on the elevator, then put back together. A tedious process, but it was paying off. The digger drill was pushing through the soft sedimentary earth, and the chief engineer felt he would be hitting pay dirt within two weeks.

AIR DEFENSE RADAR INSTALLATION, ROSS ISLAND

In the saddle between Mount Erebus and Mount Terra Nova on Ross Island, the wind came off the ocean in a brutal gale, pummeling the air defense brigadier with invisible haymakers that almost knocked him into the snow. There was no way his helicopter was going to land and retrieve him in this weather, so he grabbed his division chief by the arm and shoved him back toward the safety of the launch van. Once inside, they savored the warmth they had left only minutes ago, and took sustenance from some freshly brewed tea.

Greedily the major swallowed the hot brew, then wiped his mouth. "I have never experienced wind like this, General. Not even on the steppes."

"Nor have I, Valery," confessed the brigadier. "Do you think the antennae can withstand this weather?"

The major took another gulp before replying, "They were not built to endure this kind of wind, General. We can only pray they will hold."

The tall, slender brigadier with the Gallic nose had designed his air defense of Williams Field (Leopard Base) in layers—like a Russian *matryoshka* doll, one inside the other. The outside layer comprised the orbiting Mainstay radar planes and the combat air patrol, which electronically scanned the territory around Leopard Base for a radius of eight hundred kilometers. The brigadier felt the Mainstays would provide ample warning to scramble his fighters and bombers. But if the Americans penetrated that outer layer, they would have to grapple with his missile net, and that was what brought him to the windblown saddle of Ross Island. The brigadier had ringed the island with radar antennae to provide a 360-degree sweep—north to the sea, west over McMurdo Sound, east along the cliff of the ice shelf, and south toward the Windless Bight and the ice shelf proper. The antennae were wired into the SA-12 Gladiator missiles—which had an extraordinary range of eighty kilometers, but relied on a complex radar system. The Gladiators used a large, flat, phased-array antenna called a "billboard" for target search/acquisition, a radar link with the launcher, and a smaller "grill pan" radar that illuminated the target while guiding the missile to an intercept. But despite the Gladiator's complexity, the brigadier was quite pleased with the positioning of his antennae, for they were placed high on the slopes of Ross Island and gave him a "look down" scan to the horizon. That is, they gave him a look-down capability if they were not blown down by the horrendous gales shooting through the island's saddle.

Yet even if the Americans were able to penetrate his fighter umbrella and the Gladiators, they would have to deal with the final defensive layer of the SA-11 Gadfly missiles that absolutely bristled around Williams Field. Except for Hut Point Peninsula, the terrain surrounding the airfield was extraordinarily flat, giving the missiles a clear field of fire. The air defense brigadier was one of a handful of people who knew the true capabilities of the Gadfly missiles and how devastating they could really be. They gave him a feeling of confidence, and allowed him to look toward the next rung on his career ladder. If he brought this Snow Leopard business to fruition, he would certainly be one step closer to his dream of becoming Commander in Chief of the Soviet Air Defense Force.

THE *KHARKOV*

"Depth?"

"Nine-eight-three meters...nine-eight-five...nine-eight-seven..."

"Up scope," ordered Toomas Mizim, and the metallic tube rose. The pilot yanked down the brass handles and said, "Illumination."

Once again the exterior lights came on as Mizim pressed his face against the rubber eyecups of the viewer and clicked on the light amplifier.

"Depth nine-nine-three," chanted the diving officer. "Nine-nine-four . . ."

Captain Kasimir Bodin listened to his ship groan under the weight of the ocean as it pressed against the titanium hull at 1,450 pounds per square inch. The *Kharkov* was cruising along the downward-sloping ceiling of the Passage, approaching the Hump, which was the deepest part of their transit through the chamber—deeper than the *Kharkov*'s maximum depth limit as set forth in the ship's manual. Bodin had always been told the specifications in the manual were conservative, and he hoped that was true.

Mizim tilted the periscope head up slightly to ensure that it would not clip the rocky ceiling. He felt it was uncomfortably close as he ordered, "Increase dive angle to twenty degrees."

"Dive angle to twenty degrees, aye."

Bodin held on to the brass railing as his submarine pitched forward an additional five degrees.

"Depth?"

"One-zero-one-three meters . . . one-zero-one-five . . ."

Over a thousand meters in depth now. Bodin felt his grip involuntarily tighten on the brass railing. If the double titanium hull gave way, the ship would probably implode so quickly they wouldn't have time to utter a prayer. So the captain prayed silently now.

"Depth one-zero-two-three . . ." The diving officer's voice was growing taut. He had difficulty believing the gauge he was reading. "One-zero-three-one meters."

The pressure was now generating a wailing or singing sound that permeated the submarine like the mating call of a humpback whale.

The diving officer was sweating as the seconds ticked by and the submarine continued to descend. The red light on the digital depth-gauge readout had come on, indicating they had passed the *Kharkov*'s maximum dive limit. "Depth one-one-zero-five meters . . . one-one-one-five . . . one-one-two-five . . ." The young *starshiy* lieutenant looked at Bodin with a pleading face. "Captain, the ship will not take—"

"Belay that, diving officer!" snapped Mizim as his face remained mashed against the viewer. "And keep those reports coming!"

On one of the panels another red light came on, followed by a *buzzzz! . . . buzzzz! . . . buzzzz!* The damage-control officer shut off the annunciator and held his headphones against his ears, then said, "Damage control reports breach in seal integrity in missile tube number fifteen! The tube is beginning to flood!"

"The tubes are probably the strongest part of the ship," Bodin replied, trying to make his voice sound calm for the ears of his officers in the control room. "Number fifteen is empty. We can compensate for it easily with the buoyancy tanks and repair it once we are out of the Passage. Mr. Mizim still has the conn."

"Depth one-one-five-five . . . one-one-five-*seven* . . ."

In the viewer, Mizim saw the rocky green ceiling fall away into nothingness. He slapped the handles together and yelled, "Down scope! Trim the planes to horizontal! Ahead one-third for two minutes, then twenty degrees up angle and take us up to nine hundred meters."

"Aye!"

Mizim looked to Bodin. "We are passing under the Hump, Captain. The remainder of the Passage can be negotiated with relative ease. I transfer the conn to you."

"Transfer accepted," replied the captain, as he contemplated the sweat-soaked pilot. "Do you suppose our *Alfa*-class submarine, the *Tashkent,* was lost while diving below the Hump?"

Mizim shrugged. "Possibly . . . probably."

Bodin nodded. "I have been in submarines for thirty years, and this is the greatest depth I have ever reached."

Mizim nodded. "And we are still almost four thousand meters from the bottom. The sea is a treacherous place."

THE *CARL VINSON*

The twin engines of Sweet Thang's F-14 Tomcat spooled up to full military power, causing the image of the Pacific moon to ripple as it passed through the thermal waves blooming around the jet blast deflector. The catapult officer in the bubble gave a green-shirted crewman a signal, who passed it to Sweet Thang, who lit the Tomcat's dual afterburners, which bathed the jet blast deflector with a blue and yellow flame.

The catapult officer then punched a button that sent a signal to the catapult controller, who hit another button, and in the time it takes to snap a finger, the Tomcat was hurtling down the catapult track.

Once airborne, Sweet Thang retracted his gear and trimmed out his F-14 before pointing it straight up toward the stars. The Tomcat he was "driving" was different from his favorite *Nellie Belle* in the Screaming Eagles Squadron, but he and his backseater, Wrangler, had taken a number of practice runs in this specially modified F-14 and had become familiar with it. Although the newer F-14s didn't need afterburner to get airborne on a catapult launch, this particular one did, because of the weight of its payload.

Wrangler was in actuality a native Chicagoan with bristly red hair, who had never been on a horse in his life. But he loved watching Western B-movies on late-night TV and he always wore cowboy boots when out of uniform. Ergo, the call sign of Wrangler.

"So how's it looking?" asked Sweet Thang.

"We're in the envelope," replied Wrangler as he began punching buttons on his armament panel.

The Tomcat's speed was approaching supersonic as it burned off fuel and maintained its vertical climb. Slung beneath the aircraft's belly was a single missile that resembled an old-time butter churn, in that it had a thick base and a narrow top.

Wrangler was intently watching a CRT screen that was spitting out the F-14's speed, angle of ascent, rate of climb, altitude, and position, and telling him where the Tomcat was in relation to the programmed parameters. It was within the "envelope" as they climbed past thirty thousand feet.

Sweet Thang was watching his own altimeter and figured it was time. "You got it?" he asked, louder than he had to.

Wrangler moved a switch from MAN to AUTO and said, "I've got it!"

Sweet Thang let go of the stick and kept his feet off the rudder pedals as the target-acquisition computer took over control of the aircraft. To the pilot it was an eerie, uncomfortable feeling to be flying combat, at night, straight up, in afterburner, with no hands or feet on the controls.

At 48,000 feet the F-14 began arcing over on its back, and the two crewmen felt the vibration as the missile detached itself from the aircraft's belly. Wrangler waited three seconds, then said, "You got it," as he pulled the switch back from AUTO to MAN.

Sweet Thang grabbed the stick and rolled the Tomcat upright so they could both search the indigo sky. "There it goes!" yelled Sweet Thang as he watched the antisatellite missile streak into the night.

OCEAN RECONNAISSANCE CENTER, RED BANNER PACIFIC FLEET HEADQUARTERS, PETROPLAVASK, KAMCHATKA PENINSULA

The atmosphere in the Ocean Reconnaissance Center was permeated with tension and cigarette smoke. The nonsmoking chief of the surface division found he could handle the tension, but the secondhand smoke from Russian cigarettes was particularly odious. If he could just hold his nose for the next eight hours . . .

He sighed and set his tea glass down at his console station in the gymnasium-sized room that was dominated by a large backlit screen. The Pacific and Indian oceans were pictured with multicolored dots scattered about, representing friendly warships, enemy warships, neutral warships, and commercial vessels. Submarines were there, too, of course.

Information on surface ships came into the Center from reconnaissance aircraft, trawlers crammed with electronic gear, submarine detections, and observations by surface warships and commercial transports. But most of the information came from the radar ocean reconnaissance satellites (RORSATs) and electronic ocean reconnaissance satellites (EORSATs). They were similar in many respects to the American White Cloud system, except that White Cloud incorporated both capabilities into a single system.

The surface division chief settled himself into his chair and scanned the big board. The two Pacific carrier battle groups centering around the *Carl Vinson* and the *Theodore Roosevelt* were approximately seven hundred kilometers apart, and had just crossed the equator almost due south of Hawaii. The CBGs were zigzagging, of course. The last RORSAT pass had plotted their position, and this was noted on the screen in Cyrillic type, along with an arrow indicating their last known course and speed. Elapsed time from the last pass was noted, too. The *Eisenhower* CBG was undoubtedly heading south in the Atlantic, but that wasn't pictured here and wasn't his responsibility. He knew the higher echelons in the Kremlin had agreed to observe the exclusion zone beginning at sixty degrees south, but he wished they would unleash the submarines earlier. They had the American carriers pegged in the open sea. The time to start engaging was now. At least cause some damage. Interrupt flight operations. He sipped his tea and grumbled that this wasn't the first time politicians had gotten the military into a fine mess. This would probably turn into an Afghanistan at sea. He watched the screen carefully as the data from the current RORSAT pass trickled down the screen from north to south, updating the symbology. The big triangle denoting the *Carl Vinson* CBG was starting to move, then it disappeared from the screen.

"Captain!"

The division chief raised his hand. "I know, I know, I see it.

Electronics officer, do you have any contacts?"

"Last contact was radio traffic two orbits ago. Total emissions security since then. Next pass on electronic satellite coming up in thirty-two minutes."

The Captain shrugged. "It matters little. They have blasted our radar bird out of the air. The electronic birds will be shot down soon, as well. Then they will re-illuminate their radars. I had heard rumors the Americans possessed a carrier-based antisatellite missile. Apparently they were not rumors."

He sipped his tea while punching the intercom button to his superior.

THE *KHARKOV*

"Captain to sonar!"

The bloodcurdling shriek that came through the intercom and into the control room was unlike anything Kasimir Bodin had ever heard—and it caused him, Ryback, and Mizim to shoot down the passageway toward the sonar suite like three bullets from a Makarov pistol.

Bodin plunged inside and demanded, "What is it?"

Even in the low blue light, the heavyset *starshiy* lieutenant looked ashen. He punched a button to put the sonar reception on the speaker. "The *Magadan* is taking on water! It sounded as if he was just clearing the Hump when something gave way!"

Bodin, Ryback, and Mizim were mortified as they listened to a gurgling sound coming through the speaker, which was quickly followed by a hissing and popping noise.

"He is blowing his tanks!" cried the lieutenant.

Bodin's face remained frozen as the hissing and popping dissipated, then was soon replaced by a high-pitched whine coming through the speaker.

"He has put his engines to full power! His stern must be going down and he is trying to push himself up!"

Ryback whispered to the Captain, "If his stern is going down, that means his engine room is probably flooding."

The whine continued.

Bodin slammed his fist into his hand and growled through his teeth, "Come on, Alexei! Get that stinking boat of yours *up!*"

The whine kept on for some seconds, then came to an ominous

halt. The gurgling became more pronounced until there was an *eeek* ... *eeek* ... *eeek* ... *bloom!* noise, followed by the sound of a faucet turned wide open.

"There is another leak!" cried the *starshiy*.

Bodin, Ryback, and Mizim stood there in a daze, consumed by their powerlessness to rescue their brother vessel.

A groaning sound, then a rumble came through the speaker.

The *michman* at the console held his headphones tight and screamed, "He is going down!"

As water rushed into the *Magadan* and displaced the air, the buoyancy rapidly became negative, causing the vessel to sink. The deeper it went, the venting to the sea became more severe and the sinking gained momentum, until the *Magadan* was plummeting toward the ocean floor like a lead ball. By the time it passed 1,400 meters in depth, the vessel's titanium hull was straining against water pressure of more than 2,000 pounds per square inch.

Down and down it plummeted, and as the hull began to buckle, it sent a high-pitched wail to the *Kharkov*'s sonar—something akin to a cry or a lamentation. Then, like a heavy oak door slamming shut, there was a *CHUNNGG!* that screamed through the water so fearsomely it made the *michmany* jump in their seats.

Everyone held their breath, waiting for something more. . . . But there was nothing more, save the faint sound of a distant waterfall—created by the vessel's remains tumbling toward the bottom.

With a look of weariness, the *starshiy* took off his headphones and said, almost in a whisper, "The *Magadan* has imploded, Captain."

Kasimir Bodin covered his face with his hands and moaned, "Alexei Andreievich," for his friend, the captain of the *Magadan*. No one spoke for what seemed a very long time. But slowly the shock wore off, allowing Bodin's anger to build. "So . . . we have our first casualties," he said bitterly. "Soviet workmanship has killed our brother vessel and brother sailors. . . . Why do we worry about the Americans when we are too busy murdering our own kind? . . . Number One! Pilot Mizim! Lay in a course and take us out of this damned Passage."

15

ENTER THE DRAGON

When the final book is written on the absurdity of war, there will certainly be a chapter on the conflict that erupted between India and Pakistan in the rarefied atmosphere of the Karakoram Mountains.

The roots of this insane war go back to 1947, when Pakistan was partitioned from India. Both countries coveted then—and still covet now—the remote, princely states of Jammu and Kashmir, which lay along the high-country border with China. After the British viceroy pulled out in 1947, fighting quickly broke out between India and Pakistan over control of these territories. The combat continued until 1949, when an accord was reached between the warring parties called the Karachi Agreement. Under this agreement, a cease-fire line of demarcation was established that ran through the state of Kashmir until it abruptly terminated at map coordinate NJ9842—which was about forty miles short of the Chinese border. The negotiators never extended the cease-fire line through the Karakoram Mountains to the border because no fighting had occurred in that particular region— which was certainly understandable. The Karakoram Mountains are one of the most inhospitable places on earth—home to K-2, the second highest mountain on the planet.

The absence of a cease-fire line through this beautiful but harsh land—full of towering peaks, bitter cold, and glistening glaciers— created a no-man's-land some forty miles wide. A land that was never inhabited, and only rarely explored. Yet it became a battleground. In 1984, India launched Operation Meghdoot (Cloud Messenger) to occupy two mountain passes in the region—ostensibly to preempt a Pakistani move to do the same thing. The conflict escalated into a high-altitude version of Vietnam and Afghanistan, wherein neither side would commit the resources to prevail in this craggy mountain battleground, but neither would they yield.

To keep the war from escalating out of control, neither country would introduce the use of air power; so the fighting focused, for the most part, around artillery duels. Infantry engagements in the high country were rare, because in full battle pack at eighteen thousand feet, an infantryman can muster enough oxygen to charge about three yards.

Yet death was plentiful. If not by the sword, then by the brutal conditions. Perhaps eight of every ten casualties in the Karakoram War were the result of blizzards, frostbite in the forty-below temperatures, avalanches, or falls into the treacherous crevasses.

Into this brutal field of conflict—of which the rest of the world was scarcely aware—the United States Army prevailed upon the government of Pakistan to allow two of its observers to go in and assess the men, equipment, tactics, and the horrific conditions of the Karakoram battleground. The Pakistanis assented, and the Army sent two men who were particularly skilled in the arcane craft of Arctic warfare and battlefield intelligence. Two men who possessed a kind of sixth sense— an intangible bond, of sorts—with the mountains, the ice, the snow, and the cold.

Their names were Lt. Col. Robert Rawlings and Command Sgt. Maj. Pancho Ramirez.

THE TRANSANTARCTIC MOUNTAINS—January 30

Lt. Col. Robert Rawlings craned his neck so he could peer through the small perspex window. He had to strain and look upward in order to see the jagged edge of the mountain ridge zipping by. He guessed they were traveling two hundred miles an hour, give or take, as they were shoved left, right, then up, down, and up again in the whipsaw low-level action of nap-of-the-earth flying.

The troop compartment of the Phalanx Dragon possessed all the creature comforts of a sardine can, and Rawlings was sharing the space with Spec-4 Gates, his radiotelephone operator, and Command Sgt. Maj. Pancho Ramirez. With difficulty, Rawlings looked over Gates to catch the gaze of Ramirez, then the colonel pointed to the bulging rucksack wedged under his own legs. More often than not, Rawlings and his sergeant major seemed to communicate without speaking, and this was such a time. In the frenetic preparations for the mission, Rawlings had been unable to take the time to ensure that his rucksack was properly packed, and he was silently asking Pancho about it. Ramirez nodded, meaning of course it was packed properly.

The Phalanx Dragon aircraft was one weird-looking flying machine. If you took the front half of a dolphin and the torso of a dormant frog (such as you'd find resting on a lily pad), and married the two together, then added some stubby wings, you'd have a rough idea of what the Phalanx Dragon looked like. Its skin was made of carbon composites, and this version was slightly faceted to provide a "low observable" radar signature—especially to an airborne Mainstay radar plane. Flying nap-of-the-earth between mountain ridges shielded them from ground-based radar; but the Mainstay was flying somewhere up there, and could paint the mountain canyons, gullies, and valleys with its downward-looking radar beam.

Only twelve of the troop-carrying version of the Phalanx Dragon were ever built. They were constructed specifically with the intent of carrying members of the antiterrorist Delta Force into remote hot spots quickly and stealthily, and they were flown by special operations pilots from the 23rd Air Force, stationed at Hurlburt Field in Florida.

Rawlings and his team had climbed aboard the Dragons thirteen hours previously in the blistering heat of Diego Garcia—a tiny American outpost in the Indian Ocean. The fleet of four Dragons, two KC-135 tankers, and an escort of four F-15 Eagles traveled down the sixtieth meridian and crossed into Antarctica over Mac Robertson Land on a beeline for the South Pole. At eighty-five degrees south latitude the Dragons refueled and bade their escort goodbye, then turned toward the spine of the Transantarctic Mountains. As the four Dragons approached the Queen Alexandra Range of the Transantarctics, they descended toward the mountains. And when their radar warning receivers picked up the Mainstay's sweep, they dropped down until the peaks were almost caressing their underbellies. Then, fifty miles out from the landing zone, they dropped into the bobbing and weaving of their nap-of-the-earth flying.

Robert Rawlings was tired and hungry, and had found it impossible to sleep on the long journey. The rapid preparations, the hectic mission planning, the transport to Diego Garcia in the Indian Ocean, the interminable flight in a cramped position, all had left him and his team spent. He'd never seen a Phalanx Dragon until he was taken into a guarded hangar at Diego Garcia. Now he wished he'd never laid eyes on it, and would be glad when he parted company with the bizarre-looking machine.

He felt the aircraft slow and figured he better put on the headset.

"Coming up on the landing zone now, Colonel," said the pilot in a strained voice. "Make your exit as fast as possible. My fuel situation is going to be tight as it is."

Rawlings keyed the mike and said, "I'll be as quick as I can, but my butt's been asleep for the last three hours."

"Yes, sir. But still, make it quick."

The vector thrust nozzles on the Phalanx Dragon slowly rotated down, causing the aircraft to go from horizontal flight into a hover some six feet above the Delta Glacier, which lay inside a small canyon of the Worcester Range. As the crow flies, they were only a hundred miles from the Soviet base at Williams Field, and their chances of being detected were probably greatest right here, right now, as the aircraft hovered, giving off noise and heat on a cloudless day.

Rawlings heard the hydraulic pistons on the gull-wing doors engage, causing them to open up and reveal a cauldron of blowing snow from the jet exhaust. Rawlings hoped the damned airplane wasn't hovering over a crevasse as he shoved out his rucksack and then, with difficulty, himself. His rubbery legs plunged into the two-foot-deep snow, holding them fast as he lost his balance and fell over backward.

Sergeant Major Ramirez and Specialist-4 Gates dropped off the other side, while the cargo door in the belly of the aircraft opened up to allow skis, poles, and other assorted equipment to tumble down into the snow.

Rawlings stoically turned his face away and kept his eyes closed as the snow continued to bloom around him and pepper his face with the cold sting of the fine white crystals.

Bit by bit the blowing subsided, then finally ceased as the Phalanx Dragon rotated its nozzles back to horizontal and pulled away to head back from whence it came. Rawlings watched as three of the aircraft disappeared over a ridge in single file. A fourth Dragon lingered while six men struggled to get the AKIO sled out of the cargo bay without mishap. Once they were successful, the final Dragon turned and made its exit. The sound quickly faded, and was replaced with an unnerving silence, except for a light wind. His exhausted and emotionally drained team were now totally alone in hostile territory. The cold Antarctic stillness was broken by muffled metallic sounds as the men locked and loaded their weapons, then they stood motionless and listened to the quiet. Once convinced their insertion had not been discovered, the entire group answered a compelling call from nature, then quietly and methodically began to assemble.

Rawlings started patting down the snow around him with his white, bulbous-looking vapor-barrier boots so he could have a little room to maneuver. His team was in a glacial canyon that was about a mile across. They had been set down about two kilometers from the mouth of the canyon where the small Delta Glacier emptied into the giant Skelton Glacier. Once he had crushed down a small circle of snow, Rawlings took out his map and oriented himself while a large figure wearing "overwhite" camouflage pullovers broke through the snow toward him like a musk ox. Capt. Phillip Nye of the Long Range Surveillance Detachment (LRSD) said softly, "Everybody's off the aircraft in good shape, Colonel. We're assembling now, and will be ready to move out in about ten minutes."

"Very well, Phillip. Make sure everybody has their sea legs before we start movement. I'm just getting to where I can feel my backside again. We won't be going far—just down to the next tributary glacier—and we'll rest up there."

"Yes, sir," Nye replied, and he started back down the trail he'd broken.

"And, Phillip?"

Captain Nye turned. "Yes, sir?"

"You know that Pancho and I didn't ask to come along on this trip."

Nye smiled in understanding. "Yes, sir. I know. All the same, I'm glad you're along."

Because the temperature on the glacier was a warm seventeen degrees, the twelve men stripped down to their long-underwear tops, then helped each other with their rucksacks before clamping into their skis. Five men took positions in the pulling harness of the AKIO sled—which looked like a small landborne skiff with a smoothly-curved underside—while another soldier took up a position in the rear as a brakeman. Each man in the harness was also carrying about eighty-five pounds of equipment in his personal rucksack.

Everyone took a long drink of water from their canteens before starting off. Ramirez and two team members—with long spans of rope tied between them—took the point. They would keep a lookout

for crevasses while breaking the trail. Rawlings, Nye, and Gates the
RTO would be in the middle, and the AKIO sled team would bring
up the rear.

SPACE DEFENSE OPERATIONS CENTER, CHEYENNE MOUNTAIN, COLORADO

"Launch detection!"

Lt. Col. Lydia Strand looked at the large center screen in the Space
Defense Operations Center (SPADOC) deep inside Cheyenne Mountain, while pressing the receiver against her ear.

"Teal Sapphire is picking it up out of the Baikonur Cosmodrome."

Strand exhaled with relief that the booster was lifting off from
Baikonur (a launch facility like the Kennedy Space Center), and not
coming out of a Soviet ballistic missile silo.

The tension in Cheyenne Mountain could not have been strung
any tighter as the staff in SPADOC monitored Soviet launch facilities and satellite activity, so the U.S. could respond if and when
needed.

Strand was the duty officer in the "crow's nest" that overlooked
the cavernous room, and she quickly turned a dial on her console to
zoom in on the Kazakhstan province of the Soviet Confederation
where the Baikonur Cosmodrome was located.

"We've got a second detection, Colonel," came the voice through
the receiver.

"Put the plots up," Strand ordered, her voice sharp. Then the
striking brunette whispered to herself, "God, I'm tired." So was
everyone else in SPADOC.

"All right, Colonel . . . coming up in a moment. . . . Something
screwy here, Colonel. They're going in different directions. There's
the plot now."

Strand zeroed in on Baikonur, and sure enough, two luminescent
lines formed a V on the screen—one heading northwest and one
heading northeast. She didn't have a clue as to what the dual launch
meant, but she had to pass the word to the higher-ups, so she grabbed
the phone that was a direct line to the National Military Command
Center in the Pentagon.

SKELTON GLACIER—January 31

Fog.

Beautiful fog.

Lt. Col. Robert Rawlings had never been so glad to encounter ice fog in all his life. Because of it, he and his team were making good progress over the Skelton Glacier. After being dropped by the Phalanx Dragon, Rawlings had moved the team out of the Delta Glacier and down the Skelton, keeping in the shadows along the bluff where the exposed rock blended with snow to provide better camouflage. They had taken shelter in another small canyon, which held a body of ice called the Dilemma Glacier, and here they'd dug a snow cave to rest and recover.

After their respite, however, Rawlings knew he would have to take them across the Skelton Glacier to the Shults Peninsula, which was southwest of Mount Morning. It was twelve miles across the glacier, and they would be completely exposed the entire way. The team had taken every camouflage measure they could think of. They wore "overwhites" over their arctic gear. They had even replaced their olive drab rucksacks and webbing with white-colored versions. But still, the snow on the Skelton Glacier was shallow, so they wouldn't even be able to cover themselves up in case a helicopter appeared. One sighting by an air patrol, and the game was up.

But then the fog had moved in, and Rawlings had moved them out quickly under its protective cover.

In modern warfare, where troops can be moved swiftly by air, and state-of-the-art weapons can be employed with such shocking effect, foreknowledge of the enemy's position and movements was more vital than ever before.

It was in this environment that a small team was formed within the Sixth Infantry Division called the Long Range Surveillance Detachment (LRSD). And essentially its role was to act as the eyes and ears of the division commander behind enemy lines.

Robert Rawlings was commander of the 106th Military Intelligence Battalion, and the LRSD was one of the units under his command. In a rather heated exchange with his divisional commander, Rawlings had protested his assignment to command the LRSD on this particular outing. He felt Captain Nye and his men were well able to do the job; in fact, they were specifically trained to do this sort of thing. But Maj. Gen. Joshua Pfeiffer (inflexible in the best of times) had assumed his linebacker stance and said, "Now you listen to me, Robert. Everything, and I mean *everything,* on this Beowulf business hinges on getting your LRSD people into precisely the right place. If they don't make it, then everything craters. That's why you and Pancho are going. Period. Pick your best men and saddle up. Your XO can take care of your battalion while you're gone."

"But, General—"

"That's *it,* Colonel. I want you and Pancho on the ground."

So there it was—he and Ramirez having become victims of their own reputations among the small universe of Arctic warriors.

"How are we doing, Phillip?" asked Rawlings.

The oxlike captain, Phillip Nye, had stopped to check the map against his hand-held Global Positioning device. "Pretty well, sir. We've got about two klicks to go before we reach Fishtail Point on the Shults Peninsula. I think we should call it a day there. I've been rotating the guys on the AKIO, but nevertheless, everybody's pretty whipped."

Rawlings nodded his assent. Like Nye, he was wearing a long-handle shirt; a white stocking balaclava hat was rolled up on his head. Both men were bent over slightly by their rucksacks. "Sounds good, Phillip. It's still your team. After we break, I—"

He cut himself off and everyone froze as they heard the *whop-whop-whop* of rotor blades faintly in the distance. When the sound eventually faded, Rawlings said softly, "We must be in a low-hanging cloud. It's probably clear above that. Let's move smartly. Besides, it's getting colder."

"Yes, sir. . . . So this is what it's like to be in the real enemy's backyard."

Rawlings took a moment of bitter reflection and said, "Yes, Phillip. This is what it's like."

MOUNT DISCOVERY

From her perch on the ridgeline, Dana Harrow looked behind her at the cloud bank that had coursed through the Skelton Glacier, then she turned around and focused her binoculars back on Williams Field. She was still overwhelmed by what she saw. The place was like

O'Hare Airport in Chicago. Big planes. Little planes. One, two, three, four, *five* runways now. Lots of the little planes were hidden inside ice structures that were kind of like igloos, but not exactly. She made one last count, then took out her notebook to enter the final notation. Her supplies at the Mount Discovery seismic hut had run out, so she had packed her survival rucksack and was making a final check of Willy Field before striking out for her second hut on Mount Morning.

Dana pocketed the notebook, then hefted the rucksack onto her back, and carefully started down the mountain. She hadn't gone far before her ears picked up the *whop-whop-whop* sound, and she knew immediately what it was. As quickly as she could, she made for a rock outcropping that had a slight overhang. The *whop-whop* sound grew louder, and in the distance an object that looked like a sinister wasp rounded the contour of Mount Discovery and began cruising straight toward her. She was too terrified to move, and not moving was exactly the right thing to do, because she was in the shadow. The wasp continued toward her, then stopped and turned its nose toward the seismic hut. It approached slowly, then hovered along the slope, causing snow to billow out in the downdraft. A door slid back and two . . . three . . . four soldiers, wearing white snowsuits, jumped out with their rifles and fanned out while the wasp pulled back. One of the soldiers rushed the hut and plunged through the door. He was inside for what seemed a long time. Dana remembered something and gasped. *Don't touch the stove,* she pleaded in a silent prayer. *Please, oh please, don't touch the stove.* It would still be warm. She started to worry about footprints, but then realized her footprints were all over the place, and the helicopter downdraft would fuzz that even further. Finally the soldier came out of the hut and motioned to the wasp, which came closer so that the soldiers could climb back on board the hovering craft. Once that was done, the wasp gained altitude, flew directly over her, then turned and disappeared over the ridgeline.

Dana remained under the rock outcropping, taking deep breaths, trying to get her pulse under two hundred beats a minute. The thought of becoming a female prisoner to a bunch of Russian soldiers was repugnant as well as frightening.

She hefted her rucksack and started down the mountain.

OFFICE OF NAVAL INTELLIGENCE,
THE PENTAGON—February 1

"Whaddaya mean, we're *blind?*"

The lieutenant (jg) was tired and testy. "Just what I said, sir. The Russians had already knocked down two of our White Cloud systems with ASATs fired out of the Baikonur Cosmodrome. They blasted the last one out of the sky fifteen minutes ago. We can no longer track Soviet ship movements with White Cloud."

The captain felt a shooting pain down his left arm and reached into his desk drawer for a vial of nitroglycerin tablets.

ROSS ICE SHELF, SOUTHWEST OF MOUNT DISCOVERY

Exhausted, Capt. Phillip Nye sat down on a volcanic boulder and unlaced his air-filled vapor-barrier boots to massage his ankles. In the process, he felt his socks were moist from perspiration, and he was grateful he wouldn't have to go through the laborious process of changing them before he climbed into his sleeping bag and turned in for the "night." Changing socks while on the move was a first-class pain in the ass, but necessary to avoid frostbite.

At the end of their third full day of travel, Rawlings had halted Nye and his LRSD team at the base of the Mason Spur, which was a clifflike formation southwest of Mount Discovery, and the LRSD team was making preparations for a long rest period before pressing on. The fog had broken, but a low overcast remained. Good cover, but not the best, thought Nye. The base of the Mason Spur offered a veil of shadows and heavy snowdrifts for digging snow-cave shelters, and Nye's men were busily finishing up with their excavation chores. His team had come a long way, but had a long way to go yet. They'd had some twenty-four-carat luck with that fog on the glacier, and he wondered if that luck was going to hold. The big test would come when they crossed the open ice shelf from the Mount Discovery formation to Black Island. Staying along the periphery of the terrain—where the solid rock pushed up through the ice shelf—provided some nooks, crannies, and shadows in which to hide, as well as the occasional snowdrift to dive into, should they require some cover. But the flat open ice shelf—that was something else. Maybe they'd get lucky again. Nye hoped they would. Two weeks ago he'd been on routine duty at Fort Richardson, Alaska, outside Anchorage, buying groceries with his wife in the base PX. Then everything went loco, and now here he was—on the other pole of the earth, changing his socks. A Citadel graduate, Nye had seen a lot of bizarre things in his Army career, but he'd never figured on winding up inside the Antarctic Circle.

Nye looked up and saw Rawlings and Ramirez at the entry of the rock formation where they had taken shelter. The two men were both on their skis, surveying the ice shelf with their binoculars. Nye shook his head. Those two were a pair for the books. Both were notorious for creating paperwork log jams and having the heaviest in-boxes in Alaska. But get them out in the mountains and forests, the ice and snow, and something strange happened. They possessed a kind of mystical sense of where the adversary was hiding, and had an uncanny ability to use the terrain to their advantage. As commander of the 106th Military Intelligence Battalion of the division, Robert Rawlings had a good battalion staff. Really sharp, in fact. But ultimately the hard decisions always came down to him and Sergeant Major Ramirez. And they seemed to communicate without passing a word between them—as if some invisible coaxial cable were strung between their brain lobes.

Nye continued massaging his ankles as he watched Pancho Ramirez nod to the colonel, then ski off without his rucksack. Rawlings skied over to Nye and said, "Phillip, Pancho is taking Gates ahead for a look-see. Post one man at the mouth of our alcove here, then get everybody bedded down for some solid rest. How's the team holding up?"

"They're pretty wiped out, sir. We covered a lot of ground today. And they—or should I say we—still haven't gotten over the jet lag, I guess you'd call it. I sure wish we had some tree cover. Have you taken a drink lately, sir?"

Obediently, Lieutenant Colonel Rawlings reached for his canteen. Dehydration in the ultradry polar climate was always a danger. Captain Nye was a worse mother hen than Pancho.

After leaving her Mount Discovery hut, Dana Harrow had crossed the Eady Ice Piedmont, and when she'd reached the border of the ice shelf she'd taken a sleep break. She planned to hug the coastline—where mountain and ice shelf met—until she got past the Mason Spur. Then she would climb the slope of Mount Morning to her other seismic hut. And if a platoon of Russian paratroopers wasn't waiting at the hut to greet her, then maybe she could hold out

a little longer. She was grateful the snow was shallow here and did
not require snowshoes. But after her episode of being trapped in the
drift, she'd learned her lesson. A pair of snowshoes were sticking out
of the top of her pack, should she require them.

Dana was walking around the finger of a lava formation that
protruded along the coastline—with her head down, huffing and
puffing under the weight of her rucksack—when a white form
seemed to rise up out of the snow and knock her to the ground. The
next thing she knew, a hand was over her mouth, something very
cold and very sharp was against her throat, and she was looking into
the blackest pair of eyes she'd ever seen.

"*Vy russkaya?*"

She didn't understand what he'd said, but it sounded like Russian.
She could feel his breath against her face, and she was too terrified
to move.

"American?" he asked in a quiet but threatening voice. "Are you
American?"

Dana nodded her head very carefully so as not to have her throat
sliced open.

The blade was withdrawn but the hand remained over her mouth
as her assailant whispered, "Don't make any loud noises. I'm sorry
if I hurt you. We're Americans, too." Then he removed his hand and
drew back onto one knee, just as a second white-suited figure appeared behind him, carrying a funny-looking rifle. Her assailant
turned to the second man and said, "Go get the Colonel."

And the blade went back in the scabbard.

BRANDING IRON STATION

The digger drill ceased turning, indicating it had hit some type of
flint-hard formation. The supervisor turned the machine off, but
noise still permeated the icedome, for the skip loader was moving
excavated earth away from the mine shaft. The skip loader was
helpful, but moving the dirt around kicked up dust and, despite the
ventilation tubes, its diesel fumes hung in the air.

The drill supervisor sent for the chief engineer, who took his own
sweet time coming down in the elevator. The civilian chief's dislike
for the icedome had grown exponentially, and he preferred to remain
on the surface. When he finally arrived, his manner was brusque as
he demanded of the supervisor, "Yes, yes, what is it?"

"I believe we have hit the second lava apron, Comrade. Do you wish to try to blast?"

The chief engineer looked at the ceiling of the icedome with disdain and said, "No, you fool. I do not want to blast." He pointed upward. "You want all of this to come down on you? Besides, the mine shaft is not shored up. Blasting could collapse the whole thing. Send down the jackhammer team. We are very close now."

"As you wish, Comrade."

ROSS ICE SHELF

Dana Harrow would always remember the first time she laid eyes on Robert Rawlings. He approached on skis, then stopped a short distance away and stepped out of his bindings. He wasn't a big man. Rather small, in fact. Perhaps five foot six to five foot seven, and like the others he was wearing one of those bulky white snowsuits—but he looked like he had a sinewy build, and he approached her with a catlike walk. Dana was sitting on her rucksack as he drew close and crouched down, pulling back the hood of his anorak, which revealed a square face of tanned, somewhat leathery skin. His hair was short—almost a crewcut—and colored different shades of salt-and-pepper gray. He looked at her for the longest time with those penetrating green eyes, as though she weren't a person, but a problem that had to be dealt with—a new unknown in an equation that had to be solved. The other men obviously deferred to him, and she figured this must be the one they called "the Colonel."

Finally he asked, "Can you tell me who you are?"

Well, at least he talks. "My name is Dana Harrow."

Rawlings nodded. "I take it you are one of the scientific people at McMurdo?"

"Was," she corrected him. "Who are you, and what the hell has been happening around here? There are Russian paratroopers all over the place."

He didn't respond at once, as he was obviously formulating a reply. "Miss Harrow, I think it best we not tell you exactly who we are or what our purpose is. That's because there is the possibility you could be taken prisoner, and the less you know about us, the less you'll be able to tell a Soviet interrogator. But rest assured we are your countrymen."

His voice had a calming effect, yet there was an authoritative timbre about it—sort of like the name of one of those cocktails. What was it called? A velvet hammer? "Can you at least tell me what all this business is about?" she pleaded. "The Russians? All those airplanes? It's about to drive me crazy."

He looked out to the ice shelf, then back at her. "Something— some kind of mineral—was discovered at a geologic drill site. This mineral can be turned into an isotope and used to fashion a weapon that would make a nuclear bomb look like a cap pistol. We were digging it out when the Soviets decided they wanted it instead. . . . Now, please, tell me about yourself and how you got here. It may be important."

"I'm a geophysicist. I'm working—*was* working—on my doctoral research at McMurdo. I had a remote seismic station back there." She jerked her thumb toward Mount Discovery. "I was driving my Sno-Cat back to McMurdo when the sky opened up with Russian paratroopers. So I hightailed it back to my seismic hut, ditched the Sno-Cat, and I've been there ever since. Ran out of supplies and decided to head for my second site, on Mount Morning."

"So you've been on your own for how long? And remained undiscovered?"

Dana shrugged. "About two weeks. But just after I left my Mount Discovery station, I saw a helicopter drop a Russian search party onto my hut. I got out of there just in time." She fished in her pocket and retrieved her notebook, then handed it to him. "Here. Maybe you can use this."

Rawlings thumbed through the pages. "What is this?"

"I didn't have anything else to do, so I made some observations on what the Russians were doing. They've turned Willy Field into an airport like O'Hare. I never saw so many airplanes in one spot."

Rawlings ran his eyes down one of the pages that noted dates, times, types of aircraft—e.g., "big," "little," "big with a Frisbee on top." After scanning the page, the colonel looked upon Dana with a newfound respect. Then he made a decision. "Gates?"

"Sir?"

"Take the lady's rucksack back to base camp. Miss Harrow, please come with us. You may be able to lend us a hand."

Dana rose from her rucksack, and the boyish-looking Gates quickly adjusted the straps and hefted it onto his back. Dana then looked over at the brown-skinned man who had thrown her to the ground and placed a knife to her throat. She pointed and asked Rawlings, "Who's he?"

"That is the Sergeant Major," Rawlings replied.

The sergeant major remained silent.

As Dana dusted snow from her pants legs, she remarked, "When he knocked me down, I thought he was one of those Soviet paratroopers. But I should have realized there aren't any Hispanic sergeants in the Russian Army."

THE PENTAGON

Gen. Rodger Whittenberg, Chief of the General Staff of the United States Armed Forces, fell back into his big leather chair with all the grace of a potato sack hitting the ground. He was absolutely exhausted as he looked out his office window from the third floor E-ring of the Pentagon. It was dark, and the lights of the Jefferson Memorial were shining across the Potomac. He'd just come from a meeting of the entire National Security Council at the White House, a meeting of tired men whose sense of bewilderment was surpassed only by their profound sense of betrayal and a searing, blinding anger. They were angry at the Soviets, of course, but since no Russians were in the room, Whittenberg became the focus of their enmity. Whittenberg—the big, black, former B-52 pilot who held the Air Force Cross—had to fend off questions from a bunch of civilians who'd never heard a shot fired in anger.

Why had this been allowed to happen, General?

Why were there no forces guarding the mining site, General?

How did the Soviets get an entire carrier battle group down there under our noses, General?

How did those submarines just disappear in the North Atlantic, General?

Was this Beowulf business really going to work, General?

Whittenberg leaned back and rubbed his eyes. Then he groaned and allowed himself a moment of quiet self-reflection. To Rodger Whittenberg, the bottom of humankind's societal pecking order— which was to say, the slime of the earth—was ranked something like this:

Drug dealers.

Child molesters.

Monday-morning quarterbacks.

Although the Antarctic Treaty that had quasi-governed the continent since 1961 had fallen apart after a treaty conference in 1992, and
no new treaty had taken its place, the United States and a number
of other nations had continued to observe it. And the old SCAR
Treaty banned "any measures of a military nature." Whittenberg
had told the NSC those succinct facts, but it wasn't what they wanted
to hear.

The Secretary to the General Staff, Maj. Gen. Michael Dowd,
walked into Whittenberg's office and gently asked, "So how'd it go?"
Dowd's face resembled the picture on a package of Bull Durham
chewing tobacco, so long ago he'd been given the call sign "Bull."

Whittenberg didn't answer at once. Instead he looked out the
window for a few moments as he seriously considered, for the first
time in his life, disobeying a presidential order. "We're in a dangerous situation, Bull," he said finally. "More perilous than I could've
imagined. And quite frankly I'm at a loss as to how to deal with it."

The Bull's face scrunched up, reflecting his curiosity. "How do
you mean?"

"The President. He's new. Inexperienced. Unsure of himself."
Involuntarily, Whittenberg looked around the room. "And I hate to
say this, Bull, but there's no other word for it. The man is shallow.
He has no depth. He can't see beyond the evening newscast he used
to anchor. He thinks in ten-second sound bites. Most of his cabinet
made their careers in public relations. I'm the oldest sonofabitch in
the room. You get the picture? Well, anyway, we're sitting in the
Cabinet Room and the talk is becoming pretty acrimonious when
somebody mentions his inaugural slogan 'Bold Horizons.' Then his
highbrow national security adviser—"

"That jerkoff Winterbotham?"

"You said it. Anyway, Professor Winterbotham, who's been in an
ivory-tower think tank for so long he can't find his way to the men's
room, asks me, 'General, is there any chance we could fail to displace
the Soviets from Antarctica?' I said sure there was a chance we could
fail. There were no guarantees. Then he asks, 'General, if the Soviets
seize this rubidium deposit and fashion a scimitarlike graser weapon,
and if our intelligence is true that the Soviets are quickly running out
of oil, could they then seize the whole Persian Gulf and we would
be powerless to break their control of our vital energy source?' I said,
'That's true.' Then he said, 'This requires boldness.' Well, you can

imagine how the President picked up on that, and one thing led to another, and before you know it there's serious talk on the table about—if we don't bring it off with Beowulf—about using an Ostrich Egg on the mining site."

Michael Dowd went pale. "They can't mean it."

Whittenberg leaned forward on his massive forearms. "I've been given a direct order by the President to make contingency plans for just such a possibility. . . . And I'm thinking about sitting on it." The general shrugged. "I was looking toward retirement anyway."

Dowd began pacing the room—a sure sign he was nervous. "Hold on a minute. If the President gave you a direct order, then that jerkoff Winterbotham is bound to ride herd on this thing to make sure you don't shortstop it." Dowd, a bureaucratic Svengali if there ever was one, pondered the intricacies of the situation."Look, General, if you're determined to scuttle this order, why don't we go ahead and make the contingency arrangements? But let's get word to Tharp on the sly about what's going down. He's a clever bastard. He'll figure out a way to fudge it."

Whittenberg drummed his fingers on a little dogeared booklet on his desk. It was a copy of the Constitution he always kept nearby. "You know," he said finally, "if some lawyer got a hold of our conversation here, he could probably get a lot of mileage out of it. Charge us with conspiracy or insubordination or something. Funny thing, isn't it? We've taken an oath to uphold, protect, and defend the Constitution. Not the country. Not our homes. Not our families. The Constitution. No, Bull. We'll play it by the book. We've got a presidential order. And unless I can prove he's *mente captus,* I can only obey or resign. Period. And I'm not ready to resign. Not yet, anyway. It may come to that. We'll march to the order. Have the staff get the ball rolling to transport an Ostrich Egg down to Rumley, er, which is to say, Tharp—under hypersecret conditions."

ROSS ICE SHELF

Dana Harrow approached the rocky alcove at the foot of the Mason Spur, walking slowly behind the person on skis they called "the Colonel." As they drew nearer, a voice from nowhere said, "Halt."

The single-file line stopped.

"Tango," said the voice.

"Victor," said the colonel. "I have four people in my party."

"Advance."

Dana continued into the alcove and saw a white-suited figure crouched behind a rock bench with a black, stubby, pipelike object in his hands. As they went past, she heard the colonel say, "It's okay, Utroska. She's a friendly."

Specialist-4 Utroska had mentally prepared himself to meet Russian paratroopers. He had not prepared himself to see a strange woman—friendly or otherwise—at this particular place, at this particular time. His lower jaw dropped to around his knees.

Dana noticed that the snow around the alcove had obviously been tamped down, but other than that, there was no sign of life. Rawlings, Ramirez, and Gates stepped out of their bindings as the colonel said, "Gates, cover the skis and then bring the lady's gear inside."

"Yes, sir."

"Utroska, keep a sharp eye out. The lady has already had one brush with a helicopter. Where's Captain Nye?"

"Left cave, sir."

"Come with me, Miss Harrow."

Come where? Dana wondered. She didn't see any caves. But she followed the colonel to a snowdrift, where he knelt down and pulled out a plug of packed snow about three feet across and put it to the side. Then he went down on all fours and crawled through the portal. "I hope everybody's decent," she heard him say. "We have a lady visitor." Dana got down and followed Rawlings into a small crosswise tunnel, then turned left behind him as he crawled up onto a shelflike chamber that she found to be surprisingly large. It wasn't quite big enough to allow her to stand up, but almost. A tarpaulin was spread over the floor, and gear and weapons were stashed along the side. On top of the tarpaulin was a sleeping bag, which had the head of a large man poking out. His hair was a straw-colored crewcut, and his face, like the sentry's, expressed consummate shock at having a woman in his midst. The sound of snoring from the other chamber floated down the tunnel.

"We have a guest, Phillip," Rawlings said easily.

Captain Nye, who was in a T-shirt, came up on one elbow in his sleeping bag.

Rawlings pulled a folded sheet of paper out of one of the packs while he explained to Nye about their guest. Then he doffed his parka, sat down cross-legged, and unfolded the map while Pancho Ramirez climbed up into the chamber with them. Without speaking, the sergeant major rummaged around in one of the rucksacks and pulled out three granola bars and a canteen and set them beside Dana. She nodded her thanks.

Rawlings put his finger on the map and said, "This is where we are, Miss Harrow. At the foot of the Mason Spur. Now where was this seismic hut of yours?"

Dana pointed to a spot on the southeastern slope of Mount Discovery, near the Minna Saddle.

Rawlings nodded and said, "I see." Then he focused on the map for a few moments and added, "Captain Nye, the sergeant major, and I have to move our team from our location here"—he ran his finger across the map—"to Mount Heine on White Island."

Now it was Dana's turn to drop a jaw. "White Island? You must be nuts! That's only fifteen miles from Willy Field. I already told you, a helicopter almost landed on top of me. How can you expect to get that close?"

Rawlings moved his finger along the map as he said, "We're traveling in the open, that's true, but we have a few things in our favor. Antarctica is a big place, and there is a lot of territory for the Soviets to patrol, particularly the coastline. We will try to travel in the shadows wherever possible, and keep an eye out for drifting snow so we can take cover if necessary. But that doesn't mean we can't be spotted with a helicopter's infrared detector, or even visually. I intend to follow the edge of the Mason Spur, then go up the Eady Ice Piedmont and over the Minna Saddle. Then a bit farther north to Black Island, and across White Strait to White Island. This route should provide us with a little shadow and some snow drift along the way; and since you pointed out that the Minna Saddle area was just scouted by a helicopter, then they may leave that territory alone for a bit. What I'm worried about is here"—he tapped the map—"between the Minna Saddle and Black Island. I've been told the snow is shallow and we'll be completely exposed—just as we're getting closer to Williams Field."

Dana noticed that with so many bodies in the snow cave chamber it was warming up, so she took off her parka while looking at the map. "You intend to cross here?" she asked, pointing.

"Yes. That will keep Black Island between us and Williams Field. Not a lot of help, but a little. This is new territory for us, though, and I was wondering what you thought."

Dana studied the map for some moments and said, "Well, if I

needed a place to duck out of sight, I'd go across here." She moved her finger to a point farther north on the ice shelf, between Mount Discovery and Black Island.

"Why?" asked Rawlings.

She peeled the wrapping from one of the granola bars and ate while she spoke. "That's an area that has some crevasses, a lot of them shallow. I'm not a glaciologist, but I suppose they're caused by the narrowing and then the widening of the ice shelf as it passes between Mount Discovery and Black Island. They might give you a place to hide."

There was the muffled sound of crunching snow as Specialist-4 Utroska came in through the entry and quickly turned around to replace the plug. "Helicopter," was all he said.

Dana gasped. "A helicopter. What do we do?"

"Stay put and out of sight," said Rawlings.

The snoring from the other chamber seemed incongruous in a setting of such tension. "Shouldn't we wake them?" she asked.

Rawlings raised his hand, indicating that he wanted her silence. The faint drumbeat became slightly louder, then subsided. "Give it a few minutes before you go out again, Utroska."

"Yes, sir."

"Like I said, the fact that Antarctica is a big place doesn't mean we can't be spotted by a helicopter. Your suggestion on getting across to Black Island has merit, Miss Harrow. I think we'll take you up on it."

Dana was still dazed by it all, but she had the presence of mind to ask, "And what are you going to do when you reach Mount Heine on White Island?"

Rawlings folded up the map. "You'll find out when we get there."

"Uh . . . 'we'?"

Rawlings replaced the map and reached for his sleeping bag as the sergeant major reached for his. "Do you know how to use cross-country skis, Miss Harrow?"

"Yeah, sure, I've lived in Minnesota for years."

"Well, I could leave you here with some supplies, but you know too much about our mission now. And I can use you to guide us through the crevasse field. Technically, you can refuse. You're a civilian. A noncombatant. But if you remain behind, there's always the danger of capture. The Soviets do not embrace civil liberties quite like we do, Miss Harrow. Ask any Afghan. I think you'd be better off coming with us. You can use a backup pair of skis we brought on our AKIO sled." He pointed to her rucksack. "Lay out your sleeping bag and get some rest. We've got a long push ahead of us."

Dana was reaching for her rucksack when she heard a voice down the tunnel yelp, "A *what?*"

A few moments later, a head poked up out of the tunnel. The face was narrow, with a Roman nose. It was framed by a white-sidewall haircut and a plume of blond hair sticking up on top, and it wore a set of gold-framed glasses on the bridge of the Roman nose. The head disappeared briefly, then returned, kind of like a prairie dog scouting out the surface. Then it disappeared again and she heard muffled voices coming from the tunnel.

"Who—or should I say *what*—was that?" she asked rhetorically.

Captain Nye cleared his throat and said, "That was Sergeant de Parma. He kinda has a problem with women in the military, so he finds your presence with us . . . distressing."

THE USS *SAM HOUSTON,* IN THE ROSS SEA—February 2

The driver of Swimmer Delivery Vehicle Number One closed the canopy and locked it down. Then he tapped the floor twice with a spare weight from his weight belt. Almost immediately he heard a gurgle as water began flooding the chamber. He gave the driver in the adjoining SDV a thumbs-up sign through the perspex canopy of the cockpit, and received one in reply. Soon the water was over the canopy and the light went out, leaving them in darkness. None of the Navy SEALs was looking forward to the next hour.

The *Sam Houston* was an old, converted ballistic missile submarine rapidly approaching the end of its serviceable life. It had originally carried Polaris A2 missiles in its back, but then had gone back to the shipyard for a refit. The missile tubes were yanked out and the gutted deck was replaced with bunking quarters for a commando force, and a hangar deck for the two SDVs.

The hangar door above them slid back, allowing some light to filter in. The release catches were pulled on SDV One, and it began a corklike ascent toward the surface until the driver flooded the buoyancy tank for neutral buoyancy.

Each SDV could carry two SEALs in tandem—a driver and a "tailgunner." The SDVs were oblong in shape, with stubby little diving planes on the bow and stern, and their single propeller was battery powered. The SEALs could ride with the cockpit open and "wet," or closed and "dry." They were now operating closed and dry because the water temperature was thirty-eight degrees. To cope with the frigid waters, the SEALs were wearing dry suits rather than wet suits, because the dry suits provided better insulation by not allowing water to come between the layer of rubber and the diver's skin.

The two SDV drivers had finished several reconnaissance sorties, and this was to be the first business trip. As they drew closer, the underwater dimensions of the Ross Ice Shelf loomed toward them like a foreboding white canyon wall. The driver of SDV One slowed and came up on the diving planes just enough so that the canopy barely broke the surface. Yep. This was the place. He took the SDV back down and came alongside the underwater ice cliff so that his tailgunner could begin the first of what would be many quick, cold, and laborious sorties. The driver pulled out the mouthpiece of his breathing apparatus and said over his shoulder, "Ready?"

"Ready," replied the tailgunner.

The driver replaced the mouthpiece and opened the vent to flood the cockpit. As the frigid water swirled around him and made contact with the rubber skin, he gasped involuntarily.

Once the water pressure was equalized, the tailgunner slid the canopy back and, with aqualung strapped to his back, pushed himself out into the sea. He reached back in and grabbed the satchel charge and then took off, flippers churning the water. The tailgunner from SDV Two was close behind.

The drivers remained on station so they could make a quick retrieval. Even in dry suits, at this water temperature they had approximately thirty-five minutes to get back to the ship before hypothermia set in.

MINNA SADDLE—February 3

The young men who signed on with the Long Range Surveillance Detachment (LRSD) were cut from an unusual cloth. Many of their compatriots in the line units of the Sixth Infantry Division (Light) had the strength, stamina, and smarts to make the cut for the outfit, but did not possess the right mind-set to perform the craft of surveillance. A soldier, after all, is trained to engage the enemy and fight. To simply sit and watch and wait, goes against a warrior's grain. But sitting, watching, and waiting was exactly what the men of the LRSD were trained to do. In hostile territory. Without shooting. And here and now—on the Minna Saddle, with no tree cover—it was sort of like standing in a tiger's cage, without benefit of a whip and a chair, trying to remain unobserved.

Due to this strange job description, the men who wound up in the LRSD tended to be somewhat introspective, self-motivated, inquisitive, and fit beyond belief. In a nutshell, they were active-passive—if there was such a thing.

Dana Harrow felt like a whipped puppy when Rawlings finally called a halt—at a place close to the Mount Discovery seismic hut she'd left four days before. Crossing the Eady Ice Piedmont going uphill was a lot different from going down, even though the grade was gentle. The "boys"—as she was calling them now—had stacked their skis on the AKIO sled and pulled the contraption on foot up the long slope to the top of the Minna Saddle. The young men on the AKIO, besides carrying their own eighty-five-pound rucksacks on their backs, were pulling the sled in some kind of harness, yet Dana was having difficulty keeping up with them. They'd given her a set of overwhites for camouflage, and she had rolled the sleeves and pants up almost halfway to fit her diminutive body. After the initial introductions, the other men in the team—most of them seemed so young to her—treated her with a mixture of incredulity and protectiveness, and had put her rucksack on the AKIO sled to enable her to ski across the ice shelf unencumbered. Still, she had a hard time keeping up. One reason was that those military skis were something else. They weren't the light and flimsy cross-country skis she was accustomed to. Not at all. They were essentially long downhill skis with a binding that hinged at the toe. As the sergeant major adjusted the bindings to fit her hiking boots, he explained that the skis had to be big and strong enough to support a soldier with full military pack.

Near the top of the Minna Saddle they had found another rocky alcove, much like the one they'd left two days before, and Rawlings had called a halt.

With a sense of relief, Dana plopped down in the ankle-deep snow. She looked back toward where they had traveled. The sky was a gray overcast. To the southeast it looked darker still, and the wind was picking up. Blizzard on the way, she guessed. Too weary to move, she watched the rest of the team unstrap their sled harnesses, drop their rucksacks, and go to work. Two of them took up positions at the entry of the alcove and scanned the skies with binoculars, while several others took out their collapsible shovels and started digging out a snow cave at the direction of the sergeant major. There was little talk, due to exhaustion.

Robert Rawlings approached her and assumed his usual crouch as he held out her parka, which he'd taken off the sled. "Better put this on," he said. "The weather is getting cold again. I'd say we're about ten above zero without the wind chill." Dana was only wearing her long underwear, jeans, and the "overwhites," and while in movement on skis or hiking she was warm enough. But now she felt a chill coming on and took the parka from him. "Captain Nye's men are going to dig out a separate chamber for you, and set up a Whisper Light stove with a small pail. I want you to heat some water and—as best you can—wash out your socks and, er, undergarments and let them dry while you sleep. We have to guard against frostbite. Dirty clothes impair the insulation."

"I understand," said Dana. "I've, uh, done this sort of thing before when I was in the field, setting up my monitoring stations." Then she pointed. "Looks like a blizzard on the way." Rawlings peered over his shoulder and said, "Yes. It might cover our tracks."

With weariness in her voice, Dana asked him, "We've come so far. And we have such a long way to go. Why don't you have some kind of snowmobiles for this sort of thing? Or even sled dogs?"

Rawlings cracked a wry smile. "Well, Miss Harrow, it seems the Air Force can drum up billions for a stealth airplane, but there doesn't seem to be much of a lobby in Congress to fund a stealth snowmobile. The ones we have simply make too much noise for our kind of work. And as for dogs, if we used them we would have to silence them, and that would mean cutting their vocal cords. The Humane Society people would go nuts if we did that—and I have a problem with it myself. So we do it the old-fashioned way. On skis and on foot."

Dana thought Rawlings a most unusual man. There was something mysterious, unfathomable about him. He had a kind of empathy, a kinship, with the snow, the ice, and the mountains. When he moved, it was as though he wore some kind of mantle of authority. And the way he and that sergeant major communicated was downright creepy.

Rawlings raised his short but sinewy frame back up and said, "Drink some water. We'll break out some food after the caves are prepared." He returned to the AKIO sled and crouched down beside Sergeant de Parma. Dana watched them get into a deep discussion while Gates, the RTO, ran an antenna wire between two stakes he'd stuck in the snow.

As she struggled out of her overwhites and put on her parka, a voice from behind asked, "You doing all right, ma'am?" It was the gentle giant, Captain Nye.

"Oh, yeah, I suppose so. Considering I can't go another step."

He chuckled. "I understand. Did the colonel tell you we're fixing up a separate chamber for you in the snow cave?"

"Yes. Yes, he did. That's very kind of your men. They must be exhausted. They're carrying those packs and pulling that sled, and I can barely keep up with you."

"You're doing fine, ma'am."

Dana sighed, "Thanks," while watching Rawlings and de Parma lift the canvas cover on the AKIO and peer inside. "What's on that sled, anyway?"

"Ah . . . I guess you could say that's our payload, ma'am. But that's all I better tell you. The Colonel tells me you're a sharp lady, so I better watch what I say."

Her curiosity was aroused. "Did he now? What did the Colonel say? Exactly."

The brawny captain came down on one knee and broke into a grin. "He showed me that notebook you kept. He's an intel type. That impressed him. And the fact that you evaded the Russians. Even the Sergeant Major was impressed by that."

While keeping her eyes on Rawlings, Dana fell back on her elbows and the snow crunched under her weight. "Tell me something, Captain. Twice today I was close to the Colonel when he raised his hand and called a halt. For no reason, as far as I could see. The second time I asked him why we were stopping, and he said, 'Pancho says stop.' Well, Pancho—the Sergeant Major—had to be a half-mile ahead. I couldn't even see him. And you aren't using any radios or anything. How could he know Pancho said to stop?"

Nye chuckled again. "Ma'am, you're not the first to notice that. When those two get together, it's weird sometimes. They have some kind of wavelength—telepathy, I guess—that you can't see or hear. I went moose hunting with them one time back in Alaska. We're walking on one side of a ridgeline when they both stop at the same time. The Colonel motions the Sergeant Major to go ahead, and pulls me back the way we came. Then we start to climb the ridge. I say, 'Colonel, what are we doing?' He says, 'Pancho says there's a moose on the other side.' Well, needless to say, we had moose steaks for dinner that night. Yeah, those two have a strange . . . reputation. Some of the guys call 'em the Mountain Mystics. But like I said, you impressed them both with that notebook of yours."

Dana kept her eyes on Rawlings, then shifted them to de Parma. "And what about Sergeant de Parma? The one who doesn't think women should be in the Army, I believe you said. What does he think of me?"

Nye chuckled. "I'd say the jury was still out on that score, ma'am."

JUAN DE FUCA STRAIT, WEST OF PORT ANGELES, WASHINGTON

The half moon was playing hide-and-seek, disappearing behind the clouds, then reappearing to bathe the waters of Juan de Fuca Strait with a pale, ghostly light.

Earlier that evening the USS *Nevada* had slipped its moorings at the Bangor Naval Base and made its way under cover of darkness through the Hood Canal toward the deeper soundings of the strait. Now it cruised along like a leviathan, lingering on the surface before vanishing beneath the surface of the black waters.

To the naked eye, the *Nevada* looked like a giant Trident submarine, right down to its missile hatches. Yes, its exterior looked like a Trident in every respect.

But it wasn't.

WILLIAMS FIELD—February 3

Maj. Gen. Mitrofan Tromso walked along the perimeter of Runway Number One while watching a combat air patrol plane land across the way on Runway Number Five. The wind was stiff, for they were on the tail end of a blizzard that had brought flight operations temporarily to a halt. Tromso felt fairly secure now. He had a force of 223 aircraft of various types, spread out in a network of protective bunkers. A latticework of taxiways linked the bunkers with the five main runways. His Air Defense Force brigadier had assured him the entire complement of fighters and bombers could be airborne within twenty minutes, and the Mainstay radar planes would provide ample warning. The saddle between Mounts Erebus and Terror bristled with antiaircraft radar and missiles, and the close-in air-defense Gadfly missiles ringed the airfield in a five-mile radius. Helicopter patrols were conducted regularly, the *Tbilisi* supercarrier was on station in the Ross Sea, and his Guards regiment was dug in on Hut Point Peninsula, overlooking McMurdo Sound. All in all, it was a secure site, but Tromso knew a good soldier was never finished with his defenses; he would always improve them.

Yet Tromso had allowed his men to take a break from the defensive buildup and partake of the American supplies at the McMurdo Base. The cigarettes and liquor had been a great boost to morale, to the point where Tromso had to curtail some of the "raiding party" forays into McMurdo. As an extra morale builder, he had passed the word that if Operation Snow Leopard was successful, each man could "liberate" a radio or stereo from the American or New Zealand camps and take it back to the Motherland.

But despite the heavy defenses he now had in place, and the fact that his men were tuned to a high degree of readiness, Tromso was uneasy. Everyone was falling into a pattern of routine. Airplanes went on patrol. They came off patrol. Shore patrols watched the sea. Helicopters landed and took off. Tromso knew the American task force had been under way long enough to reach McMurdo, but where were they? Why had they not struck back? Were the Americans, perhaps, going to let Snow Leopard just finish up its business and depart? He wondered.

A captured American Sno-Cat churned along one of the taxiways, kicking up snow that was rapidly dispersed by the wind. It halted near Tromso as the passenger door opened and the portly chief engineer climbed out.

"Ah, Comrade," said Tromso, "I will wager you have come to tell me your excavation of the mineral has begun."

The portly engineer, wearing a parka and floppy-eared hat, stammered and said, "I—I am afraid not, General. The, uh, jackhammer crew I told you about is having trouble cutting through the second lava apron. They seem to be caught in some kind of lava 'bubble' and are having a difficult time breaking out."

The tall Tromso grabbed the civilian engineer by the lapel of his parka, pulled him close, and said in a whispered growl, "You have

twenty more days, Comrade. Twenty days. Then we leave. And the
failure will be on your head. Not mine. Now get back to your duties.
Where you belong."

MANZANO MOUNTAIN NUCLEAR WEAPONS STORAGE
FACILITY, KIRTLAND AIR FORCE BASE, NEW MEXICO—
February 4

Under the cloak of darkness, a package was wheeled out of the secure
storage area of Manzano Mountain and transported via armed convoy to the airfield, where it was loaded onto a V-22 Osprey tilt-rotor
aircraft. Alongside the Osprey was a Phalanx Dragon aircraft armed
with Sidewinder missiles, and together they brought their engines up
to full power and took off vertically. Quickly they changed into
horizontal flight and their crews settled down for a long trip. The two
aircraft would refuel in the air as they headed toward their rendezvous point in the Pacific Ocean, where the USS *Nevada* would be
waiting.

On board the Osprey was a small object about the size of an ostrich
egg.

ROSS ICE SHELF—**February 6**

It had been a long and arduous journey. More than once Dana
Harrow had thought she wouldn't make it. They had crossed the
Minna Bluff and followed the coastline—where rock met ice—along
the northeastern foot of Mount Discovery. They had been under way
on foot or on skis for five days—or what she guessed were five days.
The continual sunshine had made her lose track of time. She was less
of a novelty to the rest of the team now. They had grown accustomed
to her presence. Even Sergeant de Parma was cutting her a little
slack. As they traveled, she tried to help out when she could, which
wasn't often. At the last camp she'd insisted they not dig a separate
chamber for her in the snow cave, and when everyone had settled
down, her sleeping bag wound up between Rawlings's and Gates's—
the boyish RTO, who had become particularly protective of her.
She'd awakened during the "night" to hear Gates snoring like a
chainsaw—while outside the snow cave a blizzard howled. But
Rawlings remained asleep, his breathing steady and even. He was
sleeping on his side, turned away from her. Dana's gaze had lingered

on the silhouette of his head and shoulders for a time, then she had gone back to sleep.

Rawlings apparently believed in long, hard travel, followed by long rest periods to recover. He seemed not to be in any hurry, and she'd heard him say to Captain Nye, "They're not going to start without us." He never explained who "they" were, or what they were going to "start."

"All right, Miss Harrow. Take your best guess as to where they are," said Rawlings.

Dana took the binoculars and scanned the five and a half miles of flat white wasteland between the coastlines of Mount Discovery and Black Island. "I think if we take a track just a bit to the south of here, we'll run into the crevasse field."

Rawlings nodded and turned to Captain Nye. "Okay, Phillip, move them out. Pancho with the rope team, then us, then the sled."

"Yes, sir."

Dana looked up. The sky was cloudy, but it was a high overcast. "Should we maybe wait for some better cover from their helicopters?"

Rawlings shrugged. "Might get better. Might get worse. The sun's still out twenty-four hours a day. If we go now, we'll have the shortest shadows during the crossing. Maybe the Soviets won't be looking for us this close in."

Mount Melania, on the northern tip of Black Island, almost blocked her view, but Dana could see Mount Erebus, fifty-five miles away. "I hope you're right," she said glumly.

"Let's move."

The caravan struck out across the flat expanse of the ice shelf. Sgt. Maj. Pancho Ramirez was roped to two other members of the team, and he paused from time to time to probe for a crevasse that might be lurking under a snow bridge. After an hour of slow movement, he finally stopped and pointed his ski pole.

Dana heard Rawlings comment to Nye, "Pancho says he found some." The rest of the caravan pulled up and saw a field of shallow fractures in the ice. They began picking and weaving their way through the field, ears always pricked for the sound of helicopters. Occasionally, Pancho would hold up his hand to halt the caravan while he probed. The fifth time Dana saw him probe, there was a

crack! and a *whoosh!,* and then he disappeared, as if through a trap
door. Pancho was roped to Gates and de Parma, and the force of his
fall yanked them off balance and started pulling them toward the
chasm—skis, poles, packs, and all.

Rawlings and Captain Nye shot forward to help, and Dana followed. As she got close enough, she could see a gaping trench that
was easily fifty feet deep.

Sgt. Maj. Pancho Ramirez was swinging on the end of the rope,
utterly helpless. With all of his equipment he was almost three
hundred pounds of dead weight. Gates and de Parma had managed
to drag their skis to slow their advance toward the chasm. Rawlings
and Nye dropped their packs and skis and grabbed the rope. Dana
followed. The three of them heaved, giving de Parma and Gates the
chance to shed their equipment so all could pull against the rope
full-bore. Then they began to reel Pancho in. Specialist-4 Utroska
had left the sled team and hustled forward in time to help the
sergeant major up over the lip of the crevasse.

Once Pancho was safe, Dana and Rawlings let go of the rope and
collapsed beside each other. In the cold air, their huffing and puffing
turned to vapor as Rawlings remarked bitterly, "I thought you said
these crevasses were shallow."

By now, Dana was physically exhausted and emotionally brittle,
which caused her to turn on Rawlings with an anger she couldn't
control. "I said a *lot* of them were shallow. Sorry I didn't have a
detailed map survey in my pocket when the Russians landed. And
I didn't ask to come along on this . . . this . . . *expedition.*"

Rawlings remained silent as he got back on his feet and brushed
off the snow. Dana did the same, then started moving toward the
sergeant major to see if he was hurt. But she hadn't taken two steps
when Rawlings said, "Pancho says he's okay."

Dana whirled around. *"Uhhhhh!* Honestly, can't you two communicate with simple speech, like normal people? I'm going to look at
him anyway. I used to be a nurse."

VALPARAISO, CHILE

The gangway was secured against the ocean liner *Mirnyi* and the first
three passengers down the ramp were Senior U.S. Representative to
Antarctica Desmond Voorhees, Navy Capt. John Benton, and Ted
Brendan. Voorhees and Benton had welts on their faces that were

half-healed. The KGB guards had worked the two Americans over, following their short-lived hijack of the ship's radio room. They made a beeline for the first person they could find on the docks who was wearing a uniform, and through the Chilean's pidgin English, the three Americans were able to learn that he was an inspector with the Valparaiso sanitation department. Their second attempt was more successful in that they latched on to a harbor policeman, but Benton soon found that the lawman spoke no English. Like most Americans, Desmond Voorhees thought if he yelled loud enough in English he could be understood in any language, so he grabbed the policeman by the shoulders and bellowed, "TAKE-US-TO-THE-AMERICAN-EMBASSY!"

THE ROSS ICE SHELF

After Pancho's initial fall, the team had regrouped and continued their journey through the crevasse field. Despite a couple more near misses, they made good time. They were perhaps a mile from Black Island when Rawlings picked up the pace even more, anxious to get off the flat tabletop of the ice shelf. They were skirting some shallow crevasses when everyone heard it at once. . . . And froze.

Captain Nye said, "Chopper."

From behind her, Dana heard Rawlings say, "Into the crevasse."

A mini-stampede ensued as the team rushed toward the rip in the ice sheet, which was narrow and about three feet deep. Skis and poles clattered on top of each other as they were tossed in.

Sergeant de Parma had relieved one of the sled pullers and was guiding the AKIO sled into the trench. He winced as it fell over on its side with a crash. Cursing, he reached under the AKIO's tarpaulin and pulled out a tubelike object that he laid on the bottom of the trench and covered with his stocky body. It was a Stinger surface-to-air missile.

Dana was standing on the edge, trying to shed her right ski, when a pair of rawhidelike arms enveloped her and pulled her into the trench—with her ski still awkwardly attached. She heard the drumbeat of the helicopter rotor blades grow closer and closer as Rawlings yanked the hood of her white anorak over her head. The *whop-whop* sound was growing distinct now. Then it became louder. Louder still. Damn, it was getting close! Dana heard the *whop-whop-whop-Whop-Whop-Whop-Whop-WHOP!-WHOP!* There was a blast of downdraft, blowing up ice crystals that stung her face.

They found us!

But then the air blast became weaker, and the chopping sound began to fade. Dana had started to raise her head to take a peek when an iron hand grabbed her by the scruff of the neck and roughly shoved her face back down. "Ow!" she protested, but the iron grip kept her head immobile until the drumbeat sound disappeared completely.

"Clear," said Rawlings, and one by one the surveillance team slowly emerged from the crevasse, silently grateful the helicopter had passed them by.

Rawlings gave Dana a hand as she struggled to extricate herself from the trench with one ski still attached.

"I'm sorry I had to be so rough with you, Dana. But for some reason, an upturned face is like a red flag to a helicopter spotter. I had to keep your head down."

Dana shook the snow off her anorak. "That's all right, Colonel. I understand."

"And, Dana?"

"Yes?"

"Sorry I was rough on you back there when Pancho fell in. If you hadn't gotten us to this crevasse field, we might have had to shoot it out with that very same chopper."

She didn't say anything, but only nodded. A feeling of weakness was starting to pervade her body as the adrenaline rush wore off. Yet she had the presence of mind to notice he had called her "Dana" instead of "Miss Harrow." At least that was something.

ZONE OF EXCLUSION BORDER, SOUTH PACIFIC, 60° SOUTH, 127°18′ WEST—February 7

"Electronic sweep," ordered the captain.

On the sail of the *Dnepr*—a Victor-III-class attack submarine hovering beneath the surface at periscope depth—the electronic "Brick Pulp" antenna mast extended up above the light swells of the frigid sea.

The electronics officer watched the frequency scanner intently as he held a single headphone against his ear. "Virtually nothing, Captain. Some faint commercial traffic on the skywaves. That is all."

Captain, Second Rank, Aleksandr Belous said, "Very well," and pressed the intercom button. "Sonar, conn."

"Conn, sonar, aye."

"Any contacts?"

"Still nothing but the occasional marine mammal, Captain, and I picked up our brother ship on bearing zero-eight-eight three minutes ago."

Belous—blond, thin, and willowy—wiped the sweat from his upper lip and ordered, "Search periscope up."

The metallic tube rose, and he quickly pulled the brass handles down and danced around with the instrument, making a quick 360-degree sweep. There was nothing. Absolutely nothing. The sky was partly cloudy, and the light ocean swells occasionally splashed his periscope viewer. But still there was nothing but the empty sea.

"Navigator?"

"Aye, Captain."

"Tell me again the coordinates and time the American task force was supposedly going to cross into the exclusion zone."

"Sixty degrees south, one hundred twenty-seven degrees eighteen minutes west. At thirteen-fifteen hours this date."

"Extend the Glonass mast and take a reading," ordered the captain.

The navigator did so, and checked the navigational plot on the instrument panel. Then he lowered the mast and announced, "Virtually dead on, Captain. We are but a few seconds off from the intersection. And it is now thirteen-eighteen hours."

Captain Belous kept scanning with the search periscope. Still nothing. He laughed bitterly as he said, "Ha! So much for our vaunted GRU spies. Those arrogant asses! Their intelligence seems to have been completely erroneous. The Americans were supposed to be here, but where are they? Damn! What a waste of time. . . . Wait a moment." There was something bobbing out there. Like a cork in the water. Belous hit the magnifier, but still could not discern what it was. Some flotsam or jetsam, perhaps? "Come to course two-three-seven, ahead one-third. There is something out there. . . . Hardly an aircraft carrier. Probably just some debris. But it is the only thing in sight, so we might as well investigate."

The *Dnepr* turned and came to course two-three-seven while Captain Belous waltzed around with the periscope to keep the target in sight. It was coming closer now . . . closer . . . wait a moment . . . was that a . . . ?

"Captain!" screamed the electronics officer. "Strong burst transmission in the Juliet-band!"

Fear engulfed Belous as he recognized the image in the viewer and slammed the handles against the tube. "Down scope! Crash dive! Hard right rudder! That was a damned sonobuoy! It's a trap!"

As the deck pitched forward into the dive, the intercom squawked, "Conn, sonar!"

"Sonar, conn, aye!"

"Contact bearing one-seven-three. Sounded like a torpedo landing in the water and engaging its propeller. American Mark 50, I think. I lost the track in the dive."

"Hard right rudder! Continue the dive! Eject sound devices!"

"Conn, sonar, second contact bearing zero-zero-seven! Active pinging! . . . I think they have acquired us! . . . Active pinging on original contact! They have us bracketed, Captain!"

"Blow all tanks! Up on the planes forty degrees! All ahead flank! Eject more sound devices!"

The *Dnepr*'s nose pitched upward as the submarine began rising toward the surface like a dolphin, trying to evade the deadly projectiles.

But it was too late. And it was the wrong move.

The two Mark 50 torpedoes were on a down angle seeking their quarry as the *Dnepr* was rising, and they struck the bow and stern of the submarine almost simultaneously.

As the four-engined P-7A long-range antisubmarine plane banked over the drop site, the copilot leaned over and saw two giant white carnations erupt on the surface.

"Got him!" screamed the sonar operator. "Both fish hit him dead on!"

Hoots and howls went through the big turboprop aircraft as the pilot came around for a low pass. Yep. They nailed this one. Close to the surface, too. Right where the guy from ONI had said they might be. The pilot and his copilot were clapping each other on the shoulder until they saw some of the innards of the *Dnepr* bob to the surface.

Among the debris they saw the bodies of young men, very much like themselves, wearing the orange-colored escape vests they had pulled on in desperation—just before the water had entombed them.

WHITE ISLAND—February 9

Lt. Col. Robert Rawlings and Sgt. Maj. Pancho Ramirez squatted in a small, rocky pocket on the northern slope of Mount Heine. *Mountain* was really too grandiose a word for Mount Heine, which was a mere 2,500 feet high. They trained their binoculars on Williams Field, about fourteen miles away, and what they saw caused even the Mountain Mystics to become shaky. Soviet planes were everywhere.

Contrary to legend, Rawlings and Ramirez really did speak from time to time, and on this occasion Rawlings whispered, "I'm glad we didn't see this before now. I might have turned us around and headed south."

The sergeant major nodded and replied, "As always, I would have followed you, Colonel."

Rawlings allowed himself a chuckle. Nothing like a little comic relief, he told himself, as they methodically scanned the area, grid by grid. Rawlings saw the five dark strips of the runways, and the countless bunkers with dartlike noses protruding from them, but with his 8x binoculars he was having difficulty finding a Gadflylike object.

"I think I see one, Colonel," said Ramirez. "This side of the nearest runway. Toward the west end. Several miles out."

Rawlings raised his glasses. He saw something, but couldn't say for sure it was a Gadfly. "Your eyes were always sharper than mine, Pancho. I'll take your word for it. If we can peg one with field glasses, then de Parma should be able to pick them out with the scope. Let's get him up here."

"Damn, damn, double, triple *damn!*" Sergeant de Parma pulled out a shard of glass from the broken magnification mirror and threw it down on the AKIO sled in disgust.

"How bad?" asked Captain Nye.

"The damned thing is *totally* deadlined, sir. Let's hope the other one is still working. Otherwise you can write off this entire mission."

Captain Nye sighed and said, "Check it out," then he turned to RTO Gates and asked, "How long until the next communications window?"

"Twelve minutes, sir."

"Okay, prepare a message that says we're operational, but wait for de Parma and the Colonel to give the go-ahead for transmission."

"Problems?" Dana asked, as gently as she could.

Their base camp was in a craggy depression on the western slope of Mount Heine, where a heavy snowdrift had collected. The team was digging out what they hoped would be their final snow cave.

"Possibly," Nye replied. "Depends on whether or not that thing works." And he pointed.

De Parma had hefted a gizmo off the AKIO sled that looked like a long telescope. He set it up on a heavy tripod, and began punching some buttons along its side. Then he swiveled it back and forth and peered through the eyepiece.

Dana observed this diagnostic process and said, "So that's what you were carrying on the sled. What is it?"

Nye hesitated, but then decided telling her wouldn't make any difference now. "It's a long-range target-designator laser scope."

Dana stared blankly at the contraption for some time, having no idea what a laser desig-whatever-you-call-it was, and said, "Of course . . . I should have seen that."

"Looks like we're in luck, sir," de Parma announced. "This one's in good shape."

Nye let out a "Whew," just as Rawlings and Ramirez came around the ridge.

"We've found a good forward base, Phillip," said Rawlings. "How do we stand?"

"One targeting scope is out of action and beyond repair, sir. The other one is in good shape. Gates is standing by with a 'Go' message. The next commo window is coming up shortly."

"Okay, then. Sergeant de Parma, you get to carry the ball by yourself on this one. We'll have to make do with a single scope. Pancho found a Gadfly launcher with his field glasses, so you should be able to do some damage with your designation. Gates?"

"Coming up on transmit window now, sir."

"Transmit that we're operational," Rawlings ordered.

RTO Gates said, "Roger, sir," and he sat down cross-legged in the snow. He cradled a keyboard device between his knees and typed in a five-character code group, and the symbology was displayed on a small liquid crystal window. He had strung the antenna wire from the AN/GRC-193A single-sideband AM high-frequency radio along two stakes in the snow outside of the rocky depression, then up to a third stake wedged into some rocks on the ridge that encircled them. This was called a "slant wire," and the greater the angle on the wire, the greater the transmission range. Gates checked his watch, and as the second hand reached the top of the hour, he pressed the button that sent the skywave "burst" transmission toward the ionosphere, where it would be reflected back toward the earth.

SOUTH PACIFIC, 400 MILES NORTH OF THE ANTARCTIC CIRCLE

In the choppy sea, a light rain was falling as an electronic scanner mast extended out of the water for a few moments. It then disappeared and was replaced by a communications antenna that reached its full extension about forty-five seconds before Gates pushed the transmit button. Once the skywave signal had been received, the antenna was retracted and the sea closed over it, as if it had never been there.

At the proper time, another mast would appear, and Gates's signal would be relayed via satellite to CinCPAC in Hawaii.

16

. . . .

THE OLDEST TOWN IN INDIANA

During the early nineteenth century, the oceans around Antarctica witnessed a greater and greater degree of activity as whalers and sealers plunged farther and farther south on their bloody quests for furs, whalebone, whale oil, and ambergris. And as a growing number of American vessels ventured into these treacherous and uncharted waters, some suffered the misfortune of being shipwrecked. The cumulative effect of all these shipwrecks triggered a demand from the seafaring community that the government chart these unknown seas. Congress bowed to this political pressure and agreed to underwrite the United States Exploring Expedition to Antarctica.

It was a venture that seemed ill-fated from the start. Secretary of the Navy Mahlon Dickerson was opposed to it and did not want the Navy involved, so he threw up roadblocks by reappropriating ships earmarked for the journey, and assigning the expedition commander to other duties. Command of the scientific trek was then offered to a number of other officers, all of whom refused, until it was finally accepted by a forty-year-old naval lieutenant by the name of Charles Wilkes.

For this dangerous voyage, Wilkes was given a dilapidated squadron of six ships, along with some officers who were politically opposed to him. Wilkes—a resolute but hot-tempered man—was undaunted by this state of affairs and plunged forward with the expedition, setting sail in August 1838 on a journey that was to last almost four years. And in so doing, Wilkes proved his mettle. This obscure naval lieutenant charted over twelve hundred miles of Antarctic coastline. He was the first to call that frozen landmass at the bottom of the earth "the Antarctic continent," and the Wilkes Land region of Antarctica bears his name today.

But upon returning from his perilous voyage, Charles Wilkes did not receive a hero's welcome. Instead, he faced a court-martial in which a number of his officers charged that he was harsh, overbearing, and easily offended, and could become violent when excited. At the court-martial, Wilkes was able to parry and dispense with each charge save one: When a number of seamen stole some liquor from the ship's store, they received a punishment greater than the twelve lashes allowed by law.

After the legal proceedings were concluded, Wilkes would spend the next twelve years of his life writing the five-volume narrative of his incredible journey. In retrospect, it is amazing the expedition met with any measure of success at all, for it began with a broken-down squadron of six vessels, spanned almost four years, saw fifteen men meet their deaths, and finally limped home with only two ships remaining.

One of the vessels that ultimately returned home had served as Wilkes's flagship for most of the voyage. Named after the oldest town in Indiana, it was a weatherbeaten, 780-ton sloop-of-war called the Vincennes.

THE USS *VINCENNES*—February 10

The Aegis cruiser *Vincennes* was rolling severely in the heavy seas, and bitterly cold rain and spray were hitting Capt. David Erickson in the face as he hung on to the open doors of the hangar deck. The crew had sprayed the exterior of the ship with an antiphobic coating to prevent ice from forming, but the rain and sea water had rapidly washed it away. Icicles made the guard rails around the ship look like white picket fences, and ice on the electronic mast was impairing the performance of the SPY-1A radar and making the ship top-heavy. Tethered crewmen worked continually to break the ice off the superstructure and mast.

Erickson was grateful for his parka and foul-weather gear, and as ice crystals started to form on his glasses, he hoped the weather would break. At times like these, he wondered if maybe he should have gone into the submarine corps.

The Light Airborne Multipurpose System (LAMPS) helicopter came into view, and Erickson was afraid it wasn't going to make it down on the *Vincennes*'s helideck. Against the howl of the wind, the chopping sound became more distinct as the white-painted aircraft drew closer and hovered over the rolling platform. A seaman ventured out on a tether line and tried to hook the landing cable onto the helicopter's belly. Once it was attached, the winch operator could reel the chopper down to the deck. But the seaman looked like a drunk trying to keep his balance as the icy deck rolled back and forth. Twice he slipped, and Erickson was about to call the whole thing off and send the LAMPS back to the *Carl Vinson,* but then the seaman made the connection and scrambled back into the hangar as the cable engaged and pulled the LAMPS firmly down onto the helideck. It seemed an interminable time before the helicopter blades came to a halt, but finally they did, allowing the mechanical pallet to slide the LAMPS into the hangar. The doors quickly closed behind it.

Erickson wiped each lens of his spectacles with his finger as the helicopter door slid back and the smallest man he'd ever seen in uniform jumped out.

"Captain Erickson," said the tiny, parka-clad man as he saluted. "Permission to come aboard."

"Permission granted, General Tharp," said Erickson, returning the salute and extending a hand. "Good to see you again, sir. Let's get below and get a warm-up." They went through the narrow, labyrinthine passageways, shifting their weight back and forth to compensate for the rolling deck, eventually arriving at the wardroom, where they doffed their heavy gear and enjoyed the warming balm of the ship's coffee.

Capt. David Erickson was six-foot-three with reddish, sandy-colored hair. He had a distinct jawline and usually wore glasses, which he was now cleaning with a wardroom napkin. Erickson was a complex man, in that he could best be described as an imperious teddy bear. He didn't exactly command the *Vincennes.* Rather, he *ruled.* The officers and crew were constantly subjected to harangues, edicts, and proclamations that often seemed to be made up as he went along. That was because Erickson was absolutely convinced he was the smartest man on board, so his unsolicited advice rained down on everyone—from the ship's cook to the weapons officer to the pharmacist's mate. The ship's company found his autocratic, micromanagement, shoot-from-the-hip command style insufferable. They also found that he was right most of the time, which was equally galling. As if that weren't enough, the captain possessed the most easily bruised emotional fiber on the high seas—and this was an important dimension to his effectiveness as a commanding officer. Case in point: When the *Vincennes* was preparing to sail with Task Force Beowulf, a seaman was busily stacking stores in the galley pantry. Erickson appeared and immediately began pontificating on how the stores should be stacked and where, which stores should be stacked up front for easy access, which ones should be on the bottom, etc. The seaman, who hadn't slept in thirty hours, blew his stack and yelled at the captain that he knew damn good and well how to stack stores, and the captain could just butt out and let him do his job. Instead of bringing the seaman up on charges for gross insubordination to a superior officer, Erickson's face took on the countenance of a wounded puppy—showing that he was genuinely hurt that one of his people would talk to him so harshly. The seaman felt so chagrined for hurting the captain's feelings that he redoubled his efforts.

By all rights, Erickson's command style should have led to dissension at best, or mutiny at worst; but inexplicably it resulted in the ship's company having cohesion and a fierce loyalty to their captain. Perhaps the most salient element of this puzzling leadership equation was that they trusted his judgment, even though they referred to him—when he was out of earshot—as "the Mad Viking."

As Erickson and Myron Tharp sipped their coffee in the wardroom, which was rolling from side to side, the Navy captain contemplated the diminutive Marine general. Erickson would never concede that anyone was his intellectual superior—especially someone shorter than himself—but in the war-planning sessions on Operation Beowulf, Erickson got a chance to experience the firepower of Tharp's brain at close range. As a result, even Erickson had to grudgingly admit that this little Marine three-star had his act together.

"So how is your ship holding up in this weather, Captain?" Tharp asked.

"Pretty well, considering, sir. Ice is becoming a problem, as you could surely see coming in. As for the crew, the closer we get to the zone of exclusion, the higher the tension. Prolonged stress makes them jumpy and tired. The rough weather doesn't help, of course. The maintenance division has spent a lot of time breaking ice off the superstructure. The antiphobic coatings get washed off in heavy seas."

Tharp nodded sympathetically, then studied his coffee for some moments before saying, "I understand that among your peers in the task force you are known as the Mad Viking."

Erickson cleared his throat and said, "Purely a nickname, sir. Bit of a joke on my Swedish ancestry. Nothing to it, I assure you." The Mad Viking then tossed down the remnants of his cup and said, "Care to go down to CIC now, sir?"

"Certainly," replied Tharp while suppressing a smile, and they rose from the table.

After passing through several passageways and squeezing by a number of young men wearing dark blue pants and light blue work shirts, Erickson and Tharp entered the Combat Information Center of the *Vincennes*. The CIC was bathed in a soft blue light, and it was filled with seamen and petty officers hunched over their consoles. Two large aisles of consoles funneled down to a bank of four large forty-two-inch-by-forty-two-inch screens that could be called upon to display air, surface, or submarine threats. Circles on the big screens denoted friendlies, triangles were hostiles, and squares were unidentified. Right now there were no hostile triangles on the screen. The Mad Viking and Tharp took their places at the console in front of one of the screens and put on their headsets.

Within the supercarrier *Carl Vinson*'s battle group, the officers in charge of engaging air threats, surface threats, sub threats, and the battle group commander were all spread out among the various escort vessels so that all the command and control eggs were not concentrated in one basket. Myron Tharp didn't like separating himself from Vice-Adm. Hobart Rumley, the task force commander, but policy dictated they be kept apart. All of the major commanders had been over and over the Beowulf battle plan, so Tharp hoped the required intercession of Rumley or himself would be minimal once the shooting started. And if he had to, he would talk to Rumley on a voice link. He hoped it would be secure.

"Contacts?" asked Captain Erickson.

The Tactical Action Officer sitting next to Erickson said, "Nothing except a couple of icebergs within a five-hundred-mile radius. Since we figured out that Russian carrier was hiding behind a berg, we had a couple of F-14s from the *Carl Vinson* check these two out, and they were safe. Commercial shipping has virtually stopped through Cape Horn. Unless it's a berg, anything unidentified now is bound to be hostile. I wish we hadn't lost the White Cloud satellite feed, sir."

"For what it's worth, son," said Tharp through the headset, "the Soviets have got the same problem. We blinded them like they blinded us."

With his hand, Erickson rolled the little controller ball on his console and the image on the screen moved around in synchronization. Except for the task force vessels, there was nothing on the screen but the two little circles denoting the icebergs some three hundred miles to the east. Task Force Beowulf had been slowly approaching the exclusion zone, eight hundred miles west of the Drake Passage, waiting for the word to go; and the prolonged tension was getting to Erickson, causing him to ask, "So when does the shooting start, sir?"

"It already has, David," replied the little Marine general.

That caused more than a few heads to turn, and Tharp explained about the three Soviet subs that had been sunk when they took the bait on the phony crossing point into the zone of exclusion.

David Erickson grasped immediately what it meant. "So we got three subs. Okay, the opening round goes to us, but that means our communications are not secure."

"We have to progress on that assumption. That's why I had everyone drill, drill, drill on the Beowulf plan so it would keep commo to an absolute minimum. If we have to communicate by teletype, we'll have to use one-time disks or one-time pads. And if we have to communicate by voice, we'll just have to use oblique language and hope the scrambler remains secure. I can't say for certain that it will."

Erickson pondered this, then asked, "So when does Operation Beowulf kick off, sir?"

Tharp's eyes remained on the screen. "Very soon now, David. Very soon."

WHITE ISLAND—February 10

Gates, the boyish RTO, was carefully monitoring his watch for the communications time window when the radio emitted a *squeeeep!* that signaled a message had just been received. He called up the five-character cipher groups on the keyboard display screen and wrote them down. Then he deciphered the message with his one-time pad and hustled into the snow cave. Captain Nye was getting dressed after a rest period, but Rawlings was still asleep in his sleeping bag. Gates roused the colonel and handed him the deciphered message. Rawlings rubbed the sleep from his eyes and scanned the scrap of paper, which read:

BEOWULF COMMENCES 1830Z THIS DATE

17

· · · · · · · · · · · · · ·

BEOWULF

*The Scylding wise men had never weened
That any ravage could wreck the building,
Firmly fashioned and finished with bone,
Or any cunning compass its fall,
Till the time when the swelter and surge of fire
Should swallow it up in a swirl of flame.*
—Beowulf *(translated from the Old English
by Charles W. Kennedy)*

22,000 FEET ABOVE THE WESTERN ANTARCTIC ICE SHELF

"Stonebreaker Flight, Stonebreaker Flight, this is Leader. I have authenticated kickoff with receipt of Victor-Victor-Tango transmission. Verify in sequence, over."

"Stonebreaker Two, verified."

"Three, verified."

"Four, verified."

"Roger," said Leader. "Three minutes to drop. Release on individual discretion per mission plan. Combat spread."

There was a flurry of microphone clicks over the short range FM tactical radio as the four black, stilettolike B-1B bombers of Stonebreaker Flight broke up their formation and fanned out, forming a line abreast. There was no danger of their transmission being monitored, for they were eight hundred miles from McMurdo Sound, cruising twenty-two thousand feet above the flat white expanse of the western Antarctic ice shelf.

On board the lead aircraft of Stonebreaker Flight, the offensive systems officer, or bombardier, ran through his armament panel checklist for the seventeenth time. He was ensuring that the data from the Global Positioning Satellites correlated with the prescribed release point programmed into the guidance systems of the air-launched cruise missiles. Stonebreaker Flight was fast approaching the drop zone, so the bombardier threw a switch on his panel.

On the undercarriage of the B-1B, the doors of the main weapons bay opened to a howling wind, revealing a revolverlike drum nestled inside, which held eight cruise missiles. Along the external undercarriage of the bomber were fourteen additional cruise weapons, hanging on to the fuselage like remoras grasping the underbelly of a shark. The bombardier continued watching the GPS readout, and when it passed the demarcation point he shouted, "We're in the envelope! Dropping externals now!" He raised the safety cover up and pushed the button marked RELEASE.

Falling in a sequence designed to keep the B-1B in proper balance and trim, the remoralike missiles were jettisoned from the undercarriage pylons one by one.

"Externals clear! Activating rotary launcher now!"

Like something akin to a Western marshal's six-gun, the rotary launcher in the weapons bay unleashed its missiles with the staccato sound of restraints springing free and the twisting-stopping-twisting-stopping whine of the rotary motor. By the time it was all over, twenty-two air-launched cruise missiles had been dropped from the bomber, and as the projectiles plummeted toward the ice in a preprogrammed free fall, the bomb-bay doors slammed shut.

"Release report," ordered Leader.

"Two clear."

"Three clear except one hangup in the rotary launcher. We're taking it back."

"Four is clear."

"Roger," said Leader. "Let's get out of here. Form up on me. Out."

And the four B-1Bs began a 180-degree turn back toward the tankers, five hundred miles away.

Like a school of barracuda, the eighty-seven cruise missiles of Stonebreaker Flight continued their descent toward the ice shelf, deploying their wings and engaging their turbofan engines. The electronics in their guidance systems began pulling in signals from the GPS satellites and matching them with their programmed flight path, which instructed them to pull up 320 feet above the desolate ice shelf.

These cruise missiles were both similar and dissimilar to their first-generation counterparts, in that they were cigar-shaped, but did not possess a sleek aerodynamic skin. Rather, they were somewhat boxy-looking on their dorsal side, and their epidermis was constructed not of metal but of carbon-fiber composites. This gave them a radar signature about the size of a sparrow—and a small sparrow at that.

Two of the stealth cruise missiles suffered engine-start failure and crashed into the ice shelf, unseen and unheard by anyone, but the remaining eighty-five missiles from Stonebreaker Flight continued on their vector toward Williams Field, near McMurdo Sound.

One hundred twenty miles from Stonebreaker Flight, a lone B-1B also began releasing its load of twenty-two stealth cruise missiles over the western Antarctic ice shelf. The bomber dropped the missiles one by one at sixty-second intervals. These weapons looked like the missiles from Stonebreaker Flight in every respect, except that each one had a mushroom-shaped snoot sticking out of its nose.

WHITE ISLAND

Squeeeep!

Gates, the RTO, hunched over his keyboard and called up the five-character readout. He had the decipherment already memorized and didn't even bother to write it down. He just looked up at Captain Nye and said, "Kickoff, sir."

"I'll go tell 'em. You stay here with the lady and help mind the store."

Gates replied, "Yes, sir," unable to hide the disappointment in his voice at being left behind.

After Captain Nye left, Dana approached Gates and asked, "Now can you tell me what's going on?"

Nervously, Gates said, "You'll find out in about ninety minutes, ma'am."

A MAINSTAY RADAR PLANE OVER THE WESTERN ANTARCTIC ICE SHELF

The radar operator sipped tea from his glass and—with every ounce of his remaining self-discipline—tried to refocus his attention on the green screen that had become a millstone around his neck. When they'd first arrived in Antarctica, the Mainstay crew's adrenaline had been pumped up to the stratosphere, and they had monitored the green screens like fathers waiting outside the delivery room—scrambling the jets on the ground if they picked up so much as an arctic tern on their radar. But the initial fever pitch slowly gave way to routine, and routine to boredom, and boredom to mental fatigue, until the very thought of watching the screen for another seven hours made his bowels churn. He perked up for half a second when he noticed a couple of flecks on the screen, but he figured it was another flock of birds, or maybe the technicians hadn't done a proper maintenance job during the last stand-down. He thought he saw the flecks again, but then decided it was some kind of ground clutter from the Transantarctic Mountains.

WHITE ISLAND

"You got them laid in, de Parma?" Rawlings asked for the fifth time.

Sergeant de Parma swept the perimeter of Williams Field with the laser telescope, pausing each time a tracked vehicle with four darts came into view. "Yes, sir. I've got 'em laid in—in sequence. Sixty seconds between missiles should be plenty. I count sixteen Gadfly launchers altogether."

"That's almost an entire air defense regiment," observed Rawlings.

De Parma kept his eye on the viewer. "All we can do now is wait. How long since we got the kickoff message, sir?"

The colonel checked his watch. "Eighty-one minutes ago."

Rawlings, de Parma, and Sgt. Maj. Pancho Ramirez were sitting in the rocky pocket on the north face of Mount Heine, with white camouflage netting strung over their lair. Sergeant de Parma remained glued to his laser telescope, while Rawlings scanned Williams Field with his binoculars, and Ramirez kept a Stinger surface-to-air missile cradled in his arms. Captain Nye and four members of his team were dug into snow foxholes nearby, a few more Stingers sprinkled among them.

THE TRANSANTARCTIC MOUNTAINS

Like corks bobbing on the surface of a whitewater stream, the flight of cruise missiles coursed through the canyons and passes of the Transantarctic Mountains, going up, down, turning, and banking, according to their programmed flight path. The missiles were flying "cold," not using their terrain-following radar for guidance. Instead, they were relying solely on the GPS satellite data for navigational updates—for to emit a radar signal would leave an electronic footprint that might be detected.

The lead cruise missile came out of the Mulock Glacier canyon and turned left to hug the edge of the Hillary Coast along the Ross Ice Shelf. It whipped by the Mason Spur and shot across the Eady Ice Piedmont, then up and across the Minna Bluff before nosing back down to thread the needle between Black Island and White Island.

What had taken the Long Range Surveillance Detachment ten days to travel, the missile had covered in six and a half minutes.

WHITE ISLAND

Dana Harrow simply refused to retreat back into the snow cave, so Gates had relented and allowed her to take a position on the ridge of their alcove, along with the rest of the rear party. Everybody had a glum face—disappointed at coming this far and not being able to see the big finish. They sat there, staring morosely across White Strait to Black Island.

The sky was cloudless, but the air was a little windy. Dana was grateful for her overwhites, for she had become sensitive to the needs of camouflage. She noticed it was getting colder, so she patted her cheeks with her mittens—just as she looked down and spied a tiny object snaking through the air along the coast of White Island at an incredible speed. It looked like . . . it looked like . . . well, it looked like nothing she'd ever seen before.

"There's one!" Gates howled.

Perplexed, Dana asked, "What is it?"

"There's some more!" howled Gates again, this time coming to his feet with the rest of the crew.

Dana was mesmerized as a half-dozen of the objects zipped through the strait. "What *are* they?" she pleaded.

Gates was hopping up and down now. "They're cruise missiles, ma'am!"

ROSS ICE SHELF

Like lemmings rushing to the sea to embrace their own death, the cruise missiles left White Island in their wake and surged across the ice shelf toward Williams Field. Traveling at 609 mph, they would cover the final fifteen miles in about ninety seconds before throttling down to their final approach speed of 325 mph.

The bunkers on the east end of the airfield, and the two Candid fuel tankers parked alongside Runway Number One, loomed closer and closer as the missiles rushed over the ice shelf. But the cruise weapons weren't headed for the bunkers, nor were they headed for the pregnant-looking tankers parked on the ice apron.

The lead missile reined itself in, causing its speed to bleed off rapidly as it came onto a final approach to Runway Number Three of the aerodrome. Its navigational program kicked in the terminal targeting phase—which gave the missile a death wish, of sorts—and it responded by pulling up and over in a tight loop, then smashing down onto the runway—just twenty-six inches from the airstrip's exact midpoint.

There was a *Barooom!* as the thermite warhead exploded and bloomed out to immolate the aluminum-alloy runway. Its 4,400-degree-Fahrenheit flame burned through the honeycomb midsection of the airstrip like a blowtorch through butter—melting it, pitting it, cratering it, until it was a molten mass that began to liquefy the underpinning ice beneath it.

In rapid-fire sequence a flock of missiles converged on the aerodrome, pulling up, over, and down to explode with a *Barooom! Barooom! Barooom!* that sounded like the kettledrum from hell.

SCOTT BASE

Maj. Gen. Mitrofan Tromso of the 103rd Guards Airborne Division had just stepped out of the portable latrine and was zipping up his fly when he heard a muffled *boom.* Startled, he looked around and saw nothing. Then a *boom-boom-boom* struck his ears, causing him to yank out the binoculars from his pistol belt and train them on Williams Field, some ten kilometers distant. He could just make out some small mushroom clouds rising over the runways.

"It has started," he whispered to himself, becoming frozen, unable to move . . . until another muted salvo of *boom-boom-boom* slapped him out of his shock. Tromso bolted toward the air defense command post van, just as three cruise missiles came from out of the west and screamed over him. Instinctively he fell to the ground, and heard a nearby Gadfly missile pop off as the flying stealth weapons came close enough to tease the "Fire Dome" air defense radar mounted on the launcher. The Gadfly, however, went into a loco trajectory, for the radar signatures of the cruise weapons were simply too faint to lock on to.

WILLIAMS FIELD

The first *Barooom!* brought the small village of pilots and ground crews awake like a thunderclap. Bunks, chairs, tables, and chessboards were overturned, tea and food were spilled, playing cards were scattered, and bowel movements were brought up short as aviators, mechanics, and crew chiefs fumbled with their boots while running pell-mell from their tents to their airplanes in the ice bunkers. In the fog of combat, shouts, howls, and confusion reigned supreme as everyone screamed at everyone else, asking what was happening—and nobody knew.

Capt. Fyodor Tupelov had been dozing on his cot, feeling somewhat cozy under his blanket, when the first *Barooom!* brought him upright like the spring on a tripped mousetrap. Then the triple *Barooom! Barooom! Barooom!* followed, and he leapt out of his cot to tear open the tent flap. For a moment—while witnessing columns of smoke going up and a wave of flame spreading over the airfield— his stupefaction was so overwhelming that he was unable to move. But another *Barooom!* erupted, and Tupelov quickly became unstupefied. Hopping on alternate feet, he pulled on his flight boots and sprinted the short distance to his MiG-29 Fulcrum, where his crew chief was already firing up the auxiliary starter. "Where was the alert?" Tupelov demanded as he scrambled up the ladder.

"There wasn't any damned alert!" screamed the crew chief as he followed the pilot up the steps. "All hell just broke loose! They came out of nowhere!"

Tupelov jackknifed into the cockpit and the crew chief shoved the white crash helmet onto the pilot's blond head, then jumped to the ground as Tupelov retracted the ladder and turned over the twin Isotov ID-33 engines. They came to life with a screech as the crew chief yanked the starter plug and the wheel chocks, then leapt out of the path of the jet intakes as Tupelov released the brakes and advanced the throttles. The twin-tailed Fulcrum rolled out of the bunker and onto the ice taxiway as he dropped and locked the canopy while arming his ejection seat. He was in the lead flight of Fulcrums, approaching the runway, and the scene before him caused the highly trained pilot to swallow involuntarily in fear. The runways were a sea of flame and smoke, and he watched helplessly as several more dartlike projectiles flew over the runways and executed their terminal loop-crash maneuver—sending out their footprints of fire with an effect that was frightening.

Tupelov was third in the takeoff line on Runway Number Five, aching to advance, when a plea of "Get airborne! Get airborne!" came through his headphones from the air defense command post. The wall of flame on Runway Number Five was slightly smaller than the others as the lead Fulcrum rolled into takeoff position. Tupelov held his breath as one of his pilots, Lieutenant Bushkin, cut in the Fulcrum's afterburners to achieve the shortest possible takeoff roll. Bushkin's fighter was gaining momentum, and for a moment Tupelov thought he was going to make it. The nose was just lifting off when the starboard wheel reached the leading edge of the flames and plunged into a crater, snapping the landing gear off like a dry twig. Tupelov could only watch in horror as Bushkin's Fulcrum cartwheeled into the firewall, sending up a fuel-laden geyser of flame over the burning runway.

Then the final volley of thermite missiles arrived, and when they impacted, the blast sent a wave of fire toward a Candid air-refueling tanker parked alongside Runway Number One. The flames seeped beneath the aircraft's undercarriage, causing the fuselage to ignite. It burned for almost a minute before exploding in such a violent conflagration that it rocked Tupelov's Fulcrum across the field.

Excited radio chatter went back and forth between the senior pilots and the air defense command post before the order came through the headphones, "Return to bunkers! Return to bunkers!"

Tupelov looked out the back of his bubble canopy and saw almost two hundred aircraft—Backfire bombers, Fulcrum, Flanker, and Foxhound fighters—all stacked up tightly behind him, like serious drinkers in line at a Moscow vodka store. He was trapped! He couldn't go forward into the sea of flames. He couldn't go back to the shelter of the bunkers. It would take an eternity to unravel this tangled mess! He *had* to get off the ground! In desperation he looked around and spied a small bulldozer—the kind used to prepare the ice for construction of the runways. It was sitting tranquilly alongside Runway Number Five, as if oblivious of the conflagration only yards away. Upon seeing it, an idea hit Tupelov—and he instinctively knew it was his only chance. He popped the canopy, extended the ladder, unplugged his umbilicals, and slid over the side to the ground. He could feel the heat from the inferno as he started running back toward the bunkers. He hadn't taken a dozen steps when the second Candid tanker cooked off, and the force of the blast made him trip and fall to the ground. The sky was full of black smoke as he raised himself up and started running past the traffic jam of warplanes. Looking at him, his comrades probably thought Tupelov was fleeing from the war zone.

WHITE ISLAND

"Impact!" screamed Sergeant de Parma as he eyeballed the airfield through the targeting scope. "Impact again! Colonel, look!"

Rawlings put his own field glasses aside and leaned over to look through the laserscope's eyepiece. Dark puffballs were rising all over Williams Field. Fascinated, Rawlings watched as the fighters and bombers rolled out of their bunkers and queued up for takeoff . . . and then halted. After a pause, one of the planes rolled down the runway before tumbling and exploding into a fireball. Then the Candid tanker blew up in a giant black and orange mushroom cloud, causing Rawlings to pull back. "Sonofabitch, Pancho! We've got 'em! Flat on their butts, we've got 'em! Have Gates send the 'go' message!"

Pancho Ramirez dropped his Stinger and said, "Yessir!" as he scrambled out of the rocky pocket and toward the base camp.

"Okay, de Parma," said Rawlings evenly, making a conscious effort to get himself back under control. "It's your show now. Knock out the Gadflys."

Sergeant de Parma put his eye back on the viewfinder and punched the button to energize the yttrium-aluminum-garnet laser. He trained the scope on the first tracked vehicle with four darts mounted on top, and said in a warbly voice, "I've got everything under control, sir."

The second tanker blew.

WILD WEASEL FLIGHT, 32,000 FEET ABOVE THE WESTERN ANTARCTIC ICE SHELF

The backseat electronic warfare officer in the F-15G "Wild Weasel" fighter was watching the screen of his AN/APR-38 Radar Homing and Warning System (RHAWS), but he was so tired he could barely see straight. It had been a long haul from Diego Garcia, in what he figured was the most complex air logistical operation ever attempted. He'd never seen so many tankers, fighters, and bombers in the air at one time.

His F-15G Eagle fighter—specially modified to detect and destroy enemy surface-to-air radar sites—was being used at this moment to detect where the Russians' combat air patrol might be lurking. On his left were four F-15C Eagle fighters of Bird Dog Flight with freshly topped-off fuel tanks, waiting to be unleashed on their mission to provide air cover. In his wake were the three other F-15Gs of his own Wild Weasel unit. He wasn't too thrilled about their assignment. They were probably on a one-way mission, for their internal and conformational-external FAST-pack fuel tanks would be almost dry by the time they reached McMurdo in sustained afterburner flight. The backseater—known as "Bear" in Weasel jargon—had been tracking an airborne India-band emitter, but the emission was getting weaker, indicating that the source was moving away from them. If the "go" signal didn't come in pretty soon, the emission source would be out of range in short order. But then, as if someone had read his mind, the pilot in the front seat said, "We've got a 'go,' Bear!"

Bear hooted and said, "Send off the Bird Dogs! Bearing zero-one-seven. Range unknown. Tell 'em they should bag a Mainstay!"

"Roger! Bird Dog Flight. Bogey at zero-one-seven. Range unknown. Probable Mainstay. I say again, probable Mainstay. Down it."

Bear watched the tailpipes of Bird Dog Flight flare into afterburner as they spread out and took off on the assigned vector.

His own pilot—call sign "Ringtail" (as in baby golden eagle)—said, "Okay, Bear, here we go. Let's clear a path for Buckshot. Hope we don't have to punch out on the other end."

"That's a rog," replied Bear, his fatigue having vanished. "Go to it."

Ringtail cut in the F-15G's afterburner, and Wild Weasel Flight was on its way.

SOVIET AIR DEFENSE COMMAND POST, SCOTT BASE

"Launch the aircraft!" bellowed Major General Tromso. "Launch them now!"

The tall, slender air defense brigadier was scarcely listening to Tromso, for he was too busy screaming into his own headset. Finally, in frustration, he ripped it off and turned to Tromso. "Our aircraft cannot take off. The airfield is inoperative. One aircraft was lost while attempting to lift off. For their own protection I have ordered them to return to their bunkers until we can repair the damage."

In the darkened command post van, they heard a faint growl as the first Candid tanker blew.

"There isn't going to be any time for repairs, you fool!" yelled Tromso, and in his frustration the tall, athletic Guards general wailed, "How did this happen? Where did they come from? Are they from the American carriers?"

"They are not aircraft," replied the ADF brigadier while wiping sweat off his Gallic nose. "One of my regimental commanders at the airfield says they look like cruise missiles, and I have no idea where they came from. Radar! Anything?"

The radar officer looked up from his screen with a terrified face and said, "Nothing, General. Mainstay Two reported some unusual ground clutter earlier, along the Transantarctic Mountains about four hundred kilometers out. That may have been the missiles."

"Vector the combat air patrol to that sector. Maybe they can intercept something visually."

The CAP officer began muttering something into his mike when the radar officer shrieked, "General! Bogeys! Contact bearing one-nine-seven! They're making a beeline for Mainstay One!"

WILLIAMS FIELD

With the back of his gloved hand, Capt. Fyodor Tupelov slapped the hapless airman as hard as he could, then grabbed him by the scruff of his parka and shook him with a potent mixture of rage and frustration. "Now you listen to me, Comrade! We are going to be butchered like pigs if we do not get some aircraft off the ground with all possible speed!" He shook the young man again.

The airman, who was a skinny young kid, frightened to near paralysis, nervously nodded his head.

Tupelov had scoured three bunkers before he found someone who could operate the bulldozer. And now, having found one, he wasn't about to let him go. He pulled the young man roughly out of the shelter and pointed at the 'dozer resting behind a veil of black smoke. "You see that tractor out there? I cannot take off through the snow, it is too deep. But I might get off the ground if you can scrape a path through the snow so I can make a takeoff roll on the bare ice. Now get on that tractor and clear me a path!" And he shoved the airman forward so hard that he stumbled and fell in the snow.

The boy was so very young, and so very afraid. He could not bring himself to move.

Tupelov drew his Makarov sidearm out of its holster and fired a round into the snow, about a meter from the prone figure.

The airman was up on his feet and heading toward the 'dozer at double-time.

SOVIET AIR DEFENSE COMMAND POST, SCOTT BASE

"I count four bogeys in the second wave . . . five . . . six . . . seven . . . now eight. Eight hundred kilometers out. Speed in excess of one thousand kilometers per hour and increasing. . . . Uh-oh . . . what is this? Second contact! Bearing one-zero-two. Four bogeys . . . five . . . six . . . *eight* . . . speed in excess of Mach one. Seven hundred seventy kilometers out . . . Damn! *Third* contact! Bearing two-six-eight. Eight hundred twenty kilometers out. Speed, Mach one plus."

"Give me an indent on the second wave!" demanded the air defense brigadier.

The radar officer gasped. The blips he was receiving on the second wave were small. Smaller even than the radar signature of the Wild Weasels that were fast approaching. But the small blips . . . his training told him . . .

"Commander . . . I identify the second wave as"—he counted rapidly—"twenty-four American B-1 bombers approaching from three different points of the compass."

Mitrofan Tromso felt as if his stomach were sinking into his knees. How could the entire picture change so radically, so fast? He was a

Red Army man, but he knew what would happen when his air cover was stripped away. His soldiers would face the enemy naked. "We're done for," he whispered.

"*No*, General," insisted the air defense brigadier. "We are *not* done for! They must still get through our radar and missile fence. If we can hold the damage down, we may be able to repair the airfield and get some aircraft up before they send in a landing force." The brigadier turned to his radar officer. "Time to target on the lead bandits?"

"Sixteen minutes on the first wave. They must be fighters in front of the B-1s. They are traveling at almost Mach two."

The brigadier again wiped away the sweat that was dripping from his Gallic nose and said, "Order all six fighters of the combat air patrol back to base to provide a close-in defense."

"But, General," protested the radar officer. "The Mainstays will have no protection—"

"The Mainstays are dead anyway, Major! Order the CAP to return to base at once! And radio the *Tbilisi.* Tell them we need all the air cover they can spare. We have to protect our radar net."

A radar operator's screen went blank.

"General! Mainstay One is down!"

WHITE ISLAND

Dana Harrow and Gates, the RTO, were nervously clutching each other—scared about what they couldn't see—when another cruise missile whipped through White Strait.

This was the lead missile in the string that was a little different from its brethren that had just savaged Williams Field. This one packed a conventional high-explosive warhead instead of thermite, and its mushroom-shaped snoot could sniff out laser-beam reflections and home in on them like a bloodhound.

Sergeant de Parma had been holding the laser telescope on the Gadfly launcher for what seemed like hours, not minutes. And although it was cold, underneath his clothing he could feel a drop of sweat trickle down his ribs. Impatient, he muttered, "Where's the damned . . . ?"

There was a flash in his field of vision as the snow in front of the Gadfly launcher erupted in a starburst pattern—but then it dissipated, leaving the launcher and its missiles still there, unscathed.

"Dammit!" yelled de Parma. "We undershot!"

"It's the looming," said Rawlings, trying to keep his voice steady. "Compensate for it. Bracket the target."

The "looming" that Rawlings was referring to was an optical phenomenon that occurred in Antarctica, whereby objects that were at a distance could appear closer than they really were.

De Parma elevated the beam slightly so it seemed he was painting the snow behind the Gadfly launcher. A second white starburst rose from the ground, this time behind the missile but close enough to shake it.

"Almost!" yelled de Parma, as he made a minor correction and waited. It was maddeningly slow, but the seconds ticked past, and this time the tracked launcher was blasted up and into the air in a flip, before falling back on the snow, belly up.

"Got it!" de Parma howled. And he swiveled the scope to the next target.

SOVIET AIR DEFENSE COMMAND POST, SCOTT BASE

"General!" barked the officer in charge of the close-in defense systems.

The brigadier whirled around and snapped, "What?"

"We just lost the data link with one of the Gadfly missile emplacements!"

"What?"

"Now another! General, our Gadflys are being taken out!"

"Wha . . . How?" stammered the brigadier.

"I do not know, sir. I am trying to ascertain the problem now."

Mitrofan Tromso couldn't suffer the oppressive command post any longer and stormed outside. He could see smoke rising in the distance, the result of the two immolated tankers. Two hundred meters away was a Gadfly launcher installed for the defense of the command post. Tromso caught sight of a dartlike projectile as it seemed to appear out of the vast wasteland of the ice shelf. The dart married itself to the launcher in an eruption that threw up a mound of snow, just before a *whump!* reached Tromso's ears, causing him to cringe.

Then there was silence . . . a silence very different from the frenetic chaos inside the command post. A silence that cleared Tromso's mind and let his eyes wander over the white expanse of the ice shelf. His gaze lingered on White Island, then traversed to Black Island, and then to Mount Discovery—searching for something, he knew not what. But then it came to him. A sine qua non—an imperative that simply had to be. In a whisper that was a subdued counterpoint to the destruction he had witnessed, the Guards general murmured, "Someone is out there."

WHITE ISLAND

"*Hoooooeeeeee!*" hollered de Parma. "We're rockin' and rollin' now, sir! I'm knockin' these honkers out of the park!"

"Keep knockin', Sergeant," said Rawlings with a grin. "You bat a thousand and the drinks are on me. . . . Better yet, I'll carry your pack back home."

"You're on, sir!"

Another blast.

"Nine down, seven to go."

WILD WEASEL FLIGHT

The mission of the Wild Weasels was to suppress—which was to say, destroy—any remaining Gadfly antiair launchers that de Parma and his cruise missiles had missed, and to clear a path for the B-1B bombers through the long-range SA-12 Gladiator missile radars posted on the crest of Ross Island. If the Weasels could knock out the critical link of its "Grill Pan" target-acquisition antenna, then the Gladiator missiles were off the boards. It would have been well nigh impossible to take all the Grill Pans out, so Wild Weasel Flight was earmarked to blind just two of the antennae so the B-1Bs would have clear entry and exit points for their bomb run. And in order to get close enough to knock them out, the Weasels had to fly under the airspace "painted" by the radar beams . . . and that meant flying lower and faster than sanity allowed.

Ringtail screamed out of the canyon of the Mulock Glacier, which fed into the Ross Ice Shelf, then took his flight through a sharp turn to the left, like thoroughbreds coming into the home stretch. The Weasels were flying behind Ringtail, in train, as he followed the Hillary Coast toward Mount Discovery, then veered toward the Minna Bluff.

In the backseat, Bear monitored his RHAWS instruments and said, "Looks like we still have some Gadflys that are hot."

"That's a problem for Gibby and Jake. You stay on the Grill Pan target."

"Rog."

As the craggy spine of the Minna Bluff rushed toward him, Ringtail pulled back on the stick slightly and the nose of the Eagle rose. He rolled the aircraft over on its back so he could gauge when they cleared the ridgeline, coming as close as he dared.

"Signal strength is getting hotter on the Grill Pans!" cried Bear. "PRF is rising—get us down quick!" Bear was referring to the pulse repetition frequency, which was essentially an electronic drumbeat that told Bear when the radar was in "search" or "lock-on" mode.

Ringtail pulled them back down on the deck and rolled the Eagle into an upright position. In rapid sequence, the Weasels followed him over the Minna Bluff. First came his wingman Bobcat, then Gibby and Jake—and in a train they headed for the pass between Black and White islands. Ringtail keyed his mike and said, "Combat spread when we get through the gap!"

WHITE ISLAND

Dana pointed. "What are *those?*"

Gates saw the string of four fighters racing just above the ice shelf as they whipped by their position and started to flare out. He shook his head. "I'm not sure, ma'am. . . . Some kinda fighter aircraft."

WILD WEASEL FLIGHT

As Williams Field raced by them on the port side, Ringtail could see the massive smoke cloud rising from the burning Candid tankers. The Weasels were on a line abreast now, hurtling across the ice shelf toward the Windless Bight.

"Gadflys are hot!" Bear yelled.

Ringtail looked to his left and saw two of the Eagles streak up in the vertical plane. "Gibby and Jake are unmasking!" he cried, meaning the two F-15Gs were intentionally revealing themselves to the two surviving Gadfly launchers. An eyeblink later, two white, smoky trails were rising after them. Ringtail hoped his partners would win their duel with the Russian missiles, but he had to concentrate on his own problems now.

"Jammer on!" Bear shouted. This was the backseater's moment. He had to act like an orchestra conductor, telling Ringtail what to do with his instrument—the Eagle—and when to do it. "Vector to zero-zero-three." Bear felt the minor correction. "Okay . . . okay . . . range thirty-five kilometers . . . thirty . . . twenty-five . . . what . . . PRF is increasing on the Grill Pan. Dammit, it's too soon! Grill Pan is hot! They got lock-on!"

What Bear had not counted on was the Grill Pan radar's high position on Ross Island, which gave it a "look down" capability, allowing it to paint the low-flying Weasels with its beam as they raced across the Windless Bight.

On the plateau behind Sultan's Head Rock on the peninsula, two SA-12 Gladiator missiles were loosed from their launch tubes, leaving plumes of white smoke as they rose straight into the air. Ringtail saw them and yanked back on the stick, putting the Eagle in a pop-up maneuver that slammed him and the Bear back into their seats. Under the seven-G strain, Ringtail growled, "Take your shot *now!*"

Bear mashed the master switch that put the RHAWS into full automatic, and almost immediately there was a rumble as the High-Speed Anti-Radiation Missile roared off the rail to seek out the Grill Pan antenna.

At the same moment, Ringtail saw the two Gladiator SAMs nosing over—one toward the north, and one toward *him!*

It was race time.

Ringtail executed a quarter-roll and put the Eagle into afterburner while pulling back on the stick a smidge. He had an excruciatingly simple task: keep the Eagle away from the Gladiator and give the HARM missile enough time to strike home.

Tick-tock-tick-tock-tick-tock . . .

The Gladiator was gaining.

Tick-tock-tick-tock-tick . . .

Ringtail squeezed the throttle handle, as if that might give him more speed.

Tick-tock-tick-tock . . .

Sometimes the HARM didn't work.

Tick-tock-tick . . .

"Come on, you bastard! Come on!"

Tick-tock . . .

"Come on!"

Tick . . .

"Got him!" screamed Bear.

A white trail of smoke zinged in front of Eagle's canopy, and Ringtail flinched as they plunged through it.

"The HARM got the Grill Pan! We're clear, but you're getting into another hot zone. Turn around and put us into the blind spot."

Ringtail was limp, but gladly complied. "Did you see the missile trail?"

"What trail?" Bear asked.

Ringtail felt a wetness in his crotch. "Never mind. . . . Where's Bobcat?"

"Dunno. Let's nail another Grill Pan on the backside of the island. We can hit them from their blind side now. Get back down on the deck and come to zero-zero-nine."

Ringtail brought the Eagle onto the vector and pointed the aircraft down.

And it quickly came into view.

The white trail of smoke was dissipating, but it was still discernible, and it ended at a black spot on the ice of the Windless Bight.

Bobcat and his backseater were gone.

SOVIET AIR DEFENSE COMMAND POST, SCOTT BASE

"The south-sector Grill Pan radar on Ross Island is down, General!" cried the close-in weapons officer.

The air defense brigadier felt his knees wobble, and reached out with a hand to grab a chair and steady himself. His breath was coming in little gasps now, and his face had assumed the pallor of flour. Bit by bit, with the destruction of each Gadfly launcher, the brigadier had seen his meticulous plans, his painstaking defenses, and finally his bejeweled career turn to ashes. It was like seeing a giant fir tree felled before his very eyes. And now the Americans were castrating his Gladiator missiles as well.

"North-sector Grill Pan is down!"

A lesser man might have caved in at this point, but the brigadier was not that sort. In his other hand he held the stopwatch that timed the gap between the Wild Weasels and the B-1Bs. "So . . . they have cleared their entry and exit points. . . . Well, it is time to spring a surprise of our own. Order the reserve Gadfly crews to stand by on their launchers!"

"At once, General!"

The brigadier focused his eyes on the sweep hand of the stopwatch and said, in a low hiss, "It won't be that easy, you bastards . . . not so easy."

BUCKSHOT TWO

In the nose of Buckshot Two, the synthetic aperture radar of the B-1B intermittently cast out its narrow beam to probe the landscape ten miles ahead, then it displayed the return signal on cathode-ray screens in the cockpit, and in the avionics compartment where the bombardier and defensive systems officer (DSO) did their thing.

Like the Wild Weasels before them, Buckshot Two was skimming over the ice shelf, fast approaching the summits of the Transantarctic Mountains, which were just poking above the white mantle. On the bombardier's radar display, the preprogrammed navigational landmark of where Mount Marvel was supposed to be was thrown up on the screen as crosshairs. The bombardier read the radar signal—which almost had the definition of a photograph—and saw that the actual Mount Marvel was not aligned with the crosshairs, but slightly to starboard. With his control handle he put the crosshairs on the mountain and punched the update button. The navigational computer system then realigned Buckshot Two's flight path and put it "in the groove."

In the cockpit of the bomber, the pilot of Buckshot Two watched the mountains race toward him, with one eye on the navigational display and one eye out the window. He never enjoyed turning everything over to a computer and flying with hands off the stick. He was always afraid some programmer's glitch was going to auger them into the ground. Looking ahead through the window he could just make out the flight leader, Buckshot One, as he dropped out of sight to fly through the canyon of Mulock Glacier. Then the pilot felt his own aircraft's speed bleed off as the canyon came into view, and the B-1B jigged slightly to starboard to start its track down the glacier. The bomber followed the canyon through its descent, zipping by craggy walls that seemed to reach out for it, before coming out onto the Ross Ice Shelf. Automatically, the swing-wing aircraft banked to port, then hurtled over the Minna Bluff, before coming back down to cut through White Strait.

WHITE ISLAND

Dana Harrow and the rear party were all on their feet now, like a Cotton Bowl crowd watching a two-minute offense in a tight game. But when a black, stilettolike object screamed along the shore of White Island, they all dropped down.

Without speaking, Dana's eyes looked at Gates, searching for an answer. By now she was easy to read. "It's a B-1 bomber, ma'am. . . . And here comes another one!"

SOVIET AIR DEFENSE COMMAND POST, SCOTT BASE

The brigadier watched the sweep hand of his stopwatch go past a predetermined point and he yelled, "Uncover the reserve Gadfly launchers and activate radars *now!*"

WILLIAMS FIELD

At four stations around the burning runway, crewmen pulled off the white camouflage netting covering their Gadfly launchers. And as the four deadly darts on each tracked vehicle elevated into firing position, the launchers' "Fire Dome" radar came alive.

BUCKSHOT ONE

As Buckshot One raced past White Strait, the navigation program kicked in for the bomb run, and the B-1B automatically pulled up to eight hundred feet as the bomb-bay doors opened. The airborne rapier now had a twelve-mile dash to the release point.

As they closed on the target, the DSO in the rear electronics compartment received a flashing red light on his warning panel, causing his fingers to dance across the console. "The drop zone is hot! I say again, DZ is hot! *Missile launch!* Activating countermeasures now!"

Two Gadfly missiles streaked toward Buckshot One to intercept, and the bomber's ALQ-161 suite of defensive electronics kicked in—spitting out jamming signals in a 360-degree arc with the power equivalent of 120 microwave ovens cooking at full torque. The jamming confused and confounded the Fire Dome radar on the Gadfly launcher, sending one of the missiles straight up and the other into a spiral. But then, somewhere in the B-1B's massive array of circuits, silicon chips, wiring, backup systems, software code, and circuit breakers, something failed—simply failed—causing the system to go down for a few moments before the DSO could get it back on line. And in those moments the Fire Dome radar caught the bomber in its electronic death grip, putting the spiraling Gadfly on a track that led straight into the open bomb bay of Buckshot One.

BUCKSHOT TWO

"What the—? . . . *SONOFABITCH!*"

In a reflex action, the pilot of Buckshot Two yanked on the control stick and pumped the right rudder pedal to override the automatic flight control system. Never in his life had he seen anything like a B-1B with its fuel and 48,000-pound bomb load explode in a giant airburst moving at almost four hundred miles per hour. Buckshot Two was three miles back, and the pilot had to veer away to avoid flying through the expanding fireball in his path. He missed the debris, but his aircraft rumbled as it flew through the air-compression wave. The pilot moaned audibly and then shouted through the intercom, "Sonofabitch! One is down! One is down! DSO, make sure your gear is working!"

"His gear is okay, Skip," the bombardier snapped somewhat testily. "Get us back on track. I'll have to line it up manually."

One of the benefits of being in the closed-off electronics compartment was that the bombardier didn't see the remnants of the airburst whipping by the window.

The pilot weaved Buckshot Two back on track toward Williams Field, and held it steady as the bombardier tweaked the synthetic aperture radar up to full power. What he saw on his display defied his imagination. A forest of tail sections glistened on his screen as they were bathed by the invisible beam of the radar. "This is incredible! They're sitting flat on the ground!"

"Shut up and drop 'em!" barked the pilot.

"Yeah . . . yeah . . . okay . . ." the bombardier stammered as he punched another button. A vertical line with a little dot on the bottom appeared on his screen, and as the forest of tail sections loomed closer on the display, he put the "death dot" in the middle of the pack and engaged the targeting computer. The computer took soundings on altitude, heading, and speed, and continuously computed the optimum release point.

"The Grill Pans must be down!" shouted the DSO. "The Weasels did their job. We have a clear path. Gadfly PRF is increasing! Missile launch!"

"Hold steady!" screamed the bombardier. "Hold steady . . . steady . . ."

"Missile lock! Gadfly has got us!" Popping sounds erupted as the ALQ-161 fired off bomblets of rapid-blooming chaff to decoy the Gadfly.

"Steady!" screamed the bombardier again.

The pilot wanted to close his eyes and pray, but he couldn't. So he prayed with his eyes open.

There was a *whump!* as the tail wobbled slightly. "Gadfly took the chaff!"

Under his oxygen mask, the bombardier licked his lips. "Here it comes! . . . Here it comes! . . . *Now!* Bombs away!"

In three seconds, twenty-four two-thousand-pound Mark 84 bombs dropped from the weapons bay racks of Buckshot Two—raining down on the entrapped Fulcrums, Foxhounds, Flankers, and Backfires in a pattern that bracketed the "death dot" aiming point by six hundred feet, fore and aft.

WILLIAMS FIELD

Capt. Fyodor Tupelov had just holstered his Makarov automatic and was climbing back up the ladder to the cockpit of his MiG-29 Fulcrum when two Gadfly missiles roared off their launchers on the far side of the airfield and streaked over his head—vectoring off in the airspace above the ice shelf. Transfixed, he watched their white smoke trails as the bright dots of their burning propellant became smaller and smaller in the distance. He knew he should move, but he remained hypnotized somehow. They had just dropped out of sight when a black cloud appeared in the distant sky, then multiplied its size dramatically. It seemed to hang there, suspended, until a *POM!-POM!-brrraaaapppp!* punched through the air.

Tupelov's brain was screaming at him to move, but he remained perched on the ladder, transfixed by the spectacle of another Gadfly missile roaring off the launcher.

What followed took on a kind of surrealistic aspect for Tupelov as a black, sinister-looking V appeared up in the sky and disgorged a host of black darts that plummeted toward the airfield—and toward *him!*

This jarred Tupelov out of his hypnosis, and he surged up the ladder as the initial Mark 84 bomb sailed over him—before coming down to detonate with an overpowering *WHAM!* that pulsed across the field. The blast was distant enough to spare Tupelov's life, but the concussion wave plucked him off the ladder and tossed him through the air like a rag doll. He hit the ice—and what followed was beyond the ability of his senses to absorb. The earth shook in upheaval as wave after wave of *WHAM!-WHAM!-WHAM!-WHAM!* ripped savagely through the Fulcrums, Foxhounds, and Backfires.

WHAM!-WHAM!-WHAM!-WHAM!-WHAM!-WHAM!

The earth continued to tremble, and Tupelov cried out as he witnessed wings, tail sections, landing gear, tires, and broken fuselages shooting into the air along a path of such violent destruction that it looked as if the gates of hell had opened.

BUCKSHOT TWO

"Dead center!" screamed the bombardier. "Got them dead center!" The image from the strike camera mounted in the tail showed a diagonal slash of destruction cutting through the helpless Russian aircraft. "Oh, man! Great flying, Skipper! We ripped 'em apart!"

The defensive systems officer was not so buoyant. He was still monitoring his panel, looking for the Grill Pan radar signal. "Maintain this vector, Skipper," he ordered. "Let me know when we cross over Ross Island."

"Coming up now!"

The volcanic island sailed beneath the bomber, and the DSO held his breath . . . then exhaled. "I'm gonna kiss the ass of those Weasels! The north-side Grill Pan is dead! Maintain this heading for a hundred klicks, and then head for the lockers!"

Hoots and catcalls rippled through the cockpit of Buckshot Two as they put Ross Island in the rearview mirror and headed out over the Ross Sea.

Once they were out of range of the Gladiator surface-to-air missiles they would loop around and head back toward their covert staging area in the Falkland Islands.

WILLIAMS FIELD

The concussion waves had left Capt. Fyodor Tupelov dazed, and he tried without success to regain his balance. But then Buckshot Three roared overhead, unloading its weapons of destruction and causing the earth to quake once again with the unrelenting *WHAM!-WHAM!-WHAM!-WHAM!* of its Mark 84 bombs. The rolling thunder of death ripped through the air field anew, and tears filled Tupelov's eyes as he saw some of his comrades, in desperation, hit their ejection seats in a vain gamble to avoid the bomb path. Their chutes had barely opened when the concussion waves swatted them aside like so many mosquitoes.

At that moment, Tupelov's primal instincts gained supremacy over his pilot training, for his consciousness was consumed with a single, compelling thought—survival. His Fulcrum was on the periphery of the field, and miraculously it had remained unharmed, as if in the eye of a hurricane. With wobbly legs and arms, he climbed up the ladder and into the cockpit, applying the throttles even before he'd dropped the canopy and plugged in his umbilicals.

Another volley of black darts rained down with their devastating *WHAM!-WHAM!-WHAM!-WHAM!* as Tupelov aligned his Fulcrum with the center of the jerry-rigged airstrip of ice. Then he secured his canopy and shoved the throttles into afterburner to start his takeoff roll.

BUCKSHOT FIVE

The copilot of Buckshot Five was so engrossed in his instruments during the bomb run that he failed to notice a white, feathery dot as it loomed in the distance. It seemed to be suspended in the air, growing larger and larger as the bomber approached. But the copilot remained preoccupied with his instruments. He didn't even observe the object as it whipped by his cockpit window and slammed into the starboard intake nacelles.

After a B-1B crashed from a bird strike during a training mission, the air intakes on all B-1Bs had been strengthened to sustain similar collisions—even from large birds. But no one had counted on a B1-B flying straight into a forty-four-pound wandering albatross.

Buckshot Five's starboard engines choked off as the remains of the giant bird careened into the turbine blades, breaking them apart and sending them through the underside of the wing like shrapnel—

slicing wires and hydraulic lines until they were like the entrails of
a butchered steer.

With half its power lost and the heavy wingload of ordnance
pulling it down, Buckshot Five began to sink in the air. To compensate, the pilot tried to extend the wings to provide greater lift. The
port wing responded, but with its hydraulics gone, the starboard
wing became locked in its swept-back position—just as the cables
and hydraulics that governed the rudder were severed. Controls
frozen, the giant bomber fell into a flat spin, pinwheeling down
toward Williams Field.

WILLIAMS FIELD

Fyodor Tupelov was halfway through his takeoff roll when he spied
a black boomerang spiraling down in an arc toward his makeshift
runway. As it grew larger and larger in his canopy view, Tupelov
thought he saw four tiny chutes deploying—but then the nose of his
Fulcrum lifted up to block his vision. Once free of the ground, he put
the Fulcrum on its tail and prayed he would get clear of the giant
boomerang before it impacted beneath him.

They were the most frightening seven seconds of his life.

Then his aircraft shimmied crazily in the air—buffeted by the
giant concussion wave created when the B-1B and its ordnance load
detonated below. For a moment he thought he'd lost it, but as his
altitude increased, the buffeting slackened, and soon his adrenaline-
charged mind was savoring the safety of his perch in the air. Four
thousand meters up he killed the afterburner, pulled back on the
stick, and executed a quarter-roll. Directly below him he could see
a string of little flashes as they tore across the ice and into the
bunkers.

His consciousness was still coping with the shock when he saw a
jigging pinpoint of light at the end of a smoke trail rising up toward
him. "Damn! My own people are shooting at me!" He activated his
IFF (Identification Friend or Foe) transponder and kept the smoke
trail in view. As it came closer he screamed, "Damn you fools! You
are going to kill me!" He was about to take evasive action when it
veered off and waggled a bit before exploding harmlessly. Tupelov
gasped. How much strain could one person take? He had to be
dreaming this nightmare. It couldn't be real . . . could it? He had to
find out, so he toggled his mike switch. "Leopard Base, Leopard

Base, this is Sable One! You people almost shot me down!"

Static. "Sorry, Sable One. We did not think any friendly aircraft were airborne. It was your own fault for getting shot at. You were not squawking your IFF. You made us waste one of the few missiles we had left."

"Never mind your precious missiles! They looked useless to me. . . . But forget that. Vector me to an incoming American bomber! I want to smash those bastards!"

"Wait one, Sable One. . . ."

There seemed to be an interminable pause as Tupelov banked around over Williams Field. Again, another strip of bursts peppered the tarmac. "Dear God," he whimpered, "there is going to be nothing left." His fear had completely evaporated now, replaced by a blinding, vengeful anger. What was keeping the ground controllers so long? "Come on, Leopard Base! Give me a damned target!"

"All right, Sable One, listen carefully. You are to come to bearing three-zero-three. The *Tbilisi* is under attack. They are requesting any air cover we can give them. They are five hundred twenty kilometers out in the Ross Sea. Squawk your IFF on this same frequency, but voice communications are on three-nine-three-two-point-seven kilohertz. Move out fast. Do you have enough fuel?"

"Roger, I have drop-tanks. But what about the bombers? They are still—"

Static. "Forget the bombers, Sable One! The airfield is finished! If we are to have any chance at all, we must save that carrier! You have your orders! Is that understood?"

Tupelov winced as still another strip of flashes raced across Williams Field. With his guts turning over, the pilot growled, "Roger, Leopard Base. . . . Sable One will comply. Out."

Blind with fury, Tupelov put the Fulcrum on a vector of three-zero-three and cut in his afterburners, sending the twin-tailed fighter into supersonic flight over the Ross Sea.

18

· ·

WHITE FEATHER

THE AURORA

In the backseat of the flying black manta ray, Maj. Thomas "Pretty Boy" Floyd remained intently focused on his multifunction display, while his pilot—Lt. Col. Felix "Catman" Griggs—flew the monotonous search grids over the Ross Sea. Theirs was one of three Aurora spy planes looking for the Russian supercarrier with their passive video and infrared sensors—for to use their radars would reveal their presence.

With its 120,000-foot ceiling and its Mach 5 speed, the Aurora could easily outrun or outclimb anything the *Tbilisi* could throw at it—even though the Aurora was now cruising at 53,000 feet, at Mach 0.9, which was within the realm of a Soviet Su-27 Flanker's flight envelope. Pretty Boy was hopeful that the Aurora's stealth characteristics and its current subsonic speed would keep them concealed from the *Tbilisi*'s battle group.

Catman and Pretty Boy had just crossed over into another search grid when some small hash-mark images started appearing on the backseater's screen. "Keep on this bearing, Catman," he ordered. "I've got something."

More hash marks showed themselves. Then another image, larger than the others, was picked up by the infrared scanner, which was a kind of rectangle . . . and it was followed by a second, even bigger rectangle. Pretty Boy quickly switched on the video camera and zoomed in on the larger rectangle.

There was no mistaking what it was.

"Well, well, well . . . lookee what we got *heah.*"

"What's the word, Pretty Boy?" asked Griggs.

"We got ourselves one U.S.-government-certified Russkie flattop right under our ass. . . . I'm sending down the video, so be prepared to scat if they get a fix on our emission."

"No problem," said Griggs. "I'll just climb till we're out of reach.

290

Now that we got 'em pegged, we ain't lettin' go."

"Roger that," replied Floyd. "Sending down video now."

THE USS *VINCENNES*

The large, futuristic Combat Information Center of the *Vincennes* was a scene of nervous exhaustion, recently charged with a dose of cautious optimism. The ship had been at general quarters for a prolonged period, and the fatigue of the young men hunched over their sensor displays was clearly evidenced by the dark circles under their eyes—circles dark enough to be seen even in the low blue light of the CIC chamber.

The ship's captain, David Erickson, and Marine Lt. Gen. Myron Tharp were sitting at their stations in front of the large display screens. They were also tired from sleep deprivation and the omnipresent tension. Tharp knew the *Tbilisi* would be somewhere in the Ross Sea, within range of the fighter cover based at Williams Field, so Tharp had held Task Force Beowulf back— well out of range of the Mainstay radar planes and the *Tbilisi*'s own Antonov-26 airborne radar platforms. But now Beowulf had kicked off, and the initial word from the Army team on the ground was that the runways were destroyed and the Soviet planes were stuck on the ground. But Tharp didn't know if a few, or more than a few, of the Russian aircraft might get airborne before the B-1Bs arrived, so he wanted to press home the attack on the *Tbilisi* while the Soviets were still grounded and in disarray. But in order to press the attack, they had to find the supercarrier first. In the meantime—in one of the ironies of combat—there really wasn't much for the head honchos to do. (Sir Bernard Law Montgomery had slept during the opening phase of the Battle of El Alamein, because he'd given his subordinates a detailed battle plan to follow. Monty felt there was little to be gained by staying awake. Better to be fresh in the morning to take charge of the situation.) So Tharp and Erickson sat in front of the big screens and waited impatiently while the damned spy planes tried to rustle up the damned target.

Aircraft and crews on the *Carl Vinson,* the *Eisenhower,* and the *Theodore Roosevelt* couldn't be wound any tighter, and this concerned Tharp—for he knew it was impossible to keep his troops on a razor's edge indefinitely.

A steward appeared, and Captain Erickson asked, "More coffee, General?"

Tharp was wearing his Marine utility uniform, and as he leaned back in the swivel chair the diminutive general's feet barely touched the deck. He took off his glasses to rub his eyes, then tapped the cup resting on the console and said, "Sure . . . why not? My system can no longer handle the absence of caffeine." The steward poured the coffee into the cup emblazoned with the USS *Vincennes* emblem. Tharp took a sip and said in reflection, "You know, David, I knew a gunnery sergeant once who went on a bender and drank eleven Irish coffees in a row. Can you imagine? Eleven Irish coffees. He told me he went to bed totally drunk on his ass, and try as he might, he couldn't fall alseep. Said it was the worst night of his life. Went clean and sober after that."

Erickson laughed a giddy, high-strung laugh—the kind of giggle that comes from someone who is severely fatigued. "A little Irish whiskey would go down pretty well now, sir. I think we could all use a shot . . . or two." In a nervous habit, the captain reached up to the crown of his sandy hair and twirled his ever-present cowlick around his finger while contemplating the Marine three-star sitting next to him. Erickson hadn't quite figured this guy Tharp out yet. He was soft-spoken but inflexible. Approachable yet remote. And he fired off zingers when you least expected them.

The tactical action officer sitting at the captain's elbow snapped upright in his chair and clamped the headphones tight against his ears. "Contact, Captain! . . . Coming in from the Aurora . . . receiving downlink signal now . . . on screen."

There was a flutter on the picture in front of Captain Erickson as the symbology of the tactical display was replaced with a hazy picture showing one big and one small rectangle with two small hash marks nearby. A ripple of murmurs went through CIC as Erickson whispered, "Sonofabitch, look at that . . . ," and he fumbled with his own headset.

"Position?" demanded Tharp.

"The Aurora's GPS position will be superimposed on the screen in just a sec. . . . There it is now, sir."

Erickson punched a button on his console and the map on a neighboring screen zoomed out, showing the entire Ross Sea and the locations of the *Vinson, Eisenhower,* and *Roosevelt* lurking beyond, in the southernmost waters of the Pacific. He rolled his controller ball, and a cursor danced across the screen as he guided it to the *Tbilisi*'s position. The three American carrier battle groups were outside the periphery of the Ross Sea, spread out in an arc. The *Eisenhower* was the closest to the *Tbilisi,* then the *Roosevelt,* with the *Vinson* the farthest away.

"Open the secure voice channel to Admiral Rumley on the *Vinson,* " Tharp ordered. The Marine general heard bleeps and buzzes through his earphones before the TAO said, "Open, sir."

"Beowulf One, this is Beowulf Two," said Tharp, his speech having lost much of its softness. "Have you got it on your screen?"

"I'll say we do, Beowulf Two." The booming baritone voice of Hobart Rumley was unmistakable, even through the fuzz of the secure voice scrambler.

"All right, Beowulf One," Tharp said urgently, "listen to me. Launch the strike force of all three carriers immediately, per the contingency plans. Because of the distance, we'll have to engage in sequence—*Eisenhower* first, then *Roosevelt,* then *Vinson.* Order them to launch immediately."

There was a pause on the other end. "Well, Beowulf Two, I don't know about that. I think we should move all our groups in closer and launch a massed strike force."

"Massing your forces is fine when you've got the luxury of time, Admiral, but we have to hit the *Tbilisi* while we know the ground-based aircraft at McMurdo are bottled up on the ground. The B-1 bombers are still"—Tharp looked at the chronometer on his console—"twenty-two minutes out from hitting Williams Field, and we don't know how that will turn out. We've got to hit our prime target now. Otherwise we may be fighting off a flock of Backfire bombers."

There was the sound of a throat clearing. "Well . . . I dunno, Myron . . . I still think maybe we should—"

The improbable warrior in the Marine uniform cut through his superior's hesitation and snapped, "Bart, just *do it.* "

THE USS *CARL VINSON*

The wind was blowing light sheets of rain across the flight deck of the *Carl Vinson* as Lt. Michael "Blackjack" Pershing felt the massive ninety-thousand-ton carrier turn into the wind. The deck crewman—wearing a green jersey over his foul-weather snowsuit—gave Blackjack the signal for an upcoming takeoff as the loudspeakers blared, *"Launch strike aircraft! Launch strike aircraft! This is no drill!"*

Blackjack's F/A-18 Hornet was in the saddle of catapult number two. He waited until a flock of crewmen had checked the catapult seam for ice, then watched them scurry out of the way. He got the signal and advanced the throttles to full military power. On catapult number one was Cmdr. George "Bossman" Barstow, wearing his distinctive black crash helmet with the gold lightning bolts. Due to a last-minute shuffle in the flight plan, Blackjack was going into battle as Commander Barstow's wingman.

The young Texan watched Bossman's Hornet roar off catapult one, and like a robot, Blackjack cut in his own afterburners to get the fighter airborne with its heavy load of ordnance and fuel. The green light came on inside the bubble canopy sticking out of the flight deck. Blackjack tensed his neck muscles and put his helmet against the headrest, while silently imploring God to keep his airplane from moving. He begged the Almighty for a broken catapult cable, a flamed-out engine, a deadlined radar, something, anything to let him stand down from the mission and retreat to the safety of the decks below.

God hears all prayers, of course, but to some His answer is simply, "No."

The catapult engaged to heave the Hornet into the air above the frothy sea.

Never in his life had Blackjack been seized by such a paroxysm of naked fear.

THE *TBILISI*

In the CIC chamber of the Russian supercarrier, *Vitse*-Adm. Gavriil Strekalov and Capt. Dmitri Vaslov were leaning over the projection table, which was a horizontal version of the vertical display screen found on the American Aegis cruiser *Vincennes*. The symbology denoting the *Tbilisi* and the antisubmarine carrier *Minsk* was pictured in the middle of the screen. Strekalov had arranged twenty-six of his escort vessels in two concentric rings, and placed the carriers in the center—along with a couple of frigates for some help with close-in defense. The outer ring of escorts had a radius of thirty kilometers from the carriers, the inner ring a radius of ten kilometers.

The diminutive but muscular admiral was standing on a footstool so he could view the screen properly. The tall, blond Captain Vaslov needed no such assistance.

The admiral had just brought the task force to general quarters in response to the flash message from the air defense command post at Scott Base, announcing that Leopard Base was under attack. Strekalov was discussing it with Captain Vaslov when a signalman flew through the hatchway waving a piece of teletype paper. "Captain! Another message from Leopard Base!"

Vaslov grabbed the paper, and together he and Strekalov read it.

```
AIRFIELD INOPERATIVE.
UNABLE TO LAUNCH AIRCRAFT.
INCOMING BOGEYS IDENTIFIED AS AMERICAN
B-1 BOMBER FORCE.
REQUEST ASSISTANCE OF ALL INTERCEPTOR
AIRCRAFT YOU CAN SPARE.
NEED IMMEDIATE.
SPEED ESSENTIAL.
                    AIR DEFENSE COMMANDER
                            LEOPARD BASE
```

Vaslov was the first to find his voice. " 'Airfield inoperative' . . . 'unable to launch.' . . . My God, Admiral, how could that happen? They have five runways and more than two hundred aircraft. They said we would have an impregnable shield—"

Strekalov held up a hand and curtly said, "Belay that, Dmitri. We have to take Leopard Base at their word." The stocky admiral gripped the side of the table screen as he wrestled with the problem.

While Strekalov and Vaslov were absorbed with the situation at hand, a *michman* stationed at the electronic warfare console picked up something on his scanner. He put the signal on his oscilloscope and saw a definite spike in the Juliet band of the frequency spectrum. It wasn't an intermittent transmission, but steady. Hmmm. That was unusual. He tried to get a bearing on the source; it seemed to originate from somewhere overhead. He put the signal on the speaker and heard nothing but a hiss. Puzzled, he called his *starshiy* supervisor for a consultation, and after some discussion they decided to check with the radar officer. But the radar officer said he had no bogeys on his screen. Perplexed, they discussed it some more between themselves, and decided it must be some kind of satellite emission.

Too bad they didn't have a video monitor wired into the receiver. They could have seen themselves on TV . . . live.

"We must assist our comrades," said the admiral. "Equip Flanker Squadrons Two and Four with air defense weapons and dispatch them, along with two tankers, to Leopard Base at once."

"But Admiral," Vaslov protested, "the blanket of ground-based air cover we were counting on for protection of the *Tbilisi* may be destroyed before our Flankers get there. If we send them Squadrons Two and Four, we will be stripping part of our own defenses. We have our own task force to think of, Admiral."

Strekalov drummed his fingers on the lip of the table screen. Captain Vaslov had a point, but if the Flankers went to afterburner, they might make it in time to save part of the Leopard Base aircraft. Then again, they might not—and the *Tbilisi*'s defenses would be perilously weakened. Gavriil Strekalov was wrestling with this dilemma when his eyes fell on the message again, causing him to reread the words:

NEED IMMEDIATE.
SPEED ESSENTIAL.

Strekalov simply could not refuse such an eloquent plea for help. "Dispatch Squadrons Two and Four to assist Leopard Base."

"But, Admiral—"

"*Launch* them, Dmitri!"

THE *EISENHOWER* STRIKE FORCE OVER THE ROSS SEA

In the rear compartment of the EA-6B Prowler aircraft, two warriors were honing their invisible sabers in preparation for the upcoming fight on the electronic battlefield. With the Mainstay radar planes shot down, the air strike force of the *Eisenhower* battle group had hastily assembled and was now approaching its quarry with a succulent advantage provided by the Aurora spy plane: the Americans knew the location of the *Tbilisi,* but the Russians didn't know the strike force was inbound. The *Eisenhower* group would go in first, to be followed by the groups from the *Roosevelt* and the *Carl Vinson.*

The Beowulf contingency plan called for the strike force to maintain total electronic silence as the leading elements approached the *Tbilisi*'s own Antonov-26 airborne radar platforms. When they reached the fringe of the Soviet radar coverage, the Americans would "unmask" by illuminating their own E-2C Hawkeye radar aircraft in order to peg the whereabouts of the *Tbilisi*'s combat air patrol. The F-14 Tomcat interceptors would then sprint forward at supersonic speed to engage the patrolling Sukhoi-27 Flankers with their long-range Phoenix missiles, which had a range of 120 miles. While the Soviet fighters were coping with the volley of Phoenix missiles, the Prowlers would jam the *Tbilisi*'s airborne radar while a squadron of ten A-6 Intruders moved in behind the F-14 screen and launched their sea-skimming Harpoon missiles at a standoff distance. As the Soviet escort vessels were grappling with the Harpoons, the strike force of the F/A-18 Hornets would converge on the *Tbilisi* from different points on the compass, trying to penetrate the cordon of escorts and deliver a deathblow to the Russian carrier with their laser-guided bomb loads.

A nice plan on paper, but twenty-eight escort vessels were a heavy gauntlet to run . . . a heavy gauntlet, indeed.

The senior electronic warfare officer in the backseat of the Prowler monitored the intensity of the Russian radar signals and figured it was time. He hit his mike switch and said, "Sugar Cube to Hummers One and Two. We're close enough. Light 'em up, boys! Let's smoke 'em!"

In the airspace north and west of the *Tbilisi,* the electronic spectrum sizzled and popped as two Hawkeye radar planes and six F-14 Tomcats activated their radars to probe the ether. Once the Tomcats established their targeting data links with the Hawkeyes, they went to supersonic for the high-speed run to their launch points.

THE *TBILISI*

"Emission detection!" yelled the electronic warfare *michman* in the CIC chamber. "Two emission contacts, bearing three-four-nine and two-seven-two."

"Identification?" queried Captain Vaslov.

The *michman* ran his fingers over the console. "American E-2C Hawkeyes, Captain!"

"Contact!" barked the radar *michman*. "Bogeys . . . bearing three-five-one . . . two bogeys . . . three . . . speed approaching Mach two, range five hundred forty kilometers. Altitude eleven thousand meters. Second contact! . . . Two bogeys . . . three . . . also at supersonic. Bearing two-seven-eight. Altitude nine-five hundred meters."

Admiral Strekalov ran a hand across his bristly white-sidewall haircut. There was a dryness in his throat that came from the bitter realization that he had made the wrong decision. His task force was now under attack, and half of his air cover was en route to McMurdo Sound to defend Williams Field. Involuntarily he swallowed and said, "You were correct, Dmitri. . . . I was wrong. Order Flanker Squadrons Two and Four to return at maximum speed. Launch the remainder of Squadron One and have them join their comrades on combat air patrol. Vector the CAP toward the incoming bogeys. Try to splash their radar aircraft. They will undoubtedly try to blind ours. Then launch Squadron Three and hold them overhead in reserve."

"Squadrons Two and Four will have to refuel in midair before returning on afterburner, Admiral," said Vaslov grimly.

"Jamming!" cried the electronic warfare *michman*. "Identification, probable American Prowler aircraft."

"And, Dmitri, radio Leopard Base. Tell them *we* are under attack and need all the air support *they* can spare!"

As Captain Vaslov was barking orders, Strekalov leaned over the table and watched the bogeys as they advanced toward the center of the projection screen. Their symbology kept disappearing and reappearing as the *Tbilisi*'s battle-management computer tried to cope and sift through the jammed radar inputs. A drop of perspiration trickled off the end of Strekalov's nose and fell directly onto one of the bogey triangles, which seemed to spawn a flurry of smaller triangles.

"Missile separation from the bandits!" yelled the radar officer. "They are firing their weapons at our air patrol!"

THE *EISENHOWER* STRIKE FORCE

There was a flurry of chatter between the backseat radar intercept officers in the F-14s and the controllers aboard the E-2C Hawkeyes as they prioritized targets for the long-range Phoenix missiles. One by one the missiles were released and climbed on their intercept arc.

On the Hawkeye radar plane designated Hummer Two, the air-strike commander watched in fascination as the blips of the Phoenix missiles approached the Soviet Flankers of the combat air patrol. Some of the Russian fighters started diving or turning, while others began jinking and shooting off chaff. The situation wouldn't get any better than this, mused the strike commander. Now was the time. "Have the Intruder squadron move forward and let go with their Harpoons."

"Roger, sir." Two blips on the screen merged, and then disappeared into some fuzz. "Splashed our first bandit, sir!"

The squadron of A-6 Intruders advanced—five aircraft approaching the *Tbilisi* from the north, and five from the west. Each group was accompanied by a Prowler and covered by the F-14s. The Intruders could only travel at subsonic speed—635 mph—so it took some twenty minutes for them to advance to their launch points, about a hundred miles from the *Tbilisi*.

As the bombardiers on the A-6s received target information from the controllers on board the E-2C Hawkeyes, they "dumped" the data into the Harpoons' guidance systems. Once in range, the Intruders unloaded four Harpoons apiece and then scooted away from the Russian escort vessels.

Forty Harpoons descended from their drop points at seventeen thousand feet and continued down until they were almost caressing the surface of the ocean. Three missiles malfunctioned and crashed into the sea, but the remaining Harpoons engaged their programmed flight plan to guide them toward the general direction of the *Tbilisi*'s battle group. At a predetermined point their active radars would come alive and scan the airspace for the radar signatures of their respective targets. Half of the Harpoons were programmed to search out and destroy the escort vessels—to cut a path for the incoming Hornets—and half were programmed to seek out the huge and unmistakable radar signature of the Soviet supercarrier inside the inner ring.

THE *TBILISI*

"Six Flankers down!" cried the radar *michman.* "*Seven* down! . . . Second An-26 down! We are now blind on airborne radar! Switching to ship radar network. . . . Missile separation on second wave of bandits! They are descending at subsonic speed . . . probably Harpoon missiles. . . . Good God . . . the count is . . . twenty-eight . . . twenty-nine missiles . . . still increasing . . . they will reach outer ring of escorts in six minutes. . . . Bandits that launched are turning back. We splashed two before they got away. . . . Oh, no . . . what is *this?*" The *michman*'s voice went up an octave. "More bogeys." He was trembling now. "Third wave of bogeys approaching—in excess of Mach one at seven thousand meters altitude. Range two hundred thirty kilometers. Some are starting to descend."

Captain Vaslov was finding it difficult to keep track of all the symbology prancing across the screen. The Russian captain had started the day with four Flanker squadrons of twelve aircraft each. Over half of Squadron One had just been blasted into the sea trying to intercept the Intruders, while Squadron Three remained in reserve close-in to the *Tbilisi.* And as for Squadrons Two and Four—he guessed they were on their way back. With the An-26 radar planes blown out of the sky, they were no longer pictured on the screen. "Flanker Squadrons Two and Four should be en route back from McMurdo, Admiral. But I estimate they will not make it in time."

"They are sending their fighter-bombers in behind their Harpoon missiles," said Strekalov as he pointed at various triangles on the table screen. "Engage battle-management computer to full automatic, and notify all ships to activate and fire at will with their extended-range and close-in weapons systems. And launch our two remaining An-26 aircraft. We must have airborne radar."

"Get the An-26 aircraft aloft," ordered Captain Vaslov.

The signalman shot through the hatch. "Captain! Another message."

Vaslov grabbed it and slapped it on the table screen so that he and Strekalov could read it.

AIRFIELD AND AIRCRAFT AT LEOPARD
BASE DESTROYED.

ONE FIGHTER ABLE TO GET AIRBORNE.
SENDING HIM TO YOU. SQUAWKING IFF ON TRANSPONDER.
WILL COMMUNICATE ON 3932.7 KILOHERTZ.
SAVE YOURSELVES.

AIR COMMANDER
LEOPARD BASE

"Admiral! Outer ring of escorts engaging!"

THE *ADMIRAL TRIBUTS*

When the "Cross Sword" radar on the *Admiral Tributs*—an *Udaloy*-class guided-missile destroyer—picked up five incoming Harpoons, the battle-management computer quickly assigned a target priority and antiair weapon for each threat. The Harpoons were twelve miles away when the deck of the *Tributs* lit up like a Fourth of July pyrotechnic display, shooting off five SA-N-9 missiles into the air—straight up—out of the ship's vertical launcher. At an altitude of three kilometers, the missiles nosed over as the launcher-based radar painted the assigned sector of airspace with its beam. Once their quarry was pegged, the missiles dashed down to intercept.

Two of the SA-N-9s found their mark and splashed the American antiship missiles.

Three missed, and the Harpoons headed toward the *Tributs.*

Clouds of chaff blossomed into the air as the *Tributs* turned its stern toward the incoming threat.

One Harpoon took the chaff bait and augered into the sea.

One sailed past, continuing on toward the inner circle.

But the captain of the *Tributs* had made a mistake. He'd turned the vessel too sharply, putting the chaff cloud between the final Harpoon and his ship's close-in defense radar. This blinded the ship's own defensive radar as the Harpoon flew through the chaff and rammed into the *Tributs*'s fantail.

THE *TBILISI*

"*Tributs* and *Kalinin* on the outer ring are hit, Captain!"

There was a flurry of static on the projection image as the battle-management computer raced to keep track of the rapidly changing scene of combat at sea.

"Twenty . . . twenty-one of the incoming Harpoons are down," announced the radar officer.

The images on the screen seemed like some kind of extraordinary fantasy . . . but this was no fantasy. It was reality. Brutal reality.

"Sixteen missiles are approaching the second ring now."

Vaslov and Admiral Strekalov held their collective breath as the wave of Harpoons converged on the inner ring, and once again the screen became laced with static as another volley of antiair missiles and chaff rockets were released . . . then the screen cleared.

"*Gromkiy* and *Zadorniy* on the inner ring are hit, Captain!"

"Five Harpoons incoming on *Tbilisi!*"

Vaslov shouted, "Fire control, engage at will!"

"Aye, Captain!"

The guidance systems of the Harpoons had been instructed to look for a giant radar signature, and the seeker heads in two of the incoming Harpoons were suckered away by the antisubmarine carrier *Minsk*—but the other three refused to be faked out and homed in on the massive reflection of the *Tbilisi.* As they rushed forward, a host of SA-N-9 missiles erupted along the perimeter of the supercarrier's flight deck and raced out to greet them, but only two connected to blast the incoming missiles into the sea. A final Harpoon made it through—refusing to be decoyed by the *Minsk* or the chaff cloud blooming in the *Tbilisi*'s wake. It rushed forward and started to rise up in a terminal pop-up maneuver to evade the ship's close-in weapons systems.

The Harpoon was picked up by the "Bass Tilt" fire-control radar that was wired into a six-barreled AK-630 Gatling-style gun mounted on the catwalk at the corner of the flight deck. With a sound that was more like a *whrrrrrrrrr!* than a *rat-tat-tat-tat-tat!*, the 30-mm gun elevated its muzzle and spewed out its heavy depleted uranium bullets at a rate of three thousand rounds per minute. On the rear end of each bullet was a facing of aluminum foil that reflected the signal of the radar beam back to the Bass Tilt antenna. The fire-control computer took the bullet stream and the trajectory of the Harpoon, and married the two together about 388 meters from the port side of the ship—just as the missile was starting to rise for its terminal maneuver.

Although the Harpoon disintegrated, the ensuing fireball of exploding fuel and five-hundred-pound warhead was still moving at six hundred miles an hour, causing it to sail over the *Tbilisi* and impact in the sea off the starboard side of the ship with a distinct *psssssssssssst!* And as it passed over the carrier, drips and drabs of burning propellant fell onto the flight deck, causing the senior damage-control *michman* to sound the fire-alarm klaxon. The fire truck rolled out from its parking spot near the conning tower, siren and lights blaring, and came to a halt in front of the glowing embers, which looked like a string of three small campfires. A crewman wearing a fire suit jumped off the truck and ran forward with an extinguisher, quickly dispatching the campfires with a *squirt-squirt-squirt* from the cylinder.

And that was it.

"The *Minsk* has sustained a hit . . . minor damage on aft flight deck. . . . *Letuchiy,* on the inner ring, was also hit by a Harpoon, Captain," said the damage-control officer. "Our close-in gun stopped the last Harpoon from impacting the *Tbilisi.* Only minor blast burns on the hull and flight deck."

Vaslov exhaled while Admiral Strekalov pulled out a handkerchief and wiped his face.

"Good fortune smiled on us, Admiral," Vaslov observed.

"Indeed, Dmitri. Indeed."

"Bandits approaching outer ring!" barked the radar officer. "High-low profile. Probably fighter-bombers and escorts for air cover."

"How many Flankers do we still have in the air with armaments?" asked Strekalov.

The air officer checked his tote board. "Seventeen, Admiral. Twelve in Squadron Three, which has been held in reserve, and five remaining from the Squadron One combat air patrol. Some of them have expended their missiles attacking the bandits."

"Divide those with weapons equally and vector them to the two groups of incoming bandits. Position them behind the *outer* ring of defenses. Let the ships engage both high- and low-level bandits first. Then have the Flankers dive on the low-level bandits with everything they've got. Understood?"

The air officer nodded. "Understood, Admiral."

As Strekalov and Captain Vaslov returned their attention to the screen, the bandits advanced to within twenty kilometers of the outer ring. Shortly thereafter, the symbology representing the SAM missiles started to appear, and the triangles denoting the high-level American escorts started weaving and jinking to evade, filling the air with jammers and chaff to confuse the incoming SAMs. Five of twenty-two bandits were splashed—three high, two low—and the remainder pressed on past the outer ring of ships.

"Now!" ordered the admiral. "Have our Flankers engage the bandits now!"

The Flankers dove and loosed their radar-guided AA-10 and Aphid heat-seeking missiles, wreaking havoc on the low-level strike force. Five of the low-level Hornets were downed. Five pressed on.

But the toll of cutting the enemy low-level strike force by half was great. Seven Soviet Flankers were blasted out of the air by the American fighter escorts.

Tension increased in CIC again as Strekalov ordered, "Inner ring, engage all bandits! But for God's sake, do not shoot down any friendly aircraft. We need every last one."

"Aye, Admiral!"

Vaslov and Strekalov turned grimly silent as another flurry of missiles went up from the inner ring of ships—and the incoming blips became erratic with their evasive maneuvers. Three more Hornets impacted into the sea, but two made it past the inner gauntlet and got the *Tbilisi* in their sights to begin climbing for the bomb run.

"They are climbing for an air strike!" bellowed Vaslov. "Engage surface-to-air missiles!"

Four SA-N-9 missiles sailed out of their vertical launch tubes.

The pilot of the first Hornet was concentrating too hard on lining up his bomb release and was too slow on the chaff trigger. As a result, the crew in the *Tbilisi*'s flight bridge saw a spectacular air blast—but only one.

The second Hornet evaded the missiles, and everyone in the tower held their breath as the American fighter rose, then arced over and released a slick of bombs that seemed to be aimed directly at them. Scrotums tightened across the deck as they watched the bombs continue down, down, down . . . and past them, into the sea, where they exploded, sending up a bevy of harmless geysers.

The Hornet pilot had released too late, and as he tried to break away, two more SA-N-9 missiles rose up from the *Tbilisi* and cut him down.

In the CIC chamber, Strekalov heard a rumble and felt a vibration. He was sure the ship had been hit.

"They missed!" cried the damage-control officer. "They missed! The bombs fell into the sea!"

Cheers went up through CIC as the admiral and the captain sagged against each other.

THE *VINCENNES*

Capt. David Erickson was somber as he watched the big display screen and said, "Looks like three of their escorts are out of action, General. The *Minsk* may have suffered some damage . . . but no hits scored on the *Tbilisi.* "

Myron Tharp did not acknowledge Erickson's observations immediately. He could plainly see the Russian supercarrier on the screen, still cruising along. "The *Roosevelt* strike force should be arriving on the scene shortly," he said softly—hoping he had made the right decision . . . and fearful that Hobart Rumley, of all people, might have been right after all.

THE *TBILISI*

"Oh, no," moaned the radar officer. "*More* bogeys inbound. Coming in at supersonic—again at eleven thousand meters. I am afraid it is another interceptor sweep."

Captain Vaslov wiped his face on his uniform sleeve. "We have ten Flankers left overhead, Admiral. Out of fuel, and weapons expended." He tapped the display. "Squadrons Two and Four have almost returned from McMurdo. Should we vector them to the incoming bogeys?"

Strekalov raised a hand. "No, Dmitri . . . no. We know their tactics now." The little admiral's mind raced. "No . . . this is what we will do. The high-level bogeys are undoubtedly their long-range F-14 interceptors again. Recover the Flankers overhead for rearming and refueling. Move our radar aircraft and Squadrons Two and Four to the east, out of range of the F-14s, but engage the F-14s with surface-to-air missiles to keep them at bay. We will deal with the Harpoon missiles as before, and hope for the best. When the American bomber strike force passes through the outer ring, we will bring Squadrons Two and Four in to attack as we did before."

Captain Vaslov nodded. "Very well, Admiral."

"Tactical officer, bring the escorts in tighter to close up the gaps in the rings."

"Aye, Admiral."

They had survived once. Perhaps they could survive again.

MIDAIR REFUELING OVER THE ROSS SEA

When a fighter pilot makes the progression from green-nosed cadet to combat aviator, he will, quite probably, encounter at some point along the way a phenomenon known as "the Fear." Not a generic phobia one might have of, say, spiders, or heights, or water—but a paralytic seizure of such abject terror that it can turn a grown man into a crying waif. The Fear stems from some aspect of flying that penetrates to the soul of a pilot and shoves him (or her) roughly into the face of death with such horrifying clarity that a pilot's ability to perform in the air is broken. The Fear can surface at any time—the night before a solo, while flying formation at night, or during the initial aerobatic experience.

For naval aviators, the opportunities to experience the Fear were vast—such as a cadet's first carrier landing. And if not there, it can be found lurking in the black nothingness of a *night* carrier landing.

For Lt. Michael "Blackjack" Pershing, the Fear had always been a myth. When he saw members of his flight-school class wash out after routine check rides, or when they refused to set down on that first carrier landing, Blackjack was more than a little contemptuous. He was such a natural in the air that the Fear had never entered his consciousness, and he had little patience for those who showed the white feather and couldn't stomach the rigors of naval aviation. He was the kind of flier who thought night carrier landings were fun—in a masochistic sort of way.

But here, now, as his F/A-18 Hornet drank jet fuel from a KA-6B tanker, the Fear had finally caught up with Blackjack Pershing. The image of combat—of being shot at, of missiles coming at him—was so frightening that his sensory nerves were almost numb. His throat was constricted, and his dry mouth was filled with the bitter taste of bile. Aerobatic flying had always been easy for him. A breeze. A piece of cake. But this . . . he could not swallow the thought of someone shooting at him . . . of dying.

The Fear enveloped him like a cloak.

The shuttlecock refueling cone was yanked off the Hornet's intake tube and, like a robot, Blackjack retracted the tube into the fuselage. Then, as if he were on some type of automatic pilot, he veered off and took his position on Bossman Barstow's right wing.

"Rough Rider Squadron, this is Leader." Blackjack knew Boss-man's distinctive voice. "Listen up. I've gotten word over the command net that the second strike force from the *Roosevelt* has come up short. The Russian flattop wasn't scratched. We're going in. Execute per mission strike plan. Flights Blue and Green break away. Red, follow me. Leader out."

The twelve Hornets in Rough Rider Squadron were flying in a tight wedge formation. The Blue Flight of four aircraft disengaged from the rear and headed northeast, Green Flight then broke off and continued due east, while Bossman and his Red Flight banked to the southeast. Unlike the previous strikes from the *Eisenhower* and the *Roosevelt,* which had attacked from two points of the compass and had not returned, the Rough Riders of the *Carl Vinson* would be attacking from three.

THE *TBILISI*

Capt. Dmitri Vaslov and *Vitse-* Adm. Gavriil Strekalov were absolutely limp from relief as the last attacking Hornet from the *Theodore Roosevelt* smashed into the sea. Although the CIC was cool, both men's uniforms were moist from sweat.

"Two major attacks, Admiral," said Vaslov, his voice weary from nervous exhaustion. "We have held off two major attacks."

"Perhaps sending Flanker Squadrons Two and Four away for a time was the right thing to do after all," replied the admiral, almost in a daze. "If we can hold out long enough, perhaps Leopard Base can salvage some more fighters and get them aloft. That might stall the Americans—keep them from attempting a landing from the sea until we can fly in more aircraft from Cam Ranh."

"Admiral," called the air officer. "Squadrons Two and Four require refueling and rearmament. I have a half-dozen aircraft approaching critical fuel that must be recovered immediately. Four survivors from Squadrons One and Three have been refitted and are coming up on the elevators now for launch. The other six are still being rearmed."

"Admiral!" shouted the radar officer. "More bogeys inbound. Same flight profile as before. High-level interceptors."

"I must get my aircraft down!" the air officer shouted.

Strekalov covered his face with his hands, pondering what to do.

Recover the fighters and try to rearm and refuel before the bomber force arrived? Keep the fighters aloft to meet the bombers with limited armament, knowing that many of the pilots would have to punch out and fall into the freezing sea to die?

"Where are the tankers we sent with Squadrons Two and Four to McMurdo?"

"Here, Admiral," said Vaslov, as he tapped the table. "Still a hundred seventy kilometers out. The Flankers left them behind when they went to afterburner."

"And the Americans shot down our other two tankers," moaned Strekalov, as he wiped his face with his sopping handkerchief. He contemplated the board and asked, "The damage to the *Minsk* was minor, was it not?"

"*Da,* Admiral," replied Vaslov.

The former weightlifter gripped the edge of the table with his powerful hands . . . and made his decision. "Clear the flight deck and recover the aircraft. Then bring up and launch the Flankers that are ready to go. Refuel and rearm the recovered aircraft with all possible speed. If we have to, we will use the Forger aircraft on board the *Minsk* to assist in intercepting the enemy strike force."

"Aye, Admiral."

The twelve Yak-38 Forgers that operated off the antisubmarine carrier *Minsk* were stubby-winged vertical-takeoff jets. Their more notable features were their limited range, subsonic speed, and short-range armament.

In the frosty air, Flanker after Flanker slammed onto the steel flight deck of the *Tbilisi,* their tailhooks snagging the arresting wires. At a frenetic pace, flight crews hustled the fighters onto the giant elevators and struck them down to the hangar deck below, just as fresh missile loads started coming up from the magazines.

THE MIG-29 FULCRUM

As Capt. Fyodor Tupelov jettisoned his empty external fuel tanks into the Ross Sea, he remembered the parked Candid air-refueling tankers that had been destroyed back at Williams Field. And undoubtedly the Americans had destroyed the airborne tankers as well. So how was he going to make a landfall after drinking so much fuel on afterburner? He didn't know how to land on a carrier—even if the *Tbilisi* was still afloat. Did the carrier have tankers? He hoped so, shuddering at the thought of punching out over the frigid waters below. He had hit the silk once before in combat, and it was not an experience he wished to repeat. Shaking off the thought, he dialed his radio to the naval TAC AIR frequency and keyed his mike. "Sea Leopard One, Sea Leopard One, this is Sable One inbound from Leopard Base. I should be a hundred eighty kilometers southwest of your position at nine thousand meters. Am coming out of afterburner now. Request instructions, over."

"Roger, Sable One. We need your help badly. How many aircraft in your flight, over?"

"Just me, Sea Leopard. I am alone."

"Damn . . . wait one . . . all right, listen to me, Sable One. We have beaten back two major air attacks, and a third is apparently forming up. We are launching four Flankers now, but we must recover the remainder of our own aircraft for refueling and rearmament. I am going to vector you to the incoming strike force when it appears. What is your armament?"

"Air-to-air missiles. Radar-guided A-10s and Aphid heat-seekers."

"Excellent. We only have one radar platform still up, and he is not in your sector. We must rely on the radar of the escort vessels . . . wait . . . I think I have you on screen. . . . Damn! Those American Prowlers and their jammers. Are you squawking IFF?"

"Roger, Sea Leopard."

"We are interrogating you now, Sable One. . . . Yes, we have you now. . . . Sable One, we have incoming Harpoon missiles. If the Americans stay true to form, their strike force will follow the Harpoons in. Stand by for a target assignment . . . and make every shot count. . . . And be alert! F-14 interceptors may be in your area, making a sweep for the strike force."

A red light appeared on Tupelov's panel, and he heard a warble in his headphones from his radar threat receiver—a kind of airborne "fuzz buster." Bitterly he said, "Thank you for that timely warning, Sea Leopard."

AN F-14 TOMCAT FROM THE *CARL VINSON*

On the green tactical information display screen in the backseat of
the Tomcat, Wrangler watched for returns from the interceptor's
powerful AWG-9 radar, which was sweeping the airspace in its
pulse-Doppler search mode. "We got a contact, Sweet Thang. Bearing zero-nine-nine, approaching our beam at an angle. Range one-
one-five miles—or thereabouts."

"Interrogate him," ordered Sweet Thang. "There may still be
some friendlies in the area."

Wrangler hit the switch that sent a radio signal to interrogate the
bogey's IFF system.

"Negative return on IFF," said Wrangler. "I make it a hostile."

"Lock him up and splash it."

The fire-control computer provided Wrangler with the bandit's
heading and altitude, and gave it a target priority of "1" on the TID
screen. "The return is faint. He's coming across our beam almost at
a right angle. . . . I may lose him." The pulse-Doppler search mode
of the AWG-9 radar was blind to targets moving at right angles to
the path of its beam, because right-angle targets eliminated the Doppler shift. "Hold it . . . he's turning into us . . . and he's illuminated
his radar!"

"Take the shot!" ordered Sweet Thang.

Wrangler verified the computer's assignment of an AIM-54D
Phoenix missile to the bandit, then he hit the red LAUNCH button as
he yelled, "Fox one!"

The Phoenix dropped from the belly of the Tomcat, and when its
solid-fuel engine ignited, the missile streaked skyward in an arc. The
missile would climb to 101,000 feet, where it would build up speed
to Mach 3.8 in the thinner atmosphere. The F-14's AWG-9 system
would feed updated information on the target to the Phoenix, and
at the proper point it would commence a downward arc toward its
prey. Once it was close enough, the missile would activate its or-
ganic-terminal homing radar and go in for the kill.

THE MIG-29 FULCRUM

Tupelov scanned the airspace through the bubble canopy, and then
checked his radar screen for a return. The screen showed nothing,
but the Fulcrum's radar only had a range of 110 kilometers. Did an
American F-14 have him locked on or not? And what was keeping

Sea Leopard? *I came all this way for a target, and there's no . . . uh-oh . . . what's that?*

It was barely discernible on the screen, but there it was . . . a tiny blip. Coming down from a high altitude. Tupelov gulped. God, it was moving fast. . . . As the Phoenix activated its terminal acquisition radar, the warble in Tupelov's earphones turned into a screech. It was a missile! And it was locked onto his Fulcrum!

"Sable One, this is Sea Leopard. We have the strike force on screen. Vector to—"

"Not now, Sea Leopard! I am under fire!"

Tupelov forced himself not to panic and to think . . . think . . . *Doppler radar . . . the Americans use Doppler radar. . . .* The blip was screaming down on him.

"Sable One, we need you now!" pleaded the voice in his headphones.

Tupelov put the plea out of his mind and concentrated on the blip. He waited until the last possible instant, then rolled the Fulcrum onto its back and pulled it down in a powered dive while emptying his chaff magazine into the air. He cut in his afterburner and counted to five, then executed a quarter-roll and pulled up sharply into level flight—at what he hoped was a right angle to the F-14's search radar—then he killed the afterburner. He strained his neck to peer over his left shoulder, and saw a flash in the chaff cloud he'd left behind.

THE F-14 TOMCAT

"Splash one bandit!" howled Wrangler. "He tried to evade, but we got him!"

"Awright! Great shooting," said Sweet Thang. "Blackjack should have a clear shot now, if he can make it through the SAMs."

RED FLIGHT, ROUGH RIDER STRIKE FORCE

"Follow me down!" ordered Bossman Barstow, and his Red Flight of four F/A-18 Hornets dove toward the sea. Jazzman and Otter were on Bossman's left wing, Blackjack on the right.

The Fear was consuming Blackjack now, almost freezing his ability to breathe, for he was taking in air by shallow gasps—like a child on the verge of tears.

"My threat board is hot!" said Jazzman.

"Activate jammers!" ordered Bossman.

Unable to cope, Blackjack searched for a lifeline, a raft he could cling to—and he found it in Bossman's wing. Aerobatics . . . he was a Blue Angel again. . . . Everything was fine. . . . *Just stay with Lead . . . stay with Lead. Nothing can happen if you stay with Lead . . . you'll be safe . . . just don't let go.*

"Tally! Escorts ahead! Ready on the chaff!"

THE MIG-29 FULCRUM

The warble in his headphones had faded, telling Fyodor Tupelov he was clear of the F-14's radar. His Fulcrum was now in a shallow afterburner dive toward the outer ring of escorts as he responded to the carrier's plea for help.

"You are on track, Sable One! Four bandits inbound, low on the deck. Shoot them down!"

Tupelov illuminated his radar, and patches of fuzz appeared on his screen. "I have them, Sea Leopard! They are jamming, but I have them. Am engaging. Tell your damned escorts not to shoot at me!"

As the Russian armed his two radar-guided AA-10 missiles, he saw the little fuzzballs on his screen start to fan out.

RED FLIGHT, ROUGH RIDER STRIKE FORCE

"Combat spread!" Bossman barked.

Otter and Jazzman peeled off, and as the four Hornets zipped between two *Krivak*-class frigates of the outer ring, Bossman said to himself, in astonishment, "Damn, no missiles."

He couldn't know the frigates were holding their fire to avoid hitting Tupelov's Fulcrum.

Blackjack was a kind of flying barnacle, for he remained attached to Bossman's wing—unable to cut loose his only lifeline, his only shield against the Fear. So fixated was he by Bossman's wing that he took no notice of Jazzman and Otter as the Russian's AA-10 missiles struck home and blasted his friends into the sea.

THE MIG-29 FULCRUM

"Two bandits down!" screamed Tupelov. "Closing to visual range on two more!" And he armed his Aphid heat-seekers.

"Get them, Sable One! Get them!"

Tupelov sucked in his breath. He had them in sight.

RED FLIGHT, ROUGH RIDER STRIKE FORCE

Bossman winced from the double flash and glanced to his left. He couldn't find Jazzman or Otter. They had vanished. Exploded? But how? He hadn't seen any missiles leave the ships. The second ring of escorts popped into view above the horizon. *Still* no missiles. Unbelievable. He scanned the sky above, then looked to his right. What the—? He mashed his mike button.

"Combat spread, Blackjack!"

Blackjack's Hornet stayed on his wing.

Two destroyers in the inner ring zipped past.

Bossman looked again. Blackjack was still there. What the hell was that lunatic doing!? *"Dammit, Pershing! I said combat sprea—"*

There was a giant fulmination over the water as Bossman's Hornet took an Aphid missile in each tailpipe. The force of the airburst rocked Blackjack's Hornet so hard that he almost careened into the sea. The young Texan cried out in terror as his lifeline vanished and he was overwhelmed by one consuming instinct: *Run!*

With tears in his eyes and his heart in his throat, Blackjack pickled his bombs into the sea and pulled up in a vertical climb in a desperate move to flee . . . to flee . . . to flee.

THE MIG-29 FULCRUM

His missiles expended, Tupelov was closing on the final Hornet for a cannon shot when the American went nose-up into a vertical climb. It caught Tupelov by such surprise that the two aircraft almost had a midair collision before the Russian veered off to starboard and brought his Fulcrum up in a pursuit climb.

THE F/A-18 HORNET

Blackjack's mind was so choked with fear that he had lost all rational thought—as well as his sense of navigation. As he rolled his Hornet and pulled it over into level inverted flight, he thought he was running away, but he was actually heading toward the *Tbilisi* when he saw a wing come into view ahead of him.

A wing.

Aerobatics.

A lifeline.

He cut in his afterburner to close.

THE MIG-29 FULCRUM

As Tupelov climbed to pursue, he figured the American was maintaining his climb also. But the Hornet was nowhere to be found. *Where did he go?* Tupelov swiveled his head around and caught sight of the American closing on him from behind. "Oh, God," he whispered, "how did he get behind me?" He brought his MiG-29 into a tight seven-G turn to try and cut inside of the Hornet. Tupelov went around in a complete circle, then around again, groaning under the G-force. Together the two fighters cut a spiral in the sky—tighter and tighter, closer and closer—until Tupelov found the American on his wing.

THE *TBILISI*

"Two more escorts have sustained hits," announced the damage-control officer. "The *Tributs* has taken a third hit and is sinking."

The radar officer interrupted in exultation. "All low-level bandits are *down* except one coming up from the south—and Sable One is in pursuit!"

"Refueling and rearming on first flight of Flankers from Squadron Four is complete," said the air officer. "They are coming up on elevators now for launch. . . . The American Hornets ate our Forgers alive. Two of our four Flankers survived."

Captain Vaslov shook his head in amazement. "I cannot believe it, Admiral. We have held. Three major air attacks, and we have held."

The fireplug of an admiral continued watching the two triangles on the projection screen approaching from the south. They were well inside the inner ring of escorts now, moving in a serpentine track across the screen as the digital readouts changed with amazing rapidity. They were diving. Now they were climbing. Climbing some more. Now they were closing. "The bandit is almost upon us," whispered Strekalov.

"Air defense, prepare to fire!" barked Captain Vaslov.

9,300 FEET ABOVE THE ROSS SEA

Like two dragonflies in a mating dance, the Fulcrum and the Hornet bobbed and weaved, rolled and banked, climbed and dove in a dizzy progression that was paradoxical in the extreme—the Russian seeking to survive by shaking his adversary, the American seeking refuge by staying attached.

"Get off my wing, damn you!" shouted Tupelov. *"Get off my wing!"*

But, like a tar baby in the air, Blackjack refused to let go.

THE *TBILISI*

Strekalov was pleading. "Can you launch, Dmitri?"

Vaslov was on the phone. "Two Flankers from Squadron Four are moving toward the ramp now, Admiral." He looked at the screen. "But they will not launch in time. The bandit is almost on top of us. Air defense! Do you have a solution?"

"Aye!"

Strekalov raised a hand. "But we may hit a friendly aircraft."

"Admiral, I have five thousand men on my ship!"

Strekalov dropped his hand and nodded his assent.

"Engage!"

"Aye, Captain!"

On the starboard side of the carrier, two SA-N-9 air defense missiles roared out of their launch tubes—on a trajectory almost straight up.

THE MIG-29 FULCRUM

They were in a climb when Tupelov put his MiG-29 into a hard vertical scissors maneuver that caused the American to shoot ahead of him—but in so doing, Tupelov sandwiched his Fulcrum between the incoming SAMs and the American Hornet. So, by finally shaking his adversary, the Russian had turned his aircraft into a shield that took the double blast from the SAMs when their proximity fuses went off simultaneously.

The wings of the MiG-29 were sheared off as if by a cleaver, sending the Fulcrum into a tumbling roll. Inside the cockpit, Tupelov was whipped from side to side like a windsock in a gale—battered into near unconsciousness as he fought against the centrifugal force to reach the eject handles above his head. It was hopeless. The whipsaw action of the tumbling plane bloodied his arms as it threw them around the cockpit—up, down, and sideways, as if he were some kind of marionette. But then his arms were thrown under the seat—and his fingers snagged the backup ejection handle. Though barely conscious, Tupelov yanked as hard as he could.

Nothing.

Darkness closing in on his mind, he yanked again.

There was some sort of eruption, then he sailed into space as a blast of frigid air hit him. . . . Hit him with a cold so deep and piercing that it went beyond anything even a Russian could imagine.

THE F/A-18 HORNET

Blackjack was flying into a small puff of cloud when the double blast of the SAM missiles almost threw his Hornet into a flat spin. But coming out the far side, he recovered, stabilizing the Hornet in a banking turn. He feverishly scanned the airspace, searching for the wing that had been his lifeline—but it was nowhere to be found. He felt the Fear welling up inside him again, but then he looked down and saw it . . . there . . . below him . . . like a wounded Cape buffalo lying prostrate before a hungry pride of lions. It was the *Tbilisi,* in all her vulnerability.

It was at this point the Fear exerted a logic of its own upon Blackjack. To get away, to survive, the young Texan intuitively knew he must slay the beast that now lay before him, but he had jettisoned his bombs when Bossman blew up. He punched his armament panel and . . . what was this? . . . One five-hundred-pounder had gotten hung up on the belly pylon. He looked below at the *Tbilisi* again. . . . Maybe he could shake the bomb loose.

Blackjack pointed the nose of the Hornet straight down and powered up the laser target designator. A rectangle appeared on the head-up display, and he put it squarely on the flattop that was rapidly growing in his field of view. The altimeter ran backwards at a breathtaking pace as he zapped the carrier's flight deck with the laser beam. The RELEASE prompt flashed in the head-up display, and Blackjack hit the pickle switch as he pulled up out of the dive with a seven-G maneuver, growling through his teeth, "Drop . . . damn you . . . drop . . . drop . . . please drop."

A defective sprocket on the bomb rack had kept the Mk 82 Paveway bomb in place, but as the weight of the five-hundred-pounder increased sevenfold, it finally wrenched itself free and started spiraling down . . .

down . . .

down . . .

down . . .

THE *TBILISI*

"Did we hit him?" Vaslov demanded.

"A moment, Captain," said the radar officer. "We obtained missile detonation just as they flew into our radar blind spot directly above us. I am bringing the *Shaposhnikov*'s radar up on our screen now. . . . I think we must have—"

Like a set shot from midcourt that swished through the basket, the laser-guided Paveway bomb sailed through the open elevator window of the flight deck and impacted on the hangar deck below. It was greeted by a covey of armed airplanes, a web of fuel hoses, and a cartload of missiles being wheeled out of the magazine elevator.

The explosion within the hangar deck itself was staggering, but the true coup de grâce came when a flaming external fuel tank was sheared off a wing and bounced leisurely across the deck to strike the half-dozen Aphid missiles on the elevator cart. The ensuing detonation unhinged the elevator platform, causing it and the accompanying fireball to fall down the shaft toward the magazine stowage.

*Vitse-*Adm. Gavriil Strekalov was waiting for word from the radar officer when a rumble shook CIC with such force that it knocked him off his footstool and threw him to the floor, causing him to strike his head against the projection table. The lights went out, and there were cries and screams in the black void. Emergency power came back on, but only for an instant. As the dazed Strekalov struggled to get back on his feet, he felt the side of his head. There was something warm and wet. Then there was another rumble and the deck pitched up, then down, heaving him into the darkness as he cried, "Dmitri! Dmitri!"

But Captain Vaslov had been slammed against the bulkhead, and his neck was broken.

5,300 FEET ABOVE THE ROSS SEA

The freezing cold had already congealed the blood on Fyodor Tupelov's flight suit as he swayed back and forth in the air—drifting down underneath his parachute canopy. With difficulty he unsnapped the rubber oxygen mask on his face and tried to regain his equilibrium. The cold helped to revive him as he looked over and down, and saw the *Tbilisi*. The wind was carrying him away, but he had the presence of mind to hope someone would see him and dispatch a helicopter to pluck him out of the drink before he froze in minutes, if not seconds.

With his three operative, shivering fingers, he was trying to pull a flare out of the leg pocket of his flight suit when he heard a *pom-pom-pom-pom-BAH-RUMP!* that caused him to look up. He saw the *Tbilisi,* and it seemed to shudder in the water. Then, in a flash of light, the midsection of the flight deck popped off and sailed up into the air, spinning like a discus, and a *KAH-WHA-WHUMP!* washed over Tupelov—just as the forecastle of the giant vessel rose up, then sagged back down in the water.

It was an hypnotic spectacle—witnessing the death of such a magnificent ship. But as the icy waters of the Ross Sea rushed up toward him, Tupelov quickly came out of his hypnosis. Looking down, he spied a *Krivak*-class frigate steaming toward him. He yelled, "Over here!" but of course he couldn't be heard. The vessel had obviously taken a hit, for there was smoke streaming from where its radar tower had been. Tupelov's fears of freezing and drowning were quickly replaced by the fear of landing on top of the frigate. They were going to collide! But the frigate's captain was a competent seaman, and he cut the vessel's engines and veered away to give Tupelov a clear shot at falling into the sea.

Tupelov bit his lip and weakly grabbed the release straps on his parachute harness. By now his hands were almost numb as he tried to gauge the proper instant to cut the chute loose and free-fall into the water. He yanked on the straps, but nothing happened. He had to get free! If he did not, there was no doubt in his mind that he would tangle in the shroud lines and drown. He was at eye level with the smoky remains of the radar tower when he yanked again. This time Tupelov parted company with the harness, causing the canopy to deflate and drift away as he fell the final five meters into the Ross Sea.

He hit the surface and went under, emptying his lungs in an underwater scream, protesting against the knifelike cold that seized him. He had forgotten to inflate his life preserver. . . . He was sinking . . . in shock . . . he was going to die.

With consciousness fading, his numb fingers were barely able to snag the lanyard on his chest and give a little tug. A vial of compressed air inflated the vest, and Tupelov bobbed up to the surface like a cork, a moment before water would have rushed into his lungs.

Something hit him on the shoulder. With his blurred vision he could barely see it—floating next to him in the water. A white ring.

"Put it over your head!" came the voice through the bullhorn.

Tupelov got the lifesaver ring over his head . . . then under one arm . . . and under the other . . . before everything went dark in a hypothermic abyss.

THE FRIGATE *PORYVISTIY*

"Pull him in!" yelled the brawny *michman,* and along with the rescue detail he heaved on the lifeline. Once they got the MiG pilot up to the railing, the *michman* hooked his hands under Tupelov's armpits and hauled the water-logged pilot over the side. The *michman* thought Tupelov was dead, but upon feeling the aviator's neck for a pulse, he found it was still there. "Get some blankets on him and take him to sick bay! And move lively!" A litter and some blankets appeared, and Tupelov was hustled away.

Spent by his effort, the *michman* sighed and slumped against the icy rail in exhaustion. As he watched Tupelov's litter disappear through the hatch, he said, "This war is over for you, my friend."

He heard a groaning sound that caused him to turn and look in the direction of the *Tbilisi.* In horror he watched as the stern of the supercarrier pitched up in the air, where it seemed to hang, suspended, for the longest time. But then—as if it were caught in the funereal grip of a colossal pool of quicksand—the vessel slid slowly into the icy depths . . . until it disappeared, leaving nothing in its wake but bubbling foam and the filmy sheen of fuel oil.

Shaken to his soul, the *michman* whispered, "It is over for all of us."

But there was no one to hear him, save for God and the sea.

> *There Grendel suffered a grievous hurt,*
> *A wound in the shoulder, gaping and wide;*
> *Sinews snapped and bone-joints broke,*
> *And Beowulf gained the glory of battle.*

19

· · · · · · · · · · ·

WASPS

THE *VINCENNES*

"Jesus . . . oh, Jesus, look at that," whispered the tactical action officer.

On the giant display screen, a burst of light appeared in the center of the rectangle, leaving a trail of black smoke in its wake.

"The *Tbilisi* has been hit, General," said Captain Erickson. "Hit bad."

A moment before, Myron Tharp had been worried that his attack plan had failed. Now he sat mesmerized, saying nothing as he watched the rectangle slowly disappear beneath the waves in real time. There were some moments of stunned silence, until Erickson yelled, "Scratch one carrier!" And a chorus of hoots and cheers went up through CIC.

The TAO held his earphones against his head to block out the noise and said, "Secure voice channel coming in from Admiral Rumley for you, General Tharp."

Tharp nodded and heard the hiss of the scrambler.

"Myron!" came the baritone voice through the headphones. "Did you see that?"

"Roger, Beowulf One, I saw it."

"Man, oh, man, this is incredible! Myron, I have to say I was worried there for a while. We lost a passel of Hornets, but that's nothing compared to sinking a flattop! Incredible! And the airfield at McMurdo is totally pancaked! I'll just bet you, Myron—er, Beowulf Two—that you just earned yourself a fourth star. . . . Ahem, ah, maybe we both have. . . ."

Tharp took off his glasses and rubbed his eyes wearily while saying, "Let's put that aside for now, Beowulf One. There is still a lot of work to do. Order the *Wasp* to head due south at all possible speed and disembark the LCACs per the Beowulf plan. Have the surviving

Intruders and Hornets refueled and rearmed for air support if required. Then move all three battle groups south for the bombardment, but keep them away from the surviving Russian escort vessels . . . and tell the pilot who nailed the *Tbilisi* he just earned himself a Navy Cross."

"Whatever you say, Myron."

WHITE ISLAND

Lieutenant Colonel Rawlings, Sergeant Major Ramirez, Captain Nye, Sergeant de Parma, and the rest of the forward party half-slid, half-galloped down the slope of Mount Heine and tumbled into the rocky alcove, constantly muttering to each other in their excitement, "Did you see that? Did you see that? Sonofabitch! Man alive! God bless America! We hammered them, didn't we? We blew 'em away! Did you *see* that!?"

As Rawlings came into the alcove and pulled back the hood of his anorak, he didn't have to say a word for Dana to know something spectacular had happened. That whatever this little group of mostly very young men had set out to accomplish had succeeded—in spades. Dana and Gates were standing together as Rawlings threw an arm around each and hugged them tightly.

Dana hugged him back and asked, "What happened?"

Rawlings's excitement was contagious as he shook his head and said, "It was incredible, Dana. Absolutely incredible. I never saw anything like it in my life. Not even in Vietnam. Those B-1 bombers tore the airfield apart. Unbelievable devastation. Only one aircraft got off the ground, as far as we could tell." He gave Gates a slap on the butt and said, "Send the message that says 'Grand Slam.' "

Gates replied, "Roger, sir," and left to huddle over his radio while Dana remained under the colonel's arm and said, "We heard a sound like thunder. Was that the bombers we saw?"

Rawlings nodded. "That was them. They blasted the place to bits. I think three bombers got shot down. It would have been a lot worse if not for this crew getting de Parma and his laserscope in place."

"How so? I still don't understand what that was all about."

Rawlings smiled and gave her another squeeze. "I'll explain later. . . . Guess I never really told you how much your help meant to me . . . to all of us."

Dana smiled back, knowing that she looked like hell, and that she would give anything for a hot bath, clean clothes, and some makeup. "What do we do now?"

"Make some hot chocolate, sit tight, and wait for the cavalry to arrive. Shouldn't be too long."

"Message sent, sir," said Gates.

Rawlings grinned and turned to Captain Nye. "Okay, Phillip, post two men at the entrance for security and—"

They all heard it at once.

A chopping sound.

"Everybody under cover," ordered Rawlings, and somewhat roughly he shoved Dana toward the entrance of the snow cave.

Like mice trying to scurry away from a hungry cat, the LRSD team scrambled toward the opening of their shelter. Gates was bringing up the rear when he stopped and realized his radio was at the entrance to the alcove, in plain view. He turned and hustled back for it as the chopping sound grew louder. He was reaching for the set when Pancho Ramirez grabbed him and hauled him back behind the rocky walls of the alcove . . . not quite soon enough.

A HIND-E HELICOPTER

The gunner in the front seat of the HIND-E helicopter pointed and said, "I think I saw something move . . . up ahead."

The pilot dipped the nose a bit to increase the chopper's speed and ordered, "Arm your gun," referring to the twin-barreled GSh-23L cannon slung under the starboard side of the rotary-wing craft.

"My weapon is already armed," the gunner said testily, as he tightened his grip on the firing controller.

THE SNOW CAVE

Pancho Ramirez was the last one through the entryway, and it was he who replaced the plug. Then he grabbed his Stinger missile and scrambled after Gates into the chamber that housed Rawlings, Dana, Nye, and de Parma.

"I think we've been spotted," Ramirez said tersely while pulling the safety arming pin out of the Stinger trigger mechanism.

Dana was huddled against Rawlings, her heart thumping so fast she could hardly breathe as the chopping sound grew louder . . . louder . . . Louder! . . . LOUDER!

The downdraft of the hovering HIND helicopter was too much for the snow cave, causing the white, fluffy walls to collapse around the Americans in a swirl of snow and ice that stung their faces and blinded their sight.

THE HIND HELICOPTER

The HIND was hovering almost directly over the snow cave when the shelter disintegrated, revealing several white-clad figures below. The gunner could not lower the elevation of the fixed cannon—the weapon was aimed by aligning the chopper with the target—so he screamed, "Pull back!"

THE SNOW CAVE

As the HIND tilted backward for a quick retreat, Rawlings saw it through the swirling snow and yelled, *"Take him, Pancho!"*

Ramirez rose up in the churning snow and shouldered the Stinger, just as the HIND halted and began dipping its nose to bring the cannon to bear. Ramirez caught the HIND in his targeting viewer and held it for an interminable second until the ENGAGE prompt appeared.

He and the HIND gunner pulled their triggers simultaneously.

What followed had an otherworldly, surrealistic quality for Dana. The snow in her eyes abated long enough for her to glimpse a giant, deadly wasp hovering outside their alcove. Then there was a series of explosions and concussions that pummeled her backwards into the snow drift, knocking the breath from her body. Dazed, she caught sight of an orange ball as it sank from view—slowly spinning beneath its rotor blades.

It seemed the longest time, as if she were on the verge of passing out, before her lungs began functioning again. As she took progressively deeper breaths to restore the oxygen flow to her body, everything was quiet—except for the crackling sound of something burning. She saw Rawlings standing, his back toward her, as she groped up on her hands and knees. Rawlings was looking down at Pancho. Dana wobbled onto her feet and saw that Pancho, or what was left of Pancho, was lying in the snow—the middle of him nothing more than a red mass.

Dana moaned at the horrible specter, and might have screamed, but then Rawlings's knees buckled and he fell over in the snow—the left side of his overwhites a bloody crimson.

THE ROSS SEA

The giant stern gate of the amphibious assault carrier *Wasp* was slowly lowered into the icy water, and the din blaring from within its bowels sounded like the growl of a hungry sea dragon seeking its next victim. Then, one by one, the three Landing Craft Air Cushion vessels slid down the gate and onto the surface of the sea, causing the water to bloom out around them. The two large ducted propellers mounted on the fantail of each vessel pushed them along the surface as they formed up in a loose V formation. They rapidly built up speed to forty-five knots and raced across the water toward the Ross Ice Shelf.

They could have gone even faster, because except for their crews, a couple of SEALS, and a few Marines for security, the LCACs were empty.

BRANDING IRON STATION

"I am *not* going back up there!" declared the chubby civilian engineer from the Siberian coal fields. "You cannot make me," he told the Guards captain. "I am—ahem, *we are*—safer here."

The young Captain Savinykh, who was in charge of security at the mining site, said, "Nobody is safe anywhere, Comrade. The Americans have destroyed our airfield and our air cover. They will be here soon. You may rely on that."

The engineer gulped. "The Americans . . . here?"

"*Da,* Comrade. Soon."

"Oh, no," whimpered the engineer. "We have just broken through the second lava apron. The rubidium deposit is within our grasp."

Captain Savinykh bit his lip. It had been impossible to raise General Tromso on the radio net. Everybody was screaming on the airwaves at once, and their transmitters weren't getting through. But the Guards captain knew he had to make a decision. The general had put him in charge of security at the mining site because the young captain had shown initiative—a quality not overly prized in the Red Army, but it was something General Tromso admired. Savinykh slammed his fist into his palm and said, "Listen to me, Comrade. I am going topside. Get someone on that skip loader over there. Have your men use the skip loader to shovel the earth back into the mine shaft."

"*Back* into the shaft?"

"*Da.* We must do what we can to deny the rubidium to the Americans. If necessary, I will cut the elevator cables to delay the Americans and give your men time to refill the shaft."

"Cut the elevator cables?"

"*Da.*"

The engineer cleared his throat and said, "On second thought, I will come topside after all. Let me turn these matters over to my deputy."

Savinykh drew his Makarov pistol and leveled it at the engineer, saying, "You will remain here at your post, Comrade."

THE ROSS SEA

The LCAC hovercraft were racing across the Ross Sea, heading for the white Dover-like cliffs of the ice shelf. Hurtling across the surface, throwing up white spray, the LCACs looked like three enormous inner tubes just emerging from a drive-through car wash.

As they approached the skirt of the pack ice, the helmsmen slowed their vessels, and the LCACs easily made their transition from water to ice pack. Then they picked up speed again and continued on toward the white cliffs.

On the deck of the hovercraft, the LCAC crew chief turned to the Navy SEAL and shouted over the din, "Are you sure this is the right place!?"

The SEAL was looking at his hand-held GPS receiver, and replied, "This should be it! Let's find out!" He knelt down beside a contraption that looked like a portable cellular phone pack. He extended the aerial and punched some buttons, and a red light came on the panel. "Here we go!" And he punched another button.

A segment of the ice cliff seemed to rise up into a white eruption as two dozen well-placed satchel charges went off simultaneously, causing the helmsman to slow his speed reflexively.

"Yep, this is the place," said the SEAL. "I hope this works."

"We'll see," replied the crew chief.

As the hovercraft drew closer, the white cloud of ice fragments slowly dissipated to reveal a swath in the cliff that formed a kind of ramp. This section of the ice cliff had been chosen because of a natural depression in its face. The SEAL demolition team had placed the charges to blast a bigger trough.

The helmsman cut his speed to a crawl and carefully negotiated the ice debris at the foot of the ramp while inspecting the demolition handiwork of the SEALs. Then he gunned the engine, and although it was a close fit, the empty hovercraft skimmed over the chunks of ice that littered the impromptu rampway, and surged on up to the top of the Ross Ice Shelf.

The second LCAC almost got wedged in the narrow gap, but then it finally squeezed through, followed by number three. The ramp was so steep that if the hovercraft had carried any payload at all, they would not have made it.

Once again they formed up into their V and powered up to their maximum speed of fifty knots, leaving contrails of snow and ice in their wake as they headed for Branding Iron Station, some thirty-two miles away in the Windless Bight.

CRATER HILL, MCMURDO BASE

A forest of tactical radio antennae surrounded Maj. Gen. Mitrofan Tromso as he dealt with the frenetic task of moving his entire regiment out of their entrenched positions on Hut Point Peninsula and loading them onto a convoy of BMD troop vehicles and trucks.

The tall, athletic Guards general looked out over the thin pack ice of McMurdo Sound and knew the Americans could appear at any moment. His aircraft were destroyed, the *Tbilisi* sunk. If he left his men in position on the seaward side of Hut Point Peninsula, they would be exposed to savage naval bombardment. So he had ordered the Guards to load up on their vehicles and convoy across the ice shelf toward Mount Discovery. Tromso was totally at a loss as to what else to do. Without air and sea superiority, Soviet ships could not get in to evacuate his troops. The nearest friendly base was in Cam Ranh. He was utterly stranded. He had fired off a situation report to Moscow, and Moscow had replied, "Hold out as long as possible." Disgusted, Tromso knew he had to rely on his own wits.

"My battalions are ready to move out, General," said his regimental commander.

"Very well. Have them get under way. We will dig in at Mount Discovery and hold out until Moscow decides what to do. Signal officer? Have you been able to raise the mining site?"

The signal officer shook his head. "No, General, and I do not understand why our radios are not functioning."

Another frustration. "We have no vehicles to spare except one or two of the captured Sno-Cats. Put one of your men on those and send him to Captain Savinykh at the mining site. Tell him . . . tell him to hold out as best he can, but he is on his own."

"General?"

Tromso turned and saw the slender air defense brigadier as he made his way through the radio operators. He sheepishly approached and said, "I have some wounded, General. They require medical care, and I await your instructions on what you wish me to do."

Tromso looked at him with all the bitterness he could muster. "I will have my regimental medical staff attend your wounded. Load them onto our convoy vehicles. After we arrive at Mount Discovery"—Tromso grabbed his radio operator's AK-47 and flung it toward the brigadier, who caught it in surprise—"you will join A Company of the first battalion as a new rifleman."

THE *WASP*

On the flight deck of the USS *Wasp,* the noise was deafening as six V-22 Osprey tilt-rotor aircraft throttled up to full power in preparation for their vertical takeoff. At the same time, the first of six AV-8B Marine Harriers began its takeoff roll down the flight deck, the pilot hitting the vector nozzles at the right moment to achieve lift-off.

Once the Harriers were off, the V-22 Ospreys followed. Rising straight up, they gained sufficient altitude before rotating their propeller blades down to put the aircraft into horizontal flight.

With the Harriers above them acting as escort, the six Ospreys came together in a loose formation and took up a vector for the Windless Bight.

ROSS ICE SHELF

The three hovercraft were screaming across the flat expanse of the ice shelf at their maximum speed of fifty knots, heading for the Windless Bight. The helmsman—from Birmingham, Alabama—responded to the adrenaline rushing through his system and let go with the Rebel yell his granddaddy had taught him. He felt like he was in the middle of a cavalry charge.

The Navy SEAL beside him—who was from Ohio—found himself

yelling, too, as he put the powerful binoculars up to his eyes. In the distance was a towerlike object. "Yeeeaaaooowww! We got it in sight!"

And he grabbed the TAC AIR radio.

BRANDING IRON STATION

The first sergeant in Captain Savinykh's security detail was up on the derrick platform, sweeping the horizon with his binoculars, when something caught his eye. It was some kind of a . . . a . . . spout. Out on the ice shelf. Now there were two . . . three. White plumes. "Captain!"

Savinykh ran over to join him. "What is it?"

The top sergeant pointed and passed the binoculars. "Something out there, sir!"

Savinykh took the glasses and trained them out on the ice shelf. He saw them immediately. Three white plumes spewing up from three black dots. He lowered the glasses. "Those are hovercraft! Have the artillery open fire!"

"*Da,* Captain!" And the top sergeant clambered down the steel ladder to notify the arty commander.

Captain Savinykh was focusing his field glasses back on the approaching LCACs when he heard the whisper of jet aircraft above him.

Five hundred sixty feet below the derrick, the skip loader was kicking up a cloud of dust as it shoved load after load of excavated dirt back into the mine shaft.

"Commence firing!" barked the section chief, and the 122-mm artillery piece boomed its high-explosive projectile out the muzzle. Seconds ticked by until the ranging round came down two hundred meters in front of the hovercraft, causing the LCACs to break formation and scatter into random zigzag patterns.

"Right fifty!" ordered the section chief. "*Nyet!* Right one hundred! Add two hundred! *Nyet!* Add one-fifty!" The crew was spinning the elevation and traverse handles on the gun like mad, trying to keep up with their chief's instructions. "Dammit! Fire another round!" The gun responded, but the section chief saw his 122-mm shell fall ineffectually behind the fast-moving, elusive hovercraft. And rounds from the other emplacements seemed to be landing with equal impotence. Yet in those frenetic and frustrating moments of action, something struck the section chief as odd. The hovercraft did not seem interested in closing on the Soviet positions. They were staying away. Weaving back and forth. Drawing fire.

The section chief winced as two shoulder-fired SA-7 Grail antiair missiles were loosed by their gunners in the neighboring bunker.

THE HARRIERS

"Blue Leader, this is Blue Four. I see 'em. I count three . . . four arty emplacements."

"Roger, Four. I see them, too."

The six Marine Harriers from the *Wasp* were flying in a wagon-wheel pattern above Branding Iron Station, waiting for the artillery emplacements to roll back their white camouflage netting and reveal themselves.

"Blue Leader! This is Two! Missiles inbound!"

"Flares!" ordered Leader. And like a flurry of Roman candles, the brightly burning flares descended from the circling Harriers, luring away the deadly darts.

Leader doubted that the shoulder-fired missiles had lock-on before their gunmen fired. "Locking up" a target at eight thousand feet with a hand-held weapon was a long shot.

"Looks like they've got some Grails," said Leader, and he checked where the sun was hanging in the sky. "Okay, Two, Three, and Four, follow me down. Five and Six, you know what to do. Put your load to the west, I say again, to the west of the target if the wind is right. Secondary drop zone to the north. . . . Osprey flight, did you copy that?"

A faint voice said, "Copy, Blue Leader. We're ready."

"Okay, here we go." And Blue Leader pulled his Harrier out of the wagon wheel, down toward the pack ice of McMurdo Sound— on the far side of Hut Point Peninsula from Branding Iron Station.

BRANDING IRON STATION

"Cut the cable!" yelled Captain Savinykh, over the incessant *boom-boom* of the artillery pieces.

Two of his soldiers wrestled with a huge pair of wire cutters as they cut through the thick steel cable, strand by agonizing strand.

"Hurry!" Savinykh urged.

"Captain!" cried the first sergeant. "We have hit one of the hover-craft!"

Savinykh looked out on the ice shelf and saw a column of black smoke. "Excellent, Sergeant! Hold them off until we get this thing disabled. If they try to assault our position, tell the artillery to open up with flechette rounds!"

"*Da,* Captain!"

Savinykh then looked toward the sun hanging over Hut Point Peninsula, and thought he saw some dots in the sky.

THE HARRIERS

Blue Leader watched Sultan's Head Rock on Hut Point Peninsula whip by on the ceiling of his canopy as he pulled back on the stick to get himself back down on the deck. In the distance he could see the derrick, which served as an ideal landmark. The Grail antiair missiles would have a hard time locking up a target coming out of the sun, and Leader knew this as he let Blue Flight's speed bleed off to 280 knots. He brought up the "death dot" aiming point on his head-up display and began his pop-up maneuver. He had a pretty good idea where the artillery emplacements were, but with this type of ordnance, pinpoint precision wasn't a high priority.

BRANDING IRON STATION

Captain Savinykh watched the dots grow as they rose up and arced over to drop two smaller dots apiece. And as they fell toward the earth, they disgorged a host of tiny dots, like a gardener scattering seed over a lawn.

The staccato sound of overlapping *braaaaaaapppps!!!* filled the air as the twelve hundred BLU-18/B bomblets from each dispenser came down around the periphery of Branding Iron Station like a swarm of killer bees, sending some of the fragments ricocheting off the steel superstructure as Savinykh and his top sergeant fell to the floor.

Then everything was oddly silent. Savinykh ventured to raise his head and look for the Harriers, but they had disappeared somewhere over the ice shelf. The artillery was no longer firing, and the Grail missileers had not unleashed their weapons at the retreating Harri-ers. Yes, it was oddly silent. It had happened so fast. So many explosions. His artillery wiped out. And yet, except for the odd ricochet, the derrick had not been hit. Strange. Was that by design? Savinykh began to hear moans. But he quickly put them out of his mind as the sound of more Harriers filled the air. They approached like the others, but seemed to drop their canisters far short of the derrick before racing overhead. Savinykh remained semi-prone, watching the clusters of bomblets turn into a giant curtain of gray smoke.

Smoke? Why smoke?

The Russian captain got his answer as six V-22 Ospreys roared out of the gray curtain toward the derrick. Savinykh became hypnotized as he watched the Ospreys execute a pirouette just above the ground and race toward him—ass backwards. Then the pilots gunned their engines, sending up a cloud of snow as the Ospreys' tailgates dropped and a host of United States Marines began running out. The pilot of the Osprey on the far starboard of the assault line misjudged, and the tailgate submarined into the ice, causing the twin-engined craft to flop over on its back and explode in a giant ball of flame.

This shook Savinykh out of his hypnosis. He rose to his feet and cuffed the first sergeant on the shoulder, shouting, "Come on!" They scrambled over to the wire cutters, and together with the two enlisted men, they strained to sever the cable holding up the elevator.

The Marines had offloaded within the Russians' outer defense perimeter, and now that the artillery was silenced, the only thing standing between them and the Branding Iron derrick was the small detachment of twelve men dug in alongside the superstructure. While wrestling with the giant wire cutter, Savinykh heard the small-arms fire of AK-47s as his men opened up on the Marines. The Marines returned with a volley of their own fire, and the bullets pinged against the steel derrick.

Savinykh felt the cable going when the sound of a Harrier filled the air. The deadly jump jet skimmed across the ice shelf, then rotated its vector nozzles into a hover position—not a hundred yards from the derrick. Poised above the ice, engines screaming, like a deadly bird of prey looming behind a veil of snow swirling around it, the Harrier raked the steel superstructure with its 30-mm cannon.

Savinykh felt the cable cut free a split second before one of the cannon rounds passed through him.

The elevator cage crashed into the floor of the icedome after a 560-foot free-fall, causing the chubby chief engineer to jump about eight feet. "The Americans are here!" he cried.

"Shut up, you old fool!" growled the sergeant in charge, as he shoved the civilian behind the dirt berm and ordered, "Get down!"

In the background, the skip loader continued humming as it kept shoveling earth back into the mine shaft.

Minutes passed, and the tension mounted as the squad of soldiers and engineers waited for the Americans to appear. The chief engineer was curled up like a porcupine. But as the minutes dragged on, he ventured to raise his head. Nothing. The sergeant was behind the berm, AK-47 poised for firing at the elevator hole. But there were no Americans.

Clang!

The engineer recoiled as an object about the size and shape of a rugby ball bounced against the crumpled elevator and rolled toward him. His eyes grew and he became frozen. It was a bomb!

Clang! Clang! Clang!

More rugby balls dropped through the hole, ricocheting off the elevator and randomly rolling across the silty floor of the icedome.

Clang! Clang! Clang! Clang! Clang!

"They are going to explode!" cried the engineer. "The roof will cave in on us!"

But instead of exploding, the rugby ball nearest the engineer started going *pssssssssttt!*

The engineer stared at the rugby ball in horror, then felt himself growing sleepy . . . sleepy . . . sleepy. . . .

THE *CARL VINSON*

The tumultuous reception that Michael "Blackjack" Pershing received upon his return to the *Carl Vinson* was straight out of the movie *Top Gun*. He had done little more than raise his tailhook after grabbing a four-wire than the deck crew was swarming around him. His feet never touched the ground as he was hoisted up on shoulders and outstretched hands and carried to the conning tower, where he was greeted by the captain and Admiral Rumley's aide. Then he was swept up to the flag bridge, where he was told by a baritone-voiced admiral he'd never seen before that he—Blackjack—was going to receive the Navy Cross.

After Blackjack's Hornet touched down on the flight deck, the electronic wizards in the ship's public-affairs television studio lifted a copy of the videotape from his gun camera and spliced it in with the recorded imagery from the Aurora spy plane. They keyed a title over it, *The Sinking of the* Tbilisi, and put it on the ship's closed-circuit TV system, where it was played over . . . and over . . . and over . . . and over. . . .

THE *VINCENNES*

The image on the large display screen from the Aurora clearly showed the black dots of the BMD vehicles moving across the ice shelf in convoy toward Mount Discovery.

"They're pulling out, General," said Erickson. "They're heading inland. They're not even going to fight!"

The TAO listened intently to the Marine tactical net and said, "Branding Iron Station is secure, General! The Marines are down the hole and the Soviets are disarmed. They said the canisters of knock-out gas worked like a charm. Not a shot was fired down in the mine site. The prisoners are groggy but unharmed."

Captain Erickson's giant hand slammed between Myron Tharp's diminutive shoulder blades, almost knocking the Marine's glasses off. "Hot damn, General! You did it! McMurdo Sound is ours!"

The cheers that went up through CIC rattled the walls. The mood wasn't what one would call excited. Rather, it went beyond the euphoric. With fewer screw-ups than anyone had dared hope, the plan had worked. The equipment had worked. Everything had worked! In the space of a few hours a Soviet air base had been pancaked, an enemy supercarrier sunk, and McMurdo would soon be reoccupied by American forces. The euphoria was so contagious that even Tharp couldn't suppress a grin as he said, "Well, yes, I suppose things did work out rather well, didn't they, David?"

20

. . . .

WOUNDED BEAR

THE OATES COAST, ANTARCTICA—February 17

On the eastern side of the Mawson Peninsula, a small ice shelf (tiny in comparison to the colossal Ross Ice Shelf formation) came off the western Antarctic ice sheet and filled up the bulk of an inlet called Slave Bay. Extending out to the sea from Slave Bay was an apron of pack ice that was thicker than the ice found elsewhere along the Antarctic coast during the summer. That was because the winds and currents turned Slave Bay into a kind of "catcher's mitt" for the pack ice that floated along that part of the Oates Coast. As it converged in the bay, one tablet of ice might raft on top of another, forming a short stack of ice plates; or pressure ridges might be formed, making the ice ten to fifteen feet thick in spots. As a result, the pack ice in Slave Bay tended to linger, and rarely broke up during the summer. This extremely obscure piece of information was of no consequence to anyone, except maybe a glaciologist or an oceanographer. But it was one of those tidbits of data that was observed, measured, cataloged, and filed away by the small Soviet scientific base at Leningradskaya, a hundred twenty-five miles away from Slave Bay on the Oates Coast.

Captain, First Rank, Kasimir Bodin mashed his face against the periscope viewer, looking at the diffused, ghostly-lit underside of the pack ice emanating from Slave Bay. There were shallow ice keels and pressure ridges with which Bodin was intimately familiar. He probably had as much experience as any man alive at probing the underside of a floating ice sheet, looking for a *polyn'ya*—an opening—through which he could surface. The pack ice was a two-edged sword for Bodin, in that it provided concealment from deadly sub-hunter aircraft, but could also prevent the *Kharkov* from surfacing.

Unlike the American ballistic missile submarines, the *Kharkov* could not launch its missiles underwater, but only from the surface.

As the *Kharkov* cruised along at dead slow, Bodin pivoted the periscope head to inspect the underside of the ice. At this point he didn't have to bring the *Kharkov* to the surface, but he did need to find a small window through the pack. He was always a bit hypnotized by the white, translucent light that passed through the ice. He pivoted the periscope head back down and traversed it to starboard. Bodin could barely make out the underwater face of the Slave Bay ice shelf, which seemed to disappear as it traveled down into the chilling depths.

Bodin turned his attention to the ceiling once again, and was intently focused on a pressure ridge when a dark form slid by his field of vision. Startled, he pulled back for a moment, then put his eyes back on the rubber cups and traversed the scope in search of the object. Then he grinned and said to his Number One, "Avraam, have sonar report all contacts."

Ryback, the wiry executive officer, hit the intercom button and said, "Sonar, conn."

"Conn, sonar, aye."

"Report all contacts."

"One seal. Type unknown. Right on top of us now, moving away off the starboard side. We have no data in our computer on Antarctic seals. We only have data on seals native to the Northern Hemisphere."

"Very well," Ryback replied.

Bodin couldn't help but smile as he watched the bulbous creature cruise effortlessly through the water, occasionally propelling itself with a flap from its flippers. It was the biggest seal Bodin had ever seen. Indeed, it was huge, yet so graceful.

What the *Kharkov* had crossed paths with was a giant Weddell seal. An extraordinary animal of enormous bulk, it was cloaked in a thick layer of blubber that provided it with life-giving warmth. And although it weighed in at almost a thousand pounds, it could maneuver underwater like a submerged ballerina.

As it grew smaller in the viewer, an idea came to Bodin and he ordered, "Come to one-seven-zero. Ahead five knots."

"One-seven-zero. Five knots, aye."

Bodin kept the *Kharkov* just close enough to keep the creature in view, not wanting to lose it or frighten it off. If he could tail it long enough, he wagered his problems would be solved.

With the *Kharkov* in train, the Weddell seal cruised along, weav-

ing around some ice keels that protruded from above. She seemed to
be in no particular hurry, and that was understandable, for Weddell
seals can stay underwater for up to an hour, and have been known
to dive to a depth of two thousand feet.

Finally the seal halted at a point on the ice ceiling, and as Bodin
watched, the top half of her seemed to disappear. A few moments
passed, and the bottom half vanished as well. Bodin kept the *Kharkov* on track until it was under the point of her disappearance.

"All stop," ordered Bodin.

"All stop, aye."

Bodin pulled away from the viewer and rubbed his eyes. Then he
turned to the pilot, Toomas Mizim, who was now simply an observer
on board. The captain smiled and said, "I have finally found a
navigator who is your equal, Mr. Mizim. . . . Avraam, send out the
divers and prepare to release the buoy. They will find a small *polyn'ya*
directly above us."

"Aye, Captain."

In the forward torpedo room of the *Kharkov,* two frogmen
crawled awkwardly into separate torpedo tubes, pushing their aqualungs ahead of them. Once they were inside, the doors closed, and
it wasn't long before they heard the gurgling and felt the frigid water
as it closed around them in total darkness. The cold from the icy
waters stabbed through their dry suits like a dagger, and they began
sucking in air with rapid gasps. Finally the torpedo doors opened,
and they both exited into the pale, translucent light beneath the
ice—sans flippers.

They helped one another with their aqualungs, and then reached
back into their respective tubes for a nylon net bag, which they
attached to their belts.

One frogman went up to the ice ceiling and explored, and in no
time he found the Weddell seal's breathing hole, while the number
two frogman went to the top of the sail and grabbed an object that
looked like an oversized pumpkin. Pulling it by the handle, he guided
the buoyant pumpkin toward the air hole as a cable played out
behind it. He "parked" the buoy against the ceiling, and the two
frogmen reached into their bags and proceeded to strap on their foot
and hand crampons, which were specially designed for this sort of
thing.

With difficulty, the first frogman began hauling himself over the
ice ledge of the air hole. He was greeted by three female Weddell seals

lying on the ice, looking at him with mild curiosity. "Now do not get nervous," he mumbled through his mouthpiece. "I am only borrowing this little hole of yours." He struggled to grab a toehold, then heaved himself onto the surface and collapsed, looking like a fourth seal on the pack ice.

The buoy bobbed to the surface, along with his comrade, whom he helped over the ledge. Then, together, they hauled the pumpkin onto the pack.

The seals did not stir, but remained there gazing at the two intruders.

The frogmen carried the pumpkin about twenty meters away from the air hole, pulling the cable behind. Quickly they anchored the device, then unscrewed the top and flipped it over to attach the dish-shaped top to the base. One of the frogmen aligned the dish until a red light came on. Then the two Russians departed, giving the seals a wave before they disappeared back down the hole. The Soviet frogmen didn't realize how lucky they were that the three seals were all females. If the male had been present, he would have defended his air hole against the intruders.

In the communications room of the *Kharkov*, the *michman* activated the earth-station dish deployed on the ice and sent a "burst" transmission via the *Molniya* communications satellite, notifying Red Banner Black Sea Fleet headquarters in Sevastopol that the *Kharkov* had arrived on station.

It wasn't any time at all before the teletype started clattering with a brief message in reply. The *michman* tore the paper out of the machine and once again retired to the crypto-vault, where he deciphered the message on a one-time pad. When he was finished, the text read:

> *Tbilisi* **sunk.**
> **Leopard Base captured by Americans.**
> **Remain on station to await further**
> **instructions.**
> $\qquad\qquad\qquad\qquad$ **Timoshenko**

McMURDO BASE

The light first appeared as a distant star, faint and remote, like a lone beacon for an ancient mariner. But slowly it grew, becoming brighter and brighter, as if he were traveling toward the end of a tunnel, until it filled his field of vision. There was dizziness. Then grogginess. Then he saw an angel. A beautiful angel. She looked as if she were asleep, her golden hair framing a lovely face. It was so quiet. So peaceful. Was this heaven? Was he dead? He wanted to speak to the angel, to call out to her, but his throat was dry and he couldn't form the words . . . until he moved slightly and a stabbing jolt—feeling like the rowel of a spur—raked down his left side. With a new clarity of vision brought into focus by his pain, he cried out in a raspy voice, "Dana!"

Dana Harrow came awake—somewhat dazed—to see Robert Rawlings on the dispensary bed. She quickly became undazed, and was on her feet, cradling his head to help him sip some water.

She called someone, and a man appeared, wearing a long white coat over green fatigues. The white-robed man blinded Rawlings with the beam from a small flashlight and took his pulse, then checked a bottle hanging upside down, with a tube extending from it into Rawlings's arm. He lifted up the covers to check the dressing. Rawlings seemed to remember the white robe saying "Lucky," just before he disappeared.

After white robe had left, Dana heard Rawlings whisper, "Hurts." She took a syringe and injected some Demerol into his IV tube. "It will be okay soon," she said.

He seemed to be dozing, but his eyes came open again and he whispered, "What . . . happened?"

Dana retrieved another cup of water and once again cradled his head as he took some sips. Then she eased him back on the pillow and began talking softly. "You had just returned to the snow cave base. The bombing had gone well and everyone was excited. Do you remember that?"

Slowly, Rawlings nodded.

"Then . . . then the Russian helicopter came and we all ran into the snow cave. It was kind of a blur for me after that. The snow cave collapsed. . . . Pancho shot the helicopter down with that missile. . . ."

"Pancho?" he whispered.

Tears welled up in Dana's eyes, and she felt her throat tighten. She grabbed a tissue from the bedside table and said, "Pancho . . . he's gone, Robert. . . . He saved us all, but he's gone." She saw a tear roll out of his eye, and dabbed it with her tissue. "You were hit. Something—I don't know what—must have hit you under your left arm in a kind of glancing blow. Essentially, it removed one of your ribs. The actual damage wasn't that great, because it was a shallow wound. But a network of arterial vessels were severed, and you lost an ocean of blood. Went into severe shock. I was able to slow the bleeding, but couldn't stop it. Reminded me of my time in the trauma center. Anyway, the Russians pulled out. We saw them as they made their way toward Mount Discovery. Captain Nye was having Gates send a message every thirty seconds, demanding a Medevac. Finally one of those planes that can fly like a helicopter arrived."

"Osprey," whispered Rawlings.

"Yes. An Osprey. That doctor you saw earlier was on board. He said he wanted to take you back to some ship for treatment, but by this time I thought you were very close to death. I couldn't find your pulse. I knew you wouldn't survive a hundred-mile flight. So I told him about the dispensary here at McMurdo and the emergency operating suite we have. The doctor insisted we go back to the ship—I think he called it the *Wasp*—and we started shouting at each other, and that's when . . . when . . ." She hesitated.

"When . . . what?" he asked in a barely audible rasp.

"That's when Captain Nye—Phillip—leveled his gun at the doctor and growled—I mean he really growled—'You *will* do what the lady says.' Well, that doctor starts yelling about assault with a deadly weapon and courts-martial, and jail and everything, and that's when Gates, de Parma, and the rest of them started cocking their guns and pointing them at the doctor and his medics. That seemed to shut him up. We all loaded up on that Osprey and made a quick dash here. We scrubbed and got to work on you. By this time I really did think you were dead. Luckily your blood type is O. The boys ponied up about five pints in all. That doctor was—is—a real jerk, but he's also an incredible surgeon. Still says he's bringing our crew up on charges." Dana thought she detected a chuckle from him, but she wasn't sure. "Anyway, here we are. You've been semicomatose for seven days. Now that you've pulled out of it, you should heal fairly rapidly. Like I said, the actual wound wasn't that bad. It was loss of blood and shock."

Dana saw his green eyes scan the room, and he became aware that some other beds were occupied. "Who are . . . they?" he asked.

Dana followed his gaze and replied, "They're Russians. They've got four of them in here. Survivors of the bombing attack. There were others, but they were sent to the *Wasp,* I'm told." Rawlings trained his green eyes on her for a moment. She looked so different. Well scrubbed. Made up. Clean clothes. The hair—soft. As the painkiller took effect, her image began to fade, and he struggled to whisper, "Dana . . . thought you were . . . angel . . ."

She leaned closer and asked him to repeat the inaudible words, but he was already asleep.

WILLIAMS FIELD

The clouds were scattered and the wind was brisk, giving the air a distinct chill that turned Marine Lt. Gen. Myron Tharp's cheeks a rosy color. Had to be careful of frostbite, he reminded himself. Tharp had been to Norway on two Marine deployments during NATO exercises, and he'd developed a healthy respect for the cold.

Myron Tharp was alone, walking alongside one of the bomb trenches laid down when the B-1Bs had pounded the entrapped Russian aircraft. The rear half of a MiG-31 Foxhound's fuselage was lying on its side, and Tharp reached up and nudged the elevator, just to see if it would move. It wouldn't, and the Marine general continued walking. He had never seen anything like this. Even in Vietnam. There, he remembered hearing the distant thunder of some B-52 carpet bombing, but he had never seen for himself, close up, the kind of devastation such an engine of destruction could inflict.

Tharp was in a reflective mood. His Beowulf plan had succeeded beyond anyone's predictions, even his own, but the rush of euphoria that had come on the heels of the success had worn off. Now, as he walked along this trench of blackened snow, it truly came home to him—for the first time since Khe Sanh—what a bloody business he had chosen for his vocation.

Tharp heard a clanking noise that was the unmistakable sound of a tracked vehicle. He turned and saw two cubelike objects—one behind the other—rolling toward him on treads. This was a SUSV (pronounced "sus-vee"), a Sno-Cat type of vehicle manufactured by AB Hagglund & Soner of Sweden. The front cube was a cab for a driver, passenger, and equipment, while the rear cube was hooked on to the lead cube by a hitch, and it came in various configurations that could carry troops, equipment, or communications gear. The rear cube on this SUSV was sporting a forest of antennae, which told Tharp that he was about to receive a visit from Maj. Gen. Joshua Pfeiffer, commander of the Sixth Infantry Division (Light).

As the SUSV squeaked to a halt, Tharp heard the distant howl of still another C-17 transport jet taking off. Since Williams Field had been turned into a cratered cemetery, the Americans had mimicked the Soviets by assembling prefabricated runways nearby so that their transports could bring in Pfeiffer's division.

Joshua Pfeiffer stepped out of his SUSV and exchanged salutes with Tharp. Pfeiffer wasn't one for small talk, and quickly got to the crux of the matter. "General, I have my second brigade in place thirty kilometers north of the Soviet positions on Mount Discovery, along with the Second Battalion of the 17th Field Artillery. We got them pegged if they try to move, although I don't know where they would move to. My MI people are in forward observation positions, and we've been monitoring their transmissions with the Quick Fix helicopter. Within thirty-six hours I will have my First Brigade in place, along with the remainder of my division artillery. I intend to attack in approximately seventy-two hours with my two brigades and the Marine tanks in support. I will hold the Marine ground forces in reserve. They won't like it, but my people simply have more experience on this type of terrain."

The Marine general nodded. "I would agree."

Pfeiffer continued, "The armor won't help us that much. The slope leading up to their emplacements is steep and icy in patches, and the M-1s will have a tough time with traction. This is an infantry job. I plan to hammer the Soviets hard with my artillery and the Navy's air strikes, but after that, my people will have to go in and ferret them out."

Tharp sighed and decided he might as well get it over with. "Josh, I want you to continue moving your people into position, but hold off on launching any attack for the time being."

Pfeiffer blinked. "I *beg* your pardon, General Tharp?"

The diminutive Marine sighed once again and said, "As you mentioned, the Russians are bottled up. They aren't going anywhere. They have no place to go. They are probably at the tail end of their provisions. I have decided we'll starve them out."

Pfeiffer blinked again, then his stout figure assumed its linebacker stance—a sure sign that Joshua Pfeiffer was digging in. "General Tharp, sir, we may have the Russians bottled up, and they may be short of supplies, but an enemy force is an enemy force. If we don't secure the area, there's no telling what they may try. Think about it, General. What would you do if you were in the Soviet commander's place?"

"I *have* thought about it, Josh. And unless the Soviets want to up the ante, this battle is won—over and done with. In about two weeks we'll be down to the rubidium deposit. In three weeks we'll have excavated enough of it to close the book on this business, and it becomes political again. It's still a small world, Josh. We've got to live with the Soviets, and a lot of needless Russian casualties are not going to help the situation. The UN is already calling for mediation." He stopped talking as the howl of another C-17 transport filled the air, then faded. "So that's my decision, Josh. You can take it up with Admiral Rumley if you want."

Pfeiffer knew when he'd lost. "No, General. I'll let it stand. . . . But I just want you to know that I think you're dead wrong." And with that he saluted and climbed back into his SUSV. With a leg he propped open the door and said, "I would stay away from this airfield, General. My engineers made a sweep and detonated all the unexploded ordnance they could find, but there may be some live warheads still buried in the ice." The door closed and the SUSV clanked away, its antennae swaying back and forth as it churned across the snow.

As Myron Tharp watched the tracked vehicle depart, he knew that Pfeiffer had some legitimate points, but he was willing to take such a risk in order to hold down casualties on both sides. Tharp wanted only to get this rubidium business over with, and he was relieved he didn't have to use a device called an Ostrich Egg in the pursuit of that objective.

THE *KHARKOV*

"The *Tbilisi* sunk!? Leopard Base captured!?" Capt. Kasimir Bodin reached for the brass railing in the central control room of the *Kharkov* to steady himself. "How in the world did this happen?"

The *starpom,* Avraam Ryback, passed the message he'd just read aloud to Bodin and said, "I have no idea, Captain. The signal provides no additional information, except to say we are to remain on station for further instructions."

There was distilled bitterness in Bodin's voice as he barked, "Ha! Further instructions! Is this what we came twenty-three thousand kilometers for? Is this what our brothers on the *Magadan* died for? For *nothing?*"

Ryback had never seen Bodin so incensed, but knew the captain was more than justified. He waited until Bodin had vented his spleen a bit longer before asking gently, "Shall I inform the crew, Captain?"

Bodin covered his face and said wearily, "Very well, Avraam. I suppose the *Smolensk* is receiving this news with the same alacrity we are. Pass the word that we are likely to return home soon."

MOUNT DISCOVERY—February 20

Maj. Gen. Mitrofan Tromso looked through the eyepiece of the eighty-power spotting scope toward the American positions, just thirty kilometers away. They were camouflaged but still discernible—and he wondered how discernible he was to them.

On the northern slopes of Mount Discovery, Tromso's men had built a network of fortifications by hacking shallow trenches through the ice, and constructing walls and overhangs with packed snow. Surprisingly, packed-snow fortifications that were two meters thick could provide protection from small-arms fire, and battlements that were four meters thick could provide protection from artillery blasts. He speculated that the Americans had constructed similar defenses on the ice field below.

Tromso was in a quandary. It had been ten days since his Leopard Base fell, yet the Americans had not attacked him. They had not even bombarded him with artillery or air strikes. But they had him bottled up, and if he tried any mischief he knew the American planes would be upon him in a flash. Their helicopters were buzzing around constantly, out of range of his SA-7 Grail shoulder-fired SAMs. All Tromso could do was hold out until help arrived . . . *if* it arrived.

"General?"

Tromso looked over his shoulder to see his chief of staff, whose face looked gaunt and haggard. The face of a man suffering from exposure and hunger. Tromso was sure he looked the same way himself. "*Da,* Vasili. What is it?"

"It is time to release another ration to the men. You ordered that no food be released unless you gave your personal authorization."

Tromso sighed. "Very well, Vasili. We have been on half-rations for how long?"

"Full rations for six days, General. Half-rations for four days. We have two days left at half-rations. We can stretch that to four if we halve them again. It is regrettable we did not have time to load more rations before our evacuation."

Tromso bit his lip. "You are too kind, Vasili. It was a retreat, not an 'evacuation.' Any word from Moscow?"

"Just the same. 'Hold position.' "

Tromso betrayed his exhaustion and leaned against the fortification wall in his small command post. He had the dubious distinction of presiding over the worst Soviet military debacle since Afghanistan. His career, if he made it out of here alive, was finished. The Americans had him in the stranglehold of a siege. His men were tired, cold, and hungry. Morale was in the tank. But maybe, just maybe, he could endure this misery if he wasn't paralyzed by *inaction*. But what could he do? Once again he looked through the spotting telescope, and again the Americans were there—dug in, thirty kilometers away—just out of range of the rocket-assisted rounds of his 122-mm howitzers. Beyond their emplacements was the airfield, and beyond that was . . . hmmm . . . he wondered . . . was it possible? As the idea took root in Tromso's brain, he felt a small surge of energy, and decided he'd had enough of this siege crap. It was time to engage the enemy. He turned to his chief of staff and said, "Put the men back on full rations and get the commander of that *Smerch* battery—what is his name?" It was strange what hunger did to the memory.

"Major Ivanov," replied the chief.

"*Da,* Ivanov. Get him up here."

Maj. Grigori Ivanov, squat-framed and swarthy, with all the charm of a snapping turtle, peered through the eyepiece of the spotting telescope as Tromso asked, "Can you make it out? It looks like a small, dark speck against the ice pack, just below the shoreline of Ross Island."

"*Da,* General," replied Ivanov. "I see it. You are certain that is the mining site? I never saw it up close myself."

"That has to be it," replied Tromso. "There is nothing else on the ice. The question is, can you hit it with the *Smerch* missiles?"

Ivanov shrugged. "Depends."

Major Ivanov was in charge of the four *Smerch* ("Tornado") launchers that had been shipped in to defend the sea approaches to McMurdo Base. Each launcher consisted of twelve 300-mm rockets poised on top of a nineteen-ton transport vehicle. The artillery crews had labored with power winches to get the giant launch vehicles up the slopes of Mount Discovery and dug into positions. Ivanov had never understood why the Americans allowed them to do that—why they were not pounded by air strikes.

"Depends on what?" asked Tromso.

"I will show you on the map." He led the general to a small folding table in the command post, where a map of the McMurdo Sound area was spread out. "This is our position here," said Ivanov, pointing to the north slope of Mount Discovery. He moved his finger across the map to the dot representing Branding Iron Station. "The mining site is here, some eighty-eight kilometers away. My battery has the extended range version of the *Smerch* missile, and the range in the technical manual states eighty kilometers, but in fact it can usually travel up to eighty-five kilometers. Depending on the particular missile, it might reach eighty-eight kilometers."

"Why the variance?"

"Depends on how well the solid-fuel propellant is packed at the factory. That, plus our elevation relative to the target—which is in our favor. The wind direction and velocity can also have an effect."

"But is the *Smerch* accurate enough to hit it?"

Ivanov pursed his lips and said, "Pinpoint accuracy is less of an issue. The *Smerch* delivers a three-hundred-kilogram cluster-fragmentation warhead that disperses in a wide pattern. As you recall, the *Smerch* weapons were assigned to your command to engage enemy landing craft at extremely long range." Although an abrasive sort, Ivanov possessed sufficient diplomatic antennae to know it was painful for Tromso to dwell on the issue of soured plans. So he continued, "If we can coax the range out of the missiles, we should have a reasonable chance of doing some damage. But are you certain you want to hit the mining site? I can quite easily hit the airfield, or their ships unloading in the Sound. Or their positions on the ice shelf."

Tromso shook his head. "No, the Americans would only repair or replace the damage and their casualties. I want to hurt them as much

as I can, and that means going after what they came here for—what
we all came here for."

Ivanov gave a final shrug. "As you wish, General."

As Ivanov started to leave, Tromso said, "Fire a volley of all
twelve missiles, then tell your people to move out smartly. Firing
those things will give away your positions, and the American planes
will be upon you."

BRANDING IRON STATION

Lt. Col. Samuel McClure of the U.S. Army Corps of Engineers had
never thought he would see the icedome again, yet here he was. And
this time he was in charge—which was not a situation he relished.
The Russians had plugged two-thirds of the mine shaft by shoveling
the excavated earth back in. Very clever. The consistency of the
refilled earth was loose, not tightly packed like the original excavation. As a result, McClure was dispensing with the digger drill
device. Instead, he was having the loose-packed earth shoveled
into a large bucket and raised to the surface by a hoist. With the
re-excavation, the icedome was filled with dust, so McClure was
wearing a surgical mask to keep the particles out of his lungs.

McClure had heard some scuttlebutt that the task force commander was taking some heat from Washington for using knockout
gas to recapture the icedome. The engineer shook his head. Seize the
objective without causing casualties on either side, and they want to
hang you. McClure filed that piece of information away. If he ever
had to seize an objective in combat, he would always remember to
spill a little blood in the process.

MCMURDO STATION

"Care for a little dessert?" Dana asked, trying to sound cheerful.

Robert Rawlings swiveled the dinner tray aside and said, "No.
Thanks, but no."

Dana looked at his plate. It was more than half full. She was
worried. His wound was healing, but Rawlings had fallen into a blue
funk. Uncommunicative. Stoic. No appetite. And she was afraid his
morose attitude was starting to affect his physical recovery. She had
no doubt the death of Pancho Ramirez was the source of his depression. Dana had never spent any time in the psych ward, and had no
experience with something like this. She didn't know what to do,

except to bore in on the problem. Rawlings was lying there, staring at the ceiling. She began probing. "How long had you known Pancho?"

He continued staring for a while longer before responding, in a barely audible voice, "We were both in Vietnam at the same time, but we didn't know each other then. We were both a couple of kids. He was a grunt—that's a rifleman—in the First Air Cav, and I was in the Air Force."

"Air Force?"

Rawlings's face showed the glimmer of a smile. "Yeah. Sounds crazy, doesn't it? I was a tailgunner on a gunship. Some were called 'Puff the Magic Dragon,' but we called ours 'Spooky' because we operated camouflaged aircraft—at night, for the most part. I was in an outfit called the Fourth Air Commando Squadron. The gunships were old DC-3s with miniguns—Gatling-style guns—mounted sideways, pointing out the rear door. And basically it was a marriage made in hell."

Dana was taken aback at the bitterness in his voice, but felt she must probe further. "How do you mean?"

Rawlings sighed. "It taught me never to trust politicians—in uniform or out. Vietnam was a real abortion, Dana. The 'Spooky' gunship should never have happened. The DC-3 was an old transport. It was never meant to be a warplane. But I'm sure some politician advanced his Air Force career by promoting a lunatic idea like that."

Putting his hand flat, he moved it in a sweeping arc and continued, "We would fly these close air-support missions, flying around in low and slow circles over Viet Cong or NVA units, firing the miniguns down on them, or dropping flares. If you were a friendly unit on the ground, you were always glad to see us—as long as we didn't hit you by mistake—because it was effective gunfire. Devastating, in fact. We saved a lot of butts on our side, for sure. But the old DC-3 was a slow, low-flying target. And some of us got ripped to shreds by ground fire. My crew got transferred to fly interdiction missions out of Udorn, in Thailand. We were hitting the Ho Chi Minh Trail at night. My ship got shot down in Laos. I was the sole survivor, and I was on the ground in bad shape for four days before I was plucked out. Eventually I spent three months in a VA hospital. That was a real thrill. All because some politician promoted the insane idea of putting a gun in the ass of an old DC-3."

She sensed this was a sore subject and decided to guide him to something else. "Well, if you were in the Air Force, how did you wind up in the Army?"

She felt better when he chuckled a little. "Strange how things work out, isn't it? I grew up in Jackson Hole, Wyoming. I guess I never told you that, did I?"

She shook her head.

"Well, that's where I'm from. My folks ran a small lodge and some cabins. Tourists in the summer. Skiers in the winter. It was a family business. I was the youngest of five, with four sisters. Did a lot of work around the place. Trail rides in the summer. Rafting. That sort of thing. And skiing in the winter.

"After I got out of the VA hospital, I went back and kind of took up where I left off. But by now I was twenty-two and kind of restless. Decided to give college a shot, but that was expensive. The Army and Air Force were offering ROTC scholarships at the University of Wyoming in Laramie. Well, I knew I didn't want anything more to do with the Air Force, so I signed up with the Army program, thinking that by the time I got out, Vietnam would be over and I would do my time and muster out. Get a real job somewhere."

"But you didn't?"

He smiled. "No. No, I didn't. I finished school. By that time my folks had sold the place and retired, and my sisters had all married and scattered to the four winds. I got stationed at Fort Rich, outside Anchorage. I guess I was the oldest second lieutenant in the Army by that time. Spent about three weeks with a regular infantry unit before somebody found out I was a serious skier, then zingo"—he made a motion with his thumb—"before I knew it I was assigned to the Northern Warfare Training Center as a member of the Army ski team. And that's where I met up with Pancho. He'd left the Army after his tour in Vietnam. Drifted for a while. Went to Europe and joined the Foreign Legion."

"You're kidding."

Rawlings laughed. "No joke. It's true. He didn't care much for the Legion, though. Punched out after basic training and reupped in the Army after he came back to the States. Pancho hailed from Ruidoso, New Mexico. Worked part-time at the ski resort there as a kid and took up skiing, so we were already kindred spirits when we met. He's the one who talked me into transferring into intel from the infantry branch." Rawlings's eyes wandered over the ceiling. "I guess we spent about ten years together in Alaska. Our assignments always seemed to link up with each other. We'd go off for a tour in Germany, or Fort Riley, Kansas, or wherever, but we always seemed to wind up back in the north country. . . . And we both thought Alaska was the best thing this side of heaven. Hunting. Fishing. Skiing. Camping. It was great."

"Was Pancho married?" Dana asked softly.

Rawlings took a deep breath. "Yeah. His wife's name is Alena. They have two boys. One's in college. One in high school. My surrogate family, you might say."

"But you never married?" she asked, trying to sound casual.

Rawlings grinned. "You're not going to believe this, but I've been engaged four times."

She nodded. "That is hard to believe."

Robert shrugged. "Seems that whenever things got to the serious stage I would go to the field, or off on a hunting trip, and when I got back they'd married someone else."

There was a creak as the door opened, and Maj. Gen. Joshua Pfeiffer walked in, wearing a well-used set of overwhites. "So, how's the patient today?"

"Better," Dana replied. "Getting better, I think."

"Yessir," Rawlings agreed. "I think I'll be able to get back to my battalion in a couple of days."

Pfeiffer shot a glance at Dana, who gave a discreet shake of the head.

The general said, "Not for a while, Robert. The way I hear it, your blood supply was on 'empty' a lot longer than it had a right to be. It's only by the grace of God and this lady here that you're still alive. Until I say different, you're on medical. . . . Say, where are those Russians that were in here?"

Dana said, "Some Navy medics—corpsmen, I think they're called—came and took them. Said they were going to some hospital in the Philippines."

Pfeiffer emitted a "Harumpff," and said, "Nobody ever tells me a damn thing."

"Sir," said Rawlings. "One item. I understand Phillip Nye and his team used some"—he groped for the words—"heavy-duty persuasion on the Navy doctor to get me here after I was hit. I'd appreciate it if you would see what you could do to iron out any kinks."

Pfeiffer made a sound that was something like a cross between a growl and a laugh. "Robert, I'm putting Phillip Nye and his team in for the Silver Star. We lost a total of four B-1 bombers, Robert. Four out of twenty-four. If your team hadn't made it through to put the bead on those SAMs, it would've been a disaster. Since I'm the convening authority for any court-martial, I think I can guarantee the matter won't see the light of day." He looked at Dana. "And as for you, young lady, I've talked with Captain Nye and the others about what you did. Since you're a civilian, I can't award you anything. But I've spoken to Admiral Rumley, the task force commander, and he says he's going to see that the White House awards you the Medal of Freedom. It's the highest civilian honor we can bestow."

Dana blushed, not really knowing what to say. "Thank you, General. But that's not necessary. All I want is to retrieve whatever data I can from my seismic huts. When the Russians destroyed all the radios in McMurdo, my base camp receiver was totaled, too. All I have left is what's on the magnetic recording disk at each location—which isn't much. They fill up in seventy-two hours. But still, I'd like to retrieve what I can."

Pfeiffer's brow furrowed as he said, "I'm afraid we still have an enemy force out there, Miss Harrow, so that's impossible for the moment. But we'll see how things turn out. . . . I guess I should evacuate you, but I think Colonel Rawlings will have a better recovery under your care."

Dana looked at her patient. "I would agree."

Pfeiffer looked down at Rawlings, and with a gentleness in his voice that Dana found surprising, he said, "Robert, I just wanted you to know I'm putting Pancho in for the Congressional, and you for the DSC. I know you don't think much about medals, but it's the right thing to—"

Pfeiffer never finished his sentence, for the door burst open and his aide shouted, "General! There's trouble at Branding Iron Station!"

THE *CARL VINSON*

Lt. Michael Pershing was sitting on one of the folding chairs in the chapel of the *Carl Vinson,* perched forward, chin resting on hand, like a flesh and blood incarnation of Rodin's *Thinker.* He was taking solace in the quiet of the chapel—a refuge, of sorts, from his celebrity status. Blackjack was the sole aviator in the second half of the twentieth century to have sunk an aircraft carrier, and that singular

eminence had unleashed upon him an unremitting stream of hand-
shakes, backslapping, autograph hounds, and pleas for interviews.
And everywhere he turned, the chatter within the ship was the same:
"I knew Blackjack would get through." . . . "No surprise to me that
it was Blackjack." . . . "Blackjack? What a flier! Was there ever any
doubt?" It was the kind of refrain that rippled in his wake as he
walked through the passageways of the *Vinson*. And while his galac-
tic ego once would have welcomed such comments, perhaps even
expected them, he now found the chatter stifling. Oppressive. Suf-
focating. So he had come here, to the chapel, to seek some solitude
and try to grope with the reality that he was a phony hero who had
sunk a Russian supercarrier while he was in the grips of a choking
fear.

"Well, hullo, Blackjack. I guess you're the man of the hour around
here these days, aren't you? Glad you could stop by."

Blackjack raised his eyes to see the chaplain everyone called "the
Padre." Blackjack was a Roman Catholic, but the Catholic priest on
board the *Vinson* was a rather dour sort who spent the better part
of his homilies preaching how seamen had such a miserable lot in life.
He was a real downer for morale, and Blackjack never understood
why the Navy let the guy on board. It wasn't the sort of message a
congregation of sailors liked to hear. So a number of Catholic seamen
and pilots, Blackjack included, had struck up a friendship with the
Protestant chaplain named "Padre"—a Baptist pastor who hailed, as
did Pershing, from Texas.

The Padre was fifty-two, slightly stocky, with a generous middle,
a flabby neck, and thinning dark hair. He was the quintessential
father figure to whom many of the very young sailors gravitated.

"Oh, hi, Padre," Blackjack said softly.

The Padre sensed something amiss, for the aviator was not his
usual garrulous, cocky, irreverent self. Padre took a nearby seat
and said, "I suppose you've been under a glare of publicity lately."
Blackjack only nodded. "I heard that TV crew from the public
affairs shop was looking for you. Did you grace them with an interview?"

Blackjack shook his head and looked at the floor. Padre figured
something was more than just amiss, so he gently patted the young
Texan's shoulder and probed as carefully as he could. "Something
troubling you, Blackjack? Anything you want to tell me? You know
this is just between you and me."

Blackjack nodded. "Yeah, Padre. I know. It's just that . . . well, I . . . I . . ."

"Go on," prodded the Padre.

Blackjack cleared his throat and whispered in a rasp, "I choked."

The Padre waited for something more, an amplification of some kind, but none was forthcoming. Puzzled, he asked, "What do you mean, you choked?"

Blackjack cleared his throat again and said, "During the attack . . . on the *Tbilisi* . . . I choked."

The chaplain blinked uncomprehendingly. "Michael, correct me if I'm wrong, but I seem to recall it was your bombs that sank the *Tbilisi*. I would hardly call that choking."

Blackjack shook his head again. "You don't understand, Padre. I was going in, flying on Bossman's wing. I was . . . I was so scared I couldn't move. I could hardly breathe. Bossman ordered 'combat spread' and I simply couldn't let go of his wing. Well, Bossman got hit and I ran. Pickled my bombs in a panic and lost all control. I climbed, and another wing appeared in front of me. Russian, I think. I was choking with fear, and all I could think of was to hang on to that wing. Like I did with the Blues. I stayed with him for a while, then he blew up, too. The next thing I know, the *Tbilisi* is right below me, and I have a slam-dunk shot. Piece of cake. I have no idea how I got there, but it all happened because I was trying to run away— because I choked."

The Padre's brow furrowed. He was more puzzled than before. "But you said you jettisoned your bombs. How did you manage to sink the *Tbilisi?*"

Blackjack shrugged. "One got hung up on the rack, but it apparently tore free when I pulled out of the bombing dive."

"More than 'apparently,' I'd say," the Padre observed.

"Anyway, the flight back to the *Vinson* was clear. No missiles. No bandits. Nothing. I guess maybe their defensive systems were all wired into the *Tbilisi,* or something like that. I landed on the deck, and the next thing I know, I'm carried up to the flag bridge, where Admiral Rumley says I'm going to get a Navy Cross." Blackjack put his face in his hands. "I don't deserve any Navy Cross, Padre."

The preacher reached out and patted his shoulder again, and gently said, "Michael, in the fog of combat, things happen that we can't account for. Perhaps the thought of survival is so consuming that it distorts the actual course of events. Maybe what you say is

true, but I think you should look at the results, and you have to
accept that it was your bomb that sank the Russian supercarrier. The
loss of life is a tragedy. But, Michael, you had a job to do and you
did it."

Blackjack sighed. "Yeah. A job. Jazzman dead. Otter dead. Even
Bossman dead. What was it all for, anyway?"

"Ah," the Padre said knowingly. "The warrior's lament. Why do
we wage war on our fellow man? Madness, isn't it? Makes no sense
of any kind, really. But sometimes evil rises up, and we—meaning
the civilized world—must smite it down. We had to drive the life out
of Hitler, Blackjack. Had to. Or as Churchill said, Europe would
have descended into a new 'Dark Age, made more sinister . . . by the
lights of perverted science.'

"And Stalin was worse than Hitler. We had to keep him and the
old Soviet guard at the point of a sword for forty years, or they
would've consumed Western Europe. That's why men like you are
here."

Blackjack shrugged. "Here . . . in a frozen sea . . . going after some
dirt in the ground that nobody understands? Is that why Jazzman
and Otter and all those Russians had to die?"

The Padre gave him another pat and rose to leave. "I hear what
you're saying. We don't have the clarity of purpose we had when we
were striving to put Hitler in the grave. But, however blurred our
motives, Michael, you—and I—made a choice to put on these uniforms. And having done that, we're duty-bound to carry out our
orders—even in Antarctica. And there is something else I want you
to think about. When that *Tbilisi* sank, five thousand men—men just
like us—went to their deaths. We all share that responsibility, Blackjack. From the pharmacist's mate to Admiral Rumley, to the cook,
to the Air Boss, to me, to you, to the folks back home who sent us
out here. It's a collective responsibility. You can't carry it on your
shoulders alone."

Slowly, Blackjack nodded.

"Listen, I have to meet with one of the crew. Girlfriend problems,
you know. We'll talk and pray about it later. Don't get down on
yourself." And the Padre left.

Blackjack remained for a time, pondering the Padre's words—yet
even they could not take away the sting of his having choked.

BRANDING IRON STATION

Maj. Gen. Joshua Pfeiffer was beyond anger as he watched his medics lay the bodies, or pieces of bodies, onto the litters that would be taken to the grave registration detachment at McMurdo Base. One of the *Smerch* missiles had found its mark on the Branding Iron derrick, and the effect of the fragmentation warhead had been brutal—destroying the elevator hoist and cutting through the engineers on the deck like a scythe. It was particularly cruel, because some of the victims were woman soldiers.

Pfeiffer turned on Myron Tharp and bellowed, "I told you we shouldn't leave an enemy force in place, General! These are my people! Maybe you'd feel different if they were Marines! Now either we get rid of these Russians or you can get yourself another ground force commander!"

Pfeiffer's words cut into Tharp's soul like a razor, but the little Marine general knew it was useless to argue. In laying siege to the Russians—instead of attacking—his intent had been to save lives, not to take them. But Pfeiffer was on the edge of blind rage—a soldier who wanted blood for the blood of his comrades. And Tharp knew he had no choice now, so he simply said, "Secure Mount Discovery."

ROSS ICE SHELF—February 22

A battery of eight 155-mm self-propelled Paladin howitzers from the Second Battalion/17th Field Artillery Regiment—shipped in from Fort Sill, Oklahoma—rolled across the ice shelf in a line, each one spaced about a half-mile apart. At 24,000 meters from the north base of Mount Discovery, four of the howitzers halted, and immediately the gunners punched in the targeting coordinates as they were received from the fire-direction center at the battalion command post. The target data—and the howitzers' position provided by their onboard navigation systems—were digested by the Paladins' fire-control computers. Once the computations were completed, the muzzles of the weapons were rapidly brought to the precise elevation and azimuth. Working together, the assistant gunners and drivers of each section rammed the heavy, rocket-assisted rounds into the breech; and without hesitation the gunners pulled the triggers, sending the high-explosive projectiles on their way while the other four Paladin howitzers continued clanking toward the mountain, some twenty-four kilometers away.

MOUNT DISCOVERY

Maj. Gen. Mitrofan Tromso saw the high-explosive rounds erupt at the foot of Mount Discovery, sending up white geysers of snow and ice as the *Crump!-Crump!-Crump!-Crump!* sound washed over him. He looked through his high-powered spotting scope. This wasn't a major barrage, but sporadic fire. There was a pause, then four more *Crump!* sounds peppered the base of the mountain. This time closer to his position. He looked through the scope again, and he could barely make out the white camouflaged howitzers. They were leapfrogging, one group firing while the other advanced. Why?

Crump!-Crump!-Crump!

Closer.

Tromso raised his artillery battalion commander on the field telephone and asked, "Are the American howitzers in range of your guns?"

"Questionable," came the reply. "We have an advantage in range because of our elevation, but hitting such dispersed mobile targets at this distance will be difficult. Major Ivanov says he can hit them with the *Smerch* rockets."

WHUMP!

"Then engage with rockets!"

"*Da,* General!"

It was only a matter of seconds before Tromso heard the banshee screams of a volley of *Smerch* rockets taking to the air. He watched through his scope and saw the fragmentation explosions pepper two of the American howitzers. He was wondering if the fragmentation rounds would be effective against the armor on the self-propelled vehicles when a *WHAM! WHAM!* knocked him and his staff to the ground in their small command post. Tromso was stunned, but quickly realized that the last concussion was no artillery blast. It was too powerful. He clambered to his feet and looked down the mountain at the burning hulk of the *Smerch* launcher. Then he looked up at the contrails of a flight of A-6 Intruders, circling above, out of range of his shoulder-fired Grail antiaircraft missiles.

BLAM!

The artillery was almost upon his positions.

So *that* was what the Americans were doing. Drawing his fire to expose his artillery emplacements, then dropping bombs to take them out. Tromso was faced with a dilemma: hold his fire and keep

his artillery guns under cover while the American howitzers shelled
them with impunity; or return the long-range fire and let the American planes bomb his emplacements one by one. A dilemma. But
Tromso wasn't the sort of man not to shoot back. The field phone
rang, and Tromso grabbed it.

"I think they are in range of our guns now! The *Smerch* launcher
was hit by aerial bombs!"

"I know!" Tromso yelled.

BLAM! BLAM! The American artillery was crawling over his
position now.

"Save the *Smerch* launchers. Open fire with two of your guns to
keep the Americans at bay!"

"*Da,* General!"

As the American artillery crept over his position, Tromso went
back to the bunker vent and looked down at the burning *Smerch*
launcher and marveled. How did the Americans drop their bombs
with such incredible accuracy?

BROWN PENINSULA

From his camouflaged post on the southern slope of Brown Peninsula, Capt. Phillip Nye looked through his own spotting scope and
saw the puffs from the two thousand-pound Paveway laser-guided
bombs as they impacted on the *Smerch* launcher. "Excellent shot,
Sergeant de Parma," he said respectfully. "I'm sure the brass will be
impressed with your marksmanship. Perhaps you can be a character
witness at my court-martial."

Sergeant de Parma remained hunched over his laser telescope as
he replied, "I will at yours, if you will at mine, sir—Oops! Looks like
one of their howitzers just opened up, Captain. Radio the anchor-
clankers to make another pass. I've got 'em pegged."

Gates, the RTO passed the radio handset to Captain Nye, and he
immediately began to transmit.

Moments later, two more puffs erupted on the north face of Mount
Discovery, and a Soviet artillery piece was silenced.

SIXTH INFANTRY DIVISION (LIGHT) COMMAND POST, ROSS ICE SHELF

In the frenetic activity of the command tent, the air hummed with chatter from controllers on the Navy TAC AIR radio net, the artillery command net, the Marine command net, the Air Force TAC AIR net, the Army Aviation net, and the division command net.

Maj. Gen. Joshua Pfeiffer was poised over a large folding table, which had equally large recon photographs spread over it. The photos of the north face of Mount Discovery had been sectioned and overlaid with grids. Across the table was Pfeiffer's chief of staff, trying to bring order out of chaos as the frequency of reports from the various commanders, section chiefs, and liaison officers increased. Standing between Pfeiffer and his chief of staff was the division's G-2, marking the photographs with a red grease pencil each time he received a report from the LRSD of another artillery emplacement taken out.

"We have a one-five-five artillery piece out of action with wounded, General," said the chief. "Another damaged. Medevac is commencing. The remaining one-five-fives are continuing their leapfrog maneuver."

"How many emplacements do the Russians have left?"

"Their artillery appears to be battalion strength," said the G-2. "We've knocked out a baker's dozen, including two rocket launchers. I estimate they are down to approximately half-strength."

Someone whispered into the chief's ear, and he said, "Looks like they're holding their fire now. I would guess they're trying to husband what they can until we attack."

With his arms folded across his chest, Pfeiffer said, "Let's not keep them waiting. Order the rest of the one-five-fives into forward positions while the Navy hits them with area bombing. Once the Paladins are in place, commence a fifty-minute barrage. Then, when our attack begins, let's give 'em a taste of their own medicine with ICM."

"Yes, General."

"I'll be in my helicopter," he said curtly, and in an instant he'd left the tent.

ROSS ICE SHELF

The gunners, drivers, and section chiefs of the Second Battalion/ 17th Field Artillery Regiment knew they were a long, long way from their home base in Fort Sill, Oklahoma, as their 155-mm self-propelled Paladin howitzers raced forward at thirty miles an hour via a route they were told—was clear of crevasses. Usually, artillery was employed behind a terrain feature like a ridge, or a hill, or in the cover of a forest. But the Russian commander had dug in on the slope of a mountain that had an apron of flat open space at its base for many kilometers. There was no place to run, no place to hide, so that was why their compatriots had dueled with their long-range, rocket-assisted rounds—to lure the Soviet artillery out into the open so it could be destroyed. Now the sparring was over, and they were going to close to within fifteen kilometers—to bring their guns to bear on the northern slope of Mount Discovery.

21

. . . .

CRÉCY

In a major engagement of the Hundred Years War, on August 26, 1346, the army of King Edward III of Britain faced the forces of Philip VI of France, along a ridge between the two small French villages of Wadicourt and Crécy.

The battle began late in the day, after evening vespers, with Edward's forces deployed in a defensive line to meet the attacks of the mounted French noblemen. As the armor-clad knights raced up the incline on their horses to charge the enemy positions, the English longbowmen (who were massed in wedge-shaped formations) loosed their arrows in dense clouds—clouds that arced through the air and came down upon the mounted noblemen with murderous effect.

As the Frenchmen fell back and regrouped for another charge, Edward's archers ran forward to pluck their armor-piercing bodkin-point arrows from the dead and wounded. Then they returned to their formations to shoot another volley of arrows. The scene was repeated again and again and again and again. The French, who were brave to the point of lunacy, mounted something like fifteen cavalry charges against the English—all for naught.

It was almost midnight before Philip gave up the fight, his army decimated on the fields of Crécy by a devastating advance in the technology of warfare—arrow clouds fired from massed longbows.

ROSS ICE SHELF

"ICM!" yelled the battalion commander into his radio, and the order was echoed until it reached the twenty-one 155-mm self-propelled howitzer sections at the end of the chain of command. With clenched fists pressing against the bases of the ICM rounds, the assistant gunners shoved the shells home.

The order "Fire!" rippled through the battalion, and almost as one the twenty-one surviving howitzers opened up, sending their vessels of death toward the north face of Mount Discovery.

MOUNT DISCOVERY

Mitrofan Tromso and his small coterie of staff officers raised themselves off the floor of the command post as a lull in the shelling made itself felt. Tromso's ears were ringing, and he felt dazed from the concussion waves of the high-explosive rounds that had hammered his position.

His aide pulled himself up to the vent, and after retrieving the spotting scope from the floor, he trained it on the ice shelf. "They are coming!" shouted the captain. "I can see them! They are coming!" The young man's voice seemed barely audible to Tromso, who had almost been deafened by the bombing and artillery barrage. Tromso looked through the scope and could see the SUSV snow vehicles and M1 tanks advancing toward his position. They were still ten kilometers away. He wondered why the barrage had ceased. Incredibly, his command post had remained intact. As the shock from the shelling eased a bit, his composure began to return and he grabbed the field cablephone to his artillery commander. When he heard a voice on the other end, he ordered, "Open up on the Americans with everything you have left!"

The voice on the other end of the phone was obviously disoriented from the shelling as it babbled, *"Da . . . da . . .* open up . . . they stopped . . . why did they stop?"

As if in answer to his question, Tromso heard a *BOOM!-BOOM!* as the ICM rounds went off in an airburst above his position. The exploding shells scattered bundles of charges over a wide area, which hit the ground and detonated, in turn tossing up hundreds upon hundreds of bomblets at chest level that popped off with a firecracker-string *Brrraaaaaappp!!* that sent thousands of fragments slicing through the air. As the ICM bomblets peppered the north face of Mount Discovery, Tromso felt their concussion waves; but the sensation was unlike the previous artillery barrage, in that this was a succession of tightly-spaced pulses. Tromso heard a zinging sound, followed by a *pffttt!-pffttt!-pffttt!* as three scimitarlike fragments found their way through the viewing slit of the bunker and impacted in the walls of the snow bunker.

Tromso tried to raise his artillery commander on the field phone again, but now it was silent. He would have to communicate directly with his surviving artillery sections by radio. He grabbed the handset

and keyed the mike to give the order to engage, knowing he could
be signing his own death warrant by doing so.

THE QUICK FIX HELICOPTER

The electronic warfare operator monitored his scanner in the rear
compartment of the Blackhawk helicopter as it froze on 4360.5
kilohertz. "Contact!" he announced, while calling up the direction-
finding sensor. In short order, the azimuth to the target was thrown
up on his screen. "Bearing zero-seven-eight. Passing data to CP
now." And he punched another button.

The Quick Fix helicopter was crammed with electronics to monitor, locate, jam, and confuse enemy radio transmissions.

Two of the aircraft were flying on either side of the American
artillery emplacements, sniffing the air for telltale radio emissions.
The azimuths were transmitted back to the Technical Control and
Analysis Element (known as "Tee-Kay") of the intelligence battalion
where the intersect point of the two bearings were plotted. The
Tee-Kay staff passed the coordinates to the G-2 staff, who told the
G-2 himself, who passed the info to the chief of staff, who ran it by
the assistant division commander, who gave the go-ahead. The chief
passed the go-ahead to the naval TAC AIR controller, who already
had the coordinates in hand from the G-2 staff, and he radioed his
carrier strike force where to drop their bombs. At the same time—in
the interest of interservice relations—the chief of staff notified the
artillery commander to cease fire so that the low-flying Navy jets
would not be flying through a rain of 155-mm projectiles on their
way to the target.

BROWN PENINSULA

Sergeant de Parma had looked on in fascination as the bombing and
artillery barrage raked the face of Mount Discovery while the attack
formed up. There had been a pause, then the ICM barrage had
covered the mountain slope with a blanket of small eruptions. He'd
never seen anything like it, and after witnessing such destruction he
didn't know how anyone on the business end of that ICM barrage
could be left alive. The smoke from the blasts was slowly carried off
by the wind as the firing ceased, and de Parma had started searching
for any surviving artillery pieces when one, then two, F/A-18 Hor-

nets roared over him and Captain Nye—almost low enough to touch.

De Parma and Nye instinctively flattened themselves against the ground. Then, when the roar subsided, they picked themselves up, and de Parma trained his scope on the two Hornets as they raced toward Mount Discovery. "Sheeeittt! Look at that!" It was hypnotic as the lead Hornet rose up in a bombing arc and two white smoke trails rose up toward it from the mountain slope. The pilot either did not see them, or froze and did not react with his flares, as one of the trails found its mark and the Hornet disappeared in a spectacular airburst.

"Damn!" de Parma shouted. "They got one! Looks like them Russians still have plenty of fight left, sir. Take a look." De Parma withdrew and Nye looked through the viewer. Apparently the second pilot had his act together, for he did not climb in a bombing arc, but stayed low as two more smoke trails rose up. Nye watched in fascination as the Hornet released a flurry of flares, then jinked to one side, then the other, evading the Grail missiles like a broken-field runner as they veered off and took the decoys. "This is incredible!" But then Nye saw the pilot fly past the enemy positions to disappear over the top of Mount Discovery without even dropping his bombs. In the ensuing pause, Nye mumbled, "I wonder where he went?" But then the Hornet screamed back over the mountaintop, popping up, then diving down to release his slick of bombs before the Soviet missileers could draw a bead on him. Nye murmured, "You clever bastard," as the Hornet raced toward them on afterburner and screamed overhead, having left behind a volley of eruptions on the desolate face of the mountain.

THE HORNET

Blackjack Pershing saw Brown Peninsula whip underneath his aircraft, but he was unaware that Army troops were below him, appraising his performance.

The Fear had drained out of Blackjack, taking with it that dimension of the soul which defined his humanity. Warfare often dehumanizes those who are tossed into its maelstrom. So it was now with Blackjack. He no longer feared, or cared, or laughed, or cried. As the Grail missiles sailed toward him, his pulse barely rose. Blackjack had been turned into a killing machine, a man who no longer cared if he killed—or died.

It was his way of blotting out the memory that he'd choked.

ROSS ICE SHELF

The attack was closing now. The M-1 tanks and the SUSV troop transports were hurtling over the tabletop of the ice shelf like an old-style cavalry charge. The M-1s were firing their 105-mm guns as they raced along. A couple of tanks and a half-dozen SUSVs had fallen into crevasses, while another dozen had been felled by surviving Soviet artillery or *Smerch* missiles. But one by one, the enemy emplacements were taken out by the laser-guided bombs, or by the American artillery barrage, which had commenced again with unrelenting savagery.

As the SUSVs and M-1s started up the slope of Mount Discovery, the Russians opened up with the 73-mm guns mounted on top of the surviving BMD vehicles. Not many had survived, and trying to aim while receiving artillery fire was onerous, so they were not terribly effective.

The SUSV transporting the second squad of the First Platoon, Company B, Fifth Battalion/Ninth Infantry Regiment, of the Second Brigade, Sixth Infantry Division, came to an abrupt halt on the mountain slope, allowing the squad to pile out of the back and deploy into an assault line. Actually, they didn't *pile* out; they moved carefully because they were all wearing spiked crampons on the bottoms of their vapor-barrier boots. Once deployed, they began their assault march up the steep slope to the dug-in emplacements.

Pfc. Ward Chaffee—a tall, red-headed Nebraskan, felt his pulse thumping as he humped up the slope toward the barrage. He figured they were about two hundred yards from the impact area of the "friendly" artillery explosions. He prayed the forward observer for those howitzers wasn't asleep at the wheel—and that the barrage had swept away any mines placed by the Russians. Private First Class Chaffee's fire team was on the left of an M-1 tank as it advanced, on line, with the infantry. Periodically the tank would spit some machine-gun fire at a suspected position up the slope. But finally the grade became too steep and too icy at the same time, and the sixty-ton tank began skidding backward down the incline until it came to a rest.

Chaffee's fire team pressed on, carefully treading on their crampons, pausing every few steps to stop and shoot at suspected enemy emplacements within the barrage. The M-1 they'd left behind had stopped firing, for fear of hitting its own people. As they advanced, Chaffee became even more nervous. The artillery blasts were too damn close! Couldn't his pukehead squad leader see they were almost on top of their own damn barrage? The sound was no longer a distant *Crump!-Crump!* but an intimate *BLAM!-BLAM!* Where was the damn yellow smoke? The last round in the barrage was supposed to be marked by yellow smoke. Chaffee swallowed and let himself skid back a step or two. No way was he going to walk straight into that barrage. Then a cloud of yellow smoke rose up into the air from the middle of the white geysers; and almost at once, everything seemed eerily quiet—except for the small reports of the M-16s or the M-60 machine guns.

Chaffee caught up with the rest of his fire team and fell in with their advance-pause-shoot-advance rhythm. As far as he could tell, there was no gunfire coming from the Soviet positions, and that didn't surprise him, because the barrage had obviously been murderous. He continued the advance.

This was where warfare had changed little over millennia. Weapons had become more cruel in their powers of destruction, yes. Ranges had extended, yes. Mobility was greater, yes. Sensors were technically elegant, yes. But after all the high tech—the lasers, the computers, the radar, the aircraft, the thermal detectors, the radio direction finders—after all that, warfare still came down to a fundamental axiom that required a "grunt" soldier to cross those final two to three hundred yards and ferret out the enemy from his bunkers and foxholes.

Chaffee was having trouble making it up the slope, even with his crampons, for it was icy and slick. But a few more steps would put him on a tier where the grade lessened quite a bit. He had just stepped onto the next level when there was a popping sound, followed by a flash and a backwash of snow and a roar. Startled, Chaffee lost his balance and his weapon, and slid back down the slope on his back, turtle-style. By the time his forty-foot slide was arrested, the adrenaline supply in his bloodstream had increased about a pint. He sat up to see the tail plume of the Spigot missile as it headed for the M-1 tank they'd left behind down the slope. Chaffee watched the turret of the M-1 traverse as the armored giant threw itself into reverse and started back down the mountain. But the range was too short, and before the tank gunner could bring his weapon to bear, the wire-guided missile struck home. It was a small explosion at first, but then the Spigot warhead connected with the on-board ammunition, causing the M-1 to shudder in its tracks. Chaffee looked on as the turret was blasted up into the air, somersaulting several times before coming down with a sickening *clang!* Several more explosions rippled through the burning hulk as the last of the 105-mm rounds cooked off.

As the M-1 was disintegrating, Chaffee also became aware of some wounded lying farther down the slope. It was at this point that fear or anger was going to take hold of him, and he would either run up the mountain or down. Anger gained supremacy—supremacy over fear, and even over good sense—as he ignored the fire-and-maneuver tactics of his training. Picking up his M-16, he stormed up the slope, emptying clip after clip toward the bunker that had launched the Spigot. By the time he reached the tier for the second time, his adrenaline rush had expended itself, and he realized that little white puffs of snow were popping up around him. He hit the deck and continued firing at the snow bunker. Then he realized he'd outrun his own fire team, so he low-crawled backward, down over the lip of the tier, where he would have a bit more protection.

"Chaffee! Get back down here!"

Chaffee ventured a look behind him, and saw the rest of his fire team on the ground, with his fire-team leader motioning him to come back down. What? Go back down after coming all this way? He heard the M-60 machine gun from the squad's other fire team open up on the bunker to give him some covering fire as he withdrew. Cursing through his teeth, he low-crawled head-first down the slope, hoping he wouldn't take a Russian round right in the butt. The rest of the squad also started to low-crawl back toward the burning hulk of the tank, pulling their dead and wounded with them and looking like a bunch of grunion squirming up on the beach to spawn. Once they were near what was left of the M-1, Chaffee caught up with his fire-team leader—a rather muscular black gentleman from North Carolina—and demanded, "What the hell are we doing, running away? You guys left my butt hanging out up there!"

The North Carolinian growled, "Shut up, shithead. If you followed my signals, you'd be okay. That's what you get for playing Rambo."

The squad leader nearby was talking rapidly into the radio handset as Chaffee demanded, "But I don't understand why we . . ."

He heard a low drone, and looked up to see an AC-130 Spectre gunship heading straight toward him. With its four turboprops cutting through the air, the lumbering ship banked onto a course parallel to the slope of the mountain.

"Get yer damn head down," ordered the fire-team leader, but Chaffee kept looking at the aircraft until a burst of smoke erupted from the Spectre's midsection, followed by a *POM!* that reverberated through the air. Chaffee's head went down as he heard a *BLAM!* from the Spectre's 105-mm howitzer shell landing up the slope.

Chaffee kept his head in the snow as he heard the squad leader radio, "That was a little low and forty meters to the right. Give 'em an HE, and then an ICM this time, but make the ICM a little high. We're pretty close." At those remarks, Chaffee's eyes grew to about the size of silver dollars, and he scurried via low-crawl around behind the burning hulk of the M-1. He'd seen an ICM round fired at a firepower demonstration, and wanted as much protection between him and the bomblets as he could get. He looked over his shoulder and saw the Spectre finish out a slow bank in preparation for its next pass. Chaffee heard a muffled roar, and saw the white smoky trail of a Grail missile as it headed for the Spectre. But the pilot was quick on the trigger, and a host of flares dropped from the lumbering craft to sucker the missile away. Almost at the moment it detonated, there was a *POM!-BLAM!* and Chaffee's head went down again.

"Dead on!" screamed the squad leader into his headset.

Then there was a *POM!-BOOM!-BOOM!-Brrraaaaaapp!* as the ICM bomblets raked the bunker.

Then there was silence, except for the fading drone of the Spectre.

"Let's go!" yelled the squad leader, and in a flash the troops were on their feet and charging up the hill, this time shooting from the hip, not the shoulder. By the time they reached the lip of the tier, the squad leader had clamped down on the John Wayne action and got his men back under control. He ordered the "red" team to give fire support, while Chaffee's "blue" fire team advanced. Chaffee noticed they weren't taking any return fire from the bunker, which was a pillboxlike snow fortification built against an L-shaped rocky wall of the mountain's face. The high-explosive round from the Spectre gunship had caved in part of the snow wall and the bunker's overhang. The North Carolinian fire-team leader pointed at Chaffee, and at the bunker, and ordered, "Go!"

Chaffee's adrenal glands were working overtime as he rose to his feet and charged into the breach of the bunker's wall, firing his M-16 and screaming—just screaming to release the demons of fear, anger, aggression, bravado, guilt, and all the other vexations an infantry-man must conquer before he kills another human being face-to-face.

But once inside, Chaffee abruptly stopped and inspected the snow chamber. He blinked a few times to absorb the view, then turned around and walked back outside, dropped his weapon, fell to his knees, and promptly vomited.

Thinking his man had been wounded, the fire-team leader yelled, "Chaffee! Are you hit?"

Chaffee dropped his helmet while shaking his head, but his guts continued to retch.

The fire-team leader rushed forward, past Chaffee and into the bunker, rifle poised. Upon entering, he, too, blinked a few times to allow his brain to assimilate what he was seeing. The walls and floor of the white snow chamber now had a color spectrum that ranged from a light pink to several dark maroon splotches—evidence that some of the ICM bomblets had found their way into the bunker. But what had caused Chaffee to retch, and the fire-team leader to shud-der, was that on the ground lay a human head—poised perfectly upright, eyes closed, blond hair tousled and looking peaceful. It might have been mistaken for a sculptured bust of a Russian youth, had it not been for red streamers emanating into the snow at the base of the neck.

Shaken, the fire-team leader exited the bunker as the rest of the squad formed a security perimeter around their objective. Two of Chaffee's buddies were comforting him, and the fire-team leader said, "Take him back to the rear."

The squad leader came forward and asked, "Everything secure here?"

The fire-team leader replied, "Yeah. It's secure." The squad leader nodded and took a step toward the bunker, but the North Carolinian brought him up short by saying, "I wouldn't go in there if I were you, Sarge."

Maj. Gen. Mitrofan Tromso struggled to pull himself out of the snow after the command post's overhang had collapsed on him and his staff during the air strike. The staccato sound of nearby auto-matic-weapons fire told him his positions were being overrun. It was finished.

He took an assessment of himself and guessed he was badly

bruised, but with no bleeding wounds or broken bones. Further resistance was futile, he knew. His men had delayed, held out, taken more punishment, and fought harder than any desk-bound marshal in the Kremlin had a right to expect. It was time to bring the curtain down. He saw a corner of a field radio sticking out of the snow. He laboriously dug it out, becoming more and more aware of the moans around him. The radio's antenna was twisted, but Tromso hoped it would still work as he fished out the handset and keyed the mike.

A BLACKHAWK HELICOPTER OVER THE ROSS ICE SHELF

"General Pfeiffer," the aide called through the intercom. "I've got the chief of staff on the horn. He says Quick Fix is picking up a transmission from the Russian CP, telling all their troops to stand down. The spooks in the intel battalion think it's legit."

From his position above the battlefield in the left seat of the rotary-wing aircraft, Joshua Pfeiffer had directed the attack as it unfolded below him. It had been an extraordinary sight, but now it was over. "Send a message to all units: 'Soviet commander has transmitted surrender message, but some enemy units may not have received the word. Use discretion to continue advance and seize objectives, or hold position to wait for surrender. Exercise extreme caution.' "

"Right away, General."

Pfeiffer raised his field glasses and surveyed the battlefield once more. There were a number of burning hulks of tanks and SUSVs—victims of the Spigot missiles. The Russians had taken a pounding, with no air cover, and still put up a fight like a wounded Siberian bear.

As he saw the Medevac helicopters swoop toward the battlefront, he wondered how many letters he was going to have to write to wives and mothers.

And he wondered what sort of person his Russian counterpart was.

MOUNT DISCOVERY

Bit by bit, the sound of small-arms fire—and the occasional Soviet mortar that had survived—subsided, and was replaced by the *whop-whop* noise of the Medevac helicopters coming in to evacuate the wounded. The dead would have to wait for the grave-registration people.

The exact point at which the official surrender took effect—as opposed to objectives falling—was somewhat muddy. But when things cratered, they cratered rapidly; and it wasn't long before the Guards were being formed up into ranks of prisoners while Soviet and American medics worked side by side to stabilize the wounded.

Maj. Gen. Mitrofan Tromso felt excruciatingly impotent as he hobbled down the slope of Mount Discovery at the gunpoint of three very young Americans who were jabbering excitedly at the fact they had captured a Soviet general. Tromso allowed himself a smile. They were too young to realize that a general without an army was so much excess baggage.

They approached a flat plateau in the slope, where they were met by a small group of Americans. Tromso picked out the helmet insignia of an American "bird" colonel and guessed he was probably a brigade commander. His youthful captors conferred with the "bird," who inspected Tromso's insignia and was soon speaking into a radio handset.

THE *WASP*

Cpl. Alexei Protopov was twenty-one years old and possessed the body of an athlete. He had been squatting in his snow bunker, curled up in a ball against the artillery barrage, waiting for the attack. He had laid out several fragmentation and white phosphorous grenades nearby, ready to lob them when the Americans came close enough. But during the ICM barrage, some of the bomblet fragments had entered the bunker and wreaked their destruction—one sailing through the right side of his chest cavity, almost sucking his lung from his body; while another cleanly sliced off his left calf muscle; and still another managed to set off a white phosphorous grenade. The fire from the grenade ignited his uniform, and before he could roll himself over, he'd received third-degree burns over forty percent of his body. He was found, barely alive, by an American medic who put IV fluids into him as fast as possible while staunching the bleeding. He was taken to a helicopter and Medevacked to a field hospital, but the operating suites were swamped so he was transferred to a

V-22 Osprey air ambulance and flown to the *Wasp* with its six-hundred-bed hospital.

Upon unloading, he was taken to the triage area below decks, where the physicians ascertained who needed treatment in what order—i.e., those who would live if you did nothing for them, those who would die no matter what you did for them, and those who would live only if you did something for them. Protopov fell into the final category and went straightaway into one of the vessel's operating rooms.

Upon completion of his surgery and burn treatment, he was placed in the on-board intensive-care unit. But in the hours to come, the doctors would agree that his burns were beyond the ability of the *Wasp*'s medical facilities. So Protopov would be loaded onto another Osprey air ambulance and flown to Clark Air Base in the Philippines, where he would be transferred to a C-17 medical transport for a flight to Hawaii. At Hickam Field he would be transferred to another medical transport and flown to San Diego, and then on to San Antonio, where he would be admitted to the burn treatment unit of Brook Army Medical Center. At Brook he would receive state-of-the-art treatment for his burns.

Yet he would die three days later.

MOUNT DISCOVERY

Mitrofan Tromso turned his head to avoid the ice crystals blowing into his face from the downdraft of the Blackhawk helicopter. Upon landing, the rotor blades slowly wound down from their 360 rpm until they were turning with the frequency of a rather large ceiling fan.

The left-side copilot's door opened and a stocky figure emerged, wearing the overwhites and the new-style coal-scuttle helmet of the American Army. Tromso had read that the headpiece was made of a plastic called Kevlar. The stocky figure started walking toward him as the cabin door of the Blackhawk slid back and a younger man fell into place behind him. The "bird" colonel went out to the stocky man and they exchanged salutes, then conferred in low tones. Finally the new arrival—he looked quite solid to the Russian—moved forward and stopped three paces away. "You are Mitrofan Tromso?" he asked.

The Russian saw two black stars on the white camouflaged helmet. "That is correct," he replied.

"I am Major General Joshua Pfeiffer, commander of the Sixth Infantry Division. Our file on you states that you were a Red Army military attaché at the Soviet Embassy in Canada, and that you speak fluent English. I must confess, however, that our dossiers are sometimes in error. I can provide an interpreter if you prefer."

"English will be fine, General Pfeiffer."

Pfeiffer nodded and asked, "Are you the senior officer present?"

"I am—*was*—in command, yes. I regret I have no sword to offer you, General, but I hereby surrender Mount Discovery and my forces to you. I only ask that my wounded receive medical care and that my men be treated under the rules of . . . civilized warfare."

Pfeiffer pondered the words and said, "That's a contradiction in terms, but yes, your men will receive proper medical care, and I can assure you they will be treated well. My aide and a security detail will escort you back to my command post."

The Russian nodded, defeat written all over his haggard face. He started to leave with the aide, but as he was moving away, Pfeiffer asked, "Tromso—that's a Scandinavian name, isn't it?"

The Soviet general turned and said, "*Da.* My father was Norwegian, and my mother was Russian, and I hated my father." Tromso shrugged. "It's a long story."

That curious footnote over with, Tromso walked toward the helicopter.

Pfeiffer watched him go, wondering how he himself would have handled such a complete and utter defeat.

22

. . . .

TSUSHIMA

Toward the end of 1904, in the Russo-Japanese War, the forces of the Nippon Empire had Czar Nicholas II between a rock and a hard place. Port Arthur—the Russian Navy's only warm-water port in the Pacific, and the terminus for the Trans-Siberian Railway—was under seige, and the Japanese had the installation in a stranglehold of a naval blockade. In view of this dire situation, the Czar decided to send his Baltic Fleet to relieve the embattled Russian port.

Under the command of Rear Adm. Zinovi Petrovich Rozhdestvenski, the Baltic Fleet of forty-five ships embarked on their journey and crossed twenty thousand miles of ocean in seven months—quite a logistical accomplishment in view of the fact there was a dearth of friendly bases where the Russian ships could seek repair and refueling. (Ironically, one of the places the Russians were able to refuel was Cam Ranh Bay.) Yes, it was quite a feat, but once Rozhdestvenski arrived in the Pacific, his luck changed.

On May 27, 1905, Rozhdestvenski's task force of eight battleships, nine cruisers, nine destroyers, and eight auxiliaries—now renamed the Second Pacific Squadron—was in the East China Sea, preparing to make a sortie through the forty-mile-wide Tsushima Strait. It was the Russian admiral's intent to enter the Sea of Japan through the strait and then press on to Vladivostok.

Admiral Heihachiro Togo was holding the Japanese fleet at Masampo, on the southeastern coast of Korea, while his cruisers scouted for the Russian vessels. Once his quarry was spotted, Togo sortied from Masampo and intercepted the Russian squadron in the early afternoon. The Russian vessels were ill-matched with each other and some were obsolete, and this pulled the squadron's fastest speed down to about ten knots. Togo's force of four modern battleships, eight cruisers, and torpedo boats could make sixteen knots—and they had the advantage of wireless communication, used in battle for the first time at Tsushima.

The battle was joined, and the fighting continued into the next day.

When the smoke finally cleared, the Japanese had sunk or captured thirty-four Russian vessels. Rozhdestvenski himself was wounded and taken prisoner, 4,830 Russian sailors were killed, and 5,917 were wounded or captured.

The Japanese suffered 117 killed, 583 wounded, and three torpedo boats destroyed.

The Japanese victory and the Russian defeat at the Battle of Tsushima Strait were complete, and they led the way to peace negotiations mediated by U.S. President Theodore Roosevelt, which put an end to the Russo-Japanese War.

Rozhdestvenski was later absolved of blame by a Russian court-martial because he was severely wounded and unconscious during much of the engagement. Yet, in spite of the exoneration—and his logistical triumph in getting the Baltic Fleet to the Pacific—Rozhdestvenski would always be associated with the most crushing naval disaster since Nelson defeated Villeneuve at the Battle of Trafalgar.

MOSCOW—March 4

Minister of Defense Adm. Yuri Timoshenko fell into the big leather chair like a sandbag hitting the ground. He'd just come out of a seven-hour meeting of the Confederation Cabinet, and was physically and emotionally sapped. His office was chilly, and there was ice on the window due to the reduced heating-oil allotment. A sign of things to come?

Timoshenko had gone into the meeting with the full expectation of being sacked, perhaps even arrested. Snow Leopard had turned into an unmitigated disaster. Not only had the Soviet Confederation lost the prize; they had been outsmarted and—as Timoshenko was told time and again—outfought by the Americans. "It was your plan, Admiral," they said. "It is on your head." Timoshenko was amazed at how the very same men who had ordered him to go forward with Snow Leopard now were finding flaws where they'd never seen them before. And voicing disapproval as if Timoshenko had dropped paratroopers into Antarctica behind their backs. The admiral gazed out the frosty windows and tried to remember who had said it, and finally he remembered. Ah, yes, it was the American President Kennedy—how ironic! Yes, it was Kennedy who said, after the ruination of the Bay of Pigs adventure: "Victory has a thousand fathers, but defeat is an orphan."

There was a soft knock on the door, and Dr. Minos Konstantos ventured in. "By your face I would say your Cabinet meeting did not go well, Yuri Ilyanovich," Konstantos said gently. "I wondered if there was anything I could do."

With bloodshot eyes, the admiral looked up at his little Georgian-Greek friend and sighed. "Now I know how Rozhdestvenski must have felt after Tsushima. If only the Cabinet had relieved me, Minos. My life would be so much simpler. I was wishing they would do just that, but no. They said, 'You got us into this mess, Admiral. Now you get us out.'"

The physicist's goatee twitched as he asked, "Get us out? I thought you said it was over—finished. General Tromso had surrendered to the Americans. They won, we lost, and that is the end of it."

Timoshenko sighed. "It was my fervent wish that it would, indeed, be the end of it, my dear Minos. But the Cabinet will not let it die. And that is why I have not been relieved. They want the entire responsibility to be upon my shoulders."

"Responsibility for what?"

Timoshenko covered his face and said, "Our final card. It could still work, I suppose. Desperation breeds fanciful ideas, Minos."

A feeling—dark and sinister—came over Konstantos, which seemed to make the room feel even colder than it was. "What is this final card you speak of, Yuri? What are you saying?"

But Timoshenko seemed not to hear, for his eyes had fallen upon a map of Antarctica that was spread over his desk. The defense minister drummed his stubby, peasantlike fingers on the area marked ROSS SEA, and in a brooding voice he whispered, "We must wait for foul weather."

McMURDO BASE—March 6

"What the hell do you think you're doing!?"

Robert Rawlings looked up at Dana Harrow, his green eyes the picture of innocence, as he replied, "Sit-ups."

With hands on hips and steam seeming to spew from her ears, Dana growled, "You get off that floor and back into that bed this instant!"

There were times to obey and times to argue. Rawlings knew this was a time to obey. In a flash he was off the towels he'd laid down on the floor and back in the dispensary bed. Pulling the covers up to his chest, Rawlings said, "I was just doing a few to see how it felt. Honest. It feels ninety percent. I don't know why you're keeping me here. I should be back with the battalion. Besides, the war's over."

"As I recall," said Dana with more than a hint of frustration, "some fellow with two stars on his helmet said you were under my personal care until *I* say you're recovered." She lifted up the covers and opened his pajama top to investigate his rib cage. He hadn't reopened anything, but he wasn't helping matters by pulling a stunt like sit-ups. With two rigid fingers she jabbed his solar plexus, causing him to wince and cry out with an "*Ow!*"

Now it was her turn to be the picture of innocence. "Did that hurt?"

Through his teeth Rawlings hissed, "Yes, it *hurt.*"

"Good."

After the battle for Mount Discovery, Dana had thrown herself into caring for the wounded, and was able to strike up some acquaintances with some of the nurses. But now the wounded had all been moved out to the hospital ships, or to the Philippines or Hawaii, leaving Rawlings the sole patient at the dispensary.

The door opened and three men wearing overwhites entered, carrying their helmets. Captain Nye, Sergeant de Parma, and Gates the RTO walked up to Rawlings's bedside, and he greeted them. "Hullo, Phillip. How goes the battle?"

"The battle's over, sir. The last transport carrying the Russian prisoners has left. As I understand it, they're headed for New Zealand, and from there to Argentina, where they will be transferred to Aeroflot planes. Nobody here but us now. I talked with a Navy guy at the division CP. Some kinda ONI type. He said the Russian task force pulled back past the zone of exclusion and is just marking time."

Rawlings nodded. "I talked with General Pfeiffer. He said the little incident where you held the good doctor at gunpoint is all forgiven, so don't worry about it. By the way, I can't tell you how glad I am you used force to get me here."

Captain Nye grinned and nodded. "You would've done the same for me, sir."

Rawlings turned his attention to de Parma and said, "I hear you were working out with that laserscope of yours again."

De Parma shrugged. "That's what they pay me for, sir."

"Not enough," said Rawlings. "How's the weather out there, anyway?" He shot Dana a glance. "I haven't been outside in I don't know how long."

"Getting colder, sir," replied Nye. "And the sun's dipping out of sight for about eight hours a day. . . . Don't want to wear out our welcome, sir. Just wanted to stop by and let you know everything's okay. Guess we better be getting back to the battalion. There's a lot of housekeeping to be done now that the shooting's over with. I hear we won't be here too much longer. The XO says he'll get by to see you pretty soon."

Rawlings nodded his thanks, and the three men headed for the door. Sergeant de Parma, however, stopped and turned around. "I just wanted you to know, sir," he said while gesturing with his helmet, "this lady is all right." Then he turned to join the others as they filed out.

Dana saw a big grin spread over Rawlings's face as he said, "I hope you realize what a supreme accolade you have just received."

"You mean from Sergeant de Parma?"

"Yeah."

Dana shook her head. "I don't understand. Why does he not like women in the military? They seem to be everywhere."

Rawlings shrugged. "I don't know. I'll have to remember to ask his wife, next time I see her."

"The guy is married?"

The colonel nodded. "Yep. She's a Navy petty officer stationed at Adak. They're stationed apart, but seem to have a real solid marriage."

Dana looked at the ceiling, pondering the incongruity of it all, and decided she'd had enough of this place. She went to a closet and retrieved a bundle of uniform clothes, then tossed them onto the foot of Rawlings's bed.

"What's this?" he asked.

"You're the one who's gung-ho for exercise. Get dressed."

BRANDING IRON STATION

The chief geologist rode up the mine shaft by standing in the excavation bucket. He hoped the operator wouldn't open the jaws of the contraption by mistake and send him down as though he'd fallen through a trapdoor. Upon reaching the floor of the icedome, he sighed with relief and gingerly stepped over the side and made haste to locate Lt. Col. Samuel McClure. When he'd found him, the geologist said, "Colonel, I think we've got something." Both men were wearing surgical masks to keep the dust out of their lungs, and McClure motioned to the geologist to show what he had. The scientist opened a vial and emptied the contents into his hand. It looked like a mixture of salt and sand. "I'll have to run it through the lab to be sure," said the geologist, "but I think this is the carnallite. We've got the horizontal shaft extended about forty feet now, and this came from the end of it."

McClure was somewhat stunned. An invasion. A sea battle. A land battle. This mine. All for some saltlike substance the geologist now held in his hand. McClure found his voice and said, "Check it out and make sure. In the meantime, I'll notify General Pfeiffer that we may have hit pay dirt."

THE *KHARKOV*

Captain, First Rank, Kasimir Bodin was alone, walking past the tubes on the mid–missile deck that held the *Zimorodok* weapon. His arms were crossed in contemplation, his eyes focused on the deck. This voyage had been soured ever since the *Magadan* broke up in the Passage. They have traveled halfway round the world, after their transit of the Passage, only to learn everything was lost. . . . He stopped and leaned against one of the missile tubes. What kind of a world would he find when the *Kharkov* returned home? All of the promise of peace and the fruitful economy would have turned to ashes. He hadn't a clue as to what he would do upon his arrival back at Polyarny, except that he would leave the Navy. It was time for younger men like Ryback and Mizim to take the helm of vessels like the *Kharkov*.

Bodin heard the metallic sound of approaching footsteps, causing him to look up and see the communications *michman* walking toward him with a folder in his hand. "This just came in for you, Captain. One-time pad. I deciphered it myself."

Bodin took the folder and nodded, and the *michman* withdrew. Bodin opened the folder and scanned the brief message, which read:

Prepare to go operational.
Launch order may come at
any moment.
                                    Timoshenko

NEW YORK

"From our newsroom in New York, this is 'The CBS Evening News'
with Catherine Crier."

The blond judge-turned-journalist looked into the teleprompter
and read aloud, "Good evening. The word from Antarctica this
evening is that the last Soviet prisoner has left McMurdo Sound via
Air Force transport and will be repatriated to the Soviet Confederation through Argentina.

"In a statement from the White House this evening, President
Blakely said the conclusion of hostilities closes a sad chapter in
Soviet-American relations—a chapter that has thrust us back into
the hottest days of the Cold War.

"The Soviet Foreign Ministry and the Soviet Ambassador in
Washington had no comment."

HUT POINT, WINTER QUARTERS BAY

There were about a half-dozen of the Adelie penguins hanging
around on the sea ice by the water's edge. Most of McMurdo Sound
had a thin film of ice now, since the early days of the austral autumn
had arrived. Dana estimated the temperature at somewhere between
five and ten degrees Fahrenheit, and the wind was brisk off the
Sound. The sun was about to go down—they had about sixteen hours
of sunlight now. She felt they had spent enough time chasing around
and should call it a day, but Robert wanted to linger with the
penguins. He was glad to get outside again, and the cold seemed to
have little effect on him.

"Hey, let's go in. It's too frosty for me." Dana moved her arms
back and forth to keep her circulation going, and her parka made a
swishing sound from fabric rubbing against fabric.

Robert Falcon Scott's Discovery Hut, erected in 1902, was nearby,
but Rawlings showed no interest in it when they walked past. He
found the penguins a delight, however.

"Look at that!" he cried, pointing.

Dana followed his lead and saw four of the Adelies spring out of the water and onto the ice as if they were some kind of acrobats.

"Might be a leopard seal after them," said Dana. "Most of the Adelies in this area hang out in the Cape Royds rookery, but this little group shows up here from time to time."

"Unusual creatures. . . . Well, I guess we've had our walk. Thanks for the parole. Whaddaya say we see what our cooks have put together in your mess hall."

THE *VINCENNES*

Capt. David Erickson was again at the hangar door of the *Vincennes,* and again the deck was rolling. Ice was getting to be a serious problem now, as the incoming LAMPS helicopter made its approach. Considering the conditions, the recovery went well, and once the LAMPS was safely inside the hangar, the door to the helicopter rolled back, allowing Lt. Gen. Myron Tharp and a civilian to step out.

"Hello, David," Tharp said, saluting. "Permission to come aboard, sir."

"Permission granted, General. Who is your guest?"

Tharp turned and said, "Captain David Erickson, may I present Mr. Seymour Woltman of the Associated Press. Mr. Woltman, may I present the Mad Viking."

"Pleased to meet you, Mr. Woltman," said Erickson, while extending a hand. But Seymour Woltman's right hand was occupied in holding on to the helicopter door as the ship rolled back and forth. The helicopter journey had been like a ride in a blender. *Sheesh, no wonder they call those things "egg beaters,"* he thought. With a face the color of algae, Woltman asked, "Where do you go to puke on this tub?"

With Seymour Woltman ensconced in the ship's head, Tharp and Erickson made their way to CIC and some hot coffee. Tharp looked at the big display screen and picked out the *Vincennes*'s position, about thirty miles south of the zone of exclusion at the sixtieth parallel. The *Carl Vinson* battle group was about 150 miles farther south, and the *Roosevelt* and *Eisenhower* groups were southwest of the *Vinson,* strung out in a roughly diagonal pattern toward Ross Island, while the *Wasp* and some troop ships were about a hundred miles north of McMurdo. The *Vincennes* and the *Arleigh Burke–*

class destroyer *John Paul Jones* were acting as an advance picket guard—working with the Hawkeye radar planes to keep tabs on the Soviets should they try anything belligerent.

"I hadn't seen you for a while, David. Thought I'd drop by and pay my respects."

"Glad you did, sir. I hope we're getting what we came to McMurdo for."

Tharp slurped his coffee and said, "My latest report is that the rubidium deposits should be on their way to the surface anytime now. But never mind that. What are our Russian friends up to?"

Erickson shrugged. "Nothing much, sir. They're just hanging around right outside the zone of exclusion. Licking their wounds, I guess. They're right at the limit of our SPY radar, and we've had gaps in our Hawkeye airborne coverage. The ice forming on the SPY impairs its performance, and the polar conditions have made flight operations off the *Vinson* a bitch. As a result, some of the Hawkeye sorties have been curtailed."

Tharp nodded. "I know. As you're aware, I just came from the *Vinson*. The other carrier groups are having trouble as well. We lost one of the replacement Hornets off the *Roosevelt*. It was coming down in the elevator when it slid on some ice that had formed on the platform and fell into the drink." Tharp snapped his fingers. "Just like that. No pilot aboard, thank God."

"I hope we can put this business behind us soon, sir."

"I'm sure we will, David," Tharp comforted him. "I'm sure we will."

McMURDO BASE

With a mixture of awe, respect, and—he was pleased to admit—growing affection, Robert Rawlings watched Dana dig into her shrimp salad. He couldn't get over the transformation in her appearance since their trek across the ice shelf. She was an electric combination of moxie, looks, and brains, along with a womanly softness.

"Mind if I join you?"

Rawlings looked up to see Maj. Gen. Joshua Pfeiffer standing over them with a tray of food. The mess hall at McMurdo—which had been taken over by the Army cooks—was sparsely populated with soldiers from the Sixth Infantry Division, for the dinner hour had already come and gone.

Rawlings stood and said, "Please do, sir."

Pfeiffer sat down and exhaled, obviously fatigued.

"Long day, sir?" Rawlings inquired as he returned to his seat.

Pfeiffer nodded. "You might say that. We finally got those Marines loaded back on their troop ships. That regimental commander of theirs was the most pigheaded, stubborn . . ." He caught Dana's gaze and held his tongue.

Dana finished swallowing a mouthful and offered, "Sonofabitch?"

Pfeiffer smiled. "Exactly. Sonofabitch. Anyway, they're out of here. The Navy transports will start reloading the artillery one-five-fives and the M-1s tomorrow, and elements of the Second Brigade will begin flying out on the transports."

Dana saw Rawlings's brow furrow. "Is that wise, sir? So soon?"

Pfeiffer shrugged. "Can't be helped. As Miss Harrow will tell you, the weather starts deteriorating pretty rapidly from this point. We're already down to sixteen hours of full daylight. The sun disappears for good on April twenty-first. But I want most everyone out of here before then. I've got a phased withdrawal planned so we'll have a small rear guard staying through the winter."

"What about the prize?" asked Dana.

"That should start coming up tomorrow," Pfeiffer replied. "And that reminds me, young lady, it's about time I sent you home. You've done far more than any soldier should be expected to do, and we've been honored to have your help, but I think it best we get you on a transport for New Zealand, then off to wherever your home is."

Dana turned pensive as she asked, "General Pfeiffer, now that all the Russians are gone, I was wondering if there was a way I could get back to my seismic huts and retrieve the data disks from my sensor units. The disks fill up pretty rapidly, so there won't be much information to take home. But I would like to salvage whatever I can for my dissertation. Maybe my graduate committee will cut me some slack when they hear my story."

Pfeiffer pursed his lips as he thought about his response. "Where are your sensor sites?"

"On Mount Discovery, Mount Morning, and Mount Harmsworth," she replied.

"It shouldn't be a problem, sir," Rawlings chimed in. "If we can borrow a Blackhawk, we can be out and back in no time. Besides, the war's over."

Pfeiffer still hesitated.

"We owe her, sir," said Rawlings, more firmly this time. "In spades, we owe her."

Pfeiffer nodded. "Very well. I'll have a Blackhawk pick you up tomorrow at zero-nine-hundred at the motor pool. Are you fit to go along, Robert?"

"He's fit for that," said Dana, smiling. "We won't be gone long."

"Awright," replied the general. "You escort Miss Harrow out and back tomorrow, Robert. Maybe you can talk her into releasing you back to your battalion."

When Dana and Robert exited the mess hall, night had fallen, and they were greeted by a dazzling display of the Aurora Australis—the Southern Hemisphere cousin to the Aurora Borealis. They both stopped and gaped, for nature was putting on a real show this night. The aurora looked like filmy white angel hair flowing across a night sky that was peppered with brilliant, shimmering stars. They remained transfixed as the luminous waves turned from a ghostly white to a pale, almost lime green, in a spellbinding spectacle that bordered on the hypnotic. Then something remarkable happened, as the aurora went through another transformation, changing from pale green to ruby red.

Startled, Dana said, "Oooohh . . . that's overpowering . . . I've never seen one like that before. . . ." And she turned to Robert, only to find that his face was not smiling. Instead, his countenance seemed troubled. "Robert, what is it?"

It was a few moments before he spoke, and when he did his voice had a distant, strange timbre. "In Alaska the old Inuit—the Eskimos—greatly feared the aurora. They felt it would cause pain in the head or the back. Parents would even send their children inside when it appeared. A red aurora is quite rare."

Though he was standing beside her, Dana felt Robert was far, far away, communing with someone, or something, on a level and in a manner that she sensed was beyond her grasp. She looked at the red aurora one last time, then took his arm and guided him toward the dispensary. "Come on. You need your rest."

With his free hand, Robert reached inside his parka and pulled out a small knife from the scabbard he kept looped on his belt. As he waved it behind his back, Dana thought she heard him chanting something—but it was indecipherable.

THE *KHARKOV*—March 7

"Open torpedo doors one and two."

"One and two open, aye," responded the *starpom,* Avraam Ryback.

Kasimir Bodin pivoted the periscope head and could just make out the dark figures of the *Kharkov*'s frogmen against the underside of the ice pack. "Divers are in place," said Bodin. "Eject the blister packs."

Ryback hit two red buttons on his panel and said, "Blister packs free."

On the bow of the *Kharkov,* two twenty-six-inch-diameter canisters came out of the torpedo tubes with a *whoosh* as the compressed air sent them forth. Shaped like torpedoes, but without propellers on their tails, the explosive blister-pack canisters began their ascent toward the surface, each playing out a wire behind it. When the canisters hit the "ceiling" of the ice pack, the frogmen realigned them and secured them in place using a lanyard tethered to a piton-like tool.

"Open doors three and four," ordered Bodin, and the process was repeated. When the frogmen were done, the four blister-pack canisters were arranged in a rectangle on the ice ceiling.

Bodin inspected the placement of the canisters and said, "Recover the divers." Then he pulled back from the periscope viewer and looked at Toomas Mizim. "So what do you think, Comrade pilot. Is Moscow sending us on an adventure that is too little, too late, perhaps?"

The forlorn-looking pilot remained impassive as he replied, "I have learned never to predict orders from Moscow."

Bodin barked a laugh and said, "That is a lesson I should have learned long ago." Then he silently sipped from his tin teacup, until Ryback said, "Divers secure, Captain."

Bodin drained the tin cup and set it down, then returned to the periscope for a final inspection of the four loglike objects resting against the ceiling. Satisfied with their placement, he stepped back and gently folded the brass handles against the tube while saying, "Down scope. Sail planes and aft planes to ninety degrees vertical. Flood main buoyancy tank to twenty-percent negative and take us down to two hundred meters."

"Aye."

"Aye."

"Number One," said Bodin, "make sure our people play out the canister and communications cables carefully. I do not wish to have our lines fouled and lose everything at this point."

"Aye, Captain."

"Navigator, what is your depth sounding?" asked Bodin.

The officer looked up from his chart and said, "Five hundred thirteen meters, Captain."

"Drift?"

"Minimal, Captain, but we are drifting stern first, parallel to the ice shelf, and we should not tangle the lines."

Like an angler holding five fishing poles, playing out the lines as he backs away from the pier, the *Kharkov* unreeled the wires from its bow and sail as it descended.

"Depth one-eight-five meters . . . one-nine-zero . . . one-nine-five," droned the diving officer. "Blowing main buoyancy tank. Coming to neutral buoyancy. . . . Depth two-zero-one meters, Captain."

"Number One, check with communications and ensure that our satellite earth station is still functioning properly."

Ryback muttered into his intercom receiver again, and then said, "The satellite dish is functioning properly, Captain."

"Very well. Now we wait."

KALININGRAD FLIGHT CONTROL CENTER, NEAR MOSCOW

It was a large room, dominated by projection screens on the front wall, with row after row of consoles and their operators arranged below.

Col. Oleg Malyshev was sitting at the mission commander's desk, a thin film of perspiration giving a sheen to his Slavic features and matting some of his blond hair against his forehead. Reports from various operators were trickling into the earphones of his headset, and when he finally received the one he was waiting for, he swiveled his chair toward the man standing over him. "The latest report from the Sea Leopard fleet has just come in, Admiral, and it confirms the predictions of our meteorologists based on imagery from our weather satellite. A storm of extraordinary force is building across the Ross Sea. Seas are four to five meters and increasing."

Yuri Timoshenko stood with his peasant arms folded, his features betraying his deep thought. "Are the rockets at Baikonur in readiness?"

"The primary and the reserve are prepared for fueling," Malyshev replied. "Systems on the payloads are teched out and verified as operational."

"And Leopard Wing?" asked the defense minister, his voice low.

"Prepared for takeoff, Admiral."

The defense minister looked at his twenty-four-hour watch and said, "We are still within the time parameters for Leopard Wing, but is the weather over the ice sheet forecast to remain clear long enough for our purposes?"

"Affirmative, Admiral."

Timoshenko looked up at the observation booth and saw Minos Konstantos returning his gaze. It was comforting to have a friend close by at a time like this. Timoshenko surveyed the Flight Control Center once more. He had been here a few times before, of course, on ministry tours; but this was his first visit in an operational capacity. He found it served his purposes well. It reminded him of a ship's bridge, to a degree. Timoshenko drew a deep breath and said, "Colonel Malyshev, commence Operation Snow Leopard Two."

"*Da,* Admiral," responded Malyshev, and he began muttering into his microphone.

McMURDO BASE

"What was that last night?"

Rawlings looked up from his bacon and eggs and said, "What was what?"

Dana slid her tray out of the way and put her elbows up on the mess hall table to perch her chin on her hands. "After we saw the aurora. You took your knife out and waved it behind your back, and you were mumbling something. Sort of like a chant. What was that all about?" Dana thought she detected a little pink tint to his ears, which were framed by his salt-and-pepper hairline. His hair had grown quite a bit since they'd first met, and she liked the look of it.

Rawlings took a sip of his coffee and replied, "I told you about the Inuit and the aurora. Well, there's an old legend that says waving a knife behind the back and singing will ward off the effects of the northern lights. Guess I'm superstitious. It's just a myth."

She eyed him coyly.

"Come on," he said. "Let's not keep our chopper waiting."

And they bused their trays to the kitchen.

AN F-14 TOMCAT OVER NORTHERN IRAN

Maj. Hassan Rajai was cursing as he coaxed his aging F-14 Tomcat through fourteen thousand feet. His squadron was at half-strength, and out of those, only two F-14s were operational. He and his wingman had taken off together, but the other pilot had returned to base when he received a fire warning light. Now Major Rajai's own Tomcat was limping along because its portside engine had dropped to fifty-percent power. Rajai was flying without a backseater because the F-14's old AWG-9 radar didn't work. Its only armament was two Sidewinder missiles—procured with great difficulty and at great expense through the shadowy channels of open-market munitions dealers. Major Rajai figured the Sidewinders were the only thing on the whole damn plane that worked properly.

The F-14 lurched as the port engine flamed out completely, and Rajai began cursing anew. "Scrambled in the dead of night to get this broken-down beast into the air. And for what?" To answer his own question, he hit his mike switch and said, "Green Base, Green Base, this is Blue Flight Leader." *Leader?* thought Rajai. *This is Blue Flight, period.* "I have lost my port engine. Am returning to base. Vector me to runway one-right."

Static.

"Negative, Blue Leader. We are vectoring you to an intercept. We have bogeys on screen, approaching from the north, twenty-eight to thirty-seven thousand feet. Come to course zero-one-three. Main body is a hundred twenty kilometers away, but some lead elements are almost upon you."

Lead elements? Main body? "Green Base, what are you saying? How many bogeys are inbound?"

Pause.

"We are not certain our count is accurate, but we have approximately three hundred ten bogeys on our screen, coming out of Soviet airspace."

Rajai shook his crash helmet, thinking he hadn't heard correctly. "Say again, Green Base. How many bogeys?"

"Three hundred ten. Intercept and destroy."

Rajai couldn't help but laugh a high-strung laugh. Intercept three hundred bogeys!? With two Sidewinders mounted on one broken-down F-14 that could barely get off the ground!? "Listen, Green Base, either someone is crazy or this is an invasion—"

Major Rajai never finished the sentence, for his Tomcat was blown out of the sky by an Aphid heat-seeking missile.

A MIG-29 FULCRUM

Capt. Fyodor Tupelov saw an orange and yellow flash against the black background of the mountainous terrain, but then it faded into the darkness and he took his Fulcrum back up to cruising altitude. He hadn't even jettisoned his external tanks for the engagement.

With the stars shining above him, he considered what an extraordinary odyssey this was. After being pulled out of the Ross Sea with hypothermia, Tupelov had barely warmed up before he was transferred to the damaged *Minsk* and placed in the backseat of the sole surviving Forger aircraft on board—a two-seat trainer. A Candid refueling tanker had been dispatched from Cam Ranh to nurse the little plane back to Vietnam. Upon arrival in Cam Ranh, Tupelov was placed on a transport that flew him to Vladivostok, and from there to Moscow. He got a quick shave and shower, and a new uniform at the Kremlin, then the young captain was ushered into a grand and ornate room where a convention of generals had assembled to hear, firsthand, Fyodor Tupelov's account of how Leopard Base had been destroyed. He recounted his story a half-dozen times, and when the old generals finally seemed satisfied, he was dismissed; however, instead of doing an about-face and making his getaway, Tupelov surprised himself—for he started arguing, then pleading, then almost begging for a chance to get back into the fight.

The generals were silent until one man—an admiral, of all people, a man of ample girth whose uniform was covered in gold braid, spoke in a soft voice and said, "Be careful what you ask for, Captain Tupelov. You might receive it."

So here he was. Flying air cover for the grandest air armada he'd ever seen—or would see, if it wasn't dark.

Leopard Flight had just met the only resistance they would encounter in Iranian airspace. Beyond them was the long flight across the Indian Ocean, around the American base at Diego Garcia, and then on to the cold white wasteland that Fyodor Tupelov had left behind not so long ago.

THE *VINCENNES*

Capt. David Erickson and Marine Lt. Gen. Myron Tharp were on the bridge of the *Vincennes,* watching the bow of the ship pitch up as it plowed into a nineteen-foot wave. Erickson was strapped into the captain's chair and Tharp was alongside, holding on and leaning against the pitch of the deck as it went up-down-up.

"Haven't been in one this bad in quite a while," observed Erickson. "I guess it's good we got that reporter off when we did. He would've had a rough time with this stuff."

"No doubt," replied Tharp, looking a little green himself.

"I don't like that ice forming on us," Erickson observed. "In this weather we can't get out and bust it free."

Tharp's queasiness was becoming more acute, and the storm didn't show any sign of abating. "Wha . . . what's the forecast, David?"

Erickson had one of those swivel cradles for his coffee cup that was attached to the side of his captain's chair. When the deck pitched up or down it would remain level, sort of like a hammock. Erickson prided himself that it was spillproof. He reached for the cup and took a sip, then said, "It's supposed to get worse. By the way, can we get you some coffee, General?"

Tharp's face was turning a darker tint of green as he said, "Uh, no, thank you, David. I don't think coffee would be a good idea right now."

Erickson replaced his cup in the cradle and smiled in understanding. Then he said in a low voice, "Our pharmacist's mate has some magic elixir he can give you if you're feeling a bit unsettled, sir."

Tharp smiled back and said, "Thanks, David, but I'll be okay. For the moment anyway. I'm not too proud to call for help if I need it."

"Oh, shit," whispered the helmsman in a low, tense voice that at once conveyed a message of awe and fear.

Tharp looked out the windshield, and looming through the dark spray covering the forecastle of the ship was a gargantuan twenty-five-foot rogue wave. Tharp held fast to Erickson's chair and uttered "Whooaaa!" as the deck rose up in front of him, then his feet lost their traction and slid back out from under him. Had he not held fast to the captain's chair, he would have slammed against the aft bulkhead.

The *Vincennes* rose up majestically on the towering wave, then came crashing down into the trough in a crescendo of boiling surf and howling wind. The men on the watch were pitched forward, causing some to lose their grip and tumble into the forward bulkhead. Tharp was among them, his small body having become a human pendulum that swung forward as he lost his grip on the captain's chair.

Erickson waited for the ship to recover a bit, then unstrapped himself and went to aid the vice-commander of the task force. "Are you hurt, sir? That was a bad one. I hope it didn't knock any of our circuits loose." Tharp got to his feet and steadied himself while holding on to Erickson for balance. "I believe I'm all right, David, except I think I banged my shoulder. Nothing serious . . . I don't think we jarheads have ever developed the proper respect for you ship-drivers."

Erickson was about to reply when a gong went off, and a red light started blinking next to a blaring loudspeaker, "General quarters, general quarters, this is no drill. Captain to CIC."

Erickson and Tharp looked at each other in disbelief; then, grabbing handholds where they could, they made their way toward the hatch and into the passageway leading to the Combat Information Center.

KALININGRAD FLIGHT CONTROL CENTER

Col. Oleg Malyshev held the earphones tight against his head and let the report finish, then he turned to Timoshenko. "Admiral, the Sea Leopard task force has crossed the zone of exclusion and is heading for the nearest group of American vessels. The Sea Leopard commander says no enemy aircraft are detected on his radar."

"Is the satellite booster fueled and ready for launch?"

"Affirmative, Admiral."

Timoshenko nodded. "Launch the satellite when Sea Leopard commences the engagement, and bring the *Kharkov* and *Smolensk* to the surface."

"At once, Admiral!"

THE *VINCENNES*

Erickson and Tharp made their way to the chairs in front of the large display screens. "All right, what's happening here?" Erickson demanded as he slipped on his headphones.

The tactical action officer was nervously muttering into his headset before pausing to explain, "Captain, a party of Soviet vessels that were loitering outside the sixtieth parallel have crossed over the zone of exclusion and are heading for us. We count eight vessels heading toward us—two cruisers, probable *Kirov* class, and the rest destroyers or frigates. Our radar return is sporadic due to the heavy seas and the ice. We're keeping the picture on screen updated as well as we can, but it's not in real time. The *Kirov* radars are hot, though, and that's helping us track 'em."

"Range?" asked Tharp.

"Twenty-six miles, sir," replied the TAO, "and they are closing on a right-angle course. We've been heading west into the waves. They're undoubtedly having trouble making steam, heading south."

Tharp's mind searched for a reason why the Soviets would try something like this. "Does the *Vinson* have any aircraft up?"

"Negative, sir. They're a hundred twenty miles to the southwest, in worse weather than we've got. The storm is all over the Ross Sea, and all three carriers have curtailed flight operations." The TAO punched a button, and a picture of the Ross Sea came up on the screen, showing the locations of the three carriers. "The *Eisenhower* is three hundred seventy miles south-southwest of the *Vinson,* and the *Roosevelt* is two hundred eighty miles west-southwest of the *Eisenhower.* The *Roosevelt* has a single Hawkeye up that they may divert to McMurdo because they can't recover it." The TAO stopped abruptly as the antiair warfare coordinator broke in and said, "*Separation!* I have separation detection on lead heavy! Incoming threat, probable antiship missile . . . estimate time to impact three minutes thirty seconds!"

BAIKONUR COSMODROME, KAZAKHSTAN REPUBLIC OF THE SOVIET CONFEDERATION

On pad number twenty-eight of the Soviet launch center, the starfish arms of the service gantry fell away from the SL-11 rocket as its liquid-fuel engines sparked to life, belching smoke and flame onto the exhaust apron. The booster rose slowly at first, then faster and faster, and higher and higher, illuminating the night sky like a flare. Then it began arcing over onto a southern trajectory, racing toward an escape velocity that would hurl its payload, a radar ocean reconnaissance satellite, into a polar orbit.

THE *VINCENNES*

Captain Erickson inserted his firing key in the arming controller on the console. "Weapons free! Weapons free! Activate Goalkeeper doctrine statement. Cover the heavies with bulldogs, salvo two on lead heavy. Swick, get me a solution and turn your key."

The Goalkeeper doctrine statement was one of several defensive game plans programmed into the Aegis computer.

The antiair warfare coordinator came on and said, "Goalkeeper on line. Incoming threat is tagged Track one-one-nine for Goalkeeper. Threat is offscreen. I say again, off our scope. Probable SS-N-19 sea skimmer below our horizon. Our illumination is sporadic due to heavy seas. Hold Standard fire until range closes."

Erickson watched the symbology change on the screen, and wondered how close it was to reality. Not close enough when milliseconds meant the difference between defeat and victory. Life and death. "Swick, have you got the solution?" demanded the captain.

The surface warfare coordinator, known as the Swick, said, "Aye, Captain. Salvo two with simultaneous time-on-top plotted."

"Fire!"

The Swick hit the red FIRE button and immediately a rumble was heard in CIC as two Harpoon missiles left their launch tubes on the fantail.

"Harpoons away!" announced the Swick.

Not far away from the *Vincennes,* two Harpoons also left the *John Paul Jones.* All four missiles would follow separate tracks before converging on the *Kirov*-class cruiser simultaneously in an attempt to overwhelm the vessel's defenses.

"Threat detection," announced the antiair warfare coordinator. "We now have threat detection of Track one-one-nine. Time to impact, seven-zero seconds." His hands danced across his console. "It's fading in and out because of the seas. Goalkeeper is working the solution. Captain, hold your fire, we do not have a solution. . . . Whoa, separations from heavy two! We have dual missile launch from heavy two! Boost phase ascent. Assigning threats Track one-two-zero and one-two-one. Estimate time to impact three minutes twenty seconds. Time to impact on lead threat Track one-one-nine fifty seconds. Goalkeeper has a solution! Captain, your switch is hot!"

Erickson hit the red button on his panel, and a Standard missile left the rail from the forward launcher, and this time a loud roar was heard in CIC. The missile covered the forecastle of the ship with its smoke plume, which was rapidly swept away by the violent wind. As the Standard ascended into the stormy sky, the *Vincennes*'s SPY-1A radar attempted to keep the incoming threat illuminated so the missile could follow the reflection down to an intercept. "Cover heavy two with bulldogs. Salvo two. Swick, make the solution and fire at will," Erickson ordered.

"Aye, Captain."

Tharp switched his intercom to the communications room. "Is the voice channel open to Admiral Rumley on the *Vinson?*" he asked urgently.

"Negative, sir. Somethin's wrong. It's down."

Tharp grimaced. "Then send a flash teletype message to Admiral Rumley: '*Vincennes* under attack. Engaging Soviet task force. Require immediate air support.'"

"Standard is on track for intercept. . . . Separation! New threat incoming!"

More rumbling came from the fantail as two more Harpoons were loosed.

THE *KHARKOV*

"Blister packs armed," said the *starpom,* Avraam Ryback.

"Detonate," Bodin ordered.

Ryback lifted the safety cover and punched the red button, and almost immediately there was thunder that shook the submarine.

"Damage report?" queried Bodin.

The damage-control officer muttered into his hand receiver, then looked up and replied, "Negative damage, Captain."

"Number One, cut all cables to blister packs and communications buoy. Diving officer, blow your tanks and begin your ascent. Up periscope. Fire control, stand by for targeting data." The periscope column rose, and Bodin yanked down the brass handles while mashing his sharklike face to the viewer.

THE USS *SEAWOLF*

The three operators in the blue-lighted sonar suite of the *Seawolf* all jumped in their seats simultaneously as the explosion from the *Kharkov*'s blister packs punched the sensors of the hunter-killer submarine. The three young men rapidly exchanged glances, each one saying, "You heard it, too?" Finally the senior operator hit the intercom and said, "Conn, sonar."

"Sonar, conn, aye," squawked the reply.

"Contact, bearing two-zero-two. ID unknown. Range undetermined. Apparent underwater detonation."

"Detonation?"

"Aye, sir."

"Hmmm. Let's go have a listen. Battle stations."

THE *VINCENNES*

"Lead threat Track one-one-nine is down, Captain," said the antiair chief, "but I don't know if our Standard hit it or it impacted into a wave. Track one-two-zero is down as well. Track one-two-one is still incoming. Time to impact, six-zero seconds. Goalkeeper has solution, your switch is hot."

Erickson hit the red button, and again a roar was heard in CIC as the Standard missile left the forward launch rail.

"I don't understand," said Tharp. "Why are they firing piecemeal like this? Why aren't they massing their fire?"

"They're traveling south, General," Erickson snapped. "That means they're going lengthwise through the troughs and getting hammered by the waves. Their electronics aren't as good as ours, and all that together probably means they're having trouble getting a fix on us."

"We have a Harpoon impacted in the sea, Captain," said the Swick. "Three others sixty seconds out from impact on lead heavy, and still closing."

"Separation!" barked the air chief. "Two separations on lead heavy . . . three . . . looks like they're going for our bulldogs. I ID them as defensive missiles . . . no threat, no threat . . . incoming threat Track one-two-two now under Goalkeeper solution. Captain, your switch is hot."

Erickson hit his red button again, and there was another roar. He turned to the TAO and said, "When you reload the forward launcher, don't let a wave flood the open blast door."

"Aye, Captain."

The stress was unlike anything Tharp had experienced before. The roar of the missiles, the pitch of the deck, the strained voices. And all he could do was watch. He pulled on Erickson's elbow and leaned over to say, "This weather is hurting our ability to defend ourselves. The Soviets might get in a lucky shot. Should we retire to the south to take us closer to the *Vinson*'s battle group?"

Erickson shook his head. "To go down the troughs in these seas would be bad news, General. The Soviets have got a rougher time than us. Better to stay on this track and fight it out from here."

As the deck pitched up, Tharp wondered how it could get rougher than this. Then the ship went sharply down, and the console operators held on to their chairs as the incline increased, and a commo seaman came through the hatch. He was tossed forward into a roll until he came to rest against a bank of chairs. He emitted a groan upon impact, and as the deck came back to level he grabbed the back of Tharp's chair and pulled himself upright, feeling wobbly. The Marine general asked, "Are you all right, son?"

Holding a hand against his kidneys, the seaman groaned, "Uhhh, I don't think so, sir, but never mind that," and he slapped a piece of paper down on the console. "This just came in from Admiral Rumley on the *Vinson,* sir."

Tharp took the message, which read:

CAPTAIN OF VINSON PREPARING TO LAUNCH ALERT
AIRCRAFT. SEA PERILOUS. MAY NOT SUCCEED.
RECEIVED MESSAGE VIA CINCPAC FROM SPACE COMMAND—
CHEYENNE MOUNTAIN. LAUNCH DETECTION BAIKONUR COSMO-
DROME. ORBITAL GROUNDTRACK PLOTTED BY SPACETRACK RADAR
ON DIEGO GARCIA. WILL PASS OVER OUR POSITION. SPACECOM
SPECULATES PROBABLE RECON SATELLITE. VINSON ATTEMPTING
TO BRING ASAT F-14 UP FROM HANGAR DECK TO INTERCEPT.
ALERT AIRCRAFT HAVE PRIORITY FOR LAUNCH.
                                                    RUMLEY

The deck rolled again.

"Separation! New threat inbound!"

Rumble. "Harpoons away!"

"Track one-two-one is down!"

Tharp's mind raced. What was happening?

ALTITUDE: 182 KILOMETERS, ORBITAL DECLINATION: 82 DEGREES

Above the blue expanse of the Indian Ocean—which was now black under the nighttime sky—the explosive bolts on the Soviet ROR-SAT's aerodynamic launch shroud fired, causing the cover to peel away and expose the payload. The satellite's hydrazine thrusters engaged so that the RORSAT's radar antenna was facing the earth, pointed down to penetrate the clouds and paint the sea with its inquisitive beam.

On the side of the RORSAT, a small dish antenna was deployed that would send the data to a communications satellite, which in turn would bounce the signal to Red Banner Black Sea Fleet headquarters in Sevastopol.

Now activated, the RORSAT began searching for the distinctive reflections that would betray the presence of American supercarriers.

SLAVE BAY

Like an angry sea dragon emerging from a disturbed slumber, the long black form of the *Kharkov* broke through the pack ice of Slave Bay, which had been splintered by the blister-pack charges into harmless shards.

Having retracted it just before impact, Bodin ordered, "Up periscope!" again and the tube rose. He yanked down the brass handles and once more mashed his face against the viewer. He spun around and saw nothing but white desolation. Then he checked the *Kharkov*'s turtleback and cursed. Two large shards of ice had settled onto its flat surface, and Bodin feared they would impair the missile doors. "Get the ice-clearing crew out on deck at once, Number One, and raise the satellite communications mast. I will be in fire control. Have them move quickly. There is no time to lose."

"Aye, Captain."

THE *CARL VINSON*

The ocean was unlike anything Michael Pershing had ever seen in his life on the sea. His Hornet was sitting in the saddle of forward catapult number two as the deck of the supercarrier pitched up, then down, then up again in the violent storm. Spray was lashing against his canopy, and his view of the end of the catapult trail changed from

black water to gray sky as the massive carrier plunged into a trough,
then rose up on a wave. The natural elements railed against the
Vinson with such fury that it seemed to Blackjack the forces of
nature were unleashing their wrath as a protest against the human
intruders in their midst—tossing the ninety-thousand-ton vessel
around like some kind of cork.

As the deck pitched down, the end of the catapult trail was aimed
straight into the sea, but when it pitched up, a brief launch window
for the Hornet would open. It was the diciest of situations for a
catapult officer, for he had to gauge the action of the ship and
actually fire the catapult when the deck was pointed down at the
water—so that when Blackjack's Hornet reached the takeoff skid,
the launch track would be aimed skyward. Blackjack got the signal
from the cat officer—in the bubble canopy sticking up through the
deck—and acknowledged with his flashlight.

Blackjack couldn't believe they were going for it, but they were—
and he would be the first to launch. He advanced the throttles to full
military power and braced his neck. There was nothing else to do but
wait. And watch. The gray, stormy sky filled his canopy view; and
as the engine exhaust wailed against the jet blast deflector, the flight
deck plunged into another ocean trough. It hung there, bow down,
as if frozen in time. Then Blackjack felt the catapult fire—and the
wall of the dark, menacing sea rushed toward him. He felt sure he
would hurtle into the black waters, but then the forecastle of the ship
lurched upward and the catapult power of two million horses unleashed the Hornet into the air.

Like an automaton, Blackjack retracted his gear and trimmed out
the Hornet, all the while wrestling against the buffeting wind that
relentlessly assaulted his craft. He banked to port and climbed into
a racetrack orbit around the ship—waiting for his wingman to
launch from catapult number one. The wingman was a new guy—a
replacement flown in from the States for Jazzman or Otter or one of
the others who had been blasted out of the sky during the attack on
the *Tbilisi.* Blackjack couldn't recall the new guy's name. He banked
his Hornet around again to come up alongside the *Vinson* on a
parallel track, just as catapult one fired. It was a snapshot of movement, but Blackjack saw it. His wingman's Hornet was sent headlong
into the sea, breaking into pieces just before the *Vinson*'s massive hull
crushed its remains.

The cat officer had been deceived by the random fury of the waves.

"Alert One! Alert One! This is Air Boss! We have a casualty. Launching is deadlined. I say again, launching is deadlined. You are on your own. Handing you off to Golden Eagle."

Blackjack shook his head and wearily replied, "Roger, Air Boss. Golden Eagle, this is Alert One. Request instructions, over."

The voice coming from the *Vinson*'s CIC was strained as it transmitted over the radio, "Rog . . . roger, Alert One. The Russians have crossed the zone of exclusion. The *Vincennes* and *John Paul Jones* are under attack. Vector zero-one-one. Range to *Vincennes,* one-one-eight miles. Light your burners and get there quick. Pick up tactical control from *Vincennes* on this freq."

"Acknowledged, Golden Eagle. I'm on my way. Alert One out."

Blackjack pointed the Hornet straight up to climb above the storm before heading out on the assigned vector.

The perilous launch, the destruction of his wingman, the combat awaiting him, no longer triggered any emotion in Blackjack. The Fear had vanished—replaced by a robotic psyche that turned the young Texan into a flesh-and-blood automatic pilot.

THE *KHARKOV*

"*Target acquisition!*" barked the fire-control officer into his headset. Sitting in front of the horseshoe-shaped console in the fire-control center, the officer spun in his chair and said to Bodin, "Sevastopol reports our satellite has found the carriers, Captain!" He clamped one of the headphones tight against his ear and listened, then added, "Coordinates and target assignment to follow immediately!"

"Are we clear of the ice on the deck?"

"Aye, Captain."

"Then open missile hatch number one."

"*Da,* Captain." And the fire control officer rapidly threw a series of switches.

On the turtleback of the Delta-IV submarine, the titanium door concealing the first *Zimorodok* missile yawned open like a bottle cap coming off—revealing the dome of a weapon lurking underneath.

"Missile hatch one is open, Captain. Conn confirms silo is clear of ice." The fire-control officer punched more buttons, bringing the launch sequence up to firing readiness; then he stopped and once again held the headphones tight against his head, while crisply relaying the target data to the seamen on the missile deck. "Primary target assignment! Missiles one through eight! Coordinates are . . . sixty-two degrees, eighteen minutes south. One hundred sixty-eight degrees, fourteen minutes west. Confirm data entry and clear missile deck!"

In the large missile bay, eight crewmen reached through a kind of porthole in their assigned silo tubes and rapidly punched in the coordinates on a panel inside the missile.

"Confirm launch point coordinates!" ordered fire control. And in sequence the confirmations were rattled off by the crewmen. "Clear missile deck! Quickly! There is no time to lose! We must launch before the carrier gets out of range."

The urging was not necessary, for the crewmen had thrown off their headsets and were scurrying through the hatch into the fire-control compartment.

"Close the hatch," Bodin ordered, and the men swung the heavy steel blast door shut with a *clang,* and spun the wheel to seal it.

The fire-control officer punched more buttons, inserted his key into the safety lock, and turned it while saying, "*Zimorodok* missiles armed, plotted, and ready to launch on primary target, Captain!" And his hand closed around the red pistol grip sticking out of the console.

Bodin felt the blood pumping rapidly through his body as he swallowed hard. He wasn't made of iron, and had to force himself to take a deep breath and utter the command, "Fire missile one!"

The trigger was squeezed.

The turtleback of the *Kharkov* erupted in a conflagration of smoke, flame, and deafening noise as the *Zimorodok* missile thundered out of its launch tube, scorching the deck with the blazing tail plume of its solid-fuel engine.

Bodin felt the ship shudder and vibrate as the forty-six-foot-long *Zimorodok* lifted off, then he listened as the roar faded to a dull hum.

"Missile one away! Conn confirms no hull damage."

Bodin nodded as he felt a bead of sweat trickle down his cheek. "Close hatch one. Open hatch two and fire."

"Aye, Captain!"

And in only a few moments the submarine was shaking and trembling once more from the fiery violence it had unleashed.

THE *SEAWOLF*

Again, the sonar operators sat up as though they'd all been goosed at the same time. "What the hell was that?" asked one, as glances were exchanged back and forth, and a spike appeared in the waterfall display of the sonar monitor.

"There it goes again. . . . Chief, listen in on this."

The chief sonarman—whose physique had the definition of a pear—took his personal set of headphones and shoved the plug into the socket. As he held one cup to his ear, his mouth formed an O, his eyes rolled back into his head, and his eyelids fluttered like a butterfly—a definite sign he was focusing his auditory powers on the sound coming through his earphones. After a few more crescendoes he punched the intercom button and said, "Conn, sonar."

"Sonar, conn, aye."

"We have another contact, Captain," said the chief.

"Whaddya got?"

"I'm not quite certain, sir, but it sounds like the percussion section of the New York Philharmonic—specifically a kettle-drum solo."

THE *VINCENNES*

There was another rumble as the last Harpoon left the fantail tube.

"Final Harpoon away!" the Swick shouted. "We're empty."

"Threat Track one-two-seven is down, Captain," said the air chief.

After the initial salvos, the pace of the engagement had ratcheted down somewhat. The Soviet ships had turned onto a course parallel with the *Vincennes* and *John Paul Jones* and shadowed them, firing an occasional ship-to-ship cruise weapon, which—if it did not impact in the sea—was swatted down by the Americans' Standard missiles. The *Vincennes* and *Jones* had returned the fire, tit for tat, and one of the *Kirov*-class cruisers had apparently taken a hit, for it was lagging behind the Soviet pack.

"Well, damn . . . would you look at that," muttered the TAO.

Erickson studied the symbology on the screen and said, "They're breaking off the engagement and heading back north. . . . Strange." He exhaled a deep breath. "Good thing they are, because we're out of bulldogs."

Myron Tharp opened his channel to the communications room and said, "Contact Admiral Rumley on the *Vinson*. Tell them to stand down on the air support. The Soviets have broken off the attack and are retiring." As a former aviator, they didn't want a pilot to launch in this weather if it wasn't necessary.

The TAO held his headset tight, then said, "Yeah, patch it through." He punched more buttons while saying, "Captain, General Tharp, that single Hawkeye that's orbiting the *Roosevelt* way to the southwest of us has picked up something. The *Roosevelt* is passing us the feed. Coming up on the screen now . . . there . . . looks like they have a contact coming off the coast. Two. Three bogeys. Ascending rapidly. Four. Climb rate increasing. . . . Lead element passing twenty thousand feet, twenty-five, thirty, thirty-five, forty . . . five contacts now . . . six . . . lead element at sixty thousand . . . sixty-five . . . seventy . . . what in the world is this? They aren't moving laterally very much. It's almost a straight climb. Damn! *Eight* contacts . . ."

Erickson squinted at the little squares—which denoted unidentified contacts—as their digital altitude readouts changed rapidly. His fingers drummed the console, and his mind sifted through the possibilities. Finally he said, "General, these contacts . . . their flight profile is . . . is . . ." He searched for the word.

"Ballistic," said Tharp.

Erickson gave a quick nod. "That's right. Ballistic. But here? How? Why? What could they be?"

Tharp shook his head. "I don't know, David. From a sub, maybe?"

"Sub?" replied Erickson. "Ballistic? You . . . you don't think the Soviets are going *nuclear,* do you? Here? If that's the case, why so many missiles?"

Tharp shook his head again. "I can't say, David . . . but I can't take a chance." He hit his mike switch. "Commo, flash message to all Beowulf land and sea commanders. Rig for nuclear warfare. I say again, rig for nuclear warfare. Get it out fast."

"Lead element passing through nine-five thousand feet," said the TAO, in a voice that had gone up three octaves. "It's off the Hawkeye's scope . . . second contact gone . . . so's the third . . . fourth gone. . . ."

There was a chilled silence in the blue-lighted CIC chamber as the specter of a polar Armageddon loomed before them.

98 KILOMETERS ABOVE THE ROSS SEA

After the *Zimorodok* missiles had passed out of the Hawkeye's radar sweep, they responded to the navigational commands in their microchip brains and began arcing over into a flight path above the Ross Sea. The first stage on the lead missile separated and stage two ignited, increasing the payload's velocity as the microcircuits rapidly computed time, distance, speed, vector, and altitude from the launch point; plus descent track and impact point.

Now traveling at fourteen thousand kilometers per hour, it did not take long for the lead *Zimorodok* to reach its waypoint 420 miles downrange, where it nosed over and began painting the prescribed sector of the Ross Sea with its powerful nose-cone radar. The electronic pulses went out and returned, revealing the large, definitive signature of the USS *Carl Vinson*—not far from the location plotted by the RORSAT. This triggered the missile's lock-on mode, and the computer vectored the nozzles on the second stage to fire a slight correction burn before sending the warhead plummeting toward earth.

THE HORNET

Blackjack had reached his cruising altitude and leveled off his Hornet for the dash toward the *Vincennes* when his earphones crackled. "Alert One, Alert One, your strike is aborted. I say again, your strike is aborted. Return to Golden Eagle."

Frustrated, Blackjack said, "Make up your mind. You make me take off and you kill another guy in that soup, and now you want me to come back. . . . Shit . . ." He toggled his mike and said, "Roger, Golden Eagle. Alert One will comply. Out." He rolled the Hornet onto its back and pulled it back down into the clouds from whence it came.

THE *ZIMORODOK* MISSILES

At an altitude of twenty-three miles, the second stage separated on the lead *Zimorodok*. What remained was a twenty-eight-foot-long projectile, six-and-a-half feet in diameter, plummeting down in a spin-stabilized mode. At the prescribed instant, explosive bolts blew off four side panels at the rear of the projectile, revealing four small solid-fuel thrusters that were recessed and inverted in the side of the missile. They fired simultaneously to brake the projectile with an unconventional retrofire, which at the same time reduced the rate of spin. This put tremendous dynamic pressure on the missiles, and one came apart in the air, but the *Zimorodok* had been engineered with the finest materials—and the remaining seven withstood the stress. During deceleration, the nose cone radar on the lead missile took its final fix on the massive carrier, which was moving snail-like through the stormy sea.

Its fuel expended, the small retro-stage separated and a tiny drogue parachute popped out of the tail as the twenty-four-foot cylinder continued in a free-fall past an altitude of fifteen miles. The drogue slowed the payload as the atmosphere became denser, until at seven miles the drogue yanked a large parachute canopy from the tail, which caused the cylinder's speed to bleed off radically.

At 23,000 feet, cloaked in the tumultuous storm clouds, there was another flash of explosive bolts as the nose cone on the lead missile blew off and fell away. Out of the bottom of the cylinder—which was dangling at the end of the parachute lines—an inner cylinder dropped like a telescope extending, then separated completely and fell free. It looked like something akin to a telephone pole falling from the sky, but then at its midsection two stubby wings unfolded, as did a set of tailfins on its rear. This brought the fall under control, and directed a flow of air into the air scoop on the underbelly. The turbofan blades began spinning, which brought the engine to ignition, and the telephone pole continued down in a powered dive while the search radar in the nose easily found the flight deck of the *Carl Vinson* directly below.

Like caterpillars to butterflies, the *Zimorodok* weapons were rapidly transforming from ballistic to cruise missiles as they hurtled toward the *Vinson* in a "down the smokestack" track—a track that was in the blind spot of the supercarrier's own defensive radar. If they continued on their vertical course, they would impact squarely on the *Vinson*'s flight deck.

But that was not the intent.

THE *CARL VINSON*

Blackjack popped out of the clouds at a ceiling of two thousand feet and pulled up while banking around toward the *Vinson*'s fantail. The sea was still as frothy as when he left, and as he lowered his gear and tail hook, he became worried about icing. The buffeting from the wind made his Hornet feel like a bronco as the meatball bobbed up and down with the heaving deck. Blackjack resolved to make one pass, and if he didn't hook this one he was going to divert to McMurdo—and the Air Boss could shove it. He wrestled with the stick, trying to see the flight deck through the spray that was striking his windshield. It was the most horrendous weather he'd ever approached through in his life. The deck pitched down, up, down . . . the wind railed, his airspeed dropped . . . he held the throttle tightly. The black deck of the flattop rushed up . . . then fell. In a flash, tires squealed, tail hook scraped, throttles opened, and Blackjack "bolted" off the angled deck, having failed to snag a restraining wire.

The nose of Blackjack's Hornet rose as he started to regain altitude, and he'd climbed no more than a few hundred feet when a dark, long object screamed over his canopy in a near midair collision.

Like streamers flowing out from a maypole, the seven surviving *Zimorodok* missiles pulled up a few hundred feet above the *Vinson* and fanned out in multiple directions away from the carrier.

"Just what the hell was that, tower!?" shouted Blackjack. "Are you guys trying to kill me like you killed my wingman?"

"What was what, Alert One?"

"You don't know? I almost had a midair!" Blackjack screamed.

"Wait one, Alert One. . . . Traffic is picking up multiple contacts . . . we don't know what they are."

"Dumb shit," Blackjack cursed as he jerked his Hornet around in what he thought was the direction of the bogey, and cut in his afterburner to pursue. He searched through the rain on his canopy, but could only see the white crests on the ocean below . . . But wait . . . what was that? Skimming over the waves? He killed his afterburners so as not to overshoot, and put his nose down a bit to reel in the bogey. Damn! Was that . . . ? He hit his mike. "Golden Eagle,

Golden Eagle, this is Alert One. I am in pursuit of a cruise missile. I say again, I am in pursuit of a cruise missile. Looks like a big-ass Harpoon or Tomahawk. It is headed away from the ship. Is it one of ours?"

"Uh, wait one, Alert One. We're trying to get a fix on multiple contacts. Radar tracks are hard to maintain in this weather. Where did it come from?"

"You're asking me!? I nearly collided with the sonofabitch. . . . Wait . . . it's turning."

Blackjack banked and followed the *Zimorodok* as it curved around 180 degrees until its nose was pointed directly at the *Carl Vinson*'s broadside—which was looming ahead like a mammoth leviathan that had surfaced in the storm. "Golden Eagle, Golden Eagle, listen up! This bogey has turned in to you! I'm going to down it!"

"Roger, Alert One! They're all starting to turn! Activating close-in weapons now! Shoot it down and get your ass away from here!"

"Roger, but don't shoot at me!" Blackjack cut his throttle and let the missile pull ahead as he lined up a cannon shot through his head-up display. He had the target in his sights, but was distracted by a series of flashes that peppered the deck of the *Vinson* as she fired off a volley from her Sea Sparrow air defense batteries. He didn't see any Sparrows headed in his direction, so he refocused his aim on the cruise weapon. It was an easy shot, really, and he was just about to pull the trigger when the *Zimorodok* abruptly rose about a hundred feet and leveled off. Startled, Blackjack pulled up and lined up his shot again, just as the missile cut its speed dramatically, almost causing Blackjack to fly into its rear. He veered the Hornet away and cut the throttles again, while applying the air brake. Once more he pulled back, almost at stalling speed, watching the *Vinson* approach ever closer as he lined up the shot again. "Got you this time, you sonofabitch," he growled in frustration, and began to squeeze the trigger when there was a flash at the nose and tail of the missile. The exploding bolts cleaved the nose cone and power plant from the midsection, while stripping the exterior airframe away from the final stage of the *Zimorodok* weapon. Blackjack veered off again, thinking the missile had blown up. But then he executed a half-roll and caught sight of a loglike object plunging into the ocean, with a drogue chute hanging on to its tail.

Blackjack hit his throttle and pulled around to search for the object, but it was nowhere to be found, for the sea had swallowed the *Zimorodok*—which was the Russian word for "Kingfisher."

The *Zimorodok* torpedo had received a final fix on the *Vinson*'s position from the target-acquisition radar in the missile's guidance system—just before it hit the water and began streaking along at forty-seven miles an hour beneath the violent waves.

Of the seven *Zimorodok* cruise missiles that had survived reentry, one had turbofan start failure, and three were shot down by the Sea Sparrow missiles before torpedo separation. Of the three torpedoes that hit the water, one experienced a navigational malfunction and went off on a harmless tangent. But two of them—including the one that had eluded Blackjack—closed with the supercarrier. When they reached the end of their programmed run, they did not seek to ram the side of the *Carl Vinson*. Rather, they dove—to a depth of perhaps 150 meters, then turned up toward the underbelly of the *Vinson* while flicking on their active sonars. Their *pings* were immediately rewarded, and as they pressed home—on an almost vertical trajectory—the echoes became shorter and shorter until the torpedoes impacted on the heavy steel hull.

It was here that the *Zimorodok* revealed its pièce de résistance, in the form of a triple-stage warhead. The lead element was a charge engineered to crater an opening through the carrier's thick hull, while the tail element exploded at almost the same moment, acting as a propellant to send the middle charge inside the vessel, where it might do greater damage than just a hole or an air pocket below the waterline.

Upon striking home, these two *Zimorodok* torpedoes sent their explosive payloads into the loins of the ship, where they detonated almost simultaneously—in compartments of the *Vinson* known as "the magazines."

23

. . . .

HMS *HOOD*

On May 24, 1941, at 5:35 A.M., a long hunt came to an end when Vice-Adm. Lancelot Holland of the Royal Navy spotted two German warships south of the Denmark Strait—not far from the pack ice along the Greenland coast—heading southwest. The lead German ship was the 14,000-ton heavy cruiser Prinz Eugen, *followed by the pride of the German fleet, the 42,000-ton battleship* Bismarck. *They were attempting a breakout into the North Atlantic to attack Britain's lifeline of convoys.*

Holland was in command of a force comprising of his flagship, the 48,000-ton battle cruiser HMS Hood, *and the battleship* Prince of Wales.

Upon sighting the German warships at a range of twenty-three miles, Admiral Holland decided to close the gap and approached the enemy vessels at an angle of almost ninety degrees—in effect allowing the Germans to cross his own "T."

At 5:49 A.M., Holland ordered the Hood *(which was in the lead) and* Prince of Wales *to open fire with their forward batteries on the lead German ship, thinking it was the* Bismarck—*but because the silhouettes of the two German ships were so similar, Holland was actually shooting at the ship with the lesser firepower, the* Prinz Eugen. *The captain of the* Prince of Wales *guessed correctly that the trailing ship was the* Bismarck. *He therefore overruled Holland's order and directed fire from his six forward guns toward the larger enemy vessel—losing a gun in the process, owing to mechanical failure.*

With limited fire falling between them, the two German warships opened up with concentrated broadsides on the Hood, *and a hit was scored, while the* Bismarck *sustained a hit from one of the* Prince of Wales's *fourteen-inch guns.*

At this point, Holland ordered the Hood *into a twenty-degree turn to port in order to bring all of his batteries to bear. In the middle of the maneuver, the ship was bracketed by a salvo, probably fired from the* Bismarck. *Moments later a fateful round, again most likely from the* Bismarck, *fell upon the* Hood *in a near-vertical trajectory— and the battle cruiser's inherent vulnerability became manifest. The armor-piercing shell smashed through the decks—which were thinly armored—and plunged through to detonate in the* Hood's *magazines, where 112 tons of gunpowder were stored.*

A colossal explosion racked the ship, cleaving it in two as it rose out of the water amidships. One of the fifteen-inch gun turrets sailed into the air, along with a flurry of shells that crackled over the vessel like a pyrotechnic display.

The amidships section fell back into the water, causing the bow and quarterdeck to rise up. Incredibly, the forward turret fired a final salvo as this happened. Four minutes after the blast, the remains of the Hood *slipped under the waves, covered by a veil of black smoke.*

Of the 1,419 officers and men on board, only 3 survived.

THE HORNET

Blackjack banked around the *Carl Vinson* in a racetrack holding pattern as he waited for word from Golden Eagle. He made sure his IFF was squawking as he toggled his mike and said, "How about it, Golden Eagle? Was that a torpedo or wha—"

Looking at the stormy sea below him, Blackjack froze in horror as the ninety-thousand-ton supercarrier seemed to convulse and shudder in the water, belching smoke and flame from the elevator bays and fantail—as if it were a submerged volcano that had just broken the surface. Frozen, Blackjack flew on for some moments before whipping his aircraft around to orbit the carrier.

He would seem to remember hearing a groan as he watched the *Carl Vinson*—caught in the grip of a violent sea—shudder again and slowly list onto its starboard side. It lingered there for a while before finally rolling over on its back, exposing a giant rupture along the hull that made the magnificent vessel look like a gutted fish.

As wave after wave of the sea's fury pounded against its steel remains, and smoke continued to pour out of the fissure in its hull, the *Vinson* did not pitch up at the stern or bow. Instead, it slowly disappeared—as a wounded whale might sink from view.

Blackjack went beyond shock. How could the most colossal warship ever afloat vanish so quickly? So completely? *Five thousand men!* Sweet Thang. Wrangler. Padre. All of them. Gone.

It was as if his soul had been wrested through a vortex, pulling him out of the straightjacket of the robotic automaton he had become, and making him human again as he wailed in grief.

Crying and wanting only to escape, Blackjack put the Hornet on its tail and lit the afterburners to blast himself out of the oppressive storm.

BRANDING IRON STATION

Seymour Woltman was grateful for the surgical mask that covered his nose and mouth as he walked with Joshua Pfeiffer along the floor of the dust-impregnated icedome. Woltman had never been in a mine before, and although the dome wasn't exactly the mine shaft proper, it was close enough for Woltman to realize he didn't like being underground, or under the ice, or under—period. The flood lights gave the place an eerie dimension, for their beams were diffused by the fine dust particles filling the air—giving it the feel of a fog bank. But at least he'd gotten off that heaving, pitching bucket of a ship, and now had Mother Earth under his feet.

Woltman was doing the reporter's gig, slipstreaming Maj. Gen. Joshua Pfeiffer as he bulldozed his way through on an inspection tour. The guy had all the subtlety of a buzz saw, and Woltman had heard the term "brown shoe" applied to the Sixth Infantry Division commander a couple of times. He made a note in his notebook to find out what "brown shoe" meant.

"Woltman, come over here," Pfeiffer ordered.

Reflexively, Woltman felt himself respond, and drew closer to the general.

"Thought you would like to watch this, Mr. Woltman, since you were the one who blew the whistle on the Soviet invasion and all." Pfeiffer was almost shouting over the noise of a hoist winding up a cable. They were standing a few yards from the mine shaft as the large bucket appeared in the opening and the hoist stopped. "Well, there it is, Mr. Woltman. That's what we came here for."

Seymour Woltman blinked a couple of times and said, "It looks like a big bucket of sand . . . or salt, I suppose."

Pfeiffer nodded. "The geologists tell me the rubidium ore is found in carnallite—some kind of mineral found in sea-salt deposits. That's it."

An engineer swung the bucket away from the shaft and discon-
nected it, allowing it to rest on a wheeled pallet. A crew pushed it
out of the way and rolled an empty bucket into its place. The bucket-
ful of sand was then wheeled over to the elevator for transport to the
surface.

Woltman whipped out a pocket camera and snapped a couple of
flash pictures, but he doubted they would come out because of the
reflection in the foglike dust.

"I can probably sweet-talk the engineer into letting you go down
the mine shaft if you want," offered Pfeiffer.

"Uh, no, that won't be necessary," Woltman replied. "I'd just as
soon head topside."

Pfeiffer snorted and motioned toward the elevator. "Then we better ride up before they press-gang the elevator to haul the ore up."
And they started walking toward it. "So how are you liking it here
in Antarctica?" queried the general.

"Great!" replied the Associated Press reporter with obvious enthusiasm. "Couldn't be better."

Pfeiffer was surprised at the gusto of his response and asked,
"What makes you so gung-ho about being in an icebox . . . where
you might have been shot at?"

Woltman smiled under his surgical mask. "The Pentagon didn't
allow TV reporters in the press pool."

The elevator door opened and Lt. Col. Samuel McClure stepped
out, looking distraught. "General Pfeiffer, your CP wants you on the
radio right away."

THE HORNET

Blackjack blasted out of the clouds and into the bright sunshine and
blue sky of the polar morning. He cut the afterburner and pulled
himself level, then brought his Hornet upright. Tears were rolling
out of his eyes and over his rubber mask as his body shook, and a
wail came out of his throat. How much could one man take?

"Beowulf Two, this is Blackjack! The *Vinson* has been sunk! Do
you hear me? The *Vinson* has been sunk! Give me a target!"

There was a maddening silence before a response came over his
headphones. "This is Beowulf Two. Say again last transmission."

"I said this is Blackjack! I was the only one to make it off the

Vinson! Some cruise missiles appeared out of nowhere, then went into the sea. I don't know what happened. They might have been some kind of missile-delivered torpedo."

"Wait one, Blackjack," came the voice through the headset. "How bad was the *Vinson* damaged? We can't raise them on the command net."

Blackjack screamed in frustration, *"Dammit, didn't you hear me? I said the Vinson was sunk! Dead! Under the water! Do you understand? Now send me to the bastards that did this!"*

There was a pause, then the voice came back, noticeably shakier this time. "Very well, Blackjack. Your report is being confirmed by other vessels in the battle group. . . . Listen up. . . . We think the source of those missiles was west of the *Roosevelt* battle group, near the coast. The *Roosevelt* cannot conduct flight operations due to weather, and we're getting reports they're under attack as well. Your target is sixty-nine degrees forty-two minutes south, one-five-five degrees fifty-two minutes east."

Blackjack quickly punched in the data on his navigational computer.

"What is your armament, Blackjack?"

"Harpoons. Two of them. Plus Sidewinders."

"You better make tracks. That's about five hundred fifty miles to target. They're not likely to hang around. Have you got the fuel?"

"I got drop tanks, and I'll be going one way," said Blackjack as he whipped his Hornet around and cut in his afterburners to speed over the Ross Sea toward the Oates Coast.

THE *KHARKOV*

"Close missile door number twelve," Bodin ordered.

The fire-control officer threw the switch, and the hatch covering the now-empty silo of the final *Zimorodok* missile swung back into place. "Door number twelve secured and sealed."

Bodin wasted no time as he hit the intercom button and said, "Conn, fire control."

"Fire control, conn, aye."

"The final missile is away, Number One. Door is secure and sealed. Send the 'mission accomplished' message to Sevastopol, then take us down to two hundred meters. I'm on my way to central control."

"Aye, Captain."

Almost immediately the sound of water rushing into the buoyancy tanks rumbled through the vessel. Bodin clapped his fire controller on the shoulder as he turned to leave, saying, "I suppose we must wait until we arrive back at Polyarny to learn if our *Zimorodok* weapons found their mark. I must say I was surprised they all achieved lift-off."

MOUNT DISCOVERY

Dana Harrow looked around the little seismic hut that had been her refuge from the Soviet paratroopers. "It seems like a hundred years ago," she said softly. "The fear. The sense of total isolation. One minute being a benign scientist and the next being anxious about your survival."

Standing behind her, Rawlings saw her petite body shiver, as if she were trying to shake off the memory. He gently patted her shoulder and said, "I think I can relate to what you feel. Better grab what you need so we can be on our way. The flyboys in the chopper are impatient types."

Dana reached out and unplugged the cables on the hard disk drive, which she hoped contained some fragments of data that would help salvage her dissertation. Hefting the ten-pound unit under her arm, she said, "Okay, on to Mount Morning."

THE *SEAWOLF*

"Conn, sonar."

Capt. Larry Saucedo punched the intercom button beside his captain's chair and said, "Sonar, conn, aye."

"Contact, Captain. Bearing two-three-five."

"Range?"

"Haven't got a position yet, Captain, but it's about thirty kilometers to the coast, so it can't be any farther than that."

Larry Saucedo was of medium height, and appeared to be solidly built, having played defensive back for the University of Oregon. But because he had spent the bulk of his career on submarines, where opportunities for exercise were limited, the solidity of his build had wavered somewhat.

Saucedo was sitting in his captain's chair in the attack center of the *Seawolf,* which was the first of a new class of hunter-killer submarines designed to replace the *Los Angeles*–class attack vessels. Thus far, however, only three *Seawolves* had been built due to the shrinking defense appropriation.

The attack center of the *Seawolf* did not look as though it belonged on a submarine. Rather, it appeared to be the bridge of a starship. The dominant periscope columns of submarines past were no longer present. Instead of a conventional periscope, the sail of the *Seawolf* possessed a mast with high- and low-light TV cameras and an infrared thermal imager—as well as masts for radar, communications, and electronic sensors. The imagery was not passed to the attack center via a tube with mirrors inside, but by fiber-optics that projected the imagery, as well as other sensor data, on video monitors.

The attack center of the *Seawolf* was an elongated chamber with a large display screen on the forewall that was controlled by the captain. He could call up any sensor data. To the left and right of the big screen were the helmsman and planesman, respectively, then along the sides of the chamber were operators at their stations for engineering, navigation, weapons, damage control, electronics, the XO, the chief of the boat, and the like. But owing to the eclectic skills of the sonar profession and the operators' need for quiet concentration, the sonar suite was purposely sequestered down the passageway.

The locus of the attack center was the captain's station. Located in the midpoint of the chamber, he could swivel around and survey a particular station, or use his console to call up data on the forward display screen.

Captain Saucedo decided to put on his headset intercom and switch off the loudspeaker, which he didn't like to do—he was old school. He opened a channel to sonar and said, "Okay, Chief, what do your ears tell you about our contact? What have we got?"

"My ears and the computer say the same thing, Captain. We make it a Soviet Delta-IV-class ballistic missile submarine."

Saucedo was stunned. "A Delta-IV? Are you sure, Chief?"

"Virtually positive, sir."

Saucedo's mind was trying to make some sense of it. "What the hell is a boomer doing down here, Chief?"

"I would suspect, sir, that they're booming. Now that we have an ID, I would guess the rumbling sound we heard was the Delta-IV firing her missiles."

Saucedo went pale. A boomer launching nuclear-tipped ballistic missiles inside the zone of exclusion? Oh, Lord, it couldn't be. No time to surface and open up a commo channel to find out the score. Besides, his rules of engagement for a Soviet sub inside the zone were quite specific. "Weapons, get me a solution. Give me forty-eights in tubes one, two, three, and four. Helm, bring us to bear on target on sonar's track at fifteen knots." He hit a couple of buttons that instructed the computer to take the *Seawolf*'s own position from the inertial guidance system and sonar's plot of the target, and throw them up on the forward display screen.

"Course two-three-five, Captain," replied the officer of the deck.

"Tubes one, two, three, and four loaded and primed, Captain," announced the weapons officer. "Sonar has a position now. Solution completed. Inserting my arming key."

Saucedo also inserted his key in the receptacle on his console. "Quartermaster, put up the sea-floor topography for this plot."

"Aye, Captain, but there are some holes in the data."

"I know that," Saucedo said testily. "What's the maximum depth on the plot?"

The quartermaster paused before saying, "Maximum depth, based on the data we have, is one-eight-seven-six feet."

Saucedo's face almost sneered as he whispered grimly, "Got you now, you bastard. Nowhere to run. Nowhere to dive. All stop!"

"All stop, aye."

"Flood tubes one and two," Saucedo ordered.

A momentary pause, then, "Tubes one and two flooded, Captain," replied the weapons officer.

"Open outer doors on tubes one and two."

Pause.

"Doors on one and two open, Captain," said the weaponeer. Saucedo turned his key.

"Confirm solution on one and two."

"Solution confirmed."

"In sequence, one and two, fire," ordered the Captain.

The weapons officer turned his key and punched the first of six red stoppers on his console.

On the bow of the *Seawolf,* a Mark 48 torpedo came out of the tube and engaged its five-hundred-horsepower, axial-flow gas-piston pump-jet engine, while dispensing a wire out its tail. It executed a quick dogleg maneuver so as not to foul the wire from the torpedo coming out of tube number two.

"One is clear," announced the weapons officer. "Running true to the enabling point." He hit the second red stopper. "Two is away . . . clear . . . running true."

"Range?" asked Saucedo, almost in a whisper.

"Twenty-eight thousand yards, Captain," replied the weaponeer. "Going to max cruise on fish one and two." He turned the controller on each torpedo and the command raced down the wire, instructing the torpedoes to increase their prop pitch and bring themselves up to their top speed of fifty-five miles per hour.

"Time to impact, eighteen minutes, ten seconds," announced the weapons officer.

THE *KHARKOV*

"Conn, engineering."

"Engineering, conn, aye."

"Captain, we must take the port reactor off-line for a moment. We are receiving an annunciator warning that one of the control rods is stuck. I would suppose it is a faulty annunciator, but I would like to be certain. We can continue on with power from the starboard reactor if you wish."

Bodin knew that his engineer's suppositions were better than a comprehensive tear-down by fleet technicians, so he hit the intercom button and said, "Very well, Grigory. I prefer to halt until we can travel with full power. All stop."

"All stop, aye."

"Go to work, Grigory, but do not linger."

"Aye, Captain."

Had the *Kharkov* not halted, they wouldn't have had so much as a chance.

THE *SEAWOLF*

"Conn, sonar."

"Sonar, conn, aye."

"She's cut her engines, Captain. My guess is that she's going silent in hopes we'll overshoot."

Saucedo looked at his weapons officer. "Is the Russian skipper correct in that assessment, lieutenant?"

The weapons officer shook his head. "Fish one and two on track to enabling point. Last position of Delta-IV boat is on the plot, within parameters of search-and-acquisition mode."

Saucedo nodded. "Okay. We hold tight. Time to impact?"

"Sixteen minutes, twenty seconds, Captain."

THE *KHARKOV*

The *michman* called for quiet as he clamped his headphones tightly to his ears. Had the *Kharkov* not halted, the rush of water over the hull would have masked the faint, high-pitched whine now caressing his ears. He slammed the intercom button. "Conn, sonar!"

"Sonar, conn, aye."

"Captain! We have one, possibly two torpedoes inbound! Range unknown. I classify as American MK-four-eights."

In the central control room, Bodin, Ryback, and Mizim couldn't keep their faces from betraying their profound shock. Bodin gulped and demanded, "Do you think they will overshoot?"

"Doubtful, Captain. Their signal strength is increasing. I identify two distinct fish now."

Bodin's mind raced through the possible countermeasures he could take, and the list was slim. "Do we have a fix on the source?"

"Negative, Captain," replied the intercom. "But at this range it would have to be another submarine."

Dead in the water. Torpedoes approaching. Source unknown. He could fire his own torpedoes down their axis of advance, but that would be the longest of shots. "Avraam, what is the sea-floor depth!?"

Ryback ran his fingers over the navigational chart as if it was on fire. "Six hundred twenty meters, Captain."

"Blast!" and Bodin struck the periscope column in frustration. The MK-48 had a maximum depth of 760 meters, while the *Kharkov,* with its titanium hull, could pass a thousand meters, as it had done in the Passage. But with a sea floor too shallow, that escape was sealed off.

"They are closing, Captain," prodded the voice through the intercom speaker—not that Kasimir Bodin needed a prod.

He smacked his fist into his palm and punched the engineering intercom button. "Grigory! Put us on-line immediately, the control rod be damned! Prepare for flank speed!" He turned to Ryback. "Make ready on the sound devices, Avraam. Helm, bring us about a hundred eighty degrees and go to flank speed!"

THE *SEAWOLF*

"Running true . . . running true . . . time to enabling point fourteen minutes, forty seconds."

"Conn, sonar!"

Saucedo barked, "Sonar, conn, aye."

"We flushed her, Captain! Her screws are cutting like a coupla egg beaters, and she's turning."

Saucedo said, "Put it on the plot." And almost immediately the square representing the *Kharkov* was moving back the way it had come—toward Slave Bay. "Sonar, the plot says she's heading back to the coast."

"Affirmative, Captain."

Saucedo turned. "Weapons, at current speed, can she outrun the fish if she turns away from us?"

The weapons officer did some rapid calculations, then looked at his console and said, "Yes, Captain. It would be close, but yes."

"Then cut the torps' speed to two-thirds. That will drop their fuel consumption and give them some extra range while maintaining closing speed."

"The target is now off our port bow, Captain," said the weapons officer. "Should we recompute the enabling point?"

"For the port fish, aye. Keep starboard fish on original track. We'll bracket the target in case she turns again."

The weapons officer eased the joystick controller on the portside torpedo so it veered off from its original path.

"She's approaching the coast, Captain," said the sonar chief.

Saucedo could see that on the plot. But why was she going into that bay? There would be no escape from there, for sure.

THE *KHARKOV*

"Sonar!" shouted Bodin. "Give me a ranging ping to the ice shelf!"

Immediately there was a *ping* sound, soon followed by its echo. "One thousand six hundred meters, Captain."

"Avraam, sea-floor depth?"

"Five hundred eighty meters, Captain, approaching a steep rise into Slave Bay, where it comes up to three hundred meters."

Bodin turned to his diving officer. "Depth?"

"The *Kharkov* is at one hundred ninety-seven meters, Captain."

"Our speed is impairing our sensors, Captain, but it sounds as if the torpedo has turned with us," said the sonar *michman.* "It must be close."

"Dive, dive, dive!" ordered Bodin. "Thirty-degree down-angle on the planes. Maintain flank speed. Up periscope."

The tubular mechanism rose as the deck pitched forward. Bodin yanked down the brass handles and shoved his face against the viewer. "Illumination!" he ordered, and the spotlight beams again pierced the darkness of the water and he flicked on the light amplifier. "Level us off at two hundred ninety meters, Avraam. Have sonar give us a second ranging ping."

"Aye, Captain."

Ping. Echo.

"Eight hundred twenty meters to the ice shelf, Captain."

Ping . . . ping . . .

Bodin cocked an ear. Those *pings* weren't from the *Kharkov*'s sonar.

"Torpedo has gone to active search mode," said the sonar *michman.* "It is sweeping, but has not acquired us."

Bodin remained glued to the viewer. "Eject sound devices." Maybe that would divert it for a bit.

On the sides of the *Kharkov,* two compressed-air vessels were released, spewing their noisy bubbles into the water in an attempt to lure the deadly torpedo away.

Bodin remained fixed on the viewer. There it was! The ice shelf of Slave Bay, extending down from the surface like the underwater face of a sheer cliff. Bodin was operating on pure guesswork and decades of experience under the polar ice cap. "Left full rudder! Ahead two-thirds!"

"Left full rudder, ahead two-thirds, aye," replied the trim officer.

The *Kharkov* banked in a turn while Bodin executed a quarter pirouette with the periscope, searching for something as his vessel came onto a parallel track with the ice shelf.

"Rudder amidships."

"Rudder amidships, aye."

Ping . . . ping . . . ping . . . ping-ping-ping-ping-ping . . .

"We have been acquired, Captain!" shouted the sonarman.

The *Kharkov* was skimming across the ocean floor now—where ice shelf and sea floor met—like a frightened flounder looking for refuge. But an 11,000-ton, 544-foot-long vessel did not enjoy the dexterity of a flounder.

Ping-ping-ping-ping . . .

Bodin searched frantically for what he hoped would be there.

The sea floor dropped and . . . *yes!* There it was! He had found one!

"Down on the planes fifteen degrees! Hard right rudder!" Bodin held on to the tube as the *Kharkov* went into a diving, banking turn, and he watched through the periscope as the giant cavelike opening swallowed up his ship. Bodin had found a gap between the sea floor and the underside of the ice shelf, and was deftly maneuvering the *Kharkov* into the cavernlike opening in search of safety.

"Rudder amidships and bring us level, helm!"

"Aye!"

Ping-ping-ping-ping . . .

The torpedo had followed them in, and as the massive sub righted itself, Bodin spied a stalactite of ice hanging down from the ceiling. The *Kharkov* was still traveling at two-thirds speed as he ordered, "Left full rudder!" to swing the ship around the stalactite in an arc. He turned the periscope as the giant undersea icicle went past. Bodin licked his thin lips and ordered, "Hard right rudder! Reverse engines! Full power!"

Ping-ping-ping-ping-piiiinnnggg!!!

Bodin and his crew lurched forward as the reverse spin on the propellers cut into the water and broke the giant vessel's momentum.

BAROOOOM!!!

The explosion rocked the *Kharkov,* pushing up its stern until it impacted on the ice ceiling. The lights in the central control room went out momentarily, then came back on.

"All stop!" shouted Bodin as he grabbed the rail and brought himself back to his feet.

"All stop, aye."

They were still in one piece, hanging at a severe down angle. "Damage report!" demanded Bodin.

Ryback was quickly on the handset intercom, demanding damage reports from his division chiefs. It took a long three minutes, but once finished he looked up and said, "Circuitry damage in engineering. Grigory is diagnosing it now. He says we can make power with starboard engine. Other short circuits reported, but no fires. Hull integrity seems to be secure, but we may have suffered rudder or propeller damage when our stern hit the ceiling. Grigory will be able to tell when we start to maneuver."

Bodin went back to the periscope and swiveled around to look aft. The rear spotlights stabbed the darkness, and the ceiling of the ice cave was only a few meters from the viewer. The periscope had survived. "Diving officer, use rear buoyancy tanks to lower our stern and level us out. Very carefully."

The diving officer did so, causing some flooding and popping noise, which made Mizim wince.

Once level, Bodin looked aft. The giant stalactite was nowhere to be seen. He had maneuvered his Delta-IV sub so the ice stalactite was inserted between it and the MK-48. The American torpedo had locked on to the giant icicle and splintered it into pieces when the MK-48's 650-pound warhead detonated.

Underwater explosions were quirky things. A sub could be quite close to a depth charge when it went off and hardly suffer a scratch, while another sub hundreds of yards away could be hammered. Bodin knew the *Kharkov* had been luckier than it had any right to expect. Now he was cornered in an underwater ice cavern, with no option but to sit and wait. Bodin returned to the light-amplified view of the periscope and said, "Avraam, left standard rudder, ahead dead slow. If we must sit here, we will do so with our teeth facing our enemy."

THE *SEAWOLF*

"*Impact!*" shouted the sonar chief. "I think we got her, sir!"

Captain Saucedo looked over at the lieutenant on the weapons station and asked, "What do you have?"

The weapons officer checked his console and said, "The torp had lock-on before detonation. I think we've got ourselves a kill, sir."

"Range to target?"

"About twenty-seven thousand yards, sir."

Saucedo tapped his teeth with his index finger. Somehow it just didn't feel right. "Okay, let's have a look. Helm, put us on track for the point of impact. Ahead two-thirds. Silent running."

"Aye, Captain."

THE *KHARKOV*

Kasimir Bodin brought the *Kharkov* to the mouth of the underwater ice cave, which was quite large. The submarine was facing bow-forward like a moray eel that was backed into its dwelling among the coral, baring its teeth to any intruder who dared trespass on its territory.

"Load tubes one through six, Avraam," Bodin ordered. "If our adversary appears, we must be ready."

As Ryback began issuing instructions, Bodin returned to the periscope. The spotlight beams continued to stab into nothingness as Bodin swept the depths with the periscope head. "Sonar, conn. Any contacts?"

"Only some distant whales, Captain, and they are fleeing from the explosion."

"Very well." Bodin stepped back and looked at Toomas Mizim, who had followed the entire engagement on the periscope monitor. "So, our rudder and propellers are still functioning, Mr. Mizim. What do you think? Have we given our adversary the slip?"

Mizim continued staring at the TV monitor that was wired into the periscope. The phlegmatic pilot with the forlorn eyes had remained silent throughout the underwater battle, and he kept his eyes on the monitor as he spoke. "It is difficult to say whether we have eluded them, Captain, but something has occurred to me."

"And what is that?"

Mizim wiped his face with his hand—a sign of fatigue and stress—and said, "American submarine commanders are often . . . aggressive. If that is the case here, then our counterpart will come after us. To confirm his kill. His trophy, you might say. If he does so, he will be careful not to probe the wall of the ice shelf with his sonar as we did—for that would reveal his position. I would imagine he has periscope sensors similar to ours, therefore he may use spotlights, just as we did, to aid his navigation once he enters this bay."

Bodin nodded. The pilot's thesis sounded reasonable.

"And if he does, in fact, use his periscope with a light amplifier, as we have done, then our lights will act as a beacon for him."

The pilot's analysis registered on the captain, causing Bodin to remark, "Your talents extend beyond navigation, Mr. Mizim. . . . Turn off exterior lights."

"Aye, Captain."

THE *SEAWOLF*

Capt. Larry Saucedo looked at the plot on the forewall display as the circle denoting the *Seawolf* entered Slave Bay at a depth of 430 feet. The chart said the bay had a sea floor of 940 feet, but he did not have high confidence in its accuracy, so he ordered, "All stop."

"All stop, aye," replied the officer of the deck.

"Sonar, take a good listen. Anything?" asked Saucedo.

After a few moments the reply came back. "Only the water slapping against the pack ice, Captain. We've filtered that out, and we have zip."

Saucedo tapped his teeth again. "Quartermaster, looks like we got an ice shelf somewhere up ahead."

"Affirmative, Captain, but its position is probably fluid. Do you want to take a sounding with active sonar?"

"In a combat situation, I don't think so. Sonar, you sure you've got zip?"

"Affirmative, Captain."

"Very well. Weapons officer, get the best fix you can on where the fish impacted. Let's see if we can spot any debris. Then launch the SPUR. Guide it with the wire and give me the optical feed."

"Aye, Captain."

On the smooth underbelly of the submarine, the *Seawolf* looked like some kind of whale giving birth as a cigar-shaped object detached itself from a recessed well in the belly, and began to sink. It was twice as long and three times as thick as one of the *Seawolf*'s torpedoes, and as it descended it sprouted four fins around its bulbous nose. It looked like something akin to a pilot whale; but unlike a whale, four high-intensity headlights were mounted in the fins. Once clear of the *Seawolf,* its electric pulse-jet motor engaged and it moved out, trailing a wire-reinforced fiber-optic cable behind.

This was the Sensor Patrolling Undersea Robot, or SPUR as it was known, which gave the *Seawolf*'s captain the means to probe hostile waters without exposing the submarine and its crew to danger. In its bulbous nose it carried passive and active sonar sensors, and in one of its fins was a TV camera that fed pictures through the fiberoptic cable to the bridge. The SPUR could be programmed to operate autonomously, or it could be controlled by acoustic signals transmitted through the water, or by the fiber-optic cable, as it was now.

It also packed a five-hundred-pound warhead for suicide missions.

THE *KHARKOV*

"We have both reactors back on line, Captain. We can engage full power again."

"Very good, Grigory," Bodin responded, with a trace of relief.

"Captain," said Mizim, tapping the monitor screen, "have a look through the periscope and see if something is out there."

Bodin's relief vanished as he returned to the viewer and tried to discern the object through the green hue of the light amplifier. Yes . . . there it was. Very faint. Off the port bow. It was diving, and Bodin tilted the periscope head down to follow it. The pinprick of light was going to the bottom. "Sonar, conn. Do you have any contacts?"

"Something, Captain. Extremely weak. Unidentified. Too faint to obtain a fix."

Bodin watched the intruder as it began to move along a serpentine path, weaving back and forth along the bottom of the bay like a deep-sea cod. It stayed close to the sea floor and passed out of Bodin's field of view—blocked by the forecastle of the *Kharkov*. It was obviously too small and maneuverable to be an attack submarine. A midget, perhaps? "What do you make of it, Toomas?" queried Bodin.

Mizim shook his head. "A small submersible of some kind? I do not know. Looking for us, I would imagine."

"For us, or for our remains," said Bodin as he remained fixed to the viewer. The pinprick of light reappeared off the starboard bow, continuing its serpentine track below the vessel.

The entrance to the ice cave was something akin to a giant outdoor amphitheater, with the *Kharkov* hovering above the lip of the stage. From the lip of the stage the entrance dropped off about fifty feet to a flat plain below, where the SPUR device was scouring. With the periscope in the sail, Bodin had tracked the SPUR as it passed in front of and below the *Kharkov,* and now—as it continued away—he was about to lose it when it halted . . . and turned toward the ice cave.

It appeared to bob up and down a few times, then it climbed toward the opening of the amphitheater. Bodin's mind was racing. Whatever that object was, it was danger. No question. Now it was approaching. The captain's mind groped for something—anything—he could do.

It was coming closer. "Toomas," whispered Bodin, not wanting to use the intercom any longer, for fear of making enough noise to attract the intruder. "Go to the torpedo room. Tell the *michman* to prepare to flood and fire all six tubes simultaneously. When I give the order to fire we will not have much time."

Silently, Mizim left.

Bodin beckoned his *starpom* to approach, and whispered to him, "Avraam, prepare all six torpedoes for autonomous launch, in a dispersal arc of ninety degrees from the bow centerline, programmed for arming and active search at five hundred meters. If we are discovered, our only chance will be to fight our way out behind a torpedo screen."

Ryback nodded and withdrew to the weapons station.

Bodin's sweaty hands gripped the brass handles of the periscope. Fortunately the handles had a knurly surface, like the grip of a pistol, so his moist palms did not slip. The periscope was looking off the starboard beam now. The pinprick of light had climbed into the amphitheater and was heading toward the rear of the ice cave—again scouring the bottom. The captain felt that the mysterious beast undoubtedly had sonar sensors of some type, which caused him to hold his breath reflexively. The light turned again—this time toward the *Kharkov*—approaching like a bloodhound, sniffing the bottom. Perhaps it would pass underneath his submarine. Bodin swallowed hard and hoped that it would. The light stopped, turned toward the rear of the ice cave once more, and started to rise. Bodin exhaled with relief that the light had turned away from him, but then—as if deciding it had done enough spelunking—the probe did a 180-degree turn to exit the ice cave, and in so doing its lights flashed directly into Bodin's periscope viewer. The captain caught his breath as the beacon continued its traverse back toward the mouth of the amphitheater. But then it halted, like a man doing a double take, and reversed itself to bask the *Kharkov* in its spotlights.

"Flood tubes one through six, open the doors and fire!" screamed Bodin. "Ahead flank!"

THE *SEAWOLF*

"What the heck is that?" murmured the weapons officer, looking at his monitor.

"Conn, sonar! SPUR is picking up flooding tubes! Doors opening! Christ, torpedo away . . . two away! Three! Four!"

"Skipper! I think I had a sub on the SPUR viewer, but it just moved out of sight. Did you see it?"

"Active pinging on torpedo." The sonar chief had settled down a bit. "Range five thousand yards . . . we're plotting it between us and the SPUR sonar. Six torpedoes away."

Saucedo had the old feeling of being double- or triple-team blocked while trying to stop an end-run sweep. "Snapshot two-one! Give me an AT torp in tube two, pronto! All stop!"

In the torpedo room of the *Seawolf,* movements reached a frenetic pace as the torpedomen yanked open tube number two and engaged the hydraulic piston that rammed the 3,400-pound anti-torpedo-torpedo into place. The crewman slammed and sealed the tube hatch, activated and slaved the fire-control system to the weapons station in the attack center, then flooded the tube to equalize the pressure with the sea water and opened the door for launch.

From the time the captain said, "Snapshot two-one," to the time the anti-torpedo-torpedo was ready to fire, forty-five seconds had elapsed.

"Sonar, what have you got?" demanded Saucedo.

Pause.

"Let's hear it, sonar!"

"Right, Captain . . . this is it. We've got six fish on scattered bearings. Range about three thousand five hundred. They're on active search, but they seem to be scattering. Looks like a shotgun spread. And our Delta-IV is coming behind the screen."

"Any of the fish coming at us?" demanded Saucedo.

"One is coming right down our throat, Captain. Bearing one-eight-seven. Range three thousand now, and closing."

"Is the AT torp loaded?"

"Loaded, flooded, and door open, sir," replied the weaponeer.

"Launch and put it out three hundred yards and hold!"

"Aye, sir!"

"Then get me a solution on the Delta!"

The lights on the fire-control panel for tube number two had barely changed from red to green when the *whoosh* of the launch was heard by the torpedoman.

The anti-torpedo-torpedo sailed out of the tube and engaged its propeller, which sent it knifing through the water at forty miles an hour, playing out the controlling wire behind. After three hundred yards the propeller shut down and the weapon drifted at neutral buoyancy.

The anti-torpedo-torpedo, or AT torp, as it was known on the *Seawolf*-class vessels, loaded like a standard MK-48 torpedo in almost every respect, but its innards were somewhat different.

The *Seawolf* was lying still in the water, like a tethered lamb acting as bait for a prowling tiger. The idea was to let the Russian torpedo approach with its active sonar head pinging away. Then, like a moth drawn to a flame, the AT torp's guidance would home in on the pinging, and engage its own active sonar in a terminal targeting phase to intercept. It was an exercise requiring a deft hand, for the intercept closing speed of the two torpedoes could exceed a hundred miles an hour. The AT torp might not hit the incoming weapon dead on, but the explosion from its warhead could disrupt or dismember the incoming threat.

In essence, the AT torp was a high-tech flyswatter that operated underwater.

"Range two thousand yards," chanted the sonar chief, while watching the digital chronometer that computed the closing range and speed.

Ping.

"Seventeen hundred."

Ping.

"AT torp has acquired incoming threat," said the weapons officer.

Ping.

"Cut it loose," ordered Saucedo.

Ping.

"Range twelve hundred yards."

The passive sensor in the nose cone of the AT torp received each successive *ping* like a stallion growing restless in the starting gate. Finally, at a range of seven hundred yards, its propeller engaged and it streaked off on an intercept track, activating its own sonar head. The sound in the water became a *ping-ping-ping-ping-pi-pi-pi-pi-nngg-nng—BLOOOOM!*

"I think we got it, Captain!" howled the sonar chief. "A couple of the other fish have detonated, too. Ran aground or hit some ice, I suspect, and that has garbled the water. But I'm almost certain we got the incoming."

"What about the Delta?" demanded Saucedo.

"She's behind the compression wave in the water. She's shielded until it dissipates or she passes through it."

Saucedo drummed his fingers on the arm of his chair. They'd been lucky. And he didn't want to face another volley of six torpedoes. The other guy had a pair of brass nuts. You had to give him that.

"Uh, Captain?" ventured the sonar chief.

"What!?" barked Saucedo.

"The Delta is coming through on the SPUR sonar again. It's on the far side of the compression wave. The Delta must be going at flank speed. You want us to chase it with the SPUR?"

The SPUR! He'd forgotten. "How much fuel left in the SPUR, Lieutenant?"

"About half-full, sir," said the weaponeer. "I was bringing it back for refueling when I spotted the Delta."

Saucedo did some quick mental calculations. A Delta's max speed was twenty-four knots. A SPUR could manage fifty in a sprint. He mentally thrashed through the numbers and shouted, "Arm the warhead on the SPUR! Hit its active sonar and push it to max speed! Ram it up the Delta's ass before it makes it through the compression wave!"

"Aye, Captain!"

THE *KHARKOV*

The fourth explosion from the shotgun spread of torpedoes rumbled over the hull as the giant Delta-IV sub raced through the cold, dark waters of Slave Bay.

"All tubes reloaded and flooded, Captain," reported Ryback.

Bodin nodded. "Maintain course and speed. Be prepared to fire in an instant." He hit the intercom. "Sonar, do you have anything?"

"Difficult to say, Captain. We can pick up little at this speed and the explosions have muddied the sounds considerably. We may have struck an enemy submarine dead ahead. I simply cannot say."

"Very well, when we pass through the concussion wave, prepare to go to active sonar in a hundred-eighty-degree sweep. If our enemy is still alive, I intend to shoot our way out." He switched intercom channels and said, "Engineering, conn."

"Conn, engineering, aye."

"I need everything you can give me, Grigory."

"You have that and more, Captain. We are beyond red line on both reactors."

Ping.

Bodin looked at Ryback. "What was that?"

Ping . . . ping . . . ping . . .

"Sonar, conn, we are being scanned. . . ."

Ping-ping-ping-ping!

"We have been acquired, Captain!" screamed the sonar *michman.*

Where did it come from? Had they overshot the American? There wasn't time. "Eject sound devices! Forty-degree up-angle! Blow all tanks, emergency surface!" Perhaps they could hide in the shallow ice keels of the pack ice.

The water was violently displaced as air was forced into the buoyancy tanks, and the giant vessel bobbed toward the surface, goosed by its wide-open throttle. The hull might suffer ice damage, but Bodin couldn't worry about that now. They were fighting for their lives. They were closing toward the surface, the deck pitched up severely, when . . .

Pi-pi-pi-pi-p i i i i i n n n n g g g g ! ! !

As his ship was whipped by the electronic lashes of the SPUR's sonar, Kasimir Bodin knew he was beaten, and his final thoughts turned not to his vessel or his crew, but to an eight-year-old girl named Marlenya, whose photograph rested in his cabin's safe. His only wish was that he could gaze upon it one last time. But then the *Kharkov* lurched as it struck the pack ice, just as the SPUR's warhead detonated on the submarine's cruciform tail section, venting the engine compartments to the sea—and sending the giant vessel down into the cold, black depths of Slave Bay.

The final image Kasimir Bodin saw beheld the forlorn brown eyes of Toomas Mizim as he appeared in the hatchway, and they seemed to say he understood.

Then the lights went out for the last time.

THE HORNET

Blackjack had just flown past the pack ice of Slave Bay, so he did not see the white carnation of the explosion, or the leviathanlike object breaking through the ice, then disappearing beneath the white veil for its final descent.

Blackjack had crisscrossed the sea and shore, searching for the engine of war that had felled the *Carl Vinson*. Little did he know he'd missed witnessing his enemy's demise by scarcely more than a heartbeat. But now his fuel warning light was blinking a bright red. The afterburner flight and low-level search had drained his tanks until they were almost dry. He rapidly went through his options, of which there were only two: punch out over the snow-covered ice, or try to land on it. He didn't have the fuel to make it to McMurdo. In fact, he had to set it down now. He didn't want to land on the ice shelf, for the snow's depth was unknown to him. Maybe under the veneer of snow there was an ice formation hidden that could crumple his airplane—and him along with it. Punching out into the elements with just his survival kit had little appeal either, but he was more inclined to try that. He had begun going through his ejection checklist when he spied in the distance, locked in the pack ice, one of those large, flat-topped, tabular icebergs that looked like a giant, ghostly aircraft carrier. It seemed to beckon to him.

Intuitively, Blackjack banked toward the iceberg, and as it grew in his sight he hoped it would be large enough. He took a slow pass over it—he knew he'd only get one—and searched for any obstructions, but the tabular berg looked as smooth as a billiard table. Blackjack made his decision and came around on a landing approach. He jettisoned his Harpoon missiles, lowered his gear and extended his flaps, then cut his airspeed for final approach. As the white tabletop rushed up toward him, he remembered something and hit his emergency channel radio button. "Mayday, Mayday. This is Blackjack, flying off Golden Eagle. I'm going down off the coast"— he hit his emergency transponder that was wired into his Global Positioning System to provide a navigational fix—"squawking my emergency locator. Does anyone copy, over?"

There was no response, but he had to concentrate on other things at the moment. As the rear wheels of his tricycle gear touched down, his port engine gave out from fuel starvation. But it didn't matter now, as he cut both throttles and settled the nose wheel down to begin a lengthwise run down the iceberg. There was a thin layer of snow on the tabular berg that helped slow the landing roll. The touchdown felt rougher to Blackjack than a concrete runway, but not by much. The Hornet possessed no drag chute, so Blackjack had to hit the air brake and let the momentum bleed off of its own accord. He was loath to try the wheel brakes, for he didn't want to put the aircraft into a skid that would send it careening toward the edge. But he was rapidly running out of iceberg, so he began to pump the brakes lightly. It helped, but was it enough? He kept one hand on the stick to steer the nose wheel while his left hand slipped over the eject handle. He felt a washboard-type rumble, which he guessed was a series of small pressure ridges, and this seemed to slow him and give him the confidence to lean hard on the brakes. The wheels locked up and the Hornet went into a low-speed skid, yawing to the left and throwing up sheets of snow as the tires scraped through the powder. Then, like a skier coming to an abrupt halt, the Hornet reined itself in—some thirty feet from the edge of the precipice.

Blackjack went limp with relief, and it took a few minutes to recover his equilibrium. He kept his starboard engine going to fire his generator and cockpit heater, and he kept transmitting his navigational fix. When the fuel ran out, he unstrapped himself, popped the canopy, and extended the ladder. The cold air hit him like a shock wave, and by the time his foot touched the ice he was almost shivering. He took his hand-held survival radio and extended the aerial, then turned on the emergency pulse transponder that would, he hoped, lead a rescuer to the source of the 243.0 megahertz tone-modulation signal. He took it a few paces away from his Hornet and propped it up in the snow. Then he stepped back and surveyed the cold, white wasteland that surrounded him.

His carrier sunk, his shipmates dead, stranded on an iceberg in a frozen sea, Michael Pershing felt like the loneliest man on earth.

OFFICE OF NAVAL INTELLIGENCE, THE PENTAGON

The bookish-looking lieutenant (jg) was walking down the hall toward the operations officer's office when he saw a stretcher roll out into the passageway—with the chief on it. There were tubes stuck into the patient's arms as the paramedics rushed past the young officer. The lieutenant (jg) couldn't really say whether the man on the stretcher was alive or dead. He'd never seen a dead person before. Except at a funeral. And there you couldn't really tell because they always fixed them up so well.

Mrs. Perkins, the chief's secretary, came out into the hall, bawling into a hankie. She was one of those late-middle-aged, gray-haired Pentagon secretaries who had probably typed memos for Teddy Roosevelt when he was Assistant Secretary of the Navy. The lieutenant (jg) put a consoling arm around her plump but stooped shoulders, and she buried her face in his shoulder, getting her moist pancake makeup on his black uniform jacket. "It was horrible," she sobbed. "He was on the phone with Admiral Gainesborough, and he just collapsed. Right on his desk. Coronary (sob)."

The lieutenant (jg) patted her shoulder. "I understand," he said softly.

The phone rang and Mrs. Perkins—ever dutiful—ran inside to answer it as the bespectacled young officer looked down the hall to see his superior wheeled into the elevator.

"Lieutenant," Mrs. Perkins called. "It's Admiral Gainesborough. He wants to talk to you."

The lieutenant (jg) swallowed, and entered his (late?) boss's office. He would always look back on this moment as the point when he decided not to pursue a naval career.

MOUNT HARMSWORTH

Dana Harrow and Robert Rawlings had had a much longer day than they'd planned. Their chopper had been several hours late getting off due to a technical glitch. Then on their second stop at Mount Morning the Blackhawk couldn't set down near the seismic hut because of gusty winds. They were forced to land farther down the mountain, and Rawlings told the crew to stay put while he and Dana climbed up to the hut and retrieved the equipment. The crew didn't like the idea, but Rawlings leaned on them hard and they complied.

Now the same thing had happened on Mount Harmsworth, where

they were forced to leave the Blackhawk helicopter on a plateau below and climb up to the hut, which was inside a rocky pocket on the western slope of the mountain.

As they approached their objective, Dana pointed to a pitchfork-looking gizmo on the far ridge. "That's my radio antenna. Looks like I have a guy wire loose."

"Afraid we'll have to repair it some other time."

"Yeah, I suppose so," she said. Then she eyeballed him and asked, "Say, you doing okay?"

Rawlings stretched and twisted his torso a bit. "Yeah, I'm okay. Just a little soreness hanging with me."

"Well, if you're really okay, come with me for a minute. A little bit farther won't hurt. Our friends in the chopper can wait. Again. There's something I want to show you."

"What's that?"

"You'll see." She led him across the pocket and up on the far ridge, which took a little negotiating. Dana estimated the temperature at minus five to ten degrees Fahrenheit, but now the wind had disappeared. The day had turned sunny and the air had gone from gusty to dead calm. They climbed to the top of the far ridgeline, and after taking a few moments to refill their lungs, Dana said, "Take a look."

Rawlings took a look, and the view was spectacular. To the west was the flat white expanse of the Skelton Névé, to the southeast was the Ross Ice Shelf, and to the south was the craggy spine of the Worcester Range of the Transantarctic Mountains.

"You can just make out the summit of Mount Discovery over there to the east," she said.

Rawlings raised his hand to shield his eyes from the sun, and said, "Yes, I see it. It's magnificent, Dana. Thank you for bringing me up here . . . for sharing it with me."

Dana's mittened hand was in her pocket, and she felt the bottle of sunblock. "Oh, almost forgot." She pulled it out and said, "Here, you better slap some on. There's not much ozone left down here. The sun's ultraviolet rays can murder your skin if you're not careful."

Rawlings took the bottle and said, "Of course. The warpaint you made us wear as we were trekking over the ice shelf. Well, I guess this stuff must work. You certainly have lovely skin."

Dana's heart soared over Mount Discovery.

Rawlings rubbed on the lotion and massaged it in by feel.

"Come here, Cochise," she said, "you missed a spot." And she took off her mitten to rub in a white streak along his cheek. In that moment of contact, with her hand on his face, his green eyes locked on to her blues; and everything crystallized between them in a transcending moment. The incredible journey, the fear, the triumph, and the tragedy—the visions all came together for a snapshot in time that was intense, yet sublime. Then as quickly as they came, the images faded away, allowing Robert's feelings to rise to the surface and realize how much he loved this extraordinary woman. He was *juuuuusssst* about to make that leap of faith—across space and time—to place his lips on hers, when something invisible traveled through the air to brush against his eardrum—alerting his primal instincts in such a way that it shattered the magic of the moment.

It was a droning sound.

Dana was starting to turn her head, close her eyes, and part her lips when she intuitively felt a change come over him—as though he'd been pulled away from her and into another dimension without having physically left her presence. "Robert . . . what is it?"

He held up a hand, indicating he wanted silence, and said, "Listen."

It was barely perceptible, but she heard it too. Then it grew louder, and louder. Then specks appeared in the distance. They grew, and grew, and grew, until a vast armada of transports seemed to be almost upon them, and the sky turned black with parachutes.

"Oh, no," whispered Dana, in a voice that was almost a whimper. "I can't take this again."

As the blanket of parachutes descended upon the Skelton Névé, Rawlings's eyes remained transfixed on the unfolding scene, and he seemed to not hear her. Finally, he murmured, "The Russians have upped the ante."

A flight of transports roared over them, snapping them out of their shock and causing Rawlings to yell over the din, "Radio! We have to get back to the radio!" He plucked his A-2 from the snow and grabbed her arm, then they half-ran, half-tumbled down the slope, past the seismic hut, and started down again toward the Blackhawk. Dana saw a cloud of ice and snow bloom away from the rotary-wing craft as the pilot lifted off. "He's leaving us!" she cried.

They halted and saw the chopper go straight up, higher and higher. "I don't think he's running," said Rawlings. "I think he's trying to get high enough so his radio can clear the mountain. It's a line-of-sight transmission to the division C.P."

The Blackhawk rose higher and higher still, then it turned into an orange and yellow ball, just before they heard a *Baroom!* and a shower of debris began raining down.

Rawlings threw Dana to the ground and covered her body with his own as the sound of a hail storm fell about them. Dana heard Robert grunt, then a giant crash as the body of the Blackhawk hit the ground.

THE MIG-29 FULCRUM

Having expended another "Aphid" heat-seeking missile from his aircraft, Capt. Fyodor Tupelov banked his twin-tailed fighter around so he could witness the burning hulk of the American helicopter on the slope of Mount Harmsworth. Then he continued banking around toward the landing zone of the Skelton Névé. He hoped the engineers would have the runway assembled soon. He was bleary-eyed, on the fringe of exhaustion, and he did not see the two Americans as he flew over them.

MOUNT HARMSWORTH

Rawlings rolled off Dana and grabbed his left calf muscle.

"Are you hurt?" she asked.

His overwhites were blackened where a charred piece of debris had landed. Rawlings rubbed the muscle and said, "I think it's okay. Doesn't seem to be broken. No bleeding . . . but never mind about this. Our pilot may not have raised the alarm. We need to get to a radio and get the Navy in for an air strike before the Russians can assemble." Rawlings knew it wouldn't take the Soviets long to consolidate and be poised for an attack. He'd read reports of Soviet *desant* forces dropping an entire airborne division on the ground in seventeen minutes.

"Where did they come from?" asked Dana.

Rawlings shook his head. "Don't know. Cam Ranh maybe. Can't say, but we have to get to a radio."

Dana sat upright in the snow. "The seismic hut! There's one in there."

"Let's go," said Rawlings, getting up. Then he half-ran, half-limped back toward the plywood shelter, hanging on to his A-2 weapon and leaning on Dana for support.

THE SKELTON NÉVÉ

An Antonov-22 "Cock" transport plane—powered by four Kuznetsov turboprop engines—skimmed a few meters above the flat, white tabletop of the Skelton Névé, just a bit above stalling speed. The rear door yawned open and a small drogue chute popped out of the cargo bay, pulling a trio of larger chutes behind it. As the canopies billowed out, the braking effect yanked a cargo pallet from the gut of the plane.

The pallet hit the ground and went into a high-speed skid, sending up a cloud of ice and snow that enveloped the cargo and chutes.

Then the Cock transport plane gained altitude and banked toward the waiting tanker for refueling before it started on the long journey back to Russian soil.

The main chutes on the pallet had barely deflated before the combat engineers were rolling toward the pallets on their airdropped track vehicles.

THE SEISMIC HUT

Dana and Rawlings blasted through the door, breathless. "There!" she pointed.

Rawlings went to it and saw it was a simple FM transceiver. "This is line-of-sight. Are your repeater stations working?"

Dana shrugged. "I hope so. The Russians smashed my transceiver at the geophysics lab, so I never knew if the repeater was still functioning."

Rawlings tried to remember the frequency of his battalion command post net as he dialed in the numbers. He hoped the SOI hadn't changed since Beowulf started. "Bear Den, Bear Den, this is Black Bear One, do you read? Do you read, over?"

There was only the fuzz of static as they waited and Rawlings tried again, and finally the speaker responded with, "We read you, Black Bear One, over."

Rawlings recognized the voice. "Gates, is that you?"

"Roger, Black Bear One."

"Gates, listen to me. The Russians are back. I say again, the Russians are back. A giant air drop west of the mountains. We just saw it. Track down General Pfeiffer or the chief of staff and get 'em on the horn on this freq immediately. You got that?"

"Uh, roger, Black Bear One. Wait out."

THE SKELTON NÉVÉ

A dozen Cock transports had dropped their cargo loads, and the combat engineers were working like crazed bees to break down the pallets and move the honeycombed, aluminum-alloy plates into position so they could be assembled into a temporary runway. This runway would be smaller, narrower, and flimsier than the ones constructed during the original Soviet invasion, and it could not support transport planes. It could, however, support the small twin-tailed Fulcrums.

THE SEISMIC HUT

While waiting the interminable time for Gates to get someone on the horn, Dana nervously paced the tiny hut, murmuring, "This can't be happening. This can't be happening." Rawlings let her pace. There was nothing else to do. She stopped in midstride and, for no reason, flicked on the oscilloscope that was wired into the seismic sensor. She punched up the real time seismograph reading, and a bunch of tightly-spaced, squiggly lines filled the screen. "Whaaat . . . ?" she muttered to herself. "That can't be right."

"This is Pfeiffer," blared the speaker. "Are you there, Robert?"

Rawlings keyed the mike. "I'm here, sir, and we've got trouble. We just saw the better part of a Soviet airborne division drop on the ice shelf west of here. Fighter escorts as well. I'm sorry, sir, but one of the fighters—a Fulcrum, I think—shot down your helicopter. We need a Navy air strike pronto. We have to hit them hard before they have a chance to assemble."

There was a pause, and Rawlings figured Pfeiffer was absorbing this shocking and unbelievable information. But then Pfeiffer came back and said, "Robert, we can't mount an air strike. The three Navy carriers are out of action."

Now it was Rawlings's turn to be stunned. He looked at Dana, but she was fiddling with the knobs of the oscilloscope. "What do you mean by 'out of action,' sir?"

"We're not exactly sure what happened, Robert. I've been burning the airwaves with General Tharp trying to get a clearer picture, but the long and the short of it is that all three carriers were apparently hit by some kind of torpedo or missile that nobody had seen before. Admiral Rumley is dead. Tharp is in command now. The only operable aircraft are a half-dozen Harriers off the *Wasp*. Based on what you've seen, would they do much good?"

Rawlings thought of the Blackhawk helicopter shot out of the air and said, "Probably not worth it, sir. Like I said, they've got fighter cover. I have no idea where they came from, and to disrupt their operation now would take a heavy-duty, massed air strike . . ."

Rawlings was brought up short when Dana ripped the microphone out of his hand and started speaking breathlessly. "General! This is Dana Harrow. We're transmitting to you from my seismic station on Mount Harmsworth. Listen to me. Please listen. We may be in a dangerous situation."

"We're definitely in a dangerous situation, Miss Harrow," replied Pfeiffer.

"No, no. I don't mean the Russians. Listen to me. I'm looking at my electronic seismograph readings as we speak. I've never seen data waves like this before. I think Mount Erebus may be on the verge of an eruption . . . possibly a major eruption."

There was a pause before Pfeiffer came back with, "Are you certain, Dana?"

"No, General, nobody can be certain of these things, but the data waves are of greater intensity for Erebus than anything I've seen before. Some better data might give me a clearer picture." Her mind raced. "Tell Gates to get a radio and hightail it down to the geophysics lab. He knows where it is—I showed it to him once. And tell him to hurry. We may not have much time."

A few more seconds elapsed before Pfeiffer came back and said, "He's on his way."

THE ICEBERG

Blackjack was almost hopped out of energy as he watched the sun descend toward the horizon. He was shivering, contemplating a death by hypothermia in the Antarctic night when a dot appeared in the sky. It grew larger, causing the long, lanky Texan to begin hopping with renewed vigor, and to wave his arms as if he were trying to get airborne. The dot kept on growing until it banked around the iceberg, and Blackjack could see the distinctive outline of the Harrier jump jet. It turned and approached the iceberg length-wise, and as it drew closer its altitude dropped and its speed bled off rapidly—until it was hovering near Blackjack's Hornet with its vec-tored-thrust nozzles throwing up a cloud of snow crystals. Blackjack turned away as the ice crystals whipped around his shivering body and stung his face. But finally the snow cloud dissipated and Blackjack heard the Pegasus engine spool down. He looked up, grinning, never so glad to see a Marine in all his life.

The canopy to the Harrier popped open, and after the pilot extricated himself from the harness, he lifted himself over the side and slid down to the berg. The Texan approached and saw a major's insignia on the shoulders of the Marine's flight suit. He stuck out a hand and said, with teeth chattering, "How-howdy, I'm Blackjack from the *Vinson.* Am I gla-glad to se-see you!"

The Harrier pilot grabbed the hand and said, "Howdy, yourself. I'm Don Boles from the *Wasp.* Call me 'Prof.' " The Marine was of medium height, but Blackjack couldn't see him too well under his crash helmet, except that he had blue eyes and needed a shave. "We got your distress call and I followed the tone from your survival radio. An Osprey is on the way and it will fly you back to the *Wasp.* . . . I see by your helmet that you're an Aggie."

"Yessir," said Blackjack. "How—how about you?"

"Nah," replied the Prof. "I'm University of Oregon. But I went through Pensacola with an Aggie. The guy was a certifiable Section Eight. . . . Say, can you fly that bird of yours out of here? We're gonna need every set of wings we can scrounge."

Blackjack looked down the length of the berg while hugging himself. He wished the Osprey would hurry up. "I suppose so. . . . Say, Prof, ca-can you te-tell me what's happened? I sa-saw the *Vinson* go under. It was hit by a cruise mi-missile that turned into some kinda torpedo. All my buddies . . . my ship. They're go-gone."

The temperature was near zero and the Prof was starting to hop up and down, too. He looked at the naval aviator and could see the strain in his eyes. "Blackjack," he said consolingly, "I'm afraid we've taken a kick in the teeth."

THE MOUNT HARMSWORTH SEISMIC HUT

"Okay, Miss Harrow," came Gates's staticky voice through the radio. "I've got the gizmo in front of me."

"All right," said Dana, with a tremor in her voice. "Now listen carefully. The power switch is on the left side of the panel. Turn it on."

Pause.

"Okay, it's on."

"Good. Now then, on the face of the panel there is a knob with an arrow on it and above are labels for A, B, and C. Switch it to A."

"Done."

"All right, now what does the digital readout on the display say?"

"Ummm, it says minus nine-point-four."

Dana began to hyperventilate. "Gates, listen, are you *sure* it says *minus* nine-point-four?"

"Yes, ma'am, I'm sure."

"Switch to B. What does it say?"

"Minus eight-point-six."

"C."

"Minus ten-point-two."

Dana leaned against Robert for support and swallowed hard. Then she keyed the mike. "General Pfeiffer, did you hear that?"

"Yes, I monitored it, but what does it mean?"

Dana tried to get her breathing under control. "General, please listen to me." She was almost pleading now. "These readings are from three precision measurement laser beams that are mounted on Crater Hill. They are focused on three receiver panels placed at different points on Ross Island. The geophysics lab is wired into Crater Hill via cable. I guess that's why the Russians left them alone. Anyway, these instruments measure the deformation of the Ross Island terrain. By that, I mean that the surface of a volcano can fall depending on subsurface conditions. These deformations are unnoticeable to the naked eye. They can only be tracked by precision instruments. Before the eruption of Mount Erebus earlier this summer we recorded a deformation of two-point-two centimeters several hours before it blew. We now have a deformation reading in excess of ten centimeters. Based on that and the fact that my seismograph is jumping off the scale, I think Mount Erebus is about to erupt."

Having spent some time in Alaska, Pfeiffer had developed a healthy respect for volcanoes. "How bad could it be?" he asked.

"Ross Island could disappear!" cried Dana. "It could be worse than Mount Saint Helens! We could all be buried in ten feet of volcanic ash! You must get everyone out of here at once. I could be wrong but you can't afford to take that chance. Evacuate!"

Another pause. Then Pfeiffer came back with, "Robert, what do you say?"

Robert looked at Dana and saw in her eyes the crystallized fear that Pfeiffer could not see. And being an Alaska veteran, he also knew what a volcano could do. "I believe the lady, sir. I say we get the Navy in here and pull our people out as soon as possible. I'd advise against using air transport because the Soviets have"—he stopped in midsentence, still trying to accept the reversal of their situation—"have air superiority now."

"Miss Harrow," asked Pfeiffer, "how long have we got?"

"These things are impossible to predict with any precision, General, but it may be a matter of hours."

An interminable half-minute clicked by before Pfeiffer returned with, "All right, Dana, you've convinced me, although it's tough to swallow. We just started to hit pay dirt at Branding Iron. I'll get a signal off to General Tharp and CinCPAC requesting immediate evacuation of my division. And I'll try to get another chopper to pull you out of there."

Rawlings started to protest, to say it was too dangerous, but faced with the specter of having the woman he loved stranded among the Russians—yet again—was something he couldn't stomach. "Very well, sir. Have them fly nap-of-the-earth and come in before sunup. We'll stay near the seismic hut. Flight ops should have the coordinates."

"Okay, Robert," replied Pfeiffer. "In the meantime go keep an eye on the Russian drop zone and report in after nightfall."

Pfeiffer didn't miss a trick.

"Yes, sir," replied Rawlings.

THE SKELTON NÉVÉ

Capt. Fyodor Tupelov's MiG-29 Fulcrum touched down on the hastily assembled runway, and he deployed the braking parachute while applying the brakes. The aluminum alloy strip was flimsy and narrow, and had there been a crosswind, Tupelov doubted he could have held the Fulcrum steady. Once his aircraft rolled to a halt, a ground crewman motioned Tupelov off the runway and onto an ice apron, which had been scraped clean of snow. Two other Fulcrums were parked nearby, being serviced by their ground crews. As the haggard Russian pilot cut his engines he could see the air-dropped skip loader clearing additional apron space. Meanwhile, a number of BMDs towed pumpkin-shaped bladders of jet fuel from the drop zone toward the makeshift airfield. The Soviet airpower was a tiny fraction of the original Snow Leopard buildup, but with the American supercarriers out of commission, the air superiority pendulum had swung decisively back to the Soviets' favor. A mere dozen fighters aloft would secure the landing zone while the 6th Guards Airborne Division consolidated their position and the skip loaders cleared a strip for the ski-fitted transports to land. But for now, the sky was devoid of tankers and transports—they had turned around for the long journey home. A second wave would be arriving in a few hours for a night parachute drop.

Tupelov climbed out of the cockpit and down the ladder. He had no more touched the ground when the relief pilot—who had slept on the journey and parachuted in—pushed Tupelov out of the way and climbed up, while a ground crew began working a hand pump to move fuel through a hose from the pumpkin-shaped bladder to the wing tank.

Tupelov took time to relieve his own bladder onto the snow. The sun had just dipped below the horizon, providing a gorgeous sunset in the five-below temperature. The crew chief pointed to a tent, and Tupelov stumbled in. As the warmth washed over him he saw two pilots sprawled on cots, snoring peacefully. The young, blond Russian dropped his crash helmet on the canvas floor, and somewhere during his descent toward the cot, he fell asleep.

THE *WASP*

Blackjack was working on his second quart of coffee and felt his body temperature slowly returning to normal. After riding the Osprey back to the *Wasp,* he had been checked over by a Navy doctor and told to get his ass into a long, hot shower. He was happy to comply, and stayed in until the chills disappeared. By the time he exited, his flight suit had been cleaned in the ship's laundry and he had a fresh set of BVDs. A plate of bacon and eggs were inhaled, and now here he was in the *Wasp*'s wardroom.

The assault carrier *Wasp* had a true air, sea, and amphibious capability. Referred to as part of the "Gator Navy," the remarkable vessel possessed a flight deck, quarters for a Marine task force, a galley and mess hall, a six-hundred-bed hospital, landing craft, vehicles, Harriers, Ospreys, helicopters, a laundry, several dentists, a brig, and a chapel. The other assault carrier in the Beowulf battle group—the *Nassau*—had departed for Norfolk three days earlier.

As he sipped his coffee alone in the wardroom, Blackjack looked up and saw the Prof walk in. The Marine pilot quickly slid into a seat across from the Texan and asked, "Feeling better?"

Blackjack nodded. "Rog. I guess I'm halfway human again since you plucked me out of that deep freeze. I wouldn't have lasted much longer, Prof. I owe you."

Prof shrugged. "No sweat. I just followed your beacon."

Blackjack studied Prof for a moment. He was of medium height with salt and pepper hair—more salt than pepper—and needed a shave more than before. He apparently had gone without a break, and his blue eyes were bloodshot. He seemed to be a good-natured guy who was trying to come to grips with the fact that Task Force Beowulf had been cut off at the knees. Prof unzipped a leg pocket on his flight suit and pulled out a pipe kit. Breaking it out and preparing the pipe seemed to provide him some solace.

"So what's the situation now, sir."

Prof mashed the tobacco in hard and squinted as he talked. "Basically, what we got here, Blackjack, is the worst military disaster since Pearl Harbor. The *Carl Vinson* is sunk. The *Eisenhower* is on fire, dead in the water, and the fires are outta control. She's expected to sink before sunup. The *Roosevelt* has a nine-degree list, one of her reactors has ruptured, and of course, flight ops are out of the question. We've got ten thousand casualties at the minimum. The intel boys want to talk to you about that cruise missile–torpedo thing you told me about. That took everybody by surprise. The scuttlebutt is that they were launched by some Soviet boomers that were in the area, but nobody knows for sure. Wherever they came from, Ivan blew our doors off but good. And that's only half of it."

Blackjack leaned forward. "What else?"

"The Russians have air-dropped a large force of paratroopers near McMurdo. Seems they want this rubidium stuff worse than before." Prof tried to get his tobacco fired up. "And now I hear more scuttlebutt about how we may be pulling out."

"Pulling out?" Blackjack put his elbows on the table and held the sides of his head as if his hands were a vise. The image of the *Vinson* going under came back, and he asked, "We're going to give it back to them? After losing who knows how many men and three carriers?"

Prof tiredly puffed away on his pipe. "Looks that way, Blackjack. But now to my surprise I find that I, myself—a little pissant jarhead major—am now the air wing commander of Task Force Beowulf. And my 'wing' consists of five serviceable Harriers, five Ospreys, a few helicopters, and your Hornet stuck out on that iceberg. Somehow or other—we've got no idea where they came from—the Russians have got some fighter aircraft patrolling their drop zone. If we get the order to clear out we'll need all the air cover we can muster, and right now it ain't much. So come daylight I'm sending you and a coupla Ospreys with the ordnance, fuel, and crew to get your Hornet armed and flyable. Are you game for flying off the iceberg?"

"I'm game, Prof."

The major nodded. "Okay, get a few hours' sack time. I've got some spare bunks at the moment. Two of my Harriers are escorting one of the Ospreys on a transport mission."

Puzzled, Blackjack asked, "What kinda transport mission?"

McMURDO BASE

Joshua Pfeiffer heard the whine of the Osprey's rotor blades, but the aircraft remained hidden under the nighttime canopy of darkness. The moon wasn't up yet, but the stars were shimmering in the polar sky. The whine grew louder, and a nearby ground crewman popped on two flashlight wands to direct the extraordinary aircraft to its landing zone. The dark figure of the Osprey, without its navigation lights on, could then be discerned against the backdrop of stars. The wands began moving, and the whine turned into a low growl as the snow whirled into a cloud. Upon touching down, its cargo bay ramp lowered for a moment, then it closed up and the growl became more intense as the Osprey ascended into the night. Like an airborne chameleon, the tilt-rotor craft executed a pirouette and transformed itself from vertical to horizontal flight, leaving Myron Tharp alone on the LZ.

Pfeiffer saluted as he approached the Marine general. Tharp returned the salute halfheartedly. "Glad you made it off the *Vincennes,* General," said Pfeiffer, while noticing—even in the dark—that Tharp was withdrawn. In shock perhaps? "How are you holding up, Myron?" he asked gently.

Tharp let out a long breath, sending a vapor cloud into the frigid night. "Now I know how General Tromso must have felt. It's a lot different when you're on the business end of a surprise instead of springing it on someone else."

"What happened exactly?" asked Pfeiffer. "The reports you sent were giving me the picture piecemeal."

Tharp let out another long breath. "Exactly what, I still don't know. Apparently the Soviets fired some new type of weapon from a ballistic missile submarine. They were some kind of carrier-killer missiles, unlike anything we'd seen before, and I regret to say they worked like a top. They swarmed over the flattops before their close-in systems could respond. Anyway, we've got the Russians back with one-and-a-half carriers under the water and zero flight ops. I've ordered a squadron of F-16s to fly in from Hawaii, but I don't know when they'll get here."

Tharp's Beowulf plan had now become a victim of its own success, in that by gaining absolute air supremacy, Tharp had decided to rely on carrier-based warplanes for his close-in air support. The logistics snarl of getting the Marines and the 6th Infantry Division into place was a big enough hassle without flying in ground-based fighters, too. Particularly when they were redundant. After all, no one had ever envisioned three carriers being wiped off the boards almost simultaneously. Not even Tharp.

"God, what a mess," he said finally. "But we can't dwell on that. What's this about the volcano?"

Pfeiffer quickly relayed the seismic picture as explained by Dana Harrow, concluding with, "The bottom line, Myron, is that if she is correct, we could all be buried in volcanic ash if we don't evacuate immediately, and she means *immediately*. I've issued an operations order for my people to leave their equipment in place and move out to the ice wharf for pickup. It's being passed down now. We have five C-17 transports at the runway, and I want to fill them up and use the Harriers to escort them out of danger."

Tharp folded his arms and held his parka close. God, it was cold. As he thought of what he should do he asked, "Do you think this Harrow woman is on the mark?"

In the dark, Pfeiffer nodded. "She's one sharp lady, Myron, and I've decided I want my people out of here, but I need you to give the okay for the ships to come in so we can disembark. So how about it, General, do I get the ships?"

With the Russians back, it was a "fish or cut bait" decision for Tharp. Stay and fight, or bust ass out of McMurdo—fast. Finally he sighed and said, "Destroy your crypto gear and any electronics or documents that are sensitive. I'll send a message to CinCPAC telling them the evacuation is a 'go.' The transports from the *Wasp* battle group are already on their way here as a contingency. I guess we'll have our own little Dunkirk, won't we?" He paused for a moment, then asked, "Where is this Harrow woman? I read the reports on her, but I've never met her."

Pfeiffer explained how she and Rawlings were trapped on Mount Harmsworth.

Stunned, Tharp said, "I hope you're trying to extract them."

"As we speak," replied Pfeiffer.

THE MINNA BLUFF

The Blackhawk helicopter skimmed along the ice shelf, near the cliffs of the Minna Bluff. The flight crew were guided by their night vision goggles and could clearly see the relief of the cliffs rising out of the ice shelf. The Blackhawk's low altitude would mask the aircraft from radar, but the flight crew knew that with such a cold backdrop their hot engine would stand out brightly to an infrared sensor looking down from above. And a Blackhawk wasn't exactly the quietest bird to have ever flown.

THE MOUNT HARMSWORTH SEISMIC HUT

Robert Rawlings and Dana Harrow could see over the Skelton Névé from their vantage point on the ridge above. That is, they could see as far as the dim moonlight allowed. Once more they heard a low drone, causing Rawlings to take out his field glasses to probe the darkness, but it was of little use, even though the moon had just risen. He did see a strip of lights come on—and remain on—in the distance, and he guessed it was from the runway the Russians had built. The drone grew louder still, and more pinpoints of light flicked on in the distance. Landing zones, he guessed. As the drone continued, little flashes of light appeared around the LZ.

"Wh-what is th-that?" Dana asked, in a voice that was a blend of fatigue, fear, and cold.

Rawlings grappled with the question, then he replied, "When the Soviets drop heavy equipment—tanks, vehicles, that sort of thing— they are slung below the parachute canopy in a harness. The shroud lines run up from the harness through a ring of retro rockets that are wired to a sensor probe that dangles beneath the tank."

More flashes dotted the night.

"When the probe touches the ground it triggers the retro rockets, and the thrust breaks the fall of the tank just before it touches down."

More flashes.

"I would guess the Russians are dropping a load of their BMD personnel carriers and maybe some tanks. Looks like they mean to stay."

"It won't me-mean a da-damn thing i-if Erebus blows, Robert," Dana said through chattering teeth.

Rawlings trained his binoculars down the western slope of Mount Harmsworth to the foot of the mountain. The Transantarctic Mountains act like a dam against the giant Western Ice Shelf. Any ice that gets through this dam essentially is squeezed through the network of glaciers down to the Ross Ice Shelf, which is about three thousand feet lower in elevation than the western shelf. That means the vertical drop on the western side of the Transantarctics is much shallower than the vertical drop on the eastern side. Robert and Dana's position on the ridge down to the base of the western slope was about eight hundred feet.

Robert saw it through his field glasses. There . . . and there it was again—in a small, horseshoe-shaped alcove at the foot of the mountain. It was a light coming on and going out. He tried to fathom what it might be, but the cold was starting to numb his mind.

There it was again—same place—and finally he figured it out. It was some kind of door opening and closing.

6TH GUARDS AIRBORNE DIVISION COMMAND POST, AT THE BASE OF MOUNT HARMSWORTH ON THE SKELTON NÉVÉ

Maj. Gen. Valery Voroshin stepped into the cramped passenger compartment of his personal BMD-3M vehicle—a command version of the standard BMD troop carrier. Four of the vehicles were backed into a circle like musk oxen, and the nexus point was covered by a canvas tent that tied them all together in the divisional command post. As Voroshin sat down on a small chair, a pair of ferret eyes glared at him.

Voroshin was athletically built, like a wrestler might be. His forehead was low, his eyes deep set, and his dark features were severely pronounced, which almost gave him the look of a Cro-Magnon man.

The ferret eyes across from him belonged to a wiry man wearing a white parka over his coverall uniform. The fingers of his hands were thin and delicate, and his crew cut hair accentuated the hairlessness of his face. His knee was almost touching Voroshin's as he spoke. "So, General, what are the results of the second drop?"

Voroshin looked at the KGB colonel with undisguised contempt. "Perhaps if you had been at the landing zone you could have seen for yourself, instead of remaining in the heated headquarters."

"But your duty is to be at the landing zone, General. And my purpose is to see that everyone performs his duty in accordance with the Cabinet's orders."

Voroshin almost spat. "I know how to follow orders, Colonel. I thought *zampolits* like you were a thing of the past."

The ferret eyes of Col. Boris Bobkov flared. "Perhaps we would be a thing of the past—if soldiers like General Tromso followed their orders precisely."

Now it was Voroshin's turn to flare. "I was no friend of Mitrofan Tromso. But we were captains in the same battalion. He was a capable man, and I don't need any *chekist* giving me his opinion about a real soldier. An opinion I did not ask for . . . And I don't remember inviting you into my vehicle. You may leave at once."

Colonel Bobkov shrugged. "As you wish, General. I will go to my own vehicle and begin preparing my initial report to Moscow, which will include my assessment of your performance."

"You have my permission to take your leave, Colonel."

Bobkov shrugged again and exited the BMD, then he walked through the canvas-covered command post, hearing some excited chatter on the TAC AIR radio net. He tugged the elbow of the air defense chief and asked, "What is it?"

The air chief waved him off. "We have a single bogey—a helicopter flying low and slow toward our position. We are engaging now."

MOUNT HARMSWORTH

Robert and Dana heard an explosion somewhere behind them, but did not see the flash of the Blackhawk being hit.

"Wha-what was that?" asked Dana, teeth chattering.

"I don't know," replied Rawlings. "But we better report what we've seen. Let's get back to the hut."

McMURDO BASE

The three Quick Fix helicopters that contained ultrasophisticated signal processing equipment had been doused with aviation fuel, and they erupted into pillars of flame as the satchel charges placed in their cabins detonated.

BRANDING IRON STATION

Lt. Col. Samuel McClure was alone as he took one last look at the otherworldly icedome. The floodlights were still on, and they would stay on until the generators topside ran out of diesel fuel.

His crew had mined out only a few tons of ore and now were en route to the pier to board a transport. He shook his head, then stepped onto the elevator for the final ride to the surface.

THE MOUNT HARMSWORTH SEISMIC HUT

"More air-dropped BMDs, you say?" asked Pfeiffer through the speaker.

"Probably that, General," said Rawlings. "It may even be some heavy stuff. I guess they wanted to get most of their people on the ground before they dropped in the hardware. They could start moving toward McMurdo at sunup."

"Doesn't matter, Robert. General Tharp and I both accepted Dana's thesis. We're pulling out. The ships should be here by dawn. Has your Blackhawk shown up?"

"Negative, General."

Pause.

"Shoulda been there by now."

There was another pause, longer this time, before Pfeiffer came back with, "I'll send another one."

This time Rawlings didn't hesitate. "Negative, General. No sense losing another crew. We'll . . . we'll try and get out on our own."

As Robert spoke, Dana felt as if the blood in her body was sinking down into her ankles.

"But, Robert, Dana is with you." The speaker remained silent for the longest time. "Robert . . . I don't know what to say."

"It's best not to say anything, General. The Soviet spooks may have their ears up by now. . . . Tell Alena and her boys that Pancho saved us."

"I will, Robert."

"Get my people out safely, General. We're off the air now."

Dana couldn't find her voice at once. She flicked on the oscillo-scope, and the lines were all over the screen. She honestly felt her life was closing, and for solace she reached into the distant memory of her youth and began to softly pray the Rosary. She looked at Robert, and his eyes seemed distant, again as if he were in commu-nion with someone else. Finally, he said, "Come on," and grabbed her arm.

THE ROSS SEA

Like a giant icebreaker, the battleship USS *Wisconsin* plowed through the pack ice, the twelve-inch armor plate of its hull crushing through the frozen sea. In its wake were the transport vessels of the *Wasp*'s amphibious battle group, initially earmarked to ferry equip-ment out of McMurdo. But now they would be carrying out the men and women of the 6th Infantry Division and the artillery crews.

24

. . . .

DAWN

MOUNT HARMSWORTH—March 8

Rawlings and Dana were once again on the ridge, and the first telltale signs of the predawn twilight were starting to turn the sky from black to purple. They had spent the night alternating between their observation post on the ridge and warmup sessions in the seismic hut. Rawlings now trained his field glasses down the slope to where he had seen the light. He saw it again, then lowered the field glasses and said, "All right, listen, Dana. I think this may be our only chance. We've got to get down there before the sun goes up. Follow me down and when I tell you to do something, do it quickly without question. Be careful and try not to make any noise going down the slope, understand?"

"Yes, but—"

"Good, let's go."

CRATER HILL

Myron Tharp stood atop Crater Hill, watching the sky turn from black to purple. He searched McMurdo Sound with his night vision goggles, looking for the appearance of the *Wisconsin,* but it was still out of sight. He turned the goggles back toward the base and saw the leading elements of the 6th Infantry Division walking toward the ice wharf. Tharp was still a man in shock, trying to regain his equilibrium and comprehend how the situation could flip so radically, so fast. He heard footsteps crunching the snow behind him and turned to see the figure of Joshua Pfeiffer approaching. There was no salutation between the two very tired men. "I've spoken with my air defense chief. He's got the Soviet combat air patrol intermittently on his Patriot radar. They're just holding position. No one has flown over our position so they probably don't know we're packing it in."

Tharp took a deep breath. "Either way they'll be surprised. They

449

get the prize without a struggle or they get wiped out by a volcano. God, why did I ever get in this business."

"General!"

Pfeiffer and Tharp turned to see the division signal officer running up the hill, breathless with a piece of paper in his hand. "This just came in on a one-time disk over the blue channel from CinCPAC."

Tharp took the paper, and Pfeiffer looked on as the signal officer held a flashlight on it with a shaking hand.

TO: COMMANDER, TASK FORCE BEOWULF

FROM: PRESIDENT OF THE UNITED STATES, WHITE HOUSE, WASHING-
TON, D.C.

CLASSIFICATION: TOP SECRET UMBRA

CC: COMMANDER IN CHIEF, PACIFIC

I AM IN RECEIPT OF YOUR MESSAGE TO CINCPAC CONCERNING THE POS-
SIBILITY OF A VOLCANIC ERUPTION THAT WOULD DESTROY MCMURDO
BASE AND YOUR DECISION TO EVACUATE. WHILE I FIND SUCH A DECI-
SION RATHER SUSPECT ON THE HEELS OF THE SUCCESSFUL SOVIET
COUNTERATTACK, THE CHIEF OF THE GENERAL STAFF CONTINUES TO
EXPRESS HIS SUPPORT FOR YOUR JUDGMENT, AND ADVISES THAT I
SHOULD NOT COUNTERMAND THE DECISION OF THE FIELD COMMANDER.

THEREFORE, IF IN YOUR JUDGMENT THERE IS NO OTHER RECOURSE
THAN TO ABANDON MCMURDO, YOU ARE AUTHORIZED TO DO SO. HOW-
EVER, IF YOU ELECT TO PURSUE THIS COURSE OF ACTION, YOU ARE
HEREBY ORDERED BY THE PRESIDENT OF THE UNITED STATES TO DE-
STROY BRANDING IRON STATION PER CONTINGENCY PLAN BY USE OF
THE OSTRICH EGG DEVICE.

AUTHORIZATION AND VERIFICATION CODES FOLLOWING VIA SEPARATE
MESSAGE.

JONATHAN BLAKELY
PRESIDENT OF THE
UNITED STATES

"That sonofabitch!" Pfeiffer almost spat. "That greasy politician. He's making it sound like we're turning tail, and if we do we're the ones who are using the Ostrich Egg. Not him. That little . . . that little . . ."

"Anchorman," said Tharp.

"What?"

Tharp's eyes remained fixed on the message. "The President. He used to be an anchorman . . . but he learned the politician's trade well—always maneuvering to take any credit or avoid any blame. He thinks we won't have the nuts to use the Ostrich Egg, so we'll have to stay in place or be court-martialed for disobeying orders." Tharp crumpled the message in his hand. "Well, I've got news for our anchorman President, Josh," said Myron Tharp bitterly. "This little Marine knows how to follow orders." He turned to the signal officer and asked, "When is the next communications window to the *Nevada?*"

MOUNT HARMSWORTH

Robert and Dana carefully made their way down the slope of the mountain, taking cover wherever they could find an outcropping of rock. Rawlings was wearing his overwhites, but Dana's thermal parka and pants were navy blue. Had they not been cloaked in darkness, they would have been easily discovered as they neared the bottom. Getting closer, the sound of generators became more pronounced, and Rawlings halted them behind a boulder. Then he peeked over it and surveyed the scene. It was definitely a command post of some kind, residing inside a horseshoe-shaped pocket that faced out on the Skelton Névé. Four BMD-3M track vehicles were in a circle with their rear ends all pointing toward the center, which was covered with a tentlike canvas. There were several other objects strewn about the horseshoe, which Rawlings guessed were generators or equipment depots. And there was a fifth BMD-3M vehicle, with its rear end married to a tent, standing by itself about thirty yards from the command post.

"Robert, what are we doing?" whispered Dana.

Sentries. There would be sentries, of course, but it was doubtful they would be looking in this direction. They would more likely be posted at the entrance to the horseshoe. "I had an uncle who was a deputy sheriff," whispered Rawlings. "He said the best place to hide from the cops was in a police station. We're going to try something like that." He looked at her navy blue parka. "But we've got to get you some overwhites."

Some light appeared as the canvas flap of the command post tent opened up and quickly closed. Rawlings could barely make out a white-clad figure as it walked across the horseshoe to a point behind some rocks below them. The Russian answered a call of nature, then zipped up his fly and headed back toward the command post.

"Come on," whispered Rawlings. "Let's move down there." Heart thumping, Dana followed him as they carefully picked their way down the slope and arrived behind the rocks of the open-air latrine. She wrinkled her nose at the foul-smelling odor. "What do we do now?" she asked while shivering.

"We wait." he whispered.

"Wait? For how long?"

"Not long, I shouldn't think. To prevent dehydration in this climate, everybody drinks a lot of water. You know that. And that means someone should be along soon. When they do I want you to stand over there and get their attention."

"Get their attention?"

"Yes, get their attention. Say 'Good morning,' 'What's for breakfast?' or whatever you want. Just distract him for a moment."

"For what?"

"Just do it. . . . Get ready. Someone's coming."

Dana didn't think it was possible to be more scared as she shivered from fright as well as the cold.

Robert crouched behind the boulder, his A-2 weapon in his hands. She didn't notice, but he had collapsed the collapsible stock. The sound of snow being crunched under boots became more distinct until a figure walked around the boulder and past the crouching Rawlings. The Russian was apparently looking at the ground and didn't notice Dana as he paused to select a place to take care of his business. "Uh, hello there," she said in a high-pitched voice.

The Russian jumped about half a meter and spun toward her. He started to grapple with the AK-47 slung over his shoulder when the butt of Rawlings's A-2 weapon crashed into his temple. The Russian buckled at the knees and—assisted by Rawlings—fell backward into the snow. The paratrooper had no more than hit the ground, when Rawlings was on top of the man, straddling him and pinning him to the ground. Rawlings's back was to Dana as she saw him raise up and savagely bring down the A-2 three times, as if he were bringing the blade of an ax down on a block of wood. Dana gasped as she saw the legs of the Russian writhe helplessly, then shudder, and finally fall still. Rawlings stayed on top of his victim for a little longer, and from the back it looked as if he was pressing down. Then he came off and knelt beside his victim. "Come here," said Rawlings, as he panted from the adrenaline pumping through his system. "Help me get his overalls off."

Dazed, Dana approached the opposite side of the young man lying dead in the snow and knelt down. She was familiar with death, and had seen it in intensive care almost on a daily basis. But she had never seen one human being take the life of another, and the sight of it almost pushed her over the edge. She looked at the Russian and saw that he was young. A ski-type stocking cap concealed much of the cranial damage Rawlings had wrought with the butt of his rifle, but there was still some blood, and the eyes stared open blankly. "Oh, Robert, he was so young."

Rawlings was unbuttoning the Russian's uniform when he looked up at her. Grabbing her shoulders, he shook her—hard—and said, "Yes, Dana, he was a kid. Just like Gates. Just like Pancho used to be." He looked down. "Just like I used to be. And his death makes no sense. But if I'm going to get you—us—out of here, I had to do it. Now I need you to get your head together, and fast. Do you understand?"

She nodded, then reached over and gently closed the Russian's eyes.

"Let's get his uniform off."

"What for?"

"So you can wear it."

Dana swallowed, then set about the task of pulling a limp body— clad in thermal underwear—out of a cream-colored jumpsuit uniform. Once that was done, Dana pulled the jumpsuit on over her own parka and parka pants. The arms and legs of the uniform were a bit long and she had to fold them back. Rawlings took his own balaclava stocking hat from his parka pocket and told her to cover her head so only her eyes showed.

"Now what?" she asked.

Rawlings dropped his A-2 and picked up the AK-47, then slung it over his shoulder while saying, "Walk next to me and keep your head down. We're going to the lone tracked vehicle parked over there. Let's go. It's getting light."

Totally weak from fright, Dana walked numbly as they struck out across the snow toward the BMD. It seemed a mile away, but it was only about thirty yards. She was tempted to look up, but she obeyed Rawlings's instructions and kept focused on the snow as she trudged along.

Col. Boris Bobkov was enjoying one last French cigarette before turning out the lantern and getting a few hours' rest. His cot, and the cot of his driver, were in the tentlike structure married to the tail end of his BMD-3M vehicle. The BMD-3M had a better ergonomic design than the older command vehicles. It possessed a tailgate that lowered to provide access from the rear, where a tent could be conveniently attached. The older BMDs, and the standard ones still, could only be entered through a hatch on top. In Afghanistan, paratroopers found that climbing in and out of the vehicles made them fine targets.

The stove kept Bobkov's tent reasonably warm, and his driver was already snoring softly. He had just finished another row with General Voroshin. The third in as many hours, and Voroshin had kicked him out of the command post yet again. *Well, let the brigand have his way for now,* thought Bobkov. *When I awake I will signal Moscow about the paratroop general's bad attitude toward the Cabinet's personal representative, and then we'll see the high and mighty general toe the mark.* Bobkov had stubbed out his cigarette and he was reaching for the lantern when the flap of the tent jerked open—and all of a sudden he was looking into the muzzle of an AK-47.

"Do not move," said the rifleman in stilted Russian. "Do not make a sound. Your driver?"

Bobkov shook his head and pointed at the sleeping figure in the neighboring cot.

"Wake him and pull on your uniforms," instructed the rifleman.

Bobkov froze for a moment, then said, in English, "You are American."

"Correct. Including one-sixteenth Cheyenne. Now get your partner up and dressed. We're going for a ride."

Bobkov didn't move, but continued staring down the muzzle. "You shoot that thing and you will have hundreds of paratroopers in here on top of you."

"And you'd be dead. The choice is yours."

Bobkov pondered the muzzle a few moments longer, and then roused his slumbering driver. After the driver was given the picture, the two Russians pulled on their overalls, silently watching Rawlings—and his companion, who said nothing.

Rawlings motioned with the AK-47. "The driver up front. You in the troop compartment. My Russian's a little stale, so you inform the driver that he will follow my orders or you will receive a bullet in your forehead."

Bobkov relayed the instructions, and they all moved forward, the driver getting in the cockpit while Dana and Robert sat down on the bench seats across from Bobkov.

"Start the engine and hands off the radio," ordered Rawlings.

The driver complied.

"Now raise the tailgate and put it in gear. Drive straight out the entry and don't stop for anything."

There was a whine from the tailgate going up, then Dana felt the vehicle lurch as the gearbox engaged.

One of the radio operators who worked the TAC AIR net in the command post had taken a few steps out of the CP tent, heading toward the open-air latrine, when he saw the *zampolit*'s BMD tear out and briskly churn across the snow toward the entrance of the horseshoe, dragging the tent behind it like a car with JUST MARRIED painted on the rear window. It continued out the entry, leaving two befuddled sentries in its wake.

ICE WHARF, McMURDO SOUND

The giant screws of the USS *Wisconsin* engaged in reverse, sending up a torrent of bubbling foam at the fantail of the battleship as it backed away from the ice wharf to make room for the transports.

On the quay of the wharf were the men of the 6th Infantry Division, watching the sky grow lighter as dawn approached.

SOVIET COMMAND POST, MOUNT HARMSWORTH

"What do you mean, the *zampolit* drove off?"

"Just that, Sergeant," said the radio operator while stepping from foot to foot to console his overflowing bladder. "I was on my way to relieve myself when the *zampolit*'s BMD started up and took off, dragging its tent behind. It seemed most unusual, so I came to report it."

Not quite sure what to believe, the sergeant walked to the tent flap and looked out to where the *zampolit*'s BMD had been. There was nothing there but two upside-down cots, an overturned stove, and the sound of the generators.

It was at this point that the rigid and formal command and control system of the Red Army began to work against itself. While the radio operator was explaining what had happened, one of the sentries had entered the opposite side of the tent and told the same story to the sergeant of the guard. The sergeant of the guard didn't believe his subordinate either, and felt obliged to look out of the tent also. With that done, the sergeant of the guard reported the situation to the top sergeant of the headquarters company, and the top sergeant, of course, had to see for himself. After doing so, he went to wake the headquarters company commander, who had to get dressed and (you guessed it) had to go outside to see things for himself.

Meanwhile, on the other side of the tent, the same information had worked itself up the command structure of the radio network in much the same fashion until the officer-in-charge of communications and the headquarters company commander both approached the divisional chief of staff simultaneously. The radio operator was jumping up and down by this time because his bladder was about to burst, and he wished he'd relieved himself before making the report.

Once the chief of staff had the separate reports in hand—and had poked *his* head out of the tent to verify their accuracy—the progression of the information halted. The chief of staff knew that General Voroshin and the *zampolit* Bobkov had had a few shouting matches, and there was no one in the command structure between the commanding general and Bobkov. They both reported directly to Moscow. The chief assumed that Bobkov had left in a huff to relocate his BMD in some kind of protest. It was odd, to be sure, but the chief elected not to wake General Voroshin and tell him.

Now free, the radio operator hopped, skipped, and jumped out of the command post to deflate his bladder.

SKELTON NÉVÉ

As the heater of the BMD warmed the passenger cabin, Dana pulled off her balaclava stocking hat and shook her blond hair, causing Bobkov to betray his surprise at finding a woman in his midst. "Who are you?" he stammered. "How did you get here?"

"Never mind that," said Rawlings, as he raised up to take a peek out the viewing portal. He withdrew and said, "Take a look, Dana. It's not sunup yet. You know the terrain better than I. What's the best route?"

She raised up and looked around to get her bearings. "Keep hugging the side of the mountain and follow it around to the Skelton Glacier."

Rawlings shoved the muzzle into the back of the driver's neck and said, in Russian, words to the effect: "Make this crate go faster." He received a nod in reply and felt the speed increase.

"Robert, there's something ahead." She pulled away to let him see through the portal.

"Looks like we're approaching their defensive perimeter. Keep moving," he told the driver, "and don't even think about stopping." Rawlings looked back in the dim light and saw no one chasing them, and as they churned past the defensive emplacements he saw several paratroopers staring at the BMD with puzzled expressions.

SOVIET COMMAND POST, MOUNT HARMSWORTH

"Nevolin is dead!" screamed the radioman.

Every eye in the tent turned toward him as he pointed. "Out there! His head is crushed!"

This time the news traveled up the chain of command instantaneously as the chief of staff and several straphangers ran out of the tent to the open-air latrine. They found the dead soldier stripped to his thermal underwear. The chief of staff looked him over, then spied a tubelike object lying in the snow. He picked it up and said, "This is American!"

"Colonel!" cried a clerk running from the command post. He came up, breathless, and said, "Second battalion reports a BMD has driven past their position!"

Now everything came clear to the chief as he sprinted back toward the command post, cursing himself for not waking the general.

The ossified Red Army command structure had bought Robert and Dana a head start.

7,000 FEET ABOVE THE ROSS ICE SHELF

In the predawn sky, the Prof could see nothing but the fading pinpoints of starlight as he and two of his Harriers from the *Wasp* circled in a wagon-wheel pattern over the airfield below, flying air cover for the departing C-17 transports. The Prof knew the Harrier was superb for close air support and virtually unbeatable in a close-in dogfight, but for a long-range air superiority mission it was painfully weak. It had no radar, and its missiles were the short-range Sidewinders. In the poor visibility he had to rely on the ground radar of the Patriot air defense system to tell him if a bandit was approaching.

"Cover Flight, this is Groundpounder."

"Go, Groundpounder," replied Prof.

"The transports are off and headed for New Zealand. Vector zero-six-seven to cover their tail. We've got two bandits inbound headed for you, bearing two-three-three. Stay with the transports. We will engage bandits with Patriot."

"Roger, Groundpounder. We're on our way. Cover Flight, form up on me." Prof banked onto the assigned vector and shoved his throttle to the max, grateful the Patriot was on his side.

ICE WHARF, McMURDO SOUND

Tharp and Pfeiffer were supervising the loading of the LSD *Spiegel Grove* when they heard, then saw a flurry of Patriot missiles taking to the sky. Pfeiffer called for his RTO and spoke briefly into the handset. Then he turned to Tharp and said, "The air defense boys caught two Soviet fighters in range going after the transport escorts. Looks like they downed 'em, and the C-17s are on their way."

Tharp nodded, shivering mightily. It seemed the cold was like a lead blanket from which there was no escape. Funny how it didn't seem to affect Pfeiffer. The Marine general thought the boarding was going well. The *Spiegel Grove*'s hovercraft had been beached to make room in the hold for the infantry men and women piling on board. Leaving equipment behind was costly, but necessary to expedite the process.

A large man, built like a defensive tackle, made his way through the lines of soldiers boarding the LSD, and walked up to Pfeiffer. He was followed by a small group of soldiers. Pfeiffer returned the man's salute and said, "Hello, Phillip. . . . General Tharp, may I present Captain Phillip Nye, commander of my Long Range Surveillance Detachment. Phillip, this is General Tharp. I don't believe you two have met."

"I haven't had the honor," said Tharp, as he took off his gloves to shake hands, adding, "I've heard a lot about you."

Nye nodded an acknowledgment and turned back to Pfeiffer. "General, we know Colonel Rawlings is stranded up at one of Dana Harrow's seismic stations. I got a group here"—he pointed behind him—"and we want to try to pull them out."

Pfeiffer shook his head. "I'm sorry, Phillip. I know how you feel, but I've already got two Blackhawk crews gone, missing, probably dead. I'm not sending in another extraction mission without air cover. Besides, there isn't time. If Dana Harrow is right about Mount Erebus, they might be safer where they are. Now get your people on board."

"But, General," protested Nye, "the Colonel would do it for us...."

Pfeiffer cut him off. "Your Colonel also knew how to follow orders, Captain. Now get your people on board."

Nye sighed, then saluted with a halfhearted "Yessir," and took his small group of volunteers toward the end of the line. As he left, the divisional signal officer ran up to Pfeiffer at the double time. "General, we tried to make contact with the *Nevada* but did not receive an acknowledgment."

The two generals frowned. So much for the electronic battlefield. "When is the next commo window?" asked Tharp.

"In just under three hours, sir."

"We should be out of here by then," observed Pfeiffer. "Any further transmission from Colonel Rawlings?"

"Nothing, sir."

SKELTON GLACIER

The BMD's tracks rattled through the snow past the Delta Glacier where Rawlings and the LRSD team had initially been "inserted." It seemed like a hundred years ago to him now as he looked out the viewing portal and examined the terrain. Yes, it looked a little familiar. Just keep following the same route his group had taken before. Down the Skelton Glacier, around the Shults Peninsula, across the ice shelf, and over the Minna Saddle, then through the White Strait between White Island and Black Island, and into McMurdo.

"How fast are we going?" asked Dana.

Rawlings came down and said, "About thirty to thirty-five miles an hour, I guess. I'd say we've got maybe four hours before we make it to McMurdo."

Dana went to the portal and said, "Tell the driver to stay near the edge of the glacier."

Rawlings passed the request on to the driver in his stilted Russian.

Dana came back down and sat next to Robert on the bench seat, and together they silently eyed their captive. Bobkov gave Dana the chills. She thought he had the face of a weasel . . . and the disposition of one, too. She breathed deeply and tried to let some of the tension ebb from her body. She'd been awake for over twenty-four hours, and the lack of sleep combined with the unremitting terror made her a bundle of fatigued nerves. She was hungry, too. But at least the heater in the BMD worked well enough, enabling her to doff her parka alongside the baggy coverall uniform. The uniform Robert had killed for in order to disguise her. "Think we'll make it?" she asked.

"I'd say our chances are a lot better now than they were an hour ago," replied Robert. "I don't understand why they didn't come after us. Maybe the wind covered our tracks and we got lucky."

Whump!

Dana sat up straight. "What was that?"

Whump!

Rawlings handed the AK-47 to Dana and said, "Safety is off. Shoot our host here if he so much as hiccups."

Dana took the weapon and leveled it at the weasel, somewhat surprised that she had no reservations at the thought of pulling the trigger.

Rawlings opened the top hatch all the way, and a cold blast of air filled the BMD. He stuck his head out and saw a geyser of snow rise up in their wake just before he heard another *whump!* He pulled out his field glasses and quickly picked it out. He counted five, six, *eight* BMDs behind them, one of them firing its 73-mm cannon. Rawlings came back down and told the driver to weave, while Dana ventured up to the hatch for a peek. Without binoculars they appeared as tiny specks in the distance.

Whump!

Rawlings yanked her back in. "Wait a minute, Robert! I have to see something. Give me your field glasses."

Whump!

The BMD weaved, causing the two Americans to fall over on the weasel. Recovering, Dana repeated, "Give me your field glasses!" Rawlings complied and Dana returned to the hatch. As the BMD continued its serpentine course and the geysers continued falling in their wake, Dana surveyed their position. They were hugging the rim of the Ant Hill mountain that was the dominant feature of the Ant Hill Glacier—a tiny tributary of the giant Skelton Glacier. Then she traversed the binoculars over to the midsection of the Skelton Glacier. She was fairly certain it was over there.

Whump! The blasts were getting closer.

She climbed back down and said, "Robert, have the driver go

another mile, then cross over the glacier and continue down the opposite side."

"Why?"

Whump!

She quickly explained, and Rawlings passed the word to the
driver. The driver looked less than enthused, so Rawlings kept the
muzzle of the AK-47 in the young man's ear as the BMD pressed
on, then executed the glacier crossing. The sporadic barrage continued and Rawlings returned to the hatch. The serpentine pattern
had allowed the pursuers to close the gap a bit, but the rounds kept
falling behind them. *That's odd,* he thought. He trained the field
glasses on the BMDs that were advancing on a line abreast, changing
course to pursue them across the glacier. All of a sudden one of the
BMDs disappeared. Then another. "It worked, Dana! It worked!
They plowed right into the crevasse field!" He came back down.
"That will slow 'em up for sure."

Dana grabbed the field glasses and went to look, just as they heard
a chain-saw-like sound, accompanied by a roar, which caused the
driver to halt the BMD in its tracks.

A MIG-29 FULCRUM OVER THE SKELTON GLACIER

Capt. Fyodor Tupelov finished his strafing run in front of the BMD
and then banked around for another pass.

"Did you hit it, Sable One?" asked the ground controller. "You
must not hit it."

"No, I did not hit it. I followed your instructions and fired in front
of its path . . . hold on, I am passing over it now. *Da,* it appears to
have stopped."

"Excellent, Sable One! We have BMDs in pursuit. They will be
there shortly."

Tupelov came around again. "Uh-oh, ground control, it appears
target is moving again. Are you sure you do not want me to destroy
it?"

"*Nyet,* Sable One! Lay down another volley in its path. Someone
is on board who must not be harmed."

"Roger, ground control. Sable One will comply." And Tupelov
came around again. He lined up a shot fifty meters in front of the
advancing BMD and pressed the red button on his control stick to
fire the Fulcrum's 23-mm cannon.

THE SKELTON GLACIER

Rawlings instinctively ducked as the Fulcrum strafed the snow, but now curiosity was supplanting fear. He closed the hatch and sat beside Dana. "The Russian fighter is shooting warning shots . . . just like the BMDs chasing us . . . why don't they just blow us away?"

Dana said nothing as she kept the AK-47 muzzle against the back of the driver's head.

Rawlings eyeballed the weasel. Closer this time. His captive was wearing a white parka over the paratroop utility uniform, and in the melee of their departure, Rawlings realized he'd missed something. He reached over and yanked the shoulder of the parka back, which revealed a green-colored epaulet with two gold stripes and three gold stars.

"Whoa! . . . What, or should I say whom, do we have here?"

"What is it?" asked Dana.

Rawlings stared at the shoulder board. "We got us a government-certified KGB colonel. Isn't that right, Colonel?"

The weasel remained silent as the chain saw rippled through the snow again. Rawlings frisked the colonel and found an identity card in an inside breast pocket. "So," said Rawlings. "You are Colonel Boris Bobkov of the border guard Stavka staff. No wonder we haven't been hit. But I thought *zampolit*s were a thing of the past in the Red Army."

Bobkov said nothing.

"What's a *zam* . . . whatever you said?" asked Dana.

"Political officer. Internal security. Done away with several years ago, right, Colonel? But it looks like you're back again, and that makes it our lucky day."

The chain saw sound returned, and Rawlings broke into a grin.

"Robert, what is it?"

He clapped the weasel on the knee and said, "Nobody in the Red Army is going to grease a *zampolit*. Ain't that right, Colonel? You're our ticket out of here."

SOVIET COMMAND POST, MOUNT HARMSWORTH

Major General Voroshin had become a rogue elephant in the command tent, cursing, swearing, snarling, and kicking tables and chairs out of his path. How could he ever explain that his KGB "escort" had been snatched out from under his very nose? It was a colossal breach of security, and Voroshin had already placed his headquarters company commander under arrest.

The chief of staff was nervously monitoring the TAC AIR net. The KGB colonel was the personal representative of the Confederation Cabinet, and his capture would likely mean imprisonment for Voroshin. If the KGB weasel died, Voroshin—*and* the chief of staff— could be shot. Reforms aside, the Red Army could still be a brutal place. Even for generals.

The chief of staff looked up and said, "General Voroshin, the pilot reports he has made multiple strafing runs, but the *zampolit*'s—er, the 'escort's'—BMD refuses to stop."

Voroshin's face was contorted to the point that it looked like a prune. He was trapped, and he knew it. He took several deep breaths and said, in a guttural voice, "Do *not* harm the vehicle. Maintain pursuit with the second battalion's BMDs and monitor the situation by air. . . . What I would not give for some helicopters right now."

"*Da,* General. But we cannot allow Colonel Bobkov to fall into enemy hands."

Voroshin remained silent. It was axiomatic in the old Red Army that everyone wanted the *zampolit* dead, but no one wanted to pull the trigger.

QUICK DRAW FLIGHT OVER THE ROSS SEA

"Any of you guys see it?" asked Leader.

"Negative, Leader."

"Negatory."

"Nada."

The leader of Quick Draw Flight was at the head of a formation of four F-16 Falcons, en route from Hickam Air Force Base in Hawaii to McMurdo. They had refueled twice in midair, but when the order came down that the mission was scrubbed, Quick Draw Flight didn't get the word with the rest of the squadron. However, the tanker that was supposed to be meeting them over the Ross Sea *did* get notified of the stand-down.

Leader checked his Global Positioning System readout and his chronometer, and was convinced his flight was in the right place at the right time, but the tanker was nowhere to be seen and had not responded to a dozen calls on the radio. "Okay, listen up. Our big gas station in the sky has choked on us, but I've run the numbers, and with our tail wind we should just be able to make it to McMurdo, but only just. Jettison your wing tanks if they're already dry and continue on me at economy cruise."

"If we drown in that frozen drink down there," said Quick Draw Two, "I'm gonna kill the staff rats who planned this gig."

"Get in line," said Three.

"Pipe down on the chatter," ordered Leader. "If anyone is going to kill the staff rats, *I* get to do it."

"Roger, Leader," said Two. "All I ask is that you castrate 'em first."

"Certainly. Now throttle down."

ICE WHARF, MCMURDO STATION

Joshua Pfeiffer, Myron Tharp, and a small coterie of staff officers were alone on the ice wharf of McMurdo Sound as the sun rose into late morning. The final transport ship was waiting for them to board, and they were waiting for the commo people to bring word on the USS *Nevada*. As two SUSVs raced toward them, Pfeiffer and Tharp heard a *boom!* and in the distance saw a cloud of smoke rise up. A satchel charge had destroyed the commo center in the command post.

Four men piled out of the SUSVs, one of whom was the signal officer, who ran up to Pfeiffer and said, "We got word to the *Nevada*. General Tharp's message and presidential verification codes transmitted and acknowledged."

"Is Colonel McClure at the Branding Iron site yet?" asked Pfeiffer.

"On his way in a SUSV, sir. We gave him the word it was 'go' over the radio and he said don't forget him."

"He'll go out with the *Nevada* team," said Tharp.

"Well, that's it," said Pfeiffer. Then he turned to his aide and ordered, "Tell the Patriot batteries to blow 'em and bust ass over here. Everybody else on board."

About fifteen seconds later a series of *booms!* punched the stillness of the Antarctic morning as the Patriot missile launchers and their control centers were ripped apart by preplaced charges.

From his vantage point on the far side of Hut Point Peninsula, Myron Tharp couldn't see Mount Erebus, but he could see the clear blue sky above the volcano in the distance. As he walked up the gangway, he hoped he'd made the right decision. At this moment, it didn't look like an eruption was imminent to him.

AN ICEBERG OFF THE OATES COAST

Blackjack Pershing hopped up and down again, trying to ward off the cold—almost in the same spot he'd been before his rescue. The wind was whipping over the berg, increasing the wind chill, but improving his chances for lift-off.

Two V-22 Ospreys bracketed Blackjack's Hornet. One was pumping jet fuel into the wing tanks, and the other one had brought two extra Sidewinder missiles, giving his Hornet a total of four.

The parka-clad crew chief approached the lanky Texan and said, "Okay, Lieutenant, you can climb in now. Are you clear on your mission? You're to fly air cover over the Branding Iron mining site while an Osprey makes a delivery. Then you're to escort the Osprey back to its launch point, then fly to these coordinates in the dry valleys west of McMurdo and punch out. We'll be there to meet you and fly you back to the *Wasp*. Prof will link up with you to fly air cover with a total of three Harriers. We only got five serviceable Harriers now, and we need to keep two to fly cover for what's left of the *Wasp*'s battle group."

Blackjack took the slip of paper with the coordinates scribbled on it and said, "I'm not sure I understand. You said I'm supposed to escort the Osprey back to its launch point. Won't it be flying off the *Wasp?*"

"No, it won't. But that's all I know."

THE ROSS SEA

The sea bubbled into a frothy foam as the giant figure of the USS *Nevada* blew her tanks and broke the surface, not far from where the perimeter of the ice pack met the open water.

The sea was barely whitecapping as the massive 560-foot-long vessel cruised on the surface at five knots to maintain its trim. Besides its diving planes, two outrigger planes deployed from its keel, providing added stability. The *Nevada* looked like any other Trident ballistic missile submarine, but that false veneer was about to be exposed.

On what appeared to be the submarine's missile deck, giant hydraulic pistons engaged and the dorsal side of the vessel seemed to split down the middle, breaking open. It yawned open wider and wider, revealing not a missile deck, but a hangar deck containing two aircraft. The giant doors continued to spread until they were laid back, almost touching the sea, to give the V-22 Osprey sufficient clearance. The wing of the Osprey, which was turned parallel to the fuselage for stowage, now rotated into a perpendicular position, and its folded rotor blades unfurled like a butterfly breaking out of its cocoon. Once wing and blades were locked into position, the twin Allison engines fired up and were soon delivering their combined power of twelve thousand horses.

Behind the Osprey, a similar awakening was taking place as a Phalanx Dragon vertical takeoff jet also came up to full power. Its nozzles rotated downward and it lifted off, then went into a sideslip to clear the sub and the Osprey, before rotating the nozzles back into the horizontal plane so it could begin to climb.

The marriage of aircraft and submarines was anything but a new idea. In 1925, the American Navy had a sub called the *S-1,* which could stow a float plane (in pieces) in a cylindrical hangar on its deck. It could be reassembled and flown off for observation missions. The same was true of the French-built *Surcouf* in 1929. And during World War II the American mainland was bombed by a float plane launched from a Japanese sub (it executed an air strike over Oregon, starting a forest fire).

The *Nevada,* however, was much more sophisticated than these early crude attempts. It was a one-of-a-kind vessel designed for special operations. Built to look like a Trident, it possessed the hangar deck, which could accommodate aircraft or specially-designed hovercraft or assault boats. Below the hangar deck were berthing facilities for eighty commandos, and below that was an underwater hangar for two submersibles.

In its life span, the *Nevada* had been operationally employed four times—once in the Caribbean off the Colombian coast, twice in the Persian Gulf, and once off the Kamchatka Peninsula—but none of those affairs ever made the papers. Now it was being called on again to ferry a device known as the Ostrich Egg.

The Osprey sent up a cloud of spray as it lifted off the hangar deck and then slowly tilted its rotors down to strike out for the rendezvous point.

THE ICEBERG

Blackjack advanced the throttles into afterburner and released the brakes, allowing his Hornet to commence its takeoff roll down the giant tabular berg. His speed increased, but not rapidly. He was thankful his only ordnance load was the four Sidewinders as he squeezed the throttle handle—pretending that would coax additional speed from his craft. But the edge of the berg loomed before him . . . closer . . . closer . . . closer . . . He checked the airspeed indicator—still not enough. The light layer of snow that had helped slow Blackjack's Hornet on landing now acted as a hindrance to his lift-off. The edge rushed toward him, and the F/A-18 plunged over the side to fall toward the pack ice, just as it reached escape velocity. Blackjack raised the Hornet's nose, retracted the gear and flaps, took a deep breath—and banked onto a vector toward the rendezvous point.

MINNA SADDLE

"Six I.D. command post, do you read, over?" Robert Rawlings listened to the radio speaker intently, but he heard nothing but dull static. It was a Soviet radio set, but he was fairly certain he had it calibrated to the same FM frequency that he had used at the seismic hut. He'd waited until they crested the Minna Saddle so the line-of-sight signal could reach McMurdo; but after repeated calls there was no answer, which could only mean one thing: the Americans had pulled out. The Russian BMDs had skirted the crevasse field and resumed their pursuit as fighter planes continued to buzz overhead. His hope began to fade, until he noticed that this BMD vehicle (since it was a command version) had a second radio. Rawlings studied the Cyrillic symbols and decided the second radio had frequencies in kilohertz instead of the megahertz band—meaning it was an AM radio that could bounce a signal off the atmosphere in a skywave and have much greater range than an FM set. He turned it on as they rattled through the snow, leaving the Minna Saddle behind. He could see Black Island and White Island ahead. He set the frequency to a distress channel and keyed the mike. "Mayday, Mayday. This is Rawlings of the 106th calling anyone in Task Force Beowulf. Does anyone read, over?" There was no response and he tried again. Much to his surprise a response came back this time with, "We read you, Rawlings. This is the *Anchorage,* over."

Robert hooted and began talking rapidly. "Listen, *Anchorage.*
Listen carefully. I need to be connected to General Joshua Pfeiffer
of the Sixth Infantry Division. Tell him Rawlings and Harrow are
making an escape but we need to be pulled out by air."

There was a pause before the voice came back with, "I don't think
he's on the *Anchorage,* Rawlings."

Robert went ballistic. *What a time to run into a bureaucrat!* "Listen, stupid, I don't have time to argue! Now you pull your head out
of your ass and *find* him wherever he is and fast. We've got Russians
on top of us!"

Pause. "How do I know you're for real, Rawlings? Authenticate
Victor Alpha."

Robert nearly crushed the microphone in his hand. "I don't have
an SOI with me, you jerk! General Pfeiffer has a pet Siberian husky
named Lulu, he's got a bum knee from cross-country skiing, and he
shot a caribou in the Yukon last year. Run that by him and you'll
know I'm for real. Now you find him and get him on the horn and
tell him Rawlings is on the wire or he'll have your head on a platter.
You got that, *Anchorage?*"

Their BMD reached the bottom of the Minna Saddle, and Rawlings pointed toward the White Strait. The Russian driver nodded
wearily, as if he were a New York cabbie who had just picked up his
last fare of the day.

Time seemed to drag by until the radio squawked with, "Robert,
is that you?"

Rawlings would have jumped for joy if it wasn't so cramped.
"Yessir! Listen, this is the situation—" He quickly outlined his and
Dana's impossible predicament.

Pfeiffer took some time to absorb the report, then came back with,
"You say you have hostile aircraft overhead?"

"Roger, sir."

Another maddening pause.

"All right, Robert, listen up. Head for Branding Iron Station as
fast as you possibly can. I say again, head for Branding Iron. There
will be an Osprey putting down there soon, with what little air cover
we can muster. The Osprey won't wait for you, so get there pronto."

"Roger, sir. We'll try to connect. Rawlings out." He turned to the
driver and said, roughly translated, "Step on it."

12,000 FEET ABOVE THE ROSS SEA

Blackjack saw the dot that was the Osprey and interrogated it with his IFF. Relieved when he got the proper response, he closed on the tilt rotor craft and more dots appeared in the air. He quickly discerned three Harriers and another aircraft that was unlike anything he'd ever seen before.

"Blackjack calling the Professor. Do you copy? Over."

"That's a roger, Blackjack. How you doin'?"

"Full belly and some sleep under my belt, so I'm okay."

"No sleep and nothing but coffee for as long as I can remember," replied the Prof.

"Don't nod off," replied Blackjack. "What's the drill here, anyway?"

"McMurdo has been evacuated. In addition to the Russkies landing, it looks like that volcano is about to blow."

"No shit?" said Blackjack. "Then why are we headed back?"

"This here Osprey has to drop something off and we're flying cover. You have the only radar so I want you to scan as we approach. The landing zone may be hot. Also, I just got word there's a friendly on the ground who needs help. Form up on me and I'll give you the brief."

Blackjack complied, and the rag-tag group of scrounged fighters and the Osprey headed off toward the Windless Bight.

SKELTON NÉVÉ

After taking time to relieve his bladder and visit the flight operations tent, Capt. Fyodor Tupelov headed for his MiG-29 Fulcrum, which had been refueled and reloaded with 23-mm ammunition. He tried to explain to the dolts in flight ops that his threat warning receiver wasn't picking up any radar emissions from the Americans' Patriot missile air defense system. Nor were the sensors on his comrades' aircraft. He thought that odd, since they had lost two Fulcrums to the Patriot missiles early that morning. But the people in flight ops were preoccupied with the runaway BMD that he was going after again. He climbed into his aircraft, started the engine, and taxied onto the flimsy runway. As he lined up for his takeoff roll, he glanced out his canopy to the right and saw a ski-equipped Candid transport on the scraped-off strip of ice. A helicopter was being unloaded.

As Tupelov began his takeoff roll he hoped the Patriot missiles remained turned off. Because of their deadly presence, no Soviet reconnaissance aircraft had ventured over McMurdo to see that an evacuation had taken place.

BRANDING IRON STATION

Lt. Col. Samuel McClure thought he'd left this place for the last time. Drop everything, they said. Clear out the crew and get everybody to the pier for evacuation, they said. And once he'd done that he'd been pulled aside by this little Marine three-star and told to hop into a SUSV and head back to Branding Iron. Assist a team that would be arriving by Osprey—and he was to fly out with them.

Well, here he was. Standing on the derrick, all alone, hugging himself for warmth. No sign of any damned Osprey, and Mount Erebus didn't look like it was going to erupt. It appeared pretty benign, in fact. Not so much as a whiff of smoke coming out of the caldera. He hopped around the derrick, convinced now that somebody somewhere had dropped the ball and was leaving him here to face a Russian airborne division all by himself. Why on earth did he ever join the Army?

He saw it before he heard it. A speck coming through the gap between Mounts Erebus and Terror. It seemed to head straight for him, and he hoped it was friendly. It came closer and he could see that it was painted black. Then the howl of the rotor blades reached his ears, and it hovered before touching down about twenty yards away from the derrick in a swirl of ice and snow. The cargo bay ramp lowered and two parka-clad figures emerged. The first man was husky—like a football guard or a weight lifter. He had a small brown moustache and thinning hair, and he was carrying a large pouch in a sling that was hooked across his chest—like a bandolier so it couldn't slip off. It seemed rather heavy. The second man appeared extraordinarily thin, as if his parka were hanging from a coat hook. He had black hair greased back, an aquiline nose, and a protruding upper lip.

McClure came off the derrick to greet them. The husky one did the talking. "Colonel McClure? I'm Mr. Toomay. This"—he jerked his thumb—"is Mr. Hotchkiss. You're supposed to get us into the mine shaft at once. The Russians could be on top of us any second."

"Right," said McClure. "Follow me." He pegged the two as naval warrant officers as they climbed the derrick steps.

"You seen a lone Russian armored vehicle in the vicinity?" asked Toomay. "We were told to look out for one."

"No," replied McClure as he stepped into the elevator. "Why?"

Toomay held the pouch carefully as he and his partner entered. "There's supposed to be some friendlies on board."

The elevator cage closed.

WILLIAMS ICE AERODROME

As the BMD churned past what was left of Williams Field, Rawlings looked out the hatch and saw the charred remains of over two hundred Soviet aircraft. It seemed a lifetime ago since he had witnessed their destruction, but the soreness in his side told him it wasn't really that long. Rawlings had tied their KGB host's white parka to the BMD's whip antenna so the Americans wouldn't shoot at them, then he cut free the shelter tent they had dragged halfway across Antarctica. He raised his field glasses and could see the other BMDs still in pursuit, like an unrelenting sheriff's posse a couple of miles behind. They had about twenty miles to cover before they reached Branding Iron Station.

He closed the hatch.

SOVIET COMMAND POST, MOUNT HARMSWORTH

"No resistance?" asked General Voroshin incredulously. "What do you mean, no resistance?"

"Exactly that, General," said the company commander who was leading the pursuing BMDs. His voice was fuzzy as it came through the radio loudspeaker. "We are passing Williams Field now—where the Americans bombed our aircraft. No one has made a move to intercept us. The flight leader of our air cover says there are no emissions from the American air defense radar. It is like we are alone out here."

Voroshin rubbed his narrow brow, which had furrows that seemed permanently etched into it. What was this? Some kind of American trick? He keyed the mike and asked, "What about the *zampolit?*"

"Still four kilometers ahead. He did not head for McMurdo. He appears to be on track for the mining site."

"General!" barked the TAC AIR officer. "My pilots covering the *zampolit*'s BMD are picking up bogeys on their radars."

Voroshin was completely confounded now. No Americans on the

ground where they were supposed to be, but in the air where they were *not* supposed to be. He ran his free hand through his bristly hair and yelled at his TAC AIR officer, "This has to be a trick! Get as many aircraft up as you can and engage the bogeys. Keep them away from that mining site. Try to disable the *zampolit*'s BMD, but if that fails to stop it"—he hesitated—". . . you are authorized to destroy it."

"Understood, General." The TAC AIR chief began muttering into his headphone.

Voroshin smashed the plywood table with his fist. *What were the Americans doing?*

BRANDING IRON STATION

The elevator door opened and McClure led Toomay and Hotchkiss to the crane holding the giant bucket. Toomay couldn't help but gape at the ghostly-lit icedome, but the skinny Hotchkiss seemed oblivious to it all. "I'll have to lower you down one at a time," explained McClure. "The mine tunnel runs horizontally from the bottom of this shaft. It's still lighted, and the lights will stay on as long as the generators have fuel. And here, you'll need these," he said, while handing them some goggles and surgical face masks. "It's dusty down there."

"Okay," said Toomay, while slipping his on. "Mr. Hotchkiss will go first."

As if on cue, the skinny warrant officer climbed into the bucket, and McClure went to the controls and began lowering it down the shaft. McClure glanced at Toomay, and then to the pouch. "What have you got in there, anyway?" he asked.

Toomay acted as if he didn't hear.

THE F/A-18 HORNET OVER THE WINDLESS BIGHT

Blackjack flicked his APG-65 radar to the "range-while-search" mode and watched his cockpit display carefully to ensure he wasn't crying "wolf." He wasn't, and he keyed the mike. "Prof, this is Blackjack! We got four . . . five bandits thirty-plus miles out about angels one-zero at one o'clock. They're coming at us. . . ." A *screeee!* raked Blackjack's eardrum. "Missile lock! Missiles inbound!" Blackjack wished he had an AMRAAM missile to engage at this distance, but all he and the Harriers had were the short-range Sidewinders.

"Blackjack, you turn tail and go supersonic! Hide behind Mount

Erebus, then come around in high cover over the LZ. Use your radar to find and bounce the bandits if they head for our guys on the ground. Everybody else hit the chaff and follow me down to the deck."

"But, Prof—"

"Shut up and get undercover, Blackjack!"

The Texan watched the three Harriers and the Phalanx Dragon roll over on their backs and pull into a powered dive. He whipped his Hornet around, hit his own chaff trigger, and advanced his throttles into afterburner to hide behind Mount Erebus.

He felt as if he was running again.

BRANDING IRON STATION

Mr. Toomay eased himself over the rim of the bucket, being careful not to bang, scrape, or bobble the object in his pouch. The thing was lousy with safety devices, but why tempt it? He joined Hotchkiss and they made their way down the narrow tunnel in single file. The passageway was narrow, with a string of lights running overhead, and their footprints quickly kicked up a choking cloud of powdery dust that hung in the air, making Toomay grateful the guy up top had given them the goggles and masks. They went to the end of the tunnel, where Toomay slowly knelt down in the dust, holding the pouch steady as he set it on the ground. He unzipped it and pulled out an object that resembled an ostrich egg, but was really closer to the size and shape of a rugby ball.

Toomay rose and moved back, and Hotchkiss took his place, kneeling down in the dust. He entered a key and turned it, and the top of the egg opened up, revealing a number of buttons and lights—along with two LCD displays and two slots. With experienced hands, Hotchkiss punched in a sequence of buttons and a red light came on. He held his palm open and Toomay placed a plastic punch card—about half the size of a credit card—into it. Hotchkiss took Toomay's card and the one from his own breast pocket and inserted them simultaneously into the two parallel slots. The light went from red to green and he extracted the cards, handing one back to Toomay. He then set the timer and took the final safety catch off. One LCD panel showed the countdown running backward while the other one flashed: ARMED . . . ARMED . . . ARMED.

Hotchkiss closed the top of the egg and locked it. Then he rose, and together with Toomay the two warrants headed back down the tunnel.

Not a word had passed between them.

THE ROSS ICE SHELF

Rawlings looked through his field glasses and thought he could just make out the top of the derrick. "I think I can see it, Dana!" Then he heard something like a whisper, and he looked up in the sky. He caught a glimpse of a fighter—like a winged angel of death—coming straight at him, and he thought it was over. But then there was a flash, followed by a *boom!* And from behind the starburst, Rawlings saw the distinctive outline of a Harrier jump jet as it swooped over him, followed closely by a twin-tailed Fulcrum.

THE AV-8B HARRIER

The aerial debris of his kill whipped by Prof's canopy as he shot past it and then pulled up—close to the deck of the ice shelf. As the nose of his Harrier rose, Prof caught a glimpse of something in his cockpit rearview mirror. He kept the Harrier in tight loop maneuver—and at the top of the circle he rammed his thrust vector control forward.

It was the right move, but a half-second too late as he felt his Harrier shudder.

THE MIG-29 FULCRUM

Tupelov had just squeezed off his cannon when the American jump jet stopped—literally stopped—in midair and Tupelov's Fulcrum shot past. He thought he'd scored a hit and was bringing his Fulcrum around for another pass when an American Hornet screamed past his canopy. *God, where had all these Americans come from? The American carriers were supposed to have been sunk! And where is my wingman?*

Now out of missiles and forced to use his cannon, Tupelov cursed while banking his Fulcrum around to go after the Hornet.

THE F/A-18 HORNET

Blackjack had followed orders. He'd flown around the back side of Erebus, then came around and scanned the scene with his radar. All the action was down on the deck, so he dove for the shoreline of

McMurdo Sound and scooted along the seaward side of Hut Point Peninsula, using it for cover. Then he popped over the ridge to join the fray and nearly ran into a midair.

"Blackjack, this is Prof! My bird is hit! I got fuel coming out of my port wing."

Tupelov had lost his wingman, but now Blackjack saw the second Fulcrum—turning toward Prof's Harrier. "You got one coming around on you, Prof! Stay on the deck and get out of here!"

Blackjack watched Prof's bird head for the Sound as Tupelov's wingman began finishing out his turn to go after the wounded Harrier. Blackjack groaned under the force of eight g's as he hooked his Hornet around to fall in behind the Soviet warplane.

TUPELOV'S FULCRUM

Tupelov came out of his own eight-g turn and found his wingman sandwiched between the American Harrier and Hornet. Tupelov fell in behind Blackjack, making it an aerial train of four aircraft—the Harrier, his wingman, the Hornet, and his own Fulcrum.

THE F/A-18 HORNET

Like a roller coaster in the sky, Prof led the train of warplanes up and over Hut Point Peninsula, trying to shake whoever was behind him. Blackjack got the wingman's Fulcrum in his head-up display and began moving the targeting pipper onto the glowing dual tail exhausts of the Russian fighter. And then, in that moment, he caught sight of Tupelov's Fulcrum in his rearview mirror, bearing down on him. Time seemed to slow down—and a part of his being, like a siren's song, coaxed him to *break away, break away, break away.* But then another part of his soul exerted its own force and he remained in place, moving the pipper onto the tailpipes. He was rewarded with the distinctive growl in his earphones of the Sidewinder's lock-on, and he pressed the red firing button to send the missile off the rail, just as the 23-mm cannon fire from Tupelov's Fulcrum ripped through his cockpit.

TUPELOV'S FULCRUM

Fyodor Tupelov saw smoke pour out of the American Hornet only a moment before his wingman disappeared in a flash of light. Angry and bitter, he began to climb so he could dive on the crippled Harrier—but then an American F-16 screamed past his windshield.

THE F/A-18 HORNET

Blackjack felt something warm and he looked down. It was a dark liquid mass at his middle. Things about him seem to take on a slow-motion kind of dimension. His sense of touch started to escape him, and then the color faded from his vision, as if he'd tuned in a black and white TV. Although blood had splattered the inside of his canopy and obscured his view, he caught a glimpse of Prof's Harrier skimming over the pack ice of the Sound. His Hornet was nose up. How did it get that way? Blackjack saw the stick in his hand, but he couldn't feel it. As the horizon passed down over his blood-spattered canopy like a windshield wiper, the white nothingness of the pack ice filled his view. He reached for the eject handle under the seat, but his fingers wouldn't obey his command to grab it. Then strangely, he relaxed; and as the ice-covered sea rushed up toward him, Michael Pershing was at peace with himself—for he knew, within his own soul, that this time he had not choked.

BRANDING IRON STATION

The elevator door opened and Samuel McClure walked out, for what he hoped was the last time. He and the naval warrant officers descended the steps and strode toward the waiting Osprey. They looked up to see a number of corkscrewlike contrails painted against the cold blue sky. Then they heard some distant explosions. McClure spied the pilot of the Osprey, who pointed toward the ice shelf where a dot was approaching.

AN F-16 FALCON OVER THE WINDLESS BIGHT

Quick Draw Leader had no earthly idea what was happening. He and his flight of F-16s had flown into McMurdo on dry tanks, unable to raise anybody on the radio; and they had run smack into a passel of Soviet fighters. Leader had already fired off his two Sidewinders and was flying on nothing but fumes when he crossed paths with a

Russian Fulcrum that had just nailed an American Hornet. Dry tanks or no, Quick Draw Leader couldn't let that one pass as he armed his Vulcan cannon and pulled his Falcon around in an Immelmann.

THE FULCRUM

It had been a major air battle, and Fyodor Tupelov had fired all four of his missiles at the flock of American planes that seemed to have come out of nowhere. Now he had to tangle with an F-16 with only a few rounds left in his cannon. Tupelov brought his Fulcrum up in a climbing loop to search for his new adversary, but the American F-16 had disappeared—only to reappear in his rearview mirror. The Russian gasped, but did not freeze. At the apex of the loop he rolled the Fulcrum and pulled into a climbing "split-S" maneuver. Then he jinked, did a spiral dive, and went into a violent scissor, but the F-16 remained imprinted on his rearview mirror. *Who was this American?* Now frightened, Tupelov was going into a dive when he heard metal tearing metal and felt a sharp pain through his left knee. Smoke filled the cockpit so rapidly he lost all orientation and could do nothing but reach for the eject handles. He pulled with all his might while moaning, "Not again."

THE F-16 FALCON

Quick Draw Leader had just fired the burst from his Vulcan Gatling-style 20-mm cannon when his Pratt & Whitney turbofan engine went *chug-chug-chug* from fuel starvation. He immediately throttled down to idle to keep his generator going and his electronic fly-by-wire controls working long enough to make it down on a "dead stick" landing. He caught sight of the Russian plane as its pilot ejected from a smoke-filled canopy. Then he looked down and saw a towerlike structure and decided to set it down there.

THE WINDLESS BIGHT

The derrick was in full view now, and Rawlings could see the Osprey waiting with its rotor blades twirling, making him wish the Russian BMD had a horn to blare. He went up to the machine gun by the hatch and opened the breech, then he took out the ammo belt and tossed it onto the ice. Having come this far, he didn't want the weasel to start shooting at them when they parted company. He looked toward the derrick and could see three men in front of the Osprey, motioning him to hurry. Rawlings smiled and went back down the hatch. He nudged the weary driver and said, "Over there." Then he took the AK-47 from Dana and said, "It's been real, Colonel. Look me up if you ever make it to Anchorage. . . . Driver, halt!"

The BMD finally clanked to a stop, and Rawlings lowered the tailgate. He scooped up Dana and together they hustled down the ramp. Over her shoulder she said to Bobkov, "Would you believe this is my second grand theft auto in Antarctica!?"

As they exited the BMD they were greeted by a bizarre scene. A parachutist plunked down almost right in front of them as an F-16 touched down on the snow—in a belly landing—with a *squisssssh.* The rapier-looking jet skidded directly toward them, and Dana was about to leap out of the way when it finally came to a halt.

"Come on! Move it!" yelled the men from the Osprey.

Rawlings grabbed Dana again, but she heard the parachutist cry out. She stopped and said, "He's hurt."

Rawlings looked at their flight to freedom and at the parachutist, then said, "Okay, let's grab him." They began pulling the harness off the pilot—who was semiconscious from shock—and Dana saw his left knee was a bloody mess. Meanwhile, the canopy on the F-16 raised, and the pilot was extricating himself when a *whump!* punched through the air, throwing up a geyser of snow not a hundred yards behind him.

"Move it!" yelled one of the Osprey men. "We ain't waiting around!" As the F-16 pilot ran toward the Osprey, he overtook a man and woman helping the parachutist hobble toward the waiting rescue. He pulled the woman off and put the parachutist's arm over his neck, then the three men and the woman hustled up the ramp of the Osprey. Their reception party hustled in behind them as a *blam!* impacted beside the BMD.

The rear ramp had not even closed before the pilot had spooled the Osprey up to full power and lifted off the Windless Bight. Then, like an airborne ballerina, it executed a pirouette and raced off toward the saddle between Mounts Erebus and Terror.

Upon arrival of the *blam!* Colonel Bobkov and his driver ran like hell from the BMD, and kept on running until they were out of breath. By that time the pursuing BMDs had their target ranged in, and the colonel got to watch the vehicle he had just left get ripped apart by multiple 73-mm hits.

When the pursuing BMDs clanked up to the remains of the vehicle, Bobkov stalked back. Having gone light-years beyond blind rage, he grabbed the nearest soldier by the throat and screamed, *"What the hell are you trying to do! Get me killed at all cost?"* He let go of the choking youth and made a sweeping motion with his arm. "You are all under arrest! I will see you all hang! You will all be shot!"

The company commander dismounted his vehicle and strode over to Bobkov, saying, "I am glad we were able to rescue you, Colonel. We were afraid the Americans had escaped with you as prisoner."

"Rescue me?" The weasel struck the brawny captain with all the strength he could muster, but succeeded more in hurting his delicate hand than inflicting pain. As he wailed and shook his hand, Bobkov screamed, "I will shoot Voroshin myself!"

The captain wiped a drop of blood from the corner of his mouth, and said, "It appears you will have the opportunity, Comrade Colonel."

The sound of distant rotor blades could be heard.

THE OSPREY, 7,000 FEET OVER THE ROSS SEA

With the help of the two warrant officers and the Osprey's crew chief, Dana and Robert moved the wounded parachutist forward in the cabin and began to work on the bloody knee. "You got a first aid kit?" she asked.

"Yes, ma'am," said the crew chief, and he quickly fetched one.

"Belt," ordered Dana. "I need a belt."

The crew chief was wearing a flight suit and had no belt, so they appropriated one from Mr. Toomay. It was at that point the crew chief exclaimed, "Hey . . . this guy's a Russian!"

"Yeah, and they bleed like everyone else," said Dana. "Here, Robert, hold this tourniquet tight." Rawlings complied while Dana dressed the wound. The knee was a mess, but she got it bandaged as best she could while the pilot faded further into unconsciousness from shock. After she'd done all she could, she used some hand wipes from the first aid kit to get the blood off her fingers, while telling the crew chief to relieve Robert and keep firm pressure on the tourniquet. Then, emotionally and physically spent, she moved over and collapsed on one of the canvas-webbing seats along the bulkhead, while Robert stuck his head up in the cockpit to confer with the pilot.

Four men sat across from her. McClure, the two naval warrant officers, and the Air Force pilot who had belly-landed his F-16. McClure looked at her passively, while the naval warrants seemed tight-lipped and withdrawn, saying nothing and eyeballing her suspiciously. It was the Air Force pilot who seemed to match her measure for measure in strain and fatigue, for it was evident in his face. He had angular features, and his tanned skin seemed drawn. His hair was black as a raven's feather, except for a dash of gray at the temples, and it was matted with sweat. But the most notable features were his incredible blue eyes. Quite unusual to find striking blue eyes in someone with such dark features. He looked at Dana yet seemed not to see her, as if he were still in shock.

Robert fell in beside Dana and sighed. "Pilot says we're headed for the *Wasp*. Our Russian patient will be in their surgery soon."

Like Dana, Rawlings quickly took an inventory of their fellow passengers, and his gaze landed on the Air Force pilot. The man who had belly-landed the F-16 was clearly wiped out, and Rawlings noticed a single star on each shoulder of his flight suit. That made him the senior officer present, so Robert broke the ice by saying, "General, let me introduce myself. I'm Robert Rawlings, commander of the 106th Military Intelligence Battalion of the Sixth Infantry Division."

The pilot stared at him for a few moments, then shook his head and took off his flight glove to wipe his face. "Forgive me," he said finally. "I'm a little . . . shaken up. My name is Peter Lamborghini. I've been in the air a long time, and at the end of the haul my flight ran right into a swarm of Russian planes. . . . I'm the commander of the air task force that's flying in from the States, and I came down with the lead squadron from Hawaii." He wiped his face again. "I don't know what happened to the rest of my flight. I need to get a search-and-rescue team after them at once."

"No way," said Toomay, the naval warrant.

Lamborghini turned his head. "What do you mean, 'no way'? Those are my men."

"General," said McClure over the noise of the rotors, "we've pulled out of McMurdo. Totally. We are the last ones to leave."

"And nobody's going back in," said Toomay. "By presidential order."

Dana looked at Lamborghini as he put his head back against the bulkhead and closed his eyes. He was the picture of a man who'd just reached the end of the trail. She turned to Robert, and for a moment their eyes locked. Then he raised his arm to put it around her, and in a flash she was locked tightly in his embrace—neither one about to let go.

BRANDING IRON STATION

The HIND helicopter touched down, and it wasn't two seconds before Major General Voroshin was struggling out of the gunner's compartment, no doubt a little perplexed by the American F-16 parked alongside the group of BMD vehicles.

Bobkov was on him in an instant. "You incompetent fool!" he screamed. "First you can't guard your own headquarters! And then to cover your blunders you order your men to kill me! I will have your head for this, General!"

"Shut up, Comrade," replied Voroshin. "If anything, I will be the first soldier to receive the new Confederation Medal for Gallantry."

"What!?" screamed Bobkov, approaching a stroke.

"Look around you, Colonel. Do you see any Americans? No. They are gone. Pulled out. They took one look at our airborne forces and realized we were determined to prevail. So"—he made a sweeping motion with his hand—"we have won our objective. The Confederation Cabinet will no doubt be impressed."

"The only shots you fired were at me!"

Bobkov would have continued his harangue, but another helicopter—also freshly off-loaded from a Candid transport—flew in for a landing, and the rotor blades drowned out his tirade. This time it was a light Mil Mi-2 helicopter, carrying a detachment of combat engineers who jumped out.

"Up there, quickly," Voroshin ordered the detachment commander. "Check for booby traps." A veteran of Afghanistan, Voroshin knew a great deal about booby traps—his units had sown many of them there.

The engineers were quick and methodical, leaving no stone unturned as they checked the superstructure and electrical wiring for any sign of danger. There was none, so a team of three went down the elevator and began scouring the icedome below. As the minutes ticked by topside, Voroshin became impatient and demanded, "What is the status? It seems to be taking a long time."

The detachment commander—a major—was on the elevator telephone, talking to his men below. "It appears clear in the icedome, General. I have a man preparing to enter the mine shaft now."

"Very well. I will go down to the dome. I want to see it for myself."

"I would not advise that, General, until the entire site is secure."

"You said the dome was secure. I will stay out of the shaft until that is pronounced safe."

The major shrugged. "As you wish, General."

Voroshin and the major rode the elevator down together and entered the icedome for the first time. Like all first-timers, they were somewhat entranced by the eeriness of it all. Since the work in the dome had ended, the dust had settled somewhat, allowing Voroshin a reasonably clear view. As he walked through on an inspection tour he found the place was cluttered with silent equipment, and he paused here and there to take a closer look at whatever caught his eye. Yes, it was eerie. Approaching the mine shaft he saw the major talking on a cablephone to his men below. The major turned to Voroshin and said, "It is extremely dusty below, General, but it appears to be secure."

"Excellent. I shall see for myself."

"As you wish, General," said the major. One of his men rewound the bucket and Voroshin climbed in. As it lowered into the cold earth he passed a string of lights. The vertical shaft was much deeper and colder than he thought it would be, and he was now sorry he'd elected to travel to the bottom. But he wanted to report to Moscow that he had personally inspected the objective and that the prize was secure and well in hand.

As he neared the bottom the dust became noticeable, and then irritating. Upon hitting bottom it was like a pea soup fog, being stirred up by the engineers' footprints.

"I am General Voroshin. Who are you?" he asked, coughing.

"Sergeant Lamantov, sir."

"Show me this mine and let us get out quickly." He coughed again.

"Put this over your nose and mouth, General," said the sergeant, giving him a handkerchief.

Voroshin took it and said, "Lead on."

The sergeant complied, but there was little to see. Voroshin had no goggles and had to squint to keep from being blinded by the fine particles as the sergeant led him down the tunnel, crouching to avoid

the lights hanging from the ceiling. Not really able to tell how far
they'd gone, they stumbled past the other engineer, who was on his
hands and knees, feeling the wall for any unnatural protrusions.
Voroshin took several more steps down the tunnel before the engineer on the ground snapped at him, "Do not go any farther. I have
not examined the rest of the tunnel."

"Very well," said Voroshin, coughing again. "I have seen enough
. . . not that I can see anything in this dust bowl." The general turned
to leave, and as he did, the toe of his boot struck something heavy.
He stepped back and looked down, waving some of the dust away
so he could see. It helped a little, allowing him to discern a hazy
ball-shaped object on the ground. Voroshin was calling to the sergeant to notify him of his discovery, when the 1.7 kiloton nuclear
weapon went off.

25

....

THE SEPTEMBER 22 EVENT

On September 22, 1979, a Vela *reconnaissance satellite detected a brilliant flash of light in the desolate waters of the Southern Hemisphere, between South Africa and Antarctica. This "event," as it came to be known, exhibited the trademark "double pulse" burst of light of a nuclear explosion; and a few weeks later high levels of radiation were found in the thyroid glands of slaughtered Australian sheep— evidence they had been exposed to radioactive fallout.*

It seemed an open-and-shut case that a nuclear detonation had taken place, and speculation was rampant as to whose bomb it was— e.g., South Africa had the bomb. Israel had the bomb (they'd already had it for years). It was an Indian nuke. France had pulled off another atmospheric test—in a place where the radioactive fallout wouldn't cause political fallout like their tests in Polynesia.

But despite the evidence and the speculation, there remained one piece of data that just wouldn't square with the premise that the "September 22 event" was a nuclear blast.

The Vela *satellite system orbits about 60,000 miles above the earth with the specific mission of detecting atmospheric nuclear detonations. Each satellite possesses two sensors on board called "Bhangmeters" that observe and record abrupt changes in the intensity of incidental light. While the event in the Southern Hemisphere demonstrated the trademark double pulse footprint of light, the Bhangmeter recordings of the footprint fell outside the known parameters for nuclear detonations. In short, the September 22 event looked like a nuclear duck, walked like a nuclear duck, quacked like a nuclear duck; but according to the anomalous Bhangmeter recording, it wasn't a nuclear duck.*

So what was this mysterious burst of light in remote waters of the Southern Hemisphere?

The answer was painfully simple: The flash was actually two nuclear devices detonated simultaneously—their blasts separated only by a few microseconds and enough distance to kick the Bhangmeter reading out of the established envelope.

Two explosions?

Then to whom did they belong?

In the mid-seventies France and Israel were pursuing their own nuclear programs and ran into some problems at roughly the same time. France wanted to develop a neutron weapon but just couldn't make it work in their underground tests in Polynesia. Israel wanted to expand the size and scope of its nuclear arsenal but needed a long-term source of fissionable material to do so.

A bargain was struck.

Israel provided France with its expertise in theoretical physics and supercomputers (which was, and is, considerable), and France supplied Israel with a covert source of uranium and weapons-grade plutonium.

The key to this relationship, of course, was secrecy. If the words "France–Israel–Neutron Bomb" were ever leaked to the Arabs, then the oil spigot to France might be turned off permanently. So, for a time, the relationship blossomed. With Israel's help, France did develop a neutron weapon, and Israel began developing a new type of nuclear weapon that was earmarked for their ongoing war against terrorism. This new type of weapon was to be small, low-yield, low-fallout, and man-portable so it could be smuggled in on the back of a camel and used on, say, a guerrilla training camp in the Libyan desert.

As France and Israel pursued their respective neutron bomb and "Camel Bomb" programs, they came to a point where they both needed the same thing: an atmospheric test to assess the real-world effectiveness of their new weapons. Therefore they put together a test in the French Kerguelen Islands (in the southern Indian Ocean) where France has long maintained a small scientific station. The neutron weapon and the Camel Bomb were suspended below helium-filled balloons about twenty miles apart and detonated simultaneously at dawn on September 22, 1979, confusing the Vela satellite.

Several years later the Defense Intelligence Agency dug out the whole story on the Franco-Israeli collaboration, but kept the lid on it—for two reasons: one, the U.S. had never conducted a neutron bomb test in the atmosphere and wanted the French data on the Kerguelen blast; and two, they were intrigued by the Israeli Camel Bomb, which was much more man-portable than anything the U.S. had stored in its nuclear warehouse at Manzano Mountain in New Mexico. France and Israel agreed to cooperate with the Americans in return for their silence.

So, with the Israeli model, the Americans embarked on their own Camel Bomb program. If some flashpoint flared up in a distant trouble spot, the Americans could infiltrate an agent with a Camel Bomb and let it be known, discreetly, to their adversary that a nuclear weapon was in town—across the street, in fact—so why don't you just release those hostages. Or—if the Cold War became very hot—agents could be smuggled in and pre-positioned near command and communication centers to "decapitate" the Soviet leadership from their armed forces.

Yes, the Camel Bomb had considerable appeal, but because of the sensitivity of its potential use, and the fragile veil of secrecy around the Franco-Israeli pact, the Americans always treated the Camel Bomb program with hypersecurity—and gave it a different code name.

They called it the "Ostrich Egg."

The plastique explosive that lined the interior of the Ostrich Egg detonated, sending the plates of plutonium into the target sphere of plutonium. Once the plates and target sphere were compressed, they reached supercritical mass and triggered a nuclear chain reaction. In the first one-millionth of a second the force of seventeen hundred tons of TNT was released, creating a fireball of over a million degrees and a bubble of hot gas that compressed the air around it to several million atmospheres. In the initial microseconds Voroshin and the engineers in the tunnel were vaporized, and the surrounding rock was melted as the compression wave expanded in all directions. The high pressure of the expanding gases created a cavity around the point of detonation and an upward shock wave that began fracturing and crushing the rock in a cylindrical pattern called a "chimney." By the time the shock wave reached the floor of the icedome (some 240 feet above the detonation point) much of the fracturing wave's energy had dissipated, but there was enough force left to splatter a layer of earth and the remaining engineers against the ceiling of the icedome.

But the engineers were already dead, for a column of expanding gas and earth had raced up the mine shaft ahead of the fracture wave, filling the chamber with superheated air that instantaneously melted the ice and turned the dome structure into a cauldron of boiling mud.

Then the fracture wave lost its "uumpff," and the chimney collapsed back in on the detonation cavity, leaving a cratered depression where the floor of the icedome had been.

On the surface of Branding Iron Station the men of the Red Army were knocked off their feet as the earth trembled and the derrick shook, just as a column of gas, earth, and boiling mud belched out of the elevator shaft. Some of the men were hit by the scalding, irradiated slime and began screaming, while the uninjured soldiers looked at each other in shock, trying to fathom what had happened. Those who were able raised themselves off the ground to tend to the injured—who were still alive and able to scream. But then they heard something that overpowered the wailing of the wounded. It was a distant thunder that rolled over them like an approaching storm. They all turned and looked at Mount Erebus, and the screams of pain were soon joined by the cries of fear.

The shock wave from the Ostrich Egg had dissipated into a seismic wave that, by the time it reached the base of Mount Erebus, was rather puny. But it was just enough—the proverbial straw that broke the camel's back—to cause the country rock plug in the volcano's column to shear, giving the gases that had been building in solution for so long an avenue of escape. Once free, the gas, ash, and pyroclastic material raced up the column to expand and rise in the atmosphere, creating a colossal dark column that rose with a force that dwarfed the little man-made firecracker that had destroyed the mining site.

The prevailing winds off the Ross Sea took the expanding ash cloud and carried it inland, and as it began looming toward them, the men at Branding Iron Station hefted the injured into their BMDs and raced away.

It was all they could do.

Mount Erebus continued erupting for the next four days.

The gusty cold winds cooled the hot ash, causing it to fall as it moved inland, coming down on the Soviet positions and covering them with a choking blanket. Cut off from the air and sea, there was little the Russians could do except try to move inland, but with their general vaporized, the ossified decision-making machine of the Red Army kept them in place until it was too late to begin an escape.

The eruption of Mount Erebus followed the Santorini model—the eruption that wiped out the Minoan culture in the Aegean Sea about 1500 B.C. It was not like Mount Saint Helens, where the top half of the mountain blew off. Instead, it was a progressive eruption, where the interior matter of the mountain was expelled as ash and pyroclastic material over several days. This left the mountain as a hollowed-out shell that could no longer support its own weight, and the exterior of Mount Erebus collapsed back into its own caldera. The hole that was left was about ten cubic miles in volume, and as the Ross Sea rushed in to fill the gaping void, the water displacement created a tsunami wave of gigantic proportions. With nothing to break its path, the wall of water that was 300 feet high surged across the flat ice shelf and up into the Koettlitz Glacier, which acted as a funnel that channeled the torrent of water into a mammoth spout that shot onto the Skelton Névé, forming a massive lake of water and ash.

And since the volcano's ash plume had long since blotted out the sun, temperatures plummeted further, and it wasn't long before the once proud Sixth Guards Airborne Division was encased in a tomb of frozen mud.

26

. . . .

TRUCE

VERSAILLES, FRANCE—July 20

The blond anchorwoman spoke a few words into the microphone to get a voice level, and then received a "stand by" from the remote director. It was already dark, as she stood in front of the Versailles Palace. It was illuminated with spotlights, making it a much more magnificent backdrop than any studio set could be.

She was wearing a heavy coat, for the weather was cold—even for July. As will happen with violent volcanic eruptions, the sulfur dioxide that was belched into the upper atmosphere by the demise of Mount Erebus turned into sulfuric acid, creating a veil that covered the earth and diffused the sun's heat. Brutal winters would follow for a couple of years—shortening growing seasons and reminding man how frail this vessel of the earth could be.

The director pointed to the anchorwoman and she began. "Good evening. This is Catherine Crier with a special live report from the Soviet-American summit at the Versailles Palace. We received word just moments ago that a final 'agreement in principle' has been reached between the President and Soviet Confederation Chairman Vitali Kostiashak on a treaty governing all future rubidium discoveries, and on the future of Antarctica. These negotiations, which have been mediated by U.N. Secretary General Syed Khatak, will now—we are told—result in a treaty not only between the superpowers, but one that will be submitted to the United Nations General Assembly for ratification, and will be binding on all members who elect to sign.

"We will have more on our regularly scheduled newscast later this evening."

"Cut," said the director. "That was good, Catherine. We'll redo it at the beginning of the program feed—"

There was a crashing sound as one of the klieg lights fell onto the brick walkway. The set director spun round to see what had happened, and found a rather dumpy, middle-aged man with unkempt

489

hair sprawled alongside the broken equipment.

"What the hell do you think you're doing!?" screamed the set director.

The supine figure growled, "I was going to the press conference, Bozo! Maybe if you sound-bite turkeys didn't put trip wires all over the place some of us real reporters could get a little work done around here!" He struggled to his feet, straightening his overcoat around his paunch while trying to regain a semblance of dignity.

The set director picked up the light stand and hissed, "And who are you, Mr. Hotshot, that you can't see a simple cable?"

"Woltman. Seymour Woltman with the AP, smartass."

The director placed the lamp stand up right and hissed, "Well, listen, Seymour, I hate to be the one to tell you this, but you're paying for this light."

"That's rich, Bozo, that's really rich. I'm gonna sue your ass for causing a public hazard with these booby traps you got strewn all over everywhere—"

"Oh, yeah, well, I hate to take the wind out of your sail, Seymour," sneered the director, "but before you call your lawyer you'd better pick up your flask."

Crier rolled her eyes and walked off toward the press conference, thankful she was no longer the judge who would eventually have to sort it all out.

In the ornate Hall of Mirrors, the Secretary General of the United Nations sat at the head of the long table, and down each side were the opposing principals and their aides. It had been an arduous negotiation, but at last the basic provisions had been agreed upon and the fine print could be left to their respective staffs.

Syed Khatak, the Secretary General, was a Pakistani economics professor turned diplomat. He had a small body, but a correct and distinguished voice that spoke with resonance and authority. He scanned his paper one last time, then looked down the table and said, "Very well, then. We are in agreement. The mining site of any future discoveries of rubidium-96, on the soil of any treaty members, will be turned over to the United Nations as a protectorate territory. The Security Council of the U.N. will then take responsibility for the actual extraction of the mineral and will entertain applications from treaty members for research and development using said extracted mineral.

"All uses of rubidium-96 are to be for peaceful scientific or medical purposes, subject to a comprehensive program of U.N. inspection. Any use of the isotope for military purposes is to be banned, and this provision is subject to the full enforcement powers of the Security Council.

"Further, Antarctica is to become a world park, closed to commercial development of its resources, and closed to the presence of any military force. . . ."

As the Secretary General continued, Rodger Whittenberg, Chief of the General Staff of the United States Armed Forces, took off his reading glasses and rubbed his eyes. It wasn't that he was disinterested. Rather, he'd drafted much of the agreement and knew it chapter and verse. The superpowers had turned the world on its ear down in Antarctica. Now the superpowers were trying to put Humpty-Dumpty back together again. In squaring off against each other, the Soviet Confederation and the United States had succeeded in alienating the entire world. Even Great Britain had only grudgingly let the Americans use the Falklands as a staging area. The Philippines had only allowed Clark Air Base and Subic Bay to be used for medical purposes. Now here we were, mused Whittenberg, standing at the altar of what was a shotgun wedding, of sorts.

The big, black Air Force general surveyed the other side of the table. The Russians lacked polish but they were capable men. The Confederation Chairman, Vitali Kostiashak, Whittenberg knew. He was a diminutive Ukrainian with high cheekbones and a penchant for English-tailored clothes. He was a man of immense intellectual power, a grandmaster of chess, but to Whittenberg it seemed he had lost much of his old vitality. His hair—which he combed straight back—had turned almost white, and Whittenberg noticed the Chairman no longer smoked like a chimney. He guessed that the CIA report he'd read about Kostiashak having a lung removed was correct after all.

Whittenberg's gaze then turned to the admiral at Kostiashak's elbow named Timoshenko. Now that guy was a piece of work. The kind of person Whittenberg would have liked to have met under other circumstances.

Finally, Whittenberg shot a glance to his right toward his own President. He was the former Vice President, and before that the governor of Missouri. Not a flashy guy. Rather plodding, in fact. But solid. And honest. The anchorman President Jonathan Blakely had resigned from office, in lieu of facing certain impeachment over the first wartime use of a nuclear weapon since Nagasaki.

To his own surprise, Whittenberg had survived. The former Vice President had been to all the National Security Council meetings and knew the score on the decision to go nuclear. Ordering the use of a nuclear weapon requires a lot of inconvenient documentation. And the paper trail leads to one place and one place only: the Oval Office. It had been Jonathan Blakely's call, and when the shit hit the fan in the aftermath, there was no "plausible deniability" for him to hide behind. No subordinate to take the fall.

". . . very well," said the Secretary General, bringing Whittenberg back to the matters at hand. "We stand adjourned. The press conference will commence in forty-five minutes." As the Secretary General rose to leave, the Hall of Mirrors filled with the sounds of chairs moving, papers shuffling, and briefcases closing. And as the President and his aides joined the group moving toward the door, Whittenberg stayed behind, gathering his memoranda together. Turning to his left, he asked Robert Rawlings, "Well, what did you think of your first summit?"

Rawlings stood as well, stretching his legs. "Not my sort of thing, I'm afraid, General. I prefer to be outside. And I think you, me, and the Soviet Chairman are the only ones in the entire room who don't smoke. I could use some fresh air."

"Can't say I blame you. I had mixed feelings about bringing you here, but since you saw most of the events at McMurdo I thought it might be a good idea to have you around." Whittenberg's gaze went from the new eagles on Rawlings's epaulets to the rows of ribbons on the left breast of his jacket. He saw the new ribbon denoting the Distinguished Service Cross—which he had awarded personally—and noticed the one denoting the Distinguished Flying Cross. Whittenberg tapped the DFC and said, "One of these days you'll have to tell me how a groundpounder like you got that one."

Rawlings shrugged. "Long story."

"I'm sure. . . . Well, where would you like to go from here, Colonel? You can pretty much have your pick of assignments. I'll cut the orders myself. What'll it be? Back to Alaska?"

Rawlings shook his head. "No, sir. I think a change of scenery is in order. I think my wife and I would like Hawaii. It will be my last tour before I retire, so I'd like it to be a peaceful one."

"Retire?" asked Whittenberg.

"Yes, sir."

"Very well, Colonel. I'll talk to CinCPAC and see what I can do. Perhaps something in intelligence at IPAC."

"That would be fine, sir. . . . If you won't be needing me any longer, I'll be heading back to the embassy."

"No, Colonel, I'd say that's a wrap. I might catch you for a drink later."

"Sounds good, sir. I'll buy a round."

Whittenberg nodded and Rawlings departed. He went through a few more papers before noticing that Adm. Yuri Timoshenko was standing next to him.

"So, General," said Timoshenko. "Our proceedings are concluded here. An end to an unfortunate business."

"Unfortunate to be sure, Admiral. And we still have our energy problems to work out," said Whittenberg.

Timoshenko nodded and remarked, "Yes, but perhaps in Antarctica we all looked into the abyss of Armageddon—and found we did not care for the view. Perhaps that is reason to hope." He held out his hand and said, "You have conducted yourself with honor, General. It is regrettable we had to meet for the first time in circumstances such as these."

"Regrettable," agreed Whittenberg.

"I could not help but notice the colonel who sat beside you during the negotiations. He speaks Russian. Was he your interpreter?"

"Not exactly."

"Your aide-de-camp?"

"Not exactly that either."

"Well," chuckled Timoshenko, "he seemed quite disinterested in the whole proceedings."

Whittenberg nodded. "He's the kind of man who appears not to pay attention but misses nothing."

"Indeed?"

"Yes, indeed. He's the one who told me you were ambidextrous."

Timoshenko laughed. "Amazing! It is a skill I developed as a boy when I broke my right arm twice the same year. It almost kept me out of the Navy. I have written with either hand quite naturally ever since." He laughed again.

"And he noticed that you are color-blind."

Timoshenko quit laughing. "How did he know that?"

Whittenberg pointed at the table. "The pens provided by our

French hosts. A black, blue, and a dark green pen in front of every seat. Everyone else stayed with one color for the most part. The Colonel noticed you varied your choice and guessed you had some trouble discerning color."

Timoshenko pursed his lips and replied, "A recent problem with my eyesight, General. . . . My compliments to your Colonel—?"

"Rawlings. Robert Rawlings. I will pass your compliments along." Whittenberg held out his hand. "Goodbye, Admiral. Perhaps our paths will cross again."

Timoshenko shook it. "Perhaps, General."

Whittenberg left and the Russian watched him depart. Alone in the Hall of Mirrors now, Timoshenko looked down at the scratch pad that the mysterious colonel had incessantly doodled upon during the entire summit. He held the pad closer and saw that Rawlings had scribbled three entries, over and over: DANA, PANCHO, and HIN-MATONYALATKIT.

The Russian admiral had no idea what they meant.

27

· ·

HINMATONYALATKIT

Who was the greatest American military leader who ever lived? Surely the list from which to choose is long and distinguished: George Washington, Chester Nimitz, George Smith Patton, John Paul Jones, Red Cloud, James Doolittle, John Joseph Pershing, Creighton Abrams, and Stonewall Jackson, to name but a few. But if nobility is the handmaiden of greatness, then perhaps the greatest of all was a Native American named Hinmatonyalatkit.

Hinmatonyalatkit—which means "thunder coming up over the land from the water"—was of the Nez Percé tribe in what is now the state of Oregon. He was the son of a Nez Percé chief named Tu-Elakas, who underwent a conversion to Christianity and took the Biblical name of Joseph, which he passed on to his son.

In 1863 Joseph (the elder) refused to accept the terms of a renegotiated treaty between the U.S. government and other Nez Percé tribes concerning the status of their lands, but the government decreed the treaty was binding on all the Nez Percé. The situation simmered until the government ordered the nontreaty Nez Percé off their beloved Wallowa Valley in 1877. By then Joseph (the younger) had become chief, and he yearned for a peaceful settlement with the white man—his nature was that of a diplomat rather than a warrior. But an incident occurred where several whites were killed, and Army troops moved in to capture his and several Nez Percé bands that had rejected the treaty.

The Nez Percé resisted and fought back, defeating the U.S. Army at White Bird Canyon, Big Hole River, and Canyon Creek. But with unlimited manpower and supplies, the Army gained the upper hand. Yet the Nez Percé refused to surrender, and proceeded to embark upon a retreat that remains one of the most incredible campaigns in the history of warfare.

Rather than surrender, this group of 750 Nez Percé men, women, and children—over the course of eleven weeks—executed a retreat that covered 1,600 miles through four states. They engaged ten separate U.S. commands in thirteen battles or skirmishes, and crossed the Rocky Mountains twice. They were thirty miles from sanctuary in Canada when an Army force under Col. Nelson A. Miles finally nailed them at Bear Paws, Montana, in the final battle of the campaign.

A reputation developed around Chief Joseph that he was an "Indian Napoleon" who single-handedly masterminded this campaign of the Nez Percé. But Joseph was one of several Nez Percé chiefs (White Bird, Looking Glass, Toohoolhoolzote, Lean Elk, Hahtalekin, Husishusis Kute) who presided over their own bands, and it is more likely that the military decisions for the retreat were made in council.

Joseph surely contributed mightily to the military venture, but the true mantle of greatness descended upon him not during the campaign, but at the end—where in defeat at Bear Paws he elected not to escape to Canada, but to remain with his wounded and lay down his arms. He surrendered to Colonel Miles and Gen. Oliver Howard on October 5, 1877, and his final words of the campaign were taken down by Howard's adjutant at the scene. His speech was an epitaph to his struggle, a reflection of his character, and the eloquent lamentation of a man whose heart had been broken asunder. They were the words that secured Chief Joseph's place in history:

Tell General Howard I know his heart. What he told me before I have in my heart. I am tired of fighting. Our chiefs are killed. Looking Glass is dead. The old men are all killed. It is the young men who say yes or no. He who led the young men is dead. It is cold and we have no blankets. The little children are freezing to death. My people, some of them, have run away to the hills and have no blankets, no food; no one knows where they are, perhaps freezing to death. I want time to look for my children and see how many of them I can find. Maybe I shall find them among the dead. Hear me, my chiefs! I am tired. My heart is sick and sad. From where the sun now stands, I will fight no more forever.